PRINCES OF CHAOS

ROYALS OF FORSYTH U

ANGEL LAWSON
SAMANTHA RUE

FOREWORD

Dear Queens,

If this is your first Royals of Forsyth book, we suggest going back to the beginning, *Lords of Pain*, to prepare for the full experience of *Princes of Chaos*. Each series is set in the same world of Forsyth U and although they can be considered standalone/a separate harem, this world bleeds like a face wound. It's messy and hard to contain.

If you are a friend or family member looking to be supportive, we appreciate it! But it's better for everyone, and future family dinners, if you just skip this series. This is not the place for you. Or anyone with any real sensibilities.

Now that we're all ready to proceed, let's talk content.

Queens, it's hard to know where to begin. Like, we literally are unsure if we can fully explain what you're about to experience in *Princes of Chaos*. This book is about breeding. Contractual, dubiously consensual, breeding. That takes place in a house of horrors filled with three trauma monsters and a ruthless King. It's rough. Poor Verity has no f-ing clue what she's about to get into. And therefore, neither do you.

These guys are... well, you're about to find out. You're going to hate them, but we know you love them that way. Absolutely, 100%, irredeemable.

Until, of course, they are.

Princes of Chaos contains: breeding, non/dub, insertion, inflation, medical kink, edging and withholding, and some light-dick touching for our readers' pleasure. They're spoiled, mean and controlling. Also, if you're sensitive to issues surrounding torture, prior childhood sexual abuse, drug addiction and use, degradation, public humiliation/exposure, physical abuse/punishment, and misogyny, you may want to sit this one out.

If you haven't already, click on the link below and join our Monarch's group for community, book news and other goodies! Also, check out our exclusive Royals of Forsyth U website for bonus content and links to our store!

Angel & Sam

PREFACE

Did you read the foreword? Yes? Carry on. No? Go back and read
the content warnings.
—Samgel

NORTH SIDE

EX-KING: LIONEL LUCIA
CHILDREN: LAVINIA (SOLD), LETICIA (DEAD)
PLEDGES: CASH "MONEY" MALLIS (DEALER)

WEST END

KING: SY PERILINI
QUEEN: LAVINIA LUCIA
DUKES: NICK BRUIN, REMY MADDOX
DKS MEMBERS: BRUCE OAKFIELD,
BALLSACK
MANAGER: MAMA B
CUTSLUTS: HALEY, LAURA
KATHLEEN, GRETA
FAMILY:
TIMOTHY MADDOX (DAD)
LOCATIONS: THE GYM (TRAINING/FIGHTS)

KING: TIMOTHY MADDOX

EAST END

KING: RUFUS ASHBY
PRINCES: WICKER ASHBY (KAYES),
PACE ASHBY, LEX ASHBY
PRINCESS: VERITY SINCLAIRE
STAFF: STELLA (HANDMAIDEN)
DANNER (SERVANT)
FRANK (DRIVER)
FAMILY: FELIX ASHBY
(MURDERED BY NICK)
LOCATIONS:
THE PURPLE PALACE
THE GENTLEMAN'S CHAMBER (STRIP CLUB)
NU ZOO (PARTY HOUSE)

SOUTH SIDE

KING: KILLIAN PAYNE
LORDS: TRISTIAN MERCER,
DIMITRI RATHBONE
QUEEN/LADY: STORY AUSTIN
FAMILY: DANIEL PAYNE (DAD/FORMER KING/DEAD AF)
WORKERS: MRS. CRANE (BAMF), AUGUSTINE (MANAGER)
LOCATIONS: THE VELVET HIDEAWAY (BROTHEL)
THE LDZ BRWONSTONE

1

erity

IT'S NOT CROSSING the boundary into East End that does it. Lots of students go into East End, which has the best shops in Forsyth, plus, every kingdom has its more neutral spaces closest to the campus. I wring my hands into my sweatshirt–*DKS* emblazoned on the front–but feel mostly fine. Aside from the fancy luxury car, whose driver I don't even know, it could be any other outing to the pristine streets of Ashby's kingdom.

It doesn't really hit me until the car approaches the bridge.

The water is murky, dark, and perfectly still, reflecting the afternoon sun like a mirror as we cross it. Part of me is fascinated, wanting to press my face to the glass and soak in the details. The Princes live in a sprawling estate. It's tucked away on the outskirts of their territory, the most eastward thing *in* Forsyth, and it's completely surrounded by brackish water. I could probably count the West End girls who've been invited here on one hand, and for good reason. The Princes are the enemy, and I don't belong here.

Alone.

Isolated.

On an actual fucking island.

My phone dings just then, reminding me that I'm not *really* alone. It's not my actual phone–I'd left that behind, just in case. This is one Story smuggled to me just for this purpose, and it only has two contacts.

Chrysalis: You there?

Vivarium: Going over the bridge now.

Chrysalis: Keep us in the loop!

Instar: Don't take any bullshit. Remember who your King is.

Some of the panic falls away at Lavinia's reminder. She's right. I may be in East End, but I have the power of the DKS frat behind me. The cutsluts. The Dukes, including Simon Perilini, their new King. Not to mention *two* Queens.

The Monarchs.

I put my phone away to keep focused on my surroundings. Seeing the large, ornate Victorian mansion rising in the distance, I straighten my back and remain alert, eyes scanning the property. It's surrounded by a fence, and the car comes to a stop at an enormous, wrought-iron gate. Both gates have an intricate letter "P", but they're mirrored so that one is backwards, and everyone knows what they stand for.

After a moment of stillness, the gates swing open, and as the car crawls through, I see a whole bank of cameras pointed at us.

I begin gnawing at my thumbnail. The Lady hadn't mentioned it being this heavily surveilled, but who knows? Tonight is the Royal masquerade, and just like Friday Night Fury, it's open to any Forsyth elite, no matter which kingdom they're from. Security will be heightened.

It's *fine*.

Probably.

Rolling up the drive, I begin noticing the other cars, identical to the one I'm in, parked in a perfect row along the path. And the house...

The mansion.

The *palace.*

It's breathtaking.

The imposing stone structure is even more beautiful than everyone said it'd be. Its big turrets and slender chimney stacks soar above me, the roofline a collection of glass, tile, and stone that stands regally against the clear sky overhead. The fine detail and heavy ornamentation puts even the West End's signature clock tower to shame.

The moment I step out of the car, it's easy to forget how this place gets its name.

The *Purple* Palace.

It's not the pale stone facade. It's the vines that crawl up like capillaries to the bright roofline. Right now, the wisteria and roses covering the side of the building are dormant and wilted, gray and brown, lifeless in the January winter. But I've heard that when they're blooming, it turns the mansion a deep purple with stipples of white.

Today, it just looks sickly and anemic.

A lot like I feel.

Shutting the car door behind me, I steel myself, squaring my shoulders as I face it down. East End's palace is tall, but West End's clock tower is taller. As I glance over my shoulder to scan Forsyth's skyline, I can see the clock face all the way from this beautiful, wilted island.

It's never felt so far away.

THE DRESS IS MASSIVE. Yards and yards of glaring white fabric, covered in a thick spread of beads and sequins greets me when I'm ushered into my dressing spot. The skirt curves out from the waist like a bell, stuffed with crinoline, and grazes the floor. The strapless bodice has a scalloped design edging across the chest. The lace accents are beaded with tiny crystals that catch the light. It's expensive for sure, the designer's tag hand-stitched in gold in the back.

It's pristine.

Bridal.

Virginal.

It's not the first time I've felt that little swell of excitement at the prospect of being chosen, but it's the first time I've felt it this tangibly. Cutsluts aren't made for silk, brocade, lace, and crystals. We're made for Lycra and denim, skin-tight and frayed around the edges.

As much as I hate to admit it, just looking at this dress makes me feel like a Princess.

By the end of the night, maybe that's what I'll be.

The Princess. The house girl for Psi Nu Zeta.

God, it feels wrong to even think it.

"Oh my god," a girl gasps. "I can't believe they got Velma Kang to design our dresses."

I blink, brought back to the fact I'm not alone in the room. There are eleven other girls who all arrived at the Purple Palace doorstep at the same time that I did. Each is beautiful, each bubbling with excitement, all clutching that same golden ticket in their hand—an invitation to the Prince's Royal masquerade: an opportunity to be chosen as the next Princess.

I don't need to pull mine out, because I've already memorized every square inch of it, from the foiled edges to the dark ink.

Verity Sinclaire has been cordially invited to attend the Princes' seventy-eighth Masquerade ball, which will be celebrated at the Purple Palace on January 6th.
As an esteemed guest of honor, you'll have the opportunity to become Forsyth's next Princess, a position of the highest prestige.
Your attire and accommodations will be provided.
Respond by January 3rd.

The other girls and I have been escorted to the third floor, where a lushly decorated room has been designated, at least for the night. From the looks of the tall stained glass facing westward–a thorn-clad baby being crowned with a halo, surrounded by three wise men–I'm guessing this room probably served as a chapel back in the early days of Forsyth.

Or maybe it's just a depiction of the Princes.

Bigger egos have happened.

Twelve matching dresses hang on the wall, positioned next to twelve floor length mirrors. Everything is uniform, from the shoes to underwear.

A beaded, feathered mask is attached to the top of the mirror, looking down with vacant, watchful eyes.

The girl next to me is already in her corset and panty set, an evil-looking contraption that makes her waist seem dramatically narrow and her breasts abnormally full. Other than a small blue bow tied between the breasts, it's the same shade of white as the dress.

"They're gorgeous," the girl next to her agrees, gushing. "I heard a custom Kang dress is a minimum of twenty grand." Her dark, shiny hair falls over her shoulders as she tugs at the top of her identical corset. Her breasts spill out of the top, at least a cup size bigger than everyone else in the room. Her skin is perfect, too—a warm, rich, dewy brown. The tag attached to her mirror says her name is Lakshmi.

"Just imagine what the wardrobe allowance will be if one dress costs thousands of dollars." I clutch my robe at the waist and lean over enough to see that the girl next to me is named Heather. "Piper had the most adorable boots from Freebird."

"Yeah, well Piper fucked up," a voice chimes in from behind us. In the reflection, I see her name is Gina. "She fucked around *and* found out."

The room erupts into laughter but there's a nervous tinge to it. Piper had been the Princess in the fall, and we're here to replace her. She'd gotten pregnant well within the three-month deadline, but when the mandatory paternity results came in, the baby wasn't one of the Princes'. She and her men had been booted from the Palace, opening up the positions of three new Princes and one new Princess. All to be chosen by the Prince King himself: Ashby.

"I can't believe my father refuses to pay for a boob job," Heather goes on, frowning as she cups her breasts. "I told him that these B-cups were going to keep me from success one day."

"If it helps, my mother's sister's yoga instructor said that Ashby has a thing for blondes," Lakshmi says.

Heather snorts. "Girl, he doesn't give a rat's ass about what anyone looks like. He wants a functioning womb. Three out of the last four Princesses were failures, which means they've only had *one* baby in five years. My uncle was a Prince when he was at Forsyth," she brags, fluffing her hair, "and he says Ashby is panicking."

"Even if that's true," Gina says, nudging close to lower her voice, "there's no fucking way he's picking that girl over there with the tattoos. How'd she even get an invite? I know for a fact they don't allow women with tats or extra piercings."

"Connections I'm sure."

They talk as easily to one another as the cutsluts do. I can't decide if they know each other or if I'm the only one who feels awkward and alien, fumbling a tube of mascara from my makeup bag. It's not that I'm not used to pretty girls, because the cutsluts have that sexy, hot girl vibe down to a science. Their entire duty at DKS is to be there for the guys, whether that means being their cheerleader in the ring, a study partner to get through a hard class, or a quick fuck in between bouts.

But these girls are different. They're... classy? Sorority girls, probably. Royal adjacent stock—nieces, cousins, granddaughters of former members. They may look pretty, but there's no doubt that under the thick layers of mascara and shiny waxed skin, there's a cutthroat bitch who will do anything to become Princess.

One appears pretty quickly. "Hey, you. Redhead." Heather says, her voice suddenly right beside me. "Don't you belong to one of the Dukes?"

Stiffening, I realize Lakshmi and Gina are both watching,

aggressively expectant. Trying to keep my voice strong and even, I answer, "I don't belong to anyone."

Lakshmi arches an eyebrow. "But you were supposed to be Duchess, weren't you?"

Well.

That was the plan.

Mama B groomed, educated, and *preserved* me for the Dukes. While the other girls around me, the cutsluts, could wear whatever they wanted—whatever the DKS liked best—I wasn't allowed. I needed to be different. Special. The kind of girl men wanted but couldn't have. The kind of girl coveted in Forsyth.

I think it would've happened too, if Nick Bruin hadn't been assigned to handle Lavinia Lucia.

That job, that one assignment by Daniel Payne, had set the dominoes in motion. One that ousted me as the next Duchess and inserted Lavinia as their Queen. I'd be more upset if Lavinia wasn't a perfect fit for her Dukes, or if she wasn't such a good friend.

"No," I answer, sighing. "That's, uh, not in the cards anymore."

There's nothing in my cards, and that's half the reason I came here. The one time I gave dating a shot, it was before I started Forsyth U and it was clear I needed at least a little experience if I was going to be Duchess. It involved a dating app, a clever profile name–*Rosilocks*–and a ten-minute conversation with a guy that ended with him sending me a video of himself jerking off. It was the first time I'd seen a penis like that. Thick and taut and somehow aggressive. I blocked him immediately, but the videos kept coming, each more graphic than the last. Moral of the story: that's what happens when non-Royals try dating in Forsyth. You attract the dregs of society and end up calling the police.

Heather crosses her arms. "Still, your connection to DKS should disqualify you."

My pulse quickens, from anger just as much as embarrassment. "I was invited," I say, voice clipped.

"That means she passed the medical exam," Lakshmi says to Heather, mouth slanted skeptically.

I freeze, caught off guard. "Medical exam? I-I didn't take any exam."

Heather smirks. "You don't take it, honey. Ashby does."

"Your medical records." Lakshmi gives me this indulgent look, like she's speaking to a toddler. "Ashby consults all the offices and clinics, and they refer girls to him–only the cream of the fertilest crop."

My face goes slack at the realization. So *that's* why my gyno appointment last month was so weirdly involved. I argued with the receptionist for twenty minutes about not needing any STD testing. I told her over and over again that I'm a virgin. I wonder, "Isn't that, like... illegal?"

Lakshmi barks an obnoxious laugh, Heather following suit. "Oh, that's adorable."

"So you must have pedigree," Gina guesses, scrutinizing me. "An uncle or something?"

I know what she's asking, and the truth makes me squirm under the weight of their eyes. At first, I thought the invitation was a joke —an elaborate prank set up to humiliate one of West End's girls. A plot to get back at the Dukes for a deal gone wrong, maybe someone bitter about losing a fight.

But why me?

Why Verity Sinclaire? Good medical records or not, I'm not special enough. I'm just a regular twenty-year-old West Ender who was raised by a single mother: Mama B, the wrangler of a den of Bruins. She's gorgeous, seductive, and absolutely badass. But she isn't Royal—not that it stopped Saul Cartwright from fucking her. The ex-King of West End was a snob, but cutsluts get a pass, and my mother is the Queen of them. Mama B isn't precious when it comes to the men she invites in her bed. I've watched them come and go, enthralled by my mother, but Saul was always wary of me. The look he gave me was distasteful, like I was some sort of parasite he was afraid would attach to him if I got too close.

I'm not a bit sad that Simon Perilini put a bullet in him.

"No," I crisply answer. "No uncles. No aunts. No grandprinces. Just... me."

Lakshmi and Heather share a knowing look. "Right," Heather says, her slow smile dripping with condescension. "Well, I'm sure you'll be the one to beat!" They don't even wait until they get out of earshot before she tells the others, "Well, that's two out of the running: the punk bitch and the redheaded step-bastard. Ashby may be desperate, but he's not lowering himself to the gutter of West End for a pair of functional ovaries."

I spin, fist clenching as I snap, "Excuse me?"

They don't even look back, ignoring me altogether. "What about me?" Lakshmi asks. "You have anything to call me out on?"

Heather sighs. "No. Your tits are fabulous, your skin glows like an angel, and your hips are perfect for childbearing. You've got a solid chance." A bubble of laughter follows. "I should slit your throat right here, but then I wouldn't get to wear that fantastic dress."

Gina raves, "I hear we get to keep them, and everything else, even if we aren't chosen!"

The reality of what I'm doing here slams home and I turn, walking past the room full of girls to the bathroom. It's predictably huge, a brightly lit, gilded mirror towering over a large countertop that's been piled with every kind of makeup imaginable. Hairspray, curling and flat irons, gels and nail polish. It reminds me of the cutslut lounge, and for a moment, I'm caught off guard by a wave of homesickness.

If that exchange had happened in the gym's lounge, there would have been a panty-clad fist fight. It doesn't matter that I've never been much for the fighting part of West End. My knuckles still go white with the impulse, blood thrumming with rage.

It's just another reminder that I don't belong here.

Unable to look at myself right now, I avoid the row of mirrors and duck into the shower. I keep thinking that if I get a moment alone, time to catch myself and remember why I'm here, I'll calm down. It's the same thing I've been doing since I arrived an hour ago. Deep steadying breaths, followed by a single word: Sisterhood.

That's why I'm here. For the Monarchs.

I know Lavinia and Story asked me to do this, but the Dukes? The cutsluts—my other sisterhood? God, my *mother*. If they find out I agreed to this cattle call...

Betrayal.

That's how they'd see it.

Deep breaths, Verity.

It helps a little, but it's not what gives me the strength to walk back out there, head held high.

One interaction in this house has proven to me why Story and Lavinia need someone on the inside. East Enders don't throw fists. They make little cuts from afar, smiling all the while, and if the three of us want to see any kind of change in Forsyth, this is where we start.

Walking out of the bathroom, I march past the other girls already in the process of getting dressed. I stop at my mirror, taking in my mother's green eyes and her mother's red hair. Unlike the bitches around me, my pedigree comes from real women.

Women who aren't afraid to stand on their own.

Eyes on the mirror, I drop my robe and reach for corset and panties. It's a challenge not to cover myself—to show my nerves— but I square my shoulders and shimmy my legs into the soft, satin panties that fit like a glove. The corset is a bitch, and it feels like it's stabbing into my ribs, but whatever. I grew up in a gym with fight- ers. No pain, no gain.

Once I'm hooked in, my tits look spectacular, and it's not just me that notices. I see it in the reflection, Heather's narrow eyes sweeping over me. *That's right, bitch.* I'm a solid C-cup.

It's not just silk and lace I'm wearing. It's armor.

This isn't a party. It's a battle.

And there can only be one winner: The Monarchs.

2

W icker

I EXHALE a thick plume of vapor, lounging back. "Fuck, I missed this."

Pace is a couple feet away, fingers tapping away at a keyboard. "You missed watching me hack into the Palace's feed?" he asks, and even though I'm behind him, sprawled out on the bed, he still reaches back at the exact moment I pass the dab pen. "You would. Without me around, you and Lex practically live in the stone age."

I'm lost for a moment in the fog of what just happened. Lex and I are on a wavelength that's different from the one me and Pace share, and *that*.

That's what I really missed.

"I can navigate my way through Father's servers," I insist, kicking out a foot. "I meant the weed. Lex hasn't so much as touched a cup of coffee since..." I bite back the words, already seeing the tension in Pace's shoulders. We both know what I mean, though. Lex got hooked on Viper Scratch after Pace got sent away, which was bad.

But when Pace got out, Lex had to stop.

Cold turkey.

Honestly, I'm not sure which was worse.

The silence settles with a heaviness that I try to ignore as the THC takes hold, dragging me further into the mattress.

But Pace's room is never silent for long.

"*Who's a dirty bird?*" There's a long trill, and then, "*Suck my balls.*"

Pace sighs, long and beleaguered. "Thanks for teaching her that, fuckface."

Laughing, I watch his bird–an overly excitable, inky mynah–pluck a key from his keyboard before running victoriously up the length of the desktop with it. She's been eyeing that key-cap all night. He doesn't bother to stop her from flinging it off the edge, singing out, "*Who's a dirty bird?*"

"Yeah, yeah," he mutters, pulling another key-cap from the drawer beside it and clicking it on. I don't need to ask what she took. Effie has been taking the same key off his keyboard since he got her, back in middle school. It's how she got her name.

F12.

The two of them are practically inseparable. I think Pace's prison stint was harder on her than anyone else. Lex and I took care of her while Pace was away, but she never really stuck to either of us. The day he came home, she got so worked up that she bit the fuck out of anyone who tried to re-cage her.

Brightly, she sings, "*Suck my balls. Suck my fuck. Wicker. Wicker. Suck.*"

I cringe at the way my name sounds when she says it, the 'r' never quite right.

It sounds like 'wicked'.

Huffing, Pace brings up an image on the monitor closest to her. It's the view from the highway sky cam. "Perch somewhere and settle down, you dirty-mouthed bitch."

She flaps a wing when she sees the monitor, giving another long trill. But never one to let the last word go, Effie gives one last, "*Suck my balls.*"

I crack the fuck *up.*

Pace's room in the PNZ townhouse we share is a lot like mine and Lex's with its dark, oversized furniture and a wall of built-in bookshelves. Similar trophies and awards line the wall–hockey mostly, although when Pace went to lockup, mine changed to lacrosse and Lex quit sports entirely. The ones up on Pace's shelves are dusty, just another reminder of how different things are now. The other difference in our rooms, aside from the large bird cage, is the elaborate bank of monitors against the back wall. There are a variety of computer towers stuffed beneath the desktop, their internal fans whirring away. It's always hot in here, and I feel it now, tugging at my collar.

Pace still hasn't resumed his typing, hitting the vape pen again. "Good thing you waited for me. Last time we trusted you to hook up, we spent six days smoking Mr. Rosenstein's glaucoma prescription."

I extend my middle finger. "Fuck you. Mrs. Rosenstein was really generous to give that to me, considering she didn't get a piece of my gold-plated dick." The woman in question was a forty-something ex-dancer. In her prime, she thought marrying a rich geezer was a fast and easy way to a fat life insurance payout. Unfortunately for her, Mr. Rosenstein became Forsyth's longest living citizen. His decrepit ass is probably running off nothing but pure spite.

Gotta respect that.

Pace turns his head, his dark eyes narrowing. "He still making you do all that?" I know without asking exactly which *he* Pace is talking about.

"Only sometimes," I answer.

Pace knows I'm lying. He *always* knows. "I bet the Lords would pay you better," he says, and the touch of derision in his voice isn't meant for me, but it still makes my buzz turn sour. "South Side knows how to treat their whores."

"Please," I scoff, knitting my fingers behind my head. "I'm the best paid whore in Forsyth." It's not usually sex. Sometimes this town's female–occasionally male–elite require an escort to public events, and honestly, who better? I'm young, athletic, well-connected, and leagues hotter than anyone else in this town. "If Father needs me to dress up every now and then to be someone's arm candy, then that's what I do." I give Pace a meaningful look. "Clearly you're not above it."

Pace is dressed in a full tux. He grimaces without even looking away from the monitor. "Fucking dog and pony show."

A quick glance down at my own tux brings it all back to me, and I laugh. "Oh, shit. That's why I came in here. I need a tie."

Right.

Shit to do.

Pace passes the vape pen back, coughing. "What, you don't have one?"

"Not a bowtie," I explain, taking another hit. "I lost it at the Christmas party at the country club."

"How?" He never looks away from the screen. "Or is it better I don't know?"

I grin, blowing my vape cloud into the back of his head. "Miranda Weller is a screamer. Shoved it in her mouth to keep her quiet."

A screamer *and* fucking flexible. Had her bent halfway over the back staircase to the upstairs ballroom. Of course, Miranda wasn't who I'd come with. My job for the night was to play escort to a recently divorced ex-congresswoman. Something about making her ex jealous.

Bet it worked, too.

But what can I say? Something about having a woman on my arm–no matter her age or beauty–makes the others want me even more. Hence, my fucking Miranda over a banister.

Pace jerks his head toward the back wall. "Top drawer. I think."

Struggling to my feet, I walk over to the dresser and open the drawer. All I see are socks, so I push them aside, revealing a stash of worn, wrinkled porn magazines. I pull one out. The date on the cover is faded but I can just barely make it out: 1968. Flipping it open, I see that it's all bush and full, natural tits. Yeah, there's a reason to go old school.

Pace glances over. "Hands off, pervert. Other drawer."

I snort. "*I'm* the pervert. Who keeps skin mags nowadays, anyway? Just use the internet like the rest of us, you fucking grandpa."

"Vintage porn is better," he mutters, only halfway paying attention. "It's not like I was getting broadband in lockup."

I pause, giving him a closer look. The vintage porn isn't the only holdover from Pace's eighteen months in prison. He's quieter than he used to be. Deathly still. Sophomore year, he was bouncing off the goddamn walls at the prospect of getting out for a night, chasing some tail, and getting wasted. He's been back for two months, and aside from the bullshit process of re-enrolling him into Forsyth's comp-sci program, he's only been out once, which was for my bout at the Duke's Friday Night Fury.

All he does is sit behind those screens—usually in the dark—and talk to his bitch of a bird.

He hasn't even made an effort to get any pussy.

Looking into the mirror over the dresser, I pop the stiff collar of my shirt and loop the tie around my neck. Even in the dim gloom Pace keeps his room in, my tux looks awesome. It's the darkest of blues, only noticeable when the light hits it right.

The three of us weren't raised in Ashby's house until we were teenagers, but it'd been a crash course after that. Cotillion, etiquette lessons, tutors, long, boring cocktail parties followed by tedious dinners. There was a time Pace did it better than us, the superior brother. *Poised*, all the older ladies would say, which was doublespeak for 'cute and facilitating'.

Now, he's got dark circles around his eyes, the curve of his shoulders heavy and defeated.

Sighing, I begin, "Pace..."

But I'm interrupted. "Are you two ready?" Lex asks, sticking his head in the room.

"Almost." I pull the ends of the tie, but they slip through. "Dammit."

"You seriously haven't figured out how to do that yet?" Glaring, Lex steps in looking like he stepped out of a catalog. A crease appears in his forehead as he looks around the dark room. "Have you considered–oh, I don't know–turning on a fucking light so you can see it?"

"I'm working on it." I make another attempt, but it's as lame as the last. While I struggle, Lex stops by the bedside table and turns on a lamp, then another by the dresser.

"Hey!" Pace barks, frowning at the light. "Screen glare, motherfucker!"

"Turn around," he tells me, ignoring our brother. When I don't move fast enough, he grabs my shoulders and spins me toward him, always happy to manhandle anything that isn't going his way. He picks up the limp tie and levels the ends, but pauses, tugging down my collar. "What's this from? A girl?"

"No." I wince when he touches my throat, the cut still raw and tender. "It's from the job last night. He still alive?"

Lex looks unhappy about the scratch, but he prods at the edges with a clinical precision. "Yes, he's alive. That *is* my job."

"That's a shame," I reply, remembering the burning hatred in his eyes when the switchblade swiped my flesh. "That little bitch is lucky I didn't stick him harder."

Still caught up on the wound, Lex asks, "Did you even disinfect this? And why isn't Effie in her cage yet? I swear to god, you two are hopeless."

"I see you got your hair under control." I eye the knot it's been pulled into at the top of his head, wondering not for the first time why he doesn't just cut it. He only ever lets it down when he's sleeping, and it's a bitch to tame in the mornings. Every time I bring it up, he just gestures to my own hair, which I dedicate a solid thirty minutes each day to perfecting.

Fair.

He grunts at me, then cinches the knot, yanking the edges tight.

I inhale sharply. "Jesus, be careful! That's not the kind of choking I had in mind for tonight."

Ignoring me, Lex looks down at my tux, his mouth tensing. "And what's with the blue suit? Father's not going to like it."

Our father has a strict, black-only tuxedo rule for these things. He likes his functions to be perfectly uniform, everyone matching, like a little collection of figurines. But... "Bitches like me in blue. It brings out my eyes." I know what they want and I'm happy to give it to them.

Lex frowns disapprovingly. "Tonight isn't about you, Wick."

I brush a speck of lint off Lex's lapel. His suit is, of course, the blackest of blacks. Always toeing Daddy's line. I snort when he jerks away from my touch. "It's fine. Father should be too occupied with announcing his new set of cuckold Princes and picking his next heifer to care what color I'm wearing."

Lex jabs a finger at me, turning to approach Effie. "Don't call her that."

"What? That's what she is. A prized cow specifically for breeding." I check myself out in the mirror. I look good. Fantastic even.

"She's a vessel and a symbol," Lex agrees, coaxing the bird to jump to his arm. "And if anyone hears you say that, there'll be hell to pay."

"I can occasionally keep my thoughts to myself, you know." I turn my face, inspecting my jaw line for any missed patches of stubble. Pristine, as always. "I feel more sorry for the poor bastards Father ends up choosing to rail her. All those fucking rules about... well. *Fucking.*"

I'll admit there's some sour grapes between me and every new set of Princes, but it's not because I want to be one. Sure, the position comes with a lot of perks, especially if the chick gets knocked up. 'Set for life' is what they call it. But even if I did want it, as with most things in our lives, the odds are decidedly not in our favor.

Lex is too old, about to graduate in five months, and then he'll head straight into the medical program here at Forsyth. Pace, as a convicted felon, is definitely not up to the standards our father has for appointed positions. And me? Well, I've been his prized cow since high school. Taking me off the market is a net negative for us both. There's absolutely no chance I'm narrowing down my options to one pussy for the next year just to be straddled with a baby and responsibilities, no matter how good the perks may be.

"Fucking shouldn't have rules," I decide, fiddling with my hair in the mirror.

The thought of being a Prince repels me, but watching Father butt-pat three stuck-up, Royal morons for a year repels me even harder. They're mostly all the same, each set eager to remind us that adopted or not, in the eyes of Forsyth, all three of us are bastard mutts who lack any Royal blood. Pace entered the system the moment he was born, Lex's parents weren't even from Forsyth, and mine...

Well.

My blood might be Royal, but aside from my brothers and Father himself, no one knows. Even if they did, being the descendant of the Barons' highest Royal lineage would just make me even *less* accepted in East End.

We were raised on these ideals: bloodlines, legacy, heirs, paternity, building up the Kingdom, all of it hammered home by our adoptive father, the current heirless King. And every lesson ended on the same note.

Our job isn't to be Royal.

It's to serve the ones who are.

Hearing the tone of my voice, Lex stiffens, pinning me with a hard look. "Wicker, can you please behave, just for tonight? This is a big deal. He expects us to be on our best behavior." His jaw tenses as he puts Effie into her cage, closing it up tight. "*I need* you on your best fucking behavior."

I roll my eyes. "We do this every year, Lex. It's a *party*. We're talking champagne, wine, molly, women in sexy dresses cosplaying as chaste virgins, and best of all?" I reach out to adjust his bowtie, smirking. "Losers. Eleven of them, all sad and desperate, gagging at the chance to taste some Prince cock, and we're the silver medal, brother. Next best thing."

"So much for having a gold-plated dick," Pace mutters.

Gesturing to Pace, I say, "Plus, we need to get our baby brother laid, or else he's going straight-up Unabomber. He hasn't gotten any in almost two years–"

"Fuck you, Wick," Pace doesn't even turn around to offer his weak protest. "I just got head the other day."

"*Suck my balls*," Effie screeches, pecking at the cage door.

I point out, "You got blown six weeks ago, after my fight, by a girl who didn't even look happy about it." Shaking my head, I tell Lex, "Come on, it's his first party since–"

Lex slams his fist down on the dresser, making the mirror rattle. "Goddamn it, Wick! Aren't you listening?" The ensuing silence is heavy. Pace's back is rigid with tension, and even Effie goes quiet. Lex fumes, "It's our first real appearance together since Pace got sent to fucking prison, and the two of you are in here getting stoned!" Just as quickly as it came, the anger plummets from his expression. His shoulders shift in a careful, awkward way, as if the weight of his tux is painful. Quieter, he asks, "Do you want him to give me another appointment?"

"No," I answer instantly, startled at the implication. "What kind of fucking question is that?"

"An honest one," Lex replies, glancing at Pace, who's so motionless, he could be a statue. Lex sighs, "Pace. You know I don't blame you. I'm just saying... let's not flirt with disaster."

Raising my palms, I relent, "Fine. I'll be a good boy until the clock strikes midnight. You have my word."

"Everything should be over by then," he agrees, seeming mildly appeased. "At least for us."

He's right. Once they anoint the new Princes and Princess, they'll go off to their private ceremony and the rest of us will be cut free. Cue all the sad, rejected hot girls.

Lex steps into the middle of the room. Things have been weird between them since Pace got back. I keep waiting for the *click*, just like earlier when Pace took the vape pen without even needing to look. It's a rhythm between us. A synchronicity. They've been off-tempo and it makes my temples throb.

"Has Father talked to you yet?" Lex asks.

Pace just shakes his head. "Not one word."

Lex takes this in slowly, as if he's rolling it around in his head. "That could be a good thing."

"Could be," Pace agrees, tapping on the keyboard. "But we're smarter than that."

Lex and I share a look. Pace is plugged into that thing twenty-four-seven. It's been worse since he got home, as if he's living life *through* the monitors. The campus is on one screen. On another, the Avenue. Another screen shows an infrared shot of the Palace's gates.

Jittering nervously, Lex says, "Come on, Pace. Father wants us at the Purple Palace by seven."

Pace leans closer to the screen, raising a hand. "Hold up, things are getting good."

Annoyed, Lex starts toward the set-up with the obvious intention of shutting it off, but as he gets closer, he stops short.

"What..." He runs his hand through his hair, loosening the product. "Oh. *Oh.* Damn."

Curious, I walk over. The monitor they're looking at is split into four separate video feeds—each showing a female in various stages of dressing. The footage is in black and white, the camera mounted at a perfect height to catch their cleavage in high-definition.

"Are those the girls?" I ask, already feeling the horny tickle in my balls. "Father rigged their dressing room?"

"Yep. One on every mirror." Pace taps a few buttons and the camera zooms in a little, giving a better view of one girl as she threads her feet through her panties. She loses her balance, twisting around and flashing her plump ass at the hidden camera. My fingers twitch, craving the feel of all that flesh in my hands. It's been at least forty hours. My blood is humming with the itch.

Pace watches with heavy eyes. "Nice selection, don't you think?"

I shoot Lex a grin over Pace's head, surprised to see my brother return it.

Twenty months without sex.

Yeah, baby bro is thirsty as fuck.

Leaning closer, I shrug. "Well, you know Father Dearest. Only the finest specimens for his collection." My eyes jump from screen to screen. "I just wonder which one is the best."

"Or genetically superior," Lex adds. "Something extraordinary."

"Something fun to play with," Pace adds, wetting his lips.

Laughing, I tell Lex, "Guess we better call our dibs."

The three of us grow still as we watch these women squeeze themselves into tight corsets and sheer panties. They're all different shapes, sizes, skin tones. My gaze is drawn to a pretty, dark-skinned number with massive tits. "Fuck, I want to bury my face in those."

"Mmhmm," one of the guys agrees. I'm too distracted to figure out which one.

"What about her?" Pace asks, gesturing to the top screen. She's got ink on her lower ribcage. "You think Dad changed his rules?"

"Doubtful," Lex says, frowning as his eyes flick to Pace's forearm. Only a few months into lockup, he managed to get some ink. Lex has never been a fan of tattoos, but Pace's especially.

He has tally marks of each day he spent in lockup.

"Father probably owed someone a favor," Lex muses, paying that one no further mind. He'd never openly admit it, but I know what his weird appreciation for our house's Princesses is all about. Lex likes his girls all prim and coy, blushing and curvaceous, busty and soft.

Someone ripe to take a man's fat load and do something with it.

Pace hums in agreement, while my eyes dart from one screen to another as they come in and out of view.

Lex snorts. "Poor girls, so excited. I almost feel bad for them."

"They have no fucking idea what they're about to get into," Pace adds. His hand falls to his lap, and he shifts his cock. "In four hours, one of them will sign their life away."

"Yeah, they get no sympathy from me," I say, noticing a new face emerge in the bottom left screen. "They're just like all the other bitches in this town. Greedy gold-diggers, selling their body for the hope of experiencing the spoiled, lavish lifestyle of a Princess. They know what they're doing." I rest my hands on the back of Pace's chair, trying to get a better look. The black and white video makes it impossible to confirm much about her features, like hair color. It's not dark like the girl with the big tits, or the glaring white of some of the platinum blondes. Her face is cast down, but there's something familiar about her.

"Okay, time's up." Lex says, taking a step back. "We need to get going."

Pace moves to shut off the monitors, but I grab his shoulder. "Wait."

The girl I've been watching shrugs out of her robe revealing a perfect, tight body. My limbs grow heavy as I watch her dress. First putting on a pair of those sexy panties, then the corset. When she reaches for the dress, I get a good look at her face and it hits me. "Red."

Pace notices at the same time I do. It's the *click* again, the feel of him tensing, the knowledge that his eyes are boring into her like lasers. I can practically hear his tongue running along the sharp edge of his teeth as the tendons in his wrist flex.

I know what he's going to say before he even opens his mouth.

"This one." Pace flicks the screen and rises from his seat. "This one is mine."

3

 erity

I'VE NEVER BEEN in a house with its own ballroom, but the Purple Palace is rumored to be as close to a castle as anyone will find in a town like Forsyth. Everything is ornate, dipped in gold or draped in crystal. The ceilings are high, held up by round, Roman columns, and painted like a pale blue sky.

I can't help but imagine the Dukes in here, like bulls in a china shop. They'd destroy it in a heartbeat.

My eyes can't settle on any one thing. From the finely painted, antique ceilings to the chandeliers, the marble floors and the candelabras, it's a while before my gaze even begins taking in the crowd.

Everyone in this room looks just like the tapestries on the walls. Decorations.

A waiter passes, and I clumsily snag a glass of champagne from his tray—mostly to give my hands something to do. The dress hangs heavy and uncomfortable, the stays of the corset digging sharply into my ribs. The mask is secured behind my head and covers the majority of my face, curving over the bridge of my nose, leaving my mouth and eyes clear. Although it's foolish, it makes me feel bold, as if no one knows who I am or where I'm from. Like maybe, only for tonight, I can be just another one of the potential Princesses.

And the thing is, it works. Whenever someone passes me, I can feel them looking, their eyes taking me in curiously, wondering if it'll be me.

Easing back against the wall, I take a moment to observe them. There are eleven other girls in the running for Princess, but there are plenty of other women too. Some of their dresses are shimmery and metallic, but others are just a flat orange-yellow. Most seem older, maybe even past Princesses, and I realize they're probably following an unspoken rule. The other candidates and I are in a pristine white, but every other woman is wearing gold.

Men outnumber us two-to-one. They're all dressed in tuxedos, faces covered with the same basic black mask. It causes them to merge into one indistinct, shadowy blur.

Across the room, even in her mask, I recognize Lakshmi. She's standing near a column, hand demurely toying at the neckline of her dress, eyelashes batting up at the man speaking to her. His forearm is pressed against the column and he leans into her–leers really, eyes zeroed in on her chest. He lifts his chin, giving me a better look at his face, the cut of his sharp jaw, and I'm struck with recognition. There are handsome men all over Forsyth, but none carry themselves with the same level of arrogance as golden-haired Whitaker Ashby.

I recoil at the memory of the night he cornered me after his win at Friday Night Fury. The wild intensity in his eyes. I couldn't name it at the time, not when Nick and Lavinia stopped whatever he had planned to come next, but now I recognize that look for what it is; a dark mixture of anguished want.

No man had ever looked at me like that before.

The strains of a violin fill the room, the orchestra in the corner beginning a new song. A few men use this as a cue to ask women to dance. I watch curiously as a few decline, probably because they don't know the mechanics of the waltz. I swallow the rest of my drink, the dry fizz burning the back of my throat, and look for a place to leave my empty glass.

"I'll take that."

Startled, I almost drop the glass, looking up to find a man. A tall, lean, but somehow still imposing man. His skin is pale, but other than the way his auburn hair is pulled up into a tidy knot, he looks like every other man here. His eyes are amber, lips turning up in a half smile that feels neither natural nor forced. *Practiced.*

I hand him the glass. "Thank you."

"Of course." He offers me his other hand, eyes dipping downward to my chest for the briefest of moments. "Would you like to dance?"

Wringing my hands, the urge to run is fierce. Every step into this situation seems closer to something I can't come back from. But I came with a purpose, so I square my shoulders and look him in the eye. "That'd be nice, thank you."

When he extends his palm, I only give it a brief glance before sliding my hand into it. I almost flinch again when I do, because his hand is cold.

Freezing.

Trying to hide my shiver, I follow him onto the marble dance floor, watching as he coolly drops the champagne flute off on a passing waiter's tray. He moves with both a tight precision and a fluid ease, and it hypnotizes me. The men at DKS are large and athletic, made of hard muscle and sharp reflexes. They're physically intimidating because of how they're built.

This man is physically intimidating because of how he moves.

Finding a vacancy in the whirling crowd, he turns to me, posture perfect as he places a hand on my waist. When I meet his gaze, there are no words. No instruction. No giggles or awkward laughter. With a bland expression, my partner falls into the music, his feet adeptly leading me in the steps of a traditional waltz.

It takes every ounce of my concentration to keep up with him. Maybe that's why the first comment I choose to make is so unbelievably stupid. "You know how to dance."

The dullness of his eyes suggests he wasn't expecting anything else. "Yes, I know how to dance." He spins me and my body follows, already knowing the moves. "So do you."

Trying to salvage a thread of dignity, I explain, "My mother forced me into lessons as a child." Another preparation for Royal life. A Duchess should be ready for anything. Wouldn't want to embarrass my Dukes at an official Royal function, would I?

"As did mine." His shoulders remain straight and poised, cold fingers gripping mine. "Well, my father."

It's almost impossible to form a complex thought, my mind battling to keep rhythm. I resolve to try, though. "Is this your first Royal masquerade?"

"No." He answers, voice blandly polite. "It's my twelfth."

It's the tone of the response just as much as his bored, wandering eyes that gives me the realization. "You hate them."

His gaze snaps to mine. "No, I don't."

"Yes, you do," I argue, grinning. "You'd rather be anywhere else."

"So would you." His eyes flash, and at first I'm not sure why. Then he spins me, hard and fast, making my head rattle with the snap of it. His next words are like venomous silk in my ear. "But then you'd be missing out on the opportunity to become Forsyth's next pampered whore." When he leans back, the song flutters to an end, and his smile is hard and empty. "I guess we all make sacrifices."

He steps back, bowing.

And then he's gone.

I stare after him in shock, my stomach twisting at yet another glimpse of ugliness in this beautiful place. All around me, people are smiling beneath their masks, and I wonder how many of those masks are figurative, plastered on to hide derision and jealousy. To think West End is looked down on by these people, even though we're *real*. We don't hide. We don't wear masks. We look our enemies in the eye when we wound them.

Flustered, I scurry off the dance floor, desperate for one morsel of something authentic and clear.

I find it out on the balcony.

The wind is frigid, cutting against my face as I look out over the Palace grounds. It's just as breathtaking as the house itself, the garden to the south still striking even in the dead of winter. I gulp in the air greedily, stomach churning at the man's words.

Being a Princess is Forsyth's highest honor. Everyone knows it. It's the Royal position girls want most of all. Princess first, Lady second, Countess third, Baroness fourth, and Duchess...

No one wants to be Duchess except West Enders.

Maybe that's what makes it so different. We don't have to compete like banshees. We just have to be...

Loyal.

The thought makes my stomach churn with guilt.

I walk along the railing, into a darkened corner, pushing further away from the music and dancing, attempting to compose myself. I'm doing the right thing, I tell myself. I belong here as much as any of those other girls.

"Shouldn't you be inside with the rest of the chattel?"

My eyes snap behind me to where a man is lounging on a marble bench. The first thing I notice is how long his legs are, magnified by the dark lines of his tuxedo. They're sprawled out in front of him. His hands and face are partially obscured by the shadows but I can make out his hair, twisted into fine, loose twists that frame his face. That, and the tone of his skin—a deep, trans-fixing brown.

"Jesus," I gasp, hand rising to my chest. "You scared me." I try to temper my alarm with a light laugh, but it's creaky. That's another thing about DKS. They're loud. You always know when you're not alone.

This guy is a barely visible shadow.

"Did I?" he asks, his subtle shift audible in the rustled fabric of his suit. His voice is deep, the rumble of it settling uneasily in my gut. "You know, my father hasn't spoken to me in almost two years–not since they took me away."

I frown. "Your father?"

The man sighs in a quiet, casual way. "But he loves to send a discreet message, that's more his style."

"I don't know what you're talking about." I take a step forward, narrowing my eyes to get a better look. "Do I... know you?"

"Parts of me," he replies. At this distance, I see his elbow moving slowly, and I squint, trying to make out what he's stroking. "But it's been a while. You've been in school. Living life. Being free. You've probably forgotten all about the guy you stole that from." Before I can argue that he has me confused with someone else– maybe he's drunk–he tips forward. "Haven't you, *Rosilocks*?"

I stiffen at the name, his voice like ice against my neck. "You're..." The guy on the dating app. The video of him masturbating. *Videos*, plural, the later ones showing him holding a photo of me, spilling his thick, ropey seed on my face.

Later on, Laura and Haley would laugh about it in the dressing room with me. "They're called tributes, sweetie," they said in that fond way of theirs, as if I was so naive and young, and they found it adorable. But before that came the panic and the disgust, and me turning everything over to the campus police. That was almost two years ago, and I never heard a word about it again.

"You're that... that *pervert*." It's all I can manage to say past my heart being lodged in my throat.

He replies, "And you're the uptight bitch who didn't know how to take a compliment." His right leg falls to the side, another rustle of fabric the only sound between us. "You see, Rosilocks, my father is the master manipulator. Setting up people like pieces on his chessboard is a sport for him. All this time, I thought I was being punished." After a pause, "Well, I am. But the minute I saw that you were one of the prospective Princesses, I knew he'd been waiting to make his move–to get me back in the game."

I slide back, too confused with his words to question the movement of his arm. "W-what are you talking about?"

And then he stands, making it all too clear.

His pants are unbuttoned, fly down, his thick cock gripped in his large hand.

The tip is gleaming and wet.

My belly drops and I spring for the door, but just as quickly as the instinct arrives, his body is there, swift and tall–so fucking tall that it's practically nothing for him to block my escape, herding me back.

His voice comes low and venomous, eyes two narrow blots of shadow. "I've thought about this night for two years, Rosilocks. Imagining you out there, living it up while I was locked away, rotting in a cell. Do you know what it's like to hear grown men–men bigger and scarier than me–crying for their mothers at night? Do you know how fucking bleak that is?" He bears down on me like a storm, his fist sliding up and down his shaft.

The motion isn't all that unlike watching a Duke load their weapon.

He gives a soft, dark laugh. "Of course you don't. The jewel of West End cunts, all safe and sound in her fortified gutter, wouldn't know the first thing about the consequences of her own fucking actions."

I avert my eyes, face twisting. "I don't know what the hell you're talking about!"

His free hand reaches out, fingers snagging the curve of my neckline. With a quick downward yank, he exposes my breast, the back of his knuckles rolling over my nipple as he struggles against my protest. "You might not remember, but I do. All I did for a year and a half was remember. Your face. Your lips. The way your cheeks looked with my cum dripping down them." A shudder rolls through him, and when I plant my palms on his shoulder, shoving frantically, his fingers move from my breast to my neck, pulling me into him with an iron grip.

"What's wrong with you?" I ask, anger now warring with fear. "I-I reported you, but I didn't–nothing happened!"

He leans forward, hips pinning me to the railing of the balcony. "Everything happened," he growls into my ear. His hand jerks, dragging up and down my dress. The ring he's wearing snags on the beads. "You fucked up my life. You ruined *everything*. Now, I'm going to get a little taste of what I paid for, and you're going to–" Whatever he means to say gets lost in a strangled grunt, the cords in his neck visible. His grip on my neck tightens, teeth gnashing as he hisses, "*Fuck*, yes."

He rears back, head bowed as he squeezes his cock in one hand and my neck in the other, as if he's forcing me to look down–to watch. I gape as it surges in his palm, spurting milky ropes of cum onto my white dress. I'm so stunned by it that I forget to keep pushing, my palms flat but inert against the warmth of his chest.

I gasp in a hard lungful of chilled air when his grip loosens, the man's shoulders sagging. There's a moment of horrific stillness, and then he gives a soft, disappointed sigh, tucking his cock back into his trousers.

"Should have been your face, but best behavior and all that." His black eyes reflect the glittering lights of Forsyth when he looks up, catching a lock of my hair between two slender fingers. "If I were you, Rosilocks," he says, leaning in to whisper, "I'd think twice about reporting me again. A guy like me with Royal connections? Let's just say I made a lot of useful contacts in prison." To anyone else, it might look like he's flirting. A roguish Romeo to my Juliet, twirling my hair as he gazes deep into my eyes. But I feel the quiet, creeping menace in his words as his lips brush against the shell of my ear. "Next time, I won't be so generous."

He's gone just as quickly as he came, stepping into the light as he zips his pants. It's then that I see his face for the first time. Pace Ashby. One of Ashby's sons.

He's gone before I can react, reattaching his mask, and striding back into the party. I look down at my dress, the splotch of semen darker than the rest of the white. A glob sits just above where the crinoline flares out. I try to shake it out but it's too thick and with a frantic grimace, I wipe it off.

The cool, sticky pool clings to my fingers, and I fight a wave of nausea.

My only thought is singular and focused: I've got to get out of here.

I need to get back home. Lavinia will understand. There has to be another way.

A chime comes from inside the house, followed by a smooth, commanding voice. "Good evening, everyone." Ashby's amplified voice carries to the balcony. "It's time for the announcement of our Princes and Princess."

Panicking, I dart back into the ballroom, noticing the other eleven girls already lining up. I fix my bodice as I join them, stumbling in my heels in my urgency. I notice the heads turning to watch as I scurry forward, whispered insults drifting to my ears, but when I reach the line of girls, I just exhale and pretend as though I belong.

The man in front of us looks different than I'm used to. I've never seen Ashby, their King, in anything else but his pristine white suits. Tonight, he's in an all black tuxedo. Collar, shirt cuffs, even his socks are black. It looks more like an outfit suited for the Baron King than him.

Ashby doesn't even look at me as he addresses the room, his graying blond hair shining in the light of the chandelier. "Some are of the mind that tonight is a solemn occasion. A Royal masquerade twice in one year can only mean one thing." He raises a finger, his beady eyes passing over the crowd. "Failure."

I shudder at the glint in his eyes. For all Ashby is known for being prim and proper, right now he looks sharp with malice, his eyes absorbing the darkness.

It falls away as he lifts his glass. "But that's behind us! Tonight isn't about failure. On the contrary–a second masquerade is actually about renewal. The renewal of promises. The renewal of legacy. The renewal of pride." His pause is dramatic and loaded, and the people all around me read it for what it's meant to be.

They all begin clapping.

Ashby smiles indulgently. "And pride is exactly what I feel tonight. Our house is the strongest in Forsyth, and for too long I've been unable to fill it with my name. My dear son..." This pause isn't like the other one. It's not intentional, nor meant to be filled with cheers. This one is Ashby's throat tightening with a swallow, his eyes filling with grief as he stares down into his glass of champagne. "My dear son, Michael, who we lost all too soon, would have led this house with such power and grace." I can feel the anger in his words. The bitterness. He visibly struggles to shake it off. "But since tonight is about renewal, that's what I intend to do. Renew my pride in the Ashby name."

"No fucking way."

The whisper comes from behind me, low and full of stunned dread, but when I twist to find who said it, all I see are the wide, amber eyes of the man who danced with me before.

"This is why I'm particularly excited to announce our three new Princes," Ashby continues, regaining his picture-perfect composure. Gesturing to the crowd, he lets loose a wide, beaming smile. "My sons, Whitaker, Pace, and Lagan Ashby."

There's a long, bewildered silence from everyone, but it's not long before we begin turning to find them.

The first to drop his mask is the man behind me–amber eyes belonging to none other than Lagan–Lex–Ashby. He's staring up at his father with a stupefied expression, mask clenched tight in a fist.

The next is the devil himself, Whitaker, who throws his mask off to reveal a furious, incredulous stare.

Lastly is Pace, the weight of his stained semen still dragging at my skirt. He's over by the orchestra when he lifts a slow, heavy hand to the mask covering his face, plucking it off with such dispassion that I get the impression he's not exactly happy about the news, either.

I gape at each of them, completely baffled.

The three adopted sons of Ashby aren't blood. They aren't *Royal*. They aren't even leaders. They're just random kids Ashby spent a few years playing house with. All I've heard since arriving is how my blood isn't good enough. My parents aren't prominent enough. My lineage isn't established enough.

But when it comes to the men...

The room erupts into a cheer that's stilted at first, but quickly grows exuberant and celebratory. These people have no issue accepting three 'bastard' men to lead their house.

The hurt is unexpected, but the shame isn't. Suddenly, I know just why I was invited to this charade. It really was a joke, all along. A game, like Pace said–machinations by his father. People of East End are seeing exactly what blood means: Nothing–not if you're already rich and connected to the elite. But for people like me, the lack of it is all that matters.

For the first time, I let myself acknowledge the pang of disappointment. A part of me, hidden deep inside, had been hoping that maybe Lavinia taking the role of Duchess didn't close the door on my potential to be Royal. Hoping I'd been picked because someone finally saw something special in me.

Hoping I was good enough.

The new Princes meet in the middle of the room–some strides more willing than others–before joining Ashby at the forefront. Lex stands awkwardly stiff, while at his side, Pace ducks his head, glaring daggers into the toes of his shiny shoes.

Whitaker looks murderous.

I'm so caught up in the injustice–the secret, scandalous disappointment of knowing I've let the Queens down–that I forget Ashby still has another announcement to make.

"Princess isn't a title that just any mere woman can wield," he's saying, ignoring his sons. "It's a crown in and of itself. A mark of a strong, unique, powerful woman. To be chosen as Princess means that you, my lovely girls, are the best of the best. This is not a decision I make lightly." His dark eyes pass over all of us, turning serious. "Our next Princess will also be one of renewal, as the girl I've chosen tonight has something the rest of you don't." He lifts a hand, listing off, "Class. Poise. Strength. Chastity. *Fire*."

It's the fourth word that causes a chorus of frightened exhales to my left and right.

Chastity.

I can feel the semen on my dress like a physical burn.

"You're all beauties," Ashby assures, sending us a superior grin. "But the fact is, only one of you is fit to sit on our throne tonight. So without further ado," he motions at the orchestra, "please join me in welcoming your next Royal Princess."

The violins begin swelling, and to my left, one of the girls–Gina–blindly grabs my hand, squeezing hard as she gapes up at the King.

And, robustly, he announces, "Verity Sinclaire!"

Well, clearly I've gone crazy. Auditory hallucinations? I should really ask Sy about that tomorrow.

If it weren't for the way everyone looks around, expectant and stunned, I might even go on believing that. Through the rising volume of cellos and clarinets, the realization grips me like a fist around my lungs.

Beside me, Gina turns, regarding me with slack-faced awe. "It's you. You're the Princess."

Me?

It's me.

All I can wonder is if they see the stain on my dress.

It takes a long time until I can get my limbs to work, frozen so stiff that my joints begin aching. With rusty joints, I lift my hand to remove my mask, looking around me at the shocked faces and confused stares.

It doesn't happen all at once.

The first one to clap is an older man lingering at the front, his hands a blur as he frantically applauds. "Welcome home, Princess!" he cheers, and beside him, another man does the same, their mouths pulling into wide, exuberant grins.

The second round of cheers comes from the rest of the men, glasses raised jubilantly into the air. "Welcome home!" they all echo. "Our Princess!"

It's only then that the confetti happens.

I'm not expecting it, even though it seems everyone else has a pocket of the stuff. Glittery gold is shot into the air, only to rain down on me, the rest of the attendees joining in the celebration.

And the thing is...

None of them look *mad*.

All that injustice and anger I felt when the Princes had been announced is absent in all of their faces. One by one, their masks fall off, and they're simply...

Smiling.

That must be why I smile back, laughing as another shower of golden confetti hits me. All around me, people are clapping, cheering, and when I'm swept up by two of the burlier PNZ members and hoisted on their shoulders, my squeal isn't even born of panic.

I'm *flying*.

Hands reach out to touch me as the men carry me to the front, whooping loudly, and all I can do is reach back, grazing their fingers with my own. As I look down into their adoring eyes, I suddenly understand everything.

I get what it's like to be Royal.

To be special.

To be wanted.

I'm so drunk on it, full to the brim of astonished joy, that it's easy–*so easy*–to forget what it all means.

Until I'm carried straight through the doors.

As soon as the doors close behind us, the cheers are gone.

I'm panting with exertion, still perched on the shoulders of two masked men as they walk me down a corridor, and it's a shamefully long length of time before I hear the footfalls behind us. Twisting my neck, I see them.

Pace, Lex, Whitaker.

And Ashby.

Their eyes are all fixed straight ahead, none of them deigning to award me with a glance as I'm taken to a large set of wooden doors. Once there, one of the PNZ members performs some sort of intricate knock. After it swings open, the men ducking to carry me through, I regret not memorizing it.

I regret not remembering why I'm here.

The room is dark, only it also isn't. Tall candelabras illuminate an enormous parlor, revealing several rows of chairs, but there's no other light. More disconcerting is the fact the seats are all filled. Maskless PNZ fraternity brothers sit straight-backed in each, as if they've been waiting. These are young men, I can tell by the set of their shoulders and jaws. Some probably thought they'd be chosen tonight, yet here they are: observers.

Coming from the rowdy celebration of the ballroom to this dark, muted eeriness startles me. The tension creeps in like ice running through my veins, but before I can break the silence to ask what's happening, the men bend, placing me smoothly on my feet.

I hug my middle, feeling chilled in the hush of the room. "What–what now?"

"Now," one of the two PNZ members, young enough to have pimples scattered across his exposed forehead, says, "you take off your panties."

I jolt, stepping away from them. "I *what*?!"

"For the throne," Ashby says, standing back to gesture to the front of the room.

It's only now that I see it. The throne is enormous. There are flowers carved into the wood–delicate but stately roses–but also real ones, draped all around it. White roses are arranged around the arms and back, filling the room with wafts of sickly floral sweetness. The throne is gilded, the gold bearing an aged patina. Not knowing what that has to do with taking off my fucking panties, I begin, "But why do I–"

And then I see something rising from the seat of the throne.

It's blatantly phallic, about five inches tall, and gleaming in the candlelight.

I snap my gaze around, finally landing on Lex, who's perfectly expressionless as he explains, "It's to break your hymen."

Casually, Pace adds, "So none of us have to compete. For the *honor*." The word is said with such derision that it makes me wince.

One of the PNZ members who carried me in gives the seat an excited pat. "This throne has broken in every Princess since the very first. Sitting on it is a privilege almost no one gets."

I give a slow, dazed nod. "A privilege."

Crazy.

This is fucking crazy.

I've been keeping my virginity intact for a Royal since the day I learned it existed, so it's not the fact of it that makes my stomach turn.

It's the coldness of it.

A Duke would never let some horrifying, antique, golden dildo 'break in' his Duchess. He'd fight for it. He'd touch her. He might not make love to her, but he'd damn sure *feel* her.

He'd *win* her.

"Princess," Ashby says in his lilting voice. "By walking through our gates tonight, you agreed to follow our traditions." The tone suggests his patience is already wearing thin, and I gulp, looking around me. There must be well over forty men here–not a woman in sight–and they're all at least twice my size. I could try to run, but would they let me go?

And do I want to?

The answer is obvious enough. As much fun as it'd been to be hoisted into the air and celebrated for a couple minutes, the last thing I want to do is give myself up to the likes of Ashby and his wayward sons. Whitaker has tried to assault me, Pace is a perverted creep who already fucking has, and Lex? I don't even want to know.

Princes are supposed to be sweet and doting, handsome and charismatic, indulgent and adoring. When I agreed to this, that's what I pictured. A Princess and her devoted Princes. Not three of the worst men in Forsyth.

But even then, it was a lie I made to myself.

Because I'm not here to become a Princess. I never was.

I'm here to become a Monarch.

Clenching my jaw, I gather up my skirts, fishing through the crinoline and silk to find the bare skin of my thighs. My hand lands in a wet spot, but there's no time to recoil. Working upward, I grab the edge of my panties and drag them down, face heating at the feel of eyes on me, watching, waiting. When I've stepped out of them, I clutch the panties in a tight fist, body already trembling with adrenaline.

"This way," Lex says, his voice lacking any of the charming politeness I'd heard earlier on the dance floor. This version of him is strung taut, his cold hands like manacles as he leads me to the throne, ordering, "Sit."

He and Pace stand on each side of the throne, while a hard-faced Whitaker stands behind it, not meeting my worried gaze.

Dragging in a long, shaky breath, I turn to the room, seeing the faces of PNZ. Each man is watchful, all of them dressed in black tuxedos of their own, but some are looking more eager than others.

Some are fucking smiling.

I tell myself it's not a big deal as I lift my skirts, glancing behind me to judge the distance. My virginity was always meant for something like this. I never had a chance to get attached to a perfect, romantic first-time experience. I tell myself it's worth it if it means being able to call Story and Lavinia tonight, a victor with all my spoils.

Somehow, I did it. I'm in. When this weird ceremony is over, I'll be an East Ender behind the pretty, secure walls.

Except when I look up again, Ashby stands in front of me, his gaze as reverent as his voice. "Verity Sinclaire, tonight embarks your journey as the vessel for the next great heir. Any woman can have a womb, but yours has been chosen." He steps forward and presses a hand to my stomach. "Blessed."

It takes everything in me to not physically flinch.

"Pierce your body, dear girl," he whispers, eyes flashing with an intensity that frightens me. "Spill your blood, and agree to the covenants of this honor."

Feeling movement behind me, I turn, finding a man draped in a black cloak. It's the man from the ballroom, I realize–the first one to clap for me. He's holding a small golden vial, the mouth tipped into his palm. I watch as he dips his finger inside, then uses it to rub the tip of the phallus in a thin coat of oil. He looks to Ashby, nodding as his deep voice says, "It's been anointed."

"Very good," Ashby commands. "Sit, Verity."

I bend my knees, reluctantly lowering myself toward the seat. I feel the tip of the... *thing*... graze my backside, hard and cold, so I readjust, grasping the arms of the throne to pull myself further back. My face screws up into a grimace as I shimmy, getting it into position.

The moment the tip settles against my entrance, I take a long, steeling breath, eyes sliding closed.

And people thought the Barons were weird...

I'm so preoccupied with hyping myself up to the fact this is actually happening, preparing myself to just *take it*, that I barely feel the gentle weight of two hands settling on each of my shoulders.

If I thought they were there to soothe my anxiety, then I'm the biggest fool in Forsyth.

Because they *shove*.

White-hot agony rips through me as I meet the seat, eyes flying wide. The ensuing scream is feral, clawing wetly from my throat as I fight against the grip. Whitaker's hands clamp down hard, forcing me flush with the throne. My skin tears, the device ripping through me, cold and foreign and excruciatingly invasive. I reach up to frantically pry his hands away, but Pace and Lex each take one of my own, pinning them to the arms of the chair.

The thorns of the roses stab into my wrists.

"Stop!" I cry, struggling against their holds. "It hurts, stop!"

Whitaker just presses harder, fingertips digging into me.

I kick out, but that just makes it worse, all my weight driving me down. I plant both feet on the floor, feeling the heel of my shoe snap as I buck, trying desperately to get away from the piercing *hurt* of it.

Hot tears instantly fill my eyes, brimming over with my shrieks of torment. Every second I'm on it scorches through me like a searing, hot poker. It's an urgency I've never felt before–the all-consuming instinct to *get away*.

"Breathe, child," comes Ashby's voice, but even though he's right in front of me, crouched down to catch my gaze, I can't see him.

All I see are stars.

"Let me go," I sob. "It hurts, it *hurts*–please! Please, I'll do anything." It smarts to know I'm begging, but I can't feel the shame of it. The only thing I can feel is the fire between my legs.

"The longer you fight, the longer it'll take," comes a voice at my side. *Lex.* "Relax, Princess." He sounds calm, assured, and I use that to take a deep breath and force myself to calm down–to get through this.

It takes a Herculean effort to still my body, to ignore the throb as I pry my eyes open to meet Ashby's gaze.

He's doubled over, and I don't understand why at first. He seems to be doing something beneath the throne, and when he snaps back, he's holding a small glass vial up to the candlelight, scrutinizing the red inside of it.

Ashby's mouth tips up into a soft grin. "We were right," he tells the cloaked man. "Look how much she's bled. The Princess arrives to us pure of body." Bile rushes toward my throat as I realize what he's holding.

My blood.

Blood from the *thing* invading my body.

He hands the other man the vial, standing as it's poured into an antique inkwell. "Now, you must come to us pure of spirit," Ashby says, retrieving a sheaf of papers from a nearby table.

"Is it over yet?" I gasp. Sweat is beading up on my brow, but I fight to remain still. The more I move, the more it hurts. "Can I get up now?"

"Very nearly," Ashby replies, placing the stack of papers in my lap. "All that's left is for you to sign the covenant."

I sob, fingers curling into tight fists as I look down. The stack of paper is thick, the first page bearing mine and the Princes' names. It shudders from my shaking legs. "I-I can't r-read it."

Ashby commands, "Pace, Lex, let her hands free. Our Princess needs to read the contract. After she's done, we'll let her up." He gives me a smile that's as sickly sweet as the roses crushed beneath my arms. "Take *all* the time you need, Verity."

My face goes slack in horror.

There must be a hundred pages.

Hot, defeated tears track down my cheeks as I try, reaching down with a trembling hand to uncover the second page of the covenant. The black ink blurs through my tears and I blink them away, heart twisting as I realize it's impossible. No one could remain in this much agony for the length of time it'd take to fully comprehend what I'm agreeing to.

As if to solidify this point, Pace's hand joins Whitaker's on my shoulders, *pushing*.

I cry out, slamming my fist into the arm of the chair. "Stop!"

Ashby forces something into my palm, saying, "You can make it stop, Princess. All we need is your signature on the last page. It'll be your explicit agreement to abide by everything within."

When the black spots have cleared my vision, I'm left panting and exhausted, clawing my fingers around the fountain pen. "Where?" I gasp impatiently, body quaking. "Tell me where!"

Smoothly, he extracts the last page from my lap, laying it on top. "Well, right here, of course."

When the inkwell filled with my blood appears in front of me, I can't even think about it. There's no space in my body–my mind–for anything except pain and the desperation to rid myself of it.

I dip the metal tip of the pen into the inkwell and fling my hand toward the paper, messily scrawling my name across the line. There's no time to really consider what I've just signed away. I lift the pen, watching through watery eyes as a drop of blood falls from the tip, landing on my white dress.

The stain blooms out like a crimson flower.

Ashby collects the papers, beaming. "Congratulations. All done."

The hands on my shoulders leave, only to wedge themselves beneath each arm, wrenching me upward and off the device.

The absence of the intrusion is almost worse. My vision swims as I fling myself away, tumbling gracelessly to the floor in front of the throne. Ashby steps back, but all I can see are the toes of his shoes, as polished as black mirrors.

"Exceptional," he breathes, and though I can't find the strength to look up, I can still feel Ashby's eyes on me as I curl into a ball, hands wedged between my thighs. "Not many women could withstand being throned as well as you have. Such an effort is worthy of reward. I'll make sure my sons understand that."

Fuck your reward, I want to say, pressing hot, humiliated tears into my knees.

But I don't.

I lay there and try to feel grateful that the worst of it is over.

And then Ashby says, "Fetch me the knife, would you, Danner?" and I'm clutched with panic as my eyes snap up, watching the new Princes move to the front of the throne.

Luckily, the next hurt isn't meant for me.

One by one, they prick their forefingers, squeezing the blood into the same inkwell that holds mine. The only break in the solemn hush of the room is when Whitaker pauses, the edge of the knife centimeters from his flesh.

His blue eyes jump up to Ashby's. "Father," he starts, the line of his shoulders tense. And then quieter, downright pleading, he adds a strained, *"Dad."* The room grows thick with an uncomfortable silence, and I get the sense this is as close to begging as Whitaker has ever come.

Ashby's eyes flare angrily. "Is something about this confusing to you? It shouldn't be. You've borne witness to several ceremonies. You prick the finger and sign your name." When Whitaker just stands there, frozen and edgy, Ashby sighs, glancing at his other son. "Lex, what are you doing Friday?"

Whitaker lurches forward, barking, "No!" At the expectant curve of Ashby's brow, Whitaker sucks in a sharp breath, nostrils flaring wide as he finally presses the blade to his finger. "I'll do it," he says through clenched teeth.

Watching them sign the covenant makes me want to vomit.

A prick of their finger.

That's all.

There's no crying or pain. Aside from one word and a long look, there's no begging. No *torture*. There's just the long line of their backs as they curve over the table, signing their names below mine.

When it's all done, Ashby gathers up the sheaf of paper, tucking it beneath an arm. "You have three months," he tells them. Not one of his sons meets his gaze. "I trust none of you will disappoint me. And Wicker," he adds, already heading for the door, "tonight is your responsibility."

Whitaker's head snaps up, forehead puckered. "Tonight? But I was going to–" His words clip off at his father's stare.

"Oh, I know what you were going to do. However..." Ashby stops, hand poised over the knob, and gives his son a visible once-over. His next words make my stomach drop. It's the PNZ motto. The prayer of their house, just as much as West End has its victors and spoils–just as much as the Lords keep what's theirs. "To create," he says, "is to reign."

Whitaker fists the fountain pen like it's a dagger–like he'd really prefer to bury it into someone's throat.

Ashby seems nonplussed about it. "Oh, and keep it clean, son. Wouldn't want to stain such a fine blue suit, would you?" With a chilly grin, his father strides from the room, closing the door behind him.

Whitaker's distant gaze takes in the audience, all the PNZ members still waiting. That should be my second clue for what's going to happen next. The sting between my legs, deep inside, still throbs, but I fight to read the situation. Whitaker's blue eyes lock on mine, filling with a fury that makes me press my thighs together harder. I might not know what's next, but one thing becomes very clear.

I'm going to like it even less than he does.

"Get up," he sneers, marching over to where I'm laying, fetal on the floor.

I shake my head, still quivering with the aftershocks of pain. "I can't," I lie.

Violence fills his eyes. I'd know it anywhere. I see it in the DKS boys every day, but somehow it's more frightening on someone as composed as Whitaker.

"Get her up," he growls.

Before I can even think to flinch back, Lex and Pace move toward us, each of them grabbing my arms and hauling me up. The instinct is to fight–to struggle and scream and kick–but I don't. I let them drag me toward the table between us and the audience, limp and anxious.

I've made it this far.

I can make it just a little farther.

That's the idea, at least. To persevere. To endure. To get through it and come out the other side, because this is just one night.

One horrible night.

And then in a hard, icy voice, Whitaker commands, "Show me her cunt."

I do fight then, gasping as I try to wrench my arms from their grip. "Wait, you can't–"

"Yes, he can," Pace hisses into my ear, palm planted into the middle of my back. Ruthlessly, he shoves me down, my chest pressed to the table. "You signed the covenant. You agreed to this."

Lex explains, "They need to see," and when my panicked eyes find him, he nods to the room–to the other men. "We need to prove that one of us has claimed you." A sharp, bitter smile appears. "We signed the covenant, too. We agreed to this."

My body goes slack as comprehension dawns. These three don't want this. I'm not sure how, and I have no fucking idea why, but some part of me is suddenly very sure that these guys are being just as forced into this as I am.

Lex and Pace begin lifting my skirts, shoving handfuls of the fine dress fabric up around my waist, and when the cold air brushes against my backside, I know I'm exposed to them.

My Princes.

There's a short pause, Whitaker's harsh breaths audible from behind me, but when I begin hearing the telltale sounds of him unfastening his pants, I stiffen.

"Hold her," he says, and their grips tighten.

"Don't," I plead, forcing my body to go lax, eyes sliding shut. "I won't–I won't fight."

After a moment of what's probably quite heavy suspicion, Lex and Pace let me go. "Of course you won't." Lex's scoff drips with contempt. "I guess even West End girls give up the fight for the right price."

Whitaker says, "Spread her," and Pace's palm pushes into my ass cheek while Lex takes the other. Roughly, they spread me open for their brother.

"Just make it quick," Pace says. "We've got a long night ahead of us, Wick."

Whitaker grunts, and when I twist to look, he's got his cock out, hand stroking angrily at the shaft. I snap forward when his gaze meets mine, but that's not much better. Some of the PNZ guys in the audience are cupping their own crotches.

I groan, low and miserable as I feel Whitaker coming forward, snugging the head of his cock up against my abused entrance. I hold my breath, muscles seizing in anticipation of more hurt, and that's exactly what I get.

He slams forward just as his hand grips a tight fistful of my hair.

I bury my cry into my own forearm, tasting blood as Whitaker fucks into me, fast and thoughtless. It's nothing like I thought sex would be. There's no kissing. No touching. There's no shared heat or the bloom of lust quickening my way to orgasm.

It's hard and painful and so cold that I'd reach out to any of the forty men in the room to save me, if I thought any of them would care.

I can't see Whitaker behind me, but I can feel him—the anger rolling off of him in waves. His grip is bruising on my hip as he fucks me, these little punches of breath punctuating each thrust. There's a moment where I try to get away from the intrusion, inching closer and closer to the table.

But he follows me.

Any space I gain is punished with a sharp growl and a harder thrust, his hips crashing against mine, until eventually, there's no more room to run with. The edge of the table digs into my pelvis as he pins me to it, banging me into the wood.

The pain isn't even the worst part.

It's the sight of the other men—the PNZ men—sitting there and watching, feeling pleasure from the tears that race down my cheeks. The worst part is knowing that anything could happen to me in this room and they'd all go along with it.

I try not to look. To close my eyes and drift away. To pretend I'm back in West End, drinking with the cutsluts on top of the gym. To imagine the streets spread out before us like limbs, beckoning us home.

In the end, it could be two minutes or all damn night before Whitaker finally comes. His punches of breath turn to grunts, wild and tight, until eventually he slams into me one last time, pushing hard and deep as his cock swells.

He bends to hiss into my ear, "Take your reward, *Princess*," and then I feel it. He pulses thick inside, filling me with his cum, and it *stings*. God, it stings like fire—like salt in a wound—and I bite my lip to avoid giving him the satisfaction of a yelp.

He shoves me forward more than he pulls away, slipping from my center with a wetness I'm afraid to think of. "Danner," he says, breathing hard. "Take the Princess to her bed."

Draped over the table like a defeated, broken thing, Pace and Lex don't even bother lowering my skirts. Conversation starts around the room, the entertainment apparently over, and slowly they filter back out the main doors to the ball still going on outside.

When they're gone, I push to my elbows and use one hand to shove down the netting and crinoline, the other to lift myself off the table.

"Goddamn fucking son of a–" an earsplitting crash follows. Looking back, I see a tall candelabra tipped over on the floor, candles snapped in pieces.

"Fuck!" Wicker shouts, fist punching into the wall. "He fucking did this just to–" His words fade out as Pace pushes him through a back door. Lex stops to pick up the piece of metal, attempting to put it back in place. It wobbles, just like my legs, unsteady and mangled. Another victim of Whitaker Ashby's rage.

I stare as Lex follows his brothers out the door until I notice a figure next to me. Dark eyes peer out at me from behind the mask. Danner. He gives me a slight bow, and juts out the crook of his arm. "Princess, allow me to escort you to your rooms."

I make the final push upright, and a searing burn rips through my lower body. Lifting my chin, I smooth my dress, fingers running over the drying red spot from the ink pen, and link my arm with Danner's.

Remember who your King is.

Lavinia's words give me strength not because of Sy, but because of where I come from.

I'm from West End.

I'm a fighter.

As Danner leads me from the room, I pretend Whitaker Ashby's 'reward' isn't dripping down my leg, along with blood, sweat, and the last remaining shreds of my dignity.

4

V erity

SLEEP DOESN'T COME.

I want it to, but every time I close my eyes, I see a sea of faceless men in their dark tuxedos, feeling the pain of the throne all over again. I relive the feeling of heavy hands on my shoulders and wrapped around my wrists. I feel that *thing* tearing inside of me.

I feel the sticky warm heat of Whitaker's cum.

So instead, I stare up at the ceiling from the massive bed, counting the crystals hanging from the chandelier overhead. Yes, there's a chandelier over the bed, and giant, gilded columns framing the four corners. The fabric is both soft and itchy–golden thread woven through purple silk. The room is cavernous, ridiculous, and completely on brand with these lunatics.

I absorb the sounds of my room, the sigh of the bedsprings when I move, the wind rattling the doors to my balcony, a faucet dripping in the bathroom. I memorize the texture of the air, cold and crisp and somehow old. I let my thoughts gallop toward anything that isn't the memory of the ceremony, and sometimes those thoughts gallop right off this island and back to the Dukes.

Because I can always run back home.

Eventually, the soft glow of dawn appears through the windows.

A pang in my lower belly forces me to roll to the side. Across the room, the dress–the Velma Kang twenty-thousand dollar dress–hangs on a floor-to-ceiling mirror like a hovering ghost. In the pale morning light, I can see how the bodice is bunched, twisted from where Pace grabbed me on the balcony. The semen is dry now, invisible to the eye, but I know it's there, just like how I know the reason the hem is frayed and the skirt is a wrinkled mess isn't from a night of dancing and fun. Each tear, each bit of damage, tells a story, but none more so than the dark red spot just below the waistline. My blood. Blood used to sign away my life. In the dead-still quiet of my rooms, the words of the covenant come swimming back: *the Princess will serve & obey her Prince, she will sever all other Royal ties, she'll treat her body as a temple...*

These were the only parts I could bring myself to read before admitting defeat, and that's exactly what it was. A loss. No victor, no spoils. Just me, caving the moment things got too rough. It smarts to accept how much I've underestimated the Princes' depravity. A better woman–a *Royal* woman–would have come prepared for something that vicious. She wouldn't have fallen for the shiny facade, the veil of golden glitter.

Just as the sun begins to rise, there comes a knock on my door.

I jolt upright in panic, my wide eyes fixed to the knob. I'd locked it the night before, fully aware that nothing can keep these men out if they truly want in. I'm not foolish enough to think that. But after having everything stripped away, I needed some kind of barrier between myself and them.

A second knock comes, this time louder.

I find my voice, calling out, "Just a minute!" Scrambling to the edge of the bed, I wince with each movement, a sharp pain radiating outward from my vagina. Easing my legs over the side of the mattress is a feat in and of itself, not just because of the pain, but the enormity of the bed, and it takes a moment for me to work up the courage to stand.

When I do, my whimper emerges low and pained. It's a different sort of hurt from the night before, as if the sting has had time to settle into my flesh, making itself a home there. The throb is deep and dull as I pad carefully across the room, just short of a waddle.

I press my ear to the door. "Who is it?"

"It's Stella!" replies an obnoxiously chipper voice. She says her name like it's an intro to her own sitcom. The exclamation point is an audible thing. "I'm your handmaiden."

My face scrunches. "Handmaiden?" *What the fuck.*

"I'm here to help you get ready," she clarifies.

I give the door a dubious stare. "Er, thank you," my hand twists in the cotton of the nightgown that had been laid out for me on the bed when I got to the room the night before, "but I can do it myself."

There's a pause, and then, "But... Princess, it's my job to assist you."

My perplexed stare shifts to a glower as I turn the lock, easing it open just a crack. I flinch back at the sight that greets me.

Stella is right up against the crack, face snapping into a wide, beaming grin as she stumbles back. "Oh! There you are! Gosh, you really are pretty." She's short and petite, maybe even younger than I am, but she feels as big as a fucking h-bomb, posture straight and vibrating with energy. "Everyone said so, but you know, it's East End. No one would ever call a Princess anything less than stunning." Dark, almond-shaped eyes smile back at me just as much as her thin lips, and the pair of glasses perched on the bridge of her nose doesn't lessen the effect. "But here you stand like a ray of light! I'll just pop right in and get you started."

"Look," I try, taking a deep breath. "I really don't need help getting ready, so you don't need to bother yourself."

Stella's happy expression plummets. "Oh." Her long black hair is plaited into a loose braid that hangs over her shoulder. She twirls it around her hand as she casts her eyes away, shoulders drooping. "Okay then. I guess I'll just find something to keep me busy. King Ashby doesn't like idle people. Maybe there's something I can clean, or someone else I can..." she swallows loudly, "... serve."

The implication makes my stomach turn, and before I know it, I'm swinging the door open. "*Ugh*, fine, just–"

Stella prances past me, her miserable expression immediately exploding into a sunny grin. "Wow, look at your room–it's *gorgeous*! And freaking huge!"

I turn, taking it in for the first time in the daylight. It is gorgeous. And huge. I knew that from the sheer size of the bed and the chandelier but, really, it's extraordinary.

And I'd rather be anywhere else.

In the daylight, the columns are so thick they look like they must be holding up the ceiling–a ceiling, I realize, that is made of marble. Just like the floor. The bed sits on a platform and the entire wall behind it is a tufted, thick cushion, framed in an intricate golden design. In the center, just over the middle of the bed, is an inlaid design of metalwork and jewels. A crown.

At the foot of the bed is a long bench, the fabric a deep purple velvet. Sconces the size of floor lamps hang on either side of the bed.

I've heard of this bed–or gossip that I thought was perhaps an urban legend. The Crown Bed. The Princes and Princess may change, but the bed remains.

This, I know, is where I'm meant to be bred.

"It's west-facing, too," the girl says, babbling along. "Do you think that's a coincidence? I doubt anything here is a coincidence. Oh," she gasps, pressing her face to the window. "You can see the clock tower from here! Isn't that neat?"

I gape in her zipping wake, feeling the distinct suspicion I've just been played like a goddamn fiddle. "I hadn't noticed," I mutter, using the back of a settee to help guide me back to the bed.

Stella bounds up the platform and reaches for the comforter,

"This bed is enormous. Look at all those pillows! You could suffo-cate under there. I bet it's for your Princes, too. They must be–" Her enthusiasm slams into silence as she freezes, arms suspended in the air where she was gathering up the bedding.

What she inevitably sees–what I see–is the bloody stain on the pristine white sheets. My hand drops between my legs, and I feel the crusty, dried spot on the crotch of my panties.

"Shit."

Her gaping mouth snaps shut. "Well, it could be worse, I guess." She tosses me a grin that's a touch more subdued. "I'll start you a bath."

"That's not..." but my argument fades out. My vagina feels like it was assaulted by a battering ram. My insides feel even worse. A bath is probably the *only* necessary thing. Following her across the room, we enter the bathroom, and I concede that I don't really have another choice. This is my life now.

As she begins running the water, she babbles on, "Wow, a real clawfoot tub! These fixtures are probably older than my nan. Do you think that's real gold? Are you still bleeding much? Whoa, look at this mirror."

I get whiplash just watching her zip around the room, my head beginning to throb with exhaustion. "Say, uh... Stella? I'm going to assume you've had some coffee." There's no way that much energy is natural. "Is there possibly... any left? In Forsyth? Or earth?"

She whirls around to nod, very urgently. "Oh, yes. I'll take you right down to breakfast once we've got you all fixed up. But I don't think they'd let you have any coffee. Maybe some orange juice, though?"

My face falls. "What? Why?"

She pushes the bridge of her glasses up her nose, a flash of something apologetic in her eyes. "Well, it wouldn't be good for the baby, of course. It's a part of the covenant."

My stomach churns. "Oh. Right."

The water runs furiously into the big tub. There's also a shower, a large vanity, and dressing table area. The toilet, as I discovered last night, is cloistered away in a closet near the back. The floors are marble, the walls papered in a soft lavender flower pattern. Another elegant chandelier hangs over the bathtub.

It strikes me then. This is the trade-off. A servant and the fanciest bathroom in Forsyth; this is what you get for signing those papers. It sits heavily in my gut as she pulls something out of the cabinet, digging inside with a large scoop. Humming a peppy tune, Stella pours a cup of white powder into the tub.

"What's that?" I ask, watching it dissolve in the steaming water.

"Epsom salt," she answers, looking a little proud. "It should ease some of the pain and any swelling. It's very natural."

I shift uncomfortably. The sound of salt, *down there*, seems like a terrible idea. "Oh."

She grabs a series of bottles next, pouring more and more things into the water. The fragrance is floral and delicate, and soon enough the water begins churning into a fluffy foam. Methodically, Stella places more bottles on the edge of the tub. Shampoo. Soap. Body wash. A loofah. A razor.

Glancing at me, she makes an eager gesture. "Well, go on! Go ahead and undress. Get in here while it's hot and comfy."

I realize I'm still clutching the nightgown, knuckles white from my grip. The last thing I want to do is change in front of this stranger, but she makes no move to leave, fixing me with another one of those toothy grins. Turning, I lift the dress, and then far more carefully, work my panties over my hips, down my legs.

Both the nightgown and the panties are stained an ugly brown.

I ball them up frantically, as if they're crime scene evidence.

"Don't worry about those," Stella insists. "Just leave them on the chair, if you want. I'm a pro at getting blood out of linens–you have no idea." This is punctuated with a chipper laugh, like she's remembering something funny.

Taking a deep breath, I turn, covering my breasts with my arm. She seems unaware of my self-consciousness, though. Her eyes fall to my waist, her mouth forming a surprised little 'o'. Confused, I follow her gaze, finding dark bruises blooming from hip to hip, the result of Whitaker slamming me into the edge of the table over and over. There's also the matter of my forearms, which bear small scabbing cuts, vivid and angry against my pale skin. It's a while before I remember how they even happened.

The rose thorns.

"Wow," Stella chirps, beaming at me. "That's messed up."

My cheeks burn and I propel myself into the water, ignoring the stinging burn on my skin in an attempt to hide beneath the suds. "Jesus," I hiss, biting down on my bottom lip. *God*, it burns–the heat and the salt awakening all the sting that'd settled overnight.

"It always has to get a little worse before it gets better," Stella says, still flitting around the bathroom. "That's what my sister says, and she's really smart. A total boss babe! And a *legit* boss babe too, not the kind of boss babe that's a capitalistic farce engineered from a faceless corporation that's hoping a single mother will shell out twenty bucks for a coffee mug to feel the thin veneer of independence it gives her. Here, take these." She barely catches her breath, holding out a glass of water and five pills. "Two of them are painkillers, and the rest are prenatal. Weird combination! The Princes really want you to be healthy, though. It'll take a few days for you to heal."

I don't tell her that I don't have a few days to heal, just swallow the pills with a gulp of water. She exits the room and I exhale, allowing my eyes to flutter shut. I'm so tired. The last twenty-four hours was an exhausting whirlwind that I feel bone and muscle deep, and Stella's frantically positive energy is draining what little I have left.

The scrape of the chair across the marble floors snaps my eyes open.

"I'm going to wash your hair now," Stella brightly announces.

I give a tight grin. "Kill me."

She grins back. "Can you sit up?"

Sagging in defeat, I relent, using the edge of the tub to pull myself upright. To my surprise, the experience isn't the worst. Stella pours water over my hair, humming all the while, and when she lathers it up, her fingers massaging my scalp, my face slackens in ecstasy.

Afraid I might actually drift off, I clear my throat and struggle to keep alert. "How long have you been a handmaiden?"

She hums pensively, rinsing the suds from my hair. "About five hours."

Blinking the water from my lashes, my brow furrows. "You mean–"

"I was hired to be *your* handmaid, specifically," she confirms, working her fingers through my hair. "I doubt it was anything like your audition, but I had to compete with a few other girls. Gosh, were you lucky you got me! This one girl had super bad breath, and another kept knocking things over."

Another dump of water. I sputter, water getting in my mouth. "Isn't the term handmaiden a little antiquated?"

She leans in, scrubbing my hair with strong, firm fingers, but I hear her muse, "Isn't everything in Forsyth?" She places a hand on top of my head. "Hold your breath."

I'm dunked, fully submerged and when I come back up, she's pouring clean water over my head again. "So is everything like this in East End, or is it just... here?" Walking into the Purple Palace is as close as I've ever come to entering an entirely different world.

"I wouldn't know." She wrings my hair, reaching over my shoulder to grab a bottle of conditioner. "I get the sense that the position of handmaiden isn't a very sought-after gig in East End. Most of the candidates came from the other corners."

"*Really.*" This is intriguing news, although I suppose it makes sense. The women of East End probably wouldn't dare lower their ambitions to become a mere servant. "So where are you–"

"South," is all she says, standing to grab a towel. For someone as obnoxiously chatty as Stella, the ensuing silence is conspicuous, drawing my eyes to hers. Water drips down my forehead, and our eyes meet for a second, but I catch it. A flicker of something before she turns away. "Dry off and I'll get your clothes ready." She checks her watch, face paling at what she sees. "You need to be downstairs and ready for breakfast in thirty-minutes, and we still need to get you dressed!"

"I'm not hungry."

The smile she gives me is tense and too bright. "It's not a request, Princess."

There's a heaviness to her words—a warning.

The Princess shall wear the wardrobe provided to her.

I step out of the tub and dry off, thankful for the privacy when she flits out into what appears to be a closet. I use the opportunity to cautiously tuck a hand between my legs, fingers brushing over my sore entrance. I'm so relieved when they come away without blood that I almost don't hear her quick feet growing closer.

"Here we are," she announces, holding a pale pink dress aloft. The shoulders are tiny poofed caps, with a scooped neckline and an empire waist. It looks like something out of an old TV show from the 1950s. "Pretty, right?"

"Those aren't mine," I say, as though that's not already obvious. "I had a bag. It was in the room where we prepared for the ball."

She gives a quick, understanding nod. "Oh, that. It's all been returned to your home. This outfit, along with the rest in the closet, have been picked out for you by the King himself."

Not my Princes. The King.

The distinction about who I'm here to serve is clear, and a chill runs up my spine with the realization. I keep further thoughts to myself as I dress in the prim, pink dress, and have my hair and makeup attended to by Stella. I ask nothing when she hands me a thick pad to put in my underwear—there to absorb any remaining blood. Her chatter becomes background noise, and once I grow aware that she's not expecting any replies, I begin to find it oddly soothing. Back home, I'm used to the noise of rowdy boys and catty girls, but here in the Palace, everything feels unbearably hushed.

Still, I don't let myself forget who chose this girl to pamper me. I'm starting to understand now that beneath every luxury lurks something terrible. Stella seems nice, if obnoxiously sprightly. But she's still a part of this machine.

"How do I look?" I tiredly ask, smoothing the dress down my thighs. It's flattering, I'll admit that. It makes my waist look tiny and my tits look perky. It's a far cry from the leather and lace of the cutsluts, and I'm hit with yet another certainty that I don't belong in it.

"You look like a Princess," she says, opening the door and marching right through it. For someone from South Side, she has no reservations about traversing the Palace like it's home. Given no other choice, I follow her down the wide hall, past closed doors, and walls adorned with oil paintings of past PNZ Royalty. My instinct is to observe my surroundings, but Stella's stride is too fast and I struggle to keep up, wincing with every step down the staircase.

I'll have to wait for another opportunity to scope the place out.

When we reach the first floor, I'm struck by a wave of unsteadiness. Some of it's the ache between my legs, the distance between my rooms and the dining room practically a football field. But a lot of it is the sudden swell of nerves about facing the men.

A lot of it is fear.

I press a hand to the wall, breathing in short, panicked bursts, and for a moment, I don't hear anything at all.

There's a soft sigh, and then Stella rests a gentle hand on my hip, her voice uncharacteristically quiet. "I know last night must have been really hard, but the best thing to do—the *only* thing to do—is to put on a good face and get through it." When I turn, she's giving me yet another smile. This one, however, radiates a sympathy I'm not expecting. "One step at a time. We'll make it through, because that's what we do."

The words themselves are generic and trite, but the look in her eyes when she says them...

I suspect Stella knows a thing or two about needing to push through pain.

Taking a deep breath, I nod. I can show good behavior at the breakfast table. Sure, I grew up around the chaos of Family Dinner, but I'd been trained for this. Today is the time to put all those lessons into action.

MY BACK ACHES from how stiffly I'm sitting in my chair, eyes fixed to the box sitting in front of me. It's big enough to cover the whole plate it's resting on, wrapped with a golden bow.

"Go on," Ashby says from the head of the table. It's startling to see the King sitting there–plate full, cup of coffee in one hand, the New York Times in the other. Even though his gesture is politely encouraging, I take it for the demand that it is.

The King has filled his plate, but the Princes, I'm told, can't eat before their Princess does.

Pace is glaring daggers at his empty plate.

With an unsteady hand, I reach out, gently plucking the end of the bow. Everyone in Forsyth talks about the Princess getting all her gifts. How they're elaborate and expensive, indulgent and amazing. The cutsluts love to gossip about them on Fridays as they're getting ready for the Fury. With stars in their eyes, they always gush over the jewelry, the cars, the flowers, the bling. Usually, this would be followed by grumpy mutters about the Dukes not favoring material possessions, because romance looks very different to a fighter.

I won't deny being one of the girls who'd daydream. It always seemed so luxurious, thinking of being showered with the Princes' riches. Now that it's actually happening, I look at this ornately wrapped box, and all I feel is numb.

Ashby sips his coffee. "Typically, the Princes would give their Princess something truly exceptional the morning after her throning. Since they didn't have time last night to procure you an appropriate gift, I've taken it upon myself to raid the Royal coffers for something... fitting."

They all watch as I mechanically unwrap it, pulling the top off to reveal a purple velvet box nested inside. My heart sinks, and I don't really understand why–not at first–but when I pull up the top, my stomach churns with dread.

Looking frighteningly pleased with himself, Ashby explains, "That tiara belonged to the very first Princess."

It's gold, with delicate filigree and crystals–maybe even *diamonds*–inset like glitter. The center comes up to a curving point that frames a large purple amethyst gem. Around it are smaller amethysts–three of them–and at the very tip of the center point sits another. The metal combs on the back are weathered with age. Maybe it'd be different if it were something new, but this isn't just any old tiara. This is a *relic*.

I look up into Ashby's eyes. "I can't accept this." *Too much*, my mind is screaming. Something this important comes with a price, and given as this is a priceless object, I don't want to even fucking imagine.

"You can," he says, lifting his coffee to his mouth. "In fact, it's one of the covenants that you *will* accept it. This, and all other gifts."

Strangely, the Princes seem more bothered by the gift than I am, Lex's expression full of stiff confusion. Pace tries to be subtle when he turns his head, eyes rolling, but even if his father doesn't see it, I do. Wicker's face pinches, like he's smelled something off-putting.

"Er... thank you, King Ashby." Slowly, I close the box, but his sharp *ah-ah* makes me freeze.

Eyebrows raised, he orders, "Put it on."

Flustered, I tuck my hands close, not even wanting to touch it. "But... I wouldn't want to break it. It's basically a piece of Forsyth history."

"No," Lex corrects me, his amber eyes blazing. "It's a piece of *East End* history."

Ashby argues, "Pretty things are meant to be worn by pretty girls," and stands. "Allow me."

It takes more restraint than I think myself capable of to not cringe away when Ashby rounds the table, plucking the tiara from its bed of molded silk. It's almost worse when he's behind me, his presence looming above like a distressing shadow.

I remain rigidly still, eyes cast down as he places the tiara on my head. I feel the combs making purchase, the prickly tug on my scalp, and force down a shiver.

It's heavy.

"There," Ashby says, rounding the table to assess me. I muster up the closest approximation to a smile I can, fighting the urge to squirm. "Aren't you a vision?" he simpers, eyes sparkling. When silence follows, his gaze cuts to his sons, voice sharpening. "I said, *isn't she a vision?*"

A chorus of 'yes sirs' follows, each of them unique. Lex's is crisp, while Pace sounds annoyed.

Whitaker mostly sounds bored. "Can we eat now?"

Sighing, Ashby returns to his seat. "You'll have to forgive my sons, Princess. They're terribly untutored in the art of flattery. I've been assured their proficiency will improve." The dispassionate flick of his eyes toward Wicker makes it clear that this assurance wasn't given freely. Ashby gestures to the now empty velvet box. "And with luck, that may be a ring very soon."

His hopeful grin makes me want to heave.

A Princess only receives her ring once she's conceived. I've glimpsed it a couple times on past Princesses, the ring gold and simple, the silhouette shaped much like the tiara on my head. To be given the ring is a ceremony more serious than marriage. It means your fate is sealed–that a woman's life will be inextricably linked to her Princes for eternity.

Apparently losing interest in the show, Ashby flicks a hand. "You may serve yourself now, Verity."

No one looks at me as I stand, setting the box aside and producing my plate. The sideboard is filled with a dozen dishes of breakfast food, and approaching it, I fill my plate with dazed disinterest. A tablespoon of oatmeal, a slice of melon, a scoop of scrambled eggs. I take my seat again without even processing the food in front of me.

My stomach roils at the idea of consuming anything.

The sons go next, lurching from their seats and descending on the spread like vultures. The uncharacteristic lack of manners doesn't seem to bother the King, who sips primly at his coffee, eyes fixed on the paper in front of him.

Lex and Pace return to the table in short order, but Wicker...

He hovers over the sideboard, his blonde hair messier than I'm used to seeing as he glares down at the offerings. "Is there a reason there are no bagels?"

"I can add that to the grocery list, sir." This comes from the old guy I'd seen last night–Danner. He hadn't said one word to me as he led me to my rooms, not bothering to help when I stumbled, tears still tracking down my face. He just stood a careful arm's length away, waiting patiently as I gathered myself.

Now, he's standing by the entrance to the kitchens, so unobtrusive that he could be a part of the golden damask wallpaper. With his hands folded behind his back, the man seems more like a butler than anything. Old, balding, black suit, and apparently in charge of ordering food.

"Wicker will choose from what has been made available to him," Ashby announces, shaking out his paper to a new page. "Stop making a scene."

With tight, angry movements, Wicker scoops a heaping pile of eggs on his plate, shoving two pieces of toast into his mouth at once before returning to the table. His seat is directly across from mine, giving me an involuntary view of his jaw tensing as he scoots his chair up. I get the sense there's an arrangement to the table–that if Ashby had a Queen, she'd be sitting at the seat closest to me, across from her King.

It's just empty.

Lex is next to Wicker, eating his sausage with a surgical precision that lacks any enjoyment. Every stroke of the knife, every fork tine being delicately stabbed into the meat, each shift of his jaw as he chews, feels painstakingly deliberate.

If it weren't for Pace, the whole breakfast might feel like a performance, but the brown-skinned man beside me is shoveling food into his mouth at a dizzying speed. More than that, he's got his arm curled around his plate, as if he's expecting someone to reach over and swipe his slices of bacon. In stark opposition to Lex's tidy meal, Pace doesn't even use a napkin, licking out to catch any wayward crumbs. I hesitate to make any fast movements, almost certain he'd give a possessive snarl.

It makes a wave of homesickness spark in my chest.

He eats like a Duke.

The sound of paper crinkles, and Ashby sets it on the table. "How did you sleep, Princess?"

I flinch, head snapping up. "Fine, thank you." The answer is rapid and automatic, as if my brain recognizes this as the path of least resistance.

"Excellent. An expectant mother should always be well-rested." His eyes survey me, and unsettled by the implication of his words, I look down, picking at my food. "I see you met your handmaiden. I've been assured she's a perfect fit for your specific needs."

Wicker snorts. "He means she's a South Side whore—a Hideaway reject." He takes another bite out of his toast and gives me a cold smirk. "She's experienced in the business of overworked pussies."

Ashby frowns at him in disapproval. "Son, I'm aware that my announcement was unexpected, and things aren't going exactly as you planned, but that doesn't make this kind of language appropriate for the breakfast table."

Wicker's fist curls around his fork. "Sorry, Father. Should we take it elsewhere? The library perhaps? The bowling alley in the basement? Possibly the wine cellar? Oh!" He snaps his fingers. "The graveyard out back."

Lex stiffens next to him. Even Pace drags his eyes from his food. But all Ashby does is fold his paper and meet Wicker's gaze. A low boiling tension bubbles under the surface. Silent conversation jumps around the room, a language I don't understand, but I do get the sense it's dangerous.

"Wick." Lex's quiet, but no less sharp voice cuts through the silence. I watch as Wicker drops his eyes, and I've been around fighters long enough to recognize what's just happened here.

"Sorry, sir," he mutters.

A defeat.

My heart begins hammering before I've even cleared my throat, all my nerves flaring to life as Ashby's attention is drawn to me. "I was wondering..." My voice cracks and I wince. I'd spent all night up in that bed crafting the most diplomatic way of asking, but the request emerges stilted, as if my tongue finds it foreign and unwieldy. I try again, strengthening my voice. "I was wondering if I could get a copy of the covenants. I'd like to... familiarize myself with my responsibilities and Royal obligations."

Ashby holds my gaze for a long moment before sliding his gaze to Pace, who's frozen stiff, somewhere in the middle of dunking his toast into a puddle of red jam. He straightens, an odd cautiousness in his posture. "We were up all night moving," Pace says, glaring at his toast. "I haven't set up her email yet."

I look around the table, realizing now how exhausted the three of them look.

Ashby's only response is a long, disconcerting stare.

Pace drops his fork. "It took a while to get Effie settled down. I didn't even get my computers into the Palace until a couple hours ago," he insists, glancing at his brothers. After a suspended pause, Pace stands, huffing. "I'll do it now."

Anxiety prickles the back of my neck at the fury in his eyes, and I stammer out, "I-it can wait."

But before Pace can answer, the phone beside his plate glows to life, chiming loudly. His expression giving nothing away, Pace swipes it up, tapping at the screen. His eyes harden at whatever he sees there. "There's someone attempting to breach the front gate." His gaze slides to Lex. "I use the word 'breach' very lightly."

"Who is it?" Lex asks, tossing his cloth napkin on the table and pushing his chair out.

Pace's eyes meet mine. "Looks like your feral gutter rats came looking for you."

Startled, I ask, "My... what?" But that can only mean one thing.

The Dukes.

Shit.

The boys all jump up, but I'm frozen as I watch them parade out of the room, their strides strong and worryingly confident. The Dukes, as much as I love them, aren't exactly known for their subtlety and restraint. Even if they have weapons, they're still on someone else's territory.

Double shit.

Looking at me, Ashby dabs his mouth with the napkin, saying, "You may want to get your cubs under control, Princess. There are consequences for this kind of thing, you realize."

"Y-yes, sir," I say, rising as quickly as I can with the limitations of my lower body. Adjusting the tiara, I try to follow the path his sons took, making two wrong turns before I finally find the foyer and front door. Throwing it open, I limp down the driveway, hoping to catch them before there's bloodshed.

My heart leaps as I get closer, seeing the three of them. Sy stands in the middle, shoulders tense, body stiff. One look at the girth of his biceps and you know he could snap a man's neck with one twist. Nick stands beside him, fingers laced through the wrought iron gates above his head. Someone who isn't studied in Nickology would think he looks downright casual, the curve of his body lean and laconic, but I can sense the agitation rolling off him in waves. It doesn't help that the gun tucked into his waistband is conspicuously visible.

Remy is already halfway over the gate.

They're my family—my big brothers–and as much as I know that them showing up here is a terrible, stupid idea, my chest blooms with affectionate warmth at the knowledge they came.

Loyalty.

I only hope they understand that what I'm doing isn't a betrayal.

"Verity!" Remy shouts when he spots me. His body jerks wildly when Pace opens a security box and presses his thumb against the screen, looking annoyed.

"Must be something about West End that makes you people unable to read a map," he snipes.

The gate slides open and Remy jumps off before he gets crushed. As soon as it's open enough to squeeze through, all three march inside without an invitation.

"Verity, what the hell is this?" Sy holds out a phone, showing me the screen. It's a post on social media, announcing the new Royalty. I knew telling them about this would be hard, but now that it's here, I feel sick with guilt.

I wring my hands, grimacing. "Uh, well, you see..."

Nick pushes past him, chin raised as he stares the Princes down. "If this is revenge for what happened with Felix—"

"This was a legitimate process," Lex says, looking just as composed here as he did at the dinner table. "The Princess received an invitation and accepted. But you're right." The smile he gives them is chilling in its sharpness. "We're not even when it comes to Felix. *Yet.*"

"This is bullshit," Remy says, pacing back and forth, his frame long and lithe. "Verity would never agree to anything with you assholes, which means this is a kidnapping."

Wicker laughs, looking deceptively boyish as he struts to my side. "We invite our women to come to our ball. Unlike the rest of you animals, there's no kidnapping, trafficking, or bartering in our process. They have the free will to accept or not." He tosses an arm over my shoulders, jarring me. "Miss Sinclaire accepted our invitation." I feel his cold gaze when he looks at me, lifting his free hand to sweep an obscene caress down my breast. "Didn't you, Princess?"

The weight of his arm on my shoulders brings it all back to me. The force of his grip as he pushed me down on that phallus. The way he drove me into the table. The stinging heat of his semen as it filled me. A wave of nausea rolls over me, and I'm unable to answer.

I know from the flare of white-hot fury in their eyes that this is going to be bad.

"Get your fucking hands off of her," Sy demands, voice low and deadly.

But Nick's the one who breaks frame first. His face twists into something murderous at the accusation of kidnapping. The truth about how he won Lavinia is widely known, just as much as how hard she resisted it. "That stupid polo shirt you're wearing is going to look so much better when it's stained with your own goddamn blood." Sy gets his hands on his brother before he lunges at Wicker. "You think you're better than me?"

Wicker shrugs. "Obviously. That's not really in question here."

Nick strains against Sy's taut, massive arms. "Then prove it. You may have beaten Bruce in the ring, but I will stomp your ass until you beg for fucking mercy."

As if heeding a call, Pace pushes up his sleeves, revealing the intricate lines of his tattoos. He jerks his chin at Nick. "Give me a reason to go back to prison. I dare you."

"Stop!" I shout, breaking away from Wicker to plant myself between them, arms held out. "They're right, okay? I agreed to this." I square my shoulders, trying to muster a resolve I don't feel. "I received an invitation to the ball, and I decided to take it. I understood the consequences of that decision." My lower body screams at that lie. Nowhere on the shiny gold foil invitation had it said that being crowned Princess would require me to have my hymen broken by some archaic dildo, only to then be contractually raped by one of these monsters. I take a deep breath and look the three Princes in the eye for the first time since last night. "Can I talk to them for a minute? Alone?" I add a quiet, begrudging, "Please?"

Wicker snaps, "Fat fucking chance," but Lex rests his hand on his shoulder and gives him a firm squeeze.

"Five minutes." Lex nods at a fountain twenty feet away. "We'll be right there."

Pace's eyes flick to mine. "If you try anything, we'll know." My eyes follow his to the bank of cameras above. The eyes in the sky. "*I'll* know."

I watch them walk off, and when they're a good distance away, I turn, trying to come up with the words to explain myself. But before I can, Remy has instantly closed the distance, taking my face between his hands. His hard eyes study me intently.

"Remy," I ask, "what are you doing?"

"I've already found the red," he seethes, snatching up my wrist. He holds it out, as if he's showing me the cuts there, telling me something I didn't already know. "Now, I'm looking for the orange," he bites out, "because that's the only fucking way this is happening."

"They're telling the truth." I turn my hand, catching his finger in my palm. "I was invited, and I came here of my own free will. I promise."

It's so much worse than I could have imagined, watching Remy's face sink as he steps back, releasing me. "So you're East End now." The words are harsh, even if the tone they're given with is soft. "You know what they are, don't you?" A hard, tense jaw gestures to the tiara on my head. "Everything in there is gold, Verity. *Everything.*"

He's not being literal. "I know," I tell him, hoping he'll understand. "I'm not stupid. A lot of it's a lie. But..."

Jesus, it's hard—so hard not to just tell them the truth. That I'm doing this, in some ways, for them as much as me and the Monarchs. That I want to see Forsyth become the kind of place that doesn't turn sweet boys like Remy into these hard, violent, distrusting men.

But I can't.

"I know you," Nick says, head shaking. "You're not doing this for the money or the gifts, so there must be *something*–"

"It's the only available Royal position," Sy tells his brother. There's a sad surety in his eyes that I never thought would be reserved for me. "That's it, isn't it? Verity, I know you were disappointed when we chose Lav—"

"No, I wasn't," I insist, but when his eyebrow lifts, I relent. "Okay, I *was*–for like a minute. But Lavinia is the most amazing Duchess, and she's the best Queen for you. I really do believe that.

Plus, I think we all know you guys view me more as a sister than... well, anything else."

Sy shakes his head, still looking pissed. "Duchess isn't the only place for you, Verity. You keep the cutsluts in line. They respect you. And you're more familiar with the history of the club than anyone else, keeping track of all those dates and traditions." He levels those blue eyes at me. "I'm pretty sure your mom is going to want to retire one day, and then who's going to manage the club—"

"Or us," Remy cuts in.

"—when she does?" Sy finishes.

In one rambling, run-on sentence, Simon Perilini just laid out my future. That would be my life with DKS. Wrangling cutsluts, managing Friday Night Fury, planning Family Dinners, and organizing charity events. It's not a bad life, it's just...

"I want to be bigger than that, Sy." I take a deep breath. "When I got that invitation, I thought it was a joke, or some kind of inter-frat prank, and... I don't know, maybe it still is, except..." I glance over my shoulder at the Princes, each of them watching us with alert eyes. "If it is, then those guys don't seem in on it. Regardless, I saw it as an opportunity." I turn back to the Dukes, trying to find the balance between truth and secrecy. "I don't want to be the next Mama B, you guys. I want to be the next Lavinia. I want to do something that matters. Something that leaves a mark on this place. Something my mother has no control over." I'm surprised to see Sy and Remy listening intently. Nick's a few feet back, arms crossed over his chest, staring at the ground. "If anyone could understand, it should be you, Nick."

His muscles flex, head tilting just so.

He's pissed but listening. They trust me enough to do that, and in return, I want to tell them everything. About the meeting with Lavinia and Story, how this is part of something that will help all of Forsyth. But we agreed not to divulge any of this—not yet. It's definitely not my place to tell them.

"Why does it have to be here?" Remy asks, fists curling as he gestures to the Princes. "Why does it have to be them?"

"Do you remember West End before Lavinia came?" I ask, arching an eyebrow. "Because I do. Cutsluts didn't have a choice in entertaining the alumni. You know what that means, right?" Narrowing my eyes, I dare any of them to say otherwise. "Maybe I can be to East End what Lavinia was to me. Maybe there's a girl out there who needs a voice in this Palace. I'm going to make sure she has one."

It's as close to the truth as I can give, and while Remy still looks baffled, and Nick still hasn't met my gaze, Sy gets it.

I can tell, because his eyes roll.

"What is it with West End and our insufferable martyrs?" he mutters, pinching the bridge of his nose. "If this is what you want, Verity, then fine, we can *grudgingly* allow it. But there are still matters to be hashed out."

I frown. "Hashed out?"

"I can't just let them have you," he insists, voice quiet but certain. "Whatever you might think, you're important to West End. We were going to make you Duchess at one point. What kind of King would I be if I turned my back and went home with nothing?"

I blink, his words surprising me in more ways than one. I never gave much thought to being important enough to require...

"Negotiations," Sy says, nodding. "Between houses. They can have you, but we require a price."

I look back over at the Princes', our five minutes clearly up. "And if they don't agree?"

Nick steps up, finally meeting my gaze. "Then the East and West go to war."

5

L ex

JUST ONE MORE DAY.

If I can make it just one more day, tomorrow will be better.

God knows it can't be worse than today. I drag a palm down my face, trying to wake myself up as my foot hits the accelerator. We're on the way to neutral territory–the courthouse–to negotiate with DKS. My father's Cadillac leads the entourage, my truck in the middle, and Pace and Wicker are two cars behind me, driving a van with heavily tinted windows. I keep an eye on the rearview mirror, making sure the van is still there. The last thing we need is to lose the upper hand before we even get to the meeting.

We just need to stay awake long enough to get there.

After the ceremony last night, we'd been forced to pack up everything and move into the Palace. *Immediately.*

"A Prince begins residing in the Palace the very moment his Princess does," Father had said.

And that was it.

There was no time to process the news. No hour spent discussing tactics with my brothers. No minute to come to terms with the fact that we'd come so close–so goddamn close to being out of this hellhole.

I dumped my belongings haphazardly into my new-old bedroom, helped Pace move his equipment, interviewed handmaiden candidates, and only got in an hour of studying before Father's mandatory breakfast. At best, I had ten minutes of sleep, and that was only because I passed out face first in a chemistry book. Before today, my plans had been to spend this afternoon working on an important paper, but that's been shot to hell.

The girl beside me shifts, wincing when I hit a bump. She's been silent the whole drive, but also unavoidably present. Her arms are folded tight, pushing the swell of her cleavage to more and more prominence. Every now and then, I catch a speck of movement out of the corner of my eye, her fingertip shifting as a badly-manicured fingernail picks at a scab on her wrist.

"Thanks for letting me come," she eventually says, voice stilted and anxious. She's probably been working herself up to speak since the moment we set off. "I know you didn't have to."

I release a small, bitter breath of laughter. "You think we brought you along to make you happy, *Princess*?" Glancing over, I curl my lip distastefully. That goddamn tiara is still on her head, as if she has the right to wear it. "Despite how it might seem, this isn't about you. You're just a tool."

Just like me, I don't say.

God only fucking knows how West End trash like her ended up being important enough to someone to even be a bargaining chip, but it's the truth. DKS isn't exactly the most strategic house. They're rabid, hot-tempered chaos goblins who'll jump at whatever threat is the most visible at any given moment. The girl is here to serve as a little reminder of who has ownership and what's at risk.

"All the same," she mutters, turning to stare out her window.

Her fingernail keeps picking, picking, picking, and it makes the tendons in my neck bulge with annoyance.

Just one more day.

The frustration is familiar–this feeling that there aren't enough hours in the day. This annoyance that my brain and body can't just keep chugging along without food and sleep. This bone-deep weariness that I never have the chance to address.

The cravings are familiar, too. One hit of Scratch would have me up and running, wired like a ticking bomb, ready to face anything Father had coming my way. I could ace these negotiations, get the Princess back to the Palace, write three different papers, and–oh, yeah.

Actually be able to fulfill my new fucking duty.

Gripping the steering wheel, I breathe, letting the craving come, and then letting it go. That's what Dusty, the group counselor at my weekly meetings, says to do. It's mostly bullshit, but following directions is what I was built to do. Yet again, I'm struck by dizzying relief that I hadn't been the one chosen to claim her in front of the frat last night. It doesn't mean it wasn't a shitshow, though.

I hit a pothole, and I don't miss the low hiss under her breath, or the way her hand grips the door handle. She was limping when she walked in the breakfast room. That, and the way she's gingerly holding herself, is a good indicator she suffered some internal bruising from both the phallus and the relentless fucking Wicker gave her afterward.

Wicker. Jesus. He's the reason I declared I would be driving the Princess to the meet up. Sure, Pace hasn't been alone with a woman in nearly two years, and I haven't been able to get a firm handle on his mental state since he returned. But Wicker? After last night, it's clear he can't be trusted to be alone with her right now. None of us are happy about this, but we all handle it differently. Wicker proved he's too fucking impulsive, and after the fiasco with the last set of Princes and their cheating whore, Father wouldn't handle losing another Princess well.

Not at all.

Wicker is a loaded fuse. Being pissy that his goal of fucking his way through Forsyth has been hamstrung by a real obligation is one thing. But this position isn't easy on any of us. Him acting like a brat will only make it worse.

I feel her eyes on me and cut my gaze to the side, irritated. "What?"

"I danced with you last night." She tilts her head, her green eyes searching my face. "I didn't realize it until just now. You said it was your twelfth ball. I guess that makes sense knowing who your father is."

I grunt in response, not wanting to talk about balls or my father, but apparently, she's not finished.

She casts her gaze to her lap, voice softening. "You didn't expect to be one of the Princes. None of you did, did you?"

"No," I admit through clenched teeth.

"And you don't..." Her voice trails off, like she's putting this all together. "None of you *want* to be a Prince."

I glare at her. "Does this feel like a celebration to you?"

Her mouth twists unhappily, but she gives a heavy nod. "That's why Wicker was so... harsh." No doubt reliving how Wick fucking railed her last night, she gulps. She'd taken the phallus better than expected. Oh, she fought. Her muscles tensed up, resisting the invasion, but she took it. It felt so good to push her down, too–to push back against something, to take control.

I snap, "Wicker rode you hard because he's Wicker." I make a sharp left, the old building in the distance. "That's the thing about you chicks. You all think Princes are going to make love to you on a bed of goddamn roses. We're *men*. If you came here looking for a romance, then you're a child. That's not how the world works, *Princess*."

There's a long stretch of silence as I search for a spot, and I feel more than see her eyes turn flinty. "I can make a few guesses as to why Wicker wants to hurt me," she says. "And Pace blames me for something I didn't even know about. But you? You don't even know me."

Shrugging, I say, "I know where you come from. That's enough."

"So you hate me for being West End," she concludes, and I'm not even surprised. Of course she'd be stupid on top of being shallow and selfish.

"Exactly." I take another sharp turn, my movements short and controlled.

Aside from the obvious lack of my having a choice, the funny thing is, if she'd been someone from East End–someone deserving of the position–I might have actually felt honored to do this. Maybe it makes me just as much of an idiot as it makes her, but there for a while, I'd actually bought into the whole Princess thing. She's meant to be resplendent. Iconic. A goddess. My first few years at Forsyth, I'd actually looked forward to making my public offerings. It's a requirement of PNZ to show appreciation and affection for the mother of our house, and since I've never been one for mediocrity, I excelled at it. Most of the guys in the frat would present her with flowers or jewelry, but not me. I'd make a real effort to find each one something extraordinary, bespoke to her interests and ambitions.

The thought of having to shower the woman beside me with gifts makes me sick.

"Well, just so you know, I didn't see this—*any* of this–coming either." A shiny tear builds in the corner of her eye, but she sniffs it off, blinking it away. "Not the invitation, or being chosen, or anything else that happened."

I press back in my seat, laughing darkly. "Sympathy? Really? Is that what you want?" She looks up, seeming startled at the callousness of my tone. "Before you delude yourself into thinking we're all in this together, let me be clear. We're not. My brothers and I are Ashby's namesakes, and you're a West End cubslut with a functioning womb. Our lives as men are fucked, but as long as those ovaries work?" I offer a cold smirk, reaching up to flick the sparkling tiara on her head. "You've just won the golden ticket."

She gapes at me, and I see the hot anger welling in her eyes. It's the fire Father had mentioned the night before. This, apparently, makes her an attractive candidate, and I can't for the life of me figure out why.

"You think what happened last night is a golden ticket?" She thrusts a finger at the tiara, voice belligerent and incredulous. "That I can be paid off with shiny things?!"

I slam the brakes, throw the truck into park, and whirl toward her, seething, "That's exactly what happened. You accepted that invitation because you're desperate for the fairytale, and worse than that? You were willing to sell out your own house–your own fucking people–to get it. I don't hate you for being West End," I clarify, pinning her with my stare. "I hate you for selling it out."

Her expression snaps into slack shock. "What?"

"You're a fucking traitor," I say, basking in the tears that swim in her eyes, spilling over. "Which makes you useless as a Princess, because you'll turn on us the second something shinier and more impressive comes along. You have no fucking concept of loyalty or allegiance. You're the worst kind of person."

She blinks, face paling, but when she looks away, it's with a clenched jaw. "You don't know anything about the reason I'm here."

"I know you came to East End for a fantasy; the Palace, the Princes, and the happily-fucking-ever-after." I reach out and grab her chin, jerking her gaze to mine. "But guess what? That fairytale you were so quick to sell your soul for? It's not real. It may look real on the outside, but on the inside, it's just more of what you got last night. Torture." I open my door. "For all of us."

MY FATHER GLANCES at his watch, which is the closest he'll come to admitting how much of an inconvenience this all is. The first day of a Princeship is full of obligations and planning and strategy, and sitting in an old courthouse, glaring across the long table at Simon Perilini and his street rats, isn't one of them.

I'm pretty sure the Baron King, the closest thing to a truly neutral party, yawns beneath his ornate mask. "Let's begin." Out in the lobby stand his Barons, who confiscated all our weapons before we were granted admittance.

Wicker's always particularly uneasy around any of the Barons, but in the presence of their King, he's downright electric. The two of them have never so much as spoken a word to one another, but the animosity rolls off my brother in waves.

That's bad enough, but now I have to sit beside the Princess of sluts as if she's worth all the hassle.

"I want to know why the girl is here," Father says, looking deceptively casual in his seat. Since the Kings love nothing more than posturing, he and Simon are on opposite ends of the table, while the King of the Barons sits behind the court bench, overseeing it. "This doesn't concern her."

"She's my Queen," Simon says with an insolence no one else would dare to show. "And you'll show her the respect a Queen deserves."

It's all I can do to hold back my snort.

Father, however, doesn't bother holding back his own, looking amused. "There's a reason East End doesn't have Queens. Princesses, sure. Mothers, all the time. But no woman has ever ascended to Royal parity in our house, and they never will."

Wicker gives a banal smile. "So much less drama that way."

"That's not the way I hear it." Lavinia Lucia is perched in one of the seats like it's a throne.

Queen of traitors, if you ask me. She sold out her Count legacy—real, organic, *blood* legacy—and if the rumors are true, even killed her own father, all to become Bruin trash. No wonder Verity Sinclaire has no sense of loyalty. Her own Queen clearly doesn't understand the concept of fealty. It grates something inside of me that the Lucia bitch has the nerve to speak, but the way she rolls her eyes makes it worse.

"Seems like all you guys have is drama. It bleeds over territory lines constantly. Autumn, her name is?"

Father answers her while looking at Simon. "Your house knows quite a lot about bleeding over territory lines, don't they?"

I almost don't catch it, the flash of panic in the Duchess' eyes, but it's gone as quickly as it came. "My boys are hot-headed," she says, glowering at the three of them. "If they'd *waited*, I could have told them that barging through your gates was a bad idea." From the nonplussed looks on their faces, I'm guessing this is an argument they've been having all morning.

Nagging.

Another reason we don't have a Queen.

Father is bad enough.

The Princess is sitting in the chair opposite Lavinia. They're a story of contrasts, the Duchess wearing a sweater that exposes both her shoulders and the Dukes markings on her back. One is a tattoo, the other the patented duke brand. She wrinkled her nose at the Princess' pink dress, but other than that, the two don't exchange much more than a small nod in greeting.

Good.

If Lucia has a shred of intelligence, she'll see Sinclaire for the Judas she is.

Sy clears his throat and says, "Look, Verity assures us that she accepted the invitation to compete for Princess of her own free will. She also claims she signed your covenant agreement and has asked us to allow her to fulfill her duties." He rests an elbow on the table, fist-up, and the large, gaudy ring on his finger gleams. "The problem is that she belongs to West End, and regardless of how freely her choices were made, we're not going to give her to you without getting something in return."

"The price has already been paid," Father says, looking bored. "Let me be very clear, Perilini. We didn't come here to negotiate."

There's a loaded silence after his words as everyone digests what that means.

Nick Bruin leans back in his seat, lacing his hands behind his head. "I was really hoping you'd say that." The look on his face is one of cruel satisfaction.

"We're the Dukes," Remington Maddox says, tapping a marker against the table. "You think we aren't ready for a war?"

Nick smirks. "Our fighters are creaming their pants for it."

"Oh, I know. We all know," Father says, looking unconcerned as he rests a hand on Verity's shoulder. "That's why Miss Sinclaire here isn't the prize." He gives the Dukes a placid grin. "She's the hostage."

Simon straightens, eyes turning murderous. "Excuse me?"

In a patronizing tone, Father explains, "You're a volatile house with a new King who possesses all the hunger and stupidity of youth. Young men want war. Those of us who are a bit more... seasoned," he glances at the Baron King, "know the score."

"It's funny you think we're playing a game," Simon says, teeth clenched. "But humor me, what score is that?"

"One to two." Father releases Verity, who looks like someone just slapped her clear across the face. "That game started the night Nick Bruin killed my kin."

"I knew it," Remy snaps. "Verity for Felix? You can't be fucking serious. He was a lowlife who bungled an exchange because he couldn't keep his mouth shut."

Felix was a frat brother, cousin to a previous Prince, and one of Father's minions. He went missing after a meetup with the Dukes. Autumn, the prior Princess, told us what–or who–happened. Felix is a dumbass, and Remy is right. He never did know how to keep his mouth shut–or his hands to himself. According to Autumn, Nick Bruin's impulsivity ended Felix before he even saw it coming.

Remy continues, "He meant nothing to East End, and you damn well know it."

"But Verity is special to the West." Father grins as the Dukes realize they've tipped their hand. "I knew that night when I found you defending her from my son. You see her as a sister. Kin. And I'm *sure* you wouldn't risk any harm coming to her."

It's all I can do to hold in the laughter I feel creeping up my chest. It's even harder when I tip back, meeting Wicker's eyes. It all makes the best kind of sense, why my Father chose Verity. Watching it sink in for her, the way her eyes go dull and cast down, face paling, is even better.

She really thought she was special. That she was chosen because there was something about her–something unique and worthy of celebration–but in the end, it's just like I told her. She's a bargaining chip.

She turned coat just to become our hostage.

Simon glares into Father's eyes. "You're saying if we step out of line, you'll kill her."

"*We* don't kill people." Pace's low voice surprises me, drawing my gaze to him. He's at my side, and up until now, I'd half suspected he'd fallen asleep. Now though, I realize he's been watching the entire volley, and his words couldn't have been more sinister if he'd threatened to slit the girl's throat right in front of them.

Because Pace–like me and Wicker–knows that there are much, *much* worse things than death.

"Well, not usually," Father, rolling his eyes at the boiling tension, flicks a hand. "Oh, you don't need to look so dire about it. We don't want to kill her. In fact, I'm completely serious about my boys putting an heir into her. She'll be taken care of, you can be assured of that." He leans over the table, fixing Perilini with a serious stare. "If it's a war you want, then we'll give it to you. And don't count your eggs before they've hatched, because we have plenty of firepower of our own. But an Ashby born from a daughter of the West?" Father lifts an eyebrow. "There's more advantages to be had in joining our houses. You might be a new King, but you know that much."

It's a good strategy–a genius strategy. He's getting older, and old Kings aren't exactly thriving in Forsyth these days. Father needs an heir, and he needs a Kingdom where it can thrive. By the looks of Simon, he's not exactly as willing to lose good men as the other two.

Father leans back, finishing, "You still have a whole lifetime to build your legacy, Perilini. Mine is running thin. I don't have time to keep patrolling my borders to ensure the safety of what little of my legacy still remains."

"Verity, just say the word." Nick watches her with eyes like steel, ignoring how his Duchess' gaze is flitting nervously between Kings. "Say the word and we'll end this."

Her head is still bowed when she shakes it. It's the only smart thing I've seen her do so far, refusing to let her people die in service of saving her from her own idiotic choices.

The Dukes look completely fucking stumped.

Remy, most of all. "Felix for Verity–that's one-one," he notes, eyes narrowing suspiciously. "You said two-one."

Father nods at Wicker and Pace before raising a forefinger. "I'm so glad you asked, Remington. There's still the small matter of your fighters sneaking into my territory." Everyone tenses when my brothers stand, moving toward the door, but a glance at the Baron King's nod makes it clear this is nothing that requires caution.

They march through it, Lavinia Lucia appearing particularly alarmed.

"Normally, we wouldn't think much of it," I speak up, drawing their attention back to the matter at hand. "Your kind aren't known for their skill at subterfuge. Unfortunately…"

The second the door swings open, they all shoot to their feet. But it's the Queen who speaks, all the blood draining from her traitor face as she cries, "Ballsy!" She doesn't go to him, but the impulse is clearly there. "Let him go!" Lavinia snarls to my father.

Pace thrusts him through the door, and this Ballsy fucker looks only half coherent, tumbling instantly to his knees. His mouth is taped, eye black and swollen, and bandages cover his fingers. He's shirtless, torso bearing little shallow cuts that look not at all unlike the ones on my Princess' arms.

We only stabbed him a little.

Wicker pats him on the head like he's a dog, not missing the irate glare Ballsy fixes him with.

Fucking DKS–they never know when to stop.

Simon stands to press his fists against the table. "Tell me," he grates out, eyes flashing, "what the fuck you're doing with my recruit."

I glare at the kid on the floor. "We spotted this one skulking around our warehouse district–meeting up with girls, drunk on the smell of his own testosterone, asking a suspicious amount of questions."

"Your warehouse district borders South Side's," Simon argues. "He was doing business. Business Payne and I personally fucking sanctioned!"

My father leans back, looking unthreatened by the way Nick Bruin is glaring bullets at him. "That meeting was on neutral territory. All deals were off the second he crossed the bridge, breached our gate's security panel, and attempted to sneak inside."

Simon's jaw tenses. "You're lying, Ashby. Ballsack would never do that." Only when he looks at his recruit for confirmation, he doesn't get it.

Ballsack just gives a small, guilty, lopsided shrug.

"For fuck's sake," Nick mutters, eyes rolling. "He's a kid. Probably chasing some East End pussy that convinced him to help her get an invite to the ball." Thrusting a hand out toward the pile of raw meat his recruit's become, Nick insists, "He's harmless. He's barely a player."

"If that's true," Father argues, head tilting, "then perhaps we'll rid you of such an obvious nuisance."

Ballsack's eyes widen, and he mumbles with alarm under the tape.

"No!" This protest comes from both girls in the room, Lavinia and Verity lurching up as if they're in any place to make demands. Annoying, but it gives us all the information we need to know who has the upper hand here. With one word and two panicked glances, the girls have revealed Ballsack's importance to the club.

Women.

Simon cracks his neck, falling back into his seat. "Fine," he snaps, rage lurking just beneath the surface. "Let's negotiate."

6

L ex

GRACIOUSLY, we allow Lavinia Lucia to attend to the prisoner as terms are made, her movements tightly controlled as she dabs his stab wound.

"First," Simon is saying, "you keep your impulses and business to the East and North. Leave the West and South out of it."

Pace looks up from inspecting the fresh bruises on his knuckles. Guess he got a few cathartic hits in on the prisoner before handing him over. "You're including South Side in your negotiations? Is there something we should know?"

"Nothing that isn't public knowledge," Sy says casually. Too casually. "We have some shared business interests, and that means our protections need to extend to them."

This is the first I've heard of this partnership, but my head has been under a pile of books. I haven't been paying attention. I didn't think I needed to, which unfortunately puts me and my brothers at a disadvantage. We haven't been groomed for this position like the rest of them. As far as we knew, our future in Forsyth was strictly background.

"We'll keep our business out of your territory as long as Miss Sinclaire is our Princess," Father says, jotting something down. "Although none of this accounts for the Felix situation. You owe us a body in return, and if it isn't her, then who's it gonna be?"

"We're not giving you anyone from DKS," Nick says with an air of boredom. "That's a non-starter."

Simon is looking suspiciously pensive however, rubbing at his chin. "Or maybe we will–something that benefits us both."

Pace leans back in his chair, arms folded. "We're listening."

"We recently had a problem in our ranks," he explains, sharing a knowing look with his Dukes. "It's been taken care of on an official level, but we'd like to tie up loose ends."

Lavinia springs up, saying, "Oh," in a tone that suggests she's liking this plan.

I laugh at the thought of the Dukes doing anything delicate, but quickly catch the subtext. "You mean you can't be seen doing the removal?" I ask.

Simon nods, looking put out. "This... problem of ours–he's challenged my leadership, not to mention–" He cuts off, jaw clenching. "But he's also a legacy. His family name holds weight in West End, and since I'm still a new King..."

"His family could organize against you," Father surmises, putting pen to paper. "What's the name?"

"Oakfield."

Father doesn't miss a beat, waving his hand. "They don't hold any power in the East."

"So we take this guy and get rid of him for you," Wicker says, looking neither for or against it. We're used to doing jobs, but they're not usually of the getting-rid-of variety.

"Make him the trespasser on your property." Nick jerks his head at the Baron King. "We'll pay the Barons' fee for disposal. Everything will look normal."

Simon adds, "Once you have him, it needs to be discreet and final."

"And hey, if it takes a while," Remy offers, shrugging, "I'm just saying, we won't lose any sleep."

I look to my brothers. Clearly this Ballsack kid means something to them, but the truth is that Felix was a dumbfuck piece of trash who didn't know how to mind himself. What the Dukes are offering–a man for a man–works. Pace gives me a slow nod, while Wicker waves his hand in the air, ready to be done with this.

Looking up to meet their gazes, Father says, "Consider it a deal. Have the details ready by six this evening. The boys will work up a plan."

"And then you'll release Ballsack?" Nick's eyes flick to his friend. "With *no* additional damage?"

"Immediately."

"Wait!" Lavinia blurts, glaring at her King. A silent conversation passes between them, and if the circumstances weren't so tense, I'd bust his balls for being so pussy-whipped. It's pretty damn clear that his Duchess wants something, and he's going to get it for her.

"Two more things." He turns back to the table, sighing. "One, we want daily, unsupervised contact with Verity."

My head snaps up, the answer hard and final. "Absolutely fucking not."

No one seems as surprised by my vehemence as my Father, who puts his pen down. He dips his chin approvingly, telling Simon, "This is for my sons to decide. She's their Princess–their responsibility. If you want contact with her, you'll have to convince them."

"Not much of a hostage if we can't regularly evaluate her safety," Simon says, cutting his eyes to Verity. He offers, "Every two days."

I remain perfectly still. "No."

Fuck no.

In no goddamn universe.

Pace is the one to lift his head, cutting in, "Weekly."

I whirl around, glaring at him. "Are you listening to me? I said–"

The look Pace gives me brings me up short. His eyes, dark and empty–just as they have been since he returned–spark with something meaningful. It's been almost two years now, but I can still read them. They're the same eyes that stared at me through the glass divider as he demanded Wicker and I stop visiting.

"It makes it worse," he'd said before marching away, back to his cell.

He's not suggesting it because he feels sympathy for her. This won't be a favor or a kindness. He's offering it because he knows how fucking awful it'll feel.

Catching on, I turn to Simon. "One hour, weekly, with a non-Royal escort."

The idiots look so pleased with themselves that it's a struggle not to smirk at my brothers. Wicker's caught on too, but he's good at hiding it, leaning forward with an intimidating look.

"We're going to tag her," he adds.

Nick shrugs. "Who wouldn't?"

"What was the second?" Father asks, returning to his paper. If he's upset at the concession, then he doesn't make it apparent, all business.

Remy's the one to pitch closer, raising his chin defiantly. "When–*if* she gets pregnant, we want to revisit negotiations."

"When she has all the leverage, you mean?" Wicker scoffs. "Not a chance."

But Father shuts his notebook, removing his pair of glasses. "I agree to those terms." Ignoring my brother's incredulous stare, he adds, "If the Princess conceives in three months, then we'll reconvene. And in the meantime, if she rebels, defects, or otherwise severs the covenants she's willfully agreed to, then all terms are off." He pauses, meeting Simon's gaze. "*All* terms."

The air in the room grows heavy as we all silently acknowledge what this would mean.

War.

Simon looks at Verity. I don't know what he sees in her face–couldn't possibly care less, if I'm honest–but whatever it is, it must assure him that she's up to the task of being a Royal cum dumpster for three months.

Simon nods. "I agree to your terms, Ashby."

The deal is made quietly, with such careful, meticulous tedium that it could only have been arranged by my father. The pages are signed, witnessed and stamped with the seal of Forsyth. This all happens around me, slow and disjointed because I'm stuck on the three month deadline, and what no one's had the guts to ask: what happens to the Princess–to *all of us*–if she doesn't conceive?

No one asks, because they don't need to.

If one of us doesn't successfully impregnate the Princess and she doesn't carry that child to term, finally giving Father an heir, we're all fucked.

~

BY FIVE-O'CLOCK, my head has settled into the fuzzy dullness of a body that's accepted sleep isn't on the menu. The only way I can make it down to lower East End is by telling myself if I make it just a few more hours, it'll all be over.

One more day.

I just need to make it one more day.

"Hey."

Blinking through the fog, I look over at Pace. He's gotten some sleep, but that's just how he is. Even before prison, he was always well-schooled in finding any place to fall asleep. The classroom. The bathroom. The trunk of a car. Once, he fell asleep on the roof of our boarding house in the middle of a storm so violent; it took out the power.

I've never envied him more.

"Hey," he says again, grabbing my shoulder. "You gonna make it, man?"

My gaze slides to the building in front of me and I startle, remembering where we are. *Right.* The valet just took the car. Walking works by putting one foot in front of the other. "Yeah, of course." I'm in my last semester of pre-med. I'm a fucking pro at going without sleep.

Wicker, on the other hand, is not. "Let's get this over with," he mutters, brushing past us and marching through the doors. Above our heads is a large, glowing sign that we're all familiar with. This isn't father's only business, but it's certainly his favorite.

The Gentlemen's Chamber.

I spend a second putting myself together. Smoothing the wrinkles from my button-down shirt. Tying my hair back. Adjusting my sleeves. Walking through the door evokes a strange nostalgia, from the scent of wood and whiskey to the richly paneled walls and crystal chandeliers. Even the way we're greeted, shuffled immediately to Father's table, is just like everything else in this town; unchanging.

Case in point, I know before even arriving that he'll have a rib eye, asparagus, and a half-empty glass of single malt sitting before him, and I'm not disappointed.

He cuts into the meat, glancing at us. "You're late."

I don't bother looking at my phone. "Sorry, sir. My fault." That's a plus about a drained battery. It can't spark enough to feel much of anything.

The signed pages of the covenant are spread out in front of him, the Princess' signature faded into a brownish red. It's Pace's first time here since going to prison, and he lingers as Wick and I each take a seat, his dark eyes intent as they track a topless brunette walking toward the back.

Being here now feels exactly the same as it always does. I could be twelve, or fourteen, or seventeen. The age doesn't matter. It's the feeling that settles in my chest that's familiar. It's the three of us sitting here, avoiding the very obviously naked women dancing on the stage, watching him slice through the red meat and methodically chew. Back then we were skinny and zit-faced, fueled by hormones and rage. Shoulders back. Spines straight. Eyes forward.

Waiting.

Finally, he puts down his fork and knife, even this being part of the ritual. He places them in the center of his empty plate, perfectly parallel. "I'm aware that your Princeships have come as a surprise. Not just to you, but everyone in Forsyth. And in the spirit of being forthcoming, I didn't expect it to happen either. There are certain criteria required for leadership roles such as this—more so for PNZ." Wiping his mouth with a heavy linen napkin, he folds it into eighths. "We're talking about heirs. Creating the next generation is top priority to this kingdom, and the three of you don't exactly meet the typical standard." He exhales, snagging his glass of whiskey. "But after the fiasco with the last set of Princes and their Princess, I needed someone in the Purple Palace I can trust. Men who have been raised correctly and understand the enormity of this position. Impregnating the new Princess is imperative. Failure is not an option." He holds each of our gazes as he tips back the glass. "Do you understand?"

We respond as a unit. "Yes, sir."

Father nods. "Very good. Now that negotiations have been settled with the Dukes, I thought we might take a moment to go over your responsibilities with the Princess." The moment he pushes his plate aside, a server descends to take it away, her small, perky tits visible through her sheer, lace top.

Wicker and Pace, one just as desperate as the other, watch her ass as she leaves.

"Eyes forward," Father commands, not ungently, and they both snap to attention. This is why he's always brought us here. Every important meeting, from our college acceptance letters to job designations have occurred in the lust-filled shadow of skin. Tits draped with delicate gold necklaces. Smooth legs covered in intricate hosiery. Dark lipstick and the cloying scent of sugar. The women never speak to us–never look at us–because they've been ordered not to, and everyone follows the rules.

This, like everything else, is an exercise in endurance.

"You're all familiar with the text by now, surely," he says, flipping through the papers. Pulling one out, he rests it on top, our signatures scrawled at the bottom. None of us spare it more than a quick glance, understanding the gesture for what it is. A reminder. "Tell me."

"The Prince's seed is exclusive to his Princess," I begin, reciting the covenants from memory. "He will not spill it for any purpose other than to fulfill his biological obligations."

Pace's laconic voice continues, "The Prince will nurture his body to provide his Princess with the strongest seed."

"The Prince will protect," Wicker grits out, "nourish, and sustain his Princess."

There are dozens of these–far more for her–but all of them boil down to a general understanding. No sex with anyone else. No masturbation. No sex that isn't done for the sole purpose of creation. A Prince spills his seed for one reason and one reason alone. The first time I read a covenant that wrapped the forbiddance of blowjobs into contractual jargon, it made me laugh. Now, I want to hit something.

The Prince might not belong to his Princess, but his dick sure as hell does.

I've barely had time to think of the covenants. I was reeling from the whole night. Father announcing we're the new Princes was whiplash enough, but it being followed by the throning of some random red-headed West Ender was almost as shocking.

Wicker shifts next to me, fuming. This is going to be the hardest on him. Pace has already gone years without sex. One woman is more than the zero he had in prison. Schoolwork, studying for the MCAT, frat responsibilities, and my reliance on Viper Scratch pushed relationships or even hookups down my priority list. But Wicker? His singular focus since turning sixteen has been consuming as much pussy as humanly possible.

He's as addicted to it as I am to Scratch.

Father adds, "Furthermore, there will be a schedule. Each of you will have two days of the week with the Princess. That time should be used for making Royal deposits and nothing more. Although there is no limit to the number of deposits she can receive each day, I don't need to remind you that she's a vessel," his eyes flick to Wicker, "not a plaything."

"Twice a week?" Wick asks, voice an octave too high. "We only get two days to fuck?"

"Language." Father frowns, glancing around him as if he can possibly be scandalized in his own fucking strip club. "And yes. She gets a day of rest, and of course, a week off during her cycle. Assuming she has one."

"But we can't have sex with anyone else either." He says this like he's trying to make two pieces of a puzzle fit together.

Father's eyes narrow in on my brother. "I know for a fact that you possess a remarkable reading comprehension. Don't test my patience with willful ignorance."

Wicker's nostrils flare wide, mouth pulling back into a snarl. "You're not doing this because you trust us. You're doing this to punish us! You're angry at Pace for Spring Break, me for having fun, and Lex for—" My brother looks me up and down, scoffing. "For *nothing*, because Lex is the cyborg you wish we'd all be. He never steps out of line. But since he's busy being Dr. Perfect Son, even he doesn't have the time to be on Princess pussy patrol." Wicker slams his palms onto the table, hotly adding, "You just wanted us back under your thumb again. Admit it! This is the only way you can keep us under your control."

Shit.

"Wick," I say quietly.

Pace's leg bounces, the movement growing more rapid with every word that comes out of Wicker's mouth. He's not wrong, but it's like the strippers. We know they're there, but we can't acknowledge them. There are things we just don't say aloud.

Father leans back in his chair, appraising my brother. Wicker's always been the first to flare up. Even a childhood spent under Father's heel couldn't wring the brattiness out of him. As always, Father's long, intense stare seems to get through Wicker's meltdown. It hurts to see it, almost worse than the possibility of me getting an appointment.

Wicker slowly pulls back from the table, back straight, eyes forward.

He falls back in line.

This. This is what I remember the most about being at this table. The waiting. Waiting for expectations to be laid out. For tantrums and breaking under pressure. For appointments to be scheduled.

Father picks up a small slip of paper.

"The schedule will be as follows: Sunday and Wednesday: Lex. Monday and Friday: Pace." His eyes meet Wicker's. "Saturday and Tuesday: Whitaker."

"Tuesday..." Wicker says under his breath. "You're saying I'm not going to get to bust a nut for two more days?"

"That is exactly what I'm saying," Father says through gritted teeth, "although with more decorum."

"You forced me to spend my last night of freedom with some DKS slut!"

"*Do not*," Father roars, standing and slamming his hand on the table, "refer to the Princess as a slut or any other derogatory term!" He leans forward, elbows locked. "And yes, Whitaker, that is the reason I had you go first. Because you do not respect me, and that means I do not have to respect you."

Wicker's gone pale, his furious expression losing all its tightness. Each of us can probably count on one hand the number of times Father has lost his composure in public. It makes Pace and I go rigid just from habit–this thing that only belongs behind closed doors.

Wicker stammers out, "W-what? I respect you! I do everything you ask me to."

Father tilts his head, a small grin twisting his mouth. "What color was your tuxedo the other night? Midnight blue or indigo?" When Wick doesn't answer, Father's gaze shifts to me. "Lex, do you know?"

I stare at his crisp white lapel. "No sir, I don't."

"I guess it will remain a mystery." He sits, finished with his tantrum, apparently. "Do you boys understand your responsibilities?"

All three of us echo, "Yes, sir."

He nods. "Lex will stay, but you two may go."

Neither of my brothers move, but I barely notice. Dread blooms in my stomach, the skin on my back feeling tight and itchy.

"Father," Wicker starts, collecting himself with an air of panic, "I shouldn't have worn the suit. Or disparaged the Princess, or—"

"You've been excused." He jerks his chin at the door. But they only get two steps before Father stops them. "Pace."

We all freeze, my palms growing clammy as Pace slowly turns, meeting our father's even gaze. My brother looks around, as if there's some kind of trap. This is the first time Father's spoken to him since...

"Sir?" Pace warily asks.

Father holds his stare, searching, and every second that passes, my lungs feel a little more constricted. Eventually, he dips his chin. "You did well today."

Pace's chest expands with a sharp inhale. "Thank you."

"It was a good idea," Father goes on, draining the last of his whiskey. "Giving the girl a visitation will show the Dukes our willingness to cooperate. I'm proud of you, son."

It's bullshit, just as much as Father suggesting why the visitation is a good idea. It's just like the other things we know but don't dare say. The visitation will put the Princess in a place where Princesses aren't welcome, and that place is her home. It'll drive her farther into East End, where erstwhile Duchess hopefuls aren't welcome, either. It'll drive her so far that the Palace will be her only place of refuge. It's a tetherless leash–Father's favorite thing in the world.

And that's why he praises Pace.

Because it makes Wicker's mouth go tight and unhappy.

They both leave, neither making eye contact. The women give them a wide berth, never breaking their practiced smiles as they serve the other patrons.

Once they're gone, I inhale slowly, bracing myself. "He shouldn't have spoken to you like that."

"No," he says, a sudden weariness filling his eyes, "but I expected it. Your brother..."

I tense at the frustration in his eyes. "He's–"

"An Ashby." Father tips his mouth into an irritated smirk. "If not by blood, then certainly by spirit. Spoiled and impudent and uncontrollably virile. I very nearly dread the prospect of him multiplying." He rolls his eyes, gesturing to a topless blonde for another drink. I don't argue when he points to me, even though the liquor will amplify my exhaustion. "If there's any seed left in his body to take, that is."

My laugh is fake and far too mild. Father senses it–I can see it in his pause–so I try to shift the discussion. "Is there something you need from me?" I ask, ready to get it over with.

Nodding, he accepts the fresh glass of whiskey with heavy movements. It's the first time that I wonder if maybe he's as tired as I am. "I need you to perform a medical examination on the Princess."

My brain shuts off and then kicks back to life, relief coursing through my veins. "An examination?" I take a small sip of the amber liquor, doing my best to fake it.

"Surely you notice the tender way she was carrying herself today."

"Yes, I noticed."

"That's my fault." It's a false sentiment. Nothing is ever his fault. "In my desire to teach Wicker a lesson, I was careless in how brutal he would be with her. I'd like to confirm that there are no internal injuries. Nothing to impede attempts at creating an heir."

"Of course," I agree, struggling to remember the scope of the Palace's meager medical accommodations. I haven't seen that part of the basement in years. "I can do that."

Casually, he adds, "I also wanted to confirm that there won't be any issues with your own performance."

As much as I will it otherwise, I feel the heat rising to my cheeks as I sputter on the whiskey. "N-no, sir. I have–everything will be under control."

It's a lie. I have no fucking idea how I'm going to make this work. Taking pills would be against the covenant, and the last time I tried fucking a woman, my dick barely even got hard. It's bad enough that he knows about it, but now it's just more pressure.

He watches me for a long moment, the scrutiny burning as much as the liquor. "Don't lie to me."

The panic returns, my last bit of energy burned away by the quiet vehemence of my promise, "I'll find a way," I assure him. "I *won't* fail."

"I suspected that was a temporary situation."

I clear my throat. "It was." Ever since I quit the Scratch, it just doesn't work. Sex. Fucking. I've taken enough chem classes to understand that chemicals can sometimes do weird shit, and using Scratch for a year apparently left me with some side effects. This one isn't even the worst. You can't miss what you don't want.

"You know, son," Father begins, leaning forward in a way that suggests he's about to tell me something secret. His cheeks tug up into a half-grimace. "The covenant about masturbation... the *spirit* of it is to not be wasteful with your seed. If you were to use it in service of fulfilling your obligations, however..." he trails off, eyebrows rising.

I blink, trying to process what he's saying. "Oh." And then, "*Oh*. I... I understand."

"Excellent." Father smiles. "Her red hair."

"Sir?"

His eyes have gone a little glassy, I'm now realizing. He must be on his third drink by now–maybe even his fourth. "Her red hair with your amber eyes," he says, watching me with an expression that makes me want to squirm.

I think it's wistfulness.

And I don't know what the ever-loving fuck to do with it.

Father isn't wistful. Sure, he runs on ritual and routine, but he doesn't sentimentalize, and if he ever did, it wouldn't be about us.

He visibly shakes it off, putting down his glass and pushing it away. "Well, I'll have the handmaiden deliver her to the clinic. You can perform the examination, and if everything is all clear, you may make your first deposit."

"Tonight?" I stiffly ask. It's a dumb question. Yesterday was Wick's responsibility and today is mine.

He waits a beat. "Is that a problem?"

The piles of homework, the paper that needs to get written, and every other obligation hanging over my head comes to the forefront of my mind. I need *sleep*.

I shake my head. "No, sir."

"Thank you, son. I can always count on you."

I recognize the look he gives me is one of dismissal, and I stand, adding, "I'll go directly to the clinic and get everything ready for the Princess."

"One last thing," he says, triggering a tremor up my spine. Father always has the last word. "When I said earlier that failure is not an option, that wasn't an idle threat. Verity Sinclaire will be with child, one of *your* children, at the end of three months."

I nod, well aware of the consequences of not meeting Father's expectations, except even I can sense the difference here. He wants an heir. Demands it. And will get it by any means necessary.

That's what scares the fuck out of me.

7

Verity

AT THE END of the day, it takes me twenty minutes to find the way back to my room.

I'm exhausted and confused by the corridors, trying desperately to remember if the portrait I passed this morning was a man with a beard or a man with a powdered wig. It doesn't actually matter. I only find portraits of a man in a military uniform, landscapes with white roses, bland still lifes, and cherubs. God, the cherubs. Pale, pink-cheeked, creepy as hell babies can be found on any floor and in any hallway.

I'd spent most of the day out in the cold, twiggy gardens, hiding from people who probably didn't even need to be hidden from. From the looks of the place when I came in for dinner to an empty table in an empty room, the Princes and their King were gone the whole time. Now I regret not using the opportunity to explore.

I take a left at Military Man, and then a right at Religiously Grumpy Cherub, and then–

Yes, there it is.

Powdered Wig Dude.

I give him a sour glance as I retrace my steps from this morning, finally finding myself in front of a large, gilded door. Remy was right about that much. Everything in this place is covered in a thin veneer of gold, and this door in particular stands out, heavy and ornately carved. It takes me a long moment to work past the dread roiling in my stomach, but when I do, I push it open, revealing the yawning suite. It's already all lit up, the chandelier gleaming, and the first thing my gaze seeks out is the bed beneath it.

The big, lush, gloriously *empty* bed.

The knot of tension in my belly slowly unwinds. Tonight, there's also a fire in the fireplace, burning low, as if I'd been expected much, much earlier than nine-o-clock.

"You're late."

That's a clue, too.

Stella leaps from the chair, throwing aside a laptop before frantically smoothing out her sweater. It really isn't fair that she gets to wear normal people clothes–jeans and an oversized sweater–and I have to wear this ridiculous housewife getup.

"Sorry," I mutter. "Didn't realize bedtime was scheduled."

Stella looks hunted. "Everything here is scheduled, Princess. *Everything*. That's what I'm trying to tell you."

"Great." Just fucking great. "Well, I was trying to find my way around this place. Any chance there's a map or something? Because I don't think portraits of old dudes and cherubs are going to help me navigate much longer. That's pretty much every painting in this place."

Stella laughs like this is the funniest thing she's heard all day. Then again, she's probably been hanging around that Danner guy, so maybe it is. "I've been exploring, Princess! I'll give you the rundown on the way."

"The way to what?" I ask, narrowing my eyes at the box she

extends to me. It's nine. I'm sore and tired and in desperate need of eight hours to myself.

This box doesn't have a golden bow, but it still makes my stomach churn with dread. I took the tiara off before attending negotiations, and it's sitting on the vanity inside the massive dressing room off the bath. What the fuck is this one going to be?

"Prince Pace brought this for you," Stella rushes out, shoving it at me with an urgency bordering on suspicion. I half expect to find a bomb inside.

Even more scarily, it's a phone.

A shiny, brand new, meant-for-me phone.

The burner I'd come to the masquerade ball with had been confiscated before I entered the parlor, and I'd left my real phone back at the gym, secured inside my lounge locker. Still, I'm not stupid enough to think this is something I can use to talk to the Queens with. I doubt I can even add the cutsluts or my own mother. It's probably just a–

Ding!

Proving my theory, a calendar task notification pops up on the screen.

Appointment for the Princess. Sunday. 9pm. Medical wing.

It's outlined in red because it's seven after.

A leash.

Stella groans, "Oh *no*. It's going to take us forever to get down there. Maybe we'll save the tour for tomorrow, huh? We'd better move it!"

Grabbing my arm, she drags me from the room, ignoring the tight, unhappy sound I make as I struggle to keep up with her small and freakishly fast legs. "Medical wing?" I ask, trying to get a better look at the notification details through quick peeks as we descend the staircase. "There's a medical wing?"

"In the basement," she replies, leading me down the steps. "Every Princess has exceptional medical care." She tosses me a toothy grin. "Exceptional, exclusive, *private* medical care."

Before I can really process the reality of what that means, she's dumping me off by the basement door, panting with exertion. "Okay, it's down the stairs. Go left. Turn right at the freezers. It'll be all the way down that hall, you can't miss it. Put on the gown that's been laid out for you. Be quick, and good luck!"

Paralyzed, I ask, "Aren't you coming with me?"

"Come with you?" Tilting her head, she replies, "Oh, you mean into that dark, spooky, ancient basement?" She holds her smile, blinking once. "Hell no."

I gape as she pushes me through, flashing me another sunny grin before flouncing off. The phone in my hand dings again, making my blood run cold.

The basement isn't dark.

It's not very basement-like at all, in fact, and it doesn't really match the upstairs, either. This part of the Palace has had some obvious modernizations. Fluorescent lights, a lack of any signs of life, and an eerie silence give it an uncanny, discomfiting feeling. Liminal space. That's what Remy would call it.

The floors are a shiny, pristine white, my footsteps distinct as I cautiously follow Stella's directions. They lead me to a frosted glass door with a red cross on it, and when I push inside, it's just like everything else down here.

Bright and empty.

My eyes snap straight to the exam table in the middle of the room, and for a long moment, I stand there staring at it in disbelief.

There are stirrups.

"You've got to be kidding me," I whisper, approaching the table with an awed grimace. There's a thin, white, sterile gown waiting for me, and picking it up, I inspect it like crime scene evidence, sniffing the fabric. It's clearly new, but my mind still races with thoughts of other Princesses down here. Did they have their babies here? Is this the room the last Princess was in when she got her paternity results back, everything crumbling around her?

Trying not to think too much about it, I take off my dress with quick, mechanical motions, more afraid of someone walking in and catching me naked than I am of standing here in the gown, barefoot and nervous. I fold the dress, laying it neatly on a stool before swallowing thickly.

Clamping down on the urge to run out of this room–this Palace, this whole goddamn island–I reach beneath the gown and pull down my panties, hiding them beneath the dress.

Medical accommodations are good, I tell myself. That means there's a doctor. Someone objective, whose only job is to make sure I'm okay. That's what doctors do, isn't it? They take an oath?

Not that it meant very much to my last gynecologist.

I'm cautiously peeking into a metal storage cabinet when the door swings open, making me jump. The sight of Lex striding through, not even bothering to meet my eyes, makes my pulse quicken.

"Get on the table." Lex's voice is quiet but no less commanding as he pushes up his dark sleeves, revealing pale, wiry forearms.

"Is there–I mean, where's the doctor?" I ask, tightly hugging my middle.

Turning on the faucet, he begins methodically scrubbing his hands, staring unemotionally at the motion his palms are making. "I interned at Henderson's clinic last year," he responds, ripping a sheet of paper towels from a dispenser on the wall.

It hits me like a sack of bricks.

There's no sleek, gentle doctor coming into this room.

Just *him*.

My eyes track him as he opens a cabinet above the sink, pulling out a pair of latex gloves. He moves about the space like someone practiced, familiar with the instruments as he begins placing things on a rolling tray. A white tube. Some swabs. Gauze.

A speculum.

My thighs meet, squeezing as I ask, "What's this about?" The bleeding has stopped, but the pain sure hasn't, and if he thinks that thing is going inside me a mere day after what that torture device and his brother did to my vagina, then Lex Ashby is a goddamn lunatic.

The dismay settles into an inevitable doom as I watch him pull on the gloves, the latex snapping. "Get on the table," he repeats.

He hasn't met my gaze since stepping into the room, and the part of me that's thrumming with alarm is thinking it'd probably be worse if he did. That's the only thing that gives me the resolve necessary to lift myself onto the table, reclining so stiffly that I might as well be a plank of pine.

"I have a gyno," I try, voice reedy and weak as I tug my gown down over my center. "I've already had my annual."

He doesn't respond, and as he crosses the room, approaching me with those cold, empty eyes, I grow stiffer and stiffer, bracing for his touch when he stops at the table, plucking my wrists from my middle. He barely glances at the cuts on my wrists, red and raw, before extending my arms at my side, flat against the table.

Stupid.

That's what I am for not understanding. For being confused. For letting him stalk around the table with those laser-like eyes, arranging me with all the spiritless interest of someone posing a mannequin, and not seeing what comes next.

When the straps around my middle meet, a metal buckle clicking loudly into place, my stomach plummets. "Wait!" I gasp, pushing upward. I might be in a well-lit medical room, but my mind is back in that throne room, remembering the scent of the roses, the eyes of the men, the pressure of their hands as they held me down.

The cordy tendons in Lex's forearms bulge as he gives the strap a hard yank. Coolly, he orders, "Don't struggle," and his amber eyes probe me. There's nothing else to call it. He looks more interested in the jump of my throat than the sound it makes. "I need you to be still. There's no room for error."

"Error?" I ask, pulse racing. "What are you going to do?"

Instead of answering, he rolls the stool to the end of the table and sits right on my folded dress, placing his phone on the metal tray. Giving it a tap, he adjusts his gloves, reciting in a monotone voice, "January 7th, Verity Sinclaire, annotations for Father. Put your feet up." The last part, I recognize, is meant for me.

Squirming against the binds, I try again, "I've already had–"

He releases a small sigh before reaching out to seize my ankle, forcing my leg into the stirrup. As I suspected, there's a bind on it too, his muscles tightening as he secures my thigh first, then my ankle. I don't bother fighting with my other foot, letting him place it into the contraption with cursory movements.

Once it's done, I feel like a bug. An insect. Something for him to dissect as he spins a lever, spreading the stirrups painfully wide. The humiliation wars with the paralysis of fear. My first instinct is to glue my knees together, but it's impossible, my muscles straining futilely against the binds. There's no hiding, no covering myself as he pushes my gown up to my hips, exposing me with an obscene sort of indifference.

The lamp he clicks on, pointed right at the apex of my thighs, just makes it worse.

"Now, we can begin," he says, voice smooth and sober.

I want to look away, to fix my eyes to the ceiling and pretend I'm somewhere else, but for some reason, I can't seem to tear my gaze away from the angles of his face. He doesn't touch me at first. He just looks at it–my vagina–with a detached sort of analysis. There's a spark in his eyes, though–a spark of life I hadn't seen this morning or last night.

He's looking at me like a bizarre specimen he can't wait to cut into. "Hm." His arm extends, giving the lever to the stirrups two more quick revolutions, forcing my thighs impossibly wider. I gasp at the strain, but if he hears it, he doesn't care. "Patient has visible vaginal contusions," he says, clearly meant more for the recording than me. His brows pull together as he inspects me.

As he inspects *it*.

I've thought a lot about a man seeing my body for the first time. Fantasized. I'd prepared for it by waxing and cleaning and wearing pretty panties, but having one of my future lovers inspect my vagina with clinical precision is beyond what I could've imagined.

And the first touch is even worse. All those nights on the roof of the gym with the girls, listening to their stories about deft, pushy hands had given me an idea of what it might be like for a man to touch me down there for the first time. It'd have to be slow and sensual and thrilling, just like Laura said. It'd be electric. Mind blowing.

The reality is so disappointing that I blink back tears.

Lex's cold, latex-covered fingers press into my folds, prodding me as if I were a corpse. Reaching for a package on the table, he rips it open and squeezes something clear and thick onto the tips of his fingers. "Applying a numbing lubricant," he mutters.

I jump so hard at his touch that the whole table shakes. "It's cold," I rush to say, but it doesn't matter. There's a quick flick of his eyes up the length of my body, and then, shoulder shifting, he forces a slick finger into my hole. My body is wound so tightly that it's a minor miracle he can get it in at all, but the more I tense up in anticipation of pain, the more I realize it's not there.

For all his callousness and icy hands, Lex's touch is indecently gentle.

He pauses there, finger buried inside me, and fixes his eyes to a spot on my inner thigh. "Just a moment for it to take effect," he says. I don't know who he's talking to–me or the phone. Either way, the tight panic recedes to the edges of my awareness, ready to pour forth, but willing to wait for a reason.

The room is deathly quiet, nothing but my quick breaths filling the space between us, so I hear him move before I feel it, the latex of his gloves squelching as he moves his finger, sliding it out before pushing back in. The muscles in my thigh twitch, and I know he can see it, his gaze still fixed to the tendon where my legs meet my hips. His face is blank, but I can see it in his shoulder–the rocking motion as he pulls out, pushes in, pulls out, pushes in, out, in, out, in.

Is he...

Is he fingering *me?*

Just as quickly as the thought arrives, he's adjusting the lamp, looking bored. My face heats at the stupidity of even thinking it.

"Patient has minor swelling and evidence of light bleeding." The numbing agent is working, and although I can feel him prodding around down there, forehead wrinkled pensively as he spreads my folds, the sting is absent. After some swabs and prodding, he goes on, "One... two shallow tears and hymenal transection. No scarring or evidence of past trauma. Recommended patient continue a regimen of pain reliever and sitz baths as needed."

I've been here one day and the list of injuries to my body are as long as one of the Dukes after a particularly rough fight. I remain tense as he works, watching the skilled way he moves when he holds me open with one hand and casually discards one swab for a new one with his other hand. If I find myself examining him in return, then it's only because it's an effective distraction.

Lex has dark eyebrows that are perfectly arched. I imagine if he wanted to be more expressive, it wouldn't take much to show it with his brow. He has a strong jaw that's speckled with the shadow of what stubble could be if he left it for another day or two, and there's a soft spot of color on the top of each cheek. Every now and then, when he ducks his head to get a closer look between my legs, this one particular lock of his auburn hair that's escaped his careful, tied-back knot will force him to jerk his head to the side, flinging it away.

He's... cute.

It's the first time I've really had the thought. It's not the big, flashy hotness his brother, Wicker, likes to flaunt around, nor is it the dark, compelling smolder of Pace. Although Lex has a cute face and the shoulders of his shirt are tight with the suggestion of muscles, Lex's real attractiveness is in *this*: The smooth, confident way he moves when he produces a needleless syringe, studying the contents intently before ducking his head again. He carries himself the same way he had on the dance floor, hypnotizingly precise.

"Just some pressure," he says in a disinterested tone, arm shifting as something hard and cold slides into me.

I wince, eyes clenching, but then he makes a startling, gruff demand.

"Look at me."

I blink my eyes open, meeting his gaze. His expression is unreadable, so I don't know exactly why I feel so pinned down under the weight of his stare, but I know that I do. Something about it is unbearably acute, his eyes dark beneath heavy lids as his jaw tics.

Suddenly, I begin feeling... not pain. Not even pressure. Just an odd fullness of warmth in my center. My toes curl and uncurl as I endure it, and when the curve of his shoulder shifts, hand tossing the empty syringe onto the table, his eyes finally release me.

"It... stings a little." Swallowing loudly in the stillness of the room, I ask, "What was that?"

He tosses a wad of gauze toward the trash can near the door. "My semen."

My voice gets lodged in my throat and I have to struggle against it. "Your *what*?"

"Like I said." He shrugs. "There's no room for error."

"That's disgusting," I sputter, realizing that the warm slickness I feel inside is *him*. "How did you... did you jerk off before coming in here?"

When he turns to jab the button on his phone to stop the recording, the backs of his ears are flushed. Come to think of it, he looked flush when he came in here. The thought of him jerking off just to shoot it into me with a syringe is somehow even colder than what happened to me last night, and that?

That's saying a lot.

Noticing the shocked grimace on my face, he fixes me with a weary look. "Don't pretend you don't know what you're here for," he says, standing from the stool. "The rules say I have to get my semen into you. There's no covenant about how it gets there." I feel more than see his gloved fingers pushing into my clit, the latex feeling strange. "You should be thanking me," he goes on, rubbing the nub of nerves. "A whole night to rest this mangled cunt is more than most Princesses get."

Hissing, I push against the stirrups, writhing away from the sensation. "What are you doing?"

He scoffs, clasping my hip. "You really are a virgin, aren't you?" The look he gives me drips with condescension. "I'm stimulating a state of physical arousal."

I gape at him. "Why?!"

Lex's narrowed eyes hold mine as his fingers dip down, bicep bulging when he forces them inside. "Because you're clenched so tight that nothing is going to get past that brick wall you call a cervix. You need to relax and let your body accept it."

Accept it.

His semen.

"Relax?" My responding laugh is edged with hysteria. "Just relax as I'm strapped down to a table with my legs forced open so my cunt can be–what did you call it—oh, yeah, *mangled* some more. Sure, I'll just relax."

He goes eerily still, finger buried deep inside. "I was the top of my class, from grade school to junior year of undergrad. I've won seven awards, published five papers, set the new standard for Forsyth's physiology department, and have aced every test I've ever taken, so when I say I'm good at something, you know I mean it." He pitches forward, bearing down over the cradle of my spread thighs. "I'm excellent at anatomy," he says in a low, smooth rumble that shoots right into the pit of my belly. "I know every single nerve in your body. That blush rising up your neck means it's already started with cutaneous vasodilation. Next will be–"

I gulp.

His gaze jumps immediately to the movement. "Salivation." His eyes dip down, fingers rubbing my clit in faster, tighter circles. "Nipple erection. Soon, you'll begin sweating."

Too late, I think, the back of my neck already prickling with moisture.

"Physically, all that's left," he says, eyes sweeping up my neck, "are the basic genital mechanisms, such as... this." I gasp as his latex-covered finger brushes my clit in a downward motion.

He's right. No matter how much I try to fight it, I can feel every cell of my body flaring to life under nothing but two of his skilled fingers. I turn my head, unwilling to look him in the eye as my breath quickens, toes flexing in the air.

In a quiet voice, tinged with curiosity, he notes, "Your body is remarkably responsive. They'll like that." Even in the growing fog of lust, it doesn't take me long to understand who he means. *They.*

His brothers.

I wince at the whimper that escapes my throat, unable to stop my hips from squirming upward to meet the friction of his fingers.

The next time he speaks, he sounds closer. "The sensory input is already navigating to your supraspinal structures." I refuse to look, but I can feel the heat of him, his body hovering over mine. "You're close now. Wet. Expanding. Your body is preparing for the motor contractions of your pelvic floor. The only thing that's missing–and this is the most important part–is the central activation of thoughts. Psychological stimuli will induce desire."

My breath comes in short, agonized pants, and the next time he speaks, I feel the words as much as hear them.

His silky whisper is like liquid fire against my ear. "Have you ever had your pussy licked, Verity? I know you were a virgin when you came here, but that doesn't mean you haven't done other things." Whatever sound I make elicits a sigh from him. "No, of course not. But I bet you've thought about it, haven't you? How it'd feel to have a guy's tongue on you, right here." He pushes into my clit, and without wanting to, I keen. "It'd be wet and warm. You'd feel his breaths, the sounds he'd make, the vibrations. You'd grab his hair, wouldn't you? I think you would. You strike me as the type. All coy and sweet until a man's between your thighs. Look at you right now, all red and desperate for a thick cock to slide into you. It wouldn't take much. You just might have the most perfect pussy I've ever seen. So pink and tight. My brothers won't have to work very hard to fill it up."

My back arches and I turn, catching his gaze. He's close–close enough that I can feel the breath spilling from his flared nostrils. His eyes are dark and heavy-lidded, pupils blown wide as his shoulder rocks.

And he's staring at my lips.

"A few months ago," he murmurs, "Even I would've–"

My mouth opens on a sob as it explodes inside of me–a million tiny pinpricks of pleasure, blooming from the tips of my toes to my tightly clenched eyes. It rolls through me like a thunderclap, and I chase it.

Doggedly, desperately, *shamefully*, I chase it.

I strain against the straps to buck into his gloved hand, body shuddering greedily for every aftershock.

But then the pressure of his fingers is gone.

I feel the straps being released, one by one, and I'm still halfway seizing as I watch Lex walk away. He snaps off one glove, and then the other, tossing them into the trash bin. "Put the pillow beneath your hips," he says.

I blink at him, dazed. "What?"

When he turns, any trace of interest is gone. He looks bored again, mouth tight with impatience. "The pillow beneath your head. Put it under your hips. It's simple gravity."

I obey mechanically as he washes his hands, realizing that it was just a trick. His smooth voice. The words he said. Even his smoldering stare. That tinge of want I thought I saw was just... gold.

Lies.

"You can go back to your room in thirty minutes," he says, not even sparing me another glance as he exits the room.

～

"I LAID out two outfit options for school today." Stella's standing behind me, twisting a lock of hair and trying to make it curl against my cheek in a matching soft tendril to one on the other side. "Pesky bugger."

"It looks fine," I tell her. She woke me up an hour and a half ago to start my preparations for the day. A 'Big Day!' according to her, because we've got class today and it's my first public appearance as Princess. Stella's forehead creases in concentration as she tries to tame the curl. I grab her wrist. "Seriously, it looks great. All of it does."

I glance at the mirror, and the woman reflecting back startles me. The soft, but sultry eyes. A dark blush lipstick that makes my lips plump and full, yet still seemingly innocent. The way she blended colors to make my cheekbones appear sharper, my nose a little thinner. It's like magic. My handmaiden is skilled at both applying makeup and styling hair.

Mostly to get away from her, I rise from my seat and start for the dressing closet. "How did you learn to do hair and makeup?" Wicker had mentioned something about her being a 'Hideaway reject', but her skill transcends that of a whorehouse novice.

"Tech school," she chirps, squeezing past me. "I wasn't the best student in high school, so I took an alternative route. They had a cosmetology certificate, and I took to it like a duck to water."

"Well, you're very good at it."

She beams at me. "Thank you, Princess! I never thought I'd be working with someone like you when I got it."

I wither a little at the comment, mentally preparing myself for more like it. Verity Sinclaire is nowhere close to being a celebrity, but the Princess?

She is.

The dressing room is twice the size of my bedroom at home. Bigger than the ring at the gym. Closets filled with clothing, shoes, socks, stockings, bras and panties. Everything I'll ever need lines the walls. In the middle is a wide ottoman, made of the same lush material as the headboard over the bed. Two outfits are laid across the top. The first one is a pale blue dress similar in shape and style to the one I wore to negotiations. The second is a cream sweater set with pearl buttons, and it's been matched with a gray, knee-length pencil skirt.

"Do you have a preference? I mean, the dress is pretty, but the sweater is so soft—feel it." She thrusts the sweater in my hands. She's not wrong. It's amazingly soft. The tag says that it's cashmere.

"Did you also pick these out?" I ask, weighing the options. Aside from the soft sweater, neither are anything I'd choose for myself.

Stella laughs. "Gosh, no. The closet is divided into outfits for specific events. These were titled: School-Monday. They have every event or activity you could possibly attend covered." She approaches one of the doors and slides it open. Racks of clothing hang from wall-to-wall. Tags are affixed to each hanger. "School, parties, football games, weekend casual, night clothes..." She opens a door and reveals large floor-to-ceiling dress bags. "This is just your formal wear." Opening another door, her eyes widen as she pulls delicate, sheer lingerie off the rack. "*Whoa*, check this out! Even the Hideaway doesn't get stuff this nice! My sister always says seduction is something you do with your mouth, not your hosiery, which is actually super ironic, because if you've ever been gagged by a pair of stockings, you'd be really surprised how effective they are." A pensive expression comes over her face and she taps her chin, musing, "Although, thinking of it now? It's possible the mouth thing is less about talking and more about–"

"Let's go with the sweater and skirt," I say, turning quickly, annoyed at the heat rising on my skin. After my three encounters with the Ashby brothers, I don't think seduction is something any of us are going to bother with.

Also, I think, *it'll hide the cuts on my arms.*

Stella grins. "Excellent choice!"

It's weird having her hover over me, handing me each piece of clothing and making approving gestures or comments with each one. It's a relief when she sets the heels on the floor by my feet, and I slide them on, finally ready to face the day.

That is, until I arrive for breakfast. The dread at seeing Lex at the table is replaced by confusion. There's only one place set, and it's in front of the chair I sat in yesterday. There's a single white rose in the middle of the empty plate, but the table is vacant, quiet other than Danner standing near the kitchen door.

"Good morning, Princess," he says, stepping forward to pull my chair out.

I sit slowly, casting a wary glance at the white rose waiting for me. "Excuse me, but where are the, um, Princes?"

Danner smoothly eases the chair toward the table. "If I'm not mistaken, they've chosen to take their breakfast in Prince Lagan's suite this morning. He did leave you a gift, however. There's a note."

"Oh." My stomach dips as Danner gestures to the rose. There's a slim white card nestled beneath the petals and I pluck it out, turning it to reveal a short, messy scrawl.

To my beautiful Princess. May she reign. -L

I stare long and hard at the letters, my cheeks growing warm with the memory of his voice, still slithering around in my memory.

"...the most perfect pussy..."

Confused at the flutter in my stomach, I look up, asking, "He left this? Lex? Are you sure?"

If he finds the question stupid, then Danner does a good job of hiding it, dipping his chin in a nod. "Certainly, Princess. He left it here for you earlier this morning, right after delivering the staff your new nutritional requirements."

"My... what?"

"Your breakfast," Danner clarifies. "It's waiting and warming in the kitchen. Let me see to it." He vanishes through the swinging door, quickly returning with a plate of food. There's a piece of toast slathered with bright green avocado, slices of oranges and berries, a decent helping of eggs, and turkey bacon. Danner sets all of this in front of me, including a small cup filled with a colorful array of pills—vitamins. "A special diet for gestation," he explains.

Gestation. The word is just as cold and impersonal as what happened in the basement last night. I had to lay there with my hips propped up, imagining Lex's weird robot sperm slithering through my uterus, and now I freeze. Could I be? Already?

No.

I'd know. Wouldn't I? Some kind of biological signal? A feeling?

I stare at the plate, too discomfited to meet his eyes. "Thank you."

"Of course." He sets a small bell next to the vitamins. "Just ring if there's anything else you need."

And with that, he leaves.

My appetite left at the word 'gestation', but I know better now than to skip a meal. One of the benefits of Pace's gift–the phone–is that I now have access to a copy of the covenants I'd requested yesterday.

The Princess shall treat her body as a temple.

This covenant is one of the longest, with multiple subsections and bullet points, each driving home the reality of a single fact: My body isn't mine anymore. I'm to nourish it, prepare it to sustain another life, keep it healthy and safe, and at no point was it made anything less than clear that Ashby and my Princes are the sole authorities on what qualifies as beneficial or harmful.

The Princess shall accept the gifts she is given with the highest gratitude.

The rose sits beside my fork, its long stem smooth and thornless, and I shoot curious glances its way as I fill my churning stomach. It's gorgeous, the petals a soft cream, and even though the scent makes me stiffen with the memory of being on the throne, its presence makes me feel something not altogether unpleasant. Considering that, not even ten hours ago, he'd subjected me to the coldest display of dispassion ever, the gesture seems...

Shockingly sweet.

If it'd been material–more gems or baubles–I wouldn't have given the gift a second glance. But this is simple. Elegant. Weirdly thoughtful.

Beautiful.

It's the first time any of them have paid me a compliment before, and I find my cheeks heating at the memory of him propped above me last night, speaking those low, dirty words into my ear.

I eat in total silence, nothing but the distant ticking of a grandfather clock to fill the space. Every time my fork scrapes the china, the harshness of the disturbance makes me flinch. It feels like the entire Palace is holding its breath, suspended in animation as I finger the petals of the rose, wondering what he looked like, leaving this here. Was he wearing those glasses, hair unkempt, still rubbing the sleep from his eyes as he placed it on the table? Or was it quick— an afterthought?

I eat quickly, gulping down a small glass of juice before rising to my feet and sneaking toward the stairs. It's a silly thing to do, climbing to the second floor and checking each door. Any other Princess in my position would eat her breakfast in that strange, alien stillness and be grateful for the reprieve. But I'm not any other Princess.

I like to know where my enemies are and what they're doing.

I check three hallways and seven doors, and I mostly come across it by chance. At first, I assume it's some kind of store room, with boxes stacked up against the walls and books strewn over an old, antique secretary desk. But something about the area is disturbed. There's an energy in the air, and a scent. It smells like cologne, sharp but sweet.

The windows are tall, bearing heavy brocade curtains that have been pulled back. A beam of morning sunlight catches on something silver across the room, and I walk toward it, the hair on the back of my neck rising.

It's a door—or more accurately, a lock *on* the door. It's shiny and modern, a box with a punch keypad, and judging by the grainy sawdust I scuff with my heels, it's only just been installed. It's not so much the lock that makes my hackles rise, but the orientation of it, installed on the outside of the door.

It's meant to lock something *in*.

It's unclasped, and when I give the door a cautious shove, every cell of my body is on alert for what might greet me.

But it's just a bedroom.

I blink, taking in the space. The windows are wide open, and the old, gauzy curtains billow with a sudden breeze. Shivering, I assess the bed, noticing the rumpled blankets shoved toward the antique footboard. In the center of the mattress sits three empty plates.

Some of the tension in my chest is released on an exhale, only to be replaced with an odd sense of disappointment. This is where they ate. Together, the three of them. They probably talked about the day ahead. Maybe they even talked about me. About what I looked like on that exam table with my legs open wide. Maybe they sat here, sprawled out on Lex's messy bed, and laughed as he played that recording. But on the bedside table sits a sloppy stack of blank note cards much like the one that came with my rose downstairs. Maybe they didn't laugh at all. Maybe they sat here and struggled to find the best thing to say. What was it Ashby called them? Untutored in the art of flattery?

Most importantly, however, this is intel.

The Princes have possession of this whole Palace, with all of its bells and whistles and expansive nothingness, and instead of filling it with themselves, they settled into a small place. A hushed place. A place that's easily secured, saturated with them and little else.

They're nervous.

My phone chimes with a notification that I don't need to read. It's telling me to meet them downstairs in three minutes. I quickly obey, because I don't like it. The confusion. The uncertainty. The ember in my chest that's hoping Lex meant it, and the way it's so easily stamped out by the suspicion he wouldn't.

8

V erity

THE MASSIVE SUV idles at the curb, while a guy waits expectantly at the back passenger-side door. He's young—maybe a sophomore? Although I wouldn't guess that from the way he's dressed. Pressed slacks, a crisp button-down. There's a PNZ pledge pin on the pocket.

"Princess," he says, opening the door for me. Inside the dark vehicle, I see the brothers, but I'm too busy wrapping my head around the interior to notice their expressions. It's like a limo, the seats facing one another, and I can only assume the pledge will be the one doing the driving, because all three Princes are back there, waiting.

"We've got a meeting in Coach Reed's office in ten minutes, Red," Wicker says, glaring at me from inside. "Get your ass in the car, or I'll do it for you."

"Sorry," I say, trying my hardest not to look at Lex. Unfortunately, I realize quickly that this skirt is going to be a problem with the height of the SUV. I try twice to lift my foot up to the ledge, but the narrow fit of the skirt, plus the heels, makes it impossible.

"Um." I look to the driver, tucking the jacket I'd brought beneath my arm. "A little help?"

With a start, he takes me by the elbow and places a hand on my hip, but Lex's low, venomous voice makes the boy freeze.

"What the fuck are you doing?"

The boy stammers, "S-s-she needs–"

"The only thing she needs," Pace says, jaw tense, "is *us*." Snapping forward, he grabs my wrists and yanks me in. My knees drag across the carpet and I hiss, skin burning.

"Pick her up," Lex commands.

"I've got it!" I shout, trying and failing to fight off Pace's harsh grip. Wiggling like a worm, I manage to lever myself upright. Breathlessly, I slide into the empty seat next to Pace, cradling my knee with the hand he hasn't captured. "*Jesus.*" Each of their gazes bore into me as I catch my breath, willing the hot burn of humiliation off my cheeks.

Pace bends to pluck my jacket off the floor, his dark eyes crawling up my calves. "Your legs might look killer in that skirt, but considering what you signed on for, you might want to use your brain the next time you get dressed."

I go to grab the jacket, but much like my hand, he tightens his grip, not releasing either. "What's that supposed to mean?" I ask, disconcerted at the sight of his hand entwining with mine.

Wicker, who's sitting across from us, gives my outfit a long, disdainful look. "It means that a Prince should have easy access to his Princess' pussy, so wearing a straightjacket on your legs is a cockblock."

I shrink into myself, smoothing back that fucking curl Stella worked on for so long. "This was one of the approved outfits," I mutter, trying futilely to pull my hand back. "I followed directions."

"Burn that skirt and any other like it," Wicker says, not-so-discreetly shifting his crotch. "When my time comes, I'm not going to waste it wrestling you out of wool poly blend."

I give up fighting Pace more quickly than I think I should, fixing my eyes to my knees as he rests our clasped palms on his thigh.

The driver slams the door and Lex looks at his brothers. "Why are you going to see Coach Reed?"

"Father set up a meeting," Pace says, not sounding overly happy about it. "He wants me and Wick back on the team."

"Seriously?" Lex asks, seemingly surprised. "He never mentioned it to me. They're already in pre-season."

Coach Reed is the Forsyth hockey coach. I glance at Wicker. "Don't you play lacrosse?"

My question gets his attention, and he throws his arm over the back of the seat, giving me a smug chin lift. "So our little cubslut's a fan."

My eyes narrow. "I've just seen your banner on campus. No one can miss a head that big."

Lex makes a small, amused sound, and for the first time since last night, I look him in the eye. He's not smiling, but there is a certain mirth in his gaze when he looks at his brother. "She's got a point, Wick." Such a tiny reaction, and yet, it makes my stomach erupt in frantic flutters.

Both the rose and the note are nestled in my bag.

In any case, it's pointless to pretend I don't know Whitaker Ashby. There's not a girl or guy on campus who isn't aware of his reputation. He's devastatingly handsome, flirtatious, athletic, *smart*. His face is on one of those banners that hangs from the athletic administrative building honoring the best of Forsyth U; his body in motion, lacrosse helmet covering half his head, a perfect bead of sweat gliding down his sharp cheekbone toward his strong jaw. I think about it every time I pass it on the way to the visual arts building.

I bet it's Photoshopped.

"That's a good photo," he says, the spread of his legs beckoning any available eyes to his crotch. "We played Whittmore. I had a hat trick. Were you there?"

"No," I say, but halfway through a resolve to tell him I wouldn't be caught dead at a lacrosse game, Pace shifts our clasped hands beneath the jacket on his lap.

Right to his unzipped crotch.

Pace smoothly cuts in. "We've played hockey together since our first boarding school. Lex in the net, me in the center, Wick on wing."

Wicker looks away, all the smugness draining from his eyes. "Circumstances just made it better for me to shift to lacrosse the last few years." While Pace was in prison. For what, no one has said, although he has made it clear it's somehow my fault. Maybe for commandeering women's hands and pushing them into his open fly.

A lot like he's doing right now.

Sweat prickles up my neck as I glance over, confirming that nothing is visible to his brothers, but when I give a harder yank, he digs his fingers into my wrist, pitching close to speak into my ear.

"Today is *my* day, Rosilocks," he whispers with a breath that flutters the tendril of hair. "A Princess shall obey her Princes."

Swallowing, I feel the creep of defeat as he guides my fingers through, the shock of his smooth, hard warmth unmistakable. Is that how this goes? Each one gets me for a day? It wouldn't really matter. He's right about the covenant. The very first one–one of the only covenants I was actually able to read before signing it, so I can't even tell myself I didn't know.

I let my hand rest on his erection, limp and still, as Lex speaks.

"You know why he's doing this," he says, looking between his brothers.

Pace snorts, giving nothing away. "You mean the thing where he wants to fill my time with extracurriculars, but Coach won't take me unless he gets Wicker, too?" There's a bitterness to his tone that makes his grip tighten, pushing my fingers around his hard shaft. "Yeah, that *had* occurred to us."

Wicker laughs joylessly. "We were so close," he says, head shaking as he stares out the window. "So fucking close to getting out."

"You mean *Lex* was close," Pace replies, running his fingertip around my pinky.

"No I wasn't," Lex argues. "I'm not out until you two are." My ears perk at this, eyes flicking upward. *Out*? Out of what? Whatever they're talking about, from the way they look at each other, it's useful. Important.

I tighten my fingers around Pace's shaft, asking Lex, "Does that mean you're playing hockey, too?"

Pace inhales sharply, flexing his hips up.

Lex meets my gaze, his amber eyes tightening. "Of course not. I'm in my last semester of pre-med. My schedule won't allow it." Med school. Surely he's already applied. Has he been accepted? "I'll be too busy studying, escorting *you* around campus, working my internship, making my interviews, submitting papers, and I swear to fucking god, Pace." His glare moves to his brother. "*One drop* of cum and we're all fucked."

Pace's cock twitches in my frozen palm, a puff of laughter escaping his lips. "Relax, bro." He gives my fingers a squeeze. "Just building some hype."

"You've had almost two years of hype," Lex says, jaw tense. "Bend her over the seat and shoot your load in her. She's a Princess, not a Lady."

This time when I move to yank my hand back, Pace lets me, my body jolting with the release. The humiliation burns my cheeks yet again, but it's second fiddle to the way my stomach twists at Lex's words.

From the slow smirk Wicker gives me, I'm guessing he sees. "We're almost there. Are you ready for your first day on campus as Princess?"

I wipe my palm on my thigh, willing the lump from my throat. "Yes, I'm ready."

The car comes to a stop in front of the student union and the driver hops out, opening the door. Lex and Pace, closest to the door, get out first. I move to go next, but Wicker grabs me and yanks me back. I land next to him, half on his lap.

"Let's be sure." Wicker's hand lands on my knee, and he jerks it apart, making room for his fingers to creep under the hem of my skirt. "You're to be at one of our sides all the time unless you're in class. No speaking to other men or women outside academic obligations—especially anyone from DKS—male *or* female." His body is solid behind me, and when he speaks, I feel it wet against my neck, his lips dragging over my pulse point. "When we text, you respond. When we request your presence, you be there. When we touch you, you act like it's the biggest fucking honor you can possibly imagine."

I give a rapid nod, trying to remain as still as possible. I can feel his cock against my backside, already half hard. "Got it."

The truth is, I've watched more than one Duchess go through the system. I've watched Story with her men. I've seen the other Princesses, and I understand what's expected of me, at least in public. That was never a problem–the only parts of Royal life I've been trained for.

It's the private parts that I'm struggling with.

He doesn't withdraw his hand, pushing his fingers between my thighs. Ignoring the quiet, alarmed sound I make, he drags his lips up to whisper into my ear, hissing and urgent. "If today were mine, I'd tear this skirt off of you and make you wear the scraps of it all day. Pace is patient, and he likes a challenge. But don't you fucking dare pull something like this for me." His fingers brush against my core. "In fact, I don't want you wearing any panties tomorrow at all." Lips parting, sharp teeth pluck at my earlobe, making me flinch. "It'll be our little secret."

I scramble off his lap, lunging for the door. Pace catches me as I topple out, his biceps bulging under his T-shirt, keeping me from face planting in my attempt to get away from Wicker. I stare up into his dark eyes, swallowing at the spark of malice in them.

"Never run away from your Princes," he growls, righting me

with tightly controlled movements. There are people already watching, and Pace tracks them with spiteful glances.

Nervously, I try, "I'm sorry. I didn't–I wasn't–"

When Pace meets my gaze again, the heat of anger has been replaced with something impossibly darker. It's magnified by the way he touches my face, tender and dragging. "You see, Rosilocks, the only thing we really get out of this is you," he says, grazing a knuckle along the curve of my cheek. "Your sweet lips. Your pink cheeks. Your smooth legs and perfect tits. If you want to know the truth," he pitches closer, voice dropping to a deep rumble, "nothing has ever made me harder than watching him fuck you bloody over that table."

I lurch back, sickened by the wicked grin that quirks his mouth. "You're a pig."

"And you're our bitch." His smile hardens, the corners of his eyes growing tight. "You remember that when I call for you later, Rosilocks."

~

I'VE NEVER BEEN SPECIAL. Sure, my entire life had been centered around *becoming* special, but in reality, the position of Duchess was a pipe dream. To the outside world, at school or around town, I didn't register. Inside West End, I was barely a cutslut, the expectations on my purity higher than the needs of horny frat boys looking to blow off steam before and after a fight. And it's not like I had the freedom to rebel. My mother was everywhere, always watching, always protecting, always dealing...

It didn't matter if the guys thought I was cute, not with her hovering presence. None of them, not even the slutty, impulsive ones, would have dared to make a move. Not if they wanted to live another day with their balls attached to their bodies. No, it was known in West End that I wasn't there for them. I might have been their adorable mascot, a devoted cheerleader, a little sister, but at the end of the day, I was off limits, forbidden from becoming anything more.

I think that's why the attention I receive walking across campus feels so heavy—thick and smothering, like one of those weighted blankets. I'd waited my whole life for this moment, to be wrapped in the security of a title, for everyone to know what I'd accomplished, that I was special.

But I'm not walking with the familiarity of Bruins at my side. I'm walking with the Ashby brothers, popular and intriguing in their own right, but now elevated to Princes.

"Is it always like this?" I ask. A group of girls share a badly veiled whisper when we pass. My heart pounds in a slight panic. I feel exposed, as if everyone can sense I'm a fraud.

"You get used to it," Wicker says, arm draped over my shoulder. One girl stops dead in her tracks and gapes at him. I look up at him, just in time to see him wink at her. I swear to god, her legs clench. "And learn to reap the benefits."

Lex sternly corrects, "Your days of reaping co-ed cunt are over, Wick." With Lex on my right, Wicker on my left, and Pace's long, lithe stride leading the front, I feel trapped in, no place to go but back.

But every searing stare from a West Ender makes it very clear that's not possible.

There's no going back.

I almost feel confused until I catch a glimpse of myself in the mirrored windows of the English building. For the first time, I see what everyone's staring at. Stella's hair and makeup is a transformation, Cinderella style.

I look amazing. Elegant. Refined.

I look like an East Ender.

Pace stops at the fountain, the most visible spot on campus other than the student union, and turns to me and his brothers, raising his chin.

"Father said to give her five minutes."

I look between them, clutching my jacket close. "Five minutes? For what?"

Wicker sighs, sliding onto the concrete retaining wall. "For our fan club," he says, leaning his head back, eyes closed, not at all unlike a snake basking in the heat of the morning sun.

When I turn, my whole body stiffens. There's a line of men–PNZ members–leading all the way back to the Language Arts center. Some of them look eager and bright-eyed, while others look impatient and tired. They look like Stepford soldiers, all forty-plus of them arranged in a perfect, uniform row.

Each is holding a single white rose.

"They're here to make their public offerings," Lex mutters, joining his brothers on the fountain wall. He opens a textbook, clearly bored by what's unfolding. "Participation is compulsory."

It clicks in my memory. I've never seen it personally, but I've heard about it–the Princess getting her weekly presents from the frat. I never realized it was such a spectacle, and when I turn to them, it's clear they're awaiting my signal.

"Oh," I drop my jacket and bag, and then, dusting my hands off on my skirt, give the first guy a nod. "Uh, okay. I'm... ready."

He bounds forward, thrusting the rose toward me. Taking it, I begin, "Thank–" but he's already striding off, the next guy taking his place. They work like a conveyor belt, one man after another, and I struggle to balance the roses in my arm, not to mention the cards they all come with. Each one bears a note that looks exactly like Lex's had–a small, cream card folded in half.

It isn't until the sixth guy, a bit slower than the others, that I have an opportunity to glimpse what's written inside.

To my beautiful Princess. May she reign. -HJ

I freeze as I read the note, taking the next man's rose and unfolding the card.

To my beautiful Princess. May she reign. -MM

The next man's card is smudged, as if he'd written it while standing in line.

To my beautiful Princess. May she reign. -PT

I accept the rest of the roses with mechanical motions, tucking each inside the cradle of my elbow as I give quiet, bland thanks for each. I only glance back at Lex once, finding his eyes fixed to the book that's fanned open on his thighs.

I've never felt more like an idiot in my entire life, recalling that flutter of butterflies in my stomach at the breakfast table when I read his note. To think I'd believed for even one moment that Lex Ashby had been trying to... what?

Flatter me?

To create is to reign. That's the East End motto. Those words don't mean these men want their 'beautiful' Princess to reign in any literal sense. They just want me to hurry up and get pregnant.

The people around us watch the spectacle as the PNZ members filter through, rushed and pointed. By the time I accept the last rose, the bundle has swelled in my arms, and I cradle it like a baby, stomach roiling at the thought.

"Finally," Wicker says, jumping down from the wall and approaching me. He lets his hand travel down my back to perch on the curve of my ass. "Father had our schedules aligned so we'll have the same break. We'll meet you back here at noon."

"Fine," I say, not bothering to ease out of his grip. Wicker might be vile, but he's never been less than up front about it, and I think...

I think I might respect that.

In an odd, West End'ish way.

"I'll meet you here," I tell him, raising my eyes to his.

Looking surprised at the easy acceptance, he tilts his head. "You've figured it out, haven't you, Red?" He tucks that curl behind my ear, and then curves his palm around the base of my neck. "Father is always watching. Pretend you like it."

My eyes slide to Pace's and he nods, as if confirming his father has eyes everywhere. Looking back at Wicker, his gaze moves from my eyes to my mouth, tongue flicking out to wet his bottom lip. It's a performance, one that makes my stomach bottom out, because Whitaker Ashby is a master at seducing women, and I'm not immune. His eyes are a startling blue, even more so outside in the daylight. His features are almost otherworldly, and for the first time, I wonder where this man comes from.

I brace myself for impact, expecting the hard, relenting anger that he unleashed on me during the ceremony. But my expectations are wrong, because his lips are soft. The kiss is firm but gentle, the sweep of his tongue, a slow, toe-curling caress against mine. It's over before it begins, my heart lodged in my throat.

"Noon, Red."

He saunters off, backpack hitched over his shoulder, leaving me breathless and confused.

It's only when Lex approaches me, brows crouched low, that I realize this is just like the roses. A conveyor belt of kisses. Compulsory participation.

Lex bumps his kiss into my temple limply, without any feeling whatsoever, and the resentment twists inside of me. Not toward him—toward me, for expecting anything different.

Pace, however.

Pace is the worst.

"You're our first, you know." He captures my chin in a strong grip, fingers digging into the hinge of my jaw. His eyes aren't so dark in the harsh light of day, looking almost as amber as Lex's. "Going raw on a girl? Never fucking without a condom was one of the first rules Father made for us." His eyes dip down to my lips, pursed against the grip of his fingers. "East End can only afford so many accidents, and coming from one of his own sons? That would have been a death sentence."

The first touch of his lips on mine is exactly what I expected Wicker's to feel like: demanding and hard, tongue prying my lips apart for his invasion. He tastes like heat and the sharp edge of coffee, and even though I don't struggle, accepting it with my eyes clenched tightly shut, his fingers still press into the hollow beneath my ears, holding my jaw open.

The kiss slows, his rumble vibrating against my lips. "I wonder how it's going to feel, putting a piece of myself into you..." There's a short pause, the heat of him leaving, and then something warm and slick suddenly bursts against my tongue.

My eyes fly open at the sound, and Pace is clamping my mouth shut, trapping the wad of saliva he just spat there.

"A little something to remind you of me until later," he says, finally releasing me.

My gag reflex triggers, and the urge to vomit is overwhelming. Pace stares at me, almost daring me to fail.

Wicker's words echo in my head, *Father is always watching.*

With a smile plastered on my face, I swallow.

"Good girl," Pace murmurs as I pass him, ignoring the thorns of the roses poking through the delicate cashmere and into my flesh.

That's exactly what I am.

Good.

I'm good all the way on the walk to my first class. I'm good when I smile at the people passing. I'm good when I round the student union and weave my way through the large air compressors. I'm good right up until I find the bank of dumpsters, carelessly shoving the entire bundle of roses and cards inside.

OTHER THAN THE STARES, the walk to class is the most normal I've felt in days. This is my second year at Forsyth, and I know the campus like the back of my hand. Ever since I discovered I wasn't going to be Duchess, I changed my major from pre-med to visual arts, something that lessened the overall sting of losing the position. Pre-med in Forsyth churns out students like Sy and Lex. Driven, calculating, ambitious men. The classes are hard, but the competition is harder. I was all too happy to give that up.

I climb the stairs to the fine arts building to get to my intro to ceramics class. At the staircase that leads to the music wing, I spot a figure leaning at the bottom. Sun streams in from the windows, glinting off his piercings. I'd know those dark eyes anywhere–one of Story's Lords, Dimitri Rathbone. He must sense me watching because he turns, catching my gaze. One corner of his lip twitches downward, and judging by the disgust in his eyes, there's no doubt in my mind he knows exactly who I am: the enemy.

But it's more than that. It strikes me then. I'm one of *them,* the elite. The powerful. The envied.

The realization overwhelms me, and I spin on my heel, running down the hall. I duck behind a column and take a drink from the water fountain, trying to gather my wits.

Everything is different now.

"Thought you could hide from me?"

The voice hits like a punch. Terrifying. Domineering. *Home.*

I turn slowly, cautiously, dragging a wrist over my lips to catch a drop of water before I face her. She's standing in the hallway like some strange mirage, hand on her hips, faux leopard-print leggings hugging her curves. From the leather jacket to the stiletto boots that add five inches of height to her frame, she's almost too intimidating to take in all at once.

"Mama?" I squeak, quiet but strained. I glance around to see if anyone is watching. "What are you doing here?"

There's a wildness in her eyes, rimmed with red, that I've never seen before. "What am I doing here? I'm coming to find out what the hell my daughter is thinking." Her bark of laughter crackles with hysteria. "Defecting to East End to become a breeder? You've lost your goddamn mind."

Probably, but if anyone catches us together it could spark an inter-frat war with dire results. A girl steps out of the nearest door, the bathroom, and I grab my mother's hand, yanking her inside with me before locking the door.

She snatches my wrist in a hard grip, hissing, "Verity Marie Sinclaire, you'd better start talking or I'll—"

With a jolt, I break from her hold. "You'll what, mom? Drag me back to the gym? Punish me? Lecture me about what good girls do to get ahead in life?" I laugh, the sound shrill and panicked. "Guess what? Those lectures worked. I got it—the golden ticket. I'm a house girl just like you always wanted."

Her eyes narrow, sweeping over my outfit. "You're a *Princess*." She spits the word like a curse, like the very sound of it tastes bitter on her tongue. "No daughter of mine is going to be East End's glorified cum bunker!"

The repulsion in her voice feels like a slap in the face, but it's the disgust in her glare that makes tears sting at the corners of my eyes.

"I did exactly what you raised me to do: be a Royal." I shouldn't be so hurt, but I am. I knew she'd be upset—angry even—but my mom has never looked at me with such contempt before. "I know I failed to become Duchess, but that was out of my hands. Where else was I going to go, Mama? The Lords won't need another Lady until it's too late for me. The Counts are gone. And the Barons—"

"Don't even say it," Mama snaps, expression stricken. "I forbid it."

Shrugging, my hands fall heavily against my thighs. "I got an invitation and accepted it."

"Without discussing it with me." That's when I see it. All the hurt I'm feeling is reflected back at me in her welling eyes. "You just disappeared–turned your back on us. Do you have any idea the panic I felt when I couldn't find you?"

My chest aches. "I'm sorry for that. I just didn't think—"

"That I'd ever let you go through with it?" Her bracelets jangle as she crosses her arms.

I twine my hands around the strap of my bag. "Yeah, but also... I didn't think I'd be chosen."

She sighs, rubbing her forehead. "Well, it's not too late to figure out a way to get you out of this. I have contacts, and even if you signed something–"

"I did. I signed the covenant." *In blood.* Raising my chin, I add, "And the Dukes have already made negotiations. They've signed their own deal with the Princes. Breaking it would mean breaking the peace, which is already fragile enough. It's done."

Her face pales as she realizes this trade goes levels over her head. "The Dukes gave you up?" she asks, face twisting into furious outrage. "*My* Dukes. *My* cubs. First they reject you for that North Side tramp, and then they–"

"Hey," I say, voice sharpening. "You leave Lavinia out of this!"

"They traded you–my daughter–like a piece of fucking meat?"

I guess none of the Dukes told her about that part.

Oops.

I send a silent apology to Sy. "Mama, they only did it because I asked them to." Chancing a tense smile, I offer, "They actually came to rescue me first."

"I can see they did a bang up job!" she bursts, bracelets rattling at the fling of her hands. "For Pete's sake, Verity, do you even know what you've gotten yourself into? With Ashby? With *those* boys?"

I can't stop the incredulous laugh that punches from my chest. "Oh, now you care what kind of boy I'm serving? Because before Nick Bruin came back, we were pretty much certain Bruce Oakfield was going to be my third Duke." I raise my eyebrows, but it's unnecessary. I can tell from the shadow crossing her face that she remembers that day in the gym, dabbing my wound with antiseptic and a stoic frown. "You didn't seem to have any reservations about that."

Her shrewd eyes burn into mine. "You don't know anything about my reservations. You think Nick Bruin waltzed back into West End and took that Dukeship because of his *charm*?" The smirk she gives is slow and sharp. "That's right. The Bruins have the teeth, but baby, I've got the claws."

Mama has always overstated her influence. But it's true that Saul Cartwright was malleable to the right kind of person. "Even if that's true," I say, "even if you had something *minor* to do with Nick replacing Bruce, you still expected me to–"

"Expectations?" she snaps, eyes widening. "Yes, let's discuss expectations. Do you know what Ashby and his sons expect of you?"

"I do." Even when she laughs, unhinged and disbelieving, I remain calm, collected. "I'm not as stupid and naive as you think I am. This Princess gig? It's a farce. I'm just a vessel to them. They don't want me–they want the thing I'll create." Shrugging, I add, "I didn't go into this blindly, mother. You *trained* me for this. Every etiquette lesson. Every dance class. All those nights of staying home while the other girls went on dates. The fucking obsession over my virginity." It comes out in a rush, like a dam has broken in my chest.

"You're mad at me," she says, eyes hardening. "Fine. Be mad that I trained you to be Duchess. Hate me. Get mad, get even. But becoming Princess is a fight you're not ready for."

I scoff. "You didn't train me to be a Duchess. The Dukes, the Lords—even the Counts, before they were blown to hell and back–prefer virgins, but none of them require it. There's only one house who has that requirement. *The Princes*." I feel the ache between my legs, deep in my core where that phallus ripped my hymen apart. "That's who you groomed me to be ready for, whether you intended to or not. And if being a Princess is a fight? Then all the better, because I'm still West End." I sling my bag over my shoulder, straightening my spine. "I'll win."

My mother has always kept her emotions close, and now is no different. But she can't hide the look in her eye—something I'm not sure I've ever witnessed before.

Fear.

My mother is afraid.

Not *of* me. *For* me.

"Oh, Verity. Can't you see?" Her chin trembles as she takes me in, head shaking. "Baby, you've already lost."

9

P ace

I GRIP MY SHAFT, running my hand along the hard surface, squeezing my fingers tight. This part always feels natural, like my body and soul meet in this place of transcendence. Everything is fluid, easy, a swift rhythm that results in the best kind of euphoria.

For the first time since being back, I'm able to narrow my awareness down to nothing but the motion of my hands.

"What's the ransom on that puck, Ashby? Stop holding it hostage and shoot the fucking biscuit!"

Coach's voice gets past the filter and my eyes dart to Turner, who's open on wing, then back to the net. Wicker and I have been zipping up and down the ice all fucking day, but I haven't taken the shot yet. I was so pissed when Father told me I'd be gunning for center again, but now that I'm here, I don't want to let it go. Makes me greedy. Selfish.

I want it all to myself.

My eyes meet my brother's, and he gives me the nod. The gap closes and I take the shot, hiking my elbow back, giving the puck a hard slap. I hear the crack, the best fucking sound in the world–other than my name on a woman's lips as she's coming her brains out–and watch as the puck sails past the goalie's outstretched arms and into the net.

It's almost depressing how much I want to skate over there and take it back, get lost in the glide and push.

Back in the locker room, that sense of serenity melts away. The sound of the showers, the cold tile floor, men walking around in towels or butt naked. It's all like sandpaper to my psyche, the fringes of my awareness raw with the instinct to be alert. The locker room should be soothing. It's part of why I got on so well in lockup. After a childhood of group homes, boarding schools, and hockey, being packed in a mildew-scented sardine can with a bunch of smelly, raucous shitheads is uniquely familiar. Also familiar is the feel of my teammates' curious gazes, checking me out. In prison, that assessment was life or death, men twice my age measuring me up, wondering whether or not they could take me. A lot of them liked to test me.

A lot of them lost.

The guys here are measuring me up too, but for different reasons. These aren't heathens who are doing eight to twelve for armed robbery. These are East Enders–soft even when they're being hard. They're wondering what one of their own looks like after a stint behind bars.

Jacked, is the answer. I don't need a mirror to know the hard-packed muscle on my upper body is intimidating. I can bench any one of these assholes under the table. Bounce a quarter off my abs. That's pretty much the only benefit of prison. The lack of beer or sugar, and an abundance of time to spend in a well-appointed workout room, donated graciously by the Ashby Foundation, kept me on my toes during my stint in the Forsyth Pen.

Now it makes me a sideshow.

"Nice goal," Turner says, slapping me on the back.

My muscles tense with the instinct to whip around and take him to the floor. I stop myself–just barely. Gruffly, I say, "Thanks," and try to shake off this relentless vigilance. It's been two fucking months, and I still can't stop tracking every sound, every movement, every glance of the people around me. All I want to do is get back to the Palace, lock myself in a room, and fucking relax for five minutes.

I feel Wicker emerging from the showers, always aware of his dark, frantic energy. It buzzes in my mind like a distant cicada and I hone in on it, letting my brother's presence soothe the wild mistrust roaring through my veins.

No matter where I am, Wicker's got my wing.

He's wet as he stalks across the tiles, towel slung low on his waist. Head tipped down, his eyes scan the room as he makes his way to me. I go abruptly still at the increased buzz of awareness, knowing that simmering strain in his eyes anywhere. It's been two days since Wicker got his dick wet.

"No," I say quietly, pulling a clean shirt out of my bag.

"No what?" he asks, yanking off the towel and using it to rub down his body. I'm jacked, but Wicker's body was carved from the same marble those Greek statues came from, and I can spot a flex when I see it. The couple of guys who take the bait, flicking their eyes over Wick's perfect form, are asking themselves that sly inner question: do they want to fuck him, or do they want to be him?

"Stop causing sexuality crises." I shake my head. "Just because they don't have a pussy doesn't mean you get a pass. Father not only made this crystal clear, but you signed the covenant."

Wicker is a little something I like to call fuck-sexual. His dick is an equal opportunity lender. Chick, dude, MILF, DILF, barely legal or gender ambiguous, he doesn't discriminate. Wicker's libido is Ellis fucking Island. Give him your tired, your poor, your huddled masses.

He'll fuck their brains out.

He scowls, which somehow does nothing to make him less handsome. "First of all, that covenant is bullshit. Who cares if I waste a little cum on a shower handy? It's not like I don't have an infinite supply." He yanks open his locker and it slams against the one next to it with a bang. "Second of all, this whole thing is a trap. He's setting us up to fail so he has someone to pin his dead-as-a-doornail legacy on. Me, with the forced sexile. You, having to share a roof with your own fucking narc. And Lex," he lowers his voice, tipping closer, "because his dick's still on vacation." Wicker says this grimly, like he's referencing someone's terminal brain cancer.

I'm not worried about Lex, though. It's why I understand it had to be her. Verity. *Rosilocks*. For all our brother's oblivious disinterest, Rosilocks is Lex's type to a goddamn T, from her blushing cheeks to her curvy hips, heaving bosom and all. Fertile and ripe. She's just the kind of girl he'd avoid, because he knows he'd want her too much.

It's not what drew me to her, but I can see the appeal.

"Lex made his deposit," I point out, remembering the videos I sent him to jerk off to. All of the girls were redheads. From the basement feed–which, admittedly is just the hallway–it took him forty-five minutes, but my boy finally got that nut.

And then he gave it to her.

I hide my expression as I slip on my socks. This means that Wicker and Lex have both been inside her before I have. I've done a pretty good job of swallowing down what that's doing to me, because Wicker is right. Father knows exactly what he's doing. This is just another punishment for me, watching my brothers get handed the very thing I've wanted for so long. It's always been his second-favorite way of punishing me.

But then I remember that this is a punishment for them, too.

There are dozens of guys in East End who'd give their left nuts for the chance to be his studs, and he chose the only three who wouldn't. We were two years from being gone, out from under his thumb. Once college was done–once Wicker and I got our degrees–us and Lex were going to finally be free. No more ties. No more obligations. No more Father.

And now he's doing his damndest to make sure we're tied to PNZ for life.

Wicker drops down beside me, looking like a haunted man. "I need something to take this edge off." Elbows on his knees, head bowed, he rakes his fingers through his wet hair. "I need to *come*."

He's not the only one. All damn day, I haven't been able to think about anything except the way her hand felt on my cock. Wicker probably thinks I'm drawing it out to make her nervous, but that's not the real reason.

It's about knowing who has control.

"Even so," I thread my feet through my jeans, "the last thing you need to do on your first day with a team is have a quickie with one of these guys and ruin the dynamic. Remember Exeter?"

That, at least, gets me a grunt of agreement. Fucking teammates never works out. He's been down that bumpy, drama-filled road before.

"Listen up!" Anthony Giles, our captain, shouts over the noise. "Party tonight at the Nu Zoo to welcome the Ashby brothers back on the team."

Wick grins, snapping the waist of his black boxer briefs. "Like you need us as an excuse to party. I think you're just using us to lure back all the trim you lost when we left."

Giles laughs but doesn't deny it. "You in, Wick?"

"Fuck yes, we're in," he answers for both of us.

"You bringing your new Princess?" Turner asks, looking excited. These fuckers, all salivating for a chance to earn her favor like a nice dress and a tiara makes her *not* West End trash.

A week ago, they all would have been dogging her.

Wicker looks in the square mirror on this locker door and fusses with his hair. "Not fucking likely. She'll be tucked into bed and out of our hair by nine."

The locker room empties until it's me waiting on Wicker to finally get dressed. "I'm not going," I tell him, still twitchy about hanging back. I never would have dreamed of doing that back in the Pen. That's a recipe for an ambush, and my veins rush with the instinct to keep moving.

Wick's head snaps up. "Why the fuck not? I know you've got to bang the Princess, but it's been two years, Pace. How long do you really think that's going to last?"

My fists curl, but I shove the anger down–deep. "I've got business to handle, feeds to watch, and deposits to make."

He grimaces at the word 'deposit.' "Jesus, that term. Only Father could manage to strip every ounce of feeling from sex. And seriously, checking feeds? Is that a euphemism now?"

We both know it's not, but I do spend a lot of time looking through security, keeping track of people, and being aware of who's where. Father probably assumes I'm trying to be a good soldier, always having an eye on his assets, but the reality is, I can't stop. It's the only thing that makes this jagged torsion in my chest ease the fuck up.

Mostly, though, I have big plans for Rosilocks. Plans that are going to take a lot longer than whatever he's got in store for her tomorrow. I wasn't lying when I told her she was the only benefit for me. Knowing–not fantasizing or wishing–that my dick is going to be buried into her rosy cunt in a few hours is the only thing worth savoring.

Finally.

My turn.

Pushing my hair back, I approach my next question with quiet caution. "Are you really going? Because—"

He rolls his eyes. "I know. Keep my dick to myself. I do have *some* self-control, you know."

No, he doesn't. The Nu Zoo is East End's party house. No one lives there. The frat pools together the funds to pay for rent and repairs, and in return, it's exactly what the name describes. A zoo. Wicker's been a regular since senior year of high school.

He shrugs on his jacket, the Forsyth U hockey logo on the chest. "I can get through a party without getting off. I mean," he winks, "there's no covenant against watching."

I stare at him, wondering if he really believes that, because I don't for a minute. "It's not you who'll pay if you fuck up, Wick. Remember that."

The line of his shoulders goes tense, and he turns, fixing me with a flinty stare. "*You're* reminding *me*?" he asks, eyes narrowing. "Who do you think was piecing Lex back together after you left? I'm the one who stayed up with him every night for three fucking weeks, making sure he didn't tear his stitches or walk out into traffic. I'm the one who was going out to North Side at three in the morning to score him Scratch. I'm the one who tied him down when Father made him go cold turkey."

The guilt is the most familiar thing of all–like a knife in the stomach–and I feel the blood draining from my face. That's the only way to beat it. To be numb. To be nothing. To be gone.

Wicker goes on, "Maybe it was really fucked up for you in there. I wouldn't know–you refuse to talk about it. But when it comes to Lex, you never have to remind me what's at stake."

Averting my eyes, I try to find my voice. "I know. I only meant..."

In my periphery, I see him flinch. "*Fuck.*" He pushes forefinger and thumb into his forehead, eyes closing. "Goddamn it. I shouldn't have said that. It's what he wants–for you to think we blame you." When our gazes meet again, his eyes are full of the same bitter regret I feel. "We don't."

"You both keep saying that," I point out, offering a tense grin.

Weakly, he shrugs. "Maybe you'll start believing it."

"Maybe." Probably not.

There's a long, heavy pause, but neither of us says we're sorry. We don't need to. That's the thing about the three of us. We were molded to hurt, cut, and deceive, but no matter how much Father hoped it'd be against each other, it never has been. We made that pact years ago. In blood. In darkness. In agony.

We're a Cerberus–three heads, one heart.

That's why I can't be mad. It's why I have to watch my brother fuck Verity–hold her open for him, if I must–and keep my mouth shut. It's why I have to help Lex find the best way of getting his seed into her. It's why I have to look them both in the eye and pretend it doesn't make me want to fucking explode.

Because that's what Father would want.

Wicker's the one to break the silence, propping his shoulder against a locker. "Hey." He bobs his chin up, eyes hopeful. "You horny?"

I snort, all the futile guilt and useless anger melting away. "Not for you."

His smugness plummets into a scowl. "Sounds fake, but okay."

Gripping my bag, I drape my arm around his shoulders, leading him from the room. "Eight more hours," I assure him, "and you can have all the pussy you want."

But until midnight, Rosilocks belongs to me.

Only me.

AN HOUR LATER, it's even worse.

The edginess is amplified to a thousand as Lex parks the van in the alleyway.

"What did he do to get kicked out of DKS?" I ask, covertly scanning the area.

At least my brother looks more rested than he did yesterday, some of that frayed rawness gone from his eyes. "No clue, but if I had to guess, I'd assume a lack of allegiance." For Lex, it's always about loyalty. It may be the only thing he admires about the Dukes, and probably why he was so quick to agree to this during negotiations. "I'm just glad Wick got to kick his ass at the Fury before he got bounced."

The thing about wealthy men like Bruce Oakfield is they confuse money with power. They think they're above the rules. That only makes it easier for us to do our job.

The car is sitting in the shadow of the big house. The Hideaway is a massive mansion nestled in the heart of South Side, once owned by a rapper who infamously went down for tax evasion. I met him once when we were both in county lockup. Cool guy. Really intense about macramé. But Daniel Payne snapped up his property and turned it into the best little whorehouse in Forsyth, which is something Father's had sour grapes about since it happened. It was fine when Payne was slinging questionable cunt out of the sleazy Avenue motel, but real, high-class, luxury sexploitation?

That's supposed to be Rufus Ashby's thing.

"You sure you cleared this?" I ask, eyeing the shadows as we step out. The alley is narrow and too dark, and there aren't any security feeds this far south. This place is ripe for an ambush and my blood rushes with it, nerves flaring in instinctual alarm. "They know we're coming?"

"Perilini said we're good to go." Lex approaches the back door and knocks twice. And then once. And then twice again. His other hand is on the small of his back, resting on the butt of his pistol. "But be ready just in case."

He doesn't need to tell me. I've been preparing for this since the deal was made, hopping from one cloud to the next, looking for any signs of deception or suspicious activity coming from West End. That's the problem, though. I hadn't expected the handover to happen down here, on Killian Payne's turf.

I don't like it.

One gun in my waistband, another in my boot, I'm strung taut. When the door opens and a massive man appears, it doesn't get much better. Trust has never been one of my strong points, and walking into enemy territory? Might as well just put my gun to my own fucking temple.

"You're late," the guy says, and I recognize him as Marcus Reece from the Forsyth U football team. One of Payne's top soldiers.

"Sorry." Lex's voice couldn't have sounded less sorry if he tried. "Traffic was shit on the Avenue. We're here for the package pickup."

"You mean trash pickup." Marcus jerks his chin. "Come in." The door shuts behind us, which already has me flaring up like a live wire. And then Marcus tells us, "There's been a little snag."

My stomach drops. "What kind of snag?"

"Follow me." Music filters from the front of the house, but Marcus leads us up a back staircase. His shoulders are so wide, they graze the walls when we turn the corner to the second flight of stairs.

I shoot Lex an alarmed glance, but he just shakes his head, mouthing, "Relax."

Marcus goes on, "He's been here for a week, ever since his father made him an open-ended reservation in one of our long-term rooms." He leads us down a long hallway with doors on either side. The noises coming from each one varies. Music, soft talking, loud fucking. "Boss said no at first, not with the way he left DKS, but the Dukes made contact and asked us to let him stay until they sorted some things out. It seemed like a better idea to keep him occupied here than out on the street." He looks back at us, grinning. "Plus, his daddy's money is as good as any other."

"So he's just been living in a whorehouse for a week?" I ask. Nudging Lex in the side, I mutter, "Don't tell Wick. He'd use his whole trust fund."

Lex's mouth twitches. "He'd never pay for something he could get for free."

Point.

"Unlimited pussy," Marcus adds, as though this isn't a good thing. "It's awesome until you get bored. Which he did, two days ago. The longer he spent here, the worse his requests got, until eventually, they stopped being requests." He stops in front of a door. There's a padlock on the outside. Fishing a key ring out of his pocket, he slowly picks through them until he finds the right one.

Lex shifts, and the movement chafes my already raw nerves. If his cool facade is cracking, then I know shit is looking sketchy. "Look, I'm all for suspense," he says, "but what the fuck is going on here?"

Marcus sighs, scratching his forehead with the tip of the key. "Burns. He started burning our girls. Two of them took it, but the third?" His mouth flattens. "She was branded with his ring."

I scoff. "Playing out his fucking Duke fantasy."

Marcus looks me in the eye. "Exactly our thought." He finally opens the door, sweeping out an arm as if he's revealing a prize.

I guess in some ways it is.

Bruce Oakfield is shackled to the bed, naked, a ball gag in his mouth. One scan of the room tells me these things were part of a BDSM setup. Meant for the girls, no doubt, but now it's holding him. He has a black eye and what looks like scabbed over nail scratches down his neck. His eyes widen when he sees us, fear and hope both flickering in them.

A figure moves in the hallway. I reach for my gun, but it's Killian Payne, the King himself. He pauses in the doorway, hands up. The stern look on his face dares me to finish pulling out my weapon.

Jaw clenched, I release it.

"Thank fuck you're here," Killian says, jerking his chin toward Bruce. "One more day and I would've put the bullet in his head myself."

"Why didn't you?" Lex asks, assessing the scene.

Killian smirks. "Because Auggie gets pissed when we bloody the sheets." Marcus snorts beside him, but any levity in Killian's eyes falls away. "But mostly because you have an arrangement with the Dukes, and I know it's about more than simple body disposal." He turns his gaze to Bruce, eyes full of violent promises. "We had to burn over the brand you put on her, you know. It was the only way to get rid of your fucking initial."

I recognize the simmering fury in his eyes too well, and my eyes go to Lex. That feeling of having to hurt someone you don't want to hurt... it always lingers in the pit of my stomach, like a sickness.

Lex opens his bag and pulls out a small glass bottle, followed by a syringe. "I understand." The look he shoots me says Lex knows that feeling a bit too well himself. "Hold him," he tells me.

The Bruce guy struggles. They always do. His face is red and contorted as he bucks and thrashes, but it's easy enough to plant my knees into his chest and bear all my weight down, making him wince. Lex injects the sedative into his veiny arm, and I watch as he fades, the anger draining out of him against his will. Heavy eyelids. Sluggish limbs.

"These girls he burned..." I tilt my head, assessing Bruce's ring. It's big and gaudy, bearing an 'O' with a slash through it. Looks more like a zero to me. "They good girls? Loyal and all that?"

When I turn, Killian is standing with his arms crossed, mouth pulled into a pensive frown. He hears what I'm not asking, loud and clear.

Do you want revenge?

"Depends," he answers, eyes narrowing. "What do you want?"

I climb off Bruce, shrugging. "Access to one of your southmost cam feeds." Before he can protest, I assure, "It's not for my dad."

Killian scoffs. "Why should I believe that?"

"You probably shouldn't," I admit. "But it's the truth."

There's a beat of tense silence as Lex packs up the supplies, shooting me a curious look.

Ultimately, Killian dips his chin. "You know all those feeds are just trees and fields?" At my nod, he sighs, deflating. "In the past, we've had... incidents here at the Hideaway. Debts that never got paid."

Ah. The Duchess. Everyone pretty much knows how Bruin came to have her–by breaking into this place and violating her. I have to imagine his whores want their pound of flesh. Giving him a nod, I wager, "Loyal girls won't stay loyal very long if you let shit like this go."

Killian glowers at me. "Don't coax me, Ashby. I know how to handle my girls." Still, he looks away, thinking about it. "I'll give you one of the upper trail cams. Take it or leave it."

I take a moment to make it look like I'm considering. An upper trail cam will be nothing but sky and tree scape. Probably any sign of human life will be so distant on the ground, they'll be specks.

"Deal," I say.

Effie's gonna fucking love it.

Raising his chin, Killian glares at Bruce. "Make it slow."

I think about the outfit that's waiting for Rosilocks on her bed. Smirking, I reply, "I always do."

10

Pace

AFTER TUCKING Bruce into a safe spot down in the dungeon, I feel a sense of anticipation when I can finally sit down at my computer, flipping on the monitors and watching the screens hum to life. Effie bobs along to the beat of the song playing over the speakers, but when I open the door to her cage, she doesn't come flying out like usual.

She sees the tablet in my hand.

Her head tilts as she analyzes the blank screen, chattering, "*Settle down, dirty bird.*"

"You're a pretty bird," I correct her. "Say 'pretty bird.'"

"Pretty." She trills before throatily adding, "Pretty dirty bird."

Fucking Lex.

It bothers me in a way I know him and Wicker would chirp me for. It's not just because Effie somehow adapted without me, learning new words, getting closer to my brothers while I was away.

She's always been just a little bit theirs, too. Plus, she doesn't even really know what she's saying. She's just repeating back what she's heard.

But the pang in my chest still stings, and I reach out to gently rub her head. "You're the prettiest bird, Effie. Don't ever let anyone say otherwise."

It's that she needed me, and I abandoned her.

It wasn't intentional or voluntary, but she doesn't know that, and now whenever I leave for class, she throws a fit. I watch her on my phone sometimes when I'm in a lecture, her beak opening wide as she calls out.

"Sorry," I say, giving her feathers a light stroke. "It's been a long day, huh?" First school and hockey, then the shit at the Hideaway, then talking Lex into being Wicker's handler at the Nu Zoo party.

She preens after my touch, her yellow beak digging into her down. "*I love Pace.*"

I grin, remembering how long it took me to teach her that. I don't get to hear it as often now, Wicker and Lex having filled her head with nonsense while I was gone, but the sound of it makes something settle inside of me. "Hey, look what I scored for you."

It takes a few taps, but then the camera feed from the south upper trail fills the screen. It's a gorgeous view, the camera mounted so high that Effie can see for miles.

She squawks, turning to the screen with her wings extended. I can tell she's appropriately enthralled when the trill she emits isn't followed by any curse words. I give her one last scritch and close the cage.

"You're going to have to be quiet for a while." I drape the sheet over her cage before turning back to my own monitors. I've been letting thoughts of Verity simmer in the back of my thoughts all day, my nuts aching from the chronic tent pitching at the thought of being inside her. Any other night, I'd be hunkering down for some serious isolation, but there's one last obligation I need to attend to before the day is over.

I enlarge the screen for the bedroom and lean back in the chair.

The first thing I notice is she's wearing the night dress as I'd instructed. It's a tiny cotton dress with a scooped neck and little capped sleeves. The hem barely covers her thighs and my cock twitches at the sight. Baby Doll Magazine. Issue 24. April, 1978. Model Ivy Eden wore a very similar nightie. *That* magazine is in my bedside table, not nestled away in my sock drawer like the others. It's special to me–I traded a month of commissary funds for it. Ivy's long red hair and pink-pale skin got me through a lot of hard nights in the Pen.

Verity sits at her desk, a thick math textbook open in front of her. Calculus is a requirement, even for an art major. She tries to look busy, but I see the impatient bounce of her leg, the way she reads the same passage three times, and the unused highlighter clutched in her hand. She's anxious. *Good.*

The Princess is a fast learner, that much was obvious today. She's waiting for my call, and I spend a long time wondering what she's thinking. Is she hot for it? Thinking about how I'd jerked off in front of her at the ball? Is she daydreaming about the size of my cock? Thinking of how it felt under her hand in the car? Is she wondering how I'd taste?

Jesus, I thought I was hard when she was touching me, but that was nothing compared to watching her swallow my spit. I almost bent her over the edge of the fountain and fucked her right there. It would have been frowned upon, but I could've. It's my day, after all.

Giving my cock a squeeze, I grab my phone.

Prince Pace: Third door down. Door's unlocked.

I watch on the screen as she hears the notification, her whole body jolting at the sound. It takes her a moment to pick it up, her motions slow and wary. There's a suspended moment where I'm almost positive I can see her swallow, and then:

Princess: Coming.

Not yet, Rosilocks, but soon.

Entering in a command, I queue up a new video that fills the top right screen. It's from the day of the ceremony, from the very moment she arrived through the gates. It took me some time to hack into it that afternoon, so I missed this part–the one where she's gliding through the doors of the Palace with her head held high. Sure, she looks different than she did back in the day. A little older, sharper. Bigger tits and curvier hips. But the red hair I'd wanted so badly to feel around my fingers is the same. Shiny and long. Rosie Red. Rosi*locks*.

The hair is what got my attention on that dating app in the first place, so fiery and soft-looking. Unique. Special. Before I even swiped on her, I was imagining it between my thighs as she sucked me down, the way my fingers would look tangled in it. The name she chose seared her into my memory, and as soon as she accepted, we started messaging, exchanging a few innocent pics. When I asked her to show me her tits, she didn't quite go all the way, but still sent a fuck-hot shot of her cleavage, showing just enough of a royal blue bra to give me a raging hard-on. It was annoyingly coy, a little too innocent, but the thrill of the chase has always been just that for me.

A thrill.

I thought I'd up the ante, let her see what I could deliver if we met in person.

A girl needs to know what she's getting, right?

That video was a goddamn work of art. It wasn't a lame bathroom jerk off with the toilet and my half empty shampoo bottle in the background. I had mood lighting and clean sheets. Atmosphere. I wasn't just rubbing one off like a typical Tuesday morning. I was pumping one out to Rosilocks and her pretty, blushing tits, her cute emojis and flirty smile.

The video... too much too fast? Who the fuck knows with women. I knew by then she liked to play games–hard to get, cat and mouse–and I knew I could win her over. I just needed to let her know how I felt about her. How fucking hot she made me.

Except she blocked and ghosted me.

Pace Ashby wasn't going to let a shitty dating app security system ruin a good thing. I hacked into her account and showed her what she was missing out on. All over her face.

The worst part wasn't even campus security banging down my door a few days later. It wasn't being led out to the parking lot, shirtless and panicking, and being shoved against a police cruiser before I was handcuffed. It wasn't even the humiliating spectacle of it, the way everyone came out to watch.

It was that I heard that knock and hoped it'd be her.

It was the fact I let my guard down.

I hear her tentative footsteps outside the door, and the click of the doorknob turning, the creak of the hinges as she pushes it open. Without turning around, I order, "Shut the door behind you."

I watch her through a camera focused on the doorway. She takes a few steps into the room, eyes sweeping over my belongings. There's no bed in here, although there is a black leather couch. A coffee table sits in front of it with a stack of porn on top. Her nose wrinkles distastefully, and she quickly averts her eyes up to the bookshelves.

"That's a lot of trophies," she notes, hugging her middle. She looks small and scared on the monitor, her green eyes wide and alert.

I lean back, giving my balls some room as I fix my eyes to the image of her ass. "Father likes them on display."

She hovers near the couch, fingers picking at the piping. Something flickers across her expression. A comment about Father? Some sharp remark? Whatever it is, she holds it back.

She holds herself back too.

"Despite whatever you and Lex have done in the med clinic, I'm going to need you to get a little closer for us to fulfill my obligation."

Even on the screen, I can tell her cheeks turn pink, giving away that whatever actually *is* going on with her and Lex carries some weight. She moves closer. Nervous. She should be. This has been two years in the making.

"H-how are we going to do this?" she asks, fingers tugging at the dress hem. "I just—it'd be nice to be prepared." Lower, she mutters, "For once."

Fair, I think, considering the ceremony and the way Wicker took her. I'm sure Lex didn't prepare her at all.

Spreading my knees, I adjust my cock. "I'm going to make it easy on you, Rosilocks. All you're going to need to do is sit right here." I swivel my chair around, patting my thigh, and I take the sight of her in. Fuck, that nightie. The video screen doesn't do the real vision of her justice, all soft and shy.

I'm not the only one getting an eyeful. I've had my pants tugged down since I brought her up on the monitor. I grip the base of my bare cock in my fist, willing it to stay down. *Not yet.*

She gapes at it, stiffening. "You want me to sit in your lap?"

I give it a stroke. "You can watch me while I work."

Her eyes drag away from my erection to the monitors, throat jumping with a swallow. "What is all this?"

I shrug and beckon her over. "I monitor Father's security. Some in-house, some out."

Her movement causes the skirt of her dress to rise up, giving me a view of the cotton panties that match the top. "Do you want me to, um…" Her fingers run to her hips, embarrassment clear in the aversion of her eyes. "… take these off?"

My eyes narrow. "Well, I'm not going to fuck you through them."

Something in her face shutters, a bit of life draining from her eyes as she reaches beneath the hem, tugging the panties discreetly down her thighs. *Too* discreetly.

"Show me," I demand, stilling my hand on my cock. "Lift it up."

Turning her head away, she doesn't look at me as she plucks the end of the dress up, giving me a reluctant view of her mound. Her thighs are mashed together, so I can't see much except the shape of her.

"You're waxed." I let out a hard, frustrated breath. "Why the *fuck* are you waxed?"

Hastily, she drops the dress, glaring back at me. "What? It's a covenant. Stella–I mean, my handmaiden–she did it this morning."

"Well, never fucking do it again," I snap, feeling taut with annoyance. "Obey your Princes. It supersedes that covenant. Now, sit the fuck down."

She goes rigid at the command, eyes flicking down to my cock, swollen and ready. "Do you... does it have to be like that?" She meets my gaze, dread filling her eyes. "Again?"

It makes me grin, dark and bitter. "Remembering your throning, Rosi?" I run my hand down the shaft, emphasizing the length. "Disappointed it's not gilded? It's just as hard." When all she does is look away, face twisted, I add, "I've given my order."

She gathers up her courage gradually. A long inhale, hard sigh, chin jutting, shoulders squaring. I spend it taking the bottle of lube from the top drawer of my desk and dribbling it over my tip, exhaling loudly as I spread it with my palm.

When she finally approaches me, turning to show me her back, I almost lose it right there. She bends, the hem of her dress lifting just enough to give me the barest peek of where her ass meets her cunt. I savor it as she lowers herself, her spine a tense line, but I stop her. Lifting the dress, I wet my lips as I adjust, using one hand to point my cock right at her entrance, the other guiding her hip. I've waited so fucking long. Not just in prison, but before. I've thought about this moment a million times, in the hundreds of different ways it might unfold. This was never one of them, but it's better than nothing. I slot myself against her entrance. She's not very wet, but the first touch against her pussy makes my thighs flex instinctively.

I bat it down, pulling her in. "Torn-up pussy isn't my kink," I tell her, my voice dropping at least three octaves. "Take me nice and slow."

Her palms grip the arms of my chair, knuckles going white as she sinks down. A small noise escapes her throat, and it takes everything in me not to slam up into her, reveling in the heat. She's not wet, but the lube eases the way well enough.

For now.

"That's right, come to me," I breathe, watching as the distance between us slowly disappears. It doesn't matter that I can see her expression on the monitor, contorted with displeasure. She takes me so fucking good, every inch of my cock being sheathed by her without a protest. The second her ass finally meets my thighs, I spit a curse. "*Shit*, Wicker wasn't lying. You're tight as fuck, girl." I place a hand on her back, feeling the rise and fall of her long, deep breaths.

"I need a minute," she says through clenched teeth, and a gnarled laugh escapes me.

"Oh, you'll get more than a minute."

Her fingers don't leave the armrest, gripping it like a lifeline as I swivel us back toward the desk. I check the Palace feeds first and she notices, asking in a strained voice, "You're... watching over Ashby's assets?"

My balls are tight and I can feel my dick twitching inside of her, desperate to fuck. Clearly, she wants to be distracted, but me? I *need* to be distracted. I flip through the channels in a daze, explaining, "Front door, kitchen, your empty bedroom, the Gentlemen's Chamber, and then..."

The last one is the old tape from the ball.

She pitches forward to get a closer look, the movement making both of us tense. "Is that the dressing room?" she asks, sounding stunned. "You were watching us change?"

My cock chases her like a heat-seeking missile, and she stiffens, immediately rocking back.

The sound I make is gruff and surprised, my hands clutching hard at her hips. "Obviously." I slide my hand down her thigh, finally indulging myself in the softness of her skin. It's just as smooth as I thought it'd be, and when she shivers–or maybe shudders–I can feel it around my whole cock. "There were twelve random bitches in East End's most important asset. Had to know who you were." I finally give in to the impulse, ducking forward to graze my nose against her hair. "*What* you were."

She's still rigid. Anxious. "And what am I?"

Narc.

Traitor.

Mine.

"Too tense," I answer, trailing my hands up her body. The underside of her breast is round and heavy when I graze it with my scabbed knuckles. Her breath catches and I smile to myself. "You'll need to relax."

The weight of her in my lap is perfect, and when she turns her head, just enough for me to see the vivid spot of color on the apple of her cheek, I get a whiff of her shampoo–floral and sweet and *girl*. "No, I don't," she says, eyelashes brushing against her cheek when she blinks, slow and dejected. "I just have to take it until you're done."

"That'd be easy for you, wouldn't it?" Lowering my hand, I skate eager fingers up her inner thighs. "A little too easy." She stiffens when I brush against her center, thighs fighting to close, but I easily slide my fingers between her lips, finding her clit. "All that clenching isn't gonna get me to move."

"You're not going to, ah," she tries to shift but I grab her hip, holding her still, "move?"

"Not an inch." She'll have the urge; even if it's just to lessen the tightness, to stretch herself out. I know she's bruised in there. Lex told us so this morning. The simple pressure of my cock filling her up probably hurts like a mother. "I already told you, all I want is for you to sit." Nudging into her hair, I whisper against her ear, "Just like I did for all that time in prison."

Her jaw drops, but something catches my eye and I reach around her, minimizing all the screens but one. I leave the night of the ball in a small box in the bottom right corner. The main screen fills with the interior of The Gentleman's Chamber.

"Is that..." she wiggles, and I dig my fingers into her hip to make her stop. I'm not ready. "Is that a strip club?"

"Shhh." I'm perfectly still below the waist as I remotely shift the view, scanning over the women dancing on the stage, over to my father's table. The man sitting with him is Timothy Maddox. Maddox is known for crossing boundaries, going in and out of Forsyth with ease. There are a few wealthy, unaligned men like this in the city. Jacob Oakfield is one. Louis Mercer is another. Then there's Timothy Maddox. He doesn't just ooze wealth. He's got a calm intensity about him that makes my skin crawl.

Curiously though, the latter's' sons both hold positions of leadership in opposing frats, extending their family's reach without having to pick a side. Well, Oakfield's did, until he ended up in our basement. A waitress brings over a tray of drinks, bending to whisper something in Maddox's ear. His hand rests on her ass, fingers dipping into the curve of her booty shorts.

"What are you looking for?" she asks. In the dark part of the screen, I see her reflection, the way her eyes are focused on the video—watching—analyzing. Nosy bitch. I close it out, forcing the video of the ball to fill the space. I keep the volume off.

No words are spoken for a long time, even when I stroke her inner thighs, occasionally traveling upward to give her clit a soft rub, and then pointedly ignoring her responding flinch. The girls in the video get ready, Rosilocks among them, and we both watch as they all do their hair and makeup. My eyelids are hooded as I watch with her, my body somehow both strung tight and reduced to liquid.

It feels like practically no time has passed by the time they all filter out into the ballroom, masks affixed to their faces, but the timestamp tells me an hour has already gone by.

"Pace," she says, her voice a thin rasp as she reaches for the desk, grabbing the edge of it. "Can you–"

"No," is my flippant answer, and I adjust my legs to get some circulation back.

She's wet.

Ten minutes later, she gives a hard exhale, her back sinking. "It's getting late."

I look at the time on the leftmost monitor. Barely past ten. "I like this part," I say, dipping in to smell her hair again. I push my fingers farther between her legs, catching her slickness. "It surprised me–the way you move. I never expected that. I guess that doesn't come through in photos, does it?"

On the screen, she's dancing with Lex, their bodies moving gracefully.

She shudders when I spread her wetness over her clit. "It's been an hour," she says, thighs trembling.

"You want it to end."

"Yes." She says so bluntly that it makes my cock twitch. No softening the blow. No tiptoeing around the truth. She might as well be spitting it in my face.

Humming, I lift a shoulder. "We all want something."

Her breathing hitches at my tone, and I know she understands when she asks, "What do you want?"

Wicker has fucked her. Lex has seen the most intimate parts of her body. Both of them have filled her up, been inside of her. It's just like before, seeing her on that dating app and knowing other guys are seeing her too.

I want something that no one else has.

"Tell me you want my baby inside you."

She stiffens before craning her neck around to gape at me. "Your *what*?! I-I don't even know you."

Rubbing her clit, my lips drag against her ear as I say, "You don't have to mean it, Rosi. You just have to say it."

She tips away from my mouth, face twisted into a grimace. "That's insane."

I shouldn't let the anger take hold of me. I never expected her to do it in the first place. Things like this take time. Patience. "Your choice," I say through clenched teeth.

When I've been inside of her for an hour and a half, my fingers playing casually with her pussy, her breaths begin coming in short, closed-mouth pants. "It's uncomfortable," she tries, hips wriggling.

I pull my hand from between her legs to clamp down hard on her hips, stilling her. "I still have more than an hour."

Her jaw hardens. "I can't stay here until midnight."

"You will," I argue, curling an arm around her middle. "Unless you have something to say to me."

I hold her because I know what's coming. That flash of fire I see

in her reflection isn't all anger. Some of it's about the way she's dripping, her cunt swollen and ripe for me. Still, I bet she lies to herself.
I bet when she braces her palms on the desk and rolls her hips, that
tight pussy stroking my length, she'll tell herself it's just to end this.

But I see the way her mouth parts in ecstasy.

It's that more than anything that sends me into motion, yanking
her into my chest with a fistful of her red hair. "Do you know what
it's like spending night after night alone in a cell?" I hiss, bearing
her down on my cock. She winces, but I still feel her responding
clench. "Father claimed he couldn't get me out of a sentence, but he
did get me a room to myself. I *am* an Ashby after all." I snort
because it's both true and not. "You learn a lot of ways to entertain
yourself, Rosilocks, and my favorite fantasy was coming back here,
finding you, and making you suffer the same way I did. No pleasure. Long hours of nothing but pain and discomfort. So you're
going to sit here on my cock until midnight, or you're going to tell
me what I want to hear."

"I didn't put you into prison," she cries, chest heaving.

"You put the fucking heat on me," I burst, snapping my hips up
to punctuate it. "You're the reason they started the investigation.
You're the one who sent them to my doorstep that day." Flinging the
drawer in front of me open, I snatch up the pair of handcuffs I'd
taken from that room in the Hideaway.

Her eyes track it and she jolts, but not before I've gotten both
her wrists behind her back.

"You're the reason," I fluidly cuff her wrists, "I was handcuffed
in front of the whole frat, shoved into a car, and carted off to
county."

She twists to glare at me, her face flushed and drawn. "They
don't send people to prison because of a few perverted videos!"

I pull her arms back, snarling, "But they send them to prison for
felony wire fraud."

She freezes, her green eyes filling with confusion. "What?"

"That's what they found, Rosilocks. That's what your panicked
little bullshit tip-off led them to." I drag her forcefully against my

chest, my cock nestled so deeply inside of her that I can feel her tremble. "Wicker and Lex keep saying I shouldn't blame myself, but the truth is, I don't. I blame you for every day." I thrust my arm out in front of her, sleeve pushed up to reveal the tattoos there. "All five hundred and fifty-three of them."

She stares at it, mouth parted in horror. "Is that...?"

"A tally for each day," I confirm. The tattoos are short and crude stick-and-poke lines, each one made late at night in my cell. Sometimes, it'd take me a while to get ink, so I'd have to save them up, doing five or ten at a time. But mostly, it was routine to slump on my cot, carefully stabbing the ink into my skin. With each prick of the needle, I'd think of her.

It wasn't all anger and vengeance, though. The longer I sat in there, the more I grew urgent with the need to know what she felt like. It seemed just. Eye for an eye. I'd already paid the price. Might as well have some of the reward, too.

My dick throbs, the desire to end this racing through my bloodstream. But practice makes perfect. On the ice. In Father's office. With my tech. And even this, dragging myself to the edge of pain, until I reward myself with dark, delicious pleasure.

Willing my dick to stand down, I gain back my control and wrap my arm around her waist. I hold her tight against my body, forcing her to watch the screen as the camera view shifts from her shocked expression at being named Princess, to her long walk into the ceremonial chamber.

Every nerve in her body tenses up, inside, and out.

"I didn't know any of that was going to happen," she says, chin wobbling. "Please don't make me watch this."

"Why not?" I push my fingers between her folds, teasing over her clit again. It's hot, pulse beating under the hot skin. *Fuck.* "Because it makes you uncomfortable? Do you think I give a fuck about your comfort?"

On screen, Verity is easing herself down on the phallus, an expression of shock and horror marring her pretty face. I see myself holding her by the wrist, and then my breath catches when Wicker shoves her down. Her pussy clenches, in pain or something else, I don't know. "No clenching," I say in her ear. "What did it feel like to be ripped apart like that? To feel the blood running between your thighs?" A quiver runs through her body. "Answer me, Rosilocks. What did it feel like?"

"It hurt."

"How much?"

"M-more." She clenches around my shaft. "More than anything I've ever experienced."

The image moves along to Father bending over and gathering her blood. She looks worn out, exhausted, and traumatized. The pretty girl from the balcony transformed into nothing but blood, sweat, and tears. Her hand trembles as she signs the paperwork.

"Oh, this is where it gets really good," I whisper, feeling under her dress and roughly taking her tits in my hands. I squeeze hard, forcing her to cry out. "Goddamn, my brother–he's just... relentless, isn't he?"

A flicker runs through me. Jealousy. Wicker only ever fucked with her because he knew who she was–what she did to me. To the three of us. But she was mine first. She should have been. If things had gone differently–if she'd never reported me for those videos–I would have made her mine.

Wholly.

"I wish I could be so detached," I confess, basking in the weight of her heavy tits in my palms. "But I can't. I have a lot of rage inside of me. A lot of anger for what you did—what you started—and how it's fucked up my life."

On screen, Wicker pounds into her in that steady, manic rhythm and my hips rock upward of their own accord. I reach out and hit the volume, allowing the soundtrack of that night to join the images. The room fills with the scrape of the table as he pushes her across the floor, hips powerful. My cock thickens, stretching with every small thrust. I listen to the *thud, thud, thud,* of Wicker's beat, the soft, sad cries coming from Verity's lips with every punch.

"I don't regret it." In the reflection, she's watching with a blank expression, her eyes trained to the screen.

"You wouldn't," I say bitterly. "Even a rough fuck from Wicker is probably a good fuck."

"Not that." She shakes her head, jaw taut. "I don't regret turning you in. I wish you'd been in prison longer. I wish your brothers would have gone with you. I wish–" Her voice cuts with a cry as I suddenly stand, dumping her forward onto the desk.

I shove the flat of my palm into her head, and it's fucking amazing. "Look at you now, Rosi. Face down, ass up, hands cuffed, that flicker of fear in your eyes." I growl, grinding my cock into her. "How does it feel?"

She never gets a chance to answer. Even fucking her like I am, barely dragging an inch of my dick from her cunt, the constricting glide is too much. I'm too desperate–too fucking starved.

"Oh, fuck," I gasp, fingers clenching a handful of her hair as it begins. "Oh, god–" The first wave is like getting punched by a goddamn live wire. My body erupts with it, lips pulled back in a snarl as I seize, slamming my hips into her.

My cock pulses so hard that she feels it, her back twitching with a hitched breath. It just keeps fucking coming. My dick pumps wave after wave of cum into her, and with each pulse, I growl, the thought warming my veins like lava.

"Take it," I rumble, giving her every drop of my seed. Pumping her full of me. Leaving a part of myself inside her–maybe for the next nine months.

My cock jumps so violently at the idea that I shoot another surge into her.

I haven't had a hotter thought in my whole goddamn life.

By the time I'm drained, breathless and halfway to limp, I realize she's dripping. Pulling back, I flip up her dress, watching as the cum leaks out around my cock. "Holy shit," I breathe, fascinated. I wasn't lying before. I've never gone raw–never known the feeling of emptying myself into a hot, slick cunt.

It's like nothing I could have imagined, watching dazedly as I pull my hips back, my shaft glistening with the both of us. She twitches around me, and the moment my head slips free, her pussy *gushes,* my cum running in globs over her folds.

I rush to push it back in, finally allowing my eyes to take in the plumpness of her ass. But something higher gets my attention. Below her dress, on the small of her back, is a scar. I push the dress up far enough to see it, round, raised, and pale.

An O with a line through it.

She stays still, her eyes fixed to my keyboard as I feed the cum back into her hole. "Are we done now?" she asks, voice quiet and flat.

I pause, my fingers still buried halfway inside of her. "No." Her eyes flick up, sparking, but I'm already unlatching the cuffs and pulling up my pants. I reach for the box I've had ready and waiting since last night, uncaring when she scurries toward her panties, stepping into them with short, uncoordinated movements.

"Here," I say, sliding it to the end of the desk.

Her green eyes pass over it without even taking it in. Or so I think. "A laptop?" she asks.

Landing in my chair, I sprawl back, feeling relaxed down to my fucking marrow. "Your payment." I wave my hand. "Or as Father calls it, a *'gift.'*"

On the monitor in front of me, I watch her pick it up limply before leaving. Once she's gone, I flip back on all the other feeds; the hallway, her room, the strip club, and reboot up the video of the ceremony to watch it all over again.

11

 erity

IT's the shallow depth of sleep where everything seems all at once uncomfortably loud and too far away to care about it. That's when the voice comes, loud but inexplicably distant.

"Wake up!"

I jolt awake too fast, electricity still zinging through my nerves when I meet dark, shrouded eyes. The silhouette of the man standing at the foot of my bed is tall and lithe enough to be immediately recognizable as Pace. My stomach plummets, sure that this is another round of agonizingly drawn out torture.

His phone is glowing against his cheek. "She's up," he mutters into it, jerking his head toward my door. "Get dressed."

The last part is meant for me, but my head is fuzzy, still full of the sensation of Pace buried deep inside, pulsing and thick. "What?" I rasp, eyes wide and sticky with sleep.

Pace turns his head just enough for the light in the hallway to cut against his cheekbone. He's glaring at the floor. "We don't have much time," he says in a quiet, grave voice. "Just do what you're told."

His footsteps are loud as his long strides make for the hallway, but sitting in the bed, staring at the slice of moonlight bleeding in from my curtains, I know he's close—waiting, just outside my door. So I dress clumsily, tripping around the closet with hurried movements, and I try my hardest to ignore the slick feeling in my center. I'd come straight to bed without even cleaning him off of me. Willing the bile in the back of my throat to recede, the racks of clothes seem labyrinthine. Dresses, skirts, blouses, shoes. My pulse is a wild stampede as I pick something at random, stepping into the pleated skirt with a stumbled hop. I choose a large sweater, the kind that sags on a shoulder, and a pair of fuzzy boots. The adrenaline is still flowing through my veins as I inch toward my door, hearing Pace's voice on the other side.

"Just distract him," he's saying, the words ground out. "It's going to take me fifteen minutes to get her there." There's a pause, and then Pace sighs. "Yeah, you're right. That'll be midnight. Just... do your best." When I step out of the room squinting against the harshness of the light, Pace's tense gaze snaps to me, assessing. "Finally," he says, lips pressed into a tight line. "The skirt is good. You got any lipstick in there, or what?"

Blinking, I ask, "Lipstick? For what?" and he tips his head back against the wall, eyes rolling heavenward.

"Why'd you have to be a virgin?" He huffs, straightening to fix me with a hard look. "Go put on some lipstick. Brush your hair. Look fuckable. Be downstairs at the door in three minutes." Before I can open my mouth to ask what this is about, he snaps, "Obey your goddamn Prince!" and stalks off.

Maybe I could feel the apprehension churning in my belly if the irritation in my temples wasn't so all-encompassing. It's only been forty minutes since I left that room with his spunk running down my thighs—since I goaded him into finishing it. This morning, I wouldn't have imagined there'd be an experience that would make my previous meeting with Lex feel preferable, but sitting on Pace's cock all night did the trick.

At least Lex was quick.

I stomp into my bathroom and chuck through items in the vanity. The first lipstick I find is called Blushed Harlot and I glare at myself in the mirror, eyes hot and irate as I smear it onto my lips. Tears prickle the corners of my eyes, but I don't blink them away.

Nothing looks as fuckable to these three as my own goddamn misery.

When I get downstairs, I find Pace waiting by the door, running his fingers through his messy hair. His eyes snap to mine when he hears my approach, something dark and satisfied swelling within their depths.

"Let's go," he says, wrenching the door open and gesturing to the car idling on the drive.

I follow him with slack movements, because it doesn't matter where he's taking me. I already know what's going to happen and who's going to do it. It's nearly midnight. In twenty minutes, Wicker will have complete and total dominion over my body–for the next twenty-four hours. Between Lex's medical exam and what just happened with Pace, I haven't had time to prepare for what exactly that will entail. Probably, it'll be just like last time. Hard. Painful. Humiliating.

Just like everything else here.

Pace is quiet as we enter the car–a sleek luxury sedan that he doesn't seem to know the controls for. In his leather bomber jacket and loose sweats, he almost looks like a normal guy when he starts the car, mashing his forefinger into the button on the console. I know better, though. The lights from the dash collide with the angles of his face, illuminating the scowl that's always fixed there.

His eyes look weary. "You hear me?" he asks, fiddling with his phone.

There's a staticky sigh, and then Lex's anxious voice answers through the speakers. "This shit's about to go 237 for us, Pace. I'm not sure I can stop him." I look between the console and him, confused.

Pace hits the accelerator, pointing the car toward the gates. "We're leaving now. What's happening?"

"Some bitch is riding him," Lex answers. I can hear tinny music in the background, the sound of rowdy yells and hearty laughter. "Grinding all over his lap."

"Goddamn it." Pace hits the bridge and slams the gas, the momentum pushing me back into the seat. "We're over the bridge. Can't you just talk some sense into him?"

Lex scoffs, his voice lowering. "Not when he's like this. He's trying–I can see he's trying. But Pace, these bitches are feral. Rink skanks are bad enough when the player *isn't* a Prince."

"Fucking pucksluts." Pace growls, slamming his palm into the steering wheel. "Father knew this would happen. We all fucking knew!" I jerk, startled at the outburst and he glances at me, jaw tightening as he up-shifts. "Get the girl off his dick. I'm going as fast as I can. I don't think the highway patrol is going to care about Operation: Pussy DoorDash."

There are mumbles in the background, the sound of a girl slurring something just out of range of being audible, and then Lex's huff. "Pace?"

He makes a hard turn, knocking me sideways into the door. "I'm still here."

"Get her wet for him," Lex commands. "I don't want to spend the next three months patching up his hatchet jobs."

I wait to feel it. The heart-dragging dread. The shudder of fear. The roil in my stomach that I've grown used to since becoming Princess. I brace myself for the wave of sickening humiliation, but it doesn't come.

All I feel is defeated.

Pace glances at me, shifting the car into fourth. "Take off your panties."

"This is about Wicker, isn't it?" My voice is flat, mouth pressed into a tight line, but I'm not expecting an answer. When I reach beneath my skirt to tug down my underwear, I have the thought that I already miss my body–the dwindling sense that it's my own.

Keeping his eyes fixed on the road, Pace shifts in his seat. "Spread your legs."

I part my thighs and lift my skirt, fighting back nausea as the cool air brushes against my center. Outside the window, the lights of Forsyth sparkle and shine as Pace reaches over, his long arm crossing the distance between us. His fingers trail up my thigh and quickly find my center, invading my folds.

It'd be so much easier if my body rebelled against it, forced him out. But the reality is that Pace's fingers are deft and experienced, just like Lex's, and I turn toward the window as I begin responding. It's not like it was back in the security room. The air isn't suffocating and charged, saturating me down to my marrow. This is slow and unbearably pointed, his forefinger gliding down to enter me before trailing back up to my swollen clit.

"Status?" Lex suddenly asks, jarring me.

Pace makes another turn, but his fingers never stop stroking me. "I'm passing the shops now." There's a pause when he buries his forefinger to the second knuckle, voice growing gruff. "She's still wet from me."

I shudder at the memory of his release running down my leg as I walked back to my room. Wicker and Lex... both of them left me with a mess, but Pace...

It just kept coming, dripping out of me with every step. By the time I reached my bathroom, it was down to my calf, and still leaking out of me.

"I'll wait for you outside." Lex's words are punctuated by a crackle, and then silence.

Pace makes a low, gritty sound, spreading the slickness back up to my clit. "You just went to bed with all my cum in there, Rosilocks?"

My nostrils flare as I glare out at the city. "I'm trying to get pregnant." The lie is better than telling him the truth. I tried cleaning it up. He just came so much that it was impossible.

He hums, the glide of his fingertips making my belly clench. "We still have six minutes," he says, eyes snapping to where I'm open and exposed. "Quickies aren't generally my thing, but they're better than nothing."

When I don't answer, he huffs, snatching his hand back.

"Tell me you want my baby inside you."

His request–the deep timbre of it–still throbs in my temples like a drum.

Three minutes later, we pull up to a house just on the border where East meets North, the tires squealing as Pace slams the brakes. It sends me jolting toward the dash and I catch myself with a grunt, knees snapping closed.

He throws the car into park, turning to me with a stony expression. "You don't talk to anyone in there. You go where Lex tells you and wait for Wick." When all I do is stare out at the yard, filled with drunk co-eds and discarded hockey gear, he grabs my chin, yanking my gaze to his. "Tell me you understand."

Fifteen minutes ago, I was sound asleep, and now I'm at some hockey player's kegger with my underwear hanging off an ankle and a throbbing pussy. I don't understand *anything*. "I understand," I say, eager to climb out of the car.

When I do, flinging my panties onto the floorboard, I slam the door and start for the steps, unsurprised to see Lex's imposing figure on the porch, a bottle of cheap beer hanging from his fingers. His hair is pulled back into that same knot, and the line of his shoulders is tense, eyes two vacant blots of shadow from the dim cast of string lights above him.

The moment I reach the top steps, he's pushing a palm into my lower back, sweeping me through the doorway. "We'll make it quick," he says, voice quiet but razor-sharp. "Empty his balls long enough for me and Pace to get him out of here."

The house is packed. Despite the chill I'd come in from, the air inside is hot and stifling. A group of sweaty PNZ members have commandeered the dining room table, and they're using it for some bastardized version of beer pong that involves a hockey puck and a cluster of pots and pans. Grimacing, I cover my nose at the smell of beer and armpit, and tug down my skirt as Lex leads me past them, into a living room that's lit only with colorful beams of skittering globe lights.

It doesn't take me long to find Wicker in the writhing mass of bodies. Naturally, he's the star of the show, holding a beer aloft with one hand while the other clasps a dark-skinned girl around the shoulders. He's shirtless, jeans slung so low around his hips that I can see the dimples above his ass cheeks. The knife sheath affixed to his belt loop droops precariously low as he grinds into his partner's ass. When he turns, another girl tugging him by the neck, I see the pair of sunglasses perched askew on his nose. He grabs onto her hips as she spins to nestle up against his chest, her ass bumping against his crotch. His lips are parted, chest jerking with shallow pants of breath, and he's staring right down her chest, mouth moving against her ear.

All she's wearing is a thin, sheer bra and cut-off shorts.

The whole room reeks of lust, because her and Wicker aren't the only half-naked people here. There are about seven other guys, a couple of them down to their boxer briefs, and one of them is on a couch that's been pushed into the corner. He's openly, blatantly being fucked by a brunette who's bouncing in his lap.

Over by the sound system, a group of similarly bra-clad girls is laughing, watching their friend as she rolls her hips into Wicker's pelvis. It's clear they're waiting for a turn, sharing eager whispers with each other as they watch.

And I hate them.

God, I hate them.

I hate them so fiercely that my fingernails dig painful crescents into my palms, because *they know*. They know Wicker Ashby is off limits to any other woman in Forsyth, and they see it as a challenge. A game. Not only that, but it's a game they've already lost, because at least three of the girls are immediately recognizable.

Lakshmi, Gina, and Heather.

I'm here because of *them*. Because the only way they can get back at me is through seeing Wicker fail, and he looks right on the edge of not caring.

"Fuck," Lex mutters as he watches the girl–Lakshmi–move against his brother. One glance into Lex's amber eyes tells me Wicker isn't the only man in this room she's got by the balls. He gestures limply to her. "Well, that's just fucking great. He's getting dry humped by the walking epitome of a come shot. I don't suppose you learned anything about seducing a man while being West End's little pet virgin, did you?" He glances at me, the sarcasm visible in his flat stare. "Of course not." Mouth pressed into a thin line, he rolls his eyes. "Wait here. I'll go–"

His words clip off when I spin on my heel, marching back the way we came. I feel him reaching for me belatedly, his fingers barely catching on my sweater as I fling him off.

The PNZ members at the dining room table all freeze when I approach it, but I'm gone as fast as I arrived, swiping the handle of a frying pan, and stride back toward the living room. Lex lets out a harsh, "What–" as I pass him, but I ignore it. I see Wicker notice me in my periphery, his head rising to track my approach.

But I walk right past him.

I walk past Lakshmi.

I walk past Gina.

I walk past the guy getting ridden on the couch.

I've been around the cutsluts long enough to know how to spot a leader of a pack. I felt it that first afternoon when all of us were preparing for the ball, and I see it in her now. I make a beeline to the corner by the sound system, Heather's smoky-eyed gaze locking onto mine from across the room. Her lips spread into a slow, knowing grin and she tips her chin up, her eyes sparking in bright satisfaction. When I'm close enough to hear her laugh, she parts her lips to speak.

She never gets the chance.

I swing the frying pan with all my strength, whacking it right into her jaw. The girls around her all jolt with gasps, scattering like roaches as Heather hurtles back into the electronics, hands flailing wildly. The knock rattles the bones in my arm, and I grip the handle with both hands, swinging out again. This one slams right into her nose, a *crunch* audible through the sudden crackle of the speakers dying.

Heather cries out wetly in the abrupt silence, and it's strange. Back in West End, I never felt compelled to fight with the other girls. The idea of burying my knuckles into flesh and bone was always vaguely sickening to me.

Now, I just can't seem to stop myself.

I throw the pan aside and leap on her, pulling my fist back and slamming it into her face. She's shielding her broken nose, her hands taking the brunt of the force, but I can't seem to care. I swing out again, lips pulled back into a snarl, and everything–all of the degradation, fear, and anguish–comes pouring out. It's wild and flailing, and I'm almost glad no one from West End is here to see it, because it's sloppy–impulsive–driven by nothing but this bitter lava coursing through my veins.

Strong arms grip me from behind, tearing me away, and I know it's Wicker. I can tell from the smell of him, that sharp cologne I'd smelled earlier in Lex's room. I shove my hand back and feel for the knife clipped to his pants, easily snatching it out.

Suddenly, the arms are gone, and I'm barreling back to Heather.

Blood streams down her chin, eyes clenched tight as I grip her by the hair. Panting with exertion, I snarl out, "Maybe the last few Princesses have been so soft that you've forgotten your place, so let me be clear." Feeling the suspended energy of the party, I know everyone is watching, listening, but I wait for her pained, welling eyes to blink open before continuing. "I'm holding you personally responsible for every bitch in East End. You better tell them that the Princes are off limits, because if any of you so much as breathes near them, I'm going to find you and stick this knife into your tit." I shove the blade beneath the B-cup she'd been so eager to upgrade before. "Ask me if I'm serious."

She winces, chest bouncing with a sob, and gives a rapid nod. "They won't. They *won't!*"

My nerves are still flaring when I stagger to my feet, turning to make sure the other three also got the message.

Wicker, who's standing a few feet away, has taken off the sunglasses, eyes tracking my every movement. His jaw is slack, tongue darting out to wet his bottom lip. He's drunk, that's for sure, but not so blitzed he's not fully aware of everything that just went down. Before I can move, his hand clasps around my wrist.

"Settle down, Princess," he says, twisting it hard enough to force the knife out of my grasp.

"Okay, maybe you did learn a couple things," Lex mutters under his breath. He's not looking at me, though. He's checking the time, then fixing his brother with a relieved look. "It's midnight."

"Thank Jesus." Wicker's fingers thread between mine and he tows me from the room, every single person watching as we pass. He shoves his hand down his pants, revealing more of that curly thatch of blonde hair above his pelvis. I track the movement and see him squeeze the base of his cock. He shifts and the tip peeks obscenely out of the waistband, glistening and red. "I was hard before you got here, but fuck, Princess, watching you go after that girl, I about came in my pants."

"You're not... mad?" I stumble, trying to keep up with his long gait. Strong hands catch my hips and I realize that Lex is right behind us. He releases me with a slow drag of his fingertips over my ass.

Wicker stops at the landing, dragging me up the last two steps, then whirls around to push me up against the wall. The movement is jarring, but the shape of him pinning me in is even more disconcerting. He's still shirtless, a hand coming up to press against the wall beside my head, and I get a full view of his broad chest. Wicker might look all sleek and compact in a suit, but like this?

He's bigger and stronger than he seems.

"What can I say?" His fingers dip under my skirt, pushing between my folds. "Jealousy's a turn on." His eyes dilate, more black than blue as he invades my center. He pauses only briefly, the corner of his mouth quirking into a lazy, drunken smirk. "You're wet for me already, Red? Or did cold-cocking that girl get you hot?"

I almost say no, that Pace's cum is still inside of me, a thick reminder of earlier, or that his fingers are the ones that got me hot and bothered again. But I glance at Lex and the hard look he gives me is enough to keep my mouth shut. It's Wicker's turn. This is all about him.

"I was wrong about you not wearing panties," he says, ducking down to nip at my bottom lip. "The whole room saw your pussy when you threw yourself on Heather." He pushes a finger inside, pumping twice, and jerks his chin at Lex. "This is our pussy."

"Everybody downstairs!" Lex shouts, waving everyone past like a menacing traffic cop.

Everyone seems to know better than to gawk at the Prince and Princess as they abandon the line for the bathroom, or emerge from dark corners, lips red from making out. Still, my cheeks are on fire, every inch of my flesh burning, even though I know this is an act of power. I belong to him, and he wants everyone to know it—most of all me. The last person walks by, and Wicker pushes up my skirt. He looks down at me with dark, smoldering eyes, licking out to wet his lips. "This is for standing up for your Prince."

Then he drops to his knees.

His palms flatten against my thighs, spreading me apart, and I wobble, grabbing for his bare, muscular, shoulders. I'm already gasping in shock before his tongue even darts out, but the heat of him against my core, hot and slick, transforms it into a cry. My fingers dig into his flesh, desperate for purchase as his tongue spears into me. *Oh god.*

I close my eyes and sink back against the wall, unsuccessfully trying to catch my breath as he laps against my nub. I wonder if he even realizes what he's tasting—Pace's cum is surely still inside of me—but I quickly lose the ability to care. For all his frantic, horny energy, Wicker is downright leisurely as he draws my hips forward, making out with my pussy. That's the only way I can describe it. His sensuous licks are so intense and consuming that it's as if he's kissing a woman passionately on the mouth.

The lowest of grunts forces my eyes open and I see Lex watching us, eyes glued to where Wicker's mouth is devouring me. A jolt runs through me, and I'm hurtled back to our time together in the clinic, the dirty words he whispered in my ear.

"Have you ever had your pussy licked, Verity? I bet you've thought about it, haven't you? How it'd feel to have a guy's tongue on you, right here." Panting, I thrust my fingers into Wicker's hair, too captivated by his brother's dark stare to look away from it. *"It'd be wet and warm. You'd feel his breath, the sounds he'd make, the vibrations."*

I suck in a breath as Wicker teases me, and Lex's gaze snaps up to mine. He swallows and pushes a stray lock of that long hair behind his ear. Something in that basic, delicate move, sends a ripple of electricity from my core to my limbs. I'm robbed of all my senses, just the harsh pleasure that I can't get enough of. My hips rock forward frantically and I seize, clit pulsing against Wicker's tongue.

If I had enough sense to, I'd probably resent the sound I make, keening and agonized as I come. It feels ripped from my core, the hours of being impaled on Pace's cock as he teased me making the release all the more acute.

I float back down to earth, feeling dark, sinister laughter vibrate between my legs. Wicker rises, mouth shiny, teeth white, grin smug. "What do you say, Princess?"

My brain is lost under a cloud of fog, but the only thing I can think of is, "Thank you?"

"Good girl." He tweaks my breast with one hand and unbuckles his pants with the other. His next move is fluid. He removes the sheath and hands the knife to Lex, then grabs me by the waist, lifting me in his strong arms. He carries me down the hall, and suddenly, his mouth is on my neck, sucking with his teeth. My wet center heats against his lower belly, and over his shoulder, I see Lex tip his head back, exhaling. Relief at getting his brother under control? I don't know, because Wicker kicks open a door, enters a room, and tosses me on the bed. The door slams shut as I bounce, steadying myself with my hands.

His pants drop and I reluctantly take him in. I know it's the orgasm still zinging my nerves with aftershocks, but in a purely physical sense, a secret, guilty part of me thrums in anticipation of what's coming.

His body is a masterpiece. The hard planes of his chest. The ropey ladder of his abdomen. The deep, cut lines of the 'V' situated between his hips. My belly flutters at the lean muscle slashed down his forearm that tenses as he strokes his erection.

And then there's that.

It's the first time I've really seen his cock. The night of the ceremony he was behind me. If I'd had my wits around me that night, I probably would have been even more terrified. It's thick, wide enough for him to wrap his large hand around. The memory of the damage he did to me forces my thighs to clamp together defensively, although it's pointless.

Whitaker Ashby is a man on a mission.

He grabs my ankles, yanking me to the end of the bed. His hands roughly spread my thighs, exposing my hot, slick folds to the cool air of the room. Wicker barely looks down at me, his body moving on instinct as he props himself above me, angling his hips into the cradle of my thighs. I feel the brush of his tip against my entrance, then the hard punch inside.

I wait for the scream of my muscles, for the incomparable burn, but my body must be numb from invasion, the constant intrusion over and over again. He pumps into me with a hard expression, hips rocking in a furious motion, but he doesn't look. Not at me. His eyes are fixed to his own cock as he watches it sink inside, and then reappear, over and over. He's determined, focused, almost unaware that I'm even there.

He's a maleficent force, hovering over me, body so big he could crush me under his weight. His jaw, sharp as a knife, tightens as he nears a quick release. His grunts grow into short bursts of air. I realize then that I could be Lakshmi or Gina or Heather. I could be any girl from downstairs in this hollow moment. All Wicker Ashby wants is to get off.

"Fuck," he groans, breaking the silence, his hands grab my knees, contorting me like a pretzel. Whatever he's done it seems to please him, because he growls, "Jesus." *Thrust.* "Christ." *Thrust.* "You're." *Thrust.* "So." *Thrust.* 'Fucking." *Thrust.* "Tight."

Thrust.

His hips slam into me and he holds it, his cock buried as deep as it can possibly go. The strangled roar that's been building in his throat breaks free, and I feel it. God, I feel it the instant he releases, his seed pumping into me with a biological relentlessness.

"God-fucking-damn," he sighs, eyes fluttering closed as he surges inside of me. "Finally."

When it's over, he doesn't move. Not at first. He hovers over me for a long moment, visibly regaining his wits, and I stare at his face. Red cheeks, sweaty forehead, loose jaw.

He pulls out like he's removing a Band-Aid. A quick yank. I feel the loss of him. The intensity of his power and need. Pushing to my elbows, I feel his fingers on my center again, and I almost cry out. My body can't take any more.

He sighs at my weak, futile protest. "Can't waste a drop," he says, eyes rolling as he pushes his cum back inside, a lot like Pace had earlier. "The sooner we get you knocked up, the sooner all of this can end."

12

# Wicker

THE CAR IS WAITING outside the Nu Zoo house, the driver, a freshman relegated to after-hours pickups. Verity stands by the curb, arms wrapped around her body, shivering from the cold. My eyes drop to where her nipples press at the fabric of her top.

The pledge opens the door and she goes in first, giving me a nice view under her skirt. The pledge next to me sucks in a sharp, surprised inhale.

I elbow him in the gut. "I will end you."

Bending, he nods. "Sorry, sir. I apologize." Climbing in, I shut the door in his face.

The Princess peers out the window. "Where's Lex?"

"Pace drove him back."

Her posture is stiff—guarded. Fair. The urge to take her again is already intense, but Lex has made it annoyingly clear that her body needs time to heal. Father would be furious if we gave her an infection or something in the first week.

I lean against the door, the adrenaline of the night wearing off, and the low hum of guilt swims in through the afterglow. I know what Pace and Lex were thinking–that I was on the edge of losing my restraint with all those girls testing me. Yeah, I was rock hard and getting pretty desperate, and sure, maybe some of that rubbing was getting me close to a place that would have broken a covenant, but I didn't.

I wouldn't have.

I wouldn't.

"Can I ask you a question?"

I blink, turning my scowl on her. "I suppose."

"Why is there a lock on one of the doors in our wing?" She props her temple on a fist, looking wrung out, as she well fucking should. "Lex's bedroom, right?" My eyes narrow and she quickly adds, "Just seems like if anyone was going to get locked in at night, it'd be me."

"He sleepwalks," I say, touching the hem of her skirt and drawing it up a little to see the soft part of her inner thigh. There's a sheen there, drying cum. I graze my thumb over it. "It's better for everyone if he's secure at night."

"Oh," she says, closing her thighs slowly, cautiously, like she thinks I won't notice. "One of the girls at the gym sleepwalks. She'll wake up in the craziest places. Trying to bake in the kitchen. Once, out at her car, trying to start it, even though she didn't have a key. She kept trying to shove a pencil in the slot." She's babbling, and I can tell from the way her face twists that she realizes it.

My dick's been known to reduce women to that before.

Giving me a tight smile, she finishes, "So I can see how dangerous it can be."

I stare at her, but there's no need to tell the Princess that Lex turns into a roaming, impulsive, sex-starved beast in the middle of the night. The lock thing became imperative after a particularly bad situation at our old house in the golden row–the strip of townhouses that houses PNZ. That whole incident almost landed him in an adjoining cell with Pace.

All this sex stuff... it wasn't a problem when he was on the Scratch. Sure, he had other side effects. The paranoia, insomnia, loss of appetite, constant itching. But his dick worked like a goddamn pro exactly when he wanted it to. Everything changed when he went cold turkey.

I can still hear the sound of Mitchell's girlfriend fighting him off. Her screams. Jesus. *Piercing*. I'm good with rough sex–even when the consent is a little iffy–but crawling into bed with your frat brother's girlfriend and raw dogging her in the middle of the night? That's a hard violation of not just the bro-code, but of the Psi Nu Pact.

It took three of us to drag him off her, and if Lex weren't legally an Ashby, then god knows what would have happened. Father paid the girl off, and I put a lock on the door. I've spent the last year securing it every night.

This is the shit Pace missed out on.

The shit I *don't* blame him for.

The car pulls up to the house, and I get out before the pledge has a chance to open the door, giving him a dirty look when he offers her his hand. Danner, ever present like the sleepless vampire he is, meets me just as Verity climbs out of the car.

"Hope your evening was well," he says, taking her in.

"Splendid," I say, shrugging off my coat and tossing it at him.

"Did the Princess not have a wrap?" he asks, something pointed in his tone. His eyebrow lifts, his head nodding at my jacket. *Shit*.

"We left in a hurry," she says, rubbing her arms.

"She's fine," I say, striding toward the steps. "I warmed her up before we left."

Danner, a third-generation butler, remains stone-faced at my quip. I'd get pissed about his implication, but Danner is probably the closest thing we have to a mother. Who do you think drove us to all those lessons and practices? Certainly not Father.

This time I take the lead, not wanting to test my will with the sight of her bare pussy on the way up the stairs. We pass Pace's door, then Lex's, the new keypad firmly in place. The Princess is observant, I'll give her that.

Could be a problem.

When she reaches her door, hand reaching out for the golden knob, I sneak in behind her, covering her wrist. "My turn," I whisper.

Freezing, she spins slowly, meeting my gaze. "For?" she asks, her eyes full of wariness.

I've probably done this a thousand times, but it never gets old. First, a glance down at her lips as I hem her in against the door. Not threatening, just... imposing. Letting her assess my size, just like back on the landing in the Nu Zoo.

"A kiss goodnight," I say, keeping my voice measured in the silence of the hall. "I did give you one."

"Oh." Her cheeks blush as she remembers my 'kiss', and those nipples peak again. Fuck, those *nipples*. Are they big? Brown? Pink? Whatever they are, they're taunting me beneath her sweater, all stiff and obvious. I didn't spend nearly enough time on her body tonight. My bad.

There's a stretch of time where she gazes up at me, shoulders too stiff, but I just keep moving my gaze from her lips to her eyes. It takes her longer to get it than I'd expect, the tension swelling. When it finally clicks, some of the steel in her spine goes limp.

"Oh," she says again, dropping her gaze.

That's right.

You come to me.

With a short sigh, she tips her head back, straining up on her toes. The first brush of her lips against mine is stilted, inexperienced, but that's to be expected. I reach up to gently touch the underside of her chin, holding her still as I lick out, meeting her hesitant tongue.

I never got Forsyth's hard-on for virgins. There's nothing fun about having to walk a woman through every step of her own pleasure. Give me a whore any day. Verity kisses like she's expecting to get punched, and I'm not sure which corner of Forsyth is responsible for that. Maybe that's how they do it in West End, aggressively over-physical even during something like this. Or maybe her throning was just that bad, something that makes her flinch at the thought of my mouth on hers.

Either way, it takes a hot minute for the glide of my tongue against hers to do its magic. Slowly, she begins licking back, the kiss slick and unhurried as I wind an arm around her waist. By the time I pull back, my lips dragging against hers wetly, her eyes are hooded and dazed.

Fuck.

Mine might be a little, too.

I should spin her around and bury my cock in her right here.

Instead, I say, "My turn for a question, too."

"A... question?" Her green eyes are glazed as she watches my mouth.

Humming, I pitch forward, but it's barely a twitch. Just enough to make her think I might go in for a second kiss. "Oakfield. What did he do to get kicked out of DKS?" She stiffens, almost imperceptibly, like she's not sure if she should say something. I tisk. "I answered your question. It's only fair."

She meets my gaze, some of that lust falling away. It leaves her with a flustered aura, a lock of her hair sticking to her damp mouth. "He made a big scene at the poker game last fall. Treated the Duchess with disrespect."

The DKS poker game is the stuff of Forsyth urban legend. High stakes, lots of booze, tons of entitled alumni, and always a good show. I nod, a few pieces of the puzzle becoming clearer.

"How much disrespect?" I ask, using a finger to brush that lock of hair aside.

Her eyelashes flutter. "Enough that I'm surprised he still has a cock between his legs."

My eyebrows raise and I can't help but laugh. "Anything else?"

Her fingers curl around the doorknob at her hip, throat

jumping with a swallow. "He's bitter he didn't get a leadership spot. Nick coming back knocked him from contention."

Right. The legacy.

"Thank you, Princess." I run my hand down her neck, thumb grazing her collarbone, and I watch her pulse quicken. "That's very helpful."

"What are you going to do with him?" she asks, and something flickers in her eyes. It's not fear, or even concern, but I can't quite place it.

"What we've agreed to."

The urge to bury myself in her again overwhelms me. My dick has been hard since I drained into her an hour ago. But even I know I have to pace myself.

Speaking of...

"Oh, and Princess?" I take her hand and brush my lips over her knuckles, pinning her with my gaze. "The next time I taste one of my brothers instead of your delicious cunt, I'm not going to be so gentle." Spinning on my heel, I leave her there, gaping and outraged as I toss her a lazy wave. "Freshen it up for tomorrow, Red."

THE NEXT MORNING, I drag ass. Getting ready for class, the whispers of a hangover stab behind my temples, and I don't even bother with breakfast. The only thing that even gets me out of bed at all is the prospect of emptying my balls again. In the spirit of avoiding Danner, I jam a pair of sunglasses over my eyes and take the short-cut, ducking through a panel in the back of my closet.

Prince Whitaker: You ready for class?

Princess: Yes.

Prince Whitaker: Meet me at the upstairs landing.

I take a sharp right, my headache reluctantly waning in the soothing darkness of the passageway. It's dusty here behind the walls. Old and hushed and full of secrets. One time, when we were fourteen, we were carrying supplies down to the dungeon, and I asked Lex if we should be worried about rats. He just looked at me with that exasperated expression of his and said, "Wick, we *are* the rats." That's what being in here makes me feel like, small and a bit like a rodent, but also comfortably shrouded.

I stop at a spot I know well enough, quietly pushing aside a piece of wood. In the landing is a tall, ornately carved bookshelf, and an inch above a weathered book titled *A History of Forsyth,* is a spyhole.

I'm directly behind it.

I watch as Verity pauses on the landing, tucking a red curl behind her ear. I haven't had the opportunity to really look at her. Last night, I was drunk, and I've been so angry at Father's decision to hang this albatross over my neck that I haven't let myself indulge. But now I'm sober, the edge slightly off after having gotten some pussy a mere seven hours ago. I take a moment to study the Princess.

She's pretty enough, although sexy isn't a word I'd use to describe her. Her green eyes are clear, like bottled glass. I can already tell those soft red lips are going to feel amazing wrapped around my cock. Her tits are nice, although a little small for my tastes, but her waist is narrow. I eye her hips, wide enough to get a good handful. Her pussy tasted sweet.

I run my hand down my cock, trying to relieve some of the pressure, but it's pointless. I'm still backed up, and if I don't take my designated day by the reins, I'm going to have to wait another four days to get my dick into something warm and wet.

Fuck no.

I push my nail beneath the corner of the panel and the hidden door opens. Reaching out, I grab her by the arm. She yelps, but I'm engulfing her body in an instant, curling my palm over her mouth as I yank her inside the passageway.

"It's just me, Princess," I say, working my free hand between us to thumb the button on my jeans. "Are you going to scream?" She shakes her head and I release her mouth, finding myself under the full fury of her glare when she spins to meet my gaze. "Wouldn't be so bad if you did."

"You scared me!" She hisses, eyes assessing me in the low light. "Did you just come out of the wall? What is this place?" Her eyes squint as she scans the space, but I don't let her get too far.

I push my hips into hers. "It's the place where you're going to get fucked," I say, enjoying that flash of alarm in her eyes.

"We'll be late for class," she says, her hand curling around my shoulder. Even though it's a clutching gesture, she's pushing.

"Don't worry about it." Without warning, I lift her up, and she gasps.

"Wait!"

"No." I guide her smooth legs around my hips, pinning her against the wall. "You got off easy last night, Red." *Literally.* I reach down to pull my cock from my pants, already hard and eager. "Maybe Pace likes waiting all day to get his, but I only get twenty-four hours to make the next ninety-six bearable. Your pussy is forfeit."

Her nails dig hard into my shoulders, breath quickening. "Does it have to be here? Can't we–" Her voice chokes off when I pull the crotch of her panties roughly aside, lining myself up.

And then my phone rings.

"Goddamn it!" I keep her pinned to the wall with my hips, my erection drilling into her as I take the call. "What?"

"We're in the car," Lex says. "Where the fuck are you? Where's the Princess?"

I glance into her apprehensive eyes. "She's with me."

There's a commotion, and then Pace barks into the phone, "I have class in fifteen minutes. You know I'm on academic probation. I can't be late."

"Fuck," I growl, hanging up and dropping her to the floor. "Fucking motherfuck of a fucking *fuck*."

"Who was that?" she asks, wiggling her ass, getting those panties straight.

"Apparently we *don't* have time," I snap, stuffing my cock back into my pants. I flip the lever and the door opens, the sunlight from the stained glass window above stabbing agony into my temples once again.

Seeing her move from the corner of my eye, I grab her wrist, squeezing tight enough to watch her wince. "Later," I say, easing up my grip. "Understand?"

She flicks her eyes to my fingers, mouth pressed into a thin line. "I understand."

It strikes me that Verity really isn't so bad as a Princess. She seems to mostly do what she's told, and when I lace our fingers together, leading her down the stairs, she only looks like she wants to push me down them a *little*. It's probably because of that word. *Later*. It sapped a lot of that nervousness from her eyes, the thought that she's going to get hours to prepare herself for the next time I grace her with the privilege of milking my dick.

Cute.

"I still think the covenant is against this," Lex mutters five minutes later.

I sprawl back, wetting my lips. "There's no fucking way he possibly expects us to never get head again. Anyway, pre-cum doesn't have sperm in it. That's a fact and you know it, Dr. Ashby."

My brother grunts in defeat and pointedly averts his gaze to the window. We're in the car, one of the pledges driving us to campus. Classes start in ten minutes, and after that is practice at the rink, and after that, Father is making me go play a recital for the blue-hairs out at the club, and after *that*, we have business to deal with in the form of a Duke reject. Almost every hour of my day is spoken for, and there's no fucking way I'm not getting off at least one more time.

"If you'd been patient, we wouldn't be here right now, but you weren't, so suck it up." I reach down and shove my fingers into the fiery red locks to grab the back of her neck. "Deeper, Princess." She's on her knees, face between my thighs, I pull her forward, shoving my cock deeper. "You get me good and ready, and I'll be a one-pump-chump, giving your pussy the rest the good doctor swears you need."

She glares up at me, those green eyes watering. I'd been right about her lips. They look fantastic around my cock.

Across from me, Pace's dark, hooded eyes are fixed on her. "You've never given head before, have you?" he asks, the hand in his pocket shifting suspiciously.

Instead of answering, she pauses at the head of my cock to massage the hinge of her jaw.

"Fucking virgins," I mutter, grabbing her wrist and guiding it to my cock. Impatiently, I circle her fingers around the base. "Pump it a little." She does as she's told, fingers tightening as she jerks me, and I feel the telltale tickle rising in my balls. I slump down in the seat with a long groan. "Oh yeah. That'a girl. Fuck."

The sight of her down on her knees is better than expected. She'd looked horrified when I suggested it, and both Pace and Lex seemed annoyed at having to watch. But it's my day, and if everyone is going to keep me busy from sunup to sundown, then this is just how it's going to be.

"Check her," I grunt, the tingle spreading across my lower abdomen.

Pace gets there first, pushing his fingers between her thighs. He smirks, but lingers there, rubbing her pussy as he assures, "She's ready." When he pulls back, he lifts two long, glistening fingers to show me.

Soaked.

"Panties." I take a deep breath. "Off."

Reaching under her skirt, Pace shimmies them off her hips, fingers lingering near her ass. I get it. I'd love to play around a little bit too, explore the territory, but if I don't get her pussy now—

"Fuck. Shit!"

"Dammit!" Lex moves quickly, yanking her off my dick. Her eyes are wide, mouth still open as they lift her in the air and onto my lap. Fisting my dick, I guide the tip through her folds, finding her entrance and pulling her down.

The glide inside is tight and wet and perfect, and every inch makes her jaw loosen just a little more, those green eyes suddenly a touch hazy.

"Oh," she breathes, wriggling. "It's…"

"Warm," I mutter, holding onto her hips and rocking up. In a perfect world, she'd be riding me like a Harley, her hair swaying around us as I fondled her tits.

The reality is a lot less glamorous.

I'm gone in a pump and a half, exploding into her like a fourteen-year-old's wet dream.

I bite into the soft nook of her shoulder as I erupt, my cock surging with wave after wave of electric heat. The sound she makes is soft and surprised, but I feel the way she rocks down, that greedy pussy wanting every drop.

By the time I release her shoulder, cock spent, we're pulling into the Forsyth lot and she's scrambling out of my lap, landing clumsily on the seat beside me. My half-limp cock gives a feeble twitch at the flash of pink, dripping pussy I see before she hastily pulls her skirt down, face flushed a vibrant red.

I give a breathy laugh as I tuck myself away. "Damn, that was fucking close."

"One of these days you're going to push it too far, Wick," Lex says, eyebrow arched. "You know that, right?"

The look I give him says that I know a lot. I know the whole time I was inside her, Lex's eyes were glued to her ass, undeniably watching her pussy swallow me down. I know that his dick might not be drilling through his pants, but that it's probably achieved a bit of a chub. I know that he wishes it'd get harder–that he could have just a taste of what Pace and I have gotten, because our Princess?

Her pussy is fucking *divine*.

"Eh." I give my brother a shit-eating grin and a lazy shrug. "What's the point of being a Royal if you can't live on the edge?"

Rolling his eyes, he looks away, jaw ticcing. "Well, if you're going to live on the edge, you can at least be effective. Impaling her on your lap five seconds before her walk to class isn't going to create anything but your own afterglow."

"It's a nice afterglow," I point out, enjoying the way her face puckers.

Verity glowers at me, and then Pace. "I can't decide what's worse. Being your sentient fuckhole," pushing the car door open, she lurches out, her heels loud as she stomps onto the pavement, "or being *your* glorified petri dish." The last part is directed to Lex, but just as soon as her outburst arrives, it sinks.

Her face pales, eyes dropping to the ground.

No, not the ground.

To her inner thighs, where my cum is currently dripping.

"Shit," she curses, but when Pace clears his throat, she looks up.

He's holding her panties, mouth pulled into a wicked grin. "Want these back, Rosi?"

Her lips pucker into a tight, frustrated purse, but after glancing around the parking lot, she jerks forward to snatch them from his hands, the motion shockingly quick. She jams her feet into each hole, grinding out a low, "Fuck you," before storming off.

Pace ducks out of the car to call back, "Three more days, and I'll make good on that."

13

Wicker

It's a good thing I had the hasty fuckhole situation in the car this morning, because by the time I arrive back at the Palace that night, it's good as dead. A brutal practice and a boring two-hour performance for the slutty old biddies at the club has left me somehow both exhausted and wired, and I stand there for a long moment–too long–sipping on my caramel coffee as I stare up at the old Victorian.

Most of the windows are dark, and I think of the word 'home'. It's never really fit here. The Purple Palace could never be a real home. It's too big. Too cold. Too full of everyone else's shit. It's not home, but it's the closest we've ever come to having one, and every time I cross the threshold, that sense of having roots here wars with the knowledge that I shouldn't.

Territory.

Every man in Forsyth longs for it, whether it's in the east, west, north, or south.

But that's not in my blood. My blood–*Baron* blood–is rootless. They're everywhere and nowhere, traversing the boundaries like shadows. Maybe that's why the Purple Palace still feels like it *should* be home. I know its shadows, traverse its boundaries, walk its hidden tunnels.

Wick, we are *the rats.*

The dungeon is only accessible through two entry points; one from the outside of the house, and one from the inside. The one on the inside is only accessible through a network of dusty, hidden passageways that I know like the back of my hand. The Purple Palace is old as dirt, but while some of it has been finely maintained and constantly polished to cultivate the appearance of grandeur, there are other parts of the Victorian mansion that are neglected and crumbling.

This is one of them.

Once inside, I pull the sconce in the hall of portraits and a panel clicks open. The wood is worn lighter on the edge where my fingers instinctively pry it open, slipping through the crack and closing it behind me. My nose wrinkles at the familiar, musty smell of old wood as I make my way down the staircase. The passages are narrow, a tight fit now that I'm an adult, but they felt cavernous when we were kids, sneaking around the Palace, watching the Princes and their Princess fuck around. It was from behind these walls I got my first glimpse of real, non-virtual pussy. It was a good glimpse too; her getting cream-pied in the third-floor parlor.

Fuck.

Now I'm hard.

Again.

It's not like I haven't tried not thinking about sex. One time, Lex convinced me to try meditation, which resulted in my thoughts moving from a rushing creek to a rushing cream-pie in record time. Pace even tried back in Freshman year, taking me to the gym to work out the tension. As if putting me in a room with a bunch of scantily clad athletes was going to tame my libido.

Nothing really takes the edge off but *getting* off.

Well, almost nothing.

"You're late," Lex says, a cup of coffee in his hand, too. The room I've entered is small, meant only for observation. A cloudy two-way mirror lines the wall. We can see out, but no one can see in. On the other side of the glass is a padded cell with nothing but a bench and a bucket to keep the occupant company. My brother's eyes settle on my head. "You've got a spiderweb in your hair."

"Ah, fuck!" I jump, heart pounding, raking my hands furiously through my hair. When I look up again, Lex is smirking. "Asshole."

He sips his coffee. "Just wanted to make sure you were still awake before we get started."

Rolling my eyes, I say, "I had to play Elvis covers all night. My fingers are killing me. Not to mention Decker got in a solid hit at practice." I wince, lifting up my shirt to show him the purple spot.

His eyes flick to the mottling flesh, and since he's Lex, I fully expect those laser eyes to hone in on it as he sets his coffee down. "Let me see." He presses the area with his fingers, hard enough to make me suck in a breath.

"You done?" I wince, twisting away from his prodding fingers.

"It's just a bruise," he surmises. "Ice should work."

"Yes, sir." I drop my shirt and a whirring sound comes from the other room. We both look through the mirror. Bruce is slumped in the chair where we left him, strapped in and still unconscious.

Averting my gaze, I scratch the back of my neck. "By the way, I don't think I ever said thanks for the save last night. I owe you one."

"You owe *him* one." He nods at Pace, who's still testing the drill. "He's the one that got her there at mach speed."

Pace stands over a stainless table, organizing instruments. It's a good setup. Complete. Blades of various sizes, pliers, tacks, torches, tasers–you name it. Chains are attached to the wall and ceiling, helpful for the brute force situations. There's a drain on the floor beneath Bruce's chair and other supplies in the cabinet. Chemicals. Tarps. Locks. Anything we may need in a pinch.

"Hey." I jerk my chin, beckoning Lex closer as I watch our brother work. There's something that's been bugging me since that afternoon in the locker room. "You ever get the feeling he isn't exactly cool with Verity being our Princess?"

Lex gives me a look. "Are any of us?"

"No, I mean..." I scratch my head, trying to find the words. "Her being *our* Princess. Mine and yours. Like he'd rather not be sharing her. Catch my drift?"

Lex seems genuinely caught off guard, glancing back at Pace through the window. "You think?"

"You don't?" I ask.

He shrugs, carefully regarding our brother. "She's the whole reason he got busted. I figured he just wants to fuck some of his grudge into her."

I know he spent some time in prison, but... "Remember how he got Effie?"

She belonged to one of Father's VIPs at the Gentleman's Chamber. The guy brought her in one day, thinking she'd impress the dancers, but Pace held her for all of ten seconds and decided she'd be his by the end of the month. The whole quest was absurdly, *dangerously* single-minded.

Lex watches him, his face growing stony, and I nod. "He's still Pace, bro."

"Fuck."

"Yeah." That's basically the gist of it. Pace doesn't get his claws into just anything–or any*one*. He doesn't have flings. He has projects. Fixtures. Should have known a little thing like her getting him convicted for a felony wouldn't stand in his way.

"It's not like there's anything we could do," Lex sighs, a frown etched into his forehead. "I'm not even really fucking her. In front of him. Like other people."

The look he slides to me evokes a winced grin. "Oops."

Has to be done, though. Pace has never fucked a girl I haven't already had or eventually gotten to, and he's never made a fuss. If he asked me to, I'd do my best, but he won't. If something's going to break us, it's not going to be gutter trash like Verity Sinclaire.

"You ready?" Lex asks, draining the last of his coffee. He opens the door and I follow him into the room. Pace barely looks up to acknowledge it, focused on his work. He takes his time as he meticulously wipes each instrument down, testing and cataloging. It's an important job. A dull blade can completely ruin a contract.

I walk over and grab our new mark by the back of the neck, lifting him like a puppet. "You say he branded some chick at the Hideaway?" I ask, assessing Bruce. He wasn't exactly easy to beat at Friday Night Fury. West Enders are built like the bears on their sigils, but us? We're a finesse organization—work smarter, not harder. I had to beat Bruce with my wits, misdirecting him hit after hit.

"Payne was pissed," Pace says, breaking his silence. "Wants to send a message to his girls."

"Dumb bastard." I look down at his face. "Kicked out of his frat, crossed the Lords, and now he's in our hands."

We told the Dukes we'd get rid of him, and we will. Probably. Once we're finished.

But the truth is, executions aren't our style. As far as torture goes, the Palace's dungeon is practically a five-star resort. Almost every mark leaves this place alive, and that's something we pride ourselves on.

Professionalism.

Lex opens a cabinet and pulls out a small leather pouch. Inside are bottles and syringes. He pokes the needle into one of the bottles and withdraws the liquid. Walking over, he stabs the needle into Bruce's forearm.

"That should wake him up."

I clap my hands and rub them together, feeling the surge of endorphins. Hockey, lacrosse, sex... or this. *This* will keep the urges at bay until I can get back to the Princess.

"Or..." Angling my hand back, I slap him hard across the face.

His neck snaps, eyes fluttering open. Leaning over him, I grab the arms of the chair, grinning. "Rise and shine, Oakfield."

He blinks. "What the—" His arm moves futilely, still strapped down. "Where the fuck am I?"

I give his cheek an aggressive pat. "You're where fuck-ups go to beg for mercy."

He scans his bound arms and legs, the instrument table, me, Pace and Lex. Slowly, his eyes grow wild with panic. "Listen, whoever's paying you to do this... the Dukes, Lords... you know my father will give you double." Across the room, Pace lifts a torch and sparks it to life, the butane giving off a hiss as the room glows bright with the flame. Bruce swallows as he watches Pace coolly lift a rod to the flame. "Triple."

I give an exaggerated sigh. "Okay, that's just insulting. The three of us combined probably have more money in our trust funds than your dad's made his entire life." I jerk back and Lex drags a metal chair from across the room, placing it behind me. Always a facilitator, my big brother. "But since you seem confused, let me explain a few things for you." I sit, facing Bruce. "You've upset some pretty fucked-up people."

"Goddamn Bruins," he says, tongue darting out to lick the blood off his split lip. *Oops.*

"For example," I agree. "Do you know how much it hurts to call Simon Perilini King?" I twist up my face. "It's disgusting. A disgrace to the whole system. Saul Cartwright was a legend." I sigh, leaning back and stretching my legs out—the opposite of Bruce's position. "But Perilini is a King now,and we've got to respect that. It's just how the game is played. What you did to them? I don't know, but he doesn't just want you out of the frat, he wants you off the board completely."

Lex walks over and grabs his head, twisting it to the side. He presses his fingers against his pulse.

Because he's an absolute dumbfuck, Bruce glares up at him. "If you don't want money, then what do you want? Because I've got a date with a Phi Mu at six."

I snort a laugh, because *Jesus Christ*, this guy. "First, we're going to deal with how you treated that woman at the Hideaway."

His face screws up. "The whore? Suddenly you're protecting LDZ pussy?"

Pace moves lightning fast, pressing the red-hot metal against his bicep. Bruce's body seizes, an anguished scream tearing from his throat. Lex works just as fast, firing up his phone's camera to catch Bruce thrashing, fingers curling around the arm of the chair.

"Fuck!" he shouts once he gains the use of his tongue again. "Goddamn it!"

I give an insincere wince. "It's not nice to defile other people's property, Oakfield. That seems to be a lesson that's hard for you to learn." I lean forward, elbows on my knees, and grin. "So now that you're our property, we're going to give you a taste of your own medicine."

The torch is still lit, but Pace doesn't put the small rod back into the flame. No, this time he goes for a bigger one, making sure Bruce catches a flash of the blunt edge.

It's a skull.

An LDZ skull.

"Wait," Bruce says as he watches Pace lift the branding rod into the flame. "There has to be something you want! I can–I'll–there's information!" The words are urgent, his eyes fixed to the rapidly glowing metal.

"I'm listening," I say, sounding bored at the prospect.

Pace pulls the iron back and Bruce shoves into the right arm of his chair. "A rumor!" he insists, darting his gaze from me to the glowing metal. "There's a rumor that there's a stash of explosives left over from Lionel Lucia buried under the water tower."

"Interesting," I say, pretending to consider it. I glance at Lex.

"A rumor?" Lex asks.

Bruce nods frantically. "I believe it. Lucia told my old man personally."

I dip my chin, fixing him with a look. "But you haven't seen it yourself."

He shakes his head, a bead of sweat appearing on his temple. "But it's true–I know it's true."

Lex's lip curls up. "Does your Daddy know you go around telling all his secrets?"

Bruce's gaze jumps between us, jaw clenched. "He'd want me to do what I need to."

"Well, your Daddy would tell you that Lucia left bombs all over Forsyth. We'll be uncovering those fuckers for years." I lift a shoulder. "Everyone knows that."

Wordlessly, Pace swings the rod, shoving it right into the meat beneath Bruce's collarbone.

His next yell is like music. A little high, and then a little low. Sometimes we get guys in here who scream like little bitches. Very occasionally, we get guys who refuse to scream at all. Those ones are both the best and worst. The challenge is always a fun time, but it gets so much messier.

Bruce is a good screamer, though. Gritty. Raw.

He screams like a West Ender.

When Pace pulls the iron back, stony-faced and silent, Bruce is panting through the howls. "What the *fuck* was that for?" he roars.

"Being a useless prick!" I say, nodding at Pace, who gets a larger branding iron–this one with the imprint of a crown. Bruce's breath comes in short bursts, and I stand to lever myself over him, hands gripping the arms of the chair. "The West End. Give us something worthwhile about the Bruins."

He gives a mangled laugh. "Don't waste your time. That whole group is full of deranged, psychotic, filthy gutter rats. They're traitors—bringing in that bitch from North Side—letting her pussy-whip the three of them into letting her take control."

"You sound jealous," Lex says, still recording, even though we'll definitely be cutting this part out when we send it to Payne.

Smirking, I say, "Yeah, I heard Bruin came back and stole your spot."

"I'm not fucking jealous." Even though his face is bloodless as he watches Pace heat the iron, he still lifts his chin defiantly. "And he didn't steal my spot. You think I want to get tied down to fucking one woman for the rest of my life? Wasting my time managing a bunch of half-wit gun runners?" He shakes his head. "No fucking way. My father is on the board of the bank, the university, the hospital, and every other major player in town. Why would I want to give up the power of gliding between lines to rule over one little section?"

Lex slides his amber gaze to me. "Sounds like he's protesting a bit much, eh?"

"A little bit."

"Still," Pace approaches him, "you haven't given us one damn reason to keep you around."

Bruce doesn't scream quite as satisfyingly when Pace pushes the glowing metal into his neck. His teeth clench as he traps the howl inside his chest, the tendons in his neck popping, but nothing comes out.

I give my brothers an exasperated look.

They always scream less by the third one.

"Switch to pliers," I say, standing back and crossing my arms. "Save the rest of his flesh for the sharps."

But when Pace approaches him with the pliers, Bruce shouts, "Stop!" His bare chest is gleaming with sweat, face turning a deep, turnip red as his muscles flex. "I'll give you a reason. A good one!"

"We're waiting," I say.

"Not you." His eyes flick to Pace. "Him."

Pace's eyes narrow. "What about me?"

Panting, Bruce shifts, face drawn. "You were adopted, right? Out of foster care?"

"Yeah?" It's not uncommon knowledge, but Ashby has made it known far and wide that we're to be considered blood, as much as his own son. He grabs Bruce's hand, holding the plier up to his fingernail. "What's it to you?"

Bruce's teeth grit, and a whimper comes out of his mouth as Pace closes the metal clamp around the nail of his forefinger. "I heard something. About your father." The pliers begin tugging, and then Bruce hastily clarifies, "Not Ashby. Your *real* father."

Pace freezes.

All three of us do.

There's a moment of tense silence, but it doesn't last long–not before I lunge for him, grabbing his sweaty hair in one fist and the hot poker in the other. I put the hot metal a bare inch from his eyes, snarling, "What did you hear?"

Bruce shrieks, "He's West! West End!" When I remain there, unmoving, he stares at the poker and frantically goes on, "My dad and his buddies, I've heard them talking about it. They said Lucia– the Duchess–it reminded them of what happened back in their day with another Duke hopeful. Knocked up some chick from East End."

"What chick?" I growl.

But Bruce shakes his head. "Man, I don't know! I just heard it was a huge scandal. If I had to guess–"

I move the poker closer. "Oh, you have to."

He swallows, pushing back against my grip. "If I had to guess, I'd say she was someone important." His eyes flick up to Pace's. "Someone Royal."

Lurching back, the branding iron hangs heavily at my side as I meet my brothers' gazes. They're both thinking the same thing I am. Someone important. Someone Royal.

Someone like a Princess.

I CAN'T EVEN REMEMBER the last time I was in danger of having a wet dream.

This one is hazy but agonizing, the slow, gentle drag of red fingernails up and down my shaft. I can't see who they belong to, but I know that she's wearing a sweater and I'm pulling it up, revealing two soft, round tits. I feel more than see her mount me, my cock suddenly engulfed in wet, tight heat. That's all it is, a disconnected series of images and sensations, but even though it feels good knowing my release is on the horizon, something niggles at the back of my thoughts. It's bad. I can't remember why it's bad, but I know that I can't.

I can't come.

It's agony to stave it off as I wade through the fog to remember why. It feels urgent. Life or death. Something I'll regret later, and that's not a long list.

When it hits me, I jolt awake with a grunt, jamming my hand into my boxers to squeeze the base of my aching cock. It twitches angrily in my palm, and it hurts–god, it fucking hurts to will it back, but I try. I take deep, gulping breaths and flop back onto the mattress, feeling the fine sheet of sweat covering my bare chest.

I need it.

I need it so bad that I find myself reaching for the phone, wondering, hoping, praying...

11:55 pm.

Leaping from the bed, I cross my room and throw open my door. Uncaring of the fact that I'm marching down the hallway with my fist shoved down my boxers, I make a beeline for her bedroom. *Our* bedroom, technically speaking. That's what I tell myself as I ease the door open and duck inside. I still have five minutes–three now–until my day is up.

The room is illuminated by the fireplace, which is crackling and erratic, the fire on the verge of death. I can barely make out her form in the enormous bed–the crown bed–but there's a lump near the middle that I feel no qualms about approaching.

I'm owed this.

My weight on the bed isn't enough to wake her, but the sudden loss of blankets is. I yank them down and she startles, her entire body lurching as bleary eyes struggle to take in the room. She's wearing this soft, cream-colored nightie that isn't leaving a lot up to the imagination.

"It's me," I say, voice a touch too gruff.

Her eyes lock on mine. "Wicker?" she rasps, pulling a face. "What are you–"

"Spread your legs," I command, even though I'm already there, prying her soft thighs apart. She kicks out, heels digging into the soft sheets as she struggles to scurry back, but I grip her ankles and hold her steady.

"Get off me," she yelps, batting my hands away as I claw at her panties.

"I don't have time for this!" I snap, some of that anger at Bruce still lingering in the base of my spine as I hold her down. I force her knees apart and pull my cock out, lining it up.

She goes stiff as I thrust, barely entering her before I grunt, cock surging with my sudden release. I look down into her stunned green eyes as it pulses, liquid warmth spreading through my body. It's not a great orgasm. Actually, it's kind of fucking terrible, nothing but the tip of my dick sunk inside her tense, tight, barely-moist cunt.

That's not even the worst part.

The worst part is the way she's looking up at me with such unbridled disgust that I feel it in the pit of my stomach. The fucking *gall*. I've fucked a lot of people over the last nine years, and none of them have ever looked at me after with anything but awe and satisfaction.

Right now, she looks like she wants to murder me.

I begin, "I had to–"

But her low, venomous voice cuts me. "Every time you do this, I'm going to go out of my way to get it out." Her green bottle-glass eyes ping between mine, simmering with rage. "The thought of your baby being inside of me makes me want to vomit."

I flinch away before she kicks me, but only just. "There was only a couple minutes left before midnight," I say, tucking my dick away with curt movements. "Don't be such a drama queen."

"Get out," she growls, yanking the blankets over her chest. "Get out!"

"Jesus," I grunt when her fist connects with my jaw. If it were still my day, I'd pin her down and go again. I'd make her wet for this one–slick and desperate, until she's begging for my dick. I'd tell her about how she's mine to do with as I please, and I'd make her repeat it back to me until she's hoarse.

Instead, I stalk out of the room, not even sure where I'm heading until I reach Lex's door. With heavy, tired limbs, I punch the key code in and unlatch it, slipping inside.

Lex is still awake, his phone casting a pale glow over his features as he frowns at me from the bed. "Wick?"

"*Damn it, Wicker,*" Effie says in a nearly perfect imitation of Lex's voice.

Fuck, it's creepy when she does that.

"Yeah," I say, noticing that Pace is here, too. Effie's cage is on Lex's dresser, her little black form perched on a hammock. We do that sometimes, taking turns watching over Lex as he sleeps, making sure he stays put. Tonight, it's probably less about that, and more about what we learned down in the dungeon a few hours ago.

The information about his mother *possibly* being a Princess is big. Not that I'm buying anything that fuckwit says. If he was looking for a target though, he hit the right one. Lex and I both know our family history, but Pace has never had any information about his birth parents or where he came from. If this is true, that he's somehow tied to the Royalty? That's a lot to absorb.

"Let me in." Despite the request, I climb into the bed and start rudely nudging my way in between them before either of them can readjust.

Pace, who's barely half-awake, lets out a sharp, "Fuck, Wicker, watch the balls!"

Effie goes off, "*Damn it, Wicker. Goddamn it, Wicker.*"

"Shove over, Jolly Brown Giant." It takes a few seconds, but I finally manage to wedge my way in between them, just like old times. Lex gives this little annoyed sigh, probably because he thinks I'm here to watch over him.

"I had a wet dream," I explain, watching the color drain from his face when he turns to me.

"Did you–"

I tuck my arm behind my head, assuring, "It's fine. I got to her in time. But..." I slide him a look, and it's heavy–full of more concern than I'd like to admit. The fact that I can't control my own body is problematic, to say the fucking least.

If anyone can relate to their dick not following orders, it's Lex. "We'll wake you up," he says, nodding.

"Thanks."

I stare up at the ceiling as we all settle, and the irony strikes me. Verity is sleeping all alone in a bed meant for four people, and here the three of us are crammed into Lex's shitty double. For all the Princess gig is a bit of a veneer, it's essentially true. She's protected, coddled in her big bed with her new wardrobe and special diet.

It's bullshit.

"Do you ever think about what it's going to be like?" I wonder, turning to glance at Lex. At his puzzled expression, I elaborate, "Having a kid. Becoming a dad."

His face turns to stone. "No."

"Me either." That's exactly why I was so shaken by her words before. They're making it real. An inevitability–for one of us. I can't wrap my mind around it, and I don't fucking want to. None of us were meant to create.

We're the creations.

"We're the rats."

"What?" Lex asks, brows knitting together.

"Nothing." I shake my head, adjusting the pillow I'm sharing with Pace. "Just something you said to me once."

Lex's face grows pensive, like he's trying to remember. He clearly doesn't. "Rats are smart," is all he has to offer.

Snorting, I reply, "You say that until a pack of rats spreads disease everywhere."

"Mischief," Pace mutters. He twists to peek one annoyed eye open at us. "Their collective noun. A group of rats is called a mischief."

I laugh as Lex turns out the bedside lamp, thinking that nothing has ever been so fitting as this. "That's us," I say, the words twisting bitterly. "A mischief of Ashbys."

As we settle in together, another comparison crosses my mind. I don't express it out loud, but the idea burns into my mind, as deep as Pace's brands on Bruce's flesh. Rats also sleep together, nestled into the dark, secret, safe places.

 erity

"LOOK AT ME."

I pry my eyes open to meet Lex's gaze. I'm not sure why. Something about being strapped to this godforsaken exam table with my feet in the air makes me far too quick to follow his orders. Mostly, it's his voice, though. Not hard or demanding, nor rough and sharp.

He makes the request quietly, as if some part of him believes it to be a favor.

When I grant it, he's staring back at me with an expression more intense than I'm expecting. There's a darkness in his eyes that makes me clench around the hard plastic as I feel his semen enter me, Lex's thumb pushing the plunger.

Nothing about it is sexy or appealing. It's cold, quiet, and too bright. Beneath the harsh lights of the medical room, Lex looks too sharp as he holds my eyes. It's weird and uncomfortable, and there's no reason such a procedure should make tingles erupt in my thighs.

But that's what happens.

It's not the syringe. It's that he pulls it out, adjusting his latex gloves, and I know exactly what's coming next. I wet my lips in preparation–in anticipation, more ready for this part than I ever want to admit.

"Does it hurt?" The fingers of one hand brush over my red knee as the fingers of Lex's other hand push into my clit. "A painful reminder of my brother keeping you on your knees while you sucked him off?"

The pads of his fingers tease my inner thighs, the promise of an orgasm lulling my body into complacency. The medical room in the basement is cold, but that's not what brings gooseflesh to my skin. It's the way he watches me, those amber eyes analyzing my every twitch.

"Did you like the pain?" he wonders. Even though the question is pitched curiously, it's still done in that deep, velvety voice that makes my stomach clench. "Did it make your cunt all slippery and wet?"

"No," I say, but my body deceives me. Whimpering, my hips rise as much as they can with the straps holding me down. Something about the motion makes Lex's jaw harden, his palm skating up my thigh to push the thin gown upward. I think I must feel alarmed somewhere in the back of my senses, but I can't reach it, my teeth digging into my bottom lip as Lex exposes my belly, and then my waist, and then–

His amber eyes flick to my breasts as he bunches the gown above them, the tight knot of muscle in his jaw twitching. "Ah, yes. Look how hard your nipples are." He gives one a sharp pinch and I cry out, head digging back into the exam table. "You do like it, don't you? A little bit of pain complements your pleasure? It's nothing to be ashamed of. A lot of girls are dirty, just like you." I feel his eyes on me, studying my body, experimenting with different ways to bring me to the edge. I already feel my toes curling as he leans down to whisper into my ear. "You may be a virgin, but your body wants to be treated like a slut."

I shouldn't like it when he talks like this. It's repulsive. The demeaning and disgusting things he utters after injecting me with his sperm should make me recoil. It's not just the words that make my breath hitch, though. It's the knowledge that tomorrow we're going to go to campus, and everyone is going to see the student–the scientist, the doctor, the genius. They're going to see his straight posture and aloof eyes, and none of them are going to know what he looks like as he bends over me, whispering filth into my ear as his shoulder rolls with the motion of his wrist.

We've barely had two sessions together, and he already knows my body better than I do. How to manipulate it. How to make my belly swoop. How to turn my bones to liquid heat.

We're seeing each other's secrets.

"Wick knows it," he says, so close that I can hear the slide of his tongue against his teeth. "That's why he had you on your knees. Why he forced you to do it in front of us. You like being treated like our bitch, don't you, Verity? Same reason you didn't cry when I put that tracker behind your ear." A lock of hair slides out of his ponytail, framing his face. The look of it softens his jaw even as it tenses. "Bark, Princess. Bark for me, and I'll let you off this table."

Truthfully, having the tracker inserted ten minutes ago was the least intrusive thing done to my body this week. It wasn't even the most humiliating. In fact, it was quick and relatively painless. Not like the hours-long sex with Pace, or the multiple rounds with Wicker, including sucking him off in front of both of his brothers. Nor was it as humiliating as the gift Wicker had waiting for me at breakfast this morning; a bottle of scented lube, tucked neatly in a shiny gold box. And the tracker was quick–definitely a faster procedure than I'm experiencing right now. Legs up in the stirrups. Straps holding me down. Accepting that my body reacts to the terrible things these men do to me.

That's the worst part of all this. Feeling weak and pathetic as a man commands my body to—

I gasp, "Fuck!" and he pinches the other nipple, tugging it with a sharp yank. A jolt of endorphins runs from my tits to my clit, and I'm thrashing against the binds to chase it, body shuddering with my release. "Lex..." The sob of pleasure escapes me before I can stop it, and I can't even bring myself to care. I want to curl up in a ball, beg for mercy, jump on his cock.

At the sound of his name, Lex falters. It's barely a twitch, but my body is so magnetized to him that I sense it.

The next time he speaks, there's a gruffness in his voice that wasn't there before. "That's right, Princess," he says, fingers dropping through my folds. I cry out when two of them enter me, smooth and assured. "Let your body do the work." His lips graze my earlobe as he speaks and I seize at the possibility he'll cave. That he'll climb up on this table and just do it already, taking me like his brothers would.

But as I ride his hand, the orgasm wanes, and I tilt my head and see him moving back, securing that lock of hair behind an ear. Aside from a touch of color on his cheeks, all traces of emotion are wiped off his expression, eyes shuttered as he mechanically snaps off the latex gloves.

I'm horrifically disappointed.

"That was better," he says in a cool voice, tossing the gloves in the bin. "Expect to get finger-fucked next time, too. It'll work my semen in deeper."

"O-okay," I stutter, blinking up at the bright lights. It says something about this whole situation that Lex, the man who squirts his cum into me with a syringe, is the best of the three. He might be a threat if he actually wanted me.

He clearly doesn't.

As my breathing settles, he unbinds my arms. Like last time, I fully expect him to leave the room with instructions about allowing the sperm to swim upstream. But he doesn't. Keeping my legs strapped in, Lex moves around the room with his quiet precision, and I start to worry there's more. There are several instruments on the stainless table next to the bed. One is the empty injector that he used to inseminate me, but there's also tubing, needles, tape, and vials.

Lex picks up a long strip of rubber and ties the tourniquet around my bicep. "Pump your fist."

"What is this?" I ask, my center still throbbing with aftershocks.

He pushes at my inner elbow, checking veins. "Blood test."

"Oh." *Of course.* Princesses don't pee on sticks. They get the earliest results possible.

There's a shock of cold as he runs a sterile pad over the vein, and then he reaches over me for the needle and vial, giving me another waft of his scent. It's clean and weirdly familiar, like antiseptic and the smell of man.

I turn my head as he sticks the needle into my flesh; the prick bringing tears to my eyes. For all the blood I've seen shed at the gym, it still makes my stomach squeamish when it's coming from inside my body.

"I'm done," he says, and I look over just in time to see him dispose of the needle. "Hold this down."

It's a cotton ball. I press it against the crook of my elbow as he takes the crimson-filled vial over to the counter, setting it inside a slotted container. He returns with a Band-Aid and adheres it over the cotton.

"How long until we get the results?"

"A few days." Expressionlessly, he finally loosens the rest of my binds, freeing me from the bed.

I lower my legs, stretching my knees, asking, "So, then we'll—" But he's gone. Out the door. No instructions this time, just a quick departure.

Deposit made.

Sighing, I take the pillow beneath my head and cram it under my lower back, tilting my hips up to keep the semen inside. The only way out is through, and the sooner I'm pregnant, the sooner I'll get some of that leverage Wicker had been so threatened by during the negotiations.

A few days. That's all it'll take to know. If I'm pregnant, the horror show is over. If I'm not, I have another cycle of this. Of them.

A wave of emotion rolls over me at the thought, and I press my palms to my flat belly, sending a prayer up to anyone who'll listen.

Let this be the one.

After my thirty minutes are up, I walk upstairs from the clinic alone, through the quiet halls of the massive palace. It's late. One benefit to Lex's disinterest is that he's apparently content to make only a single deposit, and now that he has, I have a whole day of freedom stretched out before me–or as close to freedom as I'll be seeing for the foreseeable future.

Tomorrow is my day off.

I'm not sure where the Princes are. If what I experienced two days ago is accurate, Pace is holed up in his room, watching. Wicker is probably out partying or doing whatever he can to keep his dick in his pants. And Lex? Maybe he's behind that locked door, secure for the night, dreaming of things that make him wish he weren't.

The activities and the people inside the Purple Palace are nothing like they seem from the outside. The clear skin and shiny hair, the perfect teeth and expensive clothes... none of it is indicative of what really goes on here. And I don't just mean the covenant I signed—the agreement to create an heir. I mean the rest of it. The brothers clearly have their own issues from being raised in the Royalty. I've seen it before in the dark shadows of Killian Payne's eyes, in the careful way Nick watches his back, and in Lavinia's sharp anger and distrust of others.

I'd known from my mother that Ashby was ruthlessly control-ling—it's almost his brand—but I think I'm only just beginning to understand that his own sons may be ground zero for it.

When I arrive at the landing, I find myself unable to climb the last flight of stairs to reach my bedroom. If I do, I'll have to clean myself up. I'll have to look at my naked body in the mirror and ask myself what Lex has seen. I'll have to slip into that enormous, cold, empty bed and wonder if it's happened yet. Pregnancy. Motherhood. The more I think about it, the more my mind recedes at the idea, unable to grasp it.

Instead, I walk toward the wall and begin prodding curiously at the dark wood panels. I have a rare opportunity to explore, and I search all around me, knowing this is where Wicker pulled me into the passageway. The panel itself appears seamless, so there must be some lever or switch or something.

I inspect the paintings, and then the bookshelf, tugging on random volumes. East End *would* be a cliché, wouldn't they? Only none of the books are anything but dusty old tomes. Encyclopedias from the '20s. History books. Anthologies. Roster books from the days of yore.

I give up on that idea after a while, turning my eyes to the dim light of a wall sconce.

There's a spot on the bottom of it where the gold has been rubbed shiny.

Jackpot.

I strain up to grab it, yanking it down, and hear a soft *click* behind me. When I turn, I see the cut of shadow in the panel, a crack appearing.

My heart pounds, and I glance around before pulling it open.

I don't exhale until I'm on the other side.

Without Wicker here, I'm able to get a better look around. It's just a narrow hallway that goes in both directions. There's bits of anemic light, seemingly from small openings or peepholes into the house. Once my eyes acclimate, it's enough to get my bearings. The left should go down my wing. The right? I'm guessing toward the rest of the house.

Taking the right, I tread carefully, the boards beneath my feet soft and dusty. I can't help but stop occasionally to peer through the small openings, getting a glimpse of the staircase, a library, even something that I terrifyingly suspect might be Ashby's office. Someone could get lost in here.

Someone could *hide* in here.

I eventually find myself at an odd juncture that takes me a

moment to parse. One is a staircase, I realize, narrow and so dark that it might as well just be another wall. But it leads down, and after being in the clinic, the last thing I want to see is more basement nightmares. I take the turn instead, following it all the way to the end. I pause, convinced I hear the soft strains of music, but maybe it's the wind rattling in this old house, through the drafty passageway. The music guides me until it's nothing but a long note reverberating down the corridor. It stops just as I discover a shaft of pale, gloomy light filtering in. I look through a knothole in the wood. All I can see is translucent glass. With my fingers, I feel around, searching until I find a switch. It ends up being a lever just above the opening it creates, a pocket door lurching free.

I step out slowly, eyes drinking in the sight before me. Moonlight shines through the domed, milky glass above, but the dry vines tangled there do their best to cloak it. It casts a spider web of shadows onto the ground, which might have been smooth, creamy stone at one point, but now is covered with the vestiges of decayed moss and wiry weeds.

The walls are glass too, tall and regal, overlooking the garden behind the house. There's a stillness here, an odd hush that makes my neck prickle.

"That didn't take long." The voice makes me yelp and I jump, whirling around to find a figure silhouetted near the back. I have to squint to make out the squat shape of him, only he's not stooping at all. He's sitting.

There's a cello between his knees.

My heart is lodged into my throat, and it takes multiple attempts to squeak out anything. "Wicker?"

He lifts the bow in his hand, draping his arm around the neck of the instrument. The music I heard was his playing. The concept is hard to reconcile. "Found the sconce, right? I bet you checked the books first."

My mouth works around an aborted response. "I was–I mean, I got lost, and–"

"Don't bother, Red. You're a fucking terrible liar." He sighs, and something about the curve of his shoulders is a little too loose. I realize why when he reaches down to snatch up a beer bottle. "You can relax. It's not my night. You're safe from my cock for another couple days. Throw a fucking party."

I wait for the surge of anger that always seems to arrive whenever Wicker is near, but the slump of his shoulders, the caustic softness of his voice, mostly just makes me nervous.

"I'm guessing you're not here to pay your respects." He gestures with the neck of the bottle to the massive panels of windows that face the garden. When I turn to follow his gaze, I'm startled to realize the garden outside the windows isn't just a garden. A few headstones peek up in the distance, crooked like teeth. "To Michael Ashby," Wicker slurs, raising the beer in a toast. "The most annoying fucker I never met."

My brows draw together as I assess him. "You mean... Ashby's son is buried out there?"

Wicker snorts. "Buried? Yeah, right. Little shit's got a tomb, with all its special engravings and weeping angels and private fucking monthly concerts, performed by yours truly." He tips the bottle back, a bitter curve to his mouth. "When I die, Father will probably dump my ashes into the sewer. Thank god. Can't even die around here without having a schedule drawn up for you." He shakes his head, his blonde hair gleaming in the moonlight as he mutters, "Every first Wednesday of the month."

I shift uncomfortably, not used to seeing Wicker like this. "Did something happen?"

It's hard to make out his blue eyes in the darkness of the room, but I know when he looks away. I can feel the absence of that buzzing tension he always carries around. "Lex made his *deposit*?" He says the word with the same foulness I feel at hearing it.

"Yes." I tug my sleeves down anxiously, wording my next statement very carefully. "Lex... he never actually... uh, you know."

It's not a question. Not really. Which means I won't have to answer one of his.

"Disappointed?" Wicker's smirk is meant to cut. I know it before the venom even comes out of his mouth. "Wondering why my brother doesn't want to give you a taste of his magnificent cock? Maybe you're just not his type. Maybe he likes women who know what they're doing in bed. Maybe," he pitches closer, into the light, "he's just *not that into you*."

My jaw clenches, but I know what he's doing. I just shrug. "Maybe not."

Wicker scoffs, leaning back. "Don't go crying tears into your silk pillowcases," he mutters, setting the bottle down on the ground. "If he could get it up, I'm sure the good son would rail you like a fucking–"

"Princess, surely." Danner's voice makes Wicker's cut off, and I spin to find him standing in a doorway. "Sir? If you're done paying your respects, I think it's time you retire to bed."

He doesn't argue, placing his cello in a large case I hadn't seen resting on a stone wall behind him. The latches snap, echoing against the high glass ceilings. He turns to me. "Don't stay down here too long, Red. This place has a way of turning people into ghosts."

He winks, tosses his beer bottle into a thick mass of dying grass, then exits through a doorway across the room.

"Enchanting, isn't it?" Danner steps into the moonlight, lifting a mug. "I make a special effort to take my tea out here when Prince Whitaker is paying tribute."

I take deep breaths, trying to calm the thunder in my chest. Wicker has that effect on me–erratic and dangerous–seemingly everywhere all at once. And although Danner is an old man, a bit hunched, I can't forget that he was the one to 'anoint' my throne.

He's just so hard to feel threatened by.

I look up at the round dome, wondering, "What is this place?"

"A solarium," he answers, sipping his tea. "Or it was. Everything is dead now, I'm afraid." The words are said with a touch of wistfulness, and when I follow his gaze, he's looking past the overgrown, dead planters, and at the graveyard. "I suppose it seemed strange to the King, keeping this place up. A mockery of his grief, perhaps."

His gaze wanders to the opening behind me, the one that leads to the passage, and he gestures to it, eyebrow arched. "I won't keep this a secret from him."

My stomach drops and I hug my middle. "Will I get in trouble?"

"For finding this? No, I would be cautious, however." His soft smile turns somber, serious. "There are places you can't be, Miss."

"Like here?" I fret, looking around.

He shakes his head. "Quite to the contrary. In fact, I think he'll be impressed with your curiosity about the palace. Most of the past Princesses are too distracted by the shinier parts of the position to take the time to explore the more intricate parts of the property." He tilts his head. "But maybe next time, you can take the proper entrance to it, hm?"

Relief courses through my veins. "It's beautiful," I say, rubbing some warmth back into my arms. I'm not sure why–the nervousness, or Danner's aggressively innocuous nature–but I find myself reminiscing. "I had a garden back home once, up on the roof of the gym. West End doesn't have a lot of places for it, but I got some planters and everyone helped out over spring break."

It was the summer before Freshman year, right after the incident with Pace, actually. I remember how comforting it was up there with the girls; the guys hauling bags of soil and mulch up the ladder for nothing more than a peek at the cutsluts in their bikinis as they sunbathed. It was the complete opposite of this place. It was bright and warm, full of laughter and life and the promise of a future laid out ahead of us.

This place might be beautiful, but it's dark and cold, full of dead things.

My chest twists at the memory of when things were simple.

When I break out of it, Danner is looking at me with an odd sadness in his eyes. "Beautiful," he agrees, eyes flicking to the cemetery, "but haunting. It's been neglected over the years. The other Royals haven't given it much attention or thought. Out of respect, I'd wager. Or fear." He tips his head down, giving me a significant look. "And the King finds it too painful to spend much time here."

I dare a question. "Because of his son?"

"Because it brings back too many good memories–the painful kind. This used to be a place of life. King Ashby held parties out here on warm spring and summer nights. The children spent hours playing out here."

Now it's an extension of the tomb outside.

"It could use someone–a restless Princess, perhaps–to make it beautiful again."

I take an involuntary step back, head shaking. "The last thing I want to do is upset the King."

Chuffing, he frowns. "There's something you must understand about their father, Princess. He must seem to you a very cold, callous man. He is, of course, but there is one thing Rufus Ashby holds sacred above all things. Creation."

Mouth tensing, I look up at the sky, still feeling Lex's deposit drying in my panties. "To create is to reign." The words taste like bile to me.

"There's more than one way to create life." Danner nods at the dead vines and wilted things. "Perhaps this one can bring you the peace you went into that dark nook searching for."

I raise an eyebrow. "And if it doesn't?"

He winks, taking another sip. "Well, it still makes a fine tea spot for these old bones."

15

V erity

"Go around back please."

"Are you sure, Miss?" Danner's eyes meet mine in the rearview mirror.

With zero hesitation, I reply, "Yes."

I hear the flip of the turn signal, and the vehicle turns down the narrow alley. For a week I've been dreaming of getting back here —*home*—but now that the gray building is in front of me, I'm nothing but a tangled mess of nerves.

But I haven't missed a family dinner since I was a teenager, and just because I'm the Princess and my mother is furious at me, doesn't mean anything changes.

The car stops, the engine shutting off. I smooth down the gray skirt and ignore the pink rug burn still visible across my knees as I open the door.

"Princess, you're supposed to let me do that," Danner says, moving slow as... well, as slow as a really old man.

"I'm just excited," I say, meeting him around the front of the car.

"Is that why you've chosen to come in the back door?" He frowns, the judgment clear in his tone. I shouldn't be sneaking in. It's not very Princess-like of me.

"I just haven't really seen anyone since the ball." I take a deep breath, scanning the alley. "I guess I'd like my entrance to be a bit more low-key."

"Regardless," he says, looking suddenly severe, "you hold your head high. You're the Princess. The creator of the next heir."

Maybe to East End I'm those things, I think, heading to the back door, *but to everyone inside, I'm a traitor.*

He follows several steps behind. He's not just here as my driver–that much I've sussed out on my own. Danner is my chaperone. Ashby's ears. The Princes' eyes. I'd hold it against him, except he doesn't bother dressing this up as anything less.

The hallway I enter is dark, nothing but a flickering fluorescent light buzzing overhead. Even back here, I can smell the spicy scent of spaghetti sauce and garlic bread cooking in the kitchen. Everything is richly familiar and I catalog it as if it's been years instead of a mere week. The thin carpet. The scuffed walls. The badly painted Bruin logo above the locker room door.

I stop at the door of the cutslut lounge, taking a steeling breath. "Wait here."

"Miss, I can't—"

Turning to him, I shake my head. "It's the women's locker room, Danner. I can handle myself."

He stands by the wall, hands crossed at the waist like a bodyguard. What he thinks he can do to protect me here, I don't know. The man is ancient. Even the greenest DKS boys could snap him in half. But if this is what it takes to get out of that mansion, I'll take it.

Pressing my palm flat against the door, I shake off my nerves and step inside. Voices bounce off the walls, the nonstop chattering of the girls who call this their sanctuary filling the space with lively laughter. The sound feels like home, and I tuck myself in the corner by the door to bask in it, just listening.

"That blue looks good on you—brings out your eyes." I recognize Kathleen's voice among the group, my chest warming.

"Aww, thanks, babe," Maggie, a pretty brunette who joined the cutsluts last year, replies. "How's it going with Kazinski? Any progress?"

"If you call him asking me for anal progress," she laughs, "then sure, why not."

A locker slams. "At least he didn't ask for a threesome with some random girl he picked up at the last Fury. That's what he did to Laura."

I wait for Laura's cheeky response, but it never comes. Peering into the room, I look for my friend, but don't see her. My curiosity quickly reveals me, sadly. The movement catches the attention of a few of the girls. There are whispers and turned heads, and then suddenly, everything stills.

All eyes are on me.

Trying on a smile, I say, "Hey," and step into the room.

"Oh, look, everyone," Kathleen turns around, "it's the *Princess*." There's no mistaking the sneer in her tone when she says my title.

My stomach twists painfully. "I know," I laugh, trying to cut the tension, "it's weird. Like *super* weird, but I'm still just me."

"Where's your tiara?" Daphne chimes in and the girls around her laugh. The sound is mean, scathing.

"I, uh—"

"Got a princeling in there yet?" Maggie's dark eyes drop to my stomach. "You do look kind of fatter."

My cheeks heat and my hand instinctively shifts to my lower belly. "Uh, not that I know of."

A chill settles over the room and slowly they all turn away, returning to their beauty routines. Family dinner is the one night everyone puts a different sort of effort into their appearances. People here dress a little nicer. No midriffs or exposed bras, no tanks or basketball shorts. It's not quite a Princess level of formality, but it's the rule.

Mostly, however, they ignore me. Kathleen, Maggie, Andrea–who I've known since high school–Daphne, Arden, Jaden... Their eyes look right through me. It's as if I've become the ghost Wicker warned me about last night.

Steadying myself, I squeeze in next to a frosty Kathleen, where my locker is located. I jerk it open, and freeze at what I find inside.

Nothing.

It's completely empty.

"Where's all my stuff?" I panic, reaching inside, even though I know my phone and purse are clearly absent.

"Your mom tossed it." Maggie says, applying a layer of blue eyeshadow. "You know, after you abandoned DKS."

"I didn't abandon anyone," I argue. I'd love to tell them about the negotiations between DKS and PNZ. The Monarchs. The bigger goals. But I'm not at liberty to share any of that, and it cuts me like a fucking knife. Sliding my gaze to Kathleen, I say, "Don't pretend like you wouldn't take the chance if you were given the opportunity."

She slams her locker, drawing every eye back to us as she raises her chin defiantly. "No, Verity, I wouldn't. Some of us can't be bought with shallow public gestures, fancy roses, and expensive cars. I made a promise when the Dukes let me into this gym. My loyalty is to them and no one else."

Andrea sneers, "But DKS boys don't come with trust funds, so they're obviously not good enough for you."

Before I can protest, Jaden jumps in. "DKS protects us better than any pampered East End fuckboy could."

"You know what'll happen if you don't get knocked up," Kathleen offers, her eyes full of distrust, but also something else. Concern. "They'll destroy you, V. You've seen enough rejected Princesses to know better."

"And when they *do* reject you," Maggie steps toward me, only an inch away, "there won't be any crawling back to West End. Not to these men. Not to your mother. Definitely not to us."

"That's enough!" Every eye snaps to the door where Lavinia Lucia stands. There's fire in her eyes as she stares them all down, a hand propped on her hip. Her lips quirk up when she sees me. "Lurch out there tipped me off that you were here." Her eyes cut back to the girls in the room. "I'm going to pretend like I didn't just hear the nasty bullshit being spewed in here. Verity is one of us, and that's forever." Her gaze locks in on Maggie. "She's got more DKS roots than that ombre dye job on your head. Don't forget that."

"Vinny," Kathleen says, eyes wide and incredulous, "she's East End now."

Lavinia shrugs. "And I was North Side. A little part of me will always be." She lifts her foot and puts it on one of the benches, exposing her leg. A snake wraps around her calf—Remy's artistic skills having brought it to life over the past couple weeks. "We're in a new era–one where the women of Forsyth stop bashing on one another. At least as long as you're in my house."

No one says anything to this, but I see the shift as people begin packing their grudges away. West Enders have always been good at storing malice as future ammo.

Great.

She lowers her foot and throws her arm around my shoulder, telling the girls, "Verity isn't just a guest tonight. She's family. We treat her as such, got it?"

Kathleen nods, and even though she doesn't meet my gaze, leaning toward the mirror to apply some mascara, she casually asks, "So what's it like having Whitaker Ashby's perfect cock buried in your body?"

Andrea smirks. "Is it as big as his hockey stick?"

"Jesus Christ!" Lavinia shouts. "What did I just say?"

"You said treat her like family." Kathleen shrugs. "And in this family, we ask a lot of questions about cock."

"She's right," I agree, unwinding a little. "They really do."

"And our girl, Verity–the last virgin in West End–finally popped her cherry." I can't tell if Jaden's wicked grin is good-natured or cruel. "It would be rude not to ask."

Lavinia sighs, eyes rolling heavenward. "Fair, but not now. Mama is about to pitch a fit that no one's helping. Get your asses out there and set those tables up. You can interrogate Verity about her bouquet of cocks after dinner."

As they file out, it's obvious not everyone is on board with Lavinia's little speech. I'm not surprised. It took months for them to accept her as their Duchess, and even then, it wasn't easy. She had to fight tooth and nail–literally–before she proved herself. Lavinia grabs my arm once they've all gone and spins me toward her.

"Thank god you're okay." She throws her arms around me and pulls me into a tight hug. "Wait," she releases me, and looks me in the eye, "you are okay, aren't you?"

I've been so busy surviving the last week that I haven't thought much about Lavinia's early days with the Dukes, but from the dread in her eyes, she endured... something. Was it as bad for her as it was for me? Part of me thinks it couldn't have been. Remy and Sy–they were always good to me.

But I know now that the men of Forsyth aren't always what they seem on the outside.

We're both quiet for a moment, but I ultimately answer, "I'm okay."

"Are you sure?" Her gray eyes assess me carefully. "Because I can—"

She can't do anything, and we both know it. I offer her a reassuring smile. "It's fine. I'm fine. It's all just an adjustment, you know?"

A shadow passes over her features. "Yeah, I know a thing or two about that."

I glance at the door, knowing Danner is on the other side, waiting and watching. "We only have a few minutes, but here's what I can tell you." Taking a breath, I start with the ceremony. I tell

Lavinia about the throning—about the covenants—about having the illusion of a choice, but it being a lie.

The more I say, however, the darker that shadow in her eyes gets. The paler her cheeks become. I quickly suspect Lavinia doesn't have the stomach to hear it all, and since I'd rather not waste my time here dressing up the last five days of abuse into something more pretty, I switch gears.

"But that's not important," I say before Lavinia can put voice to the horror in her expression. "What's important is that the Princes are nervous—like, seriously not happy about the appointment whatsoever."

Her head snaps back in surprise. "They're not?"

I pitch closer, darting a glance at the door. "Wicker was furious, going on about his father ruining his life. Pace is paranoid, like all the time, and as far as I can tell seems to think this is his father's revenge for him being in jail. And Lex... he might have it worst of all. From what I can tell, he's totally Ashby's beast of burden. Over-scheduled, overworked. He barely seems stable."

None of them do.

Lavinia absorbs this information pensively. "I know they picked up Bruce from the Hideaway. Have they said anything about that?"

Shaking my head, I confess, "Wicker just asked me some questions about why he got kicked out." Wringing my hands, I add, "I told him."

She snorts, nudging my shoulder. "Bruce being a shithead is no secret, Ver. Anything else?"

I think about it, trying to clear my mind on everything that's happened over the past few days. I'm tired. I've had too little sleep on too much vigilance, always looking over my shoulder to find out who and what's coming next.

There is one thing that stands out in my mind, though.

"Pace has an elaborate security system set up. He watches all of Ashby's properties and assets. When I was in his room, he had the Gentlemen's Chamber pulled up."

Her brows knit together. "The strip club?"

"Yes. Ashby was there, and—" I pause to lower my voice. "He was meeting with Remy's dad."

Her eyebrow raises. "Oh, really?"

"Pace seemed curious about the meeting too," I note. "Anything I'm missing?"

Sighing, she shakes her head. "No, but when two—" she pauses, "*rich* people meet up, it's good to know."

Feeling a little more on solid ground, I nod. "I'll let you know if anything else comes up."

"Thanks, Ver." She squeezes my arm. "We should get out there, huh?"

But the thought makes my stomach lurch as I watch the door, imagining them all on the other side of it. Their cutting stares. Their acerbic whispers. "They all hate me now."

Lavinia steps forward, jaw tight. "They don't hate you. They just don't understand. And if we're being perfectly honest here, a few of them are probably jealous."

I roll my eyes. "Like Kathleen?"

Lavinia smirks. "Definitely, Kathleen. She's super pissed she's not you." We both laugh and her hand drops to mine, squeezing. "I'm going to ask one more time. Are you sure you're okay?"

A sob, along with every detail of the last week, threatens to rip from my throat, but I hold it back. This is my burden, not hers. "Positive."

Her responding grin is dimmed, but impossibly more kind. "Then let's go prove to everyone you've got what it takes to be a Royal. Teflon skin and fantastic hair."

DINNER IS... different.

It's not just Danner lurking in the back of the room like a watchful gargoyle, but the sense of being noticed so acutely. It's attention that never came my way when I was Verity Sinclaire, Mama B's daughter.

"Take my chair," Porterfield says, hopping up as Lavinia ushers us to the table where she and the Dukes sit. He almost falls, tripping over his feet, but manages to stay upright and hold the chair out.

Blushing, I insist, "You don't have to do that." The whole gesture only makes everyone look at me harder. "It's not like I'm —" I stop, because the word I'm about to say is 'royalty,' and well...

"Take the seat, Verity," Nick announces, cutting straight through my nerves. "Donating that seat to you may be the closest he'll ever get to a fine ass. That way he can brag about it for the rest of his life."

"Like that time he got you with a right hook." Sy snorts, sipping a beer.

Nick slides a dark glower his way. "That was a sucker punch. Little Bird had just walked in the gym in those tiny booty shorts that make the blood stop going to my head."

"Your big head," Remy notes, pointing his marker at Nick's face.

Nick stands, grabbing his crotch. "You want to compare again, who has the biggest head?"

"No!" Lav shouts, slamming her hands on the table. "*One* time I let you have a competition, for *scientific reasons*, and we have to talk about it for the rest of *your* lives." She winks at me and whispers. "It's idiotic. Everyone in Forsyth knows who has the biggest cock, but they still have to compete over everything."

My mother's voice cuts through the echoey room. "Dinner's ready!"

I glance up at her, but she's already headed back to her office.

And she stays there.

For the whole dinner.

I keep anxiously waiting for her, fidgeting, my eyes constantly flicking to her empty seat, but she never comes. I only begin to relax after the guys strike up a discussion concerning tomorrow's Friday Night Fury. They shout above each other, good-naturedly arguing about the odds for every matchup, and I feel myself reluctantly slipping into the comforting familiarity of it all. I glance at Lav and she rolls her eyes, clearly as bored as I am.

I haven't missed a Friday Night Fury in years.

Tomorrow, I will.

Dinner is good, and it's hard to believe that five days of cold, solitary dinners at the Purple Palace have made me forget just how much I love this. The laughter. The warmth. The way Sy chucks a garlic knot at Porterfield's head, only for Porterfield to snatch it right out of the air with his teeth, causing a raucous round of celebration that's impossible not to laugh along with.

Later, when I'm in that big empty bed, alone and grateful for it, I'll probably laugh snidely at the idea, but I feel it in my bones.

It's healing me.

The torn, wretched thing in my chest clutches onto the unabashed *life* of it all and doesn't let go. Slowly, I feel whatever poison has tangled itself around my heart loosen, and by the time the big plate of brownies is being passed around, I feel almost like my old self.

"Here," I say, holding out my hand for Porterfield's plate. "I'll clean this up."

"He's a peon," Nick says, frowning. "Don't insult him by not allowing him to do his chores." He nods over at Danner. "Plus, shouldn't he be the one wiping your ass—" Lavinia sharply clears her throat and Nick's mouth clicks shut. "I mean... mouth?"

Remy jerks his chin. "He's just here to make sure the Princess doesn't fall on some premium West End dick and get knocked up by the wrong frat." He says this casually, like my cheeks aren't flaming red.

"I'm pretty sure he's making sure we adhere to the rules of the negotiations," Sy says, giving me a kind smile. "Porterfield, take the Princess' plate."

"I've got it." I say, jumping up and stacking his plate on top of mine. I could use some space. That's the thing about DKS. There's no filter with them. Ever. Normally, I'm used to it. What I'm not used to is being the focus of the talk. I walk toward the massive tub for dirty dishes, but halfway there, I'm blocked by a guy, his frame wiry but muscular. Startled, I look up into Ballsack's eyes.

"Hey," he says, shoving his hands into his pockets. "I just wanted to thank you for helping me out." He looks like he took eight rounds in the ring with Nick. It makes it hard to hold his gaze, knowing that the men responsible have touched me. Been inside. Left parts of themselves there.

And that I've let them.

I look away. "I didn't do much." And it certainly wasn't intentional. No one even knew he was missing, least of all me.

Shrugging, he offers, "You opened the door. God knows how much longer they would have kept me there." He holds up his hand, fingers still taped together. "Or how many nails I would've had left."

"I'm glad I was able to help provide the opportunity." I give him a smile that feels forced, realizing I'd missed the sounds of his own laughter during dinner. "How are you doing?"

"Okay." His gaze darts around the room behind me, and I notice his eyes are a little haunted. "Those Princes... they're more than what they seem, aren't they?"

"They're... complicated," I admit, and maybe my eyes are a little haunted too, because his mouth twists at the word. *Complicated.* Understatement. "Just like any Royal, right?"

His eyes dart over my shoulder where I know Danner is waiting. "Are you safe there, Ver?"

It's strange to hear the question from a guy like Ballsack. If the Dukes are like big brothers to me, then Ballsack is our wily nephew, always a little too eager to serve the frat. I thought the worst part of this visit would be facing the people who don't care about me anymore, but I was wrong.

The worst part, by far, is facing the people who still do.

"Nothing I can't handle." The assurance feels a little more natural here than it did with Lavinia. I guess that's how it goes. Lies take practice. Unfortunately, Ballsack doesn't look convinced, so I swiftly change the subject. "Everything still good with you and Laura? I was looking for her earlier but haven't seen her."

"Eh," he rubs the back of his neck. "Not sure."

I frown. "What does that mean?"

He shrugs. "When I got back from my... uh, trip? She was gone."

"What do you mean gone?"

"Like, she ghosted me. Hard. Haven't seen her around here either." His shoulder lifts again. "Maybe she's mad about me taking off? Or just used it as an excuse to bolt. Who knows? Chicks are crazy." He makes a face. "Present company excluded."

I can't help but laugh. "I'm sure she'll be back. Maybe she just went on a trip or something. Or back home to her parents."

"Yeah, maybe." He looks a little sad, so I let the topic drop. I feel bad for the guy. It was obvious he really liked her, and I'm not sure how to tell him that Laura's always been kind of a free spirit. Maybe she took his absence as a chance to get some space.

I linger by the kitchen for a minute longer, making small talk with some of the guys. The girls have gone back to their dismissive, icy demeanor, which isn't a surprise. Although Lavinia has some sway with the cutsluts, there's only one person who truly leads them.

My mother.

Taking a deep breath, I cross the room and approach her office. The door is open, but I knock, tapping on the glass window. "Whatcha need?" she asks, not looking up, and I freeze.

What do I need?

I need someone to talk to who won't feel guilty about how grisly the truth is. I need someone to tell me it gets better. I need to cry and vent and punch out all the rage I'm feeling over having all autonomy over my body stripped from me, day after day. What I need is my mother, but this isn't something we can sweep under the rug. I know it before I say, "Just checking in."

"Oh," she says, glancing up over the top of her glasses. She folds her hands on her desk. "Are you still the Princess?"

And there it is. "Yes."

"Then we don't have anything to talk about."

My laugh is a quiet, broken punch of air. "You're fucking kidding me."

"Do I look like I'm joking?" I do look at her. And from the dark circles under her eyes and the gray hair sprouting at the root of her part, it's obvious she's exhausted. Stubborn, but exhausted.

"You still think I don't know what I'm doing, don't you?"

She pushes back her chair and stands. "I think you're a foolish girl who I spoiled too much. Somehow, I convinced you into thinking that all powerful, handsome men are created equal. Now you think Royals are created from the same mold, but I'm guessing you're starting to see they're not."

"You know what I think?" I ask, fists curling.

Her hands rest on the curve of her hips. "Oh, I'd love to know. Enlighten me."

"I think you're jealous." My mother's jaw drops. Speechless, for once in her life. I take advantage of the silence. "You're jealous I did this without you. That I didn't need your help getting into the Purple Palace. That I beat out every other girl in Forsyth for the position, and it had nothing to do with you."

"Listen here, missy—" Mama's eyes narrow, slitting like a snake about to snap up her dinner. A chill runs down my spine and I take a step back, crashing into a body who stumbles back at the impact.

It's Danner. "Princess, I believe it's time to leave."

My eyes dart to the clock over my mother's desk. Nine o'clock. I'm supposed to be back early, since midnight always seems to come swiftly in East End, and I'll need to be... available.

Tomorrow is Pace's day.

"Did you have something to say?" I ask her, squaring my shoulders.

She visibly gathers up whatever storm has been brewing in her eyes, shoving it down. "Go. Wouldn't want to be late for your next *deposit*, would you?"

My blood turns to ice at the use of that word.

It's *their* word. The Princes. The thought of people here

knowing it–understanding what it means–makes my spaghetti threaten to come back up. "No," I say, swallowing thickly. "I guess I wouldn't."

I walk away from her, back and shoulders straight, refusing to show her the hurt I feel. For years, I watched her usher Duchesses and cutsluts into her office, offering patient words of wisdom regarding how to best deal with her fighters. When they cried, she'd soothe them. When they screamed, she listened. When they bent, she'd teach them how not to.

It's the support she *should* be giving me. Not because of what Royal frat I belonged to, but because we're family.

Or at least we used to be.

I BARELY REMEMBER SAYING goodbye to Lavinia or the ride home.

Home.

It says a lot to consider the Purple Palace my home compared to the DKS gym.

"How was your evening?" Stella, the ever-hovering presence, waits just inside the door to my bedroom. She frowns when she sees me. "Oh, Princess, what's wrong?"

I wipe away one of the tears I tried so hard to hold back, working past the lump in my throat. "It was just hard seeing everyone—and then leaving again."

"I understand that. Come," She swoops me through the door, past the roaring fireplace and into the bathroom, "let's get you cleaned up and changed."

"Thank you," I whisper, my limbs feeling too heavy.

"Do you need a bath tonight?" she asks, giving my hand a sympathetic pat. "I've got some new salts that can help with the healing. It's also got magnesium which can soothe muscle pain."

It's a sharp contrast to the cutslut lounge, but it feels nice to wash the sticky tears off my face with someone friendly nearby.

Someone who's aware of what I've been going through and doesn't feel responsible for it.

"Today's my day off," I say casually, "so I think we can save those for tomorrow."

I've come to understand the rhythm of the calendar. Lex, Pace, Wicker. Each of them have their own day of the week, passing me around in their own humiliating ways. Lex is all about the procedure—he just wants me to get pregnant—and Wicker may actually be the easiest, because all he wants is to get off.

But Pace is different.

After last time, I have no idea what to expect when he calls me into his room. His actions are personal in a way the others' aren't. Sex with him was so... *vengeful*. He doesn't just want to fuck me, he wants to make me suffer.

After dressing for bed and washing my face, I lean back against the marble counter, wringing the washcloth in my hand. "Does it get better?" I wonder.

Stella looks up from the array of facial creams. "Does what get better?"

My mouth screws up. "Sex?"

"Oh." She blinks, brows knitting together. "It still hurts?"

I squeeze the rag, grimacing. "Sometimes. But mostly it just feels so..." I glance up at her. "Cold."

She tilts her head, obviously considering my words. "Do you want it hotter? Because I sort of got the impression you didn't."

"Maybe it'd make it easier," I say, thinking of the way it felt to have Wicker on his knees, eating me out. It's the closest I've come to having a satisfying moment, and even that was tainted. "Or maybe I'd just hate myself more."

"Verity, look at me." Stella's stern voice draws my gaze to hers. "I've never been a Princess, so I don't know what it's like. But I've been a whore." She rolls her eyes, flapping a hand. "Okay, for like five seconds, but still, I know some things." Lifting a finger, she lists off, "I know what it's like to have rough sex with rough men. I know finding pleasure in that makes it easier to get through it. And the most important thing I know is that it doesn't make you weak. It makes you the master of your fate."

"But," I say, cheeks heating, "is it always like that? Is sex just something we endure? Or can it ever be…"

"Sweet?" Stella absently twirls her braid around her wrist, eyes going dreamy. "God, I hope so. With someone nice, who really likes you. Someone who holds you afterward. Someone whose eyes you can look into, and when he looks back, you can feel how much he wants and loves you, and it'd be scary, except you can't feel scared with him, because he's the epitome of safety, and you can still feel his arms around you even when you're not together."

Blinking, I say, "… yeah. I guess."

She snaps out of the daydream, shrugging with a bright grin. "I think it's out there! Somewhere."

Suddenly, I feel bad. Even if Stella was only a whore for 'five minutes', she still probably had to put up with far more than three men. I'm just about to apologize when we hear a loud crash coming from the bedroom.

We both jump, eyes locking warily before we begin inching toward the door.

The glow of the fireplace reaches toward the bathroom, and it's the only thing illuminating the bedroom when I peek out, scanning the room. The shadows dance, swaying and flickering in time to the flames, but I can still see the figure standing beside the bed. With his back to us, I can only tell that he's tall and shirtless, standing eerily still. His loose, wild hair grazes his shoulders, and when I look downward, I see that he's only wearing a pair of white boxer-briefs.

At first, I'm convinced it's a stranger–that someone has broken in.

And then I realize.

"…Lex?"

I've never seen him like this, so bare and unfettered, and I curse my heart for ratcheting up at the sight. Because when he turns his head, the glow of the fireplace cutting his cheek in sharp relief, I have one clear, unmistakable thought.

Lex Ashby isn't just cute.

He's fucking gorgeous.

"It's not his night," Stella whispers, glancing at me. "Right?"

I shake my head. "It's *my* night–for another hour or so, at least."

A strange look passes over her face. "So, do you think he's..."

"Sleepwalking?" I know that's why he has the lock on his door.

"Oh no," she moans, but when I step into the bedroom, she grabs my wrist. Eyes widening, she hisses, "Verity, wait! You can't go out there."

I gesture to his figure, still eerily motionless. "Someone has to get him back to bed." But it's then that I finally place that odd expression on her face.

Terror.

"You don't understand, Princess. This isn't the man you know." Stella tugs me back. "He's dangerous like this."

I glance at him again, whispering, "You know about his sleep-walking?"

She nods urgently. "All of the staff has been apprised. He's not allowed to get to you when he's like this. We should lock ourselves inside and call the King."

The thought of Ashby coming in here to save me from his son makes me recoil in a way I'm not expecting. "He's my Prince. What's he going to do to me that hasn't already been done?" This is easier than the actual explanation, which is that Lex isn't like Wicker or Pace, who are aggressive and physical creatures. Lex is a storm cloud. There may be rain, lightning, and thunder, but there's no collision there.

Ignoring her frantic protest, I step out of the bedroom, approaching him slowly. That's what we did with Kathleen when she was sleepwalking. Easy. Quiet. Coaxing. She was as pliable as clay when we led her back to bed.

His back is broader than it looks beneath his nice, pressed shirts, but the closer I get, the more *off* it looks. Weirdly textured. At first, I think it's just a trick of the light, the fireplace creating shadows in places they're not meant to be.

But it's not an illusion.

When I realize what I'm seeing, it makes me freeze.

Scars. There are dozens of them criss-crossed over his back like grisly lattice-work. Some are thicker than others, the skin pulled tight around the raised, pale edges. Those look gnarled, like roots beneath his skin, but the smaller ones are just as disconcerting, the slashes thin but long.

My throat clicks with a swallow, and from my periphery, I see his hand twitch. "Lex?" I whisper, barely a breath.

But he doesn't answer.

Not until I reach out with a slow, hesitant hand, brushing trembling fingers against the ridges of his mangled skin. "Lex? Let's get you back to bed."

There's a moment where I'm sure we've got it all wrong. Lex is awake. He must be, because when he finally turns around to look at me, the movement is so fluid–so normal–that it doesn't remind me of Kathleen at all.

His eyes are a different story.

They're hooded blots of shadow, his nose flaring with a long, sharp inhale.

I barely see him move, his arm snapping upward with such haste that it could happen between blinks. Cold fingers clutch my throat, but before I can react, I'm flying, my back slamming into the mattress. I'm not sure what to grab for first, his wrist or the blankets, but it doesn't really matter.

He's on me in a flash, hair swaying wildly above me as he plants a knee on my thigh, pinning me down.

I slap at his arm, trying desperately to gasp in a breath as his vacant eyes fix sightlessly to my chest. There's anger in his movements as he reaches between us, shoving down his boxer briefs, but I don't understand it. The way his mouth pulls back into a snarl, showing his teeth, is more of a mystery to me than the hand squeezing my throat, and that's what I think about as he pulls his hard, thick cock from his underwear. His feral eyes are more gold than amber.

"Mine," he says through gritted teeth, the sound of his voice guttural and slurred–inhuman. I kick out, catching his knee, but that just makes his grip on my throat tighten. Shoving with his hips, he gets between my thighs, jamming his cock into my center.

But the tip meets my panties. The futility of the thrust brings me back to the comment I'd made to Wicker about stupid Kathleen and her *stupid*, innocent sleepwalks.

"She kept trying to shove a pencil in the slot..."

He gives it another shove, growling as he meets resistance, and then there's a *crack*.

Jolting upright, he stumbles back, hand clutching his head. "Fuck!"

Stella stands behind him, breathing heavy, the poker from the fireplace tight in her grip. "Go, Princess!"

I scramble off the bed, gulping in air as I run for the door–but not before grabbing Stella. We take off, skidding as we run into the hall. Glancing back, I see movement from my bedroom, Lex's shadow cast against the floor. "Get to safety," I tell her. "Go hide. Find Danner. Just get the fuck out!"

"What about you?" She hops on her feet, anxious, eyes darting as his shadow grows bigger.

"I know where to hide."

She runs, and I race to the spot that I know leads to the passage-way. If I get in, I can hide, at least until he wakes up or one of the guys stops him.

The thud of footsteps behind me sends a chill of terror up my spine. What if I can't find it? What will he do with me? I blink away that blank, feral look I'd seen in his eye.

A door to my left swings open, and a hand shoots out, dragging me inside.

I'm still breathing heavily when I hear the lock engage. I look up, heart thudding wildly in my chest. "Pace, oh my god."

He's shirtless too, a pair of sweats slung low on his waist, but his dark eyes are sharp as they take me in. "You look like you've been running from the big bad wolf."

I mean.

Yeah, sort of.

"Lex," I say, trying to get air, "he's lost his mind."

Pace's mouth tightens as he glances toward the door. "I've heard this happens lately."

"Didn't someone lock his door?" Straightening, I notice the way his eyes travel to where Lex tore my night dress. "Where's Wicker?"

"Out doing something for Father." He watches me carefully, eyes dipping to my throat as he ruffles the back of his hair. "Fuck. I was supposed to lock him in, but I fell asleep."

I realize now how heavy his eyes look, a crease pressed into the side of his face from the piping on the arm of the couch. Footsteps echo on the other side of the door, and I stiffen. Lex is closer. A room away. My heart pounds, beating frantically against my chest. The footsteps are slow but heavy, and looking down, I can see his shadow stopping through the crack at the bottom of the door.

The doorknob rattles.

"Can I stay here?" I whisper, since Pace isn't offering.

He's staring at the doorknob with a tense expression. "I should take care of him."

"Don't go out there," I say before he can reach for the knob, and the shame rushes inward when he looks at me, eyebrow arching.

Because he hears in my voice that I'm scared.

Scared of Lex.

Not of him.

"He could barge in," I worry.

I know it's a mistake before he even crosses his arms. "Maybe you're right. If he overpowers me and gets to you, that'd be bad for everyone—even him." Raising his chin, he peers down at me with those inky eyes. "You can stay here with me. For a price."

It's just trading one monster for the other—that much I know.

16

P ace

THE WHOLE THING WAS AN ACCIDENT. Father has us scheduled so tightly there's barely time for sleep, let alone anything else. I long ago adapted to the necessity of catching a doze wherever I could, which is something that does, on occasion, kick me in the ass.

Tonight is one of them.

Wicker is going to fucking kill me.

Scrubbing a hand down my face, I go to the monitors, searching. "Sit down."

Deep below the wild anxiety, I won't deny the moment is satisfying. The panicked girl in front of me, her chest heaving beneath that torn nightie, doesn't seem to think I'm as big a threat as my deranged, sleepwalking brother.

Things are progressing nicely.

"You want me to sit." Her eyes dart beside me, filling with dread. "In your chair? Again?"

I give her a deadpan look. "On the couch."

She hesitates, waiting for me to sit first, for this process to begin, and fuck, it's pathetic. One little week, one session with me, and she's trained, willing to do whatever we want. But that's the thing, it's important to keep people on their toes, to never allow them to get comfortable.

People are willing to do a lot for comfort.

For safety.

Release.

I gesture to the spot on the couch, and I see her confusion at me allowing her to sit first.

"Down here?" she confirms, pointing to the cushion.

"Yes."

Ultimately, she does as she's instructed, lowering herself to the seat. She flinches when the cold leather hits her bare thighs. My gaze drops down to where her nipples tighten and peak, pushing at that torn, flimsy dress.

"That was just insane," she says as I turn my back to her, leaning over the desktop to flip through the screens. "I've heard of night terrors, but nothing like that."

The first video I pull up is of the hallway, where Lex continues to roam up and down the corridor. Admittedly, I've been a bit skeptical of the whole sleep-raping thing. Wicker has a flair for the dramatic. How hard could it be to push a sleeping guy off you?

Only, I glance over at Verity, seeing the red welting around her neck, and concede that maybe Wicker had a point. I shoot Danner a quick message, hoping he can get my brother back to bed before any additional havoc ensues.

Opening another screen, it reveals the dungeon downstairs. The camera angles in on Bruce, rolled up on a cot with his back turned to the camera. Lex went in while we were at practice and checked on the brands. It's been two days, and I still can't get the scent of burning flesh out of my mind—or the little mindfuck that he dropped. My father is from West End? Bullshit. It was a hail Mary for sure, but the simple fact he came after me like that?

Brought up my past, knows my history? Well, that's something to consider.

For the third, and largest part of the screen, I pull up a recording from earlier tonight. It's a small group of well-dressed people down in the drawing room, invited for a night of music and networking. In the top corner, the camera catches the bottom curve of a cello, the bow slowly swaying back and forth. I press the volume, and the timbre of a rich music fills the room.

"*Wicker*," Effie croons in my brother's voice.

Verity gasps, her gaze jolting toward the cage as if she's just now noticing it. "What the–" Her mouth parts in shock. "You have a bird?"

Effie preens her wing. "*Dirty bird.*"

"Pretty bird," I correct her. "Effie, show Verity how pretty you are."

She turns on her perch, head bobbing and tilting. "*Mother-fucking bird.*" Lex's voice. "*Suck my balls.*" Wicker's voice.

I roll my eyes. "Show her *pretty*, Effie."

Effie pauses before raising her beak to trill out a happy melody to complement the cello. Afterward, she says in a parody of my own voice, "*Pretty bird.*"

I nod. "That's right. Good girl."

"Oh my god." Verity looks enraptured, her fingertips dragging over her throat. "Oh my *god*, it sounds just like... all of you."

I reach over for the sheet, announcing, "Time for bed, Effie."

Predictably, she doesn't take this well. "*Suck my balls*," she snaps as I reach into the cage to fire up the tablet. "*Suck, suck, suck–*" She goes silent when the screen flares to life, that South Side sky cam, her new obsession. She makes another trill, extends her wings, and then, "*Pretty bird.*"

"Good girl." Covering the cage, I say, "It's an hour until midnight."

Midnight—when Verity's day off rolls over and she belongs to me again. It smarts to have her like this, in drips and drabs. It'll delay my progress. Some marks do better with routine isolation.

Bruce, for instance. The longer we leave him alone, the more unsettled he feels. Verity isn't like that. I knew the first time we chatted, almost two years ago, that she was the type of mark who required constant attention. Did my best to give it to her, too.

I'm not one to always follow the rules, but when I drop down into my desk chair, spinning to face her, the distance between us makes my commitment to not breaking this one clear.

At least not officially.

I gesture at the tear in her gown, the rip revealing the smooth skin just below her collarbone. Red scratches mar her flesh. "He almost got you, didn't he?"

Swallowing, she reaches up to touch the skin. "Yes. If my handmaiden hadn't been there..."

It's a good thing that girl had her wits about her. I know Lex likes to roam, but I didn't actually expect him to get that physical. Aside from a few fights on the ice, it's never really been Lex's style. If he'd gotten to her—fucked her on a designated day off—father would have been livid.

"Lex has always been into tits," I say, as a way of dismissing his aggression. I lift my chin. "Let's see them."

"My—" I pin her with a hard, unrelenting look, and she deflates.

With her cheeks red from humiliation, she takes the hem in both hands and pulls the gown over her head, leaving her in nothing but white panties. My tongue darts out to lick my bottom lip, because what I just said was bullshit. *All* guys are into tits. Lex. Wick. Me...

Especially ones like Rosi's. They're full teardrops, more than a handful, the valley between them an invitation to slide a cock between and fuck relentlessly.

I shift, the erection that's been pressing against my inner thigh now twice the size as when she stepped through the door. The desk chair squeaks under my movement.

"Fuck, your areolas are huge." I sprawl back, reaching up to lazily hook an arm over the chair's back. "Does that make them more sensitive?"

"I—"

Before she can respond, I command, "Touch them."

She frowns, almost confused. "You want me to..." She cups them underneath and pushes them up. "Like this?"

My forehead creases, and something slowly dawns on me. "You've never done this before, have you? Touched yourself?"

"Yes." Her shoulders draw in, pulling her tits together. "Of course, I have."

It's a lie, and she squirms against it, skin turning the color of her hair. That, along with the music in the background, spurs me on. "No, you haven't. The little virgin Duchess-wannabe? You were a prude from day one. I bet you don't even know how to make yourself feel good. You need a man to do it for you, don't you?"

Her jaw tightens. "No, I don't."

I jerk my chin up. "Oh yeah? Then show me how you get yourself off."

I see the spitfire then, the way her eyes light up in reaction to my challenge. I heard about how she clocked that girl at the party. I remember the talks we had on the dating app before she clammed up and got shy. This girl grew up around the Bruins. No, she's not weak.

She's just innocent.

"Your nipples," I tell her, "touch them." Slowly, she draws her thumbs over the soft swell of her breasts and rolls them over the stiff peaks. Then, she swallows.

Fuck yes, she likes it.

"Did that make you wet?" I look down at her legs, clamped together. "Show me."

Her knees inch apart, and I peer between them. I felt this girl when she gave Wicker head. She was soaked. But right now, those panties are dry. That won't do.

"Even if I didn't jack off before I went to prison, that would've changed the minute I got inside." I run my hand over the outside of my sweats, down my thickening cock, pushing against the desire. I went almost two years without sex, but after having her sit on my dick for two hours, it's suddenly all I can think about. Something about finally bringing that fantasy to life... *shit*. I feel like I'm turning into Wick. It's all I want to do, be in her balls deep, round-the-clock.

Casually, I go on, "It's not a surprise really—a bunch of bored heathens, all locked up with no pussy? You learn the system quickly. When to do it. Who to hide it from. How often you can get away with it." I cup my balls, trying to suppress the twitch. "Some guys are just fucking wide open about it. Vengeful, especially with the CO's. They'll just stand in their cell, staring straight into an officer's eyes, and rub one out. They call it gunning." I lift my chin. "Pinch them."

Her fingers come down on her nipple, squeezing hard. She lets out a gasp, and that red heat spreads down her neck.

"Most guys like to do it in the shower, but that was too quick for me. We only got a few minutes, and, well..." My mouth pulls into a slow smirk. "You know I like to take my time."

Father taught us early on that what we want isn't always what we'll get. Patience is important. A necessity. I used to hate him for the days I spent down in the dungeon, nose pressed into a corner as I waited. And waited. And waited. And waited. But in the end, it made me stronger. It's why I didn't lose my edge inside. A few days spent in the hole? Man, that's just childhood nostalgia.

I'm still in control, but I'm aware.

Of the clock. The date. The time. I know when I can sink myself into her again and make her feel me inside. Make her want me as much as I want her.

Make her beg.

"Panties."

"Why?" she asks, lowering her hands protectively to her stomach. "Why are you telling me all this? Why are you making me do this?"

It's part of the process, Rosi.

I don't say that. I say this: "Because even though your entire position as Princess is about your body, you're afraid of it. You've always been afraid of it, like when you freaked out over the video I sent you."

Her brows crash together. "That was your body not mine."

"Your body caused it, Rosilocks," I give my cock a squeeze, watching the way her tits heave with a breath. "You got me so hard that finding and fucking you was the only thing I could think of."

"Because you're a pervert."

The music swells in the background, the long strains filling the room.

"Baby, you're in Forsyth." I dip my hand into my pants, grinning when her eyes instinctively follow the motion. "I'm practically a monk compared to the other men in this town. If you learned to let go of all that West End defiance, then maybe I could even teach you how to feel good."

She barks out a dark laugh. "None of you care if I feel good."

Voice firm, I say, "You're wrong." The truth is, the thought of having her beneath me, writhing with pleasure, makes my cock surge with want. Because only then will I know I've won–that I've conquered the mark.

I want her stroking that pussy until she's barreling down the edge. And then I want her to stop. To feel that denial and deprivation, how it twists her up inside and consumes any rational thought.

Quietly, she says, "It's still my day off."

"If that's how you feel, Rosilocks," I stand, cock poking out like a flag pole, "then you can take your chances out in the hall."

"No!" Her eyes flick to the computer screen. I don't have to look to see Lex still out there. I can hear him in the hall. "Fine. I'll do what you want."

I clear my throat and repeat, "Panties."

She lowers them angrily, shimmying them down her hips to the floor. Her toes are painted pink.

"Spread your legs."

Her knees part.

My cock lurches forward, twitching. "You stopped waxing."

She averts her eyes. "You told me to."

This time, I don't just feel it in my balls, but all the way up in my chest. I finally pull my cock out of my pants, the skin hot and iron-hard in my palm. With my thumb, I smear the precum over the head.

I watch as her fingers twitch against her inner thigh. "What do you want to do, Rosi?"

"Put my clothes back on."

I shake my head. "Try again."

Huffing out a breath, she replies, "Get this over with."

My eyebrow arches. "Then make it happen."

Slowly her hand slides down her thigh, toward her pussy. I know the instant she brushes over her clit, because her body goes rigid, like she's been shocked.

"Do that again," I order, and her fingers roll over that bundle of nerves, eliciting a full body shudder. "Show me your fingers."

She lifts them and they shine, wet in the light.

"Taste them."

She freezes, those green eyes peering up at me. "What?"

"Lick your fingers, Rosi."

She brings them to her mouth, sniffing first, and then her tongue darts out to get a taste. My balls clench and I fist my cock. I want that tongue on me. So. Fucking. Bad.

Leaning back, her legs part wider, and she uses her other hand to spread her folds. The fingers she licked drag down her chest and toy with her nipple. It's a move I'm not expecting, and if it weren't for the curious spark in her eye, I'd think she was putting on a show for me.

There's no artifice to it at all.

"How does it feel?" I ask, barely able to choke out the words.

Her eyes flutter shut. "Good."

"Look at me when you touch yourself."

Her eyes open, green and clear.

"What feels good?"

"When I rub my clit." She does it again, hips rising up, giving me a better view of her pretty pussy.

I'm still standing in the middle of the room, struck absolutely fucking dumb as I stroke myself. "Your fingers," I tell her, my voice dropping an octave. "Use them to fuck yourself."

Her nose wrinkles, but she pushes in one finger. Her hips rise and fall as she fucks in and out, and I try desperately to remember all those things I'd fantasized about while in prison. I can't. They pale in comparison to the reality of her squirming hips and flushed skin. I get this thought that I need to taste every inch of her. Every freckle. Every scar. Every milky, smooth swath of flesh.

I want to fucking devour her.

"Another," I command, my cock twitching eagerly. "Two fingers."

She takes a deep breath and adds her middle finger, the knuckle disappearing as it sinks inside.

I rake my lip through my teeth. "Three."

She grinds her head back into the couch, brows knitted tightly together. "I can't."

I grip my cock in my hand and say, "Trust me, Rosi. You can take three."

Her throat bobs with a swallow but she inserts a third. Her ring finger. I see the way she curves them, pushing at her walls—against her boundaries. Chip by chip, I'll make them fall.

While she stares at me, her body writhes on the leather couch, rising and falling as she fucks into her body. I put all my attention on her, forgetting my own painful desires, and watch her build and build, until her breath stutters, coming out in tight little gasps. She pushes and pulls at her breasts, leaving red marks from the rough handling of her skin. She climbs, nearing that edge and I lean forward, circling my fingers around her wrist.

Roughly, I yank her hand back.

"What?" Her eyes are wide, glazed, hips moving to chase the vanished heat. "What the hell?!"

I skate my fingertip up the slickness on her own fingers. "Not yet."

"But..." Her lips work soundlessly around her protest before, "Why not?!"

Her body is on fire. I can see it. Smell it. The scent of her dripping pussy thick in the room. I raise my hand, licking out to catch a taste of her wetness. "You know what I want."

Her eyes drop down to where my cock is hanging obscenely out of my sweats.

I snort. "You're really one-track when you're horny, aren't you." Shaking my head, I tower over her, between her spread thighs, and grip the back of the couch, gazing down into her frustrated eyes. "Tell me you want my baby in you."

Her expression immediately shutters. "No."

Shrugging, I nod at her fingers. "Then do it again. Start with one."

Her jaw tightens. She understands the game I'm playing here, and when she reaches down to emotionlessly insert a finger into herself, I sense how she means to play it.

"Two," I say, watching as she adds her middle finger, and then, when I command it, her ring finger. She's not on the edge anymore, her mind pushing her body back from the brink, knowing now what the cost of going over it will be.

Sighing, I reach down to touch her clit.

She gasps when I slide a finger in beside her own. "Wait–"

"No," I say, fucking it in against her knuckles. My thumb works above it, relentless as I stroke her clit. "Remember what you were asking your handmaiden earlier?" If she had the capacity, the question would confuse her. As it is, she just looks overwhelmed, sweat springing up on her temples. I remind her, "You wondered if sex would ever get better."

Her eyes lurch to mine, wide and frightened. "How do you...?"

"I was watching you, Rosi." I toy with adding another fingertip, her pussy so wet and warm. "Honestly, it's part of why I was only half awake. Girl talk is so fucking boring. I heard that part though, and the truth is, it *can* get better. All you have to do is say the words."

"Why? Are you..." She blinks, confusion swimming in her eyes. "Are you in love with me or something?"

It's a physical battle not to laugh right in her face. *Chicks, man.* "Would thinking I am make it easier for you to give up?" It won't. That much I can see in her expression. Sinking my finger in deeper, I say, "I don't want a girlfriend. I don't even want a Princess."

"Then why?" But the answer comes to her faster than I can reply. "You want a pet," she realizes, face twisting in outrage.

"You are a smart one."

"I'll never say it," she insists, eyes dropping to where my thumb is stroking her slick, swollen clit. "You can do this to me all you want. I'll never say it." For a third time, she stresses, "I'll *never* say it."

Yes, you will.

It's almost disappointing to know how wrong she is. That fire in her eyes? That sort of spark can be fun. Exciting. I make a promise to myself in that moment without even really meaning to.

If there's a way to avoid completely snuffing it out, I'll take it.

"We'll see."

My back aches from holding myself above her, but I endure it. The vantage is too good, gazing down at her naked body as I bring her to the edge. I know when she gets close, her clit swelling below my finger, breaths coming in short, shallow bursts. Mostly, it's the way her hips twitch upward, like she just can't help it.

Just before she comes, I tear our hands away. "Five more minutes 'til midnight."

Her inner thighs tense at the loss, but the best part is how her clit visibly twitches. I bet I could blow on it and send her screaming in release.

I don't do that.

I stand there and watch her recede, her skin beginning to glisten with sweat. She trains her eyes to the screens behind me and gulps in these long, desperate lungfuls as I gently–so fucking gently–graze the backs of my knuckles against her clit.

She cries out, thighs snapping closed.

"Nope," I say, prying them apart. "I'm just getting you ready for my deposit. Don't you want to be ready for me?"

"I don't care."

"Yes, you do." I give her clit another graze, delighting in the way she shudders. "Look at how much you're shaking. You're probably wondering if you made a mistake. Maybe Lex would have been better." Tilting my head, I assess the way her throat jumps with a swallow. "He is good at it, you know. No one knows their way around a pussy like he does."

Throwing her head back, she whimpers.

Whimpers.

Curiosity piqued, I muse, "He's shown you, hasn't he? Is that what my big brother does down there in the basement?"

Fuck, I have *got* to get a camera down there.

Her breathing ratchets up a notch, and the next time I brush against her clit, she cries out, "Please!"

Begging always makes my dick happy, but there's something about her doing it that makes it jerk eagerly, the tip leaking a fat load of pre-cum. "You know the magic words."

"I–" Her eyes slam closed as I brush it again.

Freezing, I push the flat of my thumb against her clit. "You what?"

"I want your..." She gasps and I bend closer to her parted mouth, enthralled by the flutter of her fine lashes against her cheeks. "I want your ass in a prison cell again." She opens her eyes, her defiant stare boring into mine. "Please tell me more about how I did it the first time." She tenses, probably in anticipation of my anger.

But my mouth just curls up into a loose smirk, a chuckle bouncing in my chest. "You West Enders. Always so obsessed with winning. You're in East End now, Rosi. There's only one way to reign here." When I glance back, the clock says 12:01, and I don't miss a beat.

Grabbing my cock, I notch it up against her entrance and slam my hips forward.

She screams.

Like the wideness of her eyes, it's more surprised than pained, which is good. Lex will thank me for stretching her so well. I hook my hands around the backs of her knees, shoving them up toward her shoulders, and make sure I bottom out as deep as her body will let me.

"Look at it," I snarl, some of the anger seeping through. I grab the back of her head and wrench it down, forcing her gaze to where my dick is buried inside of her. "Watch me put it into you."

I've been holding it off for the last hour, but I finally let it go, needing little more than a half a thrust before it starts. My cock visibly pulses with the first wave of my release, swelling and twitching. She makes a shocked sound, but I'm too busy erupting with ecstasy to care. This orgasm is just like the last one. It goes on and on, both of us watching as my cock surges inside of her. It's hard to hold myself up, my limbs flooded with warmth as I empty myself into her.

For some reason, I just keep *coming.*

She looks on with parted lips as it spills out from the edges of her tight cunt, as if her slender little body couldn't possibly hold it all.

"Fuck," I grunt, giving my hips a little nudge. It never used to be like this. Even when I was getting head from that girl after Friday Night Fury, I came and went. This is the second time I've fucked Rosilocks, and it's just a fucking near constant flow of spunk.

By the time I finish, the leather couch is soaked.

I pull out carefully, anticipating the stream that follows and ready to push it back in. But before I can, her fingers are there. Three of them. She catches the trail of leaking cum and quickly slides it back inside. When I glance up, she's staring right at me.

Her jaw is set, fingers holding my seed inside. "I know where I am," she says, and even though she doesn't say it, I can practically see the prayer in her eyes.

To create is to reign.

She knows only one thing can save her now.

"Oh, Rosi." Tenderly, I trace the tense line of her jaw, knowing that only one thing will truly satisfy me. "I'm going to have so much fun breaking you."

ON THE ICE, there's chaos all around me. Constant movement, the other players, the puck, the sticks. A player can't just think about what they're doing. A top player has to be three steps ahead, anticipating the next moves, and right now I'm not doing my job. I'm thinking about Rosilocks, how she looked while she was taking all of my commands. How wide her eyes got as she watched me fill her up. The look on her face when she left my room, so determined to hold her head up high, because in her mind, she'd won.

It's not that I want her to want my baby.

Love isn't real. The closest I've ever come to it is the bond I have with my brothers, but even that's too twisted and permanent for such a trite, bullshit label. People like Rosi wouldn't understand, because they're still living the lie that there's such a thing as selfless want.

It's that wanting my baby inside her–any of ours–would be her worst fucking nightmare.

Wicker would probably finesse it, because that's what he does. Lex would find a formula, something expertly designed to get him results. Me?

I'm the blunt instrument guy.

I take a whack at the puck, but my blade barely knicks it, sending it skittering left.

A whiff.

"Fuck!" I slam my fist into the glass.

Coach Reed shouts, "Get your head out of your ass, Ashby!"

"Just to be clear," Wick says, skating past, his forehead damp with sweat, "he means you."

"Fuck off," I mutter, adjusting my gloves.

He smirks. "If only."

He's trying to ease the tension, but it won't work. We both know it.

"Do it again!" Coach's whistle screeches across the ice. "From the beginning. Scoring mentality, Ashby!"

We've been running this 3-vs-3 drill for an hour, and I'm not the only one who's fucking it up. I'm probably not even the only one who's preoccupied with pussy rather than the puck. But I am the only one, other than Wicker, that has two sets of eyes watching their every move. Father showed up thirty minutes into practice and has been standing next to Coach Reed, arms crossed over his chest, speaking into his ear.

Shit.

"Don't let him in your head," Wicker says quietly, lining up next to me, puck in front of him. "We've done this a million times. We own this fucking rink."

I give him a look that I hope conveys what I'm thinking.

That shit feels so distant that it might as well have happened in another lifetime. The life before prison. Before the trial. Before the cops. Before Spring Break. Before I saw a girl online and decided to make her my next mark.

"It's on a three-count. I'll snap you the puck—you take the shot."

Frustrated, I bark, "I know."

The whistle cuts through the air, and we fall into formation–me outside of the circle, Wicker inside of it, facing off with Tommy Wright. I focus on my brother, the puck, the net at the top of the circle. I try not to let him get under my skin, try to shake her from my mind, focused only on the feel of my skates, the stick in my hands, the—

The whistle shrieks out. "You're in the circle!" Reed shouts, and

I realize I've been so focused on Wicker's stickwork that I've drifted over the drill boundaries.

All the players deflate, skating back in place.

Anxiety rips up my spine, settling in my chest. And even though I don't want to, I glance up to the stands, eyes shifting next to Coach, but Father is gone, his dark frame already exiting the rink.

The whistle blows again, but this time the sharp screech signals Reed's irritation. "Forget this. Since some of you can't seem to find a hole that doesn't have hair around it, we're finishing up with twenty suicides!"

There's a loud groan and a couple of sharp 'fuck's' muttered down the line. Baxter shoots me a dirty look. Wicker, ever the arrogant leader, pushes off the ice to yell, "Let's get started!"

By the time we're done, everyone is huffing and puffing, coated in sweat. Baxter barfs in the trash can on his way into the locker room, and Loeffler is holding his upper thigh like he might have strained something. I'm angrily stripping off my pads as I march into the gym when Wick grabs my arm. "You can't let him rattle you like this."

"I'm not."

"Sure, you're not." He sighs, pushing his sweaty hair back. "I know you're just not used to him being around, and that things are awkward as fuck between you, but ultimately he just wants us to be the best."

Not do. *Be.*

Not our. *The.*

I am used to being watched–by CO's, other prisoners, and guards around the prison. None carried the oppressive weight of Rufus Ashby.

"I liked it better when he was ignoring me." I strip off the rest of my uniform, dumping the sweaty, smelly clothes in the hamper. I'm looking forward to washing off the grime and humiliating practice when I hear my name.

"Pace!"

I look over, seeing that it's one of the assistant coaches. "Reed wants to see you."

Everyone is watching me now, but Wicker just shoves my shoulder and says, "Play nice."

When I reach the room, I half expect father to be behind the desk, but no, that would look like he cared. Coach Reed is in the chair, jerking his chin for me to shut the door. He doesn't offer me a seat.

"You want to tell me what the fuck was going on out there today?"

I shrug. "Dunno. Distracted, I guess."

He's quiet for a moment, rubbing his chin. "I'm not going to bullshit you, Ashby. You and Wick bailing on the team two years ago was a hard blow. I'd organized the entire lineup around your skills and poof," he snaps his fingers, "that evaporated. Whittaker is a good, disciplined player, but if it were up to me, I probably wouldn't let you back on the team at all. Especially with the fuck-ups you're making out there on the ice." His jaw tenses. "But it's not up to me. We both know that."

It's up to Father. He's calling the shots here with his influence and donations to Forsyth. With the former head of Athletics, Saul Cartwright, gone, it's been even easier for him to throw his weight around.

Reed jabs a finger at me. "The only fucking reason I haven't pushed back is because with you and Wick on the line, we can probably take this whole thing." He gives me a hard look. "*If* you get your shit together."

I hear what he's saying. That there's a chance to fix what happened before—when I failed the team by fucking up—no—by getting *caught*. Because that's what all of this is about. Not the action of doing, but of getting busted. That's the failure.

Coach leans back in his chair, the springs creaking under his weight. "Be straight with me, Pace, is this too much for you to handle?" He toys with the platinum ring on his right hand. A PNZ alumni ring. "It's a lot of obligation, and your father's expectations—"

"I can handle it," I say quickly. Probably too quickly. "Just getting my bearings. They don't have an ice rink down at the Forsyth Pen." At the displeasure in his eyes, I assure, "But I've kept up my cardio and weight training. I'm fit. I'll make it happen. Wicker and I can come in early for extra practice."

Oh, Wick's gonna love that.

There's a moment of tense silence as he watches me, assessing. "I'm giving you one game—this weekend—to prove yourself. Otherwise, I've got other players with less baggage that can fill the spot."

"And my father knows that?" I ask, not because I want to, but because it matters.

"It was his ultimatum." A flicker crosses his face. Sympathy? Fuck.

Nodding, I say, "I understand."

"Good." He nods to the door, and I rise, my body aching from the punishing workout.

By the time I shower and change, everyone has already left, including Wicker. I walk outside, expecting him to be in the car, but the SUV is gone.

Instead, Father's black Mercedes limo is idling at the curb.

His driver and security, a stout fucker named Frank, opens the door as I approach, and it doesn't matter that no words are spoken. The command is crystal fucking clear.

"Goddamn it," I mutter under my breath.

I get in the back, sitting across from Father. He's in a white suit, as always. A drink in a crystal tumbler sits next to him and his gaze is cast down, looking over something on his phone. God forbid he looks me in the eye.

The driver starts the car, and once we're moving, he continues tapping at his phone screen. My anxiety ratchets up, building with every passing minute, until I begin, "The mistakes I made today, those were my fault. I didn't get enough sleep last night. I already spoke to Coach Reed about putting in additional effort, going in early and—"

Without looking up, he raises his hand, silencing me. After a few more taps of the screen, he pauses, taking a sip of his drink. "Since I made you my son, you've been afforded every opportunity —just like your brothers. The best schools. Excellent tutoring. Special coaching to cultivate your skills. You're gifted in your own right, testing in the highest percentiles. You've also been given a specific type of leeway that comes from being an Ashby. A leeway I revoked when you were arrested."

Father's connections, his power and money, easily could have gotten me out of my charges. Or at the very least, I could have been given a slap on the wrist. But he decided to make an example of me. Not just to my brothers, but to East End. His wrath knows no bounds. Fail and you'll be punished, name be damned.

"Once you paid the price for your indiscretions, I wanted to wash the slate clean. Give you back the privileges of being family. I made you a Prince–the highest honor of our house. I'm giving you a shot at creating the heir, which comes with a lifetime of rewards." Before I can go through the motions of thanking him for this, he suddenly asks, "Do you know why I want you on the hockey team, Pace?"

Control.

The way he packs our schedules with obligations has always been about control for him.

But I reply, "No, sir," and it's not even a lie. I'm not sure why it's hockey instead of any other bullshit job.

He muses, "You always took isolation exceptionally well. Wicker, of course, could never suffer it. Lex might have, but I don't think I would have liked what it did to him. You, on the other hand..."

His eyebrows jump upward, probably remembering how well I took to some of his earliest punishments. There was never a dark hole Father forced on me that couldn't be quickly adapted to. I crafted stories in my mind, keeping it sharp, and I was always able to find something to make fast friends with. Once, a tiny spider named Geraldine. Another time, a shiny beetle I called Shadow.

252 ANGEL LAWSON & SAMANTHA RUE

One notable time, I managed to meet a couple of mice who I'd pretended were Wicker and Lex. I talked to them for days on end, and the next time I was put down there, they were still nesting in the vent, so I talked to them some more. I had so many conversations with those mice that I'd ended up forgetting which versions of Wicker and Lex I'd told this or that to. It'd confuse the fuck out of my real brothers whenever I'd pick up an old discussion they weren't even there for.

Father sips his scotch. "But no Prince can rule alone. I need to know your time away hasn't damaged your affinity for teamwork."

The accusation makes hot indignation flare through me. "I can be part of a team," I tell him, but it's only half true. If the team is Wick and Lex, then it's not a question. Being in prison didn't change what we are to each other.

Humming, Father inspects his cube of ice through the crystal tumbler. "Am I mistaken, or have you made the Princess one of your little pet projects?"

I freeze. "Sir, I–" There's no use denying it. That much I'm sure of.

He finally looks up, meeting my gaze. "Because if so, I approve."

I glance around the cabin of the limo, as if someone might be lying in wait to garrote me. "You do?"

"Verity Sinclaire is West End down to her very marrow. Rebelliousness, defiance, and that stubborn hunger for conflict will make her reign uncomfortable for all of us." He nods, as if he's coming to the decision at this very moment. "We'll need to be able to bring our Princess to heel."

My eye twitches. "I see."

"You will not mark her," he says, pointing his glass at me. "You will not harm her."

Unbidden, my mind flashes with the memory of Bruce Oakfield's initial, branded into the small of her back. "No, sir, I won't."

Sometimes Father has this way of looking at people like they're bugs. He's looking at me just like that when he adds, "I believe she could fall for Lex."

Every cell in my body rears back in stunned fury. "Why?"

"He's gentler than you are," he replies, "and more patient than Wicker. I can see her forming an attachment to that. Don't you think?"

"No." The answer is automatic and a little too brusque. Schooling my voice, I explain, "Lex doesn't bend enough. He's too even-keeled. Like you said, she's West End. She'd be drawn to someone emotional. Someone volatile. Someone–"

"Like you." He watches me over the rim of his glass as he takes another sip. "Your features and her eyes." The words are barely a murmur, as if he's speaking more to himself than to me. The odd dazedness of his eyes snaps to clarity when he declares, "The two of you would make an exceptional child."

I'm so fucking speechless that for a long moment, all I can do is gape dumbly into his eyes. There's a softness there that makes my stomach violently churn. "Thank you," I finally manage, because I know Father well enough to understand he's just paid me the highest compliment possible in his dead, empty soul.

He wants me to *create* with her.

The softness falls away gradually as the car crosses the bridge, both our gazes trained out the window. I can tell before we even reach the gate that the driveway is packed with cars. Tonight is our first official PNZ meeting. The whole frat is probably waiting as Danner prepares the parlor with refreshments and extra chairs. Much like Wicker had the other day, I wonder how the fuck we're supposed to get the Princess pregnant when we barely have time to breathe, let alone nail her.

Only when we enter through the gate does Father break the strange, curdled silence. "If you don't win the game this weekend," he says, sharp as broken glass, "I'll have Lex remove your index finger."

My teeth clench, sweat springing up on my brow as the car comes to a stop. "Yes, sir."

17

erity

THUMP.

Wisteria is hardy and fast-growing. That's what I'm thinking of as I pick at a golden thread on my duvet, winding it around my finger.

Thump.

It can grow in poor-quality soil, but prefers somewhere moist and fertile where it can climb. A trellis. A wall. A tree.

Thump.

It's invasive here, quick to choke out native plant species, and yet it can take decades for specimens grown from seeds to bloom. From what I've read, it's better to obtain cuttings.

Thump.

"Fuck!" Wicker growls, his fingers digging in as he slams his hips into me from behind. I feel him swell and surge as I watch the tip of my finger, which has gone purple above the golden thread.

I let the thread go, watching the blood creep back beneath my skin.

"Shit, that's good," he gasps, giving his hips a lazy nudge, like he's drawing it out. Probably is. From the reflection I see of him in the mirror above my dresser, I watch him look down at where we meet, lip disappearing between his teeth as he pulls out.

The drag is slow and slick and makes me shudder, but I refuse to confront the fact that I'm throbbing with the hope of a release I won't get.

I'm too tired to mourn it much.

Wicker came in at precisely midnight, but this time I was expecting it. Maybe that's why they make the Princess go to bed at nine–so that she can get a few hours of sleep in before whichever Prince comes barreling through her door like a sex-crazed maniac.

At least Wicker didn't try to strangle me first. He just snapped his fingers, pointed at the foot of the bed, and started unbuckling his belt. Wriggling out of my panties before being bent over the bed and driven into from behind is probably the best I could have hoped for.

Sighing, I stand and reach for my hastily discarded panties.

"What are you doing?" Wicker asks, using the t-shirt he'd come in here wearing to wipe off his dick.

"Going to clean up."

He gives me a look. "Don't bother," he says, flopping onto the bed.

I watch him stretch, my eyes narrowing at the shift and flex of his muscles, weirdly feline. "What are *you* doing?"

His blue eyes are absent of the frantic, single-minded focus he'd shown when he burst into my room. Now they're lazy and hooded as he yawns, fluffing my pillow. "Getting comfortable."

I scan the bed, and then glance at the door, and then back at him. "Here?"

He laces his fingers behind his head, eyes closing. "We'll go again in ten minutes. Like I said," he cracks an eye, "don't bother cleaning up."

Scowling, I toss my panties on the floor and lay as far from him as possible, my muscles stiff as I wait for round two of god-fucking-knows. I spend it reciting facts in my head, willing my center to stop burning with need. *Wisteria*. There was something else about it, wasn't there? What am I forgetting?

Wicker shifts, and I watch in my periphery as he fists his cock, which has already sprung back to life, hard and flushed at the tip. He makes a low, eager sound, turning his head to look at me.

"Against the dresser," he says, nodding to it. "That's where I want you this time."

Later, when I'm bent over the dresser, fingers clutching hard at the back edge as Wicker slams into me, I try not to look in the reflection to see our flushed cheeks. I try not to think about the way I push back into him, the sensations driving me mindlessly. I try not to be in the moment at all, and when he comes with a gnarled grunt, the dresser banging noisily into the wall, I remember what it was I'd forgotten.

Wisteria seeds.

They're poisonous.

He finds me at dinner.

I'm eating alone, as usual, and watching a video about rose pruning on my phone as I attempt to force down something that could either be mushrooms or tofu. I try not to think about it much as I swallow it down.

I try not to think of anything.

Which is difficult when Wicker stands beside me, unzipping his fly. "We have ten minutes before I have to leave," he says, patting the table. "Right here."

I don't know where Wicker is going, but he and Lex are in and out like a revolving door, always looking flustered and harried. Hockey. Performances. Interviews. Whatever work Ashby has them doing probably takes up what little time is left for them. This means 'deposits' made during the day are rushed and without any warmth or consideration.

Not that I get any of that at night, either.

Sighing, I stand. It's been roughly eighteen hours since I wore a pair of panties. Not because it's sexy, or because I want Wicker to have easy access. Just because it's the most practical way to be.

This will be round five for the day.

Sliding up on the table, I spread my legs.

Wicker pauses with his cock halfway out of his boxers, his blue eyes flashing in confusion. "What are you doing?" he asks, gaze dropping to my spread thighs. "Turn around and bend over."

"No," I say, voice firm. "I'm sick of being fucked into every surface in this house. My hips hurt." I raise my chin defiantly. He hasn't fucked me face-to-face since the party. *Or* gotten me off. "I want to do it like this." He looks startled by the request–so much so that he blurts out his next words with a stunning display of unfiltered, DKS-esque honesty.

"I don't want to look at you!" He seems nearly as taken aback by the admission as I feel. His eyes shutter just as quickly, and he stares at me with that cocky look on his face, chin raised just as high as mine. "But if you *really* want to look at me, then–"

Jumping down, I spin and bend over the table. "Never mind."

IT'S ALMOST TOO much to take in all at once.

I'm in the solarium the following evening, taking stock of the condition of it all. The garden has crept in, but it's all dead, leaving vines and detritus clutching at it like a skeleton to its perilously sought treasures.

The quiet here is different from the stagnant silence of the rest of the house, though. Even in the January chill, the stillness is somehow warmer. Peaceful. Restful.

I can breathe.

As much as I try to see what the garden is in its current state,

I'm so full of what it could be that it's difficult to think of much else. I snap pictures on my phone so that when I get upstairs, I can sketch over them on my laptop, making it come to life in the only way I know how. Over here, some ferns. Over there, a table for Danner to take his tea. Roses on the east end of it, naturally, because even though I've come to hate them, the Palace wouldn't be the Palace without them. Color, though. It'll need something bright and lively.

Not wisteria.

Bluebells, maybe, or morning glories.

But the peaceful nature of the solarium has its downside. It seems to constantly put me in the position of being caught off guard, which is why when I hear Lex's voice, I jump out of my skin.

"Pace lost you."

When I spin, I find him staring at me, arms crossed. "Lost me?" I ask, heart thumping wildly. Even though I know this version of Lex is awake, clothed, hair tied back neatly into a knot, it's still difficult to look at him and not see that other version.

The one with the gold eyes and feral energy.

Lex jerks his chin upward. "No cams in here."

I follow his gaze, thinking I like this solarium a little more every day. "I'm allowed to be here," I rush out, voice defensive. "Danner said–"

"Danner doesn't make the rules." Lex's eyes dip down, and I almost forget why they should. The bruises around my throat are merely faint smudges by now. "Anyway, that's not why I'm here. I have a meeting at nine, so I need you downstairs now."

My heart all at once sinks and rises. It's a confusing tangle, the anticipation and the dread, and I tuck the phone into my pocket. "I see."

Because why else would he, or any of them, track me down?

"It won't be like before," he says, the words a touch harder than I'm expecting. "That only happens when..." he swallows. "It'll be fine. I'm awake."

I look up, surprised at the defensiveness in his tone. "I know you are."

"I didn't know what I was doing."

"I know."

His nostrils flare. "You shouldn't have just walked up on me like that."

"I know."

"No, you don't," he snaps, and a darkness fills his eyes that makes me bite back a shiver. "That's what I'm trying to get through to you. You don't know everything about me. You don't know everything about my brothers. And you damn well don't know everything about this house or East End in general."

I only just manage not to tell him that I know. "I... don't," I agree.

The only thing I know is that from the outside the Princes, the Purple Palace and probably even this solarium look beautiful; shiny people and places filled with promise. When the reality is that the inside is dead and decaying–bitter and strangling the life out of everyone inside.

Lex turns, obviously expecting me to follow, and I do, dutiful and willing to fulfill my purpose, to allow him to fulfill *his* purpose: to create life in a barren landscape.

"Look at me."

My eyes fling open at Lex's command, our gazes locking. My toes curl as his semen fills me, and I wonder why he always demands it. Does he enjoy seeing my cheeks redden at the thought of what he's doing with the syringe? Is it to humiliate me? If it is, then it doesn't feel like it. There's no satisfaction in his stare as he slowly shoots it into me.

Mostly, my blood starts rushing the second he pulls it out, because I know what's coming next.

Me.

I'm just preparing myself for the pressure of his latex-covered fingers against my clit when I realize he's pulling something out of his pocket.

A *second* syringe of semen.

There's a spot of color on his cheeks as he clears his throat, spreading me to carefully slide the syringe inside. "Look at–" He doesn't finish because he doesn't need to.

I'm staring right at him.

He pushes the plunger unblinkingly, the edge of his jaw taut as he shoots another load into me. My mind races with questions. Did he whack off twice, or is it like with Pace, where there's just so much of it from one orgasm that a single syringe couldn't contain it? What does that mean?

I inhale sharply when he pulls the syringe out, because I feel the warmth of it dribbling out.

"Shit." Lex jolts, catching it with two latex-covered fingers as he guides it back to my hole.

The second his fingers enter me, I come.

It's quick and seizing, my body fluttering violently, and all I can do is gasp and let it happen. Lex's eyes fly up to lock with mine, looking almost as stunned as I feel about it, and I struggle to find my voice.

"Yesterday... Wicker was..." I clamp down around his fingers without meaning to, watching as Lex's jaw tics. "He doesn't, ugh– you know."

Somehow Lex puts it together, and even though his clinical expression returns, he still arches a brow. "He fucked you six times in one day and didn't get you off once?"

The question is rhetorical, but I glower up at the ceiling as I shrug. I can't possibly voice the frustration swirling in my lungs, which isn't even really about Wicker. It's not even about Pace, who enjoys torturing me to the point of absolute madness, and then sends me back to my room, leaking and painfully sensitive. It's not even about the fact I can't just take care of myself, because I know

now that Pace and the King have eyes in every little corner of this mansion.

It's that the orgasm Lex just accidentally gave me was fast and fleeting and utterly disappointing, and it's all I'll get until the next time I find myself back here in these godforsaken stirrups.

Pleasure doesn't live within these walls. It's not a part of the covenants. It's completely unrelated–frivolous, even–to the duty of creating an heir.

I understand that.

My body doesn't.

Lex watches me, standing as his fingers recede, and I clutch onto them without meaning or wanting to, my body clenching. "You wanted him to, didn't you?" he says, and there's something about the cadence of the question, deep and smooth, that makes my nerves flare to life.

And then, planting his free palm onto the table beside my hip, he fucks his fingers back into me, hard and pointed.

"Oh, god." I gasp, bucking into the heel of his palm.

The tendons in his wrist flex as he shifts his shoulder, fucking in deeper. "You wanted to beg for it, but you wouldn't. Not that I blame you. Wicker's ego is big enough." His amber eyes pin me as he licks out, wetting his lips. "But you're going to beg for me."

Curling my fists, I jolt my hips up. "Please."

"That easy?" His eyelids grow heavy as he watches the motions of my body, his thumb caressing my clit. "It must have been good with Wicker. I bet you didn't want it to be. You probably tried so hard not to like it–not to want his perfect cock to hit just the right place and have you screaming out his name."

My eyes slam closed as I shudder. "Oh, fuck."

He's right.

God, he's right.

Wicker might be ugly on the inside, but on the outside, he's sex incarnate. It's why it's best not to watch him when he's drilling into me, because even the way he moves is unbearably erotic. And not just him. Pace, with all his dark intensity, somehow knows exactly how far to get me before yanking the rug out from beneath my feet.

Lex's velvety voice goes on, "I could tell the second I sat down here, smelling how wet you were." I hear him take a loud inhale, his fingers twisting inside of me. The next time he speaks, his voice is closer, his body curved over the table as he husks down at me. "God, you're fucking dripping. Did you get this wet for him?" My eyes fly open and I see him hovering there, his amber eyes blazing as his fingers fuck into me. "Does he know what it feels like to see you squirming like a slut for it?"

"No." It's an unintentional moment of honesty. Wicker's never come close to seeing me like this, writhing in desperation as I clutch for my sanity.

Lex's eyes flash with surprise, but it's gone just as fast, his mouth parting to whisper, "Just me, then."

It's the thought more than anything–the implication that this is a secret we're sharing–that makes the fireworks erupt, hot and sudden, as his thumb works over my clit.

I can't stop the whimper that pours loose as I seize. "*Lex*."

When my eyes flutter open again, it's to the sight of a lock of his hair, jerking and falling with each puff of breath from his flared nostrils.

He's staring at my chest, two fingers still buried deep inside me.

And then he's gone.

I feel the absence of his heat like a shock of ice water, my knees snapping closed. It's the first time it occurs to me in any significant way that he hadn't strapped me down after taking my blood. Hastily, I tug the thin gown down over my thighs, still feeling his sticky release all over me.

Over by the door, he shucks the gloves, the broad line of his back expanding and contracting with deep breaths. "This isn't working."

My throat clicks with a nervous swallow. I can't help but picture the lines of scars on his back, knowing what's beneath the shirt, and when he turns to wash his hands, I guiltily snap my gaze up to his face. "What?"

"The gown gets in the way." He's scrubbing his hands beneath the stream of water, eyes fixed on the rough, jerky movements. "Next time, you'll undress and stay that way. We're past the need for modesty. We have a job to do."

"Oh," I breathe, detecting more of that defensive tone from before. "Okay."

If he's surprised by my easy agreement, then he doesn't show it. He tears three paper towels off the wall, rubs them between his palms, and then throws them away before marching out of the room.

He never even glances back.

Sinking heavily back onto the table, I stretch my muscles, sighing in satisfaction. "*Okay.*"

"*To my beautiful Princess. May she reign.*" -HD

I take the next rose, giving a small thanks. I ask myself a lot of idle questions as the line of PNZ members approaches me at the fountain. I wonder where all the roses come from. There must be a florist in Forsyth who looks forward to Mondays. What did the past Princesses do with all their roses? Compost?

Behind me, my Princes are audibly impatient as the frat makes their Monday offerings. Shoes scuff the stone as Pace shifts his weight. Wicker's sole taps a slow rhythm. Lex's bag rustles as he moves it from shoulder to shoulder. What makes it worse is the presence of Jaden, Kathleen, and Andrea ten feet away.

I'm just reaching out to take the last boy's rose when I realize it isn't a rose at all.

The guy, Tommy, who I recognize from my digital design class, gives me a tense smile. "I don't want to offend you, Princess. It's used, but it still works perfectly." In his hands is a product box with a photo of a graphics drawing tablet on it. "I only tried it out a couple times."

I give a series of rapid blinks. "That's... for me?"

Behind me, the Princes are suddenly still.

He nods, pushing it into my hands. "I heard you on Friday, when you were asking Professor Moore if the department had any extras."

I hold the box in my hands, stunned. "Tommy, this is–this is too much."

He gives me a strange look. "It's nothing fancy. There's some extra stylus tips, but–"

"Are you done?" Lex's hard voice is practically in my ear, the heat of him close enough that I realize he's right over my shoulder.

Tommy's mouth clicks shut. "Yes. Yessir." And then he scurries away.

"Ass-kissing little bitch," Pace mutters, appearing over my other shoulder. "What do you need a drawing tablet for anyway? I already gave you a laptop."

I clutch the box close, unable to shake the worry that they'll take it away from me. "I can't draw on a laptop," I say, thinking of the photos I have of the solarium. I'd wanted something to sketch over them with.

Pace eyes the box, mouth a flat, tense line. "It could have spyware on it or something."

"Spyware? It doesn't. It can't," I insist, backing away. "It's just a USB device."

There's a shadow in Pace's eyes that makes me shiver. "We shouldn't take the chance," he says, reaching out. "Give it to–"

Wicker's firm voice stops him. "Back the fuck off." He's sitting on the low wall, a frown etched into his forehead as he watches Pace. "It's a covenant that every Princess accepts her gifts. It's what makes all this worth it to them. It's hers, by every right." He stands, slinging his bag over his shoulder, and I'm struck speechless at the flash of protectiveness in his eyes when he looks at his brothers.

Not of them, nor of me.

He's protective of my right to keep my gift.

The whole thing is puzzling, considering the last 'gift' he gave me was a free ticket to the next home game to watch him play hockey.

"Next time you need something like this," he adds, stepping in front of me, "you ask for it. Don't go around begging for handouts. It makes us look bad."

Before I can feel any indignation at the command, Wicker is ducking in for a kiss, overwhelming me with the scent of his body, the slick taste of his tongue. The post-offering kisses are, I now know, more of a public performance than anything.

But god, he's good at it.

He reaches up to cradle my cheek as he licks against my tongue, the motion so smooth and electric that the box nearly slides right out of my arms.

He's gone just as suddenly as he came, stalking off down the path toward the Student Center. His figure cuts a confident line through the crowd, and Pace glares in his wake.

"Whatever," he mutters, grabbing my chin and wrenching my mouth up to his. Pace's isn't a performance at all. Much like last time, it's punishing and hard, the taste of him just as sharp as the teeth that graze my bottom lip when he breaks away. "Meet me here at four," he demands, dark eyes boring into mine. "Today is feeling like a multiple-deposit sort of day."

The gleam in his eyes is a pointed reminder of his first deposit, made seven hours ago, but I don't need it. The muscles in my thighs still burn from being spread open wide as I sat on his couch. Like last time, he watched me from his desk chair, counting down the minutes as he forced me, over and over again, to the edge of my sanity.

As soon as the clock struck twelve, he emptied himself into me.

Even after showering earlier, I can still feel the dampness of the remnants in my underwear, still leaking out.

Lex is last to appear in front of me, his amber eyes dropping down to the box. There's a pull of displeasure to his mouth that unnerves me. "Do you even like roses?"

I pause, thinking of the rose he'd left for me on the table this morning. Same as always. Cream-colored. Thornless. White card attached.

"To my beautiful Princess, may she reign." -L

It's currently next to the others in my bedroom, the three of them looking like some grim gradient of life. Dying, dead, deader.

The admission tastes sour. "I used to."

The weight of his stare is uncomfortable. It's almost like being on his exam table, those amber eyes analyzing me. Without another word, he bends to push a quick kiss into my temple.

It's feather light, the opposite of how he talks to me during our deposits and certainly nothing like the beast that attacked me in his sleep. It's a show, and when he steps back, on a whim, I grab his hand and stop him.

His eyebrow rises and I push up on my toes, crushing the flowers between us and brushing my lips against his.

"Have a good day, my Prince."

I turn before he can react, my gaze skimming over the cutsluts, Kathleen's expression twisted with envy. They watch me stride away with my shoulders back and my nose pressing into the heavy bouquet of roses. It's one thing for me to know the truth of my position, but it's another for the rest of Forsyth to think I'm nothing but a cumdumpster. I came to East End to play, and as I walk down the path, I feel a burst of power for the first time in a week.

I may not control what happens to me inside the Palace, but out here I can present to the world that everything is perfect.

MY JAW ACHES, and I carefully readjust, annoyed with the reminder that my knees aren't feeling that great, either.

"I'd like to make a motion about Valentine's Day," one of the frat members says.

It's eight and they're all packed into the same room I first saw them in. If I glance to my right, I can just glimpse the bottom of the throne.

I keep my eyes closed.

"Here we go again," someone else sighs.

The first guy continues in a hard, demanding voice, "I think we should consider having some dancers from the Chamber. Every year, the Princes shoot it down, but Wicker–you get it, don't you? They're one of our best assets. We should get a private show."

Lex is the one to reply. "Father will never allow it."

"We'll pay," the guy insists. "We can divert some funds from the Nu Zoo and–"

"The V-Day party is for lovers." Pace's long fingers thread into my hair as he speaks, rubbing gently at my scalp. The cock in my mouth twitches eagerly. "It's something to bring your girls to. Romance them. Make them feel special." Gently, he pushes my head down, forcing another fat inch of his cock toward my throat. "Creation doesn't happen with strippers."

I swallow a fresh wave of saliva, soaking in the information with a grimace.

Ashby wants the *whole frat* to *create*?

Wedged as I am beneath the long table, no one can see me here on my knees, my face in Pace's lap. We were the first ones in the room, Pace having already been slouched low in his chair when he thrust a finger at the floor in front of him, commanding me to get into position.

Commanding me to unzip his pants.

Get his cock out.

Put my mouth on it.

Stay quiet.

Obey your Prince.

Now I'm holding the swollen head against my tongue, fingers digging into Pace's thighs as he and his brothers oversee a frat meeting. Pace can believe it's the covenants keeping me here, breathing softly through my nose, giving his cock the occasional suckle.

But I'm here for the intel.

"I don't need to create," the guy says, an air of indignant superiority in his tone. "Kira's already six weeks pregnant." The room falls into a tense silence, Pace's muscles stiffening beneath my palms.

Wicker breaks it with an airy laugh. "Congratulations, Harker. You managed to creampie your way to excellence. Must suck to know your partying days are over, but our V-day party isn't going to be your stag night." Without waiting for a reply, he asks, "Any other motions?"

After a beat, someone speaks up. "I had a question."

In a bored tone, Lex announces, "The Royalty recognizes Dory Baxter. Ask your question."

A chair behind me scrapes as Baxter stands. "It's about the Counts."

"The Counts are toast," Pace says, scoffing. He drags me closer to his lap.

There are some hushed whispers, and then Baxter replies, "If they're toast, then why is there still so much Viper Scratch on the streets?"

My ears perk, and I give Pace another soft suck.

I can practically hear Wicker's shrug. "Maybe they left a supply in West End. Lucia's daughter is their Duchess. She's probably coasting off the inheritance of her dad's drug trade."

The accusation makes my chest flare with scorching anger. In no universe would Lavinia or the Dukes allow West End to be a home for Viper Scratch. A big part of Sy's reign has been snuffing Lionel Lucia's influence off their streets.

Baxter seems skeptical, too. "I don't think so. Loeffler says one of their Dukes is in recovery. Everyone talks about him going to that support group on campus. What does he say in there, Lex? You go to his meetings, right?"

Panic courses through my veins, because Remy needs those meetings. I know instinctively–alarmingly–that if Lex begins spilling his secrets, I won't stay silent. I'll reveal myself. I'll do whatever it takes to cut him off–to keep Remy safe.

There's another stretch of charged silence, and then Lex's rigid voice rings out. "Our support group is neutral territory, Baxter. Are you asking me to betray that so they can turn around and do the same to me?"

"We need to know," Baxter insists, not ungently.

"Then find out some other way," Lex snaps. "Maybe past Princes were okay with disloyalty, but we aren't. The next time any of you ask me to break my word, I'll submit a motion to de-crown you."

My blood rushes hot at the memory of his words during that car ride to negotiations. Lex Ashby obviously values loyalty above all else. The relief is fierce, because even in this room, among brothers and subjects of his own house, Lex is a man of his word.

A rare thing to find in Forsyth.

I keep the thought close, cherished, even though I know that on Thursday, I'm going to be spilling all of their secrets to Lavinia. The thought of betrayal should make me uncomfortable, but it doesn't. I guess having Pace's cock in my mouth for the last hour while being petted like a dog is a reminder of who has my loyalty.

The meeting continues with a brusquer tone after that. Motions arising. People recognized. Rory Livingston wants to organize a volunteer group to put up flyers for his sister, who went missing in late December. That's approved. Matt Kramus wants to organize a car meet in front of the bridge, and if Loeffler is to be believed, it's to show off his new Porsche. That's denied.

I get this niggle of thought in the back of my mind that the covenants are constantly used to keep me in line, but I'm not the only one they apply to. Moving my tongue against the bottom of his cock head, I let my hand wander up, fingers curling around the base.

Pace goes suddenly still, the fingers in my hair pausing their gentle petting motions.

Hollowing my cheeks, I pull up, lips gliding over his hot shaft.

His knee jumps. "Fuck." The curse is soft but pointed, and the men around him react with silence. Clearing his throat, I hear him say, "Just remembered I forgot my jacket in the locker room."

I wait for the conversation to resume before tightening my grip around his base, gliding my mouth back down. Pace's cock is familiar to me by now. There were the pictures and videos he sent me years ago, and then all the hours I've clocked feeling and watching it. It's thicker than Wicker's and uncut, made all the more intimidating by how complicated it looks.

But it's not complicated at all.

One firm suck is enough to make Pace's whole body jolt.

I can feel panic in the sudden clench of his fingers in my hair, scalp stinging with the force of his grip as he stalls me. The cock between my lips surges with precum, salty and warm on my tongue, and the balls against my thumb are drawn up tight.

He's close.

I squeeze my own thighs together, telling myself that it's natural to indulge in this. Pace is a man. An attractive man. A strong man. A man who smells nice as he cradles the back of my neck, feeding me his cock.

If I can make him come in my mouth, wasting his seed, then *he'll* be punished.

My next attempt–a hard jerk of my fingers, accompanied by a sweep of my tongue against his tip–ends in a wince, saliva dripping from the corners of my mouth as he grips my hair. In front of me, I can see his abs tighten and flex with the effort of staving off his orgasm.

As Lex drones on about some issue with behavior at the townhouse complex, I work my tongue faster over Pace's tip, rhythmic, looping around the swollen head in much the same way Wicker had eaten me out a few nights ago. Pace grips my hair tighter and tighter, but I spent two years as a cutslut. Hair pulling is nothing to write home about.

My scalp is basically bulletproof.

By the time they all begin standing, someone's shiny loafer

slamming into my calf, I'm sore and soaked, Pace's cock still hard as steel between my lips. If his brothers know I'm down here, then they don't show it, content to leave the room with the rest of the frat.

The moment I hear the door close, Pace is wrenching me off his cock and clambering back in his seat. "Get up," he growls, reaching down to haul me, gasping, to my feet. No sooner am I upright than he's pushing me up against the table, prying my legs open and yanking my panties aside.

He enters me with a brutal thrust.

The stretch is expected, as is the almost immediate surge of his release.

But the look on his face isn't.

Pace is always so controlled when we're doing this in his room, face schooled into various masks, but masks all the same.

Right now, he looks desperate, wild-eyed and strung tight, the tendon in his jaw twitching as his shoulders lurch with a seized, "Ah, fuck!" His brows crash together and he looks down, watching as his cock pumps into me.

I recline back on my palms and wait, eyes flicking to the window.

The weather's nice today. Maybe I'll visit the solarium.

"You fucking bitch," he seethes, grabbing my chin. His eyes are full of fire when he forces my gaze to his. "Do you have any idea what you almost–oh, goddamn..." His cock keeps surging. Pace always ejaculates a river of the stuff.

I'm getting used to it. Used to *this*.

He reaches up to palm my breast in a loose, idle gesture. His eyes are unable to hold that fire as he keeps coming, mouth parted in ecstasy. "So fucking tight," he says, rocking into me with short, choppy motions. "God, you're wet."

I could blame it on his cum.

I don't.

He never got me to the edge–never asked me to say the words. In truth, it's the first time with him I've really felt like the victor.

MY SPOILS ARRIVE the next morning in the form of a collar.

Technically, it's a golden choker composed of a stack of small links. It's elegant and pretty–or would be, if not for the fact that it's from Pace.

It's definitely a collar.

I don't have much time to dwell on it, since Wicker comes strutting into the dining room. I'm bent over the table before he can even ask, skirt flipped up to expose my bare backside. Compared to his brother, Wicker is easy to handle. All he's looking for is a convenient hole. The less back-and-forth, the better.

He makes a smug sound that's accompanied by the clink of his belt buckle, and gets to work on his second deposit of the day. It's fast and hard, my hips slamming into the edge of the table as he grunts above me. I fix my eyes on the necklace as he fucks me, thinking that I'd rather gouge my own eyes out than wear it.

Naturally, Wicker finishes and plucks the necklace from the box, winding it around my neck before I can even push myself upright.

Bending down, he gives a breathless chuckle into my ear. "Who's our good girl?"

I don't even flinch at the slap to my backside after he buckles up. I just ignore his obnoxious strut from the room and sit back down to eat.

JESUS, hockey is boring.

I'm used to shirtless, muscular, sweaty men beating the life out of one another in short, concise rounds. This? The men are covered in layers of clothes and padding. Helmets protect their heads, obscuring any recognition of who the players are. At least their names and numbers are on the back of their jerseys, Pace #3, Wicker #2.

But it's fucking freezing in here.

Lex sits next to me in the stands, pitched forward with his elbows resting on his knees. His amber eyes track his brothers like lasers, and every time one of them gets the puck, he bolts to his feet, fidgety and buzzing with an animated energy that I've never seen on him.

He looks fucking terrified.

"Pass it," he mutters, not bothering to yell out over the crowd.

Pace taps the puck, and it zips to Wicker, who catches it on the blade of his stick, legs pumping it up the ice.

"Deke, deke, shoot," Lex says, erupting into a roughly screamed cheer when Wicker sinks it into the goal. When he drops back into his seat, his face is a little blanched.

"You guys take this game way too seriously," I point out, eyeing the girl next to me, who's holding a large basket of nachos.

I miss junk food.

"How many Friday Night Furies have you been to?" he asks, mouth pressed into a tight, grim line. "It's never just about the game when it's a Royal competing. If anyone should know that, it'd be you."

I look back at the ice, wondering what's on the line. It must be pretty big, considering that Lex's intensity doesn't wane the entire first period. He rises nervously from his seat whenever one of his brothers gets the puck, like there's some kind of magnet attached to him. The opposing team nets a goal and Lex pushes his fingers into his temples, eyes trained on the floor.

All the agony is ultimately unnecessary, because the Ashby brothers?

Even to my novice eye, it's clear they're on *fire*.

Wicker glides along the ice with a grace that enthralls me, easily out-skating the boys on the other team. Pace isn't quite as nimble, but he's definitely faster, his long legs pushing harder than the rest, making space for Wicker to dart past with the puck. And the way they work together is borderline supernatural.

The brothers pass the puck back and forth like it's a choreographed dance. Around other players, beneath the blades of skates, once even bounced off of someone's knee pads. I watch them closely, but their heads don't even turn to see the other before they make a pass. Our team might have five players on the ice, but you wouldn't know it. It's a Wicker and Pace show, the stands erupting exuberantly with every goal. The other team's netminder is visibly furious, slamming his stick into the posts after the first period ends with Forsyth already up by three.

As the team rises from the bench to go back to the dressing room, a group of rowdy co-eds bends over the bleachers to touch them.

Well.

Not *them*.

Him.

"They've had sex with Wicker," I say, the sentence emerging idly, like an afterthought.

Beside me Lex snorts. "Everyone's had sex with Wicker. Those girls, several professors, most of the girl's volleyball team," he arches an eyebrow, "probably a few of the boy's volleyball team. Our senator has had sex with Wicker. Hell," he sips from his water bottle, "*I've* had sex with Wicker."

My head snaps up, eyes widening. "You and Wicker are...?"

Lex pulls a face. "Fuck no." Rolling his eyes, his gaze tracks the Zamboni. "We went through puberty playing hockey in an all-boys boarding school. Things happen." When I can do nothing but gape at him, he glances at me, catching my shocked expression. "Oh. You're a prude. I'll have to remember that."

A passing LDZ throws us a glance and Lex stiffens, shifting to throw his arm over the back of my seat. I lean into him, seeking body heat. His muscles tense, but his arm drops from the back of the seat, curling around my shoulder.

Nacho girl sends me a dirty, jealous glare.

"I'm not a prude," I say, struggling to reorient myself to this epiphany. "I just didn't realize you were gay." It makes perfect sense now why he hasn't had sex with me. Plus, Wicker's comment about Lex possibly being unable to 'get it up' makes it all click into place.

Only then, Lex says, "I'm not *gay*." The insistence is tinged with condescension. "I appreciate the scientific method. The best way to prove a hypothesis is through experimentation." He gestures up to the ceiling, where that promotional athletics banner is hanging, Wicker's intense eyes glaring down the rink. Lex explains, "Physically, Wicker is the perfect male specimen. Plus, he's flirtatious. Outrageously attractive. Fucks like a machine."

Staring at him, I deadpan, "This is the most convincing argument for heterosexuality I've ever heard."

Lex swings a glower on me. "So when I say he does nothing for me–not sexually–that's saying something."

"It's saying that you're... attracted to women?"

Despite the skepticism in my tone, Lex dips his chin in a nod. "Conclusively, without question."

"Oh."

It's all I can think about during the second period, my mind conjuring up all sorts of visions. I watch Wicker on the ice, facing off with a cocky grin as the ref drops the puck, and then I glance beside me, at Lex.

His arm is still around me, so he's close. Close enough to smell. Close enough to watch his eyes darting over the ice, the way his mouth tips down whenever Wicker passes to someone who isn't Pace. If Lex is into women, 'conclusively,' does the fact he doesn't try to fuck me on his days mean he's just not into me?

Or is it something else?

In the end, I can't help but ask, "So when you say you had *sex*..." Lex's eyes jump to mine, eyebrows knitting together. "What do you mean, exactly?"

He assesses me for a long moment, eyes scanning my face. Whatever he finds in my expression makes him snort a laugh. "I'm not giving you a play-by-play, Princess. If the thought of two guys getting off together makes you horny, then watch porn like everyone else."

"It doesn't make me–"

"Your cheeks are red. Your pulse is racing. Your pupils are widening." The words are spoken matter-of-factly, even as he looks away, back to the ice. "Ten bucks says your panties are soggy."

Any argument I have is drowned out by the sudden cheer of the crowd, Pace having sunk another goal. Down below, Wicker collides with him in an aggressive, violent, celebratory hug.

The rest of the second period unfolds in much the same way. In the end, I should have known.

"It's Wick," Lex says, staring down at his phone during the second intermission. Brow pinched, he mutters, "For fuck's sake. He needs you in the equipment room. Let's go."

I should have known *nothing* would make Wicker Ashby hornier than having a hundred people cheering for him all night.

I follow Lex where he leads, only stopping when we reach a door emblazoned with 'Equipment' to reach beneath my skirt. He turns to ask, "What are you–" but then clicks his mouth shut when I step out of my panties. "Ah."

Wordlessly, I shove them into his hand, ignoring the slack look on his face when he feels the lacy fabric, dampened with my wetness.

"Guess I'll have to get you that ten dollars later," I say. Opening the door, I disappear inside before he can reply.

Even in the dark, I can sense that Wicker has his cock out. Mostly, I hear his barely-controlled panting, the grunt he makes when he demands, "Get yourself ready."

Unabashed, I shrug. "Lex already did."

There's a short pause, and then a low curse. "Did he now?" That's when his hands find me, spinning me into the shelf. I feel the sweat dripping from his hair, smell the scent of it as he kicks my ankles apart and nudges up against my back, lining himself up.

Maybe it's the hasty silence of it. Maybe it's that the pitch black makes it impossible to see his face. Maybe it's because Wicker could be anyone, nothing but his harsh breaths and gruff punches of air to identify him as... *him*. Maybe it's that he's already fucked me three times today, and I had Pace three times before that, and Lex was right before. Stewing in the thought of him and Wicker together? After watching the brothers move on the ice, I can envision it. Fluid and masculine.

He enters me so smoothly, my pussy already slick, that a low, rough groan emerges from his chest.

Gasping, I grab the shelf and rock back into his thrusts, uncaring of the way it makes him thrust harder and faster. His mouth is a shock of fire against the side of my neck, but it's not a kiss. Not exactly. He rests his bared teeth there as he slams into me, his arms hemming me in when he rests his palms on top of mine, curling.

I match him, breath for panted breath. It's sweaty and painful, a blur of slick flesh and angry gasps, and when he comes, I feel it in the pit of my womb, my center aching for something it knows he won't give me.

There's a long stretch where we struggle to catch our breath and I'm holding him inside of me, pulsing around him, as if that could keep him there.

It doesn't.

He slips free with a sharp exhale.

Wicker must right himself, but I don't see it. I just hear the shuffle of fabric, and then the sound of the door opening as he leaves.

BY THE TIME Lex's night rolls around, I'm all but marching for the exam room in the basement. Every cell of my body feels both overstimulated and totally exhausted. How strange to think the sexual experience I'm most eager for doesn't include any sex at all.

I know there was a time that stripping off my clothes in this cold, sterile room made me shrink self-consciously in my own skin. Now, I can't get them off fast enough, slipping out of my skirt and panties, shucking off my sweater and unclipping my bra.

My eyes are trained on the exam table, though. Just the sight of it is enough to make my belly twist excitedly, like some disgusted Pavlovian response. That table means pain and humiliation, but it also means pleasure, Lex's velvety voice and dexterous fingers.

I'm just working up the nerve to climb onto it when Lex enters the room.

He's dressed more casually than I'm used to. A plain white shirt is stretched over his broad chest, and his khakis look a little wrinkled at the thighs. His hair, still pulled back into the knot at the top of his head, looks somehow more untidy than usual. Looser. Once again, he's wearing his glasses, the light flashing a reflection off the lenses when he steps closer, glancing at the empty exam table.

His amber eyes snap to where I'm standing beside it, meeting my stare for only the briefest moment before they drop, emotionlessly sizing up my naked body. His gaze settles on my breasts, pupils darkening as he yanks a pair of latex gloves from the box nestled in a compartment beside the door.

So, yeah, maybe he is into women.

"How many times yesterday?" he asks, pulling on a glove. It snaps loudly in the stillness of the room. "With Wicker."

I shift my weight, reaching over my middle to clutch my elbow in a half-hug. "Six."

Lex nods, pulling on the other glove as he approaches me. It's hard to reconcile the man I sat next to at the hockey game with the one who attacked me in my bedroom that night. But this one? I can get close to it, almost like he's halfway between the two poles. His jaw is tight, but the edge of violence isn't visible in his eyes.

"He did this?" Lex reaches out, grazing two latex-covered fingertips over my hip bone.

Looking down, I realize there are faint bruises from the dresser. The table. The counter. The shelves. Wicker has yet to find an uncomfortably hard surface he's unwilling to fuck me into from behind. "Yes," I say through a dry throat, the sensation of Lex's fingers making electricity zing into my center. "Some might be from his last day."

Lex makes a low, pensive sound as he prods the flesh, but he's not even looking at the bruises.

He's still staring at my tits.

"Turn." The quiet command is punctuated by a tap on my hip.

I shiver as I spin, stammering, "I-It's only the front." Wicker would have to actually face me to fuck my back into a table.

Only the moment I come to a rest, Lex is conspicuously silent behind me. Still. I don't feel his fingers anymore, and the longer the quiet stretches on, the more some of that petrifying shyness begins prodding at my awareness.

I gulp.

Fingers graze my backside, and then, "Get on the table."

It doesn't make much sense, but for some reason, I feel more comfortable once I've laid back and placed my thighs and feet in the wide stirrups. Perhaps it's the ritual of it, knowing that Lex has already seen these parts of me.

Unlike the other times, he doesn't bother with the stool. He steps between my spread legs, eyes sweeping down my body until his gaze comes to rest on my vagina. Reaching out, he uses two fingers to spread my folds.

"Sore?" he asks, assessing my entrance with prodding fingertips. When I shake my head, he pushes two inside, bracing his other hand on my inner thigh when I buck toward it. "I've decided," he says, burying the fingers to the knuckle, "that I'm going to have to make my deposits feel a little more organic." His tone is even and clinical. "The syringes aren't conducive to adequate arousal."

"Okay," I rush out, wetting my lips in anticipation. Organic–that means physical, doesn't it? It means his own cock. It means Lex is finally going to fuck me.

He reaches for his pants and I'm ashamed at how excited I feel, heart racing at the knowledge I'm about to finally feel him inside. Will it be gentle? Rough? Will it be fast like Wicker, or slow like Pace? Will he still want me to look at him when he–

But instead of reaching for his zipper, he pulls something from his pocket.

It's a small, flesh-colored dildo with a plunger at the bottom of the shaft. The tip of it has a hole, and he watches me as he presses it to my entrance.

Struggling to keep the plummet of disappointment off my face, I train my eyes to the center of his chest, Wicker's words ringing in my memory.

"Maybe you're just not his type. Maybe he likes women who know what they're doing in bed. Maybe he's just not that into you."

The niggling of doubt falls away like gossamer as Lex teases me with the dildo. The tip enters me, but nothing more, his thumb finding my clit.

"Wicker got you six times," Lex says, twisting the toy a little deeper. "What about Pace?"

My breath hitches, teeth sinking into my lip. "Three."

Lex hums, the sound of his voice practically droll compared to the shift of his biceps as he pushes the toy deeper. "So you've been fucked nine times in the last three days."

God, when he says it like that...

"Yes," I moan, but it's more about the push against my clit than answering his question.

"Tell me," he asks, "what was your favorite?"

"In the equipment closet at the rink."

"Why?"

"I–I don't know."

"Was it because of what I told you? Because it made you all wet and ready?" The dildo pushes in and out, stretching me with every thrust. "Or was it because I was standing outside, listening?"

"Oh God." I didn't know that, but warmth pools between my legs. Was he there for Wicker or for me?

"That's it isn't it? I heard you in there, rattling those shelves. The whole time I was standing watch, I kept my hand in my pocket, playing with those wet panties you gave me."

"Did you wish it was you?" I ask, grinding into his hand.

He stills. "What did you say?"

"Did you wish it was you in the room fucking me?" I ask,

reaching up and palming my tit. His eyes track my hand. "Or did you wish it was your brother?"

He snorts and resumes the motion of fucking me with the molded latex. "I told you, I'm not into men."

"But you're not into me either."

"You don't know anything about me." His pupils dilate, and I see it; the hunger. That, I know. I grew up around boys–men–and I know what lust looks like and I see it on Lex's face. With my other hand I reach for him, grabbing him by the belt, dragging him to me.

I expect him to hesitate but he growls, and falls forward, his large hands pushing mine aside, taking my tit into his palm. I pant at the feel of him, the way his skin feels against my sensitive flesh. But none of it compares to the sensation of his tongue, flicking over my nipple.

"Oh my God."

My toes curl and my fingers clutch his belt. Bending my knees, I want to feel him deeper. I just want to feel him inside. To hear him whisper those dirty, filthy words in my ear as I come around his cock.

We're close, his mouth and tongue working my nipple, sucking and licking me into a state of frenzy. My nerves threaten to explode after days of deprivation. "Jesus, your tits," he mutters, moving to the other. "I bet you could come just from me licking them."

He's not wrong, but it's not what I want. I want to feel full. I want his weight on top of me, I want to feel connected... I slide my hand down, below his buckle, down to his zipper–

His teeth clamp down on my nipple, hard and piercing.

"Lex!" I shout, pushing at his shoulders.

He rears back, expression dark. That hot want vanished, replaced with seething anger. "Thought you'd manipulate me? Drive me mad like you've done my brothers? Wind me up with your sloppy cunt so I'll finally give you what you so desperately want? Release?"

I expect him to plunge the dildo into me and empty the syringe but he continues to fuck it in and out, his motions growing mechanical, this thumb expertly swiping over my clit, stimulating me despite the shift in demeanor.

He bends, mouth inches from mine, pushing me closer and closer to the edge. "I have one use for you, Princess, to get you knocked up." I squirm on the table. His hand slams into my inner thigh and he spreads me open, staring down at where he's fucking the dildo into me. I feel it the minute he plunges the injection inside, and the shift in position, the hard thrust of the dildo inside, the cool air against my blistering clit, starts the shudder I've been waiting for–the release I've been craving. I cry out when it hits, back arching, hands gripping the edge of the table. It's intense, a furious ratchet through my body, and I fall back on the table, shivering as the orgasm ripples over me in waves. Once I've regained my senses I sit up, clutching my throbbing tit.

"What the fuck is your problem?" I shout as he shucks the white coat off his shoulders and hangs it on the hook.

"Oh, Princess, you have no idea how many problems I have." He laughs darkly and runs his hands through his hair. "And getting you off is the least of them."

He grabs the door handle and I probably only say it because he's not facing me. "You can't do it?" I know what I felt when I touched his crotch. Nothing. Flat and unaroused. But I also saw the look in his eye. "You do like women. And you do find me attractive." I slide off the table. "You just can't get it up, can you?"

I wait for something, a spark of denial, that angry, dirty, mouth to lay into me. But he just leaves the room–leaves me wanting once again–this time for answers. Because who the fuck appoints an impotent man to be the Prince?

18

W icker

Some girls' whole strut changes when they're in a skirt. Their asses are a little perkier. Their shoulders are a little straighter. Their legs seem a little longer. Verity always wears skirts, but she wears them like she wears pants. Just clothing. There to cover up her ass, but nothing special in her mind.

This morning, it's different.

I know the second I enter the dining room, laying my eyes on her calves, that something has changed.

She's wearing fishnet stockings.

All the blood rushes to my cock. There's something about watching a good girl try to be bad that flips my switch like no other, and right now, all I want to do is see how far she's committing to the role. Apparently pretty far, because when her kohl-lined eyes peer up at me, it's to slot a bright red cherry tomato between her lush, garnet-painted lips, and I realize why my cock surges so eagerly.

It's because she doesn't look like a Princess.

She looks like a cutslut.

People can say what they will about West End, but Jesus fuck, their girls know what's good.

I'm still soaking it in when she rises to her feet, planting her hands on my shoulders. She shoves, sending me sprawling into the chair behind me, and then she climbs into my lap, one fishnet-covered leg at a time.

"Fuck," I breathe, running my palm up a thigh. "Now this is what I'm talking about."

Finally.

Some real action.

"Stop humping my leg."

I grab her hip, pulling her close. My cock slots between her legs and—

"Goddamn it, Wicker! Wake up, asshole."

My eyes flutter open to find Lex glaring back at me. The sight of my brother's annoyed expression does nothing to quell my erection. I hear Pace snoring softly behind me.

"You were drilling into my thigh," Lex says, voice quiet. "If you come on my leg, I'll castrate you."

"Fuck." I scrub one hand over my face and the other down to my throbbing balls. "What time is it?"

He twists, the face of his watch illuminating his forehead. "Three."

"In the morning?" I ask, but I'm already moving, kicking my way out of the sheets. I hadn't even meant to fall asleep here. I'd come into Lex's room to pass the time until midnight, but these two fuckers were already asleep. No one to keep me occupied. Between hockey, cello practice, academics, Prince bullshit, and my varied obligations to Father's businesses, I'm running on an empty tank.

Time to fill that sucker up.

Pace huffs as I jostle him, grabbing the edge and rolling into his pillow. After boarding school, a few years of Father, dorms, prison fights, and non-stop noise, he can sleep through almost anything.

"Where are you going?" Lex asks, propping up on an elbow.

Rolling my eyes, I say, "Oh, I was just gonna pop out to play a game of cricket." I jab a thumb at the door. "It's three hours into my day, and I haven't nutted yet. Where the fuck do you think I'm going?"

"Wicker, I think–"

Whatever else Lex says is lost behind me as I march down the hall, my erection painfully slapping against my lower belly with every stride. My cock escaped the flap of my boxers overnight, which makes it easier now. Gripping it and giving the length a solid stroke, I enter her room. She's asleep, curled up in the bed, all pretty and warm and waiting, which surprises me. Lately, she just waits up for my first go at her. Guess I waited too long.

Pulling down the cover, I slide in, nestle into the curve of her ass, and pull aside her panties. This is all I could think about for the past two days, and I relish it. Her ass is hot, meaty enough to get a nice handful of. In another life, I'd probably get her up on her knees and pound the fuck out of that tight little hole, but this is the life of a Prince, and my cum has one destination.

I push my hands between her legs and feel slick, wet heat.

Fuck me.

"You're already wet for me," I note, looking over her shoulder at her sleeping face. I'd say she looks peaceful in repose, but she actually doesn't. There's a little crevice in her brow. "Having your own wet dream, Princess?" Smirking, I withdraw my fingers and pop them in my mouth to taste her. I pause at the tinge of copper that hits my tongue. "What the fuck?"

When I pull my hand back, I realize there's a streak of red on my fingertips.

"Ah, shit." Rucking up her gown, I search for the injury, patting her down.

She shifts, letting out a low, confused grunt. "What are you doing?" she rasps.

"Making sure you're not bleeding out." *Shit.* Maybe Lex is still awake. Father is going to blow a gasket. We've had this bitch for two weeks, and she's already broken. "Are you hurt or something?"

She sits up and winces, pushing a hand into her stomach. "Yeah, in my uterus."

My eyes widen. "Your what?"

She swings an incredulous gaze on me. "It's my period, you dumbass. I could tell it was starting last night. Guess it showed up in full force." She doesn't sound any happier about it than I feel. Because if the Princess has her period, then that means she's not—

Fuck!

The only word I can manage is, "No."

She grumbles, "Yeah," that crevice in her forehead deepening with a frown.

My cock, which has been at half-chub since I turned thirteen, deflates a little. I flop back, raking my fingers through my hair. "I can't do another month of this."

She moans, flopping back beside me. "At least three weeks, but yeah. I know."

I swing a glare on her, snapping, "You don't know shit! You've got no fucking clue what it's like to deny myself every day because of those goddamn covenants."

Her eyes flash hotly. "Then you shouldn't have signed them!"

"You think I had a choice? You think I wanted to be shackled to your subpar pussy for weeks—months?" I'm still in bed with her, surrounded by her scent. It makes me sick to my stomach. I feel like my heart is going to explode out of my chest. I'm sweaty, annoyed, and *Jesus Christ*, when she twists to move the pillow, I get a view down her shirt, and yep.

I'm hard again.

"Fuck it." Panting, I straddle a leg over her body. When her hands fling up in surprise, I grab her by the wrists and slam her body down on the mattress. "It's just a little blood."

"What are you doing?" she asks, all breathless and heaving bosom.

"Getting what I came here for." I tug at her panties, soaked with blood. "No need for that lube I got you."

She wiggles under me, only making the friction between us worse. "I don't want to!" Her face scrunches up as she struggles, kicking upward with her knee.

I catch it, with my own leg, snorting. "Did you just say no? Because nothing—not one word in that covenant—says I can't fuck you while you're on the rag."

She snipes back, "It says it's my choice! I've read the covenants front to back, and it's perfectly fucking clear. On my off-days, I have the right to decide, and I say no."

She's trapped under me, her body small and useless against my strength. Fighting back only makes my awareness narrow down to the apex of her thighs, and I wet my lips, cock surging with need. "You think you can stop me, Princess? Obeying your Prince is the only covenant that matters. Everyone knows that."

With a burst of strength, I angle into her, pushing the tip into her sticky heat. It feels so good that I groan, the heavy neediness in my balls unconcerned by her sudden cry. My hips rock back, ready to slam in, which is when the bedroom door clatters open. I know it's my brother without even needing to look over my shoulder, but I ignore him. What's he going to do? Pull me out?

Without a word, he strides over, and Verity tracks him with wide, terrified eyes. "Oh, god, not you, too."

But Lex is already grumbling, "Goddamn it, Wick. The whole wing can hear her!" Grabbing my ankles, he yanks me back with one sure jolt.

"Hey, no, just–" Panting like a dog, I claw my way back between her thighs. "Just cover me for five minutes. I'll make it quiet." Pressing a palm over her mouth, I appeal to her furious, green-eyed glare, "You already hurt, right? You won't even notice. What's the big fucking deal?"

But she shoves and bucks, her muffled scream gnashed through my fingers.

"Get the *fuck* off of her," Lex barks, clamping a hand around the nape of my neck. His next words are hissed urgently, into my ear, "He's going to see this, you idiot!"

It's like being doused with ice water.

Deflating, I drop my head to bury a groan into the crook of her neck. She smells soft and warm, and it *hurts*. It's fucking agony to feel her beneath me like this and know that I can't have her. Every nerve in my body is alight with the necessity of sinking inside, but when Lex wrenches me up, I follow, balls aching.

He looks over at Verity, who scrambles wildly up the length of the bed to curl her knees to her chest. "You're–are you awake?"

Lex's stare is flat. "Despite all efforts."

"You fucking cockblocking shithead!" I plant both hands on his chest, shoving him back. "How long is this bullshit going to last?"

Lex looks distinctly unimpressed. "Four or five days."

"Four or five—" I grip my hair, muscles rippling with need. "You can't be fucking serious."

"It's the average time, Wick," Lex says. "Some women go longer, but according to her records, the Princess' average menses lasts four to five days." He looks over at Verity. "And even if it's an inconvenience, it's an indicator that her body is shedding the lining of her uterus to prepare her for the next cycle of fertility."

"Jesus Christ," I shove my fingers in my ears, "you made my dick limp at 'shedding.' Fuck, you're as bad as Father with your clinical, boner-deflating commentary."

Verity is still bracing herself against the mattress, like either of us may change our minds and pounce on her. She's not wrong, but I'm over this bullshit. I'm so fucking horny all the time. Only getting off two days a week can't be healthy. I've never had limitations on my sexual activity. It's the one luxury I've always been given free rein over. And now Father wants to put a chastity belt on my cock.

It's the worst torture he's inflicted on me yet, and that?

That's saying a whole fucking lot.

"One." I shoot her a final look, holding up a finger. "I'm giving you *one* of my days this week. Bleeding or not, I'll be back on Tuesday to take what's owed to me."

I storm out, slamming into Lex's shoulder on the way. When I get back to his bedroom, Danner is standing in the middle of the doorway, the tray of breakfast food in his hands. I guess the whole wing really did hear us if we're getting served at three in the morning.

Through the doorway, I can see Pace still in the bed, snoring away, and I'm so sick of it. Sick of how easily he and Lex can take this. Sick of being told no. Sick of waking up every night with my heart in my throat and my dick in my fist, staving off the only morsel of satisfaction available to me in this fucked-up world.

In a fit of rage, I knock the tray out of Danner's hands, watching as it falls against the hardwoods with a loud, jarring clatter. "Fucking bullshit!"

Pace shoots upright, shirtless, hair sticking up in a million directions. Even barely awake, he looks menacing as fuck as he springs to his feet, his tattoos stretched across his muscles. "What the fuck?" he asks, surveying the mess on the floor. He looks between me and Danner, a shadow falling over his face as he comes to his conclusion. Danner doesn't fuck up. Ever.

"Are you for real?" He shoots Danner an apologetic look. "He'll clean it up."

Danner frowns at the eggs on his shoes. "I'll go get another tray—"

"No," Lex says, striding up from behind us. "We'll come down to eat later."

"Yes, sir." Danner takes a wide step over the spilled eggs and coffee, passing Lex, who manages to keep his expression in check until the minute he's gone. Then he turns to me, eyes burning with rage. "You're throwing a goddamn tantrum over something we can't control?"

I explode, "I'm throwing a tantrum because we have another three weeks of this bullshit! If not more!" I glance between them, feeling like I'm losing my goddamn mind. "How are the two of you so fucking calm about this?"

"What are you two talking about?" Pace asks, reaching up to scratch his bare chest.

"The Princess is on the rag," I snap, "bleeding like a stuck pig, *and* she's invoking her right to a dick-free cunt."

Pace's shoulders tense and he runs his hand through his hair, sliding his gaze to Lex. "She's not pregnant?"

Crossing his arms, Lex gives a small shake of his head. "Unlikely. There's still a small chance, and the blood test will confirm it one way or the other, but I doubt it."

Pace's eyes widen. "How the *fuck* is she not pregnant? We've been pumping her so full of cum, that shit should be coming out her eyeballs."

"I don't know." Lex pinches the bridge of his nose. "Maybe she ovulated before the masquerade. Maybe the conditions just weren't right. Maybe–"

"Maybe she's fucking deficient," I snarl, fists flexing. "Just our luck, we get a Princess who's been breathing in that toxic West End air her whole life."

"Or maybe you're the deficient ones," comes Verity's voice. I swing around to find her standing in the doorway, those green eyes still full of malice. "Ever think of that?"

"How do you figure?" Lex asks, the insult landing like fire in his eyes.

She's in her little white nightdress, red hair tumbling over her shoulder. Her nipples are visible through the thin fabric and my dick twitches at the sight of her. But for once, lust isn't in the forefront of my mind. Not now. A fresh wave of anger surges in my chest.

"Unless you're going to bend over that table and beg for my dick," I tell her, "*get out.*"

Pace shoves past me, knocking me into the foot of the bed. "What did you just say?" His voice is low and full of threat, and the way he towers over her almost makes my dick twitch again.

"You heard me. You're the deficient ones." Her eyes are narrowed, chin raised, and she looks a touch unhinged, something wild and unfettered burning under the surface. "If I'd gotten a set of Princes who knew how to properly fuck a woman, I'd be scheduling my coronation. But instead I get this!" She flings a hand toward Lex. "You and your crazy syringes, can't even be bothered to kiss me, let alone make a life inside of me." She flicks a hand to Pace. "Your sperm probably die off waiting for you to actually get the job done." She levels her irate eyes on me next, jaw clenching. "And *you*–"

"Don't you dare tell me I don't know how to fuck a woman," I hiss, fingers clenching into a ball at my side. "I can have a dozen on the phone in the next five minutes who'll tell you that you're the problem."

"Because Wicker Ashby is such a sex god?" She barks a sharp, maniacal laugh. "Sure, that's what they all say, but they must be talking about someone else. I'm pretty sure my uterus considers you a hostile invader at this point. Chasing me down five times a day, jumping out from the shadows, and then unloading into me like a cumdumpster isn't the suave Casanova move the rest of Forsyth seems to think it is!"

"Or maybe you don't rank the fucking effort!" I step up to her, sneering. "And while we're being critical, I think I speak for every man in this room when I say you're not exactly inspiring any letters to Penthouse."

Her jaw drops. "Excuse me?" It's the shrill pitch of her voice– that flare of outrage in her eyes–that drives me forward.

"We've fucked mattresses that acted sexier than you. Glancing across the table to watch the gardening video you've got playing on your phone isn't what I'd call active participation."

"And what the three of you do *is*?" She gapes at me, flinging a hand out toward Lex. "Your brother can't even get his dick hard!"

Lex isn't the kind of guy who loses it. In fact, the angrier he gets, the steadier he looks. That's important, with what he does–what *we* do. It's happening right now, his shoulders dropping their tension as he bites back, "Maybe *you* can't get my dick hard." His voice has this way of cutting, all low and smooth, and I watch as she goes stiff. "Wicker has a point, you know. This is all so fucking easy for you."

Her eyes bug out as she looks between us. "Easy? You're crazy!"

He reaches up to tie his hair back with short, deliberate motions, before responding. "All you have to do is spread your legs and play the victim. You're not the one doing the heavy lifting. Even when we're out in public," he gestures to me and Pace, "it's on us to put our arms around you or hold your hand. Might as well be a dead fish."

The words land like a punch. I can see it in the way her brows collide in the middle, the little flash of hurt she veils as anger. "Oh, well excuse the hell out of me for not being sexy enough!" Her incensed eyes ping between me and my brothers. "It's almost like you recruited the most inexperienced girl in the city, and then made her lose her virginity to *a chair*."

"Or maybe you already gave it up to someone else," Pace says, the knot in the back of his jaw ticcing. "I saw his mark on your back. We all have."

The three of us took our breakfast in here yesterday, which is when Lex pensively brought it up. Guess her last medical exam put her ass on full display for him. Of course, I'd seen the scar before, having bent her over plenty of surfaces, but I hadn't realized what it was. What it meant. Not until Lex and Pace explained what went down at the Hideaway.

Just figures we'd get marked goods from West End.

Pace advances on her with fire in his eyes. "I happen to know firsthand you're not the innocent little lamb our Father thinks you are. That is, after all, how we met." He takes her in with a derisive stare. "But Bruce Oakfield?"

The longer she looks between us, the more her horrified eyes begin shining with unshed tears. "You don't know anything," she says, voice cracking with disgust. "Bruce Oakfield didn't brand his ring into me because we were together. He did it to punish me."

My gaze pings to Lex. I would have thought Pace would take the idea of Verity having belonged to Bruce the hardest, but he didn't.

Lex was the one to go all quiet and gloomy about it, practically dissecting his breakfast sausage.

Now the shutters fall over his expression. "Punishment for what?"

She chews out her response. "Disobedience to my future Duke."

There's a tinge of electricity in the air, Lex's shoulders tensing up again, and it makes my nerves flare up, because *shit*. We could do that, couldn't we? Punish her for disobedience? One glance at Pace makes it clear he's thinking the same thing.

Lex, on the other hand...

He gives one sharp shake of his head.

I think I mean to tell him to stop acting above it. Just because he can't get his dick hard doesn't mean the rest of us can't. Instead, what emerges is, "You can still get pregnant on your period."

Her jaw drops in disbelief. "No, you can't!"

Lex–fucking Judas motherfucker–shrugs when I look at him. "Definitely not at the start of it."

"It doesn't matter." Pace pushes past me to jab a forefinger beneath her chin, jerking her gaze up to his. "A good Princess would let her Prince fuck her regardless," he says. There's an intensity in his stare that I might be worried about, except Pace is basically championing for my dick right now.

Her green eyes hold his, and I know before she opens her mouth that none of us are going to like what comes out of it. "Show me a Prince worth being a good Princess to," she says, low and caustic, "and maybe you'll get one."

~

THE PALACE LIBRARY has always been my go-to for a quiet spot, and since I have a paper due on Monday, I camp out there for the afternoon. No one else uses this room. Not even Lex, who prefers the science library on campus. Pace likes his walls to be filled with monitors, not books.

I'm deep in my macro econ book, headphones covering my ears, when a shadow appears over the desk.

"Jesus," I jolt halfway out of my chair, then exhale. All this semen retention is making me strung tighter than a thong. "Fuck, Danner! I told you about sneaking up on me!"

He ignores my outburst and patiently waits for me to remove the headphones. When I do, he announces, "Your Father would like to see you."

I freeze. "Now?"

"Yes, sir."

I take a deep breath and shut the laptop before rising, carefully sliding it and my notebook into my computer bag. Danner continues to lurk in the doorway, as if I need a chaperone up to the meeting. After the *incident* this morning, I guess that's fair.

Tucking the ends of my shirt into my pants, I say, "Look, Danner, about this morning—"

"No need, sir. It was a stressful situation."

"Yeah, but you didn't deserve that." Truth be told, it's easy to resent Danner, just by virtue of him being an extension of our father. Even so, I doubt Danner deserves half of the shit the three of us give him.

He looks at me for a long moment before reaching up to adjust my collar. "I remember the day your father brought you home." His shrewd eyes assess a wrinkle in my buttondown. "You were covered in blood, wailing something awful. The first time I set eyes on you, I thought Rufus was dragging in an injured animal." He steps back, nodding at his efforts to set me to rights. I hear what he's not saying. That's exactly what I was–an injured animal. "Twenty years later, you're still wailing. Even when you're quiet." He dips his chin. "He's in his office. Your brothers are already there."

"Shit." I wince. Outside of being named Prince, we haven't all been called to a meeting together in a long time. Joint meetings are always worse than one-on-one meetings. It usually means someone fucked up, and right now, that someone is probably me. Okay. Most definitely me.

"One more thing." I turn and he reaches out and straightens the shoulder seams of my button-down. "There."

I nod, searching Danner's eyes for some clue about what I'm walking into. "Thanks."

Moments later, I'm approaching the massive oak door to Father's office. Bracing myself, I knock twice and enter, finding my brothers waiting, just like Danner said.

The step over the threshold feels like straddling a canyon. It's the gulf between being a boy and man. All the emotions of childhood, the insecurities and anger, the loss and upheaval, all happened in this room. Nothing good ever happens in Father's office.

Nothing.

Straightening my shoulders, I make the long walk across the Persian rug, passing the crackling fire in the marble fronted fireplace. Over the mantle is a massive oil painting of Father and his son, Michael. The child's eerie eyes, as always, seem to follow each step.

Father looks up as I approach, although neither of my brothers do. Shoulders squared, chins held high, both of their gazes are focused on the man behind the desk. "Whitaker," he says, "take a seat."

Uneasily, I take the empty chair.

He spends a second flipping through papers. "Although I've been apprised that the Princess has had her monthly cycle, I thought I'd give you the official lab results from the most recent blood test Lex procured." He removes a slip of paper from an envelope, eyes skimming over the words, lips turned down. "Confirmed negative. The Princess is not pregnant during this round, which is unfortunate, but not entirely unexpected."

He sets the paper aside and picks up his small leather-bound notebook. He's carried one of these with him as long as I can remember. It seems to be part calendar and part diary. Habit really, since Pace has him set up with everything online. Father is nothing if not a raging traditionalist.

Sighing, he goes on, "I know you've been busy with your obligations, so I thought I'd give you a tally of each of your deposits." Verity's accusation echoes in my head.

You're the deficient ones.

This morning had been such a red-hot blur of anger, horniness, and hatred that I almost forgot to wonder if she might be right. Not that it matters. Father would agree with her regardless–because that's what we are. What we've always been.

Lesser. Deficient.

I shift my legs, propping my ankle on a knee. Next to me, Pace's leg starts that bouncing thing, jackhammering up and down. Lex, on the other hand, is as still as a statue.

Father flips the book open to a page in the middle, finger running down what seems to be a chart. "I'm sure it comes as no surprise that Whitaker is in the lead, with a record of–goodness." His eyes flick up to mine, and he sets his pen down. "Seventeen deposits." I brace myself for the admonition, the back of my neck prickling with the threat. But a threat doesn't come. Instead, he gives me a sly, pleased smile. "Well done, son."

The sense of relief that spreads through my chest is only outshined by the cringe of disgust I cover with a grin. "Thank you, Father."

He's never congratulated me on fucking before.

I need a million showers after this.

Never one to let a good criticism go to waste, he retrieves his pen and adds, "I hope you'll consider the value of quality over quantity, however." He assesses the page again. "Pace, although your numbers are a bit lower, you've had a respectable eight deposits." He looks up at my brother and gives him a rare nod of encouragement. "You may want to consider adding a few more to your days, but overall, good work."

Pace's knee slows its bounce, the tension leaving his limbs. "I'll do that, sir, thank you for the advice."

Meeting his gaze, Father asks, "And how is our mutual project coming along?"

I glance at my brother, brows knitting together. Pace gets that weird, hunted look he's had ever since returning, but he covers it well enough, giving Father a bounce of his chin. "Slow but steady."

Father jabs the point of his pen in Pace's direction. "That's the way it's done. A Princess like Verity will need a steady hand. Consistency, patience, reinforcement."

"I agree," Pace replies, nodding. "The Princess is everything you said she is. Willful, proud, combative. But she shows moments of..." Here, he seems to choose his words very carefully. "Dedication," is the one he lands on. "Being Princess is her own project. She wants to succeed."

Father's eyebrows tick up. "Is that so?"

"She seemed disappointed," Pace explains. In my periphery, I see his fingers lacing and unlacing. "That she isn't pregnant yet." Father hums, mulling this over, and the pieces click into place.

Pace is responsible for her behavioral conditioning.

A nervousness writhes inside my chest, because that should be me. I'm the one who seduces. I'm the one who finesses. I'm the talker and the extractor. But Pace always has been better at the long game. Patient to a fault. Consistent, just like Father said. I take advantage of moments of weakness, but Pace is the one who creates them.

To create is to reign.

Suddenly, all the relief and praise I felt before is drowned with uncertainty and doubt.

And I'm not the only one squirming.

The seat next to me creaks and I slide my gaze over, seeing Lex's hands grip the arms of the chair. His knuckles are white, veins tensing in the back of his hands.

When I look back, Father is staring at him. "And how many deposits did you make during this cycle, Lagan?"

Pace's knee twitches at the use of the name Lagan, and the hair on the back of my neck spikes.

Lex starts to clear his throat and then stops himself. "Four." And then, "No. Five."

Father leans back, tapping his pen against the page. "Which is it? Four or five?"

"Well, I–" Lex's fists flex, fingertips digging into the arms. "One of my deposits was comprised of two–"

"You made four." Father's voice is hard, final.

Lex deflates. "Yes, sir. One on each of my assigned days."

A chill settles over the room. There's no doubt where this is going. There's no escaping the train collision heading our —*his*—way.

"I'd like to congratulate you as I have your brothers, but one deposit per day is the bare minimum. A disappointment. *Mediocrity*." Lex pales at the word. In Father's eyes, mediocre is the worst thing a person can be. He folds the notebook and sets it in front of him, on the desk. "It's unacceptable."

"Father, I'm—"

"I thought you had your situation under control," Father snaps.

"I do." He swallows thickly. "I've made strides to compensate for any physical failings by maximizing our efforts." Lex's back is straight and he looks our father in the eye, adopting full robot mode. "In addition to my deposits, I've researched methods to encourage fertility and fertilization. I'm monitoring her diet, her hormone levels, and her ovulation cycles. I've begun genetic testing. Additionally, I'm keeping everyone on schedule and enforcing the adherence to the covenants."

Father's eyes are icy, a familiar cruelness shining through. "So what you're saying is that you're doing everything but giving the Princess a good, old-fashioned *fucking*."

Lex flounders. "I—"

"Whitaker," Father says, "get the box."

No.

Fuck no.

Every instinct I possess is screaming for me to snarl it into his face. To scream. To sweep that notebook off his desk and tell him if he wants something, he can get it his goddamn self. But I stand like a good little soldier and stride across the room to open the cabinet behind Father's desk. Inside, always waiting, is a rectangular wooden box, the top and sides carved with the PNZ crest. Bile threatens to rise in the back of my throat, but I swallow it back down, forcing myself to take the box out of the cabinet. When I turn, Lex is already standing by his chair, unbuttoning his shirt. Pace is still in his seat, staring at a spot on the floor, eyes empty— his expression impassive and still.

He shrugs off the shirt, and since he's Lex, he turns to hang it neatly over the back of the chair, giving me a full view of the criss-cross of old, puckered scars etched into his back.

"Father," I say, keeping my voice even—removing all traces of emotion, "Pace and I can contribute more deposits if—"

"This isn't about deposits, Whitaker." Father slowly rolls up his sleeves, his motions jerky and precise. It's never a good sign when his anger is visible like this. "This is about Lagan giving me his word and then failing to fulfill it. He's allowed a weakness to stand in the way of his purpose."

Pace flinches, the memory of spring break still somehow fresh for all of us.

Especially here.

Like this.

Father circles the desk, and without another glance at my brother, commands, "Fireplace."

It's always the same spot in front of the roaring flames. With his arms at his sides, Lex lowers himself to his knees, assuming the same old position. I'm still holding the box, the urge to toss it in the fireplace more powerful than any other desire in my life. More than scoring goals. More than fucking. Only one thing supersedes it: the need to grab my brothers and run from this nightmare of a hellscape.

But even that desire is tempered with harsh reality. If we left, we'd have no other family. No access to our trust funds. Nothing but the clothes on our backs, and knowing Father, he'd take those too. What's outside of these walls? The South Side? West? The rubble of the North?

The Barons' shadows?

A hysterical laugh bubbles in my chest, and I hold it back doggedly. We're fucked. We know it, Father knows it.

"Whitaker," Father says, snapping me back to the moment. He pulls a single black leather glove over his right hand. "Give your brother the box."

Pace and I make eye contact as I hand him the carved box. We both pretend not to notice the tremor in my hand as the weight shifts to him. Instinctively, I know we're both brimming with the same fear.

This isn't how it goes.

Punishing someone so directly like this isn't Father's style. I can't remember the last time Lex got an appointment for something Pace or I weren't responsible for. It's how Father's always kept us in line. Either of us fuck up, and Lex gets the punishment. And if Lex fucks up, it'd be Pace who takes the brunt of it. Shoved into one dark hole or another, cut off and isolated as Lex grieved about it.

It's been so long since Lex stepped a single foot out of line that it's easy to forget how it used to be. The way Lex would torture himself about it, desperate to search Pace out and bring him back, but just as desperate to not make it worse by being disobedient. It's been a decade since Lex last crumpled into a heap, clawing at the floorboards in an attempt to dig his way to the dungeon to get our brother.

With rigid elbows, Pace carries the box to father, opening the lid. Father reaches in and pulls out the strap, fingers flexing around the handle. The strap unfurls, three feet of razor-sharp leather. It dangles innocuously, like a sleeping viper.

Lex's body is rigid, eyes staring into the fire. Crying won't work. We all know that. Neither will pleading. Both will only lead to more trouble. As Father approaches him, the room grows unbearably hot, the collar of my shirt closing in around my throat. There's no warning, just the crack in the air, the length landing with a hard snap, the tail end of the whip biting into the backside of his bicep. Lex keels forward but stays upright, his jaw tensing from swallowing back a scream. He'd never admit it, but Father is rusty, the punishments less frequent when we were living on our own.

Father sneers out, "Four lashings for each of your deposits. And an additional four to get you to the same level as your brother." Pace flinches at the last remark. "Be thankful I'm not holding you to Whitaker's standards."

"Yes, sir," Lex replies before the whip slices through the air and cuts into his skin once again. His eyes shut, pain crossing his face. Anger wells in my blood. Hot and dangerous. The following strikes are worse than the ones before. Lex's back crisscrossed with new wounds, the flesh raw, beading with blood. Father throws himself into it, each lashing deeper than the last, until all eight have been administered. Sweat drips from his forehead, and he reaches into his pocket for a pristine, white handkerchief, which he uses to mop his brow.

Jesus Christ.

Finished, he holds out the length of leather to Pace. "Clean this," he says, then jerks his chin at Lex. "And him."

"Yes, sir." The words are low, hard, and when that strap changes hands there's a flicker of time where I think my brother may snap. Or maybe, I think, as Pace regains his composure, I just want him to do what I know I don't have the courage to do myself.

Father leaves the room. I know from experience that he won't return until all signs of his abuse have been removed. Until Lex's wounds are covered, and the box is returned to the cabinet. The instant he's gone, I fall to my knees, tears hot at the corner of my eyes. "Jesus, Lex. Are you—"

"Not now, Wick." He jerks away, struggling, but rising to his feet on his own. Once he's there, he sways, but manages to hold himself up.

"There's a kit in my room," Pace says, the words rushing out. "Antiseptic, cream, bandages."

Wincing, Lex shoves his arms into his shirt. "It's fine."

"No," I say, fists clenching, "it's really fucking not. And it's not happening again."

Lex runs his hand over his sweaty forehead. "This isn't something you can help with, Wick."

In an urgent whisper, I plead, "The covenants say I can't fuck her when it's not my day, but it doesn't say I can't deposit. I've got what you don't right now: unlimited semen. Let me come in the vials for you, and then you can tell Father you—"

"No!" he roars, but it's followed by a pained grimace and his hand coming down on the back of the chair. He twists and blood seeps through the cotton of his shirt. "That's too much of a risk–for all of us. This is my problem, and I'm the one who has to fix it." His teeth gnash, but it's not about the pain. That, Lex can handle. He's spent years being on this end of it, inflicted on account of mine and Pace's failings. Pain has never bothered my brother.

The real wound is the failure.

19

L ex

"MED WING OR OUR ROOM?" Pace asks, directing me down the hall.

"Room," I grit out, knowing once I lay down, I won't be able to get back up. He turns me toward the kitchen—where the back stairs lead up to our wing. In this house, blood on the front stairs would be unforgivable.

"Lex," Wicker starts, resting his hand on my elbow. "I'm—"

"Not now," I grunt, feeling every nerve alight as I reach the first step. The kitchen staff has vanished. The entire house is still, like everyone is in hiding. It makes the screaming in my muscles—in my head—so much louder. I lift my foot and the movement pulls at my shirt, tugging at the spots where the fabric sticks to the bloody slashes in my skin.

"Fuck," I mutter. Tears bite at my eyes. As bad as it hurts now, I know the worst is yet to come. The cleaning. The recovery. The stinging. The itching. If it was just the first part–the humiliation and pain in Father's office–it would be so much easier to swallow.

At least I don't have hockey practice like I used to.

My brothers crowd me, surrounding me with support, hands on my elbows and hips, as they help me up the stairs. It's just like the other appointments I've had throughout my life, except for one vital detail.

This time, no one but myself is to blame for it.

They're patient, avoiding the wounds, silent guilt rolling off them in waves. If I thought I could do it without snapping, I'd tell them it's not like other times. This isn't their fault. I'm the one who failed by being unable to fulfill the promises I made to Father—*to the Princess*—but it's pointless. That's always Father's goal with these things. We're intertwined. A cohesive, symbiotic unit. My pain is theirs. Their guilt is mine.

I exhale at the top of the stairs and make the turn into the main hallway. *Twenty feet*, I think, lumbering past the sitting area and portraits of former Princes.

"Do you need to sit down?" Wick asks, nose-to-nose, as I fist a handful of his shirt, pulling him toward me. The sting of the flames is already licking at my flesh, a tickle that signals I don't have much time.

"I can do it," I grind out. *Fifteen feet*. I make it six, stopping at the bookshelves, where I slump, leaning against the hard surface with my shoulder. A frame tips, knocking over with a clatter. Closing my eyes, I admit, "Fuck, I just need a minute."

I breathe in and out, trying to work past the searing pain, trying to get to that place in my head where none of it hurts. The place where I don't try to understand why Father is like this, wondering where I went wrong and how I can keep it from happening again. These issues with sex—it never happened until I got off the Scratch. I fucked. I fucked *plenty*. Freshman year, I got a little fixated with muscles and fucked my way through Forsyth's entire female diving team. Not that I can compete with Wicker in volume, but I beat him out in satisfaction. Women around campus knew they had a chance of getting a good lay when they saw either of us walk into the room.

Now I'm lucky to nut into a cup twice a week.

I knew fucking with Scratch was messy. That the Counts were flooding the market with a shitty product that hooks people too fast and too hard, leaving them with a series of side effects. It's part of the reason I tried it to begin with. It was easy to get, cheap, and gave me the energy to get through my hectic as fuck schedule junior year, but mostly it was an experiment. It wasn't just curiosity. It was the idiotic internal confidence that I was above the rest of them–equipped to handle it, more disciplined, physiologically superior.

As it turns out, I'm really fucking not, but even with all that, I'd trade Wicker's trust fund for a hit to take away this pain.

"Lex," Pace says in quiet warning. I open my eyes. There's movement down at the end of the wing. Red hair catches the light.

Stiffening, I whisper, "Don't let her see me like this."

"Cover him," Wick says before sauntering off. It gnaws at the pit of my churning stomach to watch him morph into a different person. It flips like a switch, this easy change from best friend and brother to conniving seducer. Pace shifts, blocking me from view. We stare at one another as we listen to Wicker call out, "Change your mind, Red?" There's a rustle of fabric, if I had to guess, he's cupping his junk. "I knew you'd come looking for me. I'm ready when you are."

The slam of the door is her only response.

Pace's eyebrows raise when Wick strides back to us, looping his arm under my armpit. "Guess the threat of having your cock near her one more time was enough to scare her off."

If Wicker's ego were a physical being, then Verity calling his prowess into question would probably make it look worse than me. Wicker's jaw twitches. "Please, by the end of her exile, she'll be begging me for it."

Panting, I clutch onto him. "She'll be begging *me* for it," I say, fully aware of the irony. I take a deep breath and grab Pace by the shoulder, leveraging myself back up. "I'm the only one giving her what she needs."

The pain is blinding by the time we make the final stretch to our room. Danner beat us up here, a tray of medical supplies sitting on the table next to the bed along with a clean sheet over the mattress.

I stop at the edge of the bed, a tremor running through my fingers as I try to unbutton my shirt.

"Here," Wicker says, pushing my hands aside and taking over. His longer fingers quickly run down the buttons. His movements are gentle, a complete contrast to the hulking menace that terrorizes other players on the ice. He pushes the shirt off my shoulders and carefully peels the fabric from the drying wounds. This is the side of Wicker no one else sees but us; gentle and patient.

"Okay?" he asks, looking at me from under his blonde swoop of hair.

I grunt and drop to my knees, mattress sinking under my weight. Pace helps ease me forward, helping me lay flat on my stomach. I exhale fully for the first time since stepping into Father's office.

"How bad does it look?" I ask. I could look in the mirror across from the bed, but I don't need to. I can judge the severity of wounds from my brother's expressions. Wicker's turning green, like he's fighting the urge to vomit. Pace has gone stone still. He's left us for that place inside, the one of quiet rage.

"Not as bad as... last time," he finally says, flicking a glance at Pace. The words hang between us like a ghost.

Spring break.

Nothing has ever been as bad as the night Pace got arrested. Father handed out thirty lashings. I passed out in the middle, and when I woke up, an ashen Wicker was standing over me, waving smelling salts under my nose. Beneath the scent of it was the sourness of vomit wafting from the vase in the corner where he had lost his lunch. Father told him to clean it up and put me back on my knees so he could finish the job.

Pace lowers his gaze to the tray, his dark eyes shrouded. "Is it stinging yet?" The words lack inflection.

He might as well be screaming.

Clenching my teeth, I admit, "Yes."

Before the back garden became overgrown with dead, wilted things, it used to play host to all sorts of curious plants. One of them was a type of stinging nettle–urtica. I did a paper on it in high school. Buried beneath paragraphs outlining its medical uses was a passage on urtication, sometimes used as a form of punishment, and how the fibers could be extracted, weaved with something like leather.

I got top marks.

Other than the quiet sounds of the guys opening the medical supplies, the room is silent. I don't need to look to see what's going on. We all have our roles, and we fall back into them despite the time we've been apart.

Except when Wicker moves for the antiseptic, Pace jolts forward, saying, "No." A stretch of stillness lingers, and then his determined, "I've got him."

I don't see whatever look is passed between them, but I can practically feel Wicker's frown transforming to comprehension as Pace takes the bottle. He didn't get to do this for me last time. Probably spent all those months in jail feeling responsible, imagining Wicker taking on the burden of it himself.

Gently, Pace dabs the wet cotton to my open wounds, freezing every time I flinch. Wicker sits near my head, whispering, "It won't take long. It's not that bad." And then again, as if he's trying really hard to convince both of us, "It's not–it's not so bad." He assists Pace by handing him the antihistamine first, then the antibiotic ointment, and finally the bandages.

I come in and out of it, wanting nothing more than to sleep, but the antiseptic burns worse than the urtica, sending my body into tremors. Pace leans forward, touching my forehead with the back of his fingers. "Pain check?"

I give a heavy blink, thinking. "Maybe a five."

It's an eight, but I won't show it. They're already carrying enough guilt. There's no need to pile on. The urge to protect them runs deeper than the scars on my body. Someone had to stand between them and Father's ire.

Although I'm older, Wicker was Father's first adopted son. It's hard to look at him and think that in another life, he'd be a Baron. His grandfather was Clive Kayes, King of the Barons, and his father was... well, certifiably toast. Guy never even got a chance at the crown, but was still important enough to be axed so someone else could.

My own father was a past failed Prince. As far as I know, his Princess was unsuccessful, and he was dismissed after three months. Later, he married my mother and had me. I don't remember much about being adopted myself, just that the night of my parents' deaths, in the midst of red and blue flashing lights and puddles of thickening blood, Father came and took me away in his big, fancy car. I was only two. Wicker was still just a baby himself when I arrived, not even six months old.

Looking at him now, I can't remember exactly when I started feeling so protective of him. Maybe all the way back to those early days when it was just the two of us, always seeking the other out at night, scared and needy as we hid beneath my bed, Wicker falling asleep curled around me like a vine. Or maybe it was later, the first time he was taken out of boarding school, returning the next day with a boastful story about the tall woman with razor-sharp nails who Father had ordered him to spend the evening with. More likely, it was all the time in-between, slowly figuring out that home wasn't this place made of sticks and stones, but instead *him*. The blue-eyed boy with a smile like a knife's edge.

Somewhere between the ointment and the bandages, Pace bites out, "This is bullshit."

Quietly, Wicker agrees, "Yeah."

"It's not like you can help–" Pace's words clip off, though. Futile. Useless.

Father didn't adopt him until Pace was almost six. He was small and quiet, with angry, guarded eyes that Wicker and I would know anywhere. We saw that wild, haunted look in each other every day. I don't need to remember when I started feeling protective of Pace. It happened the first second of the first minute I met him. Somehow, I just knew he was meant to be ours. Strong but fragile. Paranoid and curious. Hostile but desperately lonely.

Which is why I'm expecting it when he cautiously asks, "Have you tried fucking her?"

"Yes," I answer, but it's neither a lie nor the truth. "I've tried to try," I clarify, the words feeling inadequate.

There's a beat of silence, and then Wicker's soothing fingers are combing through my hair. "What's it like? When you try?"

My eyes flutter closed. "It's like... it's just not there anymore. The urge is, but the physical response isn't."

"So you want to fuck her," Pace says, and I don't even need to think about it. The scratch didn't take away my libido, just gave me the inability to get–and *stay*–hard.

I give a single, weak nod.

Wicker points out, "But you can jack off."

"It takes forever," I say, wincing as Pace pushes a bandage into my skin. I've thought about taking a hit, just one, but I'm not a fool. The trade-offs aren't worth it.

"Maybe I could be with you," Wicker reasons, leaning down to catch my gaze. "I could help–"

"No." My answer is immediate, unyielding. The thought of using Wicker like that makes me feel fucking sick. "I'm going to fix it."

Wicker doesn't look disappointed.

He looks worried.

"Fuck!" I rise off the bed, a sharp pain stabbing across my flesh.

"Sorry!" Pace says, eyes wide with worry. "My hand slipped."

I flop back down and grind out, "Finish it up." My eyes flutter shut, and a few minutes later, they still. "Thank you."

The mattress sinks and a hand brushes my hair back. "Take these." Wick pushes the pills into my mouth and helps me with a swallow of water. He settles in next to me, hand on my head, running his fingers through my hair in soothing strokes.

"Stay with him," Pace says, jumping off the bed. "I'll go secure the recording."

My body jostles with a silent, bitter laughter as he leaves. "Evidence," I rasp out, chuckling.

"Don't." I can feel Wicker's gaze on me as he lays at my side, and when I pry my eyes open, it's to the sight of his frown. "Don't forget the plan."

The plan to use the evidence of Father's abuse as leverage to escape was dead in the water a decade ago. Father's got so much shit on us that it's laughable. We just go through the motions of collecting it out of habit, chasing some dream of finally being free of him.

If Verity gets pregnant, we'll belong to him forever.

And that's the best case.

"She was right." My head feels heavy, fists curling as I fight the urge to scratch the wounds. "I am deficient."

Wicker's face twists angrily. "She's just some gutter slut from West End, Lex. She doesn't know us."

She will.

That's the fear in my mind, the deeper into this we go. If we'd gotten her pregnant in the first month, then maybe we could have avoided it. Sharing a space with this girl is going to pull her closer into our shadows, magnetic and inevitable.

Because I've seen her eyes.

Strong but fragile.

Paranoid and curious.

Hostile but desperately lonely.

Something inside of Verity Sinclaire is horrifyingly like *us*, and the longer she looks, the more she's going to see the truth. We grew up in East End—three lost boys, motherless, haunted by the ghost of Father's dead son. Kept in line by his obsession with perfection, lineage, and creation. As with everything, we each have our roles.

Wicker, with his attractiveness and ability to charm, was always too valuable to scar—physically, at least. Pace's calculated intelligence, his endurance for isolation and affinity for torture, made him Father's perfect tool.

But me?

I'm just a mechanic of working parts, and someone has to take the punishments we're due. Someone who can pay the debts. Someone who knows how to hurt but hide it.

Someone who can be ugly.

IT TAKES me twice the time, but I manage to get to the dungeon the next day. When I enter the observation room, my brothers look at me in surprise.

"I saw the text," I explain.

"We just wanted to keep you in the loop," Wick says, brows knitted as he assesses me. Without asking, he takes the hair tie from my wrist and steps behind me to pull my hair back. "You didn't need to come down."

But we all know that I did. There's no rest or days off when you're an Ashby, and definitely not when you're a Prince. Father was gracious enough to call us in on a Saturday—giving me a day to recover.

"Oakfield wants to talk," Pace says, but even though he nods at the man behind the glass, I can see the tight worry in his eyes.

My mouth tugs up into a cruel grin. "I bet he does."

He's back in the chair, wrists strapped to the armrests, a trickle of blood coming down his cheek. There's a process to torture–a lot of people don't get that. Pace is always first. He's so accustomed to the physical element that sometimes it's like he leaves the room entirely, leaving nothing behind but his muscles and malice. Burning. Hitting. Cutting. He's an expert at bodily demolition, which is one of the reasons he's so good on the ice.

Wicker is second. After all that pain and humiliation, sometimes all it takes is one gentle word–one trick of kindness–and people will break like fine china. Even when they don't, my brother has a way of talking information out of them.

I'm always the last resort.

If a mark finds themself on my table, they've landed themselves in some serious shit. It's the kind of thing a person just doesn't come back from. I've taken fingers. Toes. Hands. Feet. Arms, if they hold out long enough. Once, a guy's foreskin. Sometimes, if they give up the goods soon enough, I make an attempt at reattachment. Other times, I send the souvenir home with them, nestled on a bed of ice.

Then there's more passive torture. Starvation, sleep deprivation, gaslighting. The gaunt, hollow curve of Bruce's cheeks and the dark rings under his eyes indicate that phase is in effect. The physical stuff is well and good, but the best way to torture someone is psychological. Using their mind against them. That part is harder to see, and with a sociopath like Oakfield, it's almost impossible to tell if we've gotten under his skin.

"Yeah." Wick rolls his eyes. "He says he has something we may be interested in."

Nodding, I say, "Then I guess we should find out what the man wants to share." Pace swings open the door and I step aside—too quickly. I wince from the jolt of pain down my back and add, "This better be worth it."

Wicker frowns. "Lex, seriously, we can—"

"It's fine." I crack my knuckles. "I have a few questions myself."

In the long hours I laid in bed, willing my skin to knit back together, I kept thinking of that mark on Verity's back; an O with a line slashed through it. It's the same brand that landed this bastard down in our cell with a death sentence from a second King.

When I saw it on Verity that night in the med room, I'd felt a visceral disgust. It's such a West End thing, the way they voluntarily mar their flesh, and even if I'd never touched Scratch a day in my life, I still would have struggled to get hard after seeing it there.

It's different now that we know its purpose.

"Wick," I say, keeping my eyes trained on Bruce, "let me take the lead."

He hesitates, but says, "You got it."

I'm careful to control my gait when I walk in, stiff but sure, hiding the wince from the pull of my shirt fabric against my shoulder blades. Up close, Oakfield looks even worse than from afar. His skin is pale and peeling. Nails bitten to the quick. All traces of golden boy have been diminished from being locked down here for two weeks.

I grab a chair and move it in front of him, spinning it around to straddle the seat. No fucking way I can lean my back against the hard metal surface. Resting my arms on the back I say, "I hear you want to talk."

He licks his cracked bottom lip, eyes darting to Pace by the tool bench. "Yeah, but you have to promise he'll stay away from me with the branding iron."

I stare up into the corner of the room, pretending to mull it over. "Give us something useful, and maybe we can deal."

He exhales, fingers flexing and unflexing around the curve of the chair arm. "Clive Kayes is dead."

I don't blink. "The Baron King." Behind me, Wick has gone still, and I don't need to look back to know Oakfield has his attention. As far as Forsyth at large is concerned, the Barons' crown hasn't changed heads at all. The average person is under the impression Clive Kayes is still kicking.

Bruce shifts, wincing. "Former King. He got bumped off years ago in a coup inside the frat."

My eyes narrow. "How long ago?"

He shrugs. "Fifteen or so years ago."

Twenty.

He goes on, voice hoarse and dry, "Long enough that whoever's wearing that mask has way more power than anyone realizes. They're completely incognito, running that crypt with zero Royal oversight." He sniffs. "He might participate in the mandatory trials and events, but no one knows who the fuck he is, so it doesn't matter."

It takes everything in me not to roll my eyes. "So you're saying Clive Kayes was murdered, but you have no idea who killed him."

"His killer is right there!" Bruce snaps. "Whoever it is that's wearing that nightmare mask and disposing of dead bodies in Forsyth."

Wicker moves next to me, arms crossed over his chest. All pretense gone, it's a posture of intimidation, his biceps bulging against the fabric of his shirt. "What kind of proof do you have?"

Panic flickers in Bruce's eyes. "My father can corroborate."

Fuck.

Wicker scoffs. "Your father would sell his right nut to get you back. Try harder."

Groaning, Bruce squirms against his binds. "Come on, guys. My father is the financial manager for all of the Kings' personal assets. Kayes accounts haven't been touched. His social security number hasn't been used. He hasn't paid a dime in taxes." Pace makes a loud noise over by the workbench and Bruce straightens up. "That's proof, right?"

We know this already. Wicker's known the truth about his father's death since we were kids. What we don't know is *who* is behind the mask. Who killed Clive Kayes and why he's gotten away with it.

"What good is this information," Wick asks, "if you can't tell us who did it?"

"Maybe you can find out? The Dukes and Lords... they don't know. No one does–just me and my dad. That's leverage." He shifts in his seat and glances at Pace. "That's enough, right? To keep him from branding me again?"

Pace and I share a look, and the moment our gazes meet, it's as if some hidden fault line shifts, knitting the earth back together at our feet. An energy passes between us. It's a frisson. An awareness.

He dips his chin in a small nod.

"For now," I lie, scooting my chair closer. "But I've been wondering. How many women did you brand your initial into?"

Bruce's forehead furrows. "This again? Why the fuck do you care about some whores?" He nods down to where Pace branded him last time with the LDZ skull. I'd tended to the wounds, making sure that if he gets out of here alive, he'll be marked like the little bitch he is.

"I'm not talking about a whore," I say, voice curt with impatience. "I'm talking about a girl who belongs to East End. You feel me?"

His face draws blank, like he's flipping through a catalog of possible victims. "I've never touched any of your Princess bitches. At least not any who didn't get booted out of here for failing." His lips curve into something smug but Wicker clears his throat in warning. Then recognition strikes. "Wait, you mean Sinclaire? She wasn't even yours then." Bruce's gaze pings between us, flashing hot at the mention of her name, and I finally see what I've been looking for.

Bruce had gotten attached to the idea of having a Duchess. The thought of having dominion over her. Owning her.

When his lips pull back in a snarl, the bitterness is tangible. "She was supposed to be mine."

Pace's fist cracks against his jaw, snapping his head sideways. "She was supposed to be mine, actually." Despite the low, even timbre of his voice, I can sense the savage energy rolling off him in waves. It makes my blood run faster.

"And what she is," I add, rising painfully from the chair, "is *ours*."

Wicker snorts, arms folded. "Face it, Oakfield. You never had a fucking chance at being Duke."

Grabbing his bloody chin in a hard grip, I ask, "You know why? Because you have no sense of allegiance. West End is a dumpster heap of mangy hotheads, but I'll give them this: They understand the value of loyalty."

Wicker's eyes darken. "Meanwhile, you'll sell out any and all of us. DKS, LDZ, PNZ, and now BRN. Your shit list is alphabet soup."

"So what gives you the fucking right," I growl, digging my fingers into his sweaty face, "to mark up our women like a bathroom stall?"

Bruce's mouth purses in opposition to my grip, but I see the grin hiding underneath it. "Oh, her pussy must be good to get Lex Ashby this hot under the collar. It's the innocence, isn't it? If anyone gets the appeal, it's me. All naïve and eager to do her duty, with those plush lips and perfect tits." His eyes slide to Pace, and then Wicker. "Yeah, I had big plans to mold Verity into my little fuck kitten. So what if I got a little excited and pre-gamed her with my mark? You got to her first."

"I've been thinking a lot about gifts," I say, satisfied by the sense of whiplash in his stare. "You see, it's compulsory in our house to honor our Princess' burden with tokens of our affection. The problem is, we don't exactly have much of that. Affection," I clarify, glancing down at his ring. In this light, it looks dull and faded–dirty. "It's an issue. I try to excel at everything I do, but when it comes to honoring my Princess with tokens, I just can't seem to muster up the motivation. She's a narc, you see. A traitor to her house. If you'd asked me a week ago, I probably would have said she's a lot like you, actually. But you're right about one thing." I grab his finger–the one with the ring–in a tight, sure grip. "Unlike you, Verity Sinclaire does her duty. No matter how she feels about us, she shows up every night to fulfill her obligations. And I think that deserves something more special than roses. Don't you?"

The bone shears appear in front of me like magic, Bruce's eyes widening as Pace hands them over.

"Dude, wait," he rushes out, hand flexing ineffectually as I tug the finger straight. "Wait, wait, wait–I'll give you the ring, if that's what you–" His words disappear into a garbled mess of shocked screams when the shears snip right through his lower proximal phalange.

I hold up the severed finger, assessing it thoughtfully. "The faster you are, the cleaner the cut."

Bruce's pale face rapidly fills with color, turning him a deep purple. He rants through irate, pained gasps, "You motherfucking psychos! What the fuck? What the *fuck*! My father is going to put your goddamn heads on a platter! Son of a bitch, you cut off my fucking–"

Carefully laying the finger on Bruce's knee, I plug my ears.

The shot still reverberates through my eardrums like a crack of lightning, Bruce's head snapping back. Behind me, there's a wild shift in the air–Wicker jumping in surprise–but I watch the life seep from Bruce's eyes, and all I can think about is ugliness.

Ugliness and the men who inflict it on others.

I catch Bruce's finger right before it rolls off his weakly spasming knee. "Good shot."

Pace clears the slide of the pistol, shrugging. "Like shooting bears in a barrel."

"What the hell!" When I turn, Wicker is gaping at the scene, flinging a hand out in annoyance. "We could have gotten more intel out of him. We could have ransomed him to his shithead of a father. Now, he's useless!"

Glancing at Pace, I reach for a pack of gauze on the table, ripping it open. "Every second he lived was a risk not worth taking."

Tucking the gun away, Pace explains, "He knew about your grandfather, Wick. If it gets out that Clive Kayes is dead," he turns to our brother, mouth pressed into a grim line, "then people are going to start looking for his heirs."

The truth of that hangs heavily in the air between us. If people go looking for Clive's son, then they'll begin looking for his grandson soon enough. That makes Wicker a target for any number of psychopaths.

Bruce Oakfield didn't know it, but he killed himself tonight.

His father, too.

The outrage falls from Wicker's expression, leaving a distressed frown in its wake. "He could have told us more about your dad."

"Maybe, maybe not." Pace jerks a shoulder in a shrug. "I'd rather have a brother than a dad." He looks up, meeting Wicker's gaze.

All the hardness leaves his blue eyes. "Well, gee," he grumbles, "if you're going to get all fucking sappy about it, then at least wait until Oakfield's brains stop leaking out."

Pace smirks. "Ruins the moment?"

"Little bit."

Rolling the finger into the gauze, I look at Pace, "Alert the Barons. They've been waiting for our call anyway."

"What are you going to do?" Wicker asks, eyes on the package in my hand. "More importantly, what are you going to do with *that*?"

"I've got my own mess to clean up."

SHE'S NOT in the dining room when I arrive that evening.

I falter for a moment, glaring at her empty seat before placing the box and sachet on the empty plate in front of her chair. I haven't taken a proper dinner in this dining room since middle school, and my back prickles as I look around, the itch so bad that I have to curl my fingers into fists to avoid reaching back there and seeking relief. I learned a long time ago that there isn't any relief, only open scabs and pain. The restraint has become so ingrained in my mind that I'm probably the only habitual user of Scratch in Forsyth who came out of it without scars from scratching.

I take the seat across from hers–my usual–and wait.

Danner is the first to appear, coming through the swinging door with a platter of food. If he's surprised to see me, he does a good job of hiding it. "It's your favorite," he says, setting the silver dish in the center of the table. I know before he even lifts the lid what it'll be, the scent wafting out to me through the kitchens.

"Thank you," I say, looking at the pot roast with all its carrots and potatoes. My stomach burns with acidy emptiness, and for the first time since the whipping, I feel my appetite stir to life. I glance at the empty place setting in front of me. "I'll be taking dinner with the Princess tonight."

Danner nods, turning to the china cabinet. Any other night, I'd tell him not to fuss and get the dishes myself, but my back is tender, as if the smallest shift will pull apart the slowly healing slashes. He places the china and utensils in front of me before pausing. "Candles, sir? A vase, perhaps?"

My eyes jerk up to his. "What for?"

He nods toward the gift on Verity's plate. "For a more romantic ambiance, of course."

Romantic?

Princesses don't need romance. They need semen.

"That's not necessary." But then I question myself. Tonight is about showing Father I'm taking this seriously, and that means some amount of effort must be made. Stiffly, I ask, "Is it? Necessary?"

Danner laces his fingers behind him. "A young woman such as our Princess might be charmed by such a gesture."

I'm still agonizing over the decision when the young woman in question shuffles into the room, freezing at the sight of us. She's wearing leggings and a hideous, oversized sweatshirt with the DKS Bruin on it. The sight of it makes my thoughts flare red. That could be Bruin's sweater. Perilini's. Maddox's.

The disrespect is fucking galling.

The moment her eyes meet mine, they dim, hardening. "Why are you here?"

I give Danner a bored look. "Nix the ambiance for now."

He still pulls her seat out for her, but she hardly notices, going by the way her eyes are glued to the gifts on her plate. To her credit, she waits until Danner's excused himself to say, "There weren't any deposits last night." Her voice is clipped, but still oddly toneless. She looks paler than usual.

I make a mental note to test her for anemia. "Gifts aren't only for deposits," I tell her, reaching for the serving fork. It makes the skin over my shoulder pull taut, and I hiss, snatching my hand back. *Fuck.* Should have had Danner serve me the food. Instead, I stand, reaching a little more carefully.

I can feel her eyes tracking me–every aborted movement as I hide my wince. "Why are you here?" she asks again.

"To eat dinner." I slice the roast with controlled movements.

"You eat dinner in your room," she points out. "And breakfast, too."

I spoon some carrots and potatoes onto my plate. "Wicker and Pace are out. Maybe I just wanted company." In truth, they're downstairs with the Barons, cleaning up the mess formerly known as Bruce. From my periphery, I see her reach for the gifts. "Those are for after dinner."

Holding my gaze, she plucks up the sachet and completely fucking ignores what she damn well knows is an order. Rolling my eyes, I perch on the edge of my seat and await her reaction. It took a lot of convincing to make it happen.

She pulls out the foil rectangle, glancing up at me. "Is this...?"

"Yes," I confirm, draping my napkin over my lap. "I've cleared it with Father, don't worry. The covenants allow a little leeway during your cycle." I drop my eyes pointedly to her drab attire. No Princess would be caught dead in something so pedestrian. "It's a statistical likelihood that PMS is giving you cravings."

She unfolds the foil without any hesitation, her green eyes lasering in on the candy. "God, I haven't had chocolate in *weeks*."

It's obscene and stupid, her taking a huge bite of the chocolate bar as a real dinner sits in front of her, waiting to be consumed. But my frown is decimated by the moan she makes, eyes sliding closed as her face slackens in ecstasy.

This.

This is where my dick would get hard.

I tuck my hand beneath my napkin and give it a squeeze, unsurprised at the lack of hardness, but no less frustrated. The way she eats that chocolate is familiar, the rush of sugar probably not so different from me craving another hit of scratch. I feel the urge all the time, craving the sudden euphoria, the feeling that my brain is wide open and that there's no stopping me from accomplishing anything I want.

Dusty, my group leader, says that I need to avoid stressors to be successful.

Good fucking luck.

But Verity isn't me. I watch her eat it slowly, as if she's savoring the taste. Her pink tongue swipes out against her pink lips, and not for the first time, I'm struck with a ripple of fascination, wondering what makes this girl tick. It's an idle thought that no one else would understand, this idea where I could maybe slice her open to inspect what's inside. Learn her secrets.

"You like sweets," I guess, cutting into my meat. She's obviously still pissed at me, but isn't willing to sacrifice an offered pleasure. A promising trait in a Princess.

She says, "Who doesn't?" but has only consumed two squares of it when she gently re-folds the foil, placing it back in the sachet. The longing in her eyes lingers as she sets it off to the side. She clearly wants to eat more, but she won't.

She's saving it for later.

Self-indulgent, but also disciplined.

"What else do you like?" I ask, spearing a carrot. When all she does is stare at me, I clear my throat. "Wicker mentioned something about gardening."

Her lip curls back disdainfully. "Are you making small talk?"

"It's not that small."

Her grin is sharp enough to cut. "I wouldn't know."

Sighing, I put down my fork, deciding to be honest. "Look, we don't have much longer to create. Whatever grudges we're all holding, we're going to have to set them aside and try harder." At the flash of indignation in her eyes, I bitterly concede, "*I'm* going to have to try harder."

I'd meant what I said to Bruce. For all that Verity might be a narc and a traitor, she treats her duty as Princess seriously. In some ways, that's more important than a Princess who's loyal.

"Whatever," she mutters, glancing at the chocolate once again. "It's not your fault you're not attracted to me."

Her words bring me up short, and I falter, shifting as my back prickles with a wave of biting itchiness. I'd said those things the other day in the heat of the moment, striking out as sharp as a lash, because I knew precisely how badly they'd sting.

"You and Wicker go at it a lot," I say, knowing the thought seems random when her brow knits with tension. "In all kinds of places, too. The second floor landing. The backseat. The library. Right here where I'm eating my dinner." The thought almost makes me pull a face, only I'm remembering the way her body jolts with his thrusts, her slender fingers scrabbling for purchase against the dark cherry wood of the table. Raising my gaze to hers, I say, "I watch the videos when I jerk off for the syringes."

Her mouth goes slack.

They're not exactly sexy videos, either. She's fully clothed for most of them, and she always looks troubled, even when her eyes get that glazed, needy look I've become so fixated with.

Her eyes don't look glazed right now. They widen, jumping up to the ceiling as she searches each corner for a camera she'll never see. The longer she tries, the tighter her teeth clench. "Is there any privacy in this house?"

"No." Snorting, I poke at a potato. "Not even for us."

Especially for us.

"So you like watching your brother fuck me. Great." She folds her arms, pinning me with a glare. "Something you and Pace have in common."

I can feel my patience for her attitude running thin, but I bat down the ire. "I like watching you get fucked," I correct. "And you weren't wrong before. Wicker doesn't put in enough effort when he does it. If it were me, I'd–" I clamp my teeth down on the thought.

But she looks at me with a challenge in her eyes. "You'd what?"

So I ease back a little, lowering my voice in the way I know she likes. "I'd peel your clothes off and take my time. Suck your tits until you're squirming. Eat your pussy until you're dripping down my chin. I'd make you come your brains out right before I fuck you, hard and slow."

There it is.

That dazed look glazes over her eyes as she wets her lips. "Hard and slow?"

I pitch forward, resting my elbows on the table as I rumble, "And deep, too. I bet you could take all of me, couldn't you? You'd probably want more, even. Three of my fingers in your mouth as I–"

"Stop," she suddenly says, her reddening cheeks pulling into a frown. "Why do you do this to me if you don't want—"

"Because I *do* want it," I snap, pushing away from the table in a move that makes me instantly wince. *Shit.* Fire rolls across my back, making my voice emerge in a harsh growl. "Jesus, I haven't had a good fuck in months, and suddenly there's a naked woman spread out on my exam table, moaning my goddamn name. I'm still a man. Of course I want it."

Hell, I want to fuck her right now. I wanted to fuck her the moment she walked into the room. When I wake up in the mornings, it's the first thing that pops into my head. When I go to sleep at night, it's to fantasies of how hard I'd nail her on my exam table if I could. She's not special or anything. Sure, she has a great rack and a pussy that's seared into my memory like the answers to an o-chem test, and every second I have to be in her presence without pushing her up against the nearest solid surface and drilling into her like a jackhammer is actual fucking torture, but she's not.

She's not special.

She watches me with a stunned expression. "Then what's the problem?"

I keep my breathing shallow as the pain recedes. "I got addicted to Scratch," I explain. It's not a secret or anything, but it still costs me something to give this up. A token of my weakness. My failure. "Something about it wreaked havoc on my endocrine system, and now..." I offer her a tight, joyless grin. "Well, let's just say those syringes you think so little of? They take hours out of my goddamn day to fill."

She blinks, confusion filling her eyes. "But that night when you were sleepwalking..." The pink of her cheeks deepens. "I... felt you."

"I don't remember. I never remember what happens when I'm asleep." Scowling, I make sure she registers the gravity in my voice when I add, "But I always remember the aftermath."

Never breaking my gaze, she touches her throat, four delicate fingertips brushing the spot I'd bruised. "Oh."

"I'm a monster on it, and a monster off, but only one won't leave my brain scrambled."

But after feeling her come on my fingers and wanting so bad for it to be on my cock, the urge to cave is so fucking strong.

I wipe my mouth before declaring, "Open your next gift."

I'd wanted to wait until dinner was finished, but I see now that it's necessary. Those delicate fingertips of hers reach for the golden ribbon, plucking it apart. If I'm honest, I've been shit at this. I don't know what Verity wants because I don't know *her*, and I don't care to.

But I think I've figured it out.

She doesn't want flowers or sparkly trinkets. She's a daughter of the West, and there are some things they value above all others. Loyalty. Tenacity. Strength. I attended Nick Bruin's first fight to become Duke. If romance *is* necessary, then it'll need to be given in a language she's familiar with.

Violence.

The second she opens the box, she's lurching from her seat, mouth gaping in horror as she clutches her chest. "Oh my god!" she gasps, the color bleeding from her cheeks. "What the f–that's a finger!"

"I got that for you," I explain, glancing at the severed digit, "to show you that you're safe here. We'll never let anyone treat our Princess with the disrespect he did." It's on a bed of golden satin, but the fingernail is dirty. I'd spent a ridiculous amount of time earlier wondering if I should clean it up, give it a little manicure, since it's a gift and all.

Maybe I should have, because her reaction is a bit of a letdown. Her face contorts as she looks closer, chest jumping with these panicked little hitches of breath. But then she pauses, eyes zeroing in on the silver ring attached to it. She mouths a name. "Bruce?"

"Yes," I confirm. Her gasps clip off, chest stilling as she approaches the box with a gleam of curiosity in her green eyes. I point out, "He hurt you."

"I–" Her eyes flick up to mine, flashing with the memory of something painful. "Yeah, he did."

Nodding, I reach out to close the box for her, getting the feeling that she won't want to touch it. "I need you to understand that I hurt people too, Verity." Sliding the box aside, I nod to her seat, waiting until she sits again. "I'm not him–I don't do it for pleasure. Bruce Oakfield was a job, and if you and I can't agree on anything else, then we at least see eye-to-eye on the fact he deserved it."

Her answer is immediate and clear. "We do." She might not thank me, but there's gratitude in her eyes, even if it's tinged with fear.

I hold her stare. "I'm incredibly skilled at what I do to people. Talented, even. When I'm awake, I know who to inflict it on." I gesture to the box. "But when I'm asleep, I don't. Things get... mixed up. Endorphins. Adrenaline. It doesn't mean I'm not," I chew the word out, "*deficient*. If anything, it's just more proof that I am."

Her throat clicks with a dry swallow, gaze dropping to her empty plate. "I shouldn't have said that about you. I didn't know."

I shift uncomfortably, noticing that she hasn't made even one move to fill her plate. "I've ruined your appetite."

But then she glances up, all coy and sweet through her lashes. Her mouth twitches with a reluctant, tense smile. "Would you think less of me if I said you didn't?"

I give the same grin back, picking up my fork. "The carrots are really good."

I should say something more, Danner would want me to, but

talking isn't something done in the Purple Palace. We speak in threats, by inflicting pain, and through deafening silences. But this one exchange gives me more insight into why Father may have chosen this girl to be Princess. She's strong. More so than any other girl that's walked through here lately and consequently failed. He wanted a victor and he had to go to the deepest, scrappiest parts of Forsyth to find someone that had what it takes to win–to *create*–and I'm going to have to do everything it takes to make that happen.

20

erity

THE LIBRARY IS extra quiet in the middle of the afternoon, most people opting to hang out in their dorms or still in classes. Wicker and I are sharing a plaid loveseat, his arm draped across the back of it, brushing against my shoulders. He has a book fanned open on his lap, but occasionally, I feel the twist of his fingers in my hair, the smallest tug to let me know he's still there.

Today is the first day he's so much as glanced at me since I started my period, but the sudden request–order, more like–to join him in the library for a study hour wasn't exactly a surprise. I'm nervous, struggling to focus on the quiz I'm taking on my laptop. It's Tuesday–*his* day–and he'd made it very clear that he wasn't going to sacrifice more than one of his days for the sake of my reproductive system.

I'm going to tell him no.

It's my right.

It'll probably start a huge fight, which I'm not crazy about. The past few days have been so quiet and calm. My Princes have been out of the house more than usual, which is saying a lot. The only time we're all together is during the ride to campus, and just from those quick moments, it's seemed like none of them really care about me, each man appearing absorbed in his own thoughts.

Something's wrong–I know that much. It's not all terrible. They're more civil when we're in public, and no one's sneaking up on me or forcing me on my knees since I've had my period all week. It's just... something's off. There's a quiet tension that they all share. Like something happened and I'm not privy to it. Lex is acting weirder than usual, carrying himself like he's hurt. Pace seems to be hiding, even when we're in the car together, his hood pulled up like a shield. And Wicker...

His finger gives a lock of my hair another twirl, making me tense. "Christ, would you relax? I'm not going to fuck you." When I slide my gaze to him, I find his eyes still trained on the book, a highlighter marking a passage. "Even though I'd be well within my rights."

"I'd tell you no."

His eyes tighten. "You'd try."

Sighing hard, I wonder, "Why are we here then?"

"People are talking. Speculating." His gaze lifts to a group of girls over by the study room, heads leaned in close as they whisper. "Gossiping." Just then, one of the girls looks toward us, flinching when she meets my glare.

Without the constant fear of having him bend me over a table, it's easier to settle into the role of Princess in public. When a group of students strolls by, I'm quick to lean against his shoulder, placing a hand on his knee.

Wicker adds, "We need to show them you're still in the game. You looked like shit during your offerings yesterday."

The Monday morning public offerings, I've found, are worse when I'm cramping, miserable, and burdened with the disappointment of being very much *not* pregnant in front of a group of men who are asking me to be.

"I think it went fine," I argue.

He scoffs. "Well, everyone else thinks you looked unhappy."

"Gee, I wonder why."

Quiet but scathing, he mutters, "You think you're the only one who has to put aside how you feel in order to play your part? I do it every goddamn day." He finally looks at me, those blue eyes blazing with annoyance. "Kiss me." When all I do is gape at him, his jaw grows taut. "*Now.*" Hearing the threat in his tone, I clench my fist and dip forward to press our mouths together.

It's instantly scorching.

His mouth parts, tongue delving between my lips in a skilled, sensuous lick. More than that is the way he touches me, his palm reaching up to cup my cheek as he guides the kiss deeper. I don't need to wonder how it must look to everyone else, because it even feels sweet, not a trace of his ire present when he retreats only to dive back in.

If kissing is an art, then Wicker Ashby is Picasso. He's so good at this, these soft, delicious kisses. If I were standing, I know my knees would be wobbling, and for a moment, I fall into the kiss like it's a bed of fucking rose petals.

And then I reach down to cup his erection.

If I'm expecting him to freeze, then I'm disappointed. He just pulls me closer, his tongue delving deeper around a low, hungry sound. The plan is to tease him—to make him suffer blue balls until his next appointed day—but instead, I find myself intrigued, squeezing the hard length beneath my palm and enjoying the way it makes him shudder. It's like having a remote in my hand. Pressure against the tip makes his thighs flex. A squeeze against the base makes his breathing hard and gritty.

He puts his hand over mine, and somewhere between long, slick loops of his tongue around mine, he pushes it down, grinding up into my grip.

And then he snatches it away, lacing our fingers together and *squeezing*, the bones in my fingers straining against the grip.

I flinch at the pain, whimpering.

He pulls back just far enough to stare into my eyes. "Don't push me, Red. There are a lot of places in this building where no cameras reach. Every second I don't have you bent over something, crying for mercy, is a goddamn gift."

He releases me with a smug, dazed look that I know is just for show. Across the room, the girls are staring at us with disappointed expressions.

They want to see me fail, I realize.

I focus back on my online quiz, answering the last two questions quickly. Suddenly, this loveseat is way too hot, sweat beading on the back of my neck. When everything is submitted, I close my laptop and dig out the journal where I've been taking notes for the solarium. I have a list of titles to look for in the horticulture section.

"Is it okay if I go look for some books?" I ask, sitting up.

Wicker curls the strand of my hair around his finger, as if I've forgotten I'm just a dog on a leash. "Stay close," he says. "We're leaving in thirty-minutes for practice."

"Both of us?" I wanted to spend some time in the solarium before dinner.

He nods. "You and Lex can watch for the first hour. Make an appearance."

"Put on a show," I translate, even though the prospect isn't quite as daunting when it's Lex on the other side of it. He might be cold and frighteningly intense, but at least I won't have to worry about him trying to fuck me.

"Call it what you want," Wicker mutters. "Danner will come to take you home for dinner."

I'm getting the distinct feeling that no one wants to go back to the Palace. "Fine. I won't be long." But I'll take whatever time I have looking for resources on restoring the garden. Danner pointed me to some notes left by a former gardener, which led me to the library catalog and a book on heirloom seed propagation that should be in the horticulture section. It's not a big genre here, just two rows on the far wall, and there are no windows back here, making it hard to read the spines.

Still, I pause when I hear muffled voices somewhere nearby.

Guess I'm not the only one interested in the subject.

I scan the books, pausing when I finally find the title. I hook my finger in the spine and pull it out.

"That's it, sweetheart. God, you feel so good."

I freeze, growing rapidly aware I've stumbled onto someone's hookup spot.

"Harder," a voice says. A female voice. It's low and breathy and... oddly? Familiar.

Quietly, I creep down the aisle and peek around the corner.

"Like that?" Tristian Mercer has Story–the Lady, Queen of South Side–pressed into a small alcove along the back wall. His pants are unbuttoned, the top curve of his defined ass exposed as he thrusts into her. One of Story's arms drapes over his shoulders, sharp painted nails digging into his crisp white shirt. The other is over her head, clutching at a shelf as her Lord's hand wraps around her black cuff.

"Yes," she hisses, but it's less affirmation of how deep he's going and more confirmation of how he's making her feel. "Yes. *Fuck* yes."

He watches her for a minute, eyes starry, until his head dips, swallowing a groan. His hand releases her wrist, sliding down to palm her breast. His motions grow more frantic, and he drops down, pressing tiny kisses against her chest.

"Come for me, sweetheart," he murmurs into her cleavage. "You know I like to feel you clenching around me."

At the first cries of her orgasm, I duck away, pressing my back against the bookshelf.

My reaction to the scene is physical. Heart pounding. Blood thrumming. Belly twisting. The first flicker of life in days. Seeing that? The way he took care of her?

I'm not just horny from watching it, I'm jealous.

I don't move for the longest moment, just listening as Tristian finds his release, and then the two of them fight to settle their breaths.

"I love you," I hear him say over the pounding in my ears.

"I love you, too." There's the rustle of fabric. "I'm going to go clean up. Meet you by the stairs?"

"Fuck, I'd meet you anywhere," he answers.

I don't move until they're gone, and when I step out of the stacks, I see her enter the bathroom. Tristian is already focused on his phone, and I'm out of sight of Wicker. I still double check, making sure no one is watching me before I follow her in.

Story's yanking paper towels out of the dispenser when I enter. Her cheeks have a pink, post-fuck glow, and her eyebrows rise when she sees me.

"Don't worry," I assure, palms raised. "I checked. No one saw me come in."

She relaxes, running a handful of paper towels under the sink. "Then can you look out for me?"

Nodding, I stand by the door, face coloring when she pulls up her skirt to wipe down her inner thighs.

"How have you been?" she asks, ducking her head to clean higher. I can't help but get a glimpse of her pussy, waxed and pink. No panties.

I pull my gaze up. "Okay. It's my period week. I get a little time off."

"Wait, you get time off on your period?" Her eyebrows shoot up her forehead. "God, my men love a bloodbath. I think it makes them hornier."

She balls up the paper towels and I grab some more, wetting them and handing them to her. "It's in the covenants. Trust me, they're not happy about it. Especially Wicker."

She snorts. "I bet. The fuckboys always take it the worst." Her eyes land on my stomach. "Shit. I guess that means you're not pregnant."

"Unfortunately, no." I gesture to the paper towels. "You need another one?"

"Just to dry off." I pull them out and give her a couple. "You sound disappointed you're not pregnant already."

Sighing, I fold my arms, glad to have someone else to talk to. Family dinner isn't for two more days. "It means I have another month of scheduled sex, at least. It's just so exhausting. And *frustrating*. These last few days have been the first restful nights I've had yet."

She dries off and smooths her skirt down. "Lack of sleep definitely makes everything worse. Killian Payne hasn't given me a solid night's rest in over a year. Now I'm ready for it, like I take naps and stuff, but at the beginning..." She looks at me a bit too closely, and I wonder if she's seeing how worn down I am. How I'm losing control. "Verity, I know it's not easy. Talk to me. Tell me what's going on."

I weigh my words. I've signed a contract that forbids me to talk about what happens in the Palace. I'm also not allowed to speak to any other frats, especially women. But I'm struggling. Mentally and physically and if something doesn't give, I'm not sure I'll survive the next month.

"When I agreed to this, the thought of not getting pregnant was a pretty bright prospect. Now that I'm in the house, acting as Princess..." I bite my lip, wondering if I'm going to sound crazy. "This place–or maybe the Royalty, I don't know–it all has this way of blinding you, doesn't it? Like even though the last thing I want to do is bring another life into this fucked up world, day-to-day, it's all I can think about. I can't tell if I want it or if I just need to want it, in order to get by."

She watches me with a pensive frown. "Get by? Are they that bad?"

"Yes," I answer, unequivocally.

Her head tilts curiously. "I thought Princes were... you know. Sweet."

Propping a hand on my hip, I reply, "Yeah, well, arsenic can be sweet if you put it into a milkshake."

Her eyes darken, and she steps forward, pinning me with a serious look. "If we need to pull you out of there, we can. You're not pregnant yet. They might come for you, but not for long."

I stop her before she begins scheming. "I don't want to quit, Story." Looking her in the eye, I raise my chin. "I want to win."

After a moment of assessing me, she snorts. "Wow, you really are West End, aren't you?"

"I saw you out there," I finally say, embarrassed to admit it. "With your Lord."

She grimaces. "Shit. Sorry. Tris... he's super into the public stuff. It makes it worse when his father pays for all the buildings and he thinks he owns them. I figured no one would be in the heirloom seed corner of the horticulture section."

Wringing my hands, I begin, "I didn't mean to—I was looking for a book and, well, you were just there, and..."

"And what?" she asks, facing the mirror and running her fingers through her hair.

"Is it always like that for you?" I swallow, feeling my cheeks burn. "Like... do they always get you off?"

"Like it's their job." Her forehead creases. "Your Princes don't?"

I slide my eyes to the door. "Not really."

She looks stumped. "Why the hell not?"

"There's nothing in the covenants about my pleasure," I explain, eyes rolling. "And if it's not in the covenants..."

"Do you want them to," she asks. "Get you off?"

Leveling her with a look, I repeat, "Day-to-day, Lady. You told him you love him. How? How do you love a man who did that to you?" I nod at her chest.

She follows my gaze, a shadow falling over her features. "I don't love them because of this, and I don't love them in spite of it, either." Her fingertips brush over the scar between her breasts. K. One of her Lords' initials. "I love them because this changed us. All of us. It's really complicated."

"I'm not judging, I just–" I rub my forehead, trying to find the words. "They hurt you, and they put that leash on you." I point to her wrist cuff. "How do you get past that? How do you get to the point where you're fucking in a library and he's giving you amazing orgasms?"

Her head snaps back in surprise. "Is that what you want? For your Princes to love you?"

"No." I fight off a laugh, because after this first month, I don't think they're capable of loving anyone but themselves, and maybe each other. "I just don't want to be miserable all the time. And if we're going to have sex this much, maybe it could be a little less that," I nod at her scars, "and a little more *that*." I jab my thumb in the general direction of the horticulture section.

She looks at me in the mirror's reflection. "I've heard stories about the Ashby brothers. Unless they're massively exaggerated, those boys know what they're doing in bed."

"They hate me," I explain. "They hate being Princes. They all see it as some kind of punishment, and then—"

Her eyes clear. "They take it out on you."

"Yes."

"Of course they do." She rolls her eyes. "And what about you? What do you do?"

Smiling bitterly, I spread my arms. "I take it like a good little Princess."

Her answer is immediate. "Then you're going to lose." She turns, perching on the porcelain sink. "I need to ask you something important now. Chances are, you won't be sure how to answer."

Frowning, I say, "Shoot."

"Is there anything in these guys worth saving?" she asks, eyes serious. "Redeeming qualities? Moments where you looked at them and thought 'if only things were different?'"

No.

That's the word that comes up my throat, sharp like a reflex. Only I remember my dinner with Lex the other night. How his eyes shone with such earnest determination as he promised to never let anyone hurt me the way Bruce did. I think of Pace and his bird, and the way he talks to her, so sweet and soft.

Glancing at Story, I confess. "Maybe."

She nods, some of the tension in her shoulders loosening. "Then here's my advice. This isn't a sappy romcom, Verity. It's Forsyth. Royal men talk a big game about wanting submission and obedience, but you know what they really want?" She props her palms on the edge. "They want a partner. Someone who can match them. It's why they always run three or four deep. Once they find someone they can trust–someone who gets them–they don't let that person go. It's hard to find in this town."

"I'm not a bystander here." I lift my shirt and push down my skirt, revealing one of Wicker's old, yellowing bruises. "I do my duties. They have no interest in me other than being an object to rut against."

She purses her lips. "The only way to survive this is by taking control of your own life—yes, within the parameters of the system, but control nonetheless. You think our men fell for me and Lav just by us going through the motions?"

I don't know much about Story and her Lords, but I know Lavinia didn't just accept her position as Duchess. There were a lot of ups and downs. Sy never wanted her at all. Nick saw her as more of a pet than a person. Remy was so caught up in his mental illness he didn't know what was real or not. For them to get where they are now, Lavinia had to prove herself to them.

"No," I admit.

Her eyes soften. "Things were terrible when I first came into the brownstone. I knew these guys. We had a history, and it wasn't a good one. I was desperate and out of options. Although I agreed to it, I knew I couldn't take their abuse day in and day out, so the first thing I did was start being their Lady." She holds up a finger. "Not *a* Lady. *Their* Lady."

"How?"

She shrugs. "Little things, like... well, Killian likes it when I wear his jersey with his name and number on it." She taps the letter on her chest. "Marking his territory is kind of his thing. He is a Lord, after all. Dimitri likes it when I listen to him play the piano. And Tris? He's fulfilled when he's taking care of me. I stopped fighting every single thing, and they eased up."

My face screws up. "By caving?"

"By playing the game, honey." Her arms cross over her chest, making her tits push up. "Do you know the pressure these guys are under? Like *really* under, as Royals? Their Kings are breathing down their necks, unless they kill them. Then they *become* them. They've got dozens of soldiers, employees, and businesses to run, all while trying to carve out a little space in life to just be who they are, if they even can find out who that is. It clearly sounds like your guys already think you're a burden. Letting them set all the terms isn't going to make any of this easier on you."

"So you think I should... what? Romance them?" I take a deep breath. "I'm not sure I even know how to do that."

"Verity, your mother raised you to be a house girl. You grew up around the Dukes and their Duchesses. Don't tell me you have no idea how to make a man feel important."

I point out, "The Dukes aren't anything like the Princes."

She snorts. "They're Royal men, and all of them have three things in common. They're fueled on ego, nursing trauma from growing up in this godforsaken system, and always thinking with their dicks." She squeezes my arm. "*All* of them. Figure out how to meet those needs and I bet they'll start meeting yours."

"Okay." I nod, trying to work out what that even looks like. "I hear what you're saying."

She grins. "Good. I have faith in you, Ver. You'll figure this out."

Kissing me on the cheek, she walks out of the bathroom, leaving me alone and reeling from her words.

She's right. I can't just be a Princess. Not if I want to survive.

I need to be *their* Princess.

∿

FAMILY DINNER on Thursday is even more uncomfortable than usual. It's bad enough that I've become a figurehead of a rival house, but tomorrow night is going to be impossibly worse.

Remy sits across from me, drawing a large gargoyle on Lav's forearm, when he pauses and holds the marker out to me. "Here you go, Princess."

I look at the marker. "What's that for?"

"I figure you can go ahead and draw a template of my victory tatt. Save some time."

I glance at Lav, hoping she has a clue as to what he's talking about. Remy's not known for coherency. She just shrugs. "I'm going to need a little more, Rem. What are you talking about?"

"No fucking way your boy takes me out tomorrow night." He points to a spattering of stars on his ribs–one for each victory since becoming Duke. I shift uncomfortably, reminded of the stick and poke ink Pace showed me of his day tallies in prison. Remy smirks. "I know he's your Prince and all, but I've still got to stomp him."

"My Prince?" The conversation slams home how disconnected I've been the past few weeks. I hadn't even thought about one of the Princes taking a turn at the Fury, and the Princes have been so occupied that we've barely spoken. "Um, which one is fighting?"

"The felon," Nick says, licking banana pudding off a spoon. "He's up for an ass kicking. Long deserved if you ask me."

Pace.

I frown down into my own dessert. "Not sure you should count him out just yet. I've seen him play hockey. He's fast and strong." And ruthless and calculated and *mean*.

"Please, those guys are all padding and fiddling with sticks." Remy rolls his eyes. "They wear *helmets*, for Christ's sake."

"I don't know, Rem," Ballsack chimes in from down the table, "with the number of concussions you've had over the years, you may need a helmet too."

Remy points the marker at him. "That's rich coming from the dumbass who got himself trapped in the Princes' basement."

Ballsack's expression floods with outrage. "Hey! I got ambushed. That wouldn't have happened if—"

"Anyway," Lavinia says loudly, catching my eye. She's been quieter than usual tonight, an odd sadness swimming in her eyes. "That means you'll be here for sure tomorrow night, right?"

Thinking, I guess, "Probably." Especially if we're needing to stop any gossip going around. The thought captures me and I realize people are going to be salivating for the drama of this fight. No doubt attendance will rival even Nick's first match as Duke.

Lavinia grins. "Who would've thought six months ago, the two of us would be on opposing sides of the ring, supporting our men during their fights."

"Fuck," Nick says, eyes darting between us, "tell me this means you'll get in a catfight or something mid-match. These matches always lack a little girl-on-girl action if you ask me."

"No one is asking you," Lavina says.

"Hair pulling," Remy adds. "Tit slapping. Maybe a thong wedgie?"

"Leave them alone," Sy says, arm loping around Lav's neck. "No one is touching the Duchess' tits but us. And anyway, Verity's the Princess now. I'm pretty sure Ashby would lose his mind if she got in a brawl."

Every eye at the table darts to my stomach.

"Stop looking at my uterus," I say, slowly rising. "I'm not getting in a girl fight with Lavinia just to entertain you." I shoot Remy a look. "And a little advice? Don't underestimate my Princes. They're far more vicious than they look."

I grab my plates and shove my chair under the table.

"You mad?" Remy asks, brows knitted up. "You know we're just fooling. I promise not to hurt the felon's babymaker."

I shake my head. "I'm not mad. I just need..." I jerk my thumb toward the lounge. "Excuse me."

I cross the gym, making note of my mother's closed office door and the drawn shades. Danner slowly shuffles behind me, keeping me in sight.

"I'm going to the ladies' room again," I tell him.

He dips his head. "I'll be here if you need me."

I step inside and inhale the scent of hairspray, perfume, and body lotion. The girls are all out still eating, buying me a little time. Lavinia should be here in three... two... one.

The door swings open, and she struts through, latching it tightly behind her.

"Bruce is dead," I blurt, wringing my hands.

She freezes, eyes hardening. "Really?"

I nod. "It happened on Sunday, I think. I wasn't sure if the Dukes had been notified, or if they'd even tell you."

"Maybe not." She leans up against a wardrobe, its sparkly contents strewn about. "There's been a lot of disturbing news around here lately."

"What's up?" I ask, once again noticing the pall over her.

She releases a sigh, rolling her head toward me. "You know I set that explosion off, right? In North Side?"

"The one that killed your dad?"

She nods, lowering her gaze. "Turns out my father's property wasn't quite as deserted as I thought. Someone I know got caught up in it, and I just found out last week that he's really hurt."

I gape at her. "Shit. Lav..." We all heard the reports, but none of them mentioned any survivors. "Who was it?"

She meets my gaze, mouth twisting. "Cash Mallis." I know him better as Cash Money, but I know him all the same. As one of North Side's most prolific drug dealers, Cash is loved and hated in equal measure. Frowning, she goes on, "I know I chose my side and Cash chose his, and a lot of people in this town are happy to see him sidelined and not selling Scratch. But..." Lav toes at a spot of glitter on the floor. "He's not a bad guy, you know? He just never had good choices."

I remind her, "You didn't know he was there."

"I didn't care." She meets my gaze with a frankness I'm not expecting. "Don't get me wrong, I don't regret it. I just wish I'd been a little more careful." Averting her eyes, she adds, "The Dukes won't let me see him," which I am expecting. Cash is a Scratch dealer, and he's also North Side–not to mention, possibly pissed at her. If anything, I'm glad her Dukes said no. People like Cash ruin lives.

But the grief in her eyes brings me up short of saying so.

"Maybe someone can pass a message," I point out. "Where is he exactly?"

"Last I heard, he was getting released from the burn center." Just then, her head snaps up, eyes widening. "Lex interns in the surgical unit sometimes, doesn't he? Maybe you can–"

I raise my hands. "The Princes have me locked down. I can't even sleep in my own bed without being watched."

She pauses, head tilting. "That's not hyperbole, is it?" When I shake my head, she snorts. "Jesus."

"Also, I wouldn't be so quick to call Cash sidelined." I lift an eyebrow. "I overheard in a PNZ meeting that Scratch is still all over East End."

Her head jerks back in surprise. "Who's slinging it?" I shrug and she deflates, dropping her head back against the wall. "God, this has been a shitty week."

"Pretty much."

Wincing, she says, "Shit, here I am whining about my problems and you're..." She gestures vaguely toward my stomach. "Story said she talked to you. How are things in the Palace?"

"All is quiet on the Eastern front." No one's really bothered me since Wicker's little performance in the library. After a moment, I look up, casually mentioning, "Lex gave me Bruce's severed finger as a gift."

Lavinia blinks at me for a suspended moment. "To anyone else, a horrific side note. To me, a Thursday." Brows rising, she asks, "So he likes you?"

"Definitely not." Scoffing, I explain, "Lex is the leader. He stays on task and feels responsible for everything. If my Princes were a crown, he'd be those little comb things in the back, holding it on."

The smile that touches her lips is the first genuine one I've seen on her tonight. "I have one of those, too."

It takes me a second to admit, "Sometimes he's really scary, but other times..."

She gives me a slow, sly grin. "Really, who among us can resist the charm of being given your enemy's severed finger?"

A little too lightly, I wonder, "What did you do with yours?"

"I threw it back in Nicky's face." Her smile widens. "But Remy's anatomy drawing professor has this tank of beetles that cleans bones, so he put it in there for a few days, bleached them, and then mounted it in our entryway." Her brow ticks up. "A warning to the others."

"Naturally."

"What did you do with yours?" she asks.

"I buried it in the woods behind the Palace."

"Nice."

After a beat, I note, "We have really weird conversations."

She laughs, and it's a warm sound, filled with an undercurrent of happiness. "Just wait until it's a severed head."

I grimace. "Did he mount that in the entryway too?"

"Living room."

I can't help but laugh. "That has some nice irony to it."

"Remy thought so."

FRIDAY IS the first time I've ever been slightly bummed to see my period go.

The week has been energizing, though. Perspective. That's what I think about as I watch every frat get flattened by DKS from up in the balcony. My former club is on a tear, including Ballsack, who has jumped on the ropes, arms raised to the crowd in victory, while some poor kid from LDZ peels himself off the mat.

Ballsack's match is the last one before the intermission, directly preceding the main event: Pace Ashby vs. Remington Maddox.

"Tucker, get your ass off the mat!" a voice shouts. I look across the room and see Dimitri Rathbone leaning over the railing, shouting to the flattened frat boy below. Since Killian is King now, they have the right to sit with the others. Sy could too, I suppose, but those boys love the raucous energy from the stands.

Story sits next to her King, his massive tattooed arm wrapped around her shoulder, holding her close. He whispers something in her ear, and she smiles, genuine and content. She must sense my attention, because her eyes flick up and meet mine for a beat, and I can hear her words in my head. *"They want a partner. Someone who can match them."*

I'm wearing one of the approved outfits from the closet, tagged specifically for Friday Night Fury. White jeans paired with a soft, purple V-neck sweater. Appropriate but sexy, the colors representative of our house. I definitely look the part, even if I don't feel it.

My eyes dart away before anyone notices the exchange, and they land on the Baron King, mask affixed, a pretty girl sitting on his lap. The box next to him is empty. There are no Counts left to fill it. Theirs isn't the only empty box. Ashby hasn't shown up yet.

Or I thought he hadn't.

"Unseemly, isn't it?"

My heart lunges to my throat at his voice, memories of my throning rushing back like frigid, brackish water. I feel the anxiety in my gut. Did he notice Story looking at me? Could he read our minds? I put nothing past these men.

I force myself to turn.

"King Ashby." I lower into an awkward and unnecessary curtsey. "I didn't know you were here."

He moves next to me and takes in the view. "I've been watching you up here."

Freezing, I wonder if it was wrong of me to climb the stairs to the loft. A good Princess would have probably been sitting up in the VIP box with her King. "I... I was just—"

"Observing. Yes. I like to do it myself. Getting a lay of the land." He gestures to the Lords across the ring. "A good leader always knows where his opponents are." I've seen his security set up in Pace's room. This man has more eyes than a nest of spiders. He stands in his crisp white suit, eyes moving over the crowd. He's wearing an expression that drips with distaste. "I've never been much for fighting. It's a waste of a good figurehead to have him down there, using his fists. In East End, we fight with our minds. Our legacies."

Or your wallets.

"It's tradition," I say, following his gaze to where Wicker is disappearing through the doors to the back.

"It's beneath us," he argues. Even though his voice is mild and contemplative, it still makes me tense. One should never argue with their King, which makes his next words all the more stress-inducing. "I was disappointed to learn you weren't successful this cycle, Princess."

My fingers tighten around the railing. "I'm sorry, sir."

Ashby gives a bland hum. "I'm aware that the circumstances weren't exactly ideal. If anyone's apologizing, it should be me–for failing to give you Princes who understand the way to a woman's womb. They weren't bred for Royalty, you see." He meets my gaze, a shiver of disgust rolling down my spine at the gleam in his eyes. "It's divine irony that creation is a young man's game. The same youth responsible for their virility also makes them ill-equipped to wield it. I'll be more present this go around. Make sure that my boys are doing their part."

The thought makes me recoil in such a primal, fundamental way that I have to clench down the urge to physically shudder. There's no way to read those words that doesn't invoke repulsion.

"That won't be necessary," I rush out, surging with a shocking flare of defensiveness. Not for myself, but for them. "My Princes and I are going to make it work."

"I hope you're right," he says, not looking very assured. "Am I to understand that the creation schedule will resume soon?"

Recognizing this as a roundabout way of asking whether or not I'm done bleeding, I shift uncomfortably. "Er... yes, sir."

My period stopped last night.

I haven't told anyone yet.

"Excellent." There's an odd shift to his eyes. "It hasn't escaped my notice that you've been spending time in the solarium during your... break."

I freeze, the tickle of panic stealing my breath. I force out, "I have. I hope that's not a problem. Danner said—"

He waves his hand. "It's not a problem at all. On the contrary, I think it's delightful to have a Princess breathing life back into such a barren place." Despite the encouragement, there's a tightness to his grin that makes me nervous. "If there's anything you need—tools, seeds, labor—call on Danner to use my accounts."

I nod. "Thank you. I'll do that."

Then, startlingly, he reaches out to press the back of his hand against my cheek. I go stock still, breath trapped in my lungs as he rests it there for a suspended moment. "You're such a good girl, Verity. So poised and obedient. I knew you were the right choice."

The words fall from my lips like bile. "I'm here to serve." His eyebrow rises and I make the addendum. "I'm here to create."

"There's no better child than one born from duty." His smile is unnerving as he pushes a curl behind my ear, gaze falling to my belly.

"Then I should do mine," I say, springing back with wide, panicked eyes. "I'm going to go wish my Prince luck in his fight."

Luckily, Ashby just chuckles. "I suppose it's one of the better aspects of this tradition," he says, nodding toward the ring. "Go on, then. Give my boy something worth fighting for. A win tonight would be fortuitous to us all, don't you think?"

I can't escape fast enough, my heart hammering as I jog down the rickety steps. There's been this fear in my mind—more like a calculation—that Rufus Ashby may be the type of King who takes liberties with his house girls. Up until now, I haven't felt it from him. If anything, Ashby has treated me a little like a well-groomed Pomeranian.

But perhaps he's getting impatient. Perhaps—I allow the

shudder to roll over me now–he's willing to take matters into his own hands.

His praise prickles in my ear like thorns.

Poised.

Obedient.

Good.

I don't stop, pushing through the crowds at the concessions stand, gliding past couples making out against the walls, ducking around people not-so-discreetly dealing Scratch in the corners. I finally make it to the back hallway where Danner stands ever silent and stoic.

"Princess," he greets me.

"Sir." I stop in front of him, catching my breath. "I have a favor to ask."

The way Danner straightens is almost imperceptible. "I am, as ever, at your service."

I inhale, hating that it's Pace's fight—Pace's day. He'll be the hardest to crack. Taking a deep breath, I begin, "How fast do you think you can drive?"

THE THING about the gym is that it's so much more than a gym.

I basically grew up in the back halls, to the scent of sweat and adrenaline, the sounds of grunting and flesh-on-flesh. But there was also laughter. Men, five times my size, happy to lift me into the ring to play-spar with me, pretending to be taken down at the smallest nudge, falling over as if they'd been shot. Cutsluts a decade older than me, lifting me onto the vanities and curling my hair into red ringlets. Family dinners, always raucous and warm. There was paperwork for my mom, filing and scheduling. I never had to be asked to clean up at the end of the day, I just picked up the broom and got to work.

Because the gym was home.

As I walk through the back halls, that's what I feel. It's a comfort

I'll never feel inside the Purple Palace, and I hold it close, letting it lift my chin, square my shoulders. *Poised.* Ever since I stepped foot in East End, something has felt askew inside of me, but right now, it's right where it should be.

Because this is my turf.

I may not know how to act like a Princess, but I do know how to support my man at a Friday Night Fury.

There's a stutter to the sound of the crowd when I push through the doors, but I don't pause long enough to see their reactions. My gaze is trained on the ring ahead and I strut up the crimson carpet to where my Princes are waiting, Wicker and Lex by the corner Pace is sitting in.

The one time Whitaker Ashby gave me an orgasm was right after I slammed a frying pan into a girl's head for flirting with him at a party. That, and the need to claim me in public, ignited something in Wicker that's been lost these last few weeks. If Story and Lavinia are right, I'm the one in control.

I can change it.

It takes them a long time to even notice me, Pace's gaze fixed to his black high-tops as he tightens the laces. He's still wearing his sweater, hood pulled up, head down. His brothers are ducked close together, seemingly discussing strategy. Lex points to the center of the ring as Wicker shakes his head, turning to gesture at something.

Blue eyes skate over me and then snap back, Wicker's arm suspended halfway in the air. It drops slowly, and I see more than hear him say, "Holy fuck."

Lex sees me next, his amber eyes zeroing in on my breasts, which are covered by two sparkly purple triangles that don't leave a lot to the imagination. The bikini top is paired with something that can only barely be called jean shorts. They're ripped, frayed, and probably showing the entire bottom half of my ass cheeks, which are covered only with the pair of fishnet stockings I'm wearing underneath.

The final piece of the outfit is the tiara Ashby himself gifted me.

Rushed here by a very befuddled Danner, it sits proudly atop my head, my hair having been hastily pulled into two french braids.

The eyes of the crowd follow me as I approach the ring, struggling to keep my stride confident and unhurried. Although I've watched hundreds of matches, I've never been a proper ring girl. My mother never let me wear anything that may have given the slightest hint that I was anything other than virginal.

I almost falter when I see her—Mama B—across the ring. She's looking at me with such barely-restrained fury that I feel the immediate instinct to hide.

I don't.

I waltz up to my Princes and say, "Almost ready?"

It's only then that Pace looks down from his seat, his black eyes freezing as they see me.

Lex is the first to speak, the dazed shock disappearing from his gaze. "What the fuck are you doing," he growls, grabbing my arm.

"I'm being your Princess," I answer, not allowing myself to be cowed.

"A Princess would never dress like that." His gaze travels my body, and then he huffs, shrugging out of his jacket. "You look like one of those gutter rats out there. Cover yourself."

But when he goes to drape the jacket over my shoulders, Wicker's hand shoots out, pushing it away. "Hey, let's not be hasty here. I mean..." His blue eyes drop to my chest, tongue darting out to wet his lips. "I can always peel them off her later. How many hours 'til midnight?"

His words hang heavily in the air, because there's no question as to what I'm putting out here.

My break is over.

"Stop," I tell them, unsurprised at the conflicted reaction. I shoot Wicker a glare. "This isn't for you." Then shift to Lex. "*Or* you. I'm dressed to support our fighter." I lift my chin at Pace, meeting his intense gaze. "You ready?"

There's a long moment where he just stares back at me, his jaw tensing and untensing.

And then he reaches out, offering me his hand.

Relieved, I slip my hand into his, letting him lift me up into the ring. As I feel the heat of him, I try to remember that these men, for better or worse, are mine. That's what I'm thinking about as I stand before Pace. He's so tall that I have to tilt my head back to gaze into his stony expression.

"Nervous?" I ask, my own nerves shining through.

"About Maddox?" He scoffs, glancing at Remy across the ring. "Nah." His gaze returns to me, eyebrow arching. "Are you?"

"I know whose side I'm on tonight."

The corner of his mouth ticks up, but his eyes narrow with suspicion. "You even managed to say that with a straight face."

"Because I mean it." I see that now. A win for DKS is a loss for us.

All four of us.

The astonishment in his eyes when I strain up on my toes to press our mouths together is seared into my memory long after he finally reacts, his arm winding around my waist. He parts his lips to greet my tongue, licking into my mouth with a slow, sensual abandon. Behind us, the sound of PNZ members cheering swells, but I barely hear it over the rush of blood in my ears. Pace makes a low, hungry sound, yanking me up against his body as the kiss deepens. It's hard and unhurried, his fingertips digging into my flesh as he crushes me against him.

My eyes flutter open when he tears away, pulling the zipper to his hoodie and shrugging it off. Lex catches it when he tosses it aside, his dark eyes never leaving me.

"I want you ready for me," he says, "after the match."

I stare at him for a moment, taking in the hardness of him. Everything is solid, like he's carved from stone: the muscles lining his stomach and chest. The chiseled curve of his biceps, covered in a mixture of crude and intricate ink. I understand that they're marks that document his life in days, weeks and years. Much like Da Vinci's David, Pace Ashby took years to transform into the person before me.

Raising my chin, I reply, "If you win."

It's not challenge that sparks in his eyes, but instead, a sharp comprehension. Win or lose, I'm his to fuck tonight. There's nothing I can do about that.

But only I get to choose what kind of woman they're fucking.

21

P ace

THERE'S no anger in the fight for me.

There never has been. The first time Father put me into a room with a man twice my age and ordered me to hit him, I didn't know what to do. The guy was tied up, already bloody and haggard. He looked at me with a glint of a plea in his eyes. Had nothing against the guy–a banker, if I remember correctly–and I couldn't call any emotion up to put behind the force of my fist. I tried imagining the man was Father himself, but even back then, I knew that was a dangerous habit to get into.

I was twelve by the time I learned that feeling nothing at all was the most efficient way to hurt.

Wicker could never do it. Too hot-headed, driven by his impulses. Lex could–and does–but he's not one for the physicality of fists, preferring his hurt to come from the edge of a blade. The void is more effective than anger or hatred or showmanship. The

Dukes wouldn't get that. They think a man needs fire in his chest to inflict violence, but I know the truth of it.

Pain hurts more when it's empty.

My ears ring with the clang of the bell rattling against metal. It's loud, reverberating shrilly through the gym, but nothing compared to the roar of the crowd as the referee yanks my arm in the air and calls the fight.

The downside? Coming out of the void is like being thrown into a pit of needles. Every nerve sparks to life, sensation barrelling through my chest in an avalanche of shock. My heart pounds from exertion, my limbs heavy, knuckles burning. The rush of winning —of beating a Duke—is lost in the roar of the crowd.

But they don't think I've won. Not from the cacophony of boos bouncing off the metal rafters.

"Get him the fuck out of here!" someone shouts. From the back comes a loud, outraged accusation: "Cheater!"

I look around, sweat dripping to my eye, the taste of copper on my tongue. There's nothing but anger, building, *pulsing*, in the stands as I drop the switchblade. Yeah, I'd brought a knife. So what? Remington Maddox's palm is pushed into his side as blood sluggishly flows between tattooed fingers.

A red-faced DKS member is ranting, "Princes are pussies! Can't even fight with their own fists. What's wrong, worried about ruining your manicure?"

Everyone but the section reserved for PNZ is shouting down my win. Loudest of all is Remy Maddox, who despite having just been slashed, stands on the ropes with a maniacal grin, teeth white with blood, encouraging the crowd.

"Maddox! Maddox! Maddox!" they chant. Beloved even in a loss. I see his blue-haired Duchess rush into the ring with a towel, her eyes wide and concerned as she attempts to triage him. He doesn't let her get farther than pressing the towel to his wound before he captures her mouth in a bloody kiss.

That's what greets me when I surface.

The dull, throbbing sense of a loss.

I look up into the glare of lights where I know the Kings are sitting. Father, if he's still up there, is nothing but a shadow. A shadow that creeps around the edges, judging, because he won't care that I won the match.

He'll berate me for losing the war.

My heartbeat shifts, faster as the crowd throbs, crushing against the elevated ring. My hands numb, the only feeling is a tremor running through them.

"Pace," Lex says, hand on my shoulder. The contact jolts me out of my haze and I turn, squeezing through the ropes and off the mat, escaping the pandemonium.

I slam into Wicker, and he grabs my hand, clenching our fists together. "That was fucking amazing." His smile instantly falls when he meets my gaze. "Hey, man, you good?"

"No." Panting, I don't stop, only vaguely taking in the way his arm snakes protectively around Verity's bare waist. Those green eyes clock me. What does she see? A victor? A Prince? Or the empty-eyed felon who just shanked her precious Duke?

This whole fight was a mistake.

When it's the three of us down in the dungeon, my brothers know to give me time to come out of it. Space. Quiet. But those are jobs, and this is entertainment. People are everywhere, watching, crowding, pressing. Everything's too loud and unbearably bright, every sensation jacked up to eleven.

Grabbing Verity's arm, I yank her out from under Wicker and flee.

Beneath the pulse of panic and pain, I can still feel the memory of her mouth before the fight. The way she kissed me, her lips soft, tongue hot and slick against mine. I had to empty the feeling out before the match, but it comes rushing back in like a tidal wave. The way her body felt pressed to mine as she tasted me back is exactly what I've been searching for all this time–ever since the first time I saw her picture.

Mine.

"Pace," she huffs, stumbling over those fuck-me heels.

Blindly, I point myself in the direction of a door and march toward it, aware of her footsteps rushing beside me. I don't even know where I'm going, driven purely by the instincts I'd cut off while in the ring. They point me down the hall and I rush to follow, shoving through doors until I find it.

It's a broom closet, small and dark and quiet.

She stumbles as I halt, and I jerk her upright, slam my hand into the door, and toss her inside. I dive in after her like it's my fucking salvation, and maybe it is, because the second I shut myself inside, I feel the tickle of comfort at the rim of my awareness.

Unfortunately, she starts a breathless, panicked ramble. "I didn't mean to upset you with this. I did it to be supportive. For real. And that shit with Remy out there—he's just trying to save face. You beat him. No one beats Remington Maddox. He's—"

I slam my mouth over hers to shut her up, her voice as sharp as razor wire in my ears. I feel more than see her freeze, and she's probably drawing a conclusion that's all wrong. It doesn't matter that she thinks I brought her in here to fuck her. It only matters that she adjusts accordingly, winding her soft arms around my neck as I plunge my tongue between her lips.

My hands curl behind her neck, holding her still, kissing her the way she kissed me. Pressing my body into hers the way she pressed into mine. My cock grows hard, the panicked hammering in my heart shifting to sudden, pounding lust.

I go with it, because if I'm going to be ruthlessly assaulted by *feeling*, then it might as goddamn well be a good one.

With my tongue in her mouth and hands on her hips, I guide her back until she knocks into a shelf. A gasp leaves her, and my hands push at her top, greedy for her tits. They fall out, heavy and perfect, and I flatten my palm over one, causing her back to arch.

"What's that saying?" I ask her, dipping my head down to lick her nipple.

Her breath hitches. "Saying?"

I pin her with my hips, my cock drilling into her belly. "The one your fucking Dukes always say after a win." I pause over her tits, wanting to hear her say it.

Her chest rises and falls. "To the victor go the spoils."

A shudder rolls through me, fingers digging into her flesh, because I did it–I won her.

Fucking *finally*, she's mine.

I reach between us to pop the button on her shorts, impatient fingers ripping the zipper down. She moves with me, shimmying as I shove them down her hips. But when I claw at the stockings, her hand lands over mine. "Wicker actually might kill you if you shred these fishnets."

There's a careful, testing levity in her voice that I muster up the effort to match. "He probably bought you a dozen more before the first round was even over." Yanking one and then the other, the tights fall down her legs. "When he wins, he can do whatever the hell he wants. But tonight, you're mine. I won you." I drop my shorts, releasing my erection. "Say it."

There's only a short pause before she obeys. "You won me," she replies, and there's not enough light to make out all the details in her expression, but I hear the wetness as she licks her lips. "I'm yours."

My response is instant, pushing her up on the shelf to spread her legs. The crotch of her panties is already damp when I grab it, yanking it aside. A thin layer of hair is growing back on her pussy, and I grip my balls when I feel it. It's not so much the hair, but the knowledge that she follows orders that makes my cock surge with a sudden rush of precum.

I push into her before it's wasted.

She's torturously slick, her heat engulfing my cock as I slam forward, basking in her stunned gasp. Her fingers scrabble at my biceps, thighs widening to make room for me. "Oh," she breathes, pussy clamping tight around my dick. She says it in this tone, as if someone just told her the secret to the universe. Maybe she's disappointed in my unwillingness to drag this out for hours, pushing her to the brink and dragging her back again.

I don't care.

I press my sweaty forehead to hers and fuck her like she's mine, inhaling her little gasps as my hips punch into hers. The thrusts are short and sharp, more punishing than I mean for them to be. She winds her legs around my waist and holds on, a stack of something heavy and soft tumbling from the shelf beside her. I swipe out to slap it away–paper towels–before ducking in to force a hard, clumsy kiss into her mouth.

She whimpers when I reach around to grab her ass, wrenching her up against my next thrust. Her fingers slide against the sweat on my shoulders, nails digging in for purchase instead. The sting of pain sharpens my awareness of everything. Her little whimpers. The heat of her pussy. The slickness of it as I pound into her small, soft body, feeling it give and greet, so fucking open for me.

I flatten my hand on her chest, dragging it between her tits as I draw in and out. I think about how she showed up for me tonight. Sexy and strong. It was an offering, and I wonder if she realizes that. A sacrifice in front of her tribe.

I guide my hand lower, over her belly, past her bikini top bunched around her waist, down to the slick, hot nub between her legs. I brush my thumb over her clit, and her back straightens, hand gripping my shoulder.

"Yeah," she gasps, her breath ragged across my jaw. "Don't–don't stop. *Please* don't stop."

The plea just makes me drive into her harder, tasting the salt of her sweat as I duck down to suck at her neck. Her pussy tightens around me, clenching every time I touch that little delicate spot, like she wants to hold onto me forever.

I don't have forever. I'm two seconds from spilling my load.

I reach up to grasp her chin, panting into her mouth. "You gonna come for me?" The words emerge curt and raw, and her nails dig in deeper.

"You gonna let me?"

A short, mangled laugh bursts from my throat, because *fuck*.

This girl may not know who the man is under the tough, marked skin, but she knows my cock and my ways.

"Just this once." I drive in deep, continuing to rub against her.

She rises up, pressing her chest against mine, and for the shortest, brightest moment, the two of us feel like one body, writhing our way toward ecstasy. I wait for her to cry out her own release–pussy clenching wildly around me, back arching–before letting go of my own.

It's the first time the thought really strikes me.

Maybe the first time I allow it to.

I clutch her close as my cock twitches with the first wave. "Gonna make you so fucking full," I growl, feeling her grow wetter with my cum. She sobs out a needy sound and it makes me push deeper, abandoning her clit to palm at her stomach, as if I could feel it growing. My whisper tumbles into her ear, mindless and primal. "You're gonna be so round by the time I'm done with you. Do you feel that?" I ask, cock surging with wave after wave of hot cum. "Do you feel me putting my baby into you?"

She releases another long, strained whimper, her heels digging into my ass as she pulls me closer.

It goes on forever, my muscles flexing with every new swell of my release. It's only been a week since my last nut, but it seems like I've been saving it for years with how much I give her.

When it finally ends, I feel completely wrung out, too numb to feel much more than the drag of her fingers against my shoulders as I pull out. I know from experience my cum is streaming out of her, so I make a perfunctory effort to push it back in, wishing there were enough light in here to see the way her eyes flutter when I bury three fingers into her gushing cunt.

She shudders, reaching out to catch my wrist as her knees snap shut. "Stop," she gasps, flinching. "Too–too sensitive." Pausing, I pull my hand back and she stands, leaning into me for support.

I feel her reach upward, but I don't know what she's doing until I hear a click, the little closet suddenly exploding with painful brightness.

"Shit!" I hiss, staggering into a shelf as I cover my eyes. "Fucking warn a guy!"

Through my fingers, I see her wide green eyes blink back at me. "Oh my god, your knuckles." She grabs my wrist, prying it away from my squinting eyes. "Who the hell wrapped these?"

The light stabs like an ice pick through my temples, and it takes me a long moment to adjust, making out the vivid flush of her cheeks. "Wicker did."

She holds my hands in her palms, gaping at his work. "It's all wrong! Look at all these wrinkles in the tape, and he didn't even get between your fingers. You could have broken something!" When she plucks at the bloody wraps, I wince, and her mouth pulls down. "Maybe you did break something."

"It's fine," I say, tugging my hands back. That's when my eyes drop to her thighs, still bare. There's a dark streak of blood on the inside, and for a second, I wonder if she's still on her rag. Then I see the crimson smudges over her tits, realizing it's not her blood.

It's mine.

Or Maddox's.

My cum is dripping down her leg.

The blush on her face deepens as she follows my gaze, crouching to swipe the roll of paper towels from the floor. "Come with me."

THE LOCKER ROOM is bigger than the closet, but at least the light is dim as she leads me through the door, marching me up to the first shower stall. My first night with her, she looked close to bitter, humiliated tears at the mere thought of having to expose her pussy to me. Now, she undresses perfunctorily, shucking off her shorts and stockings before unfastening the bikini top.

My dick gives a feeble twitch as I watch her lean in to turn the shower knob. Water sputters out and she tests the temperature, frowning. "Why do you come so much?" She glances down at her inner thigh, which is glistening with more of my dripping release.

Shrugging, I push my own shorts down. "Because my balls are so big."

She gives my cock a dubious glance. "I don't think male anatomy works like that." But her gaze snaps back to my dick, a curious glint in her eyes. "Is it because you were never..." Swallowing, her gaze skitters away. "Er, circumcised?"

"Not used to seeing a dick uncut?" My eyebrow ticks up when her blush deepens. "I doubt that has anything to do with it."

It's only half hard now, but I've always been a show'er, my cock hanging heavily between my legs. It's something that used to add one more check to the column of things that make me different from my brothers. Different hair. Different skin color. Different height. Different eyes. Different dick. Something like that could be really alienating to a kid going through puberty with two other boys, except the first time Wicker saw it, he grew so fucking envious that I've never been able to feel anything but sort of proud of it.

Stepping beneath the spray, she beckons me in. "Let's get the tape off and clean those wounds out."

I follow her in because she's naked and wet, and no matter how fucked my mind is at the moment, I'm still a man. I fix my eyes to that smear of blood across her tit as she unwinds the wraps, pointedly ignoring the way my cock is growing harder by the second.

If it's my blood, then fine.

But if it's Maddox's?

"You didn't have to cut him, you know." The words come out tensely admonishing as she leads my knuckles under the spray. "You could have beat him without it. People in West End respect a fair fight, even if they lose."

Remembering the boos of the crowd–the sense that I lost–I bite out, "People in East End respect a sure thing."

Her green eyes flick up to me. "Then why did you run away after the fight?"

"I didn't run away," I argue, looking between the blood smear and the spray of water. My fingers twitch. "I just needed to collect my spoils."

She gives me a skeptical look. "You seemed really upset. Like you were having a panic attack or something." Her lips purse as she assesses me. "You look a little bit like that now, actually."

I snap, "I'm not panicking," and the harshness in my voice makes her flinch. I'm all too aware that I'm on the edge of losing all my progress with her. She needs to fear me. She needs to respect me. She needs to look at me and see a master–a Prince–not a victim.

She keeps her eyes cast down to my knuckles, her thumb sweeping gently over the places they've split. When she speaks, her voice is full of defeat. "I've never seen someone try so hard to make no effort."

I look at the blood smear again. Finally losing my patience, I reach out to wet my palm, splashing it on her tit before swiping it away. Something in my chest loosens at the sight of the flesh, clean and unblemished.

"That's bullshit," I say, scoffing. "You see Wicker every day." Her eyes rise to mine with a confused spark, even though amusement tugs at the corner of her lips.

"You've got me there."

As if the name itself summons him, the door to the locker room bangs open, his voice calling out, "Pace? You in here?" The shutters fall over her expression so quickly that she might as well be a china doll, stiff and wide-eyed.

The sensation courses through me like fire–this understanding that what I'm seeing here is for my eyes only. A moment that's ours. No one else's.

Holding her gaze, I reach out to snag the towel from the wall, winding it around my waist as I step out. "Go ahead and clean up," I whisper, even though the thought of her washing my cum out of her cunt makes my fists clench painfully. I stare at the trail of cum on her thigh, assuring, "I'll distract them."

Some of that woodenness leaves her spine. "Thank you."

When I walk out of the row of lockers, it's to the sight of my brothers peering down every aisle.

Wicker sees me first, the crevice in his brow disappearing the moment he sets eyes on me. "Jesus, there you are. We've been looking everywhere. This place is a goddamn maze."

"We should have known," Lex says, the crevice never leaving *his* brow. "The fight–it's a lot like..."

He doesn't say the words, but all three of us hear them. It's just like work. The dungeon. "Yeah," I reply, voice gruff. "It's a lot like that."

"You back now?" Wicker asks, and I notice the bottle of expensive champagne dangling from his fist. "Because we just had a talk with Father, and dude," he hoists the champagne into the air, smirking, "he's on cloud motherfucking nine."

Hope burns in my chest. "No shit?"

I know it's serious when even Lex grins. "A Prince hasn't taken a Fury in like two decades. He's out there stroking his ego like it's his cock."

"Fuck," I breathe, the tension falling out of me like a boulder. "I thought maybe... when everyone was booing–"

"Fuck 'em." Wicker laughs, sliding up onto the training bench. "Bunch of butt-sore losers. Rumor has it that when a Duke loses, he can't even go home. They're just trying to save face." He unwinds the foil from the mouth of the bottle, and I'd almost forgotten what this looks like.

When Wicker's unhappy–and there's been a lot of that since I got back–everyone's unhappy. But when Wicker's in a good mood? The whole fucking world sparkles. Birds sing. I once saw him smile at a girl–a genuine smile, happy and smug–and I swear to god she came on the spot.

"We've got the whole night off," Lex says, swiping the bottle out of Wicker's hands. With a skilled flick of his wrist, he uncorks it, flashing me a wicked look. "And permission to get as shitfaced as we want."

"Shit," I say, watching my brother take a long swig. "What do you think? Trap?"

Wicker snags the bottle back for his own swig, head shaking. "Nah, you just fucking owned the Dukes on their own turf. You could probably get a new car if you asked even half nicely."

"You're bleeding," Lex notes, searching through a nearby cabinet for supplies before I can even tell him not to bother.

I sit on the bench as he cleans the cuts, all three of us passing the bottle around. There's a lightness to their laughter that I clutch at like a lifeline, letting it lead me back out of the darkness. I never really forget Rosilocks is still in the room. She just blends into the background, the spray of water a comforting white noise.

Until it isn't.

The instant the water cuts, Lex's eyes dart toward the showers, back straightening as he reaches for his waistband. No one would come into Duke territory not packing.

But it's Verity who appears reluctantly around the bank of lockers, her lip trapped between her teeth as she clutches a threadbare towel around her chest. "I, uh, left my change of clothes in the cutslut's lounge," she explains, shuffling her feet.

I give Lex a look and he nods, standing to go to the door. With a twist of his wrist, he locks it, testing to make sure it's secure.

Wicker swipes his tongue over his teeth, eyes drinking her in. "Looks like someone's already collected his spoils." He glances at me. "Shower sex?"

"Broom closet."

Some of the brightness in his eyes dims. "That makes sense."

Wicker's been on edge all week, having missed two of his deposits. It's probably the longest he's gone without an orgasm since junior high. He pats the space next to him, eyes hungry and a touch wild. "Come celebrate with us, Princess. Just lose the towel first." When she hesitates, her arms folding around her middle, he arches a brow. "It's twenty minutes 'til midnight, and I gave you Tuesday."

She looks between the three of us. I have spare clothes in my bag, and I could even make it an order for her to cover herself, taking the decision out of her hands. Wicker would sulk, but he'd relent. But a part of me flares hot with the thought of them seeing her like this, all fucked out because of me.

She exhales, long and slow, eyes dropping as she unfastens the towel. All the casual aloofness about her nudity I'd seen before the shower is gone, a tremor in her shoulders as she shuffles toward us. She's not used to being bared to all of us at the same time, I realize. With Father's strict schedules, the closest we've come is Wicker's hasty backseat fuck on the way to school that one time.

Lex sits across from me sightlessly, his eyes fixed to her full, heavy tits as she approaches. Wicker perks up, sliding over to make room for her between him and Lex, but when she gets within arm's reach, I grab her hip, pulling her onto my lap.

She lands with an *oomph*, but then the strangest thing happens.

She curls into me, as if I'm her shield.

I wind my arm around her waist, tucking her close. "It's still technically my day," I tell Wicker, daring him to protest, "and I'm the one who won her."

To my surprise, he just tips the bottle toward me in a salute, eyes roving her flesh. "Fair enough."

She smells soapy and new, her skin still warm and pink from the shower. "All cleaned up," I say, a thread of disappointment in my voice.

"Kind of," she says, shifting to grab my opposite shoulder, like I won't notice it covers her tits with her arm.

"Kind of?" I ask.

She trains her eyes to a spot on her knee. "After you come, it, um, takes a while." She grimaces. "For it to all come out."

Just like that, I'm rock hard, and from one glance at my brothers, I'm not the only one. Lex is slack-jawed as he freezes with the bottle to his mouth, and Wicker, eyes hooded, reaches down to adjust the obscene bulge in his khakis.

"How long?" Lex asks, finally taking that sip.

Verity gives the smallest, cutest little shrug. "All day, sometimes." Then, with a bluntness I don't even think our Princess is capable of, she adds, "He comes like a firehose."

Wicker's eyebrows shoot up. "Does he, now?" He kicks out, catching my ankle. "You never came like a firehose for me, fuckhead."

Rolling my eyes, I point out, "You hounding me for days to trade handies, then jerking me off at lightning speed so you could hurry up and get yours never really did it for me."

Verity's head snaps up, gaping between us. "Wait, you mean– you and Wicker?" And then, at our blank gazes, "Have you *all* had sex together?"

I stroke the side of her tit, snorting. "It's the occasional handjob, not the kama sutra. And no, I was never pretty enough for Lex's freakish high school sexual experiment."

She points at my brothers. "But you and Lex..." and Wicker gives Lex a cocky grin.

"Yeah, we fucked." He jerks his chin upward, the arrogance rolling off him. "Best lay of his life."

Lex shakes his head, unimpressed. "Not even remotely. You're a selfish lover."

With a confidence he hasn't earned, Wicker decides. "Nah, I'm not."

"Yes, you are." Verity and I say the words at the same time, with varying degrees of grievance, and it makes my cock swell.

I know she feels it when she squirms, her face red as a tomato. "Did I hear something about us having permission?" She looks at the bottle of champagne hopefully.

"Us, yes. You?" Wicker snorts. "Not a fucking chance."

Her face falls. "Oh."

Lex clears his throat. "You already had permission for the chocolate bar." After a beat, he raises his gaze to hers. "It was good?"

Nodding, she says, "Yes," and a little more stiffly, "thank you," shivering when I toy with a wet lock of her hair, a drop of water falling on the swell of her tit.

The whole thing had been kind of dirty, if you ask me. No way Wicker or I can compete with a sanctioned breaking of the rules.

But we can indulge in our own.

Lurching forward, I snag the bottle of champagne, tipping it up to take a mouthful. I hold it on my tongue, fizzy and warm, and then nudge a bruised knuckle beneath her chin, tipping her face up to mine.

Her brows crash together when I thumb at her lips, but then her eyes flick down to my mouth, comprehension overtaking her features. It's not as bright as I was expecting, a dullness filling her eyes as she realizes this is the only way she can have this.

When she parts her lips, opening her mouth to me, I get the feeling it's a sacrifice she's not too happy about.

But when I spit the champagne into her mouth, she takes it.

Her throat bobs with a swallow.

"Pace," Lex says in his low, reprimanding tone.

But I'm already diving down to lick the taste of it off her tongue. Setting the bottle down blindly, I reach up to cup her tit in my palm, just to feel the weight of it–the soft warmth. The kiss tastes like bubbles and submission, and even though the man inside of me wants to push deeper, harder, I keep it light and slick, pulling away with a wet sound.

To Lex, I shrug. "She didn't drink it, technically."

Wicker's already stroking his cock through his pants, eyes flashing excitedly as he snags the bottle. "Come on, Red. Want some more?"

Her eyes are still a little glazed from the kiss, and when she turns them to my brother–currently filling his mouth with champagne–they tighten at the corners. For a second, it seems like she wants to tell him no.

She rises from my lap instead.

I wonder what it is that makes her shoulders square when she approaches him, perching stiffly on his knee. Does she really want it that bad? To be Princess? To give birth to the next heir?

Why the fuck would she?

I don't wonder for too long, because I'm too busy watching Wicker unfasten his jeans, pulling his cock out as Verity waits patiently. He grabs her hand and guides it to cup his hardness, and she does it blindly, like she's afraid to look at it.

He grunts, eyes going heavy as he beckons her close, putting his lips to hers. He doesn't spit it into her mouth so much as he pushes it, sending a stream of the champagne down their chins as he kisses her, sloppy and slow.

Verity might not be his dick's biggest fan, but she sure kisses him back like she wants to be. Her fingers tangle in the back of his hair, hips giving the smallest little writhe as their tongues tangle. If everyone in this room knows Wicker's a selfish lover, then we also all know that he's a fucking fantastic kisser. The complete opposite of how he is in bed. Unhurried and full of slow-simmering heat. He kisses our girl like he's trying to make her knees give out.

If she were standing, I'm pretty sure they would.

She pulls away first, licking the taste of champagne off her lips.

"What do you say?" Wicker asks, pushing her palm down harder on his cock.

Nudging her wrist against her chin, she mutters, "Thank you." Almost imperceptibly, her eyes dart toward Lex.

Sitting on the bench, he's leaning back against a locker, watching them a lot like I am, eyes dark and hungry. He's just better at hiding it. Usually.

Tonight, he strains over the space between him and Wicker to grab the neck of the bottle, settling back with slow, dangerous intensity. Verity stares at the bottle in his hand, and then into his eyes, a question lingering there.

Wicker sighs, giving her a small push. "Go on. We still have ten minutes before I can do anything about this."

She still looks unsure when she approaches Lex, her perky ass pointed right at me as she shifts, waiting for his signal. He gives it with a flick of his eyes downward, saying in a gruff voice, "Kneel."

I don't see her expression as she obeys, but I see Lex's as he takes a long pull from the bottle. He pitches forward as she kneels between his knees. Wicker divests him of the bottle instantly, freeing up Lex's hand to reach out, fingers knitting through the hair at the base of her skull as he guides her head back.

I see the hinge of her jaw shift as she opens wide for him, and Lex stares for a suspended moment, the fingers in her hair moving, massaging.

Then he lets it go.

The champagne streams from his mouth into hers. In the middle of it, he uses his other hand to cradle her cheek, the gesture weirdly tender considering the context.

Wicker and I share a dazed look.

I can't remember the last time Lex has intentionally participated in one of our bullshit rule loopholes.

When the stream of booze ends, Lex holds her there, sliding a thumb through her lips. "Missed some," he says, the sound ragged and low. "Stand up." As soon as she rises, standing between Lex's knees, his tongue sweeps a path from her belly button to the valley between her breasts.

"Fuck yes," Wicker says as Lex grabs her tits, squeezing them together around his face. He watches them as he strokes his cock, the head dripping already. "Get her ready for me. Shit, I'm about to blow."

It's unnecessary. Lex's fingers are already pushing between her legs. I can see them when she gasps, hastily shifting her feet to make room. She wobbles, grabbing onto his shoulders, and I can't help but reach out, sweeping a palm down the curve of her ass, spreading it.

My eyes lock in just as Lex slides two thick fingers into her cunt.

"Oh god," she whines, hips rocking.

Maybe the Princess missed getting fucked this week as much as we missed fucking her.

"Wick," Lex says, voice raw and torn as he pulls his fingers out, glistening. "Time?"

"Two minutes."

Wetting my fingers between her legs, I pull her cheeks wider and spread the slickness across her hole. She surges forward, crashing into Lex. "Let him touch you," he tells her. "Don't fight it."

I push a finger in, easing past the tight, puckered muscle of her ass. She cries out. In pain or pleasure, I don't care.

"Need a little lube?" Wick asks, tipping the bottle of champagne to dribble the liquid between her cheeks. The fluid provides a little moisture and I push in deeper, spreading my fingers to loosen her up.

"How's that feel, Rosilocks? Think you can take a little more?"

She pants, resting her forehead on Lex's shoulder. "It's too much."

"One day I'm gonna fill you with my cock, and you need to be ready." I grab the bottle from Wicker and drain the contents. I tell Wick, "Hold her open."

Verity looks over her shoulder, eyes wide. "What? No. I can't–"

"Sure you can, baby," Wicker says, running his fingers down her cheek. "Just relax."

Every muscle in her body tenses. Her thighs quiver and her asshole clenches around my finger.

I lick the rim of the bottle, tasting the champagne. The urge to fuck her with my cock is deliriously strong, but I know I'll shoot my wad the second I get in, and that goes against the rules. But this? I think, removing my finger to make room, *this* I can do.

"Wait," Wicker says, bending over and swiping his tongue over her hole. Verity lurches forward, groaning against Lex's chest. He licks and sucks, getting her nice and ready. "There." he pushes his finger in easily. "She's ready."

"I'm not," she cries, looking up at Lex. "Don't let them do this to me!"

"He can do whatever he wants," Lex says. "To the victor, remember?"

Wicker spreads her cheeks, giving me a better view of that perfect, pristine asshole. Edging the bottle up to her tight hole, I rest a hand on her back, "Breath, Rosilocks, this is just another test. Like all the others."

How much can she take?

Her breath hitches, but I feel her trying to relax. I massage the area, opening her with my fingers before nudging the bottle in. The green glass vanishes into the pink flesh and she moans in response.

"Jesus." Wicker fists his cock.

Lex's fingers are still working her cunt, and I catch up to their rhythm, pushing the neck of the bottle in a little deeper with each thrust. Her body trembles and Lex holds her upright, until the chime of a watch beeps in the room, signaling midnight.

"Wick," Lex commands. "Fuck her. *Now.*"

Wicker springs up, tearing his shirt off, and I pull out the bottle. Verity cries out and I trade places with him, finally getting a good look at her rosy face.

"Lex," she says, something both needy and morose in her tone as she grasps his shoulders.

He looks up, meeting her gaze. "Be good. I'll give you what you need."

Her fingers dig notches into his shoulders as Wicker nudges in behind her, tipping her hips back. He enters her with a rough groan, the look on his face agonized, yet euphoric. "Goddamn," he grunts, snapping his hips into her. "So fucking wet already. *Fuck.*"

"You're welcome," I say, dragging my lip through my teeth as I fist my cock. I can't come, but I don't need to. Already did. It's part of what's slicking the way for my brother as he fucks into her.

The other part probably has something to do with how Lex is mouthing at her tit, his fingers rubbing skillfully at her clit as Wicker punches into her.

"I swear to god," he grunts, yanking her hips back into him, "if either of you say anything about how quick this is, I'll cut your fucking balls off."

I laugh, but my gaze is trained on Verity, watching the little bursts of air that escape her plump lips. The sad thing about Lex's little issue is that he's actually a total fucking stud in the sack. His fingers work her over and she's like putty in his hands, using his frame for support, seeming to care more about that than Wicker's brutal thrusts into her from behind.

"Fucking fuck," Wick growls, slamming into her hard. He pumps into her, making his deposit in record time.

It's kind of hilarious–and unbearably fucking hot–that after Wicker spills inside of her and pulls out, she continues to chase her own pleasure, focusing on Lex. Wicker's barely pulled out when Lex does this little flick of his wrist, and Verity seizes, mouth falling open on a shocked cry.

Staring up into her eyes, Lex's jaw is set as he pulls the orgasm from her aggressively, like he's the one fucking her. The pained expression on his face reveals there's nothing he wants more, but one glance at his pants makes it clear that shit's still out of service.

"Bro," I say, elbowing Wicker. His chest heaves from exertion, but he looks at her, her eyes fluttering shut as she rides Lex's hand.

"Whatever," Wicker says, but he's watching, and I see the spark of jealousy in his eye. He can fuck her a dozen times a day, but he'll never hear those little cries of ecstasy falling from her lips. He's too selfish.

I'm selfish too, but *goddamn* I like seeing her like this. Begging for it. Never getting enough. Pussy so desperate for the Ashby brothers that she'll do whatever it takes. Once the tremors stop, she attempts to slump against Lex, but he's already standing, pushing her off.

"Go get cleaned up." I jerk my thumb back to the showers. She pads past me, eyes glazed, tits red and abused with two kinds of cum dripping down her legs.

Once the shower turns on again, I grab the empty bottle off the bench and hold it in the air. "We're the victors," I say, looking each of them in the eye, "but our win doesn't come from a pound of flesh."

"To create..." Lex starts,

"... is to reign," Wicker finishes.

And we drink to that.

∽

"*I'M HUNGRY,*" the statement is followed by a loud squawk. "*Feed the pretty bird!*"

"Give me a fucking minute, Effie!" I turn the knobs, shutting off the shower, and grab a towel off the bar. Barely drying off, I wrap it around my waist. She's angry that I took a shower before feeding her after the grueling training this morning. The night off to get shitfaced, my ass. Apparently Coach didn't get that memo. Six times up the cliffs and then a series of workouts at the top isn't exactly something a person wants to do twelve hours following a bloodthirsty cage fight with the Dukes. "You're lucky I have enough feeling in my limbs to feed you."

"*Thank you,*" Effie croons. "*Thank you.*"

"Don't thank me yet," I mutter, ruffling my fingers through my twists. "We're almost out of treats."

I open the cabinet in the hall, reaching for the bag, but it's not there. *Shit.* Did I use the last one? Fuck, Effie's gonna be pissed.

"Gentle," comes a soft, feminine voice I'd know anywhere. I still remember it from last night, her damp, naked body in my lap as I fed her champagne.

I straighten, hand gripping my towel, and walk into the room. "What the fuck?"

Verity, dressed in a faded sweatshirt and torn jeans, stands over Effie's cage, grinning brightly at her. I lunge, snatching the bag out of her hands, but not before Effie carefully takes a treat out of her fingertips.

"*Gentle,*" Effie croons, and I freeze.

Her voice is startlingly close to matching Verity's.

Already.

"What are you doing?" I snap, standing between her and the cage. "Who said you could feed my bird?"

Verity gestures to Effie. "After listening to her cry out in starvation for hours, I finally decided to check on her!" Her eyes shift down, drawing upward from the towel, to my bare chest, until they land on my face.

Her cheeks color.

"She's not starving." I roll my eyes, pushing between her and Effie. "She's just a drama queen." I offer Effie a treat and she takes it.

"Good girl." I run my finger down her beak.

"*Effie's a good girl*," she replies.

I dig into the bag and pull out another treat. "One more."

Verity watches with a soft glint to her eye. "She's so pretty," she says.

"*Pretty bird.*" Effie preens after eating the treat. "*Effie's a pretty bird.*"

"Don't encourage her," I sigh, closing the bag and tossing it on my desk.

"Doesn't seem like it takes much," Verity says, laughing when Effie trills out a melodic, "*Effie's a pretty, pretty bird.*" The sudden delight alters her face so much that she looks like an entirely different person. Brighter. Radiant. The sound does something to me, Verity's laughter settling into the base of my spine like electricity.

She pokes a finger through the cage to pet Effie's beak like I had. "How long have you had her?"

I look at Effie, remembering the day I finally got the old man at the Gentleman's Chamber to give her up to me. There aren't a lot of happy days in the life of an Ashby, but that definitely counts as one of them, and when I hold out two fingers, Effie skitters close to nuzzle against them. "Almost ten years now."

"Wow," she says, and her next glance is almost too much. Full of awe and sweetness. "She really loves you."

I don't like it. Last night was bad enough, letting her see me all ragged and worn thin. The celebration was nice—called for—but it can't set a precedent.

Verity isn't my girlfriend.

She's my Princess.

My project.

A job.

With this in mind, I scowl at her. "Don't ever feed my bird. She's on a specific meal plan and schedule. You're gonna fuck up her digestion."

Her mouth hangs agape in outrage. "It was one treat. She'd been crying out for hours."

I yank my drawer open before dropping the towel. "Yeah, well, I didn't know Coach was going to keep us running hills all morning."

When I turn, boxers clutched in a fist, her eyes spring up from where they'd been gawking at my ass. "So that's why Wicker hasn't been in my room yet today?"

I know for a fact Wicker made a deposit at precisely twelve last night, but nothing since. "Careful, you almost sound disappointed." Stepping into my boxers, I hold her stare, satisfied by the way she's squirming. "He was puking after the sixth run through like a little bitch. I wouldn't take it personally."

"*Goddamn it, Wicker...*" Effie calls in Lex's voice. Then in Wicker's, "*Suck my balls.*"

I swing my glare on the cage. "Effie, don't make me put you to bed."

Verity frowns as she watches Effie wobble-walk back to her tablet. It's not a live stream, since the weather's too wet and foggy for anything decent today. Instead, it's a stock video.

"Do you ever let her out?" Verity asks.

I sweep a hand toward my desk, littered with stolen, and eventually reappropriated, F12 keys. "I let her out all the time."

"Not in your room," Verity says, pointing to the tablet. "I mean *out*, to really stretch her wings."

My eyes harden. "She likes it in here. It's her home. It has all her things."

Verity looks around, pausing at the heavy, closed drapes. "It just seems sad that she's cooped up all day." Her eyes widen, snapping to mine. "Oh, maybe she could come down to the solarium with me."

I shake my head. "She wouldn't like that."

But Verity flaps a hand excitedly. "It's got those high glass ceilings and all those vines–even a few trees she can explore. I bet she'd love it!"

"And then what?" I burst, watching her flinch as I stomp forward. "Wicker or Danner would walk in, leave the door open, and she'd fly off."

"*Goddamn it, Wicker.*"

I grab the blanket and toss it over the cage. She doesn't need to be hearing all this anyway. "Effie's always been used to small spaces. She doesn't like a lot of sunlight, and she doesn't need more room. She's happy in here with me." Jaw tight, I turn my back to her, gripping the back of my desk chair, and ignore the way my heart hammers in my chest. "Why am I even explaining this to you? I don't give a fuck what you think. Get the fuck out."

There's a long moment of stillness, silence, and then Verity says, "You know, it's not normal to lock living things up all the time. Animals need sunlight, Pace. They need space and fresh air. Just because this is how it's always been for her doesn't mean that's the right thing."

By the time I form a reply, whipping around to snarl a 'fuck you' in her face, Verity is gone.

"*Gentle,*" Effie croons in Verity's low, soft voice. "*Gentle, gentle.*"

IT'S LATE when I hear a tap on my door. I check the monitor to make sure it's not Verity trying to come in here and stir up shit again. Who the fuck is she to tell me what Effie needs? She doesn't even know her.

Luckily, it's just Lex.

"Hey," he says, stepping in. His hair is down, damp from a fresh shower. He's wearing his glasses too, his contacts probably sitting in his bathroom as he gets ready for bed. "Got a minute?"

"What's up?" I ask, flipping through the monitors, pausing on the one of Father's club.

"Can you check my back? There's a few in the middle I can't reach."

I turn to look at him, the request both gutting and soothing. It hurts to see his back, but he's been letting me take care of him ever since the last punishment, and that's new.

"I've got you." I stand and he hands me the tube of ointment before pulling his T-shirt over his head. He leans over the back of my desk chair, facing the monitors, and waits. His back is a scarred nightmare, the fresh welts still red. They're healing though, scabbing over. "Does it still itch?"

"No, thank fuck, that part has passed," he says as I pick up the ointment and unscrew the cap. "I got a message from the Barons, by the way. Everything's settled."

"Good." I squeeze out a glob of the white cream.

"He said something interesting."

"Oh yeah?" I ask, my eyes flicking to the screen. One of the women dancing on the stage has on a pair of garters. My cock thickens, remembering ripping off those fishnets. I lean forward and skip to the next screen. Verity's room.

My post-fuck gift for her is still sitting on her pillow, untouched.

"He thanked me for the tip," he continues, flinching as I smooth the cream over the worst wound. "Said they'd be dealing with the 'sire' soon. Any idea what that's about?"

Mouth ticking up, I confess, "I may have let it slip to the Barons that Daddy Oakfield's been spreading rumors about Kayes."

My gaze goes back to the screen. As far as I know, she's been down in the solarium all day. There's no camera down there, at Father's insistence. Some bullshit about how he doesn't want Michael's resting place sullied by modern technology. "He needs to be dealt with, but I'm not sure we need to be the ones to do it. I figured whoever's wearing that mask probably doesn't want it out there either."

One of the live screens on the second monitor catches movement. A SUV pulls up to the front door. Wicker, in a suit and unknotted tie, gets out. I don't miss the time. 12:01. He missed his window. It's Lex's day.

"How many deposits did he make before he left?" Lex asks, reading my mind.

"Just the one."

Lex cranes his neck, looking back at me. "You're kidding?"

"Nope. I reviewed all the streams, and Verity even mentioned it earlier. You saw him last night downing all that whiskey after we left West End. He was fucked up and passed out—*hard*."

He nods. "You were both gone when I woke up."

"Coach made us jog up the trails to the cliffs. Six times." My legs still ache. Aside from our drills and the resulting misery, Father sent Wicker out to an event at the botanical garden for the evening. "Father called on the way home about Wick needing to escort someone for a fundraiser. He showered and left."

The camera follows Wicker into the foyer, and up the stairs.

"I bet he's pissed his day got ruined," Lex says, sighing.

"And about humping old ladies' legs," I scowl, smoothing a bit of cream over another angry looking wound. Sometimes I think Wicker has it worst of all of us, and this is one of them. Considering I'm staring at Lex's back, that's saying a lot.

I gently squeeze his shoulder. "Okay, all done."

"Thanks." He straightens, forehead wrinkled in worry. "Do you think he's backed off for me? To keep his numbers lower?"

I consider it. "Maybe, but down to one? Unlikely. But..."

"But what?"

I choose my words carefully. "But it's all the more reason to take him up on his offer. Let him help you out, fill a few vials. No one will know."

"*I'll* know." He reaches for his shirt, frowning. "I can fix this."

"How?" I ask, voice raising. "Nothing's worked yet. Not porn. Not watching Wick fuck Verity six times a day. Not father beating you within an inch of your life. What's the solution to this other than getting back on the Scratch?"

He opens his mouth, but from the doorway, Wicker speaks first.

"Over my dead fucking body." My brothers share a look. *The look.* It's the reminder that there's shit they went through together while I was in lockup. "Don't you even suggest it. You weren't here when he went through withdrawals."

"Insomnia. Nausea. Even some hallucinations." Lex exhales, sweeping his hair back. "The nights were the worst. If I could sleep, I'd wake up in a pool of sweat, and if I couldn't, I felt like my skin was on fire."

"Irritable as fuck, too," Wick says, then winks. "Like that's any different."

"I'm sorry I wasn't here." I should have been. If I were, Lex never would have gotten on the shit in the first place.

"You know," Wicker says, eyes flashing, "there is another answer to this."

We both look over at him, and I take him in for the first time. His hair is rumpled and there's a smear of lipstick on his white collar. I can smell lingering perfume on him—a specific scent that conjures up wealthy grandmothers—all the way across the room.

"Lex's dick is only half broken," he walks in and flops down on the couch, looking tired. "It works perfectly fine when he's asleep."

"You want to let him out of the cage," I say, catching on.

"No," Lex says, brows snapping together in a scowl. "Absolutely fucking *not.* I almost choked her out last time. If you think my punishment was bad for not fucking her, what do you think it's going to look like when I do that?"

"A choked-out girl can still get knocked up," Wicker says, inspecting his nails. "Nowhere in the covenants does it say she has to be conscious."

Lex barks, "I'm not talking about her being unconscious. I'm talking about accidentally killing her!"

"No one's dying." He rolls his eyes. "We'll supervise."

"Maybe it's not the worst idea," I say, sitting in my chair and spinning it back to face the monitors. A couple keystrokes pulls up the footage from the night he got loose. "It's either that, or let me and Wick make the deposits for you."

Lex's expression is hard, every muscle tense. I don't need him to speak to know what he's thinking: this failure? It's eating him alive. And the part he won't admit is that it's not just about failing as a Prince. It's not even really about failing as an Ashby.

It's about failing as a man.

"Maybe," Wick adds, "your cock just needs to feel a tight pussy wrapped around it to remember how good it is."

I press play on the video, and Wicker rises to come over and get a better view. In silence, the three of us watch the scene unfold. The room is dark, so it's grainy, but there's no mistaking Lex as he rolls out of bed and sits on the edge. His erection isn't noticeable until he stands, tenting out the front of his boxers.

Behind me, Lex lunges for the keyboard. "Turn it off."

"No," Wick says, batting him off like a hockey puck. "You need to see what you're capable of."

On screen, he stumbles around the room a bit before gaining his footing. It takes him two tries to get out the door, but he finally manages to turn the knob. The camera view flips to the hallway where he stumbles down the wing, toward the Princess' bedroom. I've already seen this before, when I compiled all the clips into one fluid scene, but it's the first time Wicker and Lex see him enter the room, standing motionlessly beside her bed as Verity shuffles out, reaching out to touch his shoulder.

His reaction is an explosion of chaos.

The struggle is intense, and I sense Lex behind me as the fight intensifies.

"Jesus," Wicker mutters as Lex's hands clamp around Verity's throat. Even on video, his intentions are clear. He wants to fuck her. Physically and mentally that's all he wants. He doesn't stop until the maid cracks him over the head with a vase, giving her the chance to escape to my room.

From one predator to another.

"It's too dangerous," he says, as if it's the final word.

I look between my brothers. "It's her or you, Lex. What do you think Father will do next if you don't up your deposits?" I point at the screen. "Her, we can protect, but you?"

His back tells that tale. Not just the current scars, but the road map of battle wounds from all the beatings that took place before. I see it in his eyes when it clicks, the reason he needs to do this, how important it is for him to take this step. Wicker and I don't just need Lex to do this for him.

We need him to do it for us.

22

V erity

MY BEDROOM USED to be worse at night.

Every shadow was a lurking figure. Every flicker of the dying fireplace embers danced of danger. Every skeletal gold filigree stretched like fingers, reaching out to grab me. The thick bedding was a shroud, as if I were laying on the bed of an enormous grave whose arms were waiting to pull me under, swallow me whole.

I'm not quite sure when it changed, I just know that it has. Tonight, I walk in and see comfort in the shadows, playfulness in the dancing embers. The plush expanse of the bed has transformed from a grave to a tranquil ocean of silks.

This feeling is far more terrifying than the old ones, because it's deceiving. Somewhere in this room, a camera is watching me. Perhaps even several. The lock on the door may as well be a mere decoration, considering my Princes can enter at will. These four walls and towering ceiling couldn't remotely be considered safe.

But when I fall into bed, all I can think about is how tired I am. How exhausted my body feels. I've almost forgotten what it's like to use my body for something other than the aching disappointments of their daily deposits, but I'd spent most of the afternoon and evening out in the solarium, clearing weeds and branches, and then dragging them to the bare copse of trees at the back of the garden.

And I finally met East Side's true heir.

Or rather, his tomb.

That's what I dream about as I fall into a fitful slumber. The stone and the earth, the scent of dead grass, the shivery chill of the clinging winter. And then suddenly, I'm there, standing in front of it again.

The tomb is tall and regal, with arched, gothic carvings that so perfectly match the style of the Palace that it doesn't look a day younger than a hundred. Moss has covered the flat base where his body must lay, but the name etched into the slab is still clear and stark.

Michael Claudius Ashby
Beloved son
Stolen Prince
Created in the radiance of the morning's light
May your heavenly body reign
Always

Towering over the slab is a statue of a crouching angel–weeping, just as Wicker had said–her wings folded around her like arms. The stone is pale but weather-stained, dark spots shading the grooves like charcoal on paper. As with everything else on the grounds, the wisteria is on a mission to overtake it. The wiry brown vines have coiled around the angel's feet, climbing her body and twisting up her neck like a gnarled noose. It'll probably look breathtaking in the spring, the purple flowers blooming to life like teardrop bruises, but right now, it just looks like ropes.

Her eyes are so terrifyingly empty.

In my dream, I stand there just as I did earlier in the day, staring at the angel as if she were Michael himself. I didn't speak then, and I don't speak now. I just gaze into her vacant, lifeless eyes, paralyzed with some feeling that I can't quite place. Grief, maybe.

His gravestone says he died before his third birthday.

A gust of wind rattles the trees behind the garden, the ropey vines of the angel swaying, and I hear a sound in the air. It's muffled, but shrill—not quite a howl, but more like...

Crying.

A *baby's* crying.

I look around, but it's getting darker now, the sun slouching behind the trees. Twisting to look over my shoulder, the solarium—the whole Purple Palace—feels like a dozen miles away, so it can't be coming from there. The trees, maybe? I whip back around, but I don't see any movement in the brush. All I see is...

My eyes drop to the tomb, heart kicking like a mule when I realize where the cries are coming from.

Michael.

Stumbling back, I trip on a vine—or maybe it captured my ankle—and then I'm falling—falling—falling. I jolt upright in bed, gasping at the sound, because I know that was a dream—I *know* it—but I can still hear Michael crying, trapped underground.

Creeeak.

I grasp the blankets tightly to my throat, but the slice of light widening on the floor reveals the true source of the sound: my door, opening, and the unmistakable shape of Wicker Ashby, hair flopped over his eyes, standing in its glow.

The tension falls out of me in a shivered avalanche, only to be replaced with a dull sort of irritation. I've been waiting for him since last night, forgoing panties even while working outside, figuring he'd find me at some point.

Should have known he wouldn't let his day go to waste.

Still groggy from the dream, I mentally prepare myself for the impending hasty fuck, and ask in a rusty voice, "How long do we have?"

Wicker reaches out to grab the jamb, leaning his weight there. "None." The light from the hallway cuts hollows into his lower cheeks, and for a moment, he adopts the ghastly visage of a skull. "It's one in the morning. Lex's day."

I rub my eyes, refusing to believe he'd miss his day, not after the threats and tantrum last week. "You're not going to make a deposit?"

His skull-face smirks. "Disappointed, Red?" Sniffing, he turns his head, gazing down the hall. "Don't be. You're about to get what you need."

Before I can ask what that means, he steps aside. For a long moment, the doorway is vacant, but then a shadow approaches, its towering length sharpening as it gets closer. My first glimpse of the man makes my pulse quicken, because he's naked. Unkempt hair brushes the tops of his broad shoulders. Wiry muscles lead down toned biceps, a strong chest, a ladder of abs that cuts into a V, and a thick thatch of dark hair surrounding an obscenely hard cock. When Wicker reaches out to grasp his brother's shoulder, turning him toward my doorway, my blood turns to ice.

"Go on," Wicker whispers, glancing at me from the corner of his eyes. "Take what you want."

Beneath Lex's wild hair are eyes just as empty as the angel's were.

My voice emerges in a thin, panicked rasp. "What are you doing? He's sleepwalking!"

"I know," Wicker says, glancing down. Lex's cock, thick and hard, bobs as he shuffles forward. "He needs to make a deposit."

I scramble backward, my heels slipping against the sheets. "But he'll–he'll hurt me!"

Wicker shoves Lex through, just three more steps, and then grabs the golden knob. "Better you than him."

The door closes.

I gape at it for only a short moment before seeing Lex's shape twitch in my periphery. When I gather up the courage to slide my gaze toward him, I swallow loudly in the stillness of the room. He's almost too much to take in all at once. I've had a lot of sex these past few weeks, but somehow, I've never seen any of my Princes wholly naked like this. I've spent plenty of nights on that cold exam table, watching those biceps shift and flex as Lex filled me with hard plastic, aching to know what was beneath his shirts.

And now I do.

He's hard and ready, standing there looking like something out of an erotic horror movie, and as my eyes zero in on his lips, all I can think is that it can't be so bad. Even if he fucks me hard—even if it's rough—it'll still be good, won't it? Because it's Lex. It's the man who gifted me the finger of the asshole who hurt me. It's the man who touches me with such clinical care as he draws my blood. He's the one who stroked me so skillfully as Wicker forced his seed into me last night, his amber eyes never leaving mine.

He's the only guy in this house who's ever given half a damn about giving me pleasure.

But when I raise my gaze to his, what I see there makes my stomach drop.

His eyes are as black as obsidian, honing in on me like a demon. It's a stare that promises violence, and as he takes the first step forward, I hear his warning ring in my memory.

I need you to understand that I hurt people too, Verity.

I feel the memory of his hands on my throat. Fighting... it only made him more violent. My pulse quickens and the surge that comes through me is conflicted. Fight or flight...

I could run like last time, but where? And to what end? That only aggravated him further. Fighting is futile. Wicker let him in, which means no one is going to give me refuge if I get past him.

My lips part, the words shaky and quiet. "I won't fight you, Lex," I tell him, and then I slide the covers away, revealing my thin gown and bare legs. In anticipation of Wicker's next attack, I know Lex sees everything when I spread my legs.

Or he would, if he were looking.

His eyes aren't on my body though. They're fixed to mine, dark and penetrating, his nostrils flaring with an inhale as he charges forward. It's the tension coiling his muscles that makes me brace for impact, and even though I tell myself to be still–to take whatever's coming–I still throw my hands up, gasping, as he growls, slamming into me.

It knocks the air from my lungs, but his weight bears down on me like a boulder before I can suck in a full breath. Even if I could, his fingers instantly grasp my throat, squeezing. Through the pain swimming in my eyes, I can make out his feral expression above me, mouth pulled back to show his teeth as his hips push and shove and *seek*.

"Lex," I wheeze, grabbing for his wrist, but if anything, the name makes him squeeze harder. I slam my heel into his leg, pounding my fist into his forearm, but nothing budges him. The violence I'd seen in his stare earlier has transformed to outright murder, even as he snarls, punching his hips into me clumsily.

".... when I'm asleep... things get... mixed up. Endorphins. Adrenaline."

Jolting into action, I part my thighs, reaching between us to find his cock. The skin is hot, pulled tight, and it doesn't take much to guide it a little lower, tilting my hips up to meet his next thrust.

He spears into me with a clipped growl, slamming his pelvis into me with such force that I slide up the bed. The stretch of sudden fullness is nothing compared to the rush of air that enters my lungs when I gasp, Lex's hand releasing my throat to fist the pillow beneath my head.

Some unholy satisfaction rolls through him in a wave, his chest contracting with an animalistic sound.

And then it really begins.

Looking up into his face, I watch the swinging jolts of his hair as he fucks me, but I don't see *him*. Not in his eyes. Not in his snarling mouth. Not in the fevered slump of his brow. Every inch between us hurts with the force of the meeting, and as I cry out in shock, my fingers fumble for purchase against his back, struggling to fasten his raging body to my own.

But they slide against something wet and warm, and when I pull my hand back, biting down a yelp, I realize why.

Blood.

"Lex," I whimper, fingers stuttering wetly over his bicep. "Lex, wait!"

But every time I say his name, the thrusts come harder, more punishing, the muscles in his body rippling with the force of hammering against me. It's as if he wants to beat his way into the very core of me, and I can't figure out how to stop it, grabbing for something–anything–to anchor myself.

His eyes slouch down to my chest, and then his face follows, jaw taut as his body snaps into a wild, curling thrust. He dives to the side of my breast with such clear, unimpeded intent, that for a moment, I think perhaps he's awoken.

But his lips, his tongue, aren't what I feel.

It's teeth.

My body lurches with the sudden white-hot flare of pain tearing through my breast. I scream through gnashed teeth, but not before I grab a thick fistful of his hair and *yank*.

It just makes him latch on harder.

"Lex!" I shriek, and the teeth go in deeper. If my vision wasn't spotty from being strangled, then it's definitely fizzling with the sting of his bite, my legs kicking upward ineffectually. The reflex to scream his name again mingles with the knowledge that it's only making it worse.

Which must be why the next word tumbles from my mouth in desperation.

"*Lagan.*"

Lex freezes, his hips pinning mine to the bed.

It's not a tranquil moment. His teeth don't release me, and he's panting around the bloody flesh, nostrils flared out as saliva trickles down into my armpit. But he's motionless–rigid–as if he's waiting for something, teetering on the edge of a knife's blade, and when I look into his eyes, it's not at all unlike staring down a rabid dog.

Trembling, I ease my grip on his hair. "Lagan, wake up." He

shudders when my fingers, smeared in red, flutter over his scalp, his jaw loosening just enough to give me some relief. "You like that?" I ask, swallowing down a cry as I run soothing fingers through his hair. Coaxing him with a gentle nudge, I whisper, "Please let go."

And just like that, he does.

His bloodstained teeth are all I see for a long beat, the crimson trickling down the corners of his mouth, but when I look up into his eyes, I no longer see the feral demon that climbed into this bed.

His amber eyes are hooded, an unimaginable hurt staring back at me. Suddenly, he looks so tired that I wonder how he's even holding himself up above me.

"Lagan," I try, wondering if this is it–if he's finally roused himself from the daze. But all I get in response is another of those rolling shudders, his hips rocking into me. It sends a different kind of fire through my core, and I rest my palm against the base of his skull, tugging him down. The sound he makes as he burrows against my body, face buried into the crook of my neck, is so quiet and mournful that it makes my chest twist.

It's an odd intuition, but somehow, into the very flinching depths of my soul, I realize what he needs.

I fold him into my body, arms around his shoulders, legs winding around his waist. "It's okay," I whisper, turning to brush my lips tenderly against the cut of his jaw. "You're okay, baby."

He keens, low and desperate into my ear.

The next thrust is more of a rock than anything, the drag of his cock slow and more sensual than I'm expecting. I greet it with a roll of my hips, breath hitching as I cradle him against me. "Oh, god..."

His hair is soft against my cheek, and without really meaning to, I seek it out, burying my nose in the tresses. He smells clean and masculine, the scent tinged with an edge of the sweat I can feel dampening his brow. I'm not really expecting it when he lazily rolls his head to the side, lips dragging across my jaw before catching my mouth.

It should be disgusting.

My blood is still sticky on his lips, and he's lax–clearly still asleep–so it's sloppy and uncoordinated, filled with the bitter taste of copper.

And it might be the best kiss I've ever had.

It's completely without artifice, his tongue swiping out to lick lazily against my own. It's wet and warm and somehow sweet, the perfect punctuation to his unhurried thrusts against me. I reach up to touch his cheek, softly brushing his hair away as I kiss him back.

I must be crazy, because he's not even here–driven by purely primal instincts–but I'm struck by the notion that this is it.

This is what I've been needing.

No.

This is what I've been *wanting*.

The way our bodies begin working as one, rocking together as we taste each other. The punch of his small, quiet grunts every time our hips meet. Even the sting of lingering pain, the slip of sweat and blood, is everything I always knew sex should be.

In truth, it's perfect.

I feel his cock thickening, the muscles against me coiling together, and I get a sudden sense of responsibility. Taking his face in my hands, I tug his head back, urging, "Look at me."

Lex always makes me look at him when he fills me with the syringes. I've never understood why, and though a part of me might have once suspected it was to humiliate me, the thought seems wrong now. Something about this is important to him. More important than his pride or hatred or distrust. He won't remember this in the morning, but it seems abominable for me to deprive him of it.

"Lagan, look at me," I order, guiding his head up. The moment his dazed amber eyes lock on mine, I whisper, "Come for me."

His lips part on a sharp, abrupt inhale, brows crashing together at the same time our hips do. The last thrust is as hard as the first ones, slamming me into the bed with enough force to knock a gasp from my lungs.

The groan that rips through him is followed by the hot rush of him filling me, and I resolutely keep my wide eyes fixed to his. It's nothing like Wicker, who comes aggressively, like it's a weapon.

And it's nothing like Pace, who comes and never really goes. Lex comes like a slowly rolling wave, his body rippling with every warm surge.

"Good," I tell him, never breaking his gaze as my thumb sweeps across his cheekbone. "You're so good."

I know when his eyelids flutter closed that it's over, and I have the foresight to guide him just before he collapses, his spent cock slipping wetly from me as he furls to the mattress at my side. I take a moment to arrange him, brushing the hair from his face as he stills with a long, oddly troubled sigh. There's a crevice in his brow that never really goes away, not even when I soothe it with my thumb. He looks weirdly both strong and vulnerable, his fingers clutching the pillow even when he's returned to slumber.

There's a weight to the moment that sits heavily in the pit of my chest, and I remember back to the morning I started my period.

"This is all so fucking easy for you."

If I knew then what I know now, I would have told Lex that every step of the way has been nothing but pure agony for me, but that I also understand. I see now how *not* easy it is for him. And for reasons I doubt he deserves, I feel accountable for respecting what happened here tonight.

It's why I roll to my back, grab the pillow beneath my head, and tuck it beneath my hips.

That's when I realize Wicker is in the doorway again.

I freeze, wondering how long he's had the door open like that, watching as I coaxed his brother to fill me up.

His voice is almost too quiet–too soft–to hear. I still make out the words, whispered on a slow, shaky inhale. "Thank you."

"Get out." The demand is more of a surprise to me than him. I don't mean to say it, even though it's what I feel.

This is ours.

Not yours.

Wicker doesn't look at me, though. His gaze is glued to his sleeping brother as he stands there, shoulders slumped into a tired curve. "I'll come for him in the morning," he says, finally looking away.

My jaw clenches. "Get–the fuck–*out*."

But he's already closing the door behind him, leaving me to stare at the gilded ceiling, hips tipped upward. I use my fingers to push the sticky fluid back in as I send up a silent, grim prayer.

Let this be the one.

I WAKE UP SLOWLY, drifting to the surface of a dreamless void with heavy eyes that squint against the sun pouring in through the windows. Everything seems brighter against the gilded surfaces. My first attempt at a stretch ends on a wince before it ever really begins, and when I turn my head, I'm startled to find someone else there.

Lex, I remember, the events of the previous night coming back to me in a flood of images. He's awake but eerily motionless, perched on the furthest side of the bed, his back to me as his head hangs low. He hasn't looked at me yet, and it takes a few blinks, but the broad expanse of his back finally comes into focus.

When it does, my breath hitches.

The late morning light illuminates the scars, throwing the depth of them into sharp, shocking relief. But worse than that are the raw slashes that look to be newer.

Remembering my hands sliding through blood last night, I look down, seeing dark brown stains beneath my fingernails.

Did I make those, digging my nails into his back?

But no, that's not right. Most of the wounds are well scabbed over. Only a couple seem to have reopened over the night.

I watch his back for a long time as I lay there–the rise and fall of it, even and measured, and the texture of it, gnarled and disturbing. The longer I stare, the more wrong it feels, as if I'm indulging in the sight of something I shouldn't. Something–no, some*one*–made those marks, and it only adds to the feeling that there are secrets in the Palace I don't understand.

My mouth parts with the urge to say his name, but I pause, not knowing how awake he really is. Do I call him Lex? Or should I call him Lagan? If he's awake, then maybe he won't like that.

Instead, I utter a reluctant, "Hey."

His back tenses so minutely that if I weren't staring, I might have missed it. His shoulder blade shifts as he reaches up to rake a wide hand through his hair, fingers gathering it from temple to crown as he turns to look at me. His eyes drop from my face to where the sheet is pulled to my chest. "Did I do it?"

I try to read his voice, quiet and frustratingly even, but find myself at a loss. I'm on one side of the bed, but he's on the other. A canyon between us. "Yeah," I answer, awkwardly gathering the sheets tighter. "We.... uh. You know."

His head dips in a nod, and he shifts away from me with a sigh. I get a clear view of his backside below the scars, the hard muscle of his ass, when he rises to his feet. I watch as he reaches for the night stand beside him. That's when I see the supplies by the bed. A pair of shorts he tugs on one leg at a time. A kit with a red cross on the side. When he turns next, he's wearing his glasses again.

"Where did all that come from?" I ask, looking away from the scattering of hair on his lower belly, and over at the supplies.

"I told the guys to leave it for me." His gaze darts to my throat. "I knew I'd have to check you over. Make sure I didn't leave any wounds."

If reading his voice is hard, then reading his expression is impossible. He's back to the efficient, clinical man I meet downstairs in the medical wing, even wearing nothing but a pair of boxers.

It makes it easier to let the sheet go, exposing my breasts. His eyes pin me, jaw tightening. I look down.

"Damn," I mutter when I see it. The perfect imprint of his teeth is filled with dried blood. A deep purple bruise blooms around it, but the middle is perfectly unflawed.

"I did that?" he asks, hand reaching out to inspect the wound. My skin prickles in anticipation, but he stops short. "Of course I did. I need to clean that. A bite like that could get infected."

Perching on my side of the bed, he tears open a sterile package of square gauze, pressing it to the mouth of a bottle of alcohol, and then flipping it over, saturating the cloth. "This will hurt," he says, matter-of-factly. There's no trace of apology in his voice, but when he pushes it to the wound, his touch is careful and light, amber eyes flicking up to mine.

The sting is awful, but I try not to let it show. For some reason, I feel the need to explain. "You stopped when I asked you to."

He lifts the gauze pad only to dab it back. "Not fast enough." His thumb grazes the smooth skin below the wound. There's an unhappy tightness to his mouth. "Pace and Wick said they'd keep me from hurting you."

"It didn't go too far." I think about him on top of me, feral and wild, hips thrusting, mouth hungry. "I had it under control."

"West End," he mutters, "always a glutton for punishment."

I ignore the jab, because that's what it is, a way to turn this back around on me. Instead, I ask, "What happened to your back?" This conversation, these questions are a way to distract myself from the fire stabbing its way through my breast.

Lex's eyes shutter. "Hockey accident."

It's a lie.

Worse than that, it's a really bad lie, almost no effort made to sell it.

The next time he lifts the pad, it's pink with diluted blood. He leans over, a piece of hair slumping into his face, and blows a gentle stream of air against the tender flesh.

Instantly, my nipples pebble.

Between one breath and the next, Lex's deep voice asks, "Did you climax?"

It's strange how I can have a half naked man blowing air over my boobs and not blush at all, but this question makes heat rush to my cheeks. "No," I admit. It may have actually been the first time sex with one of these men wasn't soured by the lack of it. At least for once I felt alive, like I was part of it and not just a passive participant in a medical procedure. An orgasm couldn't have made it better or worse. Unsure how to make such a confession, I add, "It was still... good, though."

He pauses halfway through smearing ointment on my breast, his eyes jumping to mine. "Getting fucked by a barely conscious man who strangled you was *good*?"

I rush to say, "Those parts weren't good. I just mean... "

God. What do I mean?

"You think I'm worried about how good of a lay I was?" he asks, brows slamming together. "I needed to make a deposit and encourage the motility of my sperm."

I sputter, totally at a loss for words. He attacked me last night. *Ravaged* me. It's so hard when he's looking like this, with his hair down and those glasses perched on his nose. Even in his rigidly clinical behavior, he looks so much softer here than the wild man who thrust into me with wild abandon. It's hard to believe this technical, competent, measured man is the same one who held me down and used his body to hurt me.

Under the baffled weight of his gaze, I blurt, "I put the pillow under my hips," needing him to know I did it right. That I didn't waste it. That I understood the gravity of it. "I didn't waste it."

His amber eyes drop, watching as his long, deft fingers screw the cap back onto the ointment. "Show me."

I blink at him. "Show you?" I suppose the pillow is around here somewhere. Probably the one wedged under my elbow. Only then I meet his gaze, and it clicks. Lex doesn't want to see the pillow. He wants to see the evidence. "Oh," I say, shifting awkwardly. "An exam, you mean."

His response is to begin peeling the sheets back, rising to his feet. "Come to the edge," he commands in his even, toneless voice. Knowing the drill, I rearrange myself, but when my thighs fall open, he reaches forward to hook his hands below them, yanking me with such casual power that a gasp pours from my lips.

It's distinctly different from the way it is in the stirrups, his warm palm landing on the inside of my thigh and parting it wider for his gaze. But I still swallow as he crouches, shirtless, with those amber eyes as intent as lasers as they take me in.

Maybe it's the instinct that's been built over weeks being on his med table, the sharp scent of antiseptic enhancing it. Maybe it's the memory of the way he felt last night. Maybe it's just that I've got a sexy guy between my legs and he's not being an ass about it.

Whatever it is, I'm suddenly horny as hell.

"Any pain?" he asks. My eyes track his forearms, strong and muscular. "Soreness?"

I take a deep breath, knowing that he can probably see my building wetness. "Maybe a little. Nothing serious."

There's a long beat where he just looks, and aside from a twitch of the tendon in his neck, he's as still as a statue.

And then he slides a finger into me.

The sound I make is a touch too breathy, and I bite it off with a hiss.

"Sorry," he says, not sounding sorry at all. "Looking for tears."

But my body doesn't feel like he's looking for tears. It feels like he's sliding his finger in and out, and when he glances up, holding my gaze, my belly clenches with want.

It doesn't get any better when he pitches forward, lips parting as he swipes out with his tongue, licking the peak of my clit.

I freeze, a whimper trapped in my throat. "What are you doing?"

Without missing a beat, he answers, "Performing cunnilingus," and latches his lips around my clit.

The move makes my whole body jolt, thighs falling open wider, and it's like a flood gate opens. My jaw drops on a long, agonized cry, and the sound seems to spur him on, a rough sound escaping his throat as he edges closer, tongue sliding wetly through my folds.

"Oh, god," I gasp. "Oh, fuck."

His hair is just as soft as I know it'll be when I knit my fingers through it, holding him close. Last night, Lex was a man possessed, but now I'm the mindless animal, rutting up into his mouth as his fingers fuck me.

I can't be blamed. Lex's tongue is just as deft as his fingers, its firm point pressing in against the side of my clit, looping around it but avoiding the sensitive center. He works me like a marionette, slick and sure, and the more I pull on his hair, the more focused his ministrations become, narrowing in on where I want him.

But it's only when I pry my eyes open to stare into his hooded eyes that he finally flattens his tongue against me, his shoulder shifting as his fingers curl.

I yell when I come.

I've never done that before, mouth hanging open as a shrill cry erupts, my fingers clenching hard in Lex's hair. My toes curl, my body quakes, and it feels like I'm being split wide open and filled to the brim with liquid warmth.

I'm still whimpering when Lex stands, swiping a wrist over his glistening mouth. "Sperm can live in your reproductive tract for up to five days," he says, coolly adjusting his glasses.

"What?" I ask, panting. I don't even realize I've pushed the heel of my palm between my legs until his amber eyes track the movement.

He reaches down to adjust his cock, which I'm just now realizing is half hard. As I'm gaping at it, he explains, "The orgasm. It'll help promote insemination."

"Promote..." When it finally hits me, my knees snap closed. "Oh."

"The syringe deposits will continue–be prepared for one later today–but my brothers will want me to do this again."

"For extra deposits." He nods, the unspoken directive hanging in the air: *To create is to reign.* That's all this is about, and I remember my prayer from the night before. I rise up on my elbows, my heart still fluttering from the orgasm. "I can handle it."

His eyes skirt over me, landing on the bandaged wound on my breast. "I know you can."

Grabbing the supplies, he leaves, and the lashes across his back are the last part of him I see. I flop back, feeling the pulsing heat wane like the sound of his footsteps, and reconcile the truth. No one lives in the Palace and emerges without bleeding.

Without scars.

I DON'T LOOK at him until he's coming, after he closes his eyes, resting his jaw on my shoulder. It's his reflection that I stare at, the bathroom counter between me and the mirror, my hips getting a fresh layer of bruises.

It sucks because he's so fucking pretty, all cheekbones and long lashes.

It also sucks because after having Lex's mouth on me, I'm desperate for more.

"Jesus, Princess," Wicker groans, cock twitching as he unloads. "If you got any tighter, I'm not sure I could get in."

He cornered me in my bathroom while I was getting ready for school, a hasty, "Beat it," directed at Stella, who scurried quickly out of the room.

I wait for the yank, the hard withdrawal as he pulls out, but he waits for a long beat, cock in place.

"Are you uh, stuck?" I ask, wondering what's going on. Wicker is the definition of 'wham-bam-thank-you-ma'am.'

His forehead presses into the back of my head. "Just giving it time."

"It." His sperm. All those little, virile swimmers, rushing toward my embryo.

I stand there, hips smarting, feeling his weight pressing down on my back, until he finally does pull out, fingers replacing his cock, pushing any wayward semen back inside.

Content, he grabs a towel off the bar and wipes down his dick. He tosses me the dirty cloth and looks past me to his own reflection. He licks his fingers and rakes them through his hair. "I need you ready tonight. Six o'clock."

Ready? I fight an eye roll. The tiny, incremental progress I've made with Pace and Lex has been impossible with Wicker. He's too fucking self-absorbed. "So no panties," I venture. "Assume the position?"

"Funny," he says, completely deadpan, zipping up his jeans. "We're going out, and I need you to be shined, plucked, and dressed appropriately." I turn as he strides across the room, flings open the closet door, and rummages through the racks.

"What are you doing?"

He pulls out a hanger and holds up a dress. It's pale pink–strapless, sheer–with a bell-shaped skirt that hits above the knees. He decides, "This'll work. The car will be waiting downstairs." He passes me, thrusting the dress into my hands with a sleazy wink. "But yeah, now that you mention it, ditch the panties. It's going to be a busy night."

That's how I end up in the back of the SUV with him, pulling at the short skirt while I ignore the layer of crinoline attempting to wedge between my ass cheeks. "Where are we going again?"

"Trudie Stein's house." He was already in the car when I got in, sprawled across the seat with his chin propped up on his knuckles. He looks bored. I sit across from him, taking in the expensive charcoal gray suit paired with a dark blue tie that matches his eyes. I shift in my seat, crossing my legs, and his eyes dart down to the exposed skin. That's when I see that he's also got a shiner, a ruddy bruise purpling at the top of his cheekbone.

"What happened?" I lean over and reach for his face, but he jerks back, giving me a hard look.

"Took an elbow from Decker during a scrimmage. Didn't stop me from scoring though." His fingers gently probe the bruise, and he pauses, asking, "Is it bad?"

The truth is that it makes him look even hotter than before, scuffing up his pretty boy looks in a sexy, dangerous way. *Not* that I'd tell him that. "It's noticeable."

"Shit." He grimaces. "I've got to perform."

My eyebrows hike upward. "You're playing the cello tonight?"

He gives me a flat, exasperated look. "Yeah, Red. Why else are we going to Trudie Steins'?"

"How would I know? You guys never tell me anything." I sigh and grab my purse. Rummaging around in the bottom, I find the makeup kit Stella stashed inside for 'touch-ups.' Pulling out the bottles of concealer, I pat the seat next to mine. "Come here and I'll cover it up."

Wicker eyes both me and the bottles skeptically, but moves across the empty space to the seat next to mine. His legs are long and take up so much space, and I feel the warm press of his calf against mine. He smells good, clean with a hint of something spicy. I take his chin in my hands and twist his face until I see the bruise.

"He got you good."

Wicker grunts in response, quiet as I squeeze a small amount of concealer on my fingertip and coat the swollen spot with a thin layer. Our skin tones are different, but it works well enough. Stella's had to cover my own bruises at times, like the ones Lex left on my throat, and the combination of tones works on any complexion. Wicker's skin is perfect, unflawed other than the bruise and a thin white scar just under his chin.

I brush against it with my thumb. "What's that from?"

His fingers meet mine as he touches it. "When I was eight, Lex, Pace, and I were playing 'iceberg' in the parlor."

"Iceberg?"

There's a surprising lightness to his grin. "Same concept as hot lava. You know, that game where you try not to touch the ground by jumping around the furniture?"

I mix in another layer of concealer. "Yeah."

"Well, back then, the parlor had this pristine white carpet."

"Gotcha."

"I tried to make this epic jump from the couch to the rocking chair—and I made it, except I didn't account for the backswing of the chair. My chin hit the edge of it, giving me a good gash. Blood just went *everywhere*."

"Ouch." I wrinkle my nose. "Facial wounds are always the worst. I bet you were scared."

"Not about the wound, but yeah." There's something faraway in his voice, and when I look at his face, expecting to see his standard smug expression, it's not there. "Anyway," he tilts his head and gives me a slow grin, "Chicks think it's sexy."

My stomach flutters at the shift in attention, although it's stupid. Wicker turns on and off the charm like a light switch. But I've been on the receiving end of his kisses, and as hard as I try not to fall for it, they still make my insides melt.

"Okay," I say, handing him a compact mirror. "I think that'll work."

He angles his face, checking out my attempt. "Good work, Red."

I toss the makeup back in the bag. "So, who is Trudie Stein and why did you invite me to come with you tonight?"

"She's chairperson of the city council, and one of Father's associates." He leans back and tosses an arm over the back of the seat. "She's having a campaign fundraiser, and I'm Father's contribution." The wording is strange, but before I can ask him to clarify anything, he adds, "Father's kept me busy as fuck lately, and we've got this tournament coming up and coach keeps giving us extra practice." He lifts his hips, grinding his cock into his hand. "If I'm not going to be home to make my deposits, you're just going to have to come with me."

The car turns down a long winding driveway, ultimately ending up in front of a brightly lit mansion. It's newer than the Palace, but no less grand. "So she's loaded," I say, peering up at the stone house. This kind of wealth... I'm not accustomed to it.

"All of Father's associates have money or power. Usually both." He looks out the window at the big house. "Tonight's the night you put all those lessons your mama paid for into practice."

The car stops and we're ushered to the walkway, where a banner announcing that we're about to enter a fundraiser for the support of the Open Hearts Adoption Agency hangs over the doorway. I smooth out my skirt while a servant goes to the back of the vehicle and removes Wicker's cello. Another attendant opens the front door, and I move to step forward, but the feel of Wicker's hand sliding into mine causes me to stumble.

"Stay by my side, Princess," he whispers, fingers tightening against mine. "We're about to be surrounded by vultures."

Inside, the party is in full swing, people—members of Forsyth—schmoozing openly. I see vaguely familiar faces from the front page of the local paper. The university president, the police chief, council and school board members, each holding a glass of wine or tumbler of liquor, all with the same false smile plastered on their faces.

These are not my people. This is not my world. The urge to run is overwhelming, but none of it is as surreal as seeing Wicker morph into another personality as he places a hand on my lower back and murmurs, "Smile," then fluidly grabs two glasses off a passing tray. "Drink, pretend to love me."

A smart retort is cut off by the sound of Wicker's name being called.

"Whitaker Ashby."

We turn, and a woman with brassy blonde hair strides toward us. She's wearing a wrap dress, the tits she bought threatening to spill out of the deep cut V. Wicker's hand returns to my back, his fingers curling around my side. I wince as he brushes against the wound left by Lex's bite.

"Christine," he says, leaning forward and kissing her cheek. "You look lovely tonight."

She giggles, but nothing on her face moves. It's as if all the natural lines of her expression have been removed. "And you look fantastic." Her hand clamps down on his bicep. "So handsome and strong."

He clears his throat, a stiffness to his smile I'm not used to seeing. "Have you met Verity? My Princess."

Her gaze cuts to me, some of the friendliness disappearing. "I haven't had the pleasure."

"Verity, this is Christine," he takes a slow sip of his drink and then adds, "Oakfield."

"Oh," I say, clicking in on who this woman must be. Bruce's mother. "I-it's lovely to meet you."

Your son is dead, I think as she returns my smile. Either she's yet to be made aware of this fact, or she couldn't care less about her son's existence. In Forsyth, either could be a possibility.

"Smart girl," she says, eyes raking down Wicker's body, "getting out of West End while you could. They've gone downhill since Saul was removed. Nothing like they were when my husband was a member."

'Removed.' Assassinated, more like. Whatever it takes for this woman to believe her son wasn't the problem. Her son, who, if I understand correctly, was possibly killed by the man she's currently eye fucking.

"Father only picks the best of the best, you know that, Christine," Wicker says, giving me a wink. "And our Verity is proving herself worthy of the title."

He leans in and kisses me on the temple, lips soft as butterfly wings.

"Oh, Whitaker, darling, you're here." Another woman comes over, a shiny gold name tag on her pale blue tweed suit jacket. *Trudie Stein.*

He leans forward to kiss her on the cheek, but she turns her head at the last minute, grazing his lips with her bold red lipstick. "Oops," she laughs, reaching out to wipe his mouth with her thumb. "Clumsy."

"Trudie," Christine says, "Whitaker was just introducing me to the *Princess.*"

Trudie's eyes shift from my face to my belly and back up. "Welcome, sweetheart. How lovely of you to support my campaign."

As these women hover around us, I try to figure out what's happening here—who Wicker is in this space. Entertainment? A contribution, he said. The way Christine Oakfield's hand lingers on his arm is a clear signal, and the smear of lipstick on the corner of his mouth is conspicuous. It's possessive. And it's an affront. For better or worse, Whitaker Ashby belongs to me.

"I came to support Wick." I lean into his side, resting my hand on his hard stomach. "I'm so eager to hear him play," I say, looking up at him sweetly, "you know, for a crowd. I'm used to solo performances, of course."

"Serenades," he laughs, charm exuding from him. "She's my muse." The women share a look, a dark flicker between them, and he pulls me closer, flush against his side, like armor.

"Well," Trudie says, her demeanor turning chilly. "I hope you've brought a little of that inspiration with you tonight, because you're the reason everyone is here."

"Nonsense," he says, blue eyes sparkling in the light of the chandelier. Wicker Ashby was made for moments like these. I see that now. "You're the reason everyone is here. I'm just a bonus."

The compliment melts a little of the ice. "We'll start in ten minutes. Sound good?"

"Yes, ma'am," Wicker replies.

A woman walks past us and Trudie grabs her arm. "Becca, darling, have you set out the donation cards yet?"

The woman stops, and there's something different about her. She's in a modest dress and comfortable shoes. Her hair is a little bit of a mess. She also has on a name tag that says, *Becca Adams: Open Hearts.*

Her smile is flustered but excited. "Yes, the twins will be stationed at the door and will give one to each patron as they depart." She gestures to the two teenagers in the foyer.

Trudie giggles. "Micha and Michaela? That's a fabulous idea. No one can say no to those adorable children."

"They wanted to come," Becca says, looking a little annoyed. "Gwen and her boyfriend are mingling as well."

A hand flutters at Trudie's pearls. "Such a family affair. The Adams' are an asset to the community."

Becca doesn't look swayed by the flattery, but says, "We appreciate you bringing attention to our program." She glances over. "You're Whitaker, right?"

He graces her with a warm smile. "Yes, ma'am."

Her eyes warm, but it's not like the other women. Becca gives off a soft, maternal energy. "Your father is one of our biggest donors. Thank you so much for coming tonight. It means so much to not only have someone talented like you perform, but to also have one of our former match-ups participate."

"Any time," he says. "I'm happy to help."

"Becca," Trudie says, steering her by the arm, "let me introduce you to a few people before Whitaker starts."

The two are swallowed in the crowd and we're left with Christine, who assesses me and Wicker closely. "Guess I'll go freshen up," Christine says. "Verity, care to join me?"

It's not a request, but Wicker holds onto me, pressing his fingers too close to the bite wound. "Sorry, Christine. I need Verity with me for a few more minutes." He gives her a pouty grin. "You wouldn't deprive a performer of his muse, would you?"

It's clear she would, but instead of arguing, she turns on her heel and walks away, hips swaying in her tight dress.

Once we're alone, I level him with a look. "I'm your *muse*?"

He grabs another drink off a passing waiter's tray, depositing the empty one. "You could be if you didn't complain so much."

I fold my arms. "You know what I think?"

"Enlighten me," he replies, throwing the drink back.

"You didn't bring me here to fuck. You brought me here as protection."

He laughs, but his expression remains flat. "How's a little girl like you going to protect a man like me?"

"Not that kind of protection." I jerk my chin at the women surrounding us. It's more than just Christine and Trudie. Every female, and possibly even a few males in spitting distance, watch him with a perverse hunger in their eyes. "They want you."

He swallows the last of his drink. It's champagne. I try not to think too hard about the last time he drank champagne in my presence. "*Everyone* wants me, Red."

Fair. "But *they* think they're entitled to it. Why?"

Something in his eyes darkens–a wildness that sends a tremor down my spine–and when he presses his hand on my back, pushing me down an empty hallway, my options are to make a scene or follow obediently.

Jaw clenched, I follow.

My heels click against the marble floors, and the second we're out of sight of the ballroom, he pushes my back against the wall, trapping me in with his body, strong and powerful. Heedless of my frightened flinch, he presses a palm to the space next to my head, hemming me in. "Let me make something clear, Princess." A casual observer might assume we're being intimate, his face leaning close to mine, but looking into his eyes, that's not what this is about. He's pissed. "I don't need a therapist. I need a Princess. Your job tonight is to look pretty and have your pussy ready when I want it."

I shove against his chest with my hand, but he doesn't budge. "My job *is* to serve you–to support you when you need it. But I can't do that while you and everyone else hides everything from me!"

His jaw tics, gaze pinging from my eyes to my mouth. My heart thunders, terrified of pushing him too far, testing his patience, because although Wicker uses me, he doesn't hurt me. Not outside of his blind lust. Not since that first night.

Something tells me he could, though.

If he wanted to.

"You know what you need to know," he replies, pitching closer when a couple stumbles, laughing, down the hall toward the bathrooms. As they pass, he brushes his lips across my cheek, making me tense up. Wicker's chest jumps with a scoff. "Except, apparently, how to properly be with a man."

Hot indignation rises, along with the memory of his accusation about me being unsexy. "Need I remind you," I grind out, "of the chair that took my virginity?"

The couple is gone now, and he jerks back, hissing, "Jesus

Christ, I'm so sick of hearing you whine about that. So you had your cherry popped and it was shitty. Boo-fucking-hoo." Flinging a hand out, he gestures to the crowd at the end of the hall. "Ask around, Princess. No one had a fun time losing their virginity. You came into the masquerade as a grown ass woman, knowing well and fucking good there might be something in store for you." His eyes rake up and down my body, lip curling in disdain. "That's a choice, and it's more than most Royal women get."

Bitterly, I ask, "And what do Royal men get?"

His eyes flash with such sudden, fiery rage that I press back into the wall, as if I could get away. "You want to know what we get?" The arm beside my head tenses as his blue eyes hold mine. "Fine. Ask me how old I was when I lost my virginity."

The words bring me up short. "What?"

"Ask me," he repeats, low and hard. The look in his eyes is a dare, and I'm not sure I should take it.

"How old were you?" I ask, searching his eyes.

I think I must be expecting some terrible boast. Wicker Ashby would probably do that–flaunt around the fact that he was banging high school bimbos left and right. Or maybe he'd brag about waiting for the right one. The perfect set of tits. The ideal lay.

What I'm not expecting is the cold, sharp smirk.

And I'm definitely not expecting his answer.

"I was ten."

I suck in a shocked breath, my heart sinking. "That's... that's *vile*," I say, face twisting as I look at him. To think of someone doing that? It makes my stomach lurch. "That's not losing your virginity, Wicker. That's ra–"

He slams his hand over my mouth and his body into mine. He's so close I can feel his hair tickle my forehead as he leans over, blue eyes piercing. "*That's* Forsyth."

Our gaze holds, and for a moment, I see past his beauty–past the smug, arrogant exterior–to the boy lurking underneath. There's anger in his eyes, frustration, even some satisfaction at my reaction. But there's also an unfathomable hurt.

With a blink, he shutters it all away, and Whitaker Ashby is in front of me again.

"Front row," he grinds out, breath hot against my cheek. "And put a smile on your fucking face."

He pushes off, releasing my wrist in the process. By the time I peel myself off the wall, he's gone.

23

icker

A SIGN of a skilled musician is that we operate not just on sound, but how the music *feels*. The vibration of the strings, the reverberation in the hollow core of the cello under my fingertips, is as familiar as the sound of a woman seizing beneath me, spine arching, breath shallow. Their bodies are as much of an instrument as this carved piece of wood between my legs.

Me? I'm just the one who pulls the strings.

Which is why I think Verity and all her disapproval and probing questions annoy the fuck out of me. Her job is to get pregnant—to create—not to talk. Not to question. Not to mindfuck me two minutes before I have to perform in front of this room full of vampires.

The most annoying part is that she was right. I did bring her for a purpose—as a shield.

There's a reason I fuck her from behind. Why I don't look her in the eye when I'm balls deep inside of her, or when she's down on her knees sucking my cock bringing me to the edge. Even now, I focus on anything but her–the strings beneath my fingertips, the way the vibrations rattle through my chest and the eyes of everyone watching me. Every woman. Every man. Everyone but the guy in the back, who can't stop looking down the front of his girl's dress. Don't blame him. She's got a killer rack.

But everyone else wants one thing: a part of me.

Time after time, I do it, because I don't have a choice. Never have. I give and fuck and smile, snatching away little parts of myself and hiding them away, because they'll be taken if I don't. It's all taken, in time. Some days I wake up and wonder how there's any of me left. Some days I seek out my brothers and just sit there as they talk, like I'm an empty battery and they're charging me up. Some days I feel like a brittle skeleton in a lake of piranhas, picked clean, nothing left to offer.

But *her*? She can have my cum. Nothing I can do about that.

I refuse to give her anything else.

I sense her in the front row, catching glimpses of her smooth legs glued together at the knee. She looks like a Princess, prim and proper except for that skirt inching up her thighs. It's four inches too short, and I chose it specifically for its accessibility.

I don't need to look at her to know she doesn't see me the way the others do. There's no hunger in her eyes. No desire. She loathes me for being a Prince. For taking her that night, bloody and torn, claiming her for me and my brothers. She despises me for hunting her down twice a week, multiple times a day, for releasing and unleashing into her to make up for my brother's failures.

She hates me for locking her in two nights ago with Lex.

After years of being used, there's a certain thrill in being able to do it to someone else.

I draw the bow back and slash across the strings, a sharp tune cutting through the air. I didn't lie about Verity being my muse. Just not in the way one would expect. I refined the piece after Father's session with Lex. Slowly plotting it out while watching over him at night, the wounds painful and oozing. A tribute to how this girl has done nothing but add conflict and turmoil in our lives.

Over the moving bow, I see her legs shift and it pulls my eyes up. She's trapped between Trudie and Christine. Her hands are folded on her lap, her thighs spread, revealing a gap in her skirt. Our eyes meet over the cello neck, the dark glint matching the small uplift of her lips in a tiny smirk.

Her knees drop to the side, giving me a full view between her legs.

As my cock swells, anger licks against my spine. She's the only woman I can have right now. The only one I can fuck with absolute abandon. The women in here, the ones eyeing me like a piece of meat, I'm for them, not the other way around.

Heat creeps up my neck, my fingers are numb from gripping the bow. The calluses are hard and thick, built up from years of practice. I never look away from her, not when she lets her fingers dangle against the inside of her knee, or when her tongue darts out to wet her bottom lip. The room is still as I draw out the last note, letting the sound reverberate against the high ceilings. When the sound ceases, I stand, barely on my feet, and dip into a tense bow before Trudie jumps to her feet, clapping furiously. Two seats over, Christine follows, leaning over to give me a view of her tits. One by one, the crowd stands, until the only one left seated is Verity.

"Thank you, Whitaker," Trudie says, snatching the microphone. She grips my bicep. "Such an incredible talent..." She drones on about donation envelopes and the children at Open Hearts, but I don't listen to her. I don't care. I step off the stage, grab Verity by the hand, and yank her out of her seat.

"Where—" she starts, but I step into a staircase, one that winds down a floor and leads to glass double doors. Swinging it open, the scent of chlorine hits my face, and I toss her inside. Verity stumbles on the tile pool deck, her pale pink dress in contrast to the aqua blue water behind her.

"You think taunting me is smart?" I shrug off my jacket, tossing it on one of the lounge chairs. "Getting me hard in the middle of a performance?"

"I don't know what you're talking about," she says innocently, eyes tracking me as I yank off my tie and loosen my collar. "You're the one who put me in this dress and told me not to wear panties. You're the one who brought me into a den of horny hyenas, playing perfect little Prince and then getting pissed when I ask questions."

"That's enough!" I shout, grabbing my belt buckle. I point at the lounge chair. "Bend over."

She has the audacity to look appalled. "No."

"No?" I laugh, easing the buckle loose. "You don't have the right to deny me, *Princess*."

"I'm not bending over." She crosses her arms over her chest. "If you want to fuck me, you can do it facing me. Look me in the eye the way you would any of those women up there."

I lunge at her, but she jumps out of the way. "You're not in control here," I say, but I sense it: the untruthfulness of that statement. "You signed the covenant and there's nothing in it about eye contact."

"Fine," she says, standing a few feet away, the lights reflecting behind her. "But tell me the truth. Are you fucking them? Are you violating *your* contract with me?"

"Jesus Christ." I snort, in complete disbelief. "You don't even want me and you're jealous? I should've known. Looks like the West End ego extends to its lesser sex."

Her pink lips purse into a scowl. "Maybe I just want to know why you can't look me in the eye while you're screwing me. Is it because I'm not one of them? I'm not rich and powerful and experienced, and I can't give you whatever it is they do?"

"What?" The accusations are wildly off base. "Don't be stupid, Red."

There's a burst of frustration in her eyes. "Then tell me! What don't I understand, Wicker? Lex makes me look at him when he makes his deposits. Pace demands that I only focus on him. But you? I could be a blow-up doll for all you care!"

I lunge again, grabbing her by the wrist, but this time she lurches backward to break away. The struggle is sudden, unexpected, and her heels slip against the tile as I tug back. It's practically slow motion, our eyes locked as she flails, shooting out both hands to clutch my lapels.

With a jerk, we both tumble gracelessly, plunging into the water.

The water is warm but still shocking, absorbed by the fabric of my shirt and pants like sandbags tied to my limbs. We're tangled together, arms and legs, and I fight against her to get loose. We both emerge at the same point, gasping for breath, but I keep one hand on her arm, holding her close.

"You fucking lunatic!" I shout, voice echoing off the low ceiling.

She blinks water out of her eyes. "You pushed me in!"

"I *grabbed* you," I say, shaking out my hair, splattering it across her face. "You're the one that pulled me in!"

She shivers, and the sheer top of her dress is completely see-through, giving me a full view of her tits. The first good look I got of them was in the locker room after Pace's win, watching my brother lick and suck them into stiff peaks. Beneath the water, my cock twitches at the vague sight of her dark, round nipples pressing against the fabric.

Sliding my hand down to her wrist, I push her toward the wall, pinning her with my hips. "Cold, Princess?"

Her jaw is utterly locked. "N-no."

My pants sag around my waist and I cup the back of her neck, holding tight. "Then why are you shivering?"

"These are tremors of rage, Wicker." She thrashes against me, water spraying upward. "Get the fuck off of me."

"Or what? You'll ruin my night? Already done, Red." Her skirt billows around us, floating to the top of the water, and it's all too easy to dip my hand underneath, immediately finding her clit. Even like this, that part of her body is warm, and she inhales sharply at my touch. "You want me to face you while we fuck? Will that make this more real to you? Less perfunctory?" I bend, breathing on one of her nipples through the fabric, eliciting a shiver. "Less of an obligation?"

Her chest jerks with hard breaths, green eyes pinning me. "It'll mean nothing, because you're incapable of feeling anything."

"You have no fucking clue what I feel." I grab the heavy fabric in my hands and yank the dress up over her head, tossing it with a wet *slop* against the deck.

She's small in front of me. Sometimes I forget that about her. She's such an enormous, fucked up presence in the Palace that she might as well be nine feet tall. But the reality is *this*.

Wet hair plastered to her face. Body bare. Lips trembling.

Vulnerable.

But the look in her eyes is searing, as if I'm the only one who feels exposed here. Until my gaze lowers to the bandage taped to the side of her breast. "What the hell is that?"

Her arm lowers, clamping down. "Nothing you care about."

"Stop telling me how I feel!" Spinning around, I pull her deeper in the water. Verity struggles against me, her hair tickling my chest. Every move is followed by a heightened sensation. I grab her by the hair in an attempt to make her stop, but the move just tilts her face, her mouth, upward. Those green eyes dart right to my lips.

It's strange.

Any other girl in this town would have been all up on me by now. They would have been clawing at me, sucking, licking, moaning. *Taking.*

Of course Verity wants me–physically, at least. She's only human. I can see it in the way her pupils blow wide, wet eyelashes fluttering with a slow, heavy blink.

She wants it, but she's waiting.

She's waiting for me to give it.

"Fuck," I groan, crashing my mouth to hers.

Her tongue greets mine more eagerly than I'm expecting, hot and slick as she surges upward to meet me. It's not the first time I've kissed her, but it might be the first time I've done it just because I wanted to. I didn't have time to prepare, and now it's all clumsy, our teeth knocking when the motion of a wave bobs us downward.

Unthinkingly, my hand flattens around one of those perfect tits, and I'm sent reeling from the jolt of electricity that zings between us. In reaction, her hands push under my shirt, wet fingers slipping greedily over my chest. Her touch sends a spark of want to my cock and I grip my shirt at the collar and yank, buttons springing off.

It's all so fucking sloppy and artless. I just know that I want to feel her hands on me—all of her against me. I'm rewarded with her palms flattening on my chest, ghosting over my nipples as she drags her nails down, our tongues still entwined. The only coordinated thing about it is that we work together to push my pants off, four determined hands shoving and sinking, freeing me from the weight.

When we have my feet free to kick and propel, I wrap my arm around her to steer us back to the wall. Her body is lightweight when her back meets it, tits floating on the surface of the water. The only reason I break away from the kiss at all is to roughly hitch her up, her legs wrapping around my hips as I line myself up.

Her mouth latches onto my neck just as I punch in.

"Shit," I hiss, fighting the weightlessness to get closer.

She gasps at the invasion, but doesn't fight it, her legs fastening our bodies together. She's just as tight this way, maybe more so because of the position, and it's quiet. So fucking quiet that I can hear everything. The water slapping around us. The sound of my panting. The distant flutter of noise from the party. The way my palm sounds meeting the tile over her shoulder to anchor us might as well be an atomic bomb for how loud it sounds.

It's not just the way she's sitting on me that feels good. It's the way she rocks back, her hips rolling against mine. It's her teeth sinking into my shoulder, her hot breaths, and her whispered little cries. I fuck into her slowly, holding her body flush against mine, nothing between us but slippery water.

Ignoring the burn in my muscles, I dip my head, taking her nipple into my mouth, licking the tip into a stiff peak. Stupid. That's what I am for depriving myself of this. Her tits are a thing of majesty, heavy and full, and I send a psychic nod to Lex.

I get it.

In for a penny and all that.

My hand travels between us and I find her clit, rubbing it in tight circles. Her body responds, back arching, tits pressed against my chest as she curses. "Oh, god."

Her eyes are closed, and that's bullshit.

"Look at me, Red," I demand, thrusting into her. Her eyes flutter open and that green is as deep as the ocean. "That's right. You wanted it like this and now I want to watch you when you take my cum. Know when I fill you up and *create* with you. I want to see the very moment you fall apart."

For a beat, I don't think she will. All that fight between us must be too intense for her to actually let go. But we're moving as one, my cock buried deep inside of her, when her breath turns shaky and her walls clench around me. It's the feel of her pussy milking me that sends me into oblivion.

I come hard, eyes pinned to hers, feeling—*watching*—as she falls too.

Shivering in the cold winter air and wrapped in towels I found in the changing room, Tommy picks us up outside the backdoor in the SUV.

"What the hell happened to you?" he asks, eyeing the two of us.

"Fell in the pool." His eyes are glued to Verity, her tits and ass barely covered by the small towel. I shove the wet clothes into his chest, hard. "Put those in the back." Gripping the towel around my waist, I point to the open car door and tell her, "Inside. Now."

Shoeless, wet, and in a too small towel, Verity stares at the high step of the SUV with skepticism. Impatient to get out of here before we're caught, I bend and sweep a forearm behind her legs, ignoring her yelp as I easily lift her into the car.

"Thanks," she says, adjusting her towel, but not before I get a view of her left nipple. Fuck, she'd tasted so good. My cock rises under the cloth, and I do nothing to hide it.

Tommy slams the front door, and he looks back in the rearview mirror. "To the Palace?"

The 'yes' is on the tip of my tongue, but I look at Verity, pausing. She's shivering across from me, arms wrapped around her body. The hair dripping down her back is four shades darker when it's wet.

"You hungry?" I ask.

Stunned eyes rise to mine, blinking. "Starving, actually."

I raise my chin at Tommy in the mirror. "Call in an order for pick up at the diner," I tell him. "Two cheeseburgers, double fries, and a milkshake." I raise an eyebrow at her. "You?"

She gives her biceps a hard rub. "Pancakes."

"That's it?"

"And b-bacon," she says through a full body shiver.

"You heard the Princess," I say to Tommy. He nods and I press the button that raises the privacy screen between the front and back of the vehicle. Cranking up the heat, I jerk my chin. "Come here."

Her eyes flick down to the tentpole poking through the towel.

"Not for that." Well, not specifically. "My metabolism runs hot. The last thing I need is Lex giving me a lecture on hypothermia."

It's probably a testament of how cold she is that she lunges across the divide and curls under my arm, flattening her body against my side. The top edge of her bandage peeks out from above the towel, the tape waterlogged, slouching downward.

"You gonna let me see it?" I ask, gently brushing my fingers over the tape.

She gives a tight shake of her head. "It's not important."

"I say it is." I tap the bruise on my cheekbone. "I showed you mine."

She frowns, but sits up, pulling away from my body with obvious reluctance. Pushing down the towel, I reveal the entire bandage and tug at the loosened tape. What I see makes my stomach turn—dried red scabs in a ridged, oval pattern. Unreasonably, I'm reminded of Lex's wounds.

For a split second, I wonder if she's been punished.

"Jesus, Red." I run my finger over the bumpy marks. "What the hell is that?"

She grimaces. "Lex bit me."

"He *bit* you?" I look between the wound and her gaze, wondering when the hell–

Oh.

He'd asked me to leave some supplies in her bedroom that night, but he never told me he used them.

Scratching the back of my neck, I muse, "Guess I'm partially to blame there."

I could say I'm sorry, but it'd be a lie.

"You did know what he was capable of," she mutters, tugging the towel up to cover it. She leans back into me, but there's a distance there that wasn't before. "It's whatever. A little collateral damage for a greater cause."

She has *no* fucking idea.

Sighing, I grab her icy hand and flatten it to my stomach. "Next time we'll set up some way for you to call for help."

She stiffens at the suggestion there'll be a next time, but she doesn't argue. There's no way around it. Until Lex's cock gets right, we're going to have to let him out on his nights. Briefly, I wonder how much of this situation she's put together. Does she know what's at stake for us? She's seen Lex's back. Has she realized the reason for it?

Awkwardly, I try, "You're... a good Princess for going through with it." I swallow, the next words even harder to say. "And for pulling that slutty thing at the Fury the other night. Pace needed it."

Her head shifts, the force of her stare like a physical nudge. "Kind of like how you needed me here with you tonight?"

I brush my hair out of my eyes. "Yeah, kind of like that."

The bright lights of the diner illuminate the interior of the car, and we're quiet as he parks and goes inside. My fingers make circles on her shoulder as we wait, and I'm not sure why, but I feel compelled to say, "I'm not fucking them." Her head tilts to look up at me and I shift my gaze, anywhere but at her. "Trudie—Christine–any of those vampires. Well, not anymore. Not since I became a Prince."

There's an uncomfortable beat before she says, "Okay."

"But..." For some reason I keep going. "There are other expectations, ones outside of the covenant, and... I just couldn't do it tonight."

"What kinds of expectations?"

I look down and skim my fingers along her chin. She doesn't look half as tired as I feel. Usually, I'd resent her for that, but tonight?

Tonight I'm glad there's someone with enough energy to steer this shipwreck.

"You don't want to know, Red."

She's quiet for a minute, fingers playing with the fine hair below my navel. "Is what you said true? That you were ten?"

The exhaustion is so heavy I barely feel the regret slamming into me. Turning to look out the window, I say, "Some dads take their sons to the Hideaway...let Augustine pick out a good match, but not Father." I laugh darkly. "God, no. Everything, including virginity, is an opportunity."

"What happened?"

I look at her, giving in to the urge to sweep the wet hair off her cheek. "It's not a story for a Princess' ears." That's what Lex would say. Pace–he'd say it's not a story for *anyone's* ears. That I should keep it all locked up tight with those meager parts of myself I've managed to salvage over the years–wind it around them like a ball of yarn.

But when I look into her eyes, there's no disgust or judgment. She's just staring at me with knitted brows, waiting.

Waiting for me to give.

Taking in a deep breath, I begin, "We were in boarding school at the time. It was a Friday, and Father came to sign me out for the week-end." Sliding her a dark glance, I stress, "*Just* me. I really wanted to stay in the dorms. Play video games with Lex and Pace. Practice my shot in the parking garage. But Father said he wanted me to perform at an event. Kind of like the one tonight, actually." Her hand stills on my stomach, but she doesn't remove it. "I'd done it before. Playing cello, getting praise and encouragement afterwards. No big deal. So I went with him, all dressed up in my tuxedo, and I played the song I knew best: Air from the 3rd Suite. Father has always approved of Bach." My mouth ticks up into a cutting smirk. "When I finished, they announced dessert, but Father kept me on the performance plat-form." Despite being cold as fuck outside and only wearing a towel, a sheen of sweat coats my skin. "That's when the bidding started."

She freezes, mouth parting in shock. "They *bid* on you?"

Shrugging, I offer, "I went for twenty-five thousand." But despite my casual, cocky tone, I find my fingers linking with hers on my stomach.

An anchor.

Her face pales. "Dollars?!"

I nod, tipping my head back against the seat. The exhaustion pushes down on me. "I rode home in the back of a car a lot like this one."

Flicking my eyes downward, I catch the flash of anguish in her eyes. "Oh, god, Wick—"

I shake my head. "Don't. *Do not* feel sorry for me. Father tapped me for my skill set. Just like Pace. Just like Lex." I look down at the bandage. "Just like you."

It's nearing midnight when we finally get home. Verity's hand-maiden is already waiting for her at her bedroom doorway, eyes wide when she spots the wet clothes in Verity's hand and the soggy towel clutched to her chest.

"Princess! What–" Her gaze darts from Verity's disheveled state to my own. She looks panicked as she snatches the clothes from her, like she thinks she should have anticipated this situation. "I'll start you a bath!"

"Twitchy little thing," I say, as she vanishes in the room.

A gentle smile touches Verity's mouth. "You have no idea." A moment later, I hear the sound of water rushing out of the faucet, her smile falling. "Wicker?" she says, looking up into my eyes. "If–*when* I get pregnant..." Her hands clutch the towel to her stomach, eyes flicking nervously down the hallway. "Should I be worried? That it'll be... an Ashby?"

Christ.

There are fewer things I hate more than the consequences of my own actions, and going by the dread in her eyes, this moment is one of them. All I did was give her the smallest, faintest glimpse of what my father is capable of, and now I have to... what, exactly? Allay her fears? Assure her that whatever pops out of there is going to have the best childhood possible? Try to present my father in a more flattering, fatherly light?

Fuck that.

"Probably," I say, a touch too flippant as her face falls. The truth is, Verity hasn't taken anything from me tonight. Maybe that's why I go on. "And if it's mine you should be twice as worried. Because it won't be an Ashby at all." Holding her gaze, I confess, "It'll be a Kayes."

Her head snaps back, confusion furrowing her brow. "Kayes?" But then it clears, comprehension slackening her features. "Your father was a Royal," she realizes, her green eyes looking me up and down, calculating. "You're the Baron bloodline?"

"Not," I add, voice hard, "as far as anyone else is concerned."

She gives a heavy, stunned nod. "Yeah, I–I understand."

"Good."

"Well..." She gives me a tight smile. "Good night."

She turns to leave and I grab her by the wrist, pulling her

against me. We're skin to skin, towel to towel, and my cock prods hard against her lower belly.

"Thanks for coming with me tonight."

"Thanks for letting me come." The corner of her mouth quirks.

I lift an eyebrow. "So the Princess does have a sense of humor."

"Sometimes." Her eyes focus on my mouth and she adds, "Are you coming in?"

We both know that if I want to get in another deposit–or two–I could pull it off.

But the thought seems vaguely uninviting. "No."

Verity looks over my shoulder, and I turn to see Pace standing in the doorway that leads to our suite of rooms. Unlike the maid, he's completely unsurprised that we're in nothing but towels. Fucker's probably been watching us since we left Trudie's with some jacked up cam in the SUV. "Lex is asleep," he tells me, then lifts his chin at the Princess. "You need to prepare yourself."

Whatever flirty vibe we had going on vanishes. Squaring her shoulders, she visibly readies herself for the battle ahead, replying, "Of course," and ducks into her room, shutting the door.

"Thanks for the cockblock," I say. "I had fifteen minutes."

"You had all day to get your dick wet." He glances down at the towel. "Although it looks like you accomplished that."

"Shut up." Brushing past my brother, I jerk off the towel and toss it in the hamper in the corner. I don't want to talk about Verity right now. Tonight was unexpectedly nice, and now I'm about to unleash a beast to hunt her down like prey.

Pace's impatience tells me there's no time to shower, so I grab a pair of shorts, tugging them on as I walk into Pace's lair. Effie's cage is covered–asleep for the night.

"How long has he been out?" I ask.

Pace stretches, looking almost as tired as I do. "Thirty minutes or so."

"So, any time now?"

Lex has a routine. He passes out, slips into REM, and once he's in deep, he rouses, still unconscious but moving. And horny as fuck.

"He left a wound last time," I say, sprawling out on the leather couch. "Did you see the bite mark?"

Humming, Pace nods to the bank of monitors. "I saw it on the video, but she didn't take her shirt off yesterday when we fucked."

"Your loss." I think about her tits, buoyed in the water, round and soft. I run a hand through my still damp hair. "I wish I could fuck them, you know?"

He grins, tapping the keyboard. "Yeah, I know. That's half the reason I keep her covered up. Too much goddamn temptation."

A groan comes from the bedroom and we pause, eyes swinging to the door. "I told her we'd keep an eye out this time. Make sure he didn't hurt her like that again."

Pace throws me an aggrieved look, but says, "I'll monitor the cameras."

He flips them on, and we discover Verity is already in bed, her handmaiden nowhere to be found. She's propped against the pillow, wearing a loose Forsyth hockey T-shirt. As much as the girl drives me crazy, she's a team player, I'll give her that.

"Time?" I ask.

He checks the clock. "Twelve-oh-one. "

Preparing myself for the alter ego of my steady, controlled brother, I head to the door. "Let's make this happen."

MY COCK WAKES me up early the next morning, throbbing from a very detailed dream about coming on Verity's tits.

Sometime after letting Lex in the room, I fell asleep on Pace's couch. He's slumped over the desk, passed out, the screen to Verity's room still pulled up. Knowing my morning wood isn't going to let me go back to sleep, I rise, stretching my arms over my head, and move behind Pace to check the feed.

Verity and Lex are also both dead to the world, tangled up in the sheets of the massive bed. It's hard to get too detailed from the camera view, but I can see the rise and fall of Verity's chest, and the twitch of Lex's exposed foot. They both survived.

Passing Effie's cage, I lift the sheet and offer her one of the little treats Pace keeps nearby.

"*Wicker*," she purrs, taking the treat.

"Morning, dirty bird," I reply quietly, running my finger over her beak.

"*Suck my balls.*"

"Would if I could, sweetheart."

I drop the sheet and head to my room, grabbing my running shoes by the closet door. Lacing them up, I notice that I feel lighter than I have in a while. I don't know if it was talking to Verity or the mind-blowing sex. With the women Father whores me out to, there's little effort put into meeting my needs, and I can admit that I was doing the same to her. But coinciding orgasms? Give and take? Holding out wasn't just depriving her—it was depriving me, too.

Satisfied everyone is still asleep, I head downstairs. I'm programming my watch for my run when Danner walks into the foyer.

I take out my earbuds. "Hey, Danner, I need you to get something for me."

"Of course. What is it you need?" Danner remains expressionless, but I sense the dread from my question. Can't blame him. Past requests have been for anything from a kilo of coke, to a strap-on dildo, to a special order of nitro-level hot wings from the shitty place down on the Avenue.

"I need something nice for the Princess. Any thoughts?"

"Oh." That perks him up a little. "There's always jewelry."

I shake my head. "Jewelry comes with expectations. Hard pass."

He hums thoughtfully. "You know she prefers to spend her time in the solarium. Maybe something for that? I noticed her gardening shears are quite rusty."

"Yeah, sure." I slap him on the chest. "Gardening whatevers. Have it ready tonight. I'll give it to her tomorrow."

"Yes, sir." I start for the door but he calls out, "Whitaker."

I brush my hair out of my eyes. "Yeah?"

"Your father is requesting your presence in his office."

"Now?" I ask, glancing up the stairs. "Just me?"

"Just you."

I must look like Verity had last night when she learned Lex was coming. Shoulders squared, a steeling breath, trapping it all away. "Okay. I should, uh, get a shirt?"

"I suggest you don't delay."

The levity I felt waking up is gone, turned into a weight in the pit of my belly. When I reach his office, I open the door and step inside, feeling a small measure of relief that the others really aren't there. "You asked to see me?"

"Whitaker," Father says. A plate is next to his calendar holding a toasted English muffin with a bite taken out of it. His eyes sweep over me. "I see I caught you before your run."

"Yes, sir. Just getting in an early workout before practice."

"Your dedication pleases me." He picks up his knife and cuts into the butter, slathering it on the bread. "Early reports say that you were a hit at the fundraiser last night."

I lace my hands behind my back. The perfect son. "I'm glad."

His eyes flick up. "Although Trudie did say she noticed you left right after your performance."

My impulsivity—and my cock—will always be my downfall. "We started late," I explain, "and with my schedule having been so hectic–and with the Princess having her monthly–I just wanted to ensure that I made my deposit."

"Sometimes we have to be resourceful." He takes a bite and chews slowly, the only sound in the room from the ticking grandfather clock in the corner. I wait, heart pounding in my chest, until he adds, "Were you successful?

"In making a deposit yesterday? Yes." *Twice.* An unfamiliar warmth spreads in my stomach at the thought of what transpired last night. "In creating an heir? The odds seem in my favor."

"Excellent." He says that, but there's a hint of disapproval in his tone. "You'll need to find a balance in your activities. I have you scheduled for additional performances. It's campaign season, after all."

"Of course." I try not to show my disappointment. Or the exhaustion.

He dusts crumbs from his hands. "Despite the limitations of the covenants, there are expectations beyond performing. You understand that, do you not?"

My balls shrivel up a little. "Yes, sir."

"Good." He clears his throat. "Trudie Stein has requested you come for a private concert tonight."

My stomach sinks. "Tonight."

He looks at me over his glasses. "Is that a problem?"

There's just practice and studying and making sure Lex didn't do any long term damage to Verity. And beyond that there's just the way my gut feels thinking about it. "Of course not. No. Not a problem."

"Excellent." The smile he gives me is wooden. "Do make sure Trudie is satisfied to the best of your abilities."

The smile I give him is steel. "I always do."

When I leave, the dismay bangs around in my chest like a sack of rocks banging against my rib cage. It's why I abandon any hope of a run, heading through the kitchen instead. It's where Danner stops me, holding out a slick, well-designed gardening catalog.

Flipping through it, he asks, "Is there something in here that you'd like me to procure?"

Staring numbly at the pictures of roses and green things, I snatch it right out of his hands, dumping it into the garbage can at my side. "Forget it."

Danner frowns, halfway to grabbing it back. "But, sir..."

Turning, I give him a hard look. "I said forget it, Danner."

I've already given Verity the only gift worth having in this place: the knowledge that my father isn't to be trusted. Not with her child.

Anything else that's left of me has already been taken.

24

L ex

FOR THE SECOND time in a week, I wake to a glaring stream of light coming through the windows, the scent of roses wafting in through my twitching nostrils.

Fuck.

Even in the soft bed, my body aches, like I'm the one who went three rounds at the Fury a couple days ago. Lifting my hand to rub my eyes, I feel the warm press of flesh against my side and pause. It's not the lack of snoring or smooth, hairless legs that tips me off that I'm not in the bed with my brothers. This body is small, soft.

Shifting, I glance down to find Verity curled into me, her head nestled into the crook of my neck. Her hand is limp against my belly, and slung over my hips is a silky, bare thigh. Unlike last time, the two of us are in the middle of the massive bed, sheets twisted around us. My skin heats, taking in her exposed flesh. Against my side, I see her tits pressed together. They're soft-looking and perfect, round and frustratingly fuckable. What I'd give to slot my cock between them and coat them in cum. Another world, one where my spunk didn't carry the weight of gold.

And where I could actually get hard.

Nudging the sheet down, I hold my breath as my eyes skim over her lax body, taking an inventory of her injuries. There's dried semen between her legs, and the healing bite mark on her breast is still red and tender-looking, but doesn't seem to have gained a twin. I spot a hickey on her collarbone though, the skin prickled pink. Her other hand is tucked beneath her cheek, but it's easy to see the blue and red marks circling her wrists. Ghosting my fingers over the discoloration, I find that they match.

Brow knitting up, I wonder if she fought me. Is that why I held her down? In that split moment between sleep and total wakefulness, I try desperately to put the pieces together. Not just to connect the dots, but to remember the feeling of taking a woman again. Of pounding into her with absolute abandon. The sound of her labored breaths as she clutched me. The rush of semen pulsing out of me as I fulfill my duty as Prince.

It's pointless, nothing comes back. It's a void. Empty and lost, from the moment I went to bed down the hall, to now.

What makes it worse is the dull ache between my legs, the slight heaviness of a half erect cock. It happens sometimes. Morning wood. An automatic biological response. As much as I want to give it a hard tug, see if I can muster it to life, I don't. I already know what will happen.

Nothing.

The first time I noticed the problem was at a Nu Zoo party in the fall. I'd been off the Scratch for a few weeks and my libido was understandably low. My days were spent vomiting in the bushes between classes. My nights, restless and sweating. Textbook withdrawal symptoms. Nothing special or out of the ordinary. But after a month, Wicker got tired of the lethargy and self-pity, and *fuck*, so was I. He figured a good time—and a little pussy—would do me good. It came in the form of a threesome with some Phi Chi chick he'd boned a few times who wanted to experience an Ashby double-dicking.

And it all seemed pretty hot. I wanted her. Even more so after watching her ride Wick. The desire was there, but the minute I saddled behind her, slotting my cock between her cheeks, my pecker deflated like a goddamn balloon in the rain.

One time's a fluke. Four months? That's a fucking nightmare.

But knowing I can fuck Verity in my sleep, that I can maintain an erection and come, means that this isn't a physical issue. It's mental. And that's unacceptable with so much on the line.

Regardless, she feels good against me. Solid but light. Gentle. It's been a while since I felt a girl touching me like this, and I bask in the moment, feeling her curves nestled against me, pressing on the thickened weight between my legs.

I'm not sure how long I stay like that, idly toying with a lock of her hair as my eyes droop, thoughts drifting to nothing in particular. Wick will buy me some time, but I've got a packed schedule today. I've got a packed schedule *every* day, but this one includes a grad school admissions interview at ten. Then, a meeting with Father at eleven to go over how it went. A study group at one. Two hours to finish a paper on DNA synthesis. At some point, a rendezvous with whatever lackey Killian Payne sends to collect the video of us branding Oakfield down in the dungeon; a gift to his whores. Then, at seven, the campus support group for fuck-ups who spend all day jonesing for a hit of Scratch. Finally, I'll need to make a night deposit, which could take fucking hours.

As I'm ruminating over whether or not I'll even have time to attend the group meeting, Verity begins rousing.

She unfurls slowly. First, her feet, rubbing against my ankle, then her head, nuzzling in a little deeper. I can tell when it hits her–that she's in bed with me–because she goes suddenly still, a breath caught in her chest.

She releases it evenly, her warm, moist exhale fluttering against my collarbone.

"Hey," she says, pushing up to meet my gaze through heavy, squinted eyes.

Unmoving, I train my gaze to the ceiling. "We did it, right?"

There's a beat of silence, and then her quiet, "Yes."

It bothers me, the way she knows everything that happened last night. She knows the way I look when I come. She knows how hard I fucked her. She can clearly remember each movement, gesture, grunt. Who even knows what I did in this bed? Did I talk? Was it fast or slow?

I should leave.

Before I can, she adds in a small, reluctant voice, "We did it twice."

My gaze jumps to hers. "Twice?"

Her hair is a fucking mess, all tangled and rumpled, and when she blushes, I can feel it in the core of my goddamn balls. She looks like the personification of ripe, fertile lust.

I've never wanted to fuck a person more than I do at this exact moment, to make a baby in that taut belly, so the whole world knows what I can do.

Her thigh shifts against my cock and I lay a heavy hand on it, stilling her. Green eyes blink open wider, mouth parting. "Oh, are you...?"

I look away. "No."

In my periphery, I see her glance down, lip trapped between her teeth. "Are you sure? Because..."

"No," I snap. "It's fucking biology. Nothing else."

"Lex." She rolls into me, putting those tits inches below my face. "Can't we at least try?"

Try?

The thought is infuriating. Every goddamn deposit I make, I've got this girl writhing and moaning, desperate for a dick I can't give her. Each time I have to pull away, frayed and useless, is the most emasculating, humiliating moment of my existence. That night after Pace's fight, looking into her eyes and knowing how much she wanted it–wondering if she was wishing Wicker's cock was mine–plays in my head on repeat.

Father thinks he has to punish me for my poor performance, but the truth is, nothing he does could hold a candle to this frenetic conflict of needing something I'm too broken and impotent to take.

So when she inches down to brush her lips against my jaw, I twitch, eyes falling closed. When she rocks against my hip, her thigh dragging heavily against my cock, I clench my fists. And when her mouth stutters upward, seeking mine, I'm powerless to stop it.

It's soft and sweet, her lips coaxing on mine as they pinch and pull. The warmth of her breath mingles with the scent of her perfume–roses, always roses–and for a split second, I hate everything she represents.

But I still open to her.

I still reach up to cup her cheek as she licks out to taste me, letting my tongue delve into the slick heat of her mouth. I still tug at her hair and clutch at her thigh when she rolls to straddle me, rocking my hips up into her.

She tastes warm and ready, her tits are a shock of heat against my chest, and I'm powerless against the urge to hold them in my palms, indulging in the soft weight of them as she releases this small, quiet, needy sound.

It'd be so much easier if she didn't want me.

But I can feel her wetness growing as she rocks against me, her slick folds gliding over my half-hard cock. It's a sensuous, womanly motion that catches me off guard, and suddenly, I'm rolling us over, the kiss deepening as I let out a raw, ragged groan.

She reacts instantly, winding her smooth legs around me, welcoming. Inviting.

It's only when her fingers tangle in my loose hair that I feel the tickle of awareness. It takes me a moment to decipher it because I'm a little busy thrusting fruitlessly against her heat, but her teeth drag against my lip and it zings through me like an electrical current.

I jerk back, staring down into her dazed, green eyes. "We kissed," I realize.

She gives me a couple heavy blinks. "What?"

"Last night," I say, jaw clenched tight. "We kissed when we were fucking."

She frowns, flushed all the way down to her tits. "Well... yeah."

It hits me like a fucking sledgehammer to my solar plexus and I roll off of her, reaching for my boxers on the nightstand.

"Lex?" Her voice is cautious, small. It just makes my muscles tense even harder. I shove my feet into the boxers, yanking them up, but I can see her in my periphery, the worried crease in her forehead deepening. "What's wrong?"

"Nothing," I lie, trying to make my voice measured and calm. "You'll need to ice your left wrist."

Her response is hard and frustrated, hands clawing at the sheets to cover herself. "*Don't* do that. Don't shut down and treat me like... like your fucking patient!" More plaintively, she demands, "Tell me what's wrong."

"Everything is wrong!" I explode, whirling on her. My chest feels tight and too full, and when she flinches, the tightness turns to fire. "You don't get to decide how I create. What gives you the fucking right?"

She stares at me, mouth agog. "Because we kissed?"

"Because this is a duty," I seethe, gesturing to the satin sheets, "and you led me into this ridiculous bed and used me to fulfill your stupid fucking Prince fantasy."

Outrage fills her eyes, and when she lifts her fists, there's no ignoring the bruises encircling them. "In what universe is *this* a fantasy?"

Unmoved, I snatch a shirt from the nightstand. "The one where only one of us wakes up with a post-coital glow."

"This is insane!" She tumbles her way off the bed, hands scrambling to cover her breasts. "You wanted to kiss me!"

I roar, "I know I did!"

The sound makes her freeze, face paling–or maybe it's the

words. Maybe it's the way I can't keep the truth off my face, the envy from my eyes, or how my hands are unsteady with rage as I pull the shirt on, my movements jerky and stiff.

"Lex," she starts.

But I shake my head. "Forget it," I say, turning for the door. "If you need those wrists wrapped, ask Pace. I'll be out all day."

It's as I reach for the door that she speaks again, voice rushed and tense. "I made sure you were looking at me." It makes me freeze, hand suspended over the knob. There's a hitch in her voice, like maybe she's fighting back tears. "It wasn't like you're thinking. I didn't–I wasn't like Wicker. I didn't just take what I wanted."

I turn just enough to meet her gaze, green eyes welling as they drill into me. It's not sadness in them, or regret, or anything like that.

She looks so fucking bitter.

If I cared enough to wipe it away–if I even understood it–I'd tell her the truth. That it should have been mine. That I'm jealous of someone who doesn't exist. That I fall asleep and become something different, and that version of me has everything that *this* version of me can't. That I've wanted to kiss her since the first time we danced at the masquerade, but I knew better.

I'd tell her that I know she didn't take what she wanted.

She took what *I* wanted.

I watch some of the resentment bleed away from her eyes when I offer a small, understanding nod. It's as close to a thanks as I can give with this fire gnawing away in my chest. "I'll see you tonight for my third deposit."

～

THE COFFEE IS TERRIBLE, just like always, but it's strong as fuck, zapping right into my veins. For that, I'll forgive it. Looking around at the familiar faces, I realize that for once, I'm not the last person here. Remington Maddox is already in his seat, a foot propped on his knee as he idly doodles something onto the side of the white sole of his shoe. The three LDZ pledges are here, as well as a cutslut and a Beta Rho–the Barons' house. There are a couple people who are house-aligned, but not a member of a frat.

And then there are the sorority girls, who started filtering in a couple weeks ago. One of them, a North Side refugee who's struggling in the wake of Lucia's destruction, is slumped over in her chair, looking about halfway to vomiting on Maddox's shoe.

The only one who hasn't showed yet is Harker. Aside from me, he's the only other PNZ member in the group. It's impossible to not feel the divisions. Even here, people flock together–the LDZs in their group by the window, the cutslut next to Maddox, and I save a chair for Harker.

Harker, whose girlfriend is pregnant.

He'd told us that during the last frat meeting.

I don't need to create. Kira's already six weeks pregnant.

It was a hard pill to swallow. Harker, not even Royal, has met Father's expectations before the three of us could. Pace and Wicker can act like they're just annoyed with his request to hire the Chamber's strippers for the Valentine's Day party, but I know the truth.

They hate him for the pressure it puts on us.

But since I'm the one who caught him buying Scratch at Wicker and Pace's first hockey game back, it was up to me to decide how to handle it. De-crown him for breaking frat covenants, or drag his ass here and make sure he quits.

"Ashby," Remy calls, looking up from his shoe. "Got a minute?"

On instinct, I look around, checking for trouble. I'd handed over the footage of Oakfield earlier in the day to the Lords, and everyone seemed pleased with the results.

"What do you want, Maddox?" I smirk. "Someone to check out that wound my brother gave you?"

"Nah. Matches the one my Duchess gave me the night we met." A slow grin tugs at his lips and he lifts his shirt revealing his heavily inked torso and skirting his fingers over a thin line of stitches. "Pauly's got a steady hand." He drops the shirt and tilts his head toward the cutslut. "Maggie was just telling me about a rumor she's heard. That a few girls have gone missing around Forsyth."

What he says rings a bell, and I think about the flyers plastered around East End that Livingston got approval for at the last PNZ meeting. His sister hasn't been seen since December. "And?"

"*And* we know you have a habit of snatching people." From the scowl set on his face, it's easy to assume he's referring to that kid, Ballsack. "Any chance you've been collecting females?"

I level him with a hard look. "Zero. We've got our hands busy with our Princess, and every girl in East End is happy to spread their legs for a PNZ." I cross my arms over my chest. "We turn them away at the Masquerade."

Maddox narrows his eyes and looks–well, not at me, but *around* me–and nods. "Blue."

"What?" I ask.

He shrugs. "Plenty of orange and gold in there, but I believe him," he says to Maggie, and she seems to take this at face value.

"Whatever," I mutter, not interested in further talk with a nut job, and start to turn away.

"Wait!"

I turn and see Maggie standing. Her eyelashes are thick, almost like feathers, and when she shifts, I see a ring glinting in her navel. "Our friend Laura has been missing for about a month. No one has heard a word from her–including the guy she was seeing. We're worried. It's not like her, and when I started asking around more, I heard that other girls, in other territories, have been disappearing, too. Like that one in your area, the Livingston girl?"

Shrugging, I reply, "We approved the flyers. I'm not sure what else I can do."

"Just..." Her eyes shine and fuck. Is she crying? "Keep an eye out, okay?" Her arms wrap around her body and she rubs her arms. "People–*women*–feel scared out there."

I look her in the eye. "The Princes don't have any interest in hurting women. We find one and keep her comfortable." I jerk my chin at Maddox. "But I'll let your Dukes know if anything comes up."

She exhales. "Thank you."

Ignoring her, I glance at my phone. The meeting should have already started, and still no Harker. When the door opens, I'm already rethinking that de-crowning.

But Dusty, our fearless counselor, is the one who walks through it. "Evening," he says in his gruff voice, adjusting the baseball cap on his head. At our murmured greeting, he stands in the middle of the room, hands propped on his hips. "Well," he starts, and from the way he's shifting, eyebrows pushed low, I get the feeling he's not too happy.

Not that he ever really is.

"Afraid I've come tonight with some bad news, folks." Here, he takes his hat off, raking callused fingers through his hair. And then he glances up at me. "I just got off the phone with campus admin. Sorry to say that Colby Harker is gone."

There's a rigid hush over the room, a dozen eyes shifting to me.

"It happened this afternoon," Dusty says, pressing his cap to his chest. "Sorry, son. That's all I know."

I blink, finally understanding. "He's dead."

Dusty gives a heavy nod. "Would you care to say something about your buddy?"

"Harker isn't my buddy," I argue, only I end up stuttering into silence.

Wasn't.

He *wasn't* my buddy.

Dusty stares before gesturing to the empty seat beside me. "Well, you're his Prince, aren't ya?"

I don't like the way he says it. *His* Prince. As if I'm responsible for every guy in our frat. Being a Prince is about creating an heir, not leading.

Only, it kind of is, isn't it?

Suddenly, I feel too hot, shifting uneasily in my seat. Harker was a prick. He was spoiled and too horny for his own good, and goddamn it, I tried. *I brought him here,* I want to say. I took him away from the Scratch and gave him an ultimatum. I'm the one who told him how to handle the withdrawals–the one who got him the meds when it got too rough.

"His girl is nine weeks pregnant," I say, thinking of Kira. I don't know her, really. Up until now, I mostly just thought of her as that bitch who got knocked up way too easily. Now, she's the girl who's going to raise Harker's kid, and she's going to do it alone. Briefly, I wonder if that means we have to take care of her now. The Princes. The Ashbys.

"Jesus," one of the LDZ guys mutters, head shaking. "What a fuckin' waste."

Harker isn't the first person the group has lost, and I doubt he'll be the last. Maggie chimes in, "Seems like a new one every couple weeks."

My skin feels pulled tight and I tug at the collar of my button-down. Harker was a prick, but he was East End. He was ours. Looking up, I admit to Dusty, "No one told me."

The hardness in his eyes is already gone. "I got that impression."

"I guess I should go," I decide, standing. I spend a moment wondering where to put my cup of shitty coffee. "Do my duty."

"Kid..." Dusty starts.

Noticing the ragged worry in his eyes, I scoff. "You don't have to worry about me using. I can't." At Dusty's unimpressed stare, I explain, "No, really. It's against the rules." More bitterly, I add, "It'd solve all of my problems, but it's off the table. Not even an option."

Maddox points out, "Pretty sure it was against the rules for your buddy, too."

But before I can offer a reply, Dusty cuts in, "Even after all these weeks, you're still on about Scratch being the answer to all your problems."

"It verifiably is," I say, growing tense with all their eyes on me. They don't know. They have no fucking idea. If I had Scratch, I could do it all. The interviews. The workload. The long nights in the dungeon, rubbing gritty eyes as Pace buries his fist into whatever sorry mark we're extracting intel from this week. I could give my brothers a break. I could ace all my finals.

I could fuck my Princess.

"Jesus, kid." Dusty pops his cap back on, sighing. "Keep thinking like that and East End's little section over there is gonna be empty."

The last glimpse I have before leaving is the disappointment etched into his frown. It doesn't bother me. Dodging Father's disappointment takes too much energy to expend any worrying about disappointing someone else.

But I am bothered.

I was Harker's Prince, and in a way, that makes me responsible. I should have been up his ass more, made sure he was clean, and the irony is that if I'd had Scratch, maybe I could have carved out a chunk of time to do that. School, Father, PNZ, East End, *creation*.

There just isn't space for anything else.

Not for life.

Not for death.

WHEN I GET HOME, I find Pace's room empty.

It's not a surprise. I already know he's downtown with Charlie, scoping out a recurring issue with some corrupt congressman.

Wicker, I know, is still down at the rink, doing a presser for the paper. Father is at the Gentleman's Chamber, handling something or other, and Danner is out back, supervising a linen delivery.

I close the door behind me as I enter, pulling the empty, sterile specimen cup from my pocket. Setting it down on the desk, I take a seat in the chair, booting up the middle monitor. It's currently showing a view of the front gate, and it takes me a moment to remember the keystrokes to pull up the server directory.

A sudden squawk makes me sigh.

"*Pretty bird*," Effie trills.

"Dirty bird," I mutter, and she echoes, "*Dirty. Dirty bird. Dirty fucking bird.*"

"Shouldn't you be sleeping?" I wonder, annoyed. Pace usually covers her cage when he goes out.

She lets out an energetic series of clicks and croons, and then, "*Gentle.*"

I whip around to gape at her, the word said in such a perfect pitch to match Verity's voice that it makes my spine rigid, like she's somewhere nearby, watching.

"Gentle?" I ask Effie.

Her little head sways side to side. "*Gentle, gentle,*" and then she switches to Wicker's voice. "*Suck my balls.*"

I exhale, realizing she's just going off on one of her tangents. For being Pace's bird, she sure is an attention whore. "Go to bed," I say, finding the sheet on the floor and covering her cage.

Once she's shut up, I go back to flipping through files, searching for the most recent recordings.

Adrenaline pumps through my veins when the video pulls up and I slide the specimen cup closer. Part of it's anxiety, part anticipation, but mostly dread. Seeing myself like this on the screen is fucking surreal. I know it's me lurching out of the bed. I know it's my cock, thick and slapping against my abdomen as Wicker lets me out of the room and leads me down the hall. My gait is a little off–a bit too lax. But there's no mistaking my scarred back.

It's not quite like the first two times I sleepwalked into her room, aimless and meandering. This time, it's almost like I know where I'm going, turning the corner and making a straight beeline right for her door.

It's already open.

Unzipping my pants, I pull out my cock, warm but limp, and try my damndest to stroke a little life into it. The response is a weak flicker of want, but mostly what I feel is *jealousy.*

I'm fucking jealous of myself in the video. Of that glorious cock. Of the way I'm approaching her bed on the screen, wild and hungry. Verity's awake, waiting for me with the covers up to her waist, but I don't wait for permission. I *pounce* on her, ripping away the sheets, tearing clumsily–viciously–at her top. It's all reckless and feral, unbelievably primal, and she fights me. I can tell from the way she was waiting that she knows she has no choice. The fight... it's probably instinct as much as anything else. I watch the two of us roll around the bed until I get the upper hand. I see the way I pin her down, my muscles flexing under the scarred flesh, my thighs powerful. My fingers tighten around her wrists as my legs spread her knees apart. She's under attack–assault–because there's no way to describe my cock in that moment but as a weapon.

I use it. *Forcefully*. Invading her cunt like I'm conquering territory.

I grip my cock in my hand and try to remember it entering her. Was it tight? It must have been tight. Was she even wet for me? Did she clench as I forced myself inside, or did her pussy remember me, let me in?

The thought brings a sudden tingle to my balls, but what makes me freeze is what she does next.

She strains upward, lips against my jaw, and speaks.

I can't hear her words, but I see her mouth moving, eyelids fluttering as I pin her with my hips, going abruptly still. I witness her fingers combing back my hair, her hands stroking my sides. She unfurls like a flower, thighs falling to the side as she welcomes me in.

With a shimmy of her hips, she grabs the globe of my ass and rolls her hips upward, taking me in, heavy eyelids blinking up at me.

Stunned, I stare at the image of us, my cock giving a small but strong twitch.

We look like two hopelessly entwined lovers, caught in a moment of slow indulgence.

That's not me–not how I fuck. When I have a girl beneath me, I command her with my hands, my tongue, my cock. Sex is a complex algebraic equation, and I've aced all the exams. Flick here, kiss there, obtain the data, find the value for x. Girls used to go wild for it–being ruthlessly analyzed to the point of utter sexual annihilation. There was a time they'd seek me out for it, flipping their hair or batting their eyelashes. Then they learned it was pointless, and I'd instead get franker and franker texts, outright asking if I'd fuck them.

My point is, this man on the screen can't be me.

He turns his head, mouth brushing hers, and when we kiss, Verity is the one guiding it. I can see the saliva glisten between our mouths as our tongues tangle, slow and luscious.

"I made sure you were looking at me."

Blood rushes between my legs, the heat surging to my cock. I grip the shaft in one hand, fingers working my balls, while I stroke with the other, trying to work it up.

Never taking my eyes off the screen, I watch as Verity slowly, gently kisses me, over and over. I kiss her in return, tongue flicking out to taste her swollen lips. My aggression wanes, this woman drawing me into something more akin to lovemaking, my hips caught in a steady rhythm.

My hand slips into the same unhurried beat.

It almost feels like the man on the screen is wasting it. He doesn't try to learn her. There's no observation or testing. Where I'd have my wits about me, this guy is utterly lost, rocking into the cradle of her thighs in a strange, primal way. If it were me–the awake version of me–I'd work her over until she was a sloppy, exhausted mess. That's what they want. To be known. Understood. Operated.

But Verity has her head thrown back, our bodies meeting like crashing waves, and I can see her nails digging divots into my biceps just as much as I feel the twinge of them still there.

I know I'm about to come when the aggression starts up again.

The muscles in my scarred back tense and flex as I slam into her, her fingers tangling in my hair. I imagine it at the same time I observe it, the way my cock must swell inside that ripe, slick pussy. On the screen, she's grabbing my face in her hands, mouth forming the words:

"Lagan, look at me."

When I do, my body seizes, ass flexing as I begin pumping into her. Filling her sweet, fertile cunt with every drop of my seed, shooting it deep into her cervix as our gazes hold.

Creating.

"Oh fuck," I grunt, reaching for the cup. It tumbles, knocking over. "Son of a *fuck!*" My eyes are transfixed on the screen, terrified to look away, but then my fingers grip the lip of the cup and I hold it under the desk, trembling with exhilaration. The groan that follows is too much for the meager amount of cum I manage to get in the receptacle, but it's enough.

I exhale, leaning back, my dick flaccid and weak once again.

It has to be enough.

~

She's in the stirrups when I arrive.

Even though I want to pause, taking in the sight of her naked body, I go fluidly for the sink, methodically washing my hands. The routine of it is soothing, calming, suds and warmth. Sometimes it's hard to remember if I always wanted to be a surgeon, or if I just wanted to be what *he* wanted me to be. Other times, like right now, glancing over at my Princess' nervously flexing toes, I can almost feel it like a calling. Something I'm good at, that's useful.

Reaching for the box of latex gloves, I ready myself for stepping between her bare, milky thighs. The room is the same. Bright white, stainless steel and chrome. Medical grade equipment and instruments are carefully organized around us. But when she looks up at me, those big green eyes and those soft pink lips, things feel different.

I keep thinking about that kiss from this morning.

"Any changes this week?" I ask, grabbing the clipboard where I document her vitals.

She nibbles for a moment on her lip. "I may be ovulating."

I turn the page to the calendar, marked with her cycle and creation schedule. "Impossible."

She clutches her hand over her stomach and shrugs. "There was some discharge when I went to the bathroom today."

I make a note and set the clipboard on the table next to her, finally allowing my eyes to drink her in. "It's possibly just regular post-menstruation. Maybe even the remains of my deposit." My gaze dips to her center at the thought of leaving a piece of myself with her. And then they rise to her flat belly at the thought of leaving *more* than just a piece. "The other option is an infection. You and Wicker did have sex in a pool, which was highly unsanitary."

Her cheeks turn pink at the mention of my brother and her having sex. I'm not sure if it's because I know the specifics or if there's something that transpired between them that's causing a flush.

Either way, I adjust my gloves. "I should check you for an infection."

"There's no infection," she says, the tendons in her thighs tensing. "I feel fine."

"Still." I edge in closer, hovering my hands over her belly, before pressing gently against her abdomen. I can't remember when she stopped flinching at my cold, clinical touch, but she doesn't flinch now. "Feel anything? Any tenderness?"

Staring up at the ceiling, she shakes her head. "No."

I go lower, pressing the soft flesh between her hips. "How about here?"

She sighs, fingers twisting together where they rest on her upper stomach. "I'm fine, Lex."

But as I inspect her body, I feel a familiar apprehension. I've never been responsible for another body before. She's laid out before me like a sacrifice, legs open, eyes guileless, and when my fingers begin wandering, I tell myself that's why. The responsibility. The weight of it. Is this bruise on her hip old or new? When I brush against her pubic mound, does her belly cave because she's ticklish, or because there's discomfort? The hair growing in–should it be thicker? Why is she so warm? Does she have a fever?

But instead of taking her temperature, I find my fingers skating lower, brain fogging over when I caress her plump labia. It's getting harder and harder to see her here like this and not think about what's happening inside.

Is my baby growing inside of her, right now?

"Okay," she murmurs, lip twitching. "Now you're just teasing me." The little squirm she makes forces my finger lower, grazing her entrance. Breaking from my daze is harder than usual, and I reach into my pocket to extract the syringe.

Her throat clicks with a swallow. "When did you get that?" she asks, green eyes fixed on the milky fluid inside.

I press my palm to her inner thigh, thumb massaging the tense tendon as I stare into her folds. "About twenty minutes ago," I explain in a voice that's dropped two octaves.

She's getting wet.

She gives me a heavy blink. "Oh."

The syringe slides in easily, and in my periphery, I can see her toes curl as I bottom it out. I don't need to ask her to look at me– haven't in weeks–so when I glance up into her green eyes, she's already staring back.

Lagan, look at me.

Her breath expands with a slow inhale as I press the plunger, and I'm hoping for that same surge of primal want that struck me as I watched myself come inside of her on the video.

It doesn't come, though.

This is not how babies are made. It's not how heirs are born. Whatever happened in her bed last night... that was warm and dirty, not cold and sterile. It was human. That's the thing about me when I sleepwalk. I'm no longer Lagan or Lex. I'm just a man searching for a woman, whittled down to my own base instincts.

And *fuck,* I want to be him right now.

Setting the empty syringe aside, I look down at her naked body, with those sweet lips and rosy cheeks. She's still as I lean over her, propping a palm on the exam table beside her elbow. I press the back of my other hand to her forehead, soaking in the warmth of it before trailing downward, over her pink cheek.

The urge to bury myself within her is fierce. Not just her pussy, but her skin, warm and soft. The little bit of give in her lower belly. The plumpness of her full, womanly breasts. Verity Sinclaire is femininity personified, and the thought slams into me like a freight train.

"You'd look so fucking good with a baby inside you."

Her mouth parts in surprise, nipples already peaked from the deposit. "I... would?"

I look at her lips, taunted by the memory of kissing her before. "Round and glowing, the personification of fertility," I explain, skating my fingertips down to her breast. "Your tits would get so full, areolas growing darker. Your hips would expand, your anatomy preparing itself for birth." I pull in a breath through flared nostrils, smelling her arousal. "It's the oldest science known to mankind."

When I look back up, her eyes are heavier, tongue darting out to wet her lips. "Creation."

The thread snaps and I dart down to take her mouth in a sudden, bruising kiss.

I can't even count how many times I've wanted to. Having her on my exam table, open and ready–it's been fucking torture. The kiss isn't as gentle as the one on the screen was, my hand jerking down to palm her warm, heavy breast. Her mouth is slick and just as frantic. It elicits a stirring deep in my chest, but wanting this girl has never been a problem. Acting on it has. It's been easier to stay away from her than to deal with the disappointment of being unable to take her. But tasting her like this–*Jesus*, it's worth the frustration. Now, her lips are yielding, a moan spilling into my mouth as my tongue delves inside to swallow it. Her breast is warm and heavy beneath my palm, my thumb sweeping over the pebbled nipple.

Her feet rattle the stirrups, soft thighs closing around my hips.

"Lex," she breathes, her nails dragging down my abdomen. "Let me," she says, tugging at my buckle. "Let me try."

I tear myself away just to push my forehead into hers, panting.

Sex.

It hasn't even been that long since I had it–while awake. Six months. I work with a few genuine nerds in the science department, and some of them are still virgins. Six months without sex is nothing, and technically, I just had it last night. Twice.

So why does it suddenly feel like years since I slid my way into a pussy?

"Lex?" she whispers, eyes blinking up at me. "Okay?"

In the end, I'm too weak to say no. Too fucking tired. Sick of the deprivation. All I want is to feel good, and that's exactly how her hands feel as she yanks the belt out of the loops, thumbing open the button. I exhale when she pulls out my cock, thumb rolling over the head.

It's what makes me a liability–I know. Whatever it is that allows me to prop my fists on the exam table and let her stroke my cock is the same weakness that got me hooked on Scratch. It'll either be my oblivion or salvation, and right now, I'd take either.

I take a deep breath and try to feel it, her hand gripping the base of my cock, hard. *Too* hard. I clamp my fingers over hers, grunting. "Softer."

She responds by loosening her grip, taking a slow glide from base to tip. I feel a rush of blood, gaze honed in on her heaving chest. "Like that?"

"Yes," I try to hold back from just thrusting. I know that won't work. Distraction. That's what I need. "Tell me..." I wet my lips, her eyes flicking down to the motion. "Tell me what it feels like when I come to your room at night."

She gives me a slow, surprised blink, stroking me carefully. "The first two times were terrifying," she admits, "I just didn't know what to expect–or frankly, that you were even coming. But last night, Pace gave me a heads up, and I was more prepared." Her motions are steady, precise, and my balls ache with so much desire that my hands curl into fists against the table. "You come in aggressive. Wild. Hair down, eyes all black and glassy. You seem awake, but also..." She looks at me, tilting her head. "But also, you seem different. Less... in control. And very, very focused on fucking me."

Her thumb strokes the ridge that lines my cock and a shiver runs down my spine.

"But it's more than fucking," she says, and there's a glint of trepidation in her eyes. I'm not sure why until she explains, "It's almost like... you want to get me pregnant. You want to plant your seed in me—your baby."

I suck in a sharp hiss as my cock suddenly begins to thicken, jaw going tight at the thought of it. Maybe I'll think to be embarrassed about that later, but right now, I dip down to lick into the seam of her lips, pushing a whisper onto her tongue. "And you like it?"

"My body reacts," she says, licking me back, her whole body arching up to seek me. "I get wet, and there's like, an ache. A feeling that I can't wait for you to get inside."

"*Fuck*." Panting, I look down to watch as a surge of clear precum dribbles across my cockhead, followed by the pump of blood to my balls. Her thumb rolls over the sticky fluid and my cock twitches, ready to bust. *Not yet.*

"Is that what you really want?" I ask, flattening my hand over her stomach. The thought of my seed growing inside of her pools liquid, animalistic heat right into the base of my spine. "Do you want my baby inside?"

Her green eyes hold mine, barely a beat for her to think about it before confessing, "More than anything." My eyes are on her face, searching for lies, but all I see is sincerity. "Sometimes when I'm alone in bed looking up at that big, ornate ceiling, or down in the solarium, digging in the dirt, I try to bring the idea to life." She strokes me a little harder this time and I grip the edge of the table, teeth clenched. "I think about what it would feel like to be pregnant, to be full with child, to carry the heir."

It's the image of it, of her swollen belly, that does it. My hips rock like I've been struck by a bolt of lightning, cum shooting across the ridge of Verity's fist. "Fuck," I groan, a surge of emotions running though me; release, humiliation, panic. Panic wins and I snap, "Don't waste it!"

Swiping the cum off her hand with my fingers, Verity falls back, spreading her legs. Frantically, I push the semen inside, pumping it in as deep as I can get it. "Keep your hips up! Give it a chance to get in there."

She's fucking *dripping* wet.

"Are you mad?" she gasps, pelvis raised. "I shouldn't have–"

"I'm not mad," I lie, taking a deep breath. I have three fingers burying my seed into her soaked cunt and all I can think about is how it should have been my cock that put it there. Why does this have to be so fucking hard? My parts go with her parts. This is a basic biological imperative. Put it in, fertilize the egg.

Jesus Christ.

This anger isn't for her. I tell myself this as I pull away, stuffing my cock back into my pants. "That was—you were—you did good," I stutter.

And fuck me if her eyes don't sparkle at the praise, color coming to her cheeks as she sinks her teeth into her lip. "Yeah?" At my scowl, she lets out this little chuckle, closing her knees. "So... maybe we can try again sometime?"

"Maybe," I agree, yanking some paper towels from the wall dispenser.

Maybe. If I can come to terms with that fact that Verity just found the key to making my dick hard.

erity

THE STRANGEST THING about all of this is how, sometimes in the middle of the day, when things are tense and stressful, I get a craving.

For Pace's cock.

Gruffly, he murmurs, "You've gotten good at this, Rosilocks," and massages my jaw.

The message came across my phone minutes after I got home from Family Dinner.

Pace: Midnight.

Princess: I'll be there.

Pace: No. Your room.

Well, that was new.

I get biology. Sexual attraction. I even understand conditioning. Is that what it is? These men have conditioned me to want them? To crave their bodies so I can find my own pleasure? It feels like it because there's something that happens to me now when I'm near them.

It's not just chemical, though.

With Wicker, sex is always weirdly akin to a fight. Our bodies have these arguments. It's hard and fast, a bit breathtaking, and always leaves me feeling either exhausted or exhilarated. Never any in between. That's how it is with him; one extreme or another, with no chance to feel grounded.

With Lex, it's this constantly confusing duality between cold, detached procedure and primal, aggressive passion. Our bodies don't argue, and maybe that's the most terrifying of all. How much I want him like that, on an unavoidably fundamental level. The woman inside of me recognizes the man in him, and she *wants*.

But Pace...

He winds his fingers in my hair, using the grip to fuck softly into my mouth. "That's my good girl."

Pace makes me mindless.

I don't have to think when I'm with him like this, because he'll tell me what to do. It was only a few weeks ago that such a thought made me furious and defiant. Now, I'm beginning to learn where my defiance is best suited.

Not here.

Not with the taste of Pace so salty on my tongue, the feel of his fingertips against my scalp, the sound of his soft sigh when my tongue slithers around the head of his cock. It's the only time I fully let myself enjoy it. The sense of responsibility I feel with Lex, and the urge to push and pull with Wicker, is replaced with something else when I'm with Pace. It's inevitability. I'm just doing what I'm told. Nothing more, nothing less.

It's the first time Pace has been in my room like this, in my bed. Inexplicably, even though we've been at this for well over two hours, he still looks like he just came in from outside. He's fully dressed, still wearing his shoes, hoodie pulled up. Even his dark wash jeans are barely pulled down, his cock spearing out of the spread zipper like it's part of the whole outfit. He looked troubled when he first came in here, ordering me out of my clothes and flopping down onto the bed. Although, with one arm bent, temple resting on his fist, and the other hand running up and down my jaw, he does look awfully comfortable.

"Get me closer," he tells me, lids heavy.

I've been suckling passively since he came in, once even nodding off with my head resting on his thigh. There's something soothing about these moments. A quiet calm. But with Pace, that never lasts.

Rising to my knees, I switch tactics, ghosting my hands over his balls and tugging at his shaft. I've gotten to know *this* cock better than any of them. Each vein, every inch of silky smooth shaft, the exact texture of his pubic hair. His hips lift, chasing my mouth, and I let him catch it, his fingers twisting around my hair to control my motions. When his cock thickens, growing between my lips, I use my tongue to cover the surface—to taste every inch of him.

It hits me just how wet I've gotten.

"What happens when you leave on Thursdays?" he asks suddenly.

I look up, cock still in my mouth, unsure if he really wants me to stop and answer. With his hood obstructing the glow of the sconce above us, his face is stonily shadowed, impossible to decipher.

He cups my chin and thumbs it open.

An assent.

I don't go far, letting the tip rest on my bottom lip when I answer. "I go to Family Dinner." He raises an eyebrow, indicating he needs more. "It's a tradition. The guys carb-load before the Fury. The cutsluts dress up and fix dinner." I shrug. "It's fun. Familiar."

He grabs the base of his cock, rubbing–teasing–the head over my lip. "Doesn't sound anything like our family dinners."

With Ashby? No, I suppose not.

"So you eat," he says, continuing to rub saliva and salty precum onto my lips like lipgloss. "Then what? You watch Bruin and Perilini jerk each other off while Maddox howls at the moon?"

I hold back a frown, swallowing my instinctual defense of the

Dukes. There's a pointed comment that could easily be made about the Ashby brothers being the ones who don't seem to have any personal boundaries with each other.

I don't make that comment.

Instead, I focus on nudging his cock with my mouth. "Sometimes the guys have a meeting afterwards. I don't know. The girls are usually cleaning up or prepping for the matches."

His dark eyes track his cock as he thumps it gently against my lip. "Isn't it weird going back now?" he asks, eyes flicking up to mine. They harden. "With everyone knowing you're a traitor?"

Abruptly, an awareness surfaces like a glowing buoy.

He's baiting me.

I know it's easier if I just work to keep him even, so I lick out, catching the tip. "I won't pretend it's not complicated or that there aren't a few people pissed about it." Including my mother. "But it's all I know. That's how I was raised."

"I guess they're used to harboring people they can't trust," he muses, hips rocking up. His cock stutters wetly against my cheek "They brought in a Lucia, after all."

"That was definitely an adjustment," I admit, feeling my stomach tighten with anxiety. He doesn't seem angry. Not yet. But it sure seems like he's looking for a reason to be. "And the circumstances were different with the Dukes and their Duchess." Nick Bruin wanted Lavinia. Fought for her. She wasn't hoisted on the Dukes the way I was with the Princes after an open cattle call.

He props up on his elbow and reaches for my breast, tweaking the nipple. "I sure as fuck wouldn't trust her. Once a snake, always a snake. Lucia blood is venom. You'd do well to fucking remember that."

I don't respond. The Dukes, West End, *Lavinia*, they're all the kind of thing that fuel's Pace's paranoia. Instead, I bend and lick the head of his cock, tasting the salty fluid at the tip. Opening my mouth, I suck him, hoping to provide the comfort I know he seeks.

Unfortunately not. "Nothing to say to that, Rosi?"

Pulling off, I sigh, already knowing I'm going to regret it. "I'd say a person is probably more than the name they're given or the DNA that made them." Arching a brow, I add, "If anyone could understand that, it should be you and your brothers."

His eyes flash in a hot, violent way that makes my spine stiffen. "What the fuck is that supposed to mean?"

"Nothing," I rush to say. "Just that family is sometimes what we make it."

He sneers, "And who's your family, Princess?" Whatever attempt I've made to placate him is too little too late, and he rises up on his knees, grabbing my hair at the base of my skull.

Wordlessly, he yanks me up.

Grabbing at his wrist, I cry out, "Pace!"

"You know the thing about snakes?" he asks, breath hot, our faces inches apart. "They live in nests. Is that why you keep going over there, Rosilocks? To slither around with a snake?"

"I-I don't know what you're talking about!" My head and neck are bent, trying to keep him from yanking out my hair. "I barely know Lavinia! She's a Royal and I'm—I *was*—just a cutslut."

He releases me with a thrust, tossing me off the bed. I land in an inelegant heap, internally berating myself for giving him this. It seems to be a pattern with the Ashby brothers. They have a bad day and decide I should be the one to pay for it.

He looms above me, nostrils flaring as he gives his cock a rough stroke. If he was hard before, now he's steel, snarling out, "Prove it. Say the fucking words."

I freeze, knowing full well what he wants. It's been a while since he's asked it of me, knowing that I'll refuse. I've been waiting for him to ask again, readying myself for whatever answer I give. The refusal is on the tip of my tongue, but when I look into his obsidian eyes, all I can think to do is comply.

Wetting my lips, I hold his gaze. "I want it," I whisper, feeling something in my chest wind itself into a tight, worried knot at the lie. "I... want your baby inside of me."

He told me once I didn't have to mean it, and I don't. It's not about sincerity for him. It's about the win. The conquered insistence. The knowledge that I'd stoop low enough to abandon my principles, even if it's only pretend. It's about subjugation.

And his eyes flash in bright, hot satisfaction at the sound of it. "Show me," he demands in a low, rough voice. "Show me how much you want your Prince's seed."

Slowly, I edge closer, knees inching toward him on the rug, and reach for him, cupping his balls in my hand. I squeeze, eliciting a hiss. His fingers curl in my hair and force my face closer. Opening my mouth, I take in the smooth, swollen crown.

"Fuck," he mutters, a tremor running through him as he holds my head close. "Knew you wanted it, Rosi." Trying not to gag, I take him deeper, flattening my tongue over the sensitive underside. Reaching around his body, I dig my nails into his ass cheeks, giving him as much pain as he's giving me. This is how it eventually goes with Pace. Manipulative and hard. Greedy and paranoid. Mood swings and epic orgasms.

His hand tilts my chin up and he looks down at me, a devilish god. "I'm going to fuck your mouth," he says, "then I'm going to come in your pussy, filling you up with so much of my seed, there's no fucking way it won't make a baby."

He pulls out, stroking his cock twice with his hand, then slots it back in with a hard thrust. He's thicker, harder, and I take him deeper than before, wincing at the ache in my throat.

"That's a girl," he says, picking up the pace. I sink my nails in deeper, anchoring myself to him, and he gives a breathy, sinister laugh. "You dirty fucking girl."

I tease him, using my tongue and my teeth, taking long licks over his sensitive slit. He fucks into my lips like a man on a mission. I guess that's what he is. But what's the mission? To terrorize me? To break me? Or do we have the same goal? To knock me up.

Over and over again, he pumps inside, and I get the sense that he's lost in it. Lost in the feel of me on my knees below him, pleasing him. I see it in the glassy haze of eyes as he stares down at me, that hood shading his face. I see it In the way his abdomen tenses with every thrust. I feel it in the thickening of his cock, his fists clenching tightly, *painfully,* in my hair.

"Oh shit," he says, spine straightening. The first hot squirt against my tongue is unexpected– just as much as the flash of panic in his eyes. The second hot spurt of semen jolts me into action, and I grab him by the shaft—like that's going to do anything—but he's already got me under the arms, lifting me off the ground, and throwing me onto the massive bed.

"Do not," he growls, wrenching my legs apart, "swallow that." The look in his eyes is wild and urgent as a thick ribbon of his cum lands on my clit, but he immediately mounts me, slamming inside. Our slickness mingles there, making his entry slick and hot, every fat inch of his cock sliding right into me. I'm propelled, both across the bed and into another world, so hot from the need he has for me, so overcome by the feel of his cock twitching with release.

Pace transforms when he comes.

His jaw gets tighter, brows tugging together with silent agony as I feel him pulsing within my core. Sometimes, like now, he twists his head, looking away with clenched eyes. "Fucking hell, Verity." Even though he's as deep as he can possibly go, his hips give these little mindless nudges into mine, like he wishes he could go deeper, and when he finally swings his eyes back to mine, they're glazed with ecstasy.

"Give it to me," he says, dipping down to fix his mouth to mine.

Reluctantly, I gather his cum to the part of my lips and push it into his warm, waiting mouth. Pace sucks it off my tongue as his cock empties another hot surge of his seed into me. It's not so strange anymore, the thought of how much cum he puts into me. If anything, it's almost beginning to make a certain kind of sense.

Pace keeps so much locked away.

When his hand dips between us, finding my clit and rolling it around, I'm confused. Lost. Suspicious. And then, I remember that I gave in.

I said the words.

Locking gazes with me, Pace brings me ruthlessly, brutally to the edge. Even when I whimper, turning away, he wrenches me back, cock twitching with another fresh round of his load.

That must be why it explodes inside of me like a nuclear bomb, my mouth falling open on a shocked cry as I spiral, spinning out.

Even after I float back down, he's still pumping the last of his seed inside.

Rolling off, he moves between my legs, scooping up the semen that drips out and pushing it back in. He's focused and intent, only stopping when he's satisfied. I'm not even surprised when he spreads my folds, purses his lips, and spits. He aims what I'd given him from my mouth right into my entrance, clamping down hard on my thighs when I flinch.

Looking up at me, he uses two fingers to push it in. "One day I'll come so hard in your mouth, it'll rattle your teeth, Rosi." He spits another glob of cum and spit onto my pussy. "But not just yet."

There was a time, not too long ago, where such an act would have been the height of humiliation for me.

Now, I just lay there, boneless.

Submissive.

I blink when he reaches into his pocket, pulling out something foreign and metallic. *Golden.* "Don't move," he quietly commands, still kneeling between my spread thighs as he slowly begins the long slide of his cock from my body.

I feel slight pressure at my entrance as he pushes the strange, small, flared object close, his dark eyes fixed to where we're connected.

I wince at the stretch. "What's–what's that?"

He pushes me back down when I rise up, keeping my thighs wide. "It's a plug." Before I can ask what that means, he acts swiftly. The loss of Pace exiting me is replaced with a sudden, thick full-ness, the object slotting inside.

I whimper, pushing against it. "A what?"

He holds my legs open, heedless of my struggle to close them. "To keep my cum inside," he explains, some of that dazed horniness returning to his eyes as he watches me flutter around it. "You're to keep it inside you until one of us takes it out."

"But—" Abruptly, he grabs me by the hips and drags me to the top of the bed, settling us into the pillows. My heart thrums as he methodically undresses himself, both from the orgasms and the weird feeling in my vagina, only adding to the sensation of my body barely feeling like my own. It's not until he settles, hand flattering over my belly, strong and wide, that I realize how close we are.

"Can you feel it?" he asks, skating his fingers just above my pubic bone. "Can you feel all my cum in there?"

Shifting uncomfortably, I answer with a weak, "Yes." It's a slick, unavoidable fullness, my body filled with the urge to push it out.

After a long beat, he asks, "Has anyone told you about this bed?"

I shake my head, breathing hard against the instinct to pull the plug out. "No."

Pace hums. "It's considered good luck. It's where the first Princess conceived."

Tipping my head back, I glance at the headboard above us. I hadn't really thought about it before, but *damn*, this bed has probably seen some fucked up shit.

Pace reaches over his head, drawing my eyes to his defined biceps, and runs his fingers along the engraved, bejeweled crown in the center of the headboard. "Each one of these jewels signals a pregnancy."

My eyes flick to the thatch of tattoos on his forearm. "A tally."

He laughs and rests his hand back on my stomach, his spent dick flopped over his hip. "Yeah, that works. Father does love to keep score. I should have taken you in here earlier," he says, pushing his hand between my legs. With two fingers, he gives the base of the plug a small, testing nudge. "Used the luck of this place to secure the deposit."

I squirm against the sensation of being stuffed too full, feeling a pang in my chest. I'd lied to Pace before. If there's a weird desire for creation to happen, it's belied by the knowledge that Pace isn't the father I'd ever want for a child. He's unstable. Violent. Codependent. If he ever had a kid, he'd probably lock it up, hold it hostage from the world, allow his paranoia to take over.

Just like Effie.

"Pace." Swallowing, I wonder, "When can I take it out?"

His palm stops rubbing my belly, only to reach over and curl around my hip, yanking me impossibly closer to the cradle of his body. "The next time I fuck you," he answers, voice hard.

"And then what?"

"Then I'll put it back in." His finger touches my chin, drawing my gaze to his. "Every drop of me is meant for you, Verity."

In another time and place those words would maybe seem romantic, but here, with his cold gaze on me, and the intrusion in my body? I hear them for what they are; a threat.

"THANK YOU FOR DOING THIS," I say, looking over at Stella. We're in a shitty old Honda that smells like mildew and oil. Every bump is jarring, reminding me of the plug still trapping Pace's release inside. Even so, it feels infinitely more familiar than the luxury vehicles the Princes drive. "I realized that I left something at the gym last night and wanted to pick it up before it got put into the lost and found."

"Of course, Princess." Her hands grip the steering wheel, smile as sunny as ever. "I'm happy to help out in any way."

Stella hadn't blinked when I asked her to drive me back to the gym. I'm not allowed to move about freely, not without a chaperone, but Stella apparently fits the description well enough, because no one had batted an eye.

I still shiver at the memory of Pace in my bed this morning, his long, lithe body stretched across my bed as he slept. We fell asleep there, and he'd only taken the plug out of me once, rousing me from slumber as he curled in behind me and eased it out of my hole, only to replace it with his hard cock. His second deposit was made slowly enough that I only remember it in flashes of dark brown skin and the vague sense of being jostled whenever he'd deign to make an actual thrust. When I woke up, hours later, the plug was back.

The way I'd had to tiptoe out of there for fear of waking him was all at once old and new.

He's never slept in front of me before.

"You need to turn—" I start, but her blinker is already on, and she makes the turn with no direction. "Oh, you know the shortcut?"

Stella sends a beaming smile my way. "Oh, yeah! My sister showed me. She knows Forsyth like the back of her knees. She actually used to take me to Furies sometimes."

There's one tonight, but I plan to be in and out long before it starts. It's stupid for me to come like this, but after last night with Pace, I have to do something.

My knee bounces as we get deeper into Duke territory. My hands run up and down my thighs. The Honda's air vents are barely sputtering out any warmth, but I still feel a prickle of sweat on my neck.

Stella glances over. "Princess, can I ask what's got you more anxious than a jackrabbit? That's usually more my thing."

I blow out a tense breath, watching out the window as the clock tower grows closer. "I left my phone at home. It's just weird." It, and my watch, are under my pillow. Abruptly, I confess. "I told Danner we were going to the stationary shop to pick out invitations for the Valentine's Day party, and this is *not* the store. If they find out—"

"They won't." Her reply is chipper and full of a certainty that nearly makes me think less of her.

"You can't know that," I argue. "These guys—"

"They're Royals. They get away with literal murder. I know." She gives me a tight, less cheery smile. "I'll get you in and out. Don't you worry your pretty little head."

We pull up to the back door and someone is already there, waiting. A man. Head bowed, cigarette hanging from his lips.

Ballsack.

Glancing up, he doesn't look surprised to see the car pull up. Nor does he looked surprised at the people inside of it. "Do you— did you..." I look between her and Ballsack, who's stubbing out the ember of his cigarette. "What am I missing?"

Stella lets out a tense giggle. "Remember when Eugene got picked up by the Princes?"

I frown. "Who's Eugene?"

She gestures to Ballsack, who waves in return. My mind reels, trying to process the fact that Ballsack has a real name, and that Stella knows him. I quickly shake that loose.

"Yeah, I remember seeing him after being captured by the Princes. What about it?"

Her grin tips into a wicked slant. "He was caught smuggling me in."

"Into East End? Why?" But slowly it all clicks into place, my jaw going slack. This is all part of some bigger plan. Stella and Ballsack, their entrance into East End, coincides with the masquerade and my throning. He smuggled Stella in for *me*, and the only person that would do that is...

"Shit," I curse, back straightening. "*God.* Turn around. Now!"

Startled, she begins scanning the alleyway. "What? Why?"

"Because I'm putting you in danger." I'm putting all of us in danger. *What was I thinking?*

The panic in her eyes is released by a snort. "I signed up for this, Princess. You don't need to worry about me." She pulls up her uniform skirt, revealing a pistol strapped to her thigh. "I'm prepared."

I gape at the gun. "Jesus."

Sighing, she says, "I get that you're freaking out, but we do need to hurry. These things have a way of going sideways when sketchy people lurk in alleyways for too long." She starts to open the door, but I grab her arm.

"You're not coming in," I insist, my voice brooking no argument. "Stay here. Lock the doors. I'll only be a minute."

She searches my eyes. "Are you sure?"

Releasing her arm, I say, "This is my home, Stella. I'm safer here than anywhere in Forsyth." But my hole is already deep enough, and I'm not dragging her in further.

I get out of the car and approach Ballsack, who's still holding the door open.

"Seriously, *Eugene*?"

His eyes widen at the use of his real name. "Sorry, Ver. I was sworn to secrecy. There was a ceremony and everything. I mean... it was pretty much just a bunch of pretty girls getting me shitfaced, but trust me when I say it all felt very official."

I roll my eyes. "Does she know I'm coming?"

He nods. "In the lounge."

I sigh and glance over my shoulder at the rusty little car. "Keep an eye on her, would you? I'll only be a minute."

He gives me a grin much like the one Stella had, crooked and wily. "You got it, Princess."

Trying to remember why I'm here in the first place, I march down the hall and enter the lounge, determined not to get distracted by the posters on the wall or the memories of romping around here as a middle schooler.

When I get there, Lavinia is waiting.

Alone.

"Hey," she says, shooting to her feet. "What's going on? Why are you here?"

I want to blast her for what I just found out. Like, lose my fucking shit. They have someone in the Palace with me? And no one said anything?

I take a deep, steadying breath.

"Officially?" I say, grabbing a sequined thong out of the lost and found box. "I forgot this last night." Knitting her eyebrows together, she stares at the thong, and I add, "Unofficially, I think I fucked up."

"Explain," she says, sitting in one of the makeup chairs. Pointing to the one across from her, she watches carefully as I take it.

Taking another deep breath, I say, "Last night, when I was... *with* Pace, he was asking me all these questions."

Her head tilts. "What kinds of questions?"

"About family dinner—and you."

Her eyebrows shoot up. "Me? Specifically?"

I look down at my hands. "He thinks you're a traitor. I mean, he thinks *I'm* a traitor, so this is pretty on brand for him, but I don't know. He just wouldn't let it go." Glancing up, I confess, "He freaked me out."

She leans back, thinking. "Pace just got out of prison, right?"

"Yeah."

She nods. "That's probably why he's so paranoid. I saw it all the time with the Counts." She says this as if that explains it all away. "A few days in lockup, and they'd get twitchy as fuck."

Pace is twitchy, that's for sure, but he was already intense before he went to prison. That, I just so happen to know personally. "The Counts were probably going through withdrawals, that's why they were so nervous."

"Verity," Lavinia says, pinning me with a serious look. "It's fine. What could they know? We barely talk. You've hardly given me any real intel anyway."

There's something in her tone that rankles me, and I straighten. "There's not much to say. My days are occupied with deposits, and sitting through hockey practices and fake presentations on campus. The other night I had to go to this stupid fundraiser with Wicker just to keep him out of trouble."

Her eyebrow raises. "What kind of trouble?"

I bite my lip, immediately feeling protective. What transpired between me and Wicker at Trudie Stein's was personal. *Too* personal—and not even relevant. Shrugging, I only halfway lie, "I don't know. The kind a super-hot rich kid gets into with a bunch of wealthy socialites?" She eyes me and I stare back. "What?"

"Huh," is all she says.

My eyes narrow. "Huh, what?"

She gives me a tense, sympathetic grin. "You're catching feelings for him."

Everything screeches to a stop. "I'm sorry, what did you say?" The accusation hits like a gunshot, reverberating in my head with a wrongness that rattles me.

She gestures to me. "You're catching feelings for your Princes. That's why you haven't been telling us anything useful, because a part of you is protecting them."

"Are you fucking with me?" I ask, stunned. Offended. *Pissed.* "I'm stuck in a house with three monsters and their insane father, as they obsessively try to fuck a baby into me—minus the orgasms, by the way–and you think I'm sheltering them?"

Her arms are crossed over her chest, and she still doesn't look convinced. Should she be? Hadn't I just felt protective over keeping Wicker's secrets?

There are just some things that should never be used against a person.

"I know how it is," she begins, her gray eyes holding mine. "When I first came into the tower, Nick and the others..."

It's as though my brain just cuts off. Her lips are moving, but I can't hear her. Not her words, at least. All I can hear, feel, see is this horrifically casual assumption that my Princes and I are anything like Lavinia and the Dukes.

Feelings? I have plenty of them. Resentment, hatred, fear, spite, disgust–the list goes on and on, and none of them are anything but negative.

"I do know something," I blurt, interrupting her halfway into some story about being locked inside an elevator. "Wicker's father is a Kayes. He's the Baron legacy."

Her expression is frozen for a second, but then she rolls her eyes. "Well, yeah. We already know that."

My eyes bug out and I lurch to my feet. "What? How? They guard that like it's gold in Fort Knox!"

Lavinia's eyes soften. "Nick Bruin has contacts all over Forsyth, across all territories. Beating him to intel is hard."

"Then what am I there for?" I hiss, physically shaking. "If it's so easy to get dirt on everyone, then why am I in there getting used and abused every day? Why not just let Nick waltz in and gather whatever information he needs?"

"Waltzing is a bit of a stretch, don't you think?" She snorts. "I'm sure there was bloodshed involved in him getting that knowledge."

"Lavinia." A wave of bone-tired exhaustion settles on me. "I don't know what you want."

But even as I say it, I do know. She wants to know their weaknesses, their vulnerabilities. Like how Lex can't get it up which implies some kind of emotional instability. Or about the scars on his back, which I don't even want to acknowledge the origin of. Or about Wicker's exploitation at the hands of Forsyth's wealthy. Or the root causes of Pace's urge to hole up and hide away. She and Story–the Monarchs–they want that kind of dirt, but there's nothing I can give them.

Or maybe I just won't.

Maybe she's right.

Shit. *Am* I catching feelings for them?

"Hey," she says, grabbing my arm. "It's okay. I understand that the role of house girl comes with a lot of mixed-up feelings. Getting that info about Wicker being a Kayes? That's fucking huge. It means they're starting to trust you, and that trust will lead to bigger revelations."

"Right." I exhale and pull away, unable to quiet the black, sick thing roiling around in my chest. "You know, speaking of revelations? On the way here, it was revealed to me that you're not being totally honest with me either."

"How so?" she asks, but the confusion is short-lived. Lavinia turns to the makeup counter and starts organizing the messy surface, lining up the nail polish bottles in a tidy row. "I have no idea what you mean."

"Vinny," I start, the name forcing her gaze to mine. "This thing we're doing? It's dangerous."

Her gray eyes grow flinty. "You think I don't know what the

Royalty is capable of doing to rebellious girls?" Before I can answer, she spins, jaw set. "If you're asking what I think you're asking, then for the record? It wasn't my idea to put her there. It's bad enough that Ballsy got caught up in this. The fewer who do, the better."

Suddenly, I feel guilty, sitting here whining about being a glorified fleshlight while Lavinia spent over two years held captive by Kings. "I want to keep her safe," I plead.

"Freedom means choice, Ver. The choice to sit down, or the choice to stand up. She's made hers." Lavinia raises her chin, and within her eyes, I see the same fight that was there the first day she walked into this gym. It's what makes Lavinia Lucia a Duchess. "Just like you and I did."

Looking down, I swallow past the lump in my throat. "I'll try to do better."

She sighs. "Verity, you're doing everything you can. I know that. I see it. You know how much you're worried about her?" Nodding toward the door, Lavinia says, "That's how worried I've been about you. I didn't want you in on this. You were my first real friend here, and I–" Her voice cracks, and when I meet her eyes, I see unshed tears. "I know you're making a sacrifice to be in that Palace. I hate it. I just want it to be worth something real, in the end."

The end.

What a strange thought.

"That's why I'm going to take a break from Family dinner for a while," I decide, squaring my shoulders. If Lavinia can believe in me, then the least I can do is commit to my role. "Just, let the air clear, in case Pace really is suspicious."

She frowns. "The guys won't like it. It's part of the deal we made with Ashby."

"They won't," I say, shrugging, "but I'm going to leave that to their Duchess to smooth over."

There's a lot on the line, for all of us. The game of shadow chess that we're playing is more than just dangerous.

Can there ever really be an end?

26

I STARE AT FATHER, his words blending into an indecipherable garble of nothingness. We're alone in his office once again. He called me in here ten minutes ago, interrupting my dinner with my brothers. Chicken and asparagus. I can feel it like a brick in my stomach, threatening to come up.

"I can't."

At first, I think these must be Father's words, so controlled and final, but going from the way he stills, face hardening, they must have been mine. Leaning back in his seat, he asks, "I beg your pardon?"

He looks so aloof.

That's the thing about Rufus Ashby, he could be plotting to have someone cut into pieces, but he'd still look them in the eye and be really polite about it.

"I can't go," I repeat. Where there should be fear, I find nothing but the bone-deep certainty that I will not be attending the event he just ordered me to prepare for. It's not rebellion. It's just that no cell in my being will allow me to do it.

So I say the words I should have said the last time I was standing here, being told about the gathering at Mayfield.

He puts down his pen. It's a dark joke between my brothers and I that the more Father divests himself of *items*, the worse a punishment is going to be. "Very well, I'll bite." Lacing his fingers on the desk, he asks, "Why can't you attend?"

There are a few different reasons I can give him. I have a game tomorrow, which means I won't even be home until ten, at the very earliest. It's a scheduling conflict. There's also the element of a Prince's reputation that might–*might*–sway him.

"I don't want to." The answer is simple, really. "I'd rather shove a hot poker into my eyeball."

He grins stiffly. "Are you giving me ideas?"

"Just being honest." Teeth clenching, I add, "Sir."

"You understand that I'm not asking." There's a very credible threat in his eyes, and I couldn't care less. "You will attend the gathering at Mayfield, tomorrow evening. You will be charming." He rises from his chair, palms flat on the desk as his eyes pin me. "You will make a dashing, well-dressed escort for Mrs. Moore. You will sit with her." Harsher–quieter–he hisses, "You will bid for her."

No, I won't.

I don't say it, but I feel it to the very pit of my being.

In a rare show of frustration, he bites out, "Don't be difficult, Whitaker. It's been a long day. I don't enjoy the thought of sending you there, nor do I appreciate being made to enjoy it even less."

I couldn't make my voice less sarcastic if I tried. "Sorry if this is difficult for you."

He slams his hand down on the desk. "That's enough insolence! Or should I call one of your brothers in here?" The threat isn't as potent as it should be. The truth is, Lex and Pace would accept the punishment if they understood why they were getting it. I'd feel guilty about it, but not guilty enough to cave.

Father must sense this, because he snaps upright, holding himself in a perfect, stick-straight posture. "Perhaps I'll invite your Princess, too."

This brings me up short. I'm half-convinced it's a bluff. He'd never really hurt her. She's too important now, full of our cum and ready to bake that bun.

He'd make her watch, though.

Taking a deep breath, I reply, "What time?"

He doesn't look nearly as suspicious as he should, re-taking his seat. "Eleven sharp. Your tuxedo will be waiting in your room." He punctuates the discussion by picking up a stack of papers and tapping them hard on his desk. "I don't know why you insist on pushing me, Wicker. I've favored you against your brothers, although god only knows why. I've spoiled you to the brink of rottenness. I've given you every opportunity to excel in this town, and you continuously spit in my face." His lips purse tightly, the skin around his mouth going white. "My only hope is that someday soon, you'll experience what fatherhood is like. Maybe then, you'll understand the hell you've put me through."

"I'm sorry, Father." The words are stiff and automatic, my mind too busy racing with a solution to this problem to feel appropriately ashamed.

With a flick of his hand, he dismisses me, not meeting my gaze again.

I take the walk back to Lex's bedroom with slow, measured steps, but it doesn't matter. I still get sidetracked darting to the powder room by the landing, the bile rising up my esophagus like claws as I slam onto my knees, heaving my half-finished dinner into the toilet.

I reach out clumsily to flush it down before rising to my feet, grabbing the sink basin to hold myself up. It takes a while for my stomach to feel... not settled, but less violently infected by this sickness roiling around inside of it.

When I flick my eyes up, I catch a glimpse of myself.

My skin is ashen, eyes rimmed with red, hair disheveled and

errant. I kick into action, blasting the faucet as hot as it'll go. The water stings inside my mouth as I swish it around, burning my hands as I frantically scrub them clean. For my eyes, I switch the water to icy cold, splashing it onto my face with prickling palms.

I don't leave until I look perfect.

Unfortunately, when I arrive at Lex's room, they're already gone, their empty plates stacked beside the bed. I find them in Pace's room instead, Effie skittering excitedly up and down the desk's edge.

"*Gentle*," she chirps, bobbing her head. "*Gentle hungry bird.*"

The voice is almost an exact echo of Verity.

I blink at her, voice a thin rasp when I ask, "When did that happen?"

My brothers startle like they've just been caught whacking off. Going by the image on the computer monitor—a video of Pace spooning Verity in her big bed, his hips rocking as he fucks into her—I'm probably not too far off base.

Pace glances at the bird. "Uh, last week. She gave her some treats. Now everything is gentle-this, gentle-fucking-that." Rolling his eyes, he returns his focus to the screen. "I was just telling Lex about the plug."

Right. The plug.

Wiping my palms on my thighs, I sink into the leather couch, remembering a couple days ago when I helped Pace pick it out. I had to talk him out of getting the widest flared base. *So she'll still be tight for me*, I argued. I got my way, but the thought of pulling the plug from her just to find Pace's river of jizz leaking out is...

Actually, pretty hot, now that I think about it.

I'd reach down to adjust my growing boner, but I know I won't find one—a testament to how revolting the thought of Father's request—*order*—truly is.

Without looking away from the screen, Lex asks, "What did he want?"

My stomach flips. "Another escort job."

Without even looking, I know Pace's shoulders go tight. He

hates the things Father makes me do, sometimes even more than I do. "Who's this one for?" he asks.

"Just... another one of the usuals." It's halfway into being a lie. The truth is, I haven't seen Mrs. Moore since high school. "Hey, do you remember that Wallis job from a couple years back?"

Lex is the one to turn to me, his full focus swinging from the sight of Verity, naked and being plugged up with Pace's cum, to my face. "Yeah," he says slowly–carefully. Then, his eyes narrow. "What about it?"

Wordlessly, I hold his gaze.

Lex snaps upright. "No." His response is hard, immediate.

The November before Pace got sent away, Father ordered the three of us to fill a time-sensitive contract for Lionel Lucia. His daughter–his *heir*–had gone missing, and North Side's King was on an absolute fucking tear to find intel as to her whereabouts. There were a lot of casualties in the path of his quest to find her, foremost being his youngest daughter, who now commands West End as Simon Perilini's Queen.

Another was Molly Wallis.

Pace's preliminary digging revealed nothing but a petty property dispute from more than a decade ago, but the blood was bad between them. We were to toss her in the dungeon, strap her down, and go through all the beats. Hot, sharp, blunt, sensory, the whole shebang. Whatever it took to get the information out of her.

But Molly Wallis was an 88-year-old war widow.

The three of us only entertained the idea for a split second before devising a way out of it, and that's exactly what we did.

Although, the results weren't exactly ideal.

Raking my fingers through my hair, I tug hard at the roots. "I need to get out of this, Lex."

"We said we'd never do that again!" He gestures to our brother. "Pace still walks funny!"

It's the only job we ever 'failed'. As far as Father is concerned, we were jumped on the way to North Side by a pack of ex-Kappa's looking to protect their neighbor.

Unofficially, the three of us stood in an alleyway after a few strategic punches, drew our tactically low-caliber pistols, and aimed the barrels at the least medically emergent location. Pace got the outside of his thigh. I took a round to my ass cheek. Lex, his bicep.

Pace swivels around in his chair to gawk at me. "What kind of fucked up job is he sending you on that you're willing to risk doing that again?"

"It's not the job," I say. The lie doesn't come naturally. In fact, getting the words out with a straight face is roughly similar to willing an organ to stop working. There's nothing I haven't told my brothers.

But if for some reason I can't get out of this and they find out what I've done?

I'd rather string myself up from the rafters than live with that. Than live with *myself*.

Instead of saying this, my shoulders sink in defeat. "Man, I'm fucking exhausted. I can't do another dinner party with another horny socialite. It's fucking killing me."

Lex's eyebrows slam together. "That's it? Dinner parties and horny bitches?" The anger in his eyes brings me up short. "That's what you're willing to risk serious physical harm to avoid? *Dancing?* And the consequences of getting caught, which won't even be aimed at you–how about that?"

Wincing, I have to admit it sounds bad when it's put like that. "I'll keep you out of it. I figured this was really more of a job for Pace, anyway."

Pace, who's watching me thoughtfully, because he'd probably lop off his own arm if it meant an end to my whoring days. "What kind of job?" he asks uneasily.

Leaning forward, I keep my voice a low, urgent hush. "Just break something–maybe my leg. Bang me around a little. Make it look legit, we can blame it on the Counts, or–"

"What?!" His face transforms to enraged horror. "I'm not breaking your fucking leg! Are you insane?"

Desperately, I beg, "Please?"

"No way!" Pace spins back to the monitors, shutting me down. "We're playing Northridge tomorrow anyway, and there's definitely no way you're getting out of that."

Sighing, Lex suggests, "Just take the Princess with you again. That helped last time, didn't it?"

Just the thought of it makes me flinch back. I get this image of Verity sitting there between me and Mrs. Moore as we watch the stage. I imagine the look on her face as she realizes what's happening—what I'm doing.

I know it'll never happen, but just the mere suggestion is enough to make another surge of bile rise to my throat.

"Never mind," I say, springing to my feet. "I'll figure it out myself."

As I storm out of the room, Lex calls, "Wicker, don't do anything stupid!"

I don't really know where I'm going when I walk out into the hallway. Not my bedroom, that's for sure. There's so little of me in it. Things, but few memories. Trophies, but not trinkets. A bed without its occupant, who prefers to sleep a room away, with the weight of Lex and Pace bracketing me in, shielding me.

But they're right.

This isn't their problem.

The Palace is loudest and busiest in the evenings. I suppose that's why I descend the stairs, seeking out an exit idly, mind still working around the problem. The door I walk through could be the main entrance or the pantry for all the mind I pay to it.

I pause when I see Verity.

The solarium is musty, the scent of earth strong in my nostrils. She's bent over a giant stone urn, digging roots from the heart of it, dirty all the way up to her elbows. Her red hair is tied back, but a loose lock of it swings across her cheek when she wrenches a thick root free, flinging it into a pile near the gate. There's a smudge of soil across her forehead, and she's wearing dirty clothes. Jeans and a flannel.

She must not hear me come in, because she doesn't turn or startle. I'm not sure how. It's deathly quiet out here. No birdsong. No wind rustling leaves. It isn't until I spot the little wireless buds in her ears that I realize why she hasn't noticed me.

Pace's gift from a couple weeks ago.

I take in the space from my place on the steps. The old, dead vines covering the glass are mostly gone. The stone floor has been picked clean of wilted weeds and old leaves. Across the back wall is a bench I've never seen in here before, a row of little pots all lined up.

Even in the fading light of dusk, it looks oddly brighter. Bigger.

I lean down and pluck the speaker out of her ear, smirking when she jumps in surprise, her jaw dropping in a gasp. "Jesus, Wicker!"

"Princess." I sit down, frowning at the thick gloves on her hands. "You know we pay people to do this."

"I like having something to do with my hands," she says, shooting me a look like she's daring me to say something dirty. I let it pass. "And occupy my mind."

I watch her work, turning over the soil diligently, while I roll the smooth plastic speaker in my fingers.

Abruptly, she says, "Thank you for the shears, by the way. They made trimming the rhododendron so much easier."

"The what?"

"The shears." She points to a large pair of garden scissors in her tool kit. Ah, the gift. Danner for the win.

"Right." I look down at my hands, clean and well-manicured, but callused from the cello. "I heard your others were rusty."

She picks up a small container from a flat of seedlings and carefully extracts it before planting it in a fresh hole. Curious, I push the speaker in my ear and the rush of music hits me. It's some chick wailing about her love life. I pull it away, grimacing. "This the garbage that you listen to?"

She reaches out, snatching the earbud back. "Sometimes."

"It's candy-coated nonsense, created for mass consumption."

"It's not non–" She stops and rolls her eyes. "You know what? I'm not justifying my taste in music to someone like you."

"Someone *like* me?" My eyebrows knit together. "And what exactly am I like?" Honestly, I want to know, because right now I feel lower than the manure piled in the corner.

She answers succinctly. "A snob."

"I'm classically trained, not a snob." I lean back on my hands, ignoring the way the dirt grits against them. "I can't help that I have impeccable taste in everything, from clothes to music to women."

Rocking back on her heels she says, "What are you doing out here, Wicker, besides insulting me? We have hours before midnight."

What am I doing out here? Looking for a distraction? A plan? An out?

Finally, I confess, "I don't know." She looks up from her project and faces me, taking me in for the first time since I walked in. Her scrutiny annoys me. "What?"

"You look tired."

"Thanks for pointing it out, Red."

"No," she moves closer, taking off her gloves one hand at a time. "Something's wrong."

I catch her scent under the permeating smell of soil. Normally being this close to a woman, being this close to *her*, would have me hard, but my dick hasn't even twitched. Jesus. I really am tired. Tired of everything.

I begin, "Do you..."

"Do I what?" she asks when I don't finish the question.

Shifting uneasily, I ask, "Do you ever wonder what it would be like not to live in this world? Under these rules and standards? Being forced into positions we don't want?" Her mother isn't Royalty, but she has power and standing in their community. "If we were just normal people with normal lives instead of being caught up in all this chaos?"

She laughs. "I have no idea what a life without chaos would look like. I grew up in a gym as the only child of a woman that played mama bear to dozens of wild cubs who settled everything with their fists. Anything could start a fight; taking the last brownie, sleeping with another guy's girl, trying to pull rank..." She rolls her eyes, but I see a warmth in her eyes at the memory. "It drove my mom crazy, but after one particularly bloody fight during Family Dinner, she had enough. A system was set into place."

None of this is surprising. DKS is filled with wild animals pretending to be men. "What kind of system?"

"If you want to fight," she says, shrugging, "you do it in the ring."

I blink. "What are you talking about, Red?"

Her gaze burns into mine. "*Controlled* chaos, Wicker. Disputes, betrayals, positions, girls... everything is solved in the ring. You want to stake a claim over someone's cutslut? You win her in the ring–and keep the blood off my mother's dinner table."

I snort but the wheels are turning. "To the victor and all that shit."

"Yep." She worries her lip for a moment, resting a hand on my knee. "So what's going on? Did something happen?"

Nothing's happened–not yet. Not if I can help it.

"Controlled chaos, huh?" I peel her fingers off and stand. "I won't be in your room at midnight."

"But," she looks up at me, stunned, "you're always in my room at midnight."

I give her a tight smile, finally giving in to the impulse to brush that stray lock of hair off her cheek, pushing it behind her ear. "Get a good night's rest, Red."

I walk off feeling the weight of the next day heavy on my shoulders, but at least now I have an idea of what I need to do.

Northridge Tech and Forsyth University's hockey programs have a rivalry that dates back to the stone age or some shit. They're a newer city up north, while Forsyth has a more rich, storied history. The whole thing is horribly cliché, but there's nothing Forsyth loves more than one of those.

The stands are a sea of purple and gold, and from the second I face-off against their team captain, Verne Weller, I know it's going to be a wild game.

"How's Theresa?" I ask, poised for the ref to drop the puck. "That is her name, right? I'm bad at remembering. Tracey? Tina?"

The puck drops and I easily snatch it with the blade of my stick, slapping it toward Pace, who pumps his leg to skate it down the ice.

The next face-off, Verne barely looks shaken.

"She still got that navel piercing?" I ask, sensing Pace's presence close by. "I hope so. It's hot."

Verne just stares at the ice, waiting for the puck. "You're not gonna shake me, Ashby."

He wins the puck this time, making me curse as I chase his left wing down.

I'm annoyed by the third face-off. The first period is almost over. "You know the best way to make your girl come? *Anal*." Smirking, I boast, "Yeah, she loves it in the ass. Screamed my name for thirty minutes straight. Kinda like her boyfriend did that one time."

The puck lands and Verne wins it, eyes dead focused as he shoots for our net.

Pace, Lex, and I bunked with him during a tournament in high school, so I know he's a level-headed guy, far too steady to send off-balance with something as minor as me having fucked his girl-friend sophomore year.

Or me having fucked *him* a couple years before that.

During the first intermission, Pace jabs his stick into my shoulder. "Stop baiting Weller. We're up by two."

"Could be up by more," I say, shrugging.

With a sigh, Pace leans across the bench to whisper, "He's not gonna beat your ass. He's a finesse player, bro. He'd never risk his hands."

I give my brother an innocent look. "I have no idea what you're talking about."

But I really crank it up in the second period, because the thing about Forsyth is that it's sometimes a really small place.

"Here's a name I remember," I say to Verne when we face-off again, two minutes into the period. "Miranda."

There it is.

Verne's eyes jump up to mine, his mouth tightening. "Bullshit."

I jerk my head up to where she's sitting in the stands. "At the Christmas party last year. Your little sister?" I tisk, head shaking. "That bitch is a *screamer*. She still has my tie, you know. I had to gag her."

The puck drops and I smoothly pluck it up, zipping away as Verne curses.

Every face-off after that, I push it just a little more. "Little sister is flexible, too," I say, watching Verne's jaw tighten. "I'm surprised she didn't tell you about fucking me, to be honest. You seem so close. She gives head *just* like you do. Is that a family thing? Should I look your mom up?"

Verne Weller loses three face-offs, and when he's swapped for one of their shitty right wingers for a small violation–his skates crossed over the hash–I can see the rage building in his eyes. It's not about me banging his sister. Not totally.

No, Verne could be from West End with how much he values winning, and right now, his team is down bad.

I almost get a little worried when the clock winds down to second intermission. Rattling a guy like Weller could take a lot of time, and as sweat beads down my temples, the panic begins setting in. It's only a few short hours until the Mayfield event.

Luckily, as I'm skating off the ice, I see Weller pull #99 aside, his gaze cutting daggers into me.

"Really wanna be pissed at you, since I know what you're doing," Pace says in the locker room, spitting out his mouthguard. "But we're fucking murdering them out there. These passes you're making on face-off? Christ, you should try to get your ass beat more often." His grin is sharp and vicious as Coach Reed claps his hands for our attention.

I don't hear what he says.

I'm too busy preparing myself for the last period, and it's got nothing to do with plays or Decker's bloodthirst on defense. Pace isn't pissed at me because he was right before. Weller isn't going to fight me, and even if he did, he wouldn't win. That's not where he excels.

But unlike Pace, after a night of scrolling socials, I just happen to know that Miranda Weller is dating Northridge Tech's biggest, most aggressive defenseman.

#99.

It's a relief to see him on the ice when Verne and I square up for the face-off. "I tried to be cool," Verne says, mouth pressed into a tense line.

Mostly just because Verne is a good player and gives fantastic head, I assure him, "Ah, don't sweat it, bro. I know what's coming to me."

He looks confused when his gaze flicks up, meeting mine, but then the ref drops the puck and we're off–until #99 suddenly drops his gloves and barrels toward me.

The crowd gives an ear-shattering roar, which is the last thing I hear before two hundred fifty pounds of pure muscle and spite slams into me. I get a flash of the guy's face pulled back into an ugly sneer, and then his fist cracks into my jaw.

It's all a bit of a blur after that.

Generally, I'm pretty good at getting my ass beat because I know how to avoid that happening. I've never been the biggest guy in the room. The brawniest. The most aggressive. A childhood of boarding school with a bunch of angry boys taught me that very quickly. A little smooth talk, some ego stroking, if necessary, and quick evasive maneuvers have always served me better than brute force.

Right now, I just take it.

Sure, I fight back a little, just to keep that fire in 99's eyes, but mostly I get smoked. A fist to my temple, a knee to my gut, an elbow to my nose. Nothing really spectacular, though.

Not until he knocks me down.

Around us, I can hear other skaters, Pace's voice among them, trying to lift the guy off me, but he doesn't budge, his knuckles slamming into me over and over, mashing my head between his fists and the ice like a goddamn mallet.

In the end, the whole thing is pretty easy.

Pace reaches for my face, his eyes filled with panic as he shouts my name. The last thing I think before oblivion takes me is that the Princess was right. Sometimes you have to rely on chaos.

It's just better when you're controlling it.

I FEEL weightless for a long while, drifting, heavy and sore.

I know there's pain, but it's too distant to worry about. Here, where everything is dark and quiet–where I can finally rest–I just allow the darkness to cradle me. I think of vacations and how nice it'd be to have one. No responsibilities. No jobs. No drills or exams. Me, on a beach, with some busty redhead. That sounds like a good time.

I'm clutching onto the thought of it as if I could conjure up a dream of my own making to get lost in when I hear familiar voices.

"... have to check him for a concussion," Lex is saying, his voice low and grim. "What the *fuck* happened out there?"

"I didn't even see him coming," Pace says, and through the fog, I feel fingers fluttering through my hair. Somehow, I know they're his. "He was jonesing for a fight all night, but I thought Weller might–"

"Verne would never drop gloves," Lex hisses.

With a growl, Pace snaps, "I fucking know! That's why I wasn't worried."

"Why would he do this?" I can practically hear Lex pacing, and I know we're all alone when he says, "Why now, when we're finally making some headway with this Prince crap? Why does he have to be such a shit all the time?"

"Just my nature, I guess." My eyes flutter open and I see them jump up, bracketing me, just like in bed. Pace on my left, Lex on my right. "How bad?" I ask, tasting blood. The lights pulse in my temples and I squint against them.

Lex looks *furious*, his teeth gnashing out his words. "Bad enough. Congratu-fucking-lations, dickbag. You got what you want-ed." His latex gloves pull at my eyebrows when he lifts my eyelids wide, shining a pen light into my pupils. "The only thing you'll be attending tonight is Pace's funeral, seeing as how Father's holding *him* responsible for your behavior."

I reach up to swat his hand away, but my whole abdomen explodes in agony. "That's not what I wanted," I groan, trying futilely to sit up.

Lex pushes my shoulder, slamming me back to the exam table. "Stay still!"

Pace is still wearing his pads, the twists in his hair plastered with sweat. "What the fuck, Wick?" He doesn't look nearly as pissed as Lex, although I kind of wish he did. Right now, Pace is gazing down at me with such a confused look of betrayal that I feel it like a hook in my gut. What's worse is the question he asks, filled with desperation. "*Why?*"

Swallowing, I blink heavily against the light Lex is shining into my eye. My nose feels like ground beef. "Mayfield." It doesn't make me feel much better to see the click of recognition in their eyes. "That was tonight's job."

Lex turns the penlight off, his face screwing up. "He was going to put you up for bid again? But you're a Prince. You can't fuck anyone–it's against the coven–"

"They didn't want me to be the product," I say, coughing around something coppery-tasting. Holding Pace's gaze, I explain, "They wanted me to escort Mrs. Moore as a bidder."

Pace looks like he's the one who just took a fist to the face, his expression plummeting. There's a long moment where he just stares at me, throat bobbing like maybe he's fighting the urge to vomit. "Why didn't you tell us? If you had, I would have found a way to take you out of the game."

Grimacing against the throb in my head, I say, "I wanted to keep you out of it. I swear, I did."

"Jesus," Lex whispers, and when I painfully haul my gaze to him, he's three shades paler. "They wanted you to...?" He rubs a gloved palm over his face. "That's beyond fucked up, even for Father."

"I'll go." Pace says it like it's simple. Just as simple as I'd known it'd be for them, accepting a punishment to rescue me from this. He pushes his hair back, and even though his eyes shutter with dread, he still nods. "I'll take the punishment. Just–just promise me you'll take care of Effie."

Voice low, Lex cuts in, "Maybe I can take responsibility. The lashes don't take long to heal, and you–"

"*No*," Pace barks, pinning our brother with a hard look. "You've taken enough lashes for me. This is mine."

But I squirm with the knowledge of how untrue that is. This is *mine*. I wanted–no, *needed*–it to be mine. As if I could wash away the guilt and humiliation of being ten years old again, up on that stage as those monsters eyed me like a piece of meat.

Father has never worked that way, though.

I squint up at Pace and grab his forearm. "I'm sorry, man."

"Don't apologize," he replies, expression softer than I'd like. My fingers lose their grip and I slump back, too tired to argue, welcoming the darkness as it swallows me.

"Oh my god."

Her voice cuts through the thickness and I try to open my eyes. Try and fail. Shit. Did #99 bruise them shut?

"How the hell did this happen?" she asks. Who let her back in the locker room?

"*Gentle.*"

Effie? I don't remember coming home. I flex my fingers and feel the soft mattress underneath, not the clinic table.

"You've got an hour 'til midnight and Wicker needs to make a deposit," Lex's voice is an urgent whisper, drawing me back to the surface.

"Like that?" She sounds horrified. "He's seriously hurt—like should-be-in-a-hospital hurt."

"The padding helped mitigate the damage," Lex says. "His ribs are bruised, and his face is mangled but there's no bone damage. He definitely has a concussion, so you'll need to be gentle."

"*Gentle.*"

When and how did I get home?

"Jesus, you just had to teach her new words." There's movement and the rustle of fabric, what I assume is Effie's cage getting covered. "Look, Verity, this isn't up for discussion. You have to acquire the deposit by midnight."

"I can't have sex with him like that,' her voice is laced with a touch of distress. "He's... unconscious. It would be unethical, especially after knowing what happened to him as a—"

"Shut up," he hisses. "*Don't* talk about that. Princess, shit hit the fan tonight—catastrophically. I'm not asking you to rob a bank. I'm asking you to ride Whitaker Ashby's dick." He's quiet. "Do you think he'd give you the same consideration if the roles were reversed?"

It's a struggle to get my eyes open, and when I do it's barely more than a slit, but I see Verity and Lex standing in the doorway. My brother has a pained, stressed expression on his face. He's panicking. Pace? He's probably already receiving his punishment.

"He'd fuck me," she admits. "Zero hesitation."

"Because he understands what's on the line."

"What exactly is on the line, Lex?" she asks, looking up at him. "What happens if we break the covenant? Is that what happened to your back? Is that from violating it?"

"No, actually, and that's why you need to understand how serious this is. Those lashings were for fulfilling my duty, but not being *enough*." His hand thrusts through his hair. "So understand me when I say that you don't want to experience the consequences. You need to climb on his cock and let him put a baby in you."

Verity pales, lowering her head so her hair falls over her face like a curtain. Unable to hold them open any longer, my eyes flutter shut.

A moment later the mattress dips and the scent of roses fills my nostrils. Farther away, I hear Lex say, "Touch him. He won't break."

"He looks pretty broken to me." The blanket lowers and I feel her take me in her hand. I regret the sharp intake of breath that follows, my ribs aching from the simple movement. Her hand feels good, soft, a sharp contrast to the needling pain coursing across my body, but even so...

"I'm sorry," she says. "It's not working. He's too injured."

The urge to laugh is squelched by the pain cinching around my body. Whitaker Ashby, too hurt to get it up.

She shifts and I feel her weight move closer to my ribs. Again, I manage to open my eyes in a small slit, seeing her red hair as it brushes over my chest, my cheek.

"What are you doing?" Lex asks.

Her fingers graze my swollen skin, then something softer—warmer. "Kissing him."

"You don't get pregnant kissing."

"Wicker likes kissing."

"Why do you say that?"

"Because he's really good at it."

Her lips are soft and cool against my overheated skin. She peppers them across the bridge of my nose, over my cheekbones and down to my mouth. My whole face aches, but she feels like a salve. She licks my lips and I part them, my cock twitching when our tongues meet.

"There we go," she says, gripping my shaft. It's not fully erect, but half a chub is better than no chub.

"Try sucking it." Lex's voice is closer, on the opposite side of the bed from Verity. My toes curl when I feel the slick heat of her mouth on my cock. "That's right, Princess. Grab his shaft and jerk up." Her touch is soft, and I feel a flutter in my balls. "Harder. He likes it harder."

"But—"

"No buts, Verity." She jerks upward and her mouth covers my tip, tongue swirling over the head.

'That's it," Lex says. "Get him good and hard, right to the edge."

She works me, and there's something mesmerizing about the little sucking and licking noises she makes. Lex is right, my cock is a programmed machine—press the right buttons and it'll come to life. Red knows my buttons.

"He's ready," she says, removing her mouth but not her hand. "I taste him."

"Then straddle him."

"What if my weight is too much?" Her hand moves lazily, tugging and taunting me. "You said his ribs are bruised."

"Then I'll spot you."

I open my eyes to see my brother's hands around her hips, bracing her as she positions herself over my cock. "Wait," she says, leveling on her knees. "The plug."

Lex's hand vanishes between her legs, and he feels around. Her cheeks turn pink and he pulls out the golden object, shiny with her juices. They move painfully slow, and as she sheaths me inside, I manage a grin, "Now I know why you think it's so hot when I wake you up in the middle of the night."

She cracks a relieved smile, a little of the worry sliding off her face. "Are you okay?"

"Never been better, Red." A sharp pain stabs at my side. "Just take it easy on me, okay? I think #99 broke everything in my body but my cock."

She nods, giving her hips the smallest of thrusts. "Like this?"

"Perfect." Running my hands up her thighs, I look at my brother. "Take off her shirt."

Lex pulls the nightshirt over her head, and I eye her full tits. My cock twitches again, this time with a little more life. Her eyebrow raises, feeling it. "Fuck, you feel good," I tell her. "Tight and slick."

I watch as this girl rides me, gentle and controlled, my brother standing a foot away, ready to pull her off if necessary. It won't be, because it's too good and with all the pain and guilt and shitty feelings surrounding the last day, something has to come out of it that's not an utter nightmare.

"Touch her," I tell him, wishing I could do it myself, but my arms ache, and whatever painkillers Lex gave me make it impossible to move. "Get her off. I want to feel her pussy clench around me."

Lex leans over, licking his fingers and then pushing them between us, quickly finding the spot that makes her back arch. Her head falls back and her jaw slacks as she exhales. She keeps her rhythm, drawing my cock deeper with every thrust. Her nipples harden, pebbling tight.

"I'm g-going to come," she breathes.

"Good," I tell her, squeezing her thighs. "Come and then I'm going to fill you up."

Her breaths turn panty, and whatever the hell my brother is doing to her clit makes her moan. I watch her, in a way I never have before, feeling her body quake and quiver over me, watching her shatter apart.

Unsure if it's the drugs or the way she's milking me, I feel high. Lex pulls his hand away, then swipes his fingers over her mouth and she greedily licks her cum off her lips. "Fuck," I groan.

Lex steps back and sits on the chair next to the bed, unzipping his pants. He's got his own half-chub, and he works it as he watches the two of us. The room falls away, he falls away, it's only me and Verity–her perfect tits, her tight pussy–my aching, about to burst balls.

"You close?" she asks, eyelids heavy, half-closed.

I grunt in response, feeling my building release. It's going to hurt. Fuck, it's going to hurt, every muscle prepared to revolt, terrified of how the orgasm is going to trigger a full body reaction. Painful but so fucking worth it.

My nails dig into her thighs bracing myself for a final thrust, I grip her, controlling her movements, wanting it to last, closing my eyes because it hurts so goddamn much. She doesn't stop riding me until my dick is limp, pulsing weakly inside.

"Look at me," I hear Lex say. I comply, thinking he's talking to me but he's got his gaze locked on Verity and she holds his back. Two pumps later he curses, "Jesus," groaning as he empties himself in a little plastic cup. "Holy shit."

Verity sighs, body lax and content. "You good?" she asks, holding my gaze until I jerk my chin. "Everyone good?"

Over the sound of our recovered breathing, Lex and I share a look.

No, not everyone.

27

P ace

WARMTH TRICKLES DOWN MY FOREARM, cooling before it hits my pants and soaks into the fabric. The gouge comes from the sharpened end of the plastic spoon delivered with my dinner. The cut fills me with a much needed hit of endorphins–a clear reminder that I'm still here. That the blood left on the floor is evidence I existed. That the time down here isn't a gap that can't be filled.

It's been a full twenty-four hours since Father had Frank, his personal security goon, toss me down here. The mark of time is easy enough to document, the lights automatically shutting off at eight in the evening, snapping back on at eight in the morning. It's pitch-black overnight. I can't see anything. Hear anything. Just the pounding of my heart and the voices in my head.

I know one thing for certain.

I'm shit company.

The first night he sent me down here, I was barely seven. I

remember crying so much I lost my voice. We'd been playing iceberg in the living room and Wicker cut his chin on the rocking chair. I'd never seen so much blood come out of such a pretty face. It was both thrilling and terrifying.

Father had called us into his office, and I waited for the punishment. All the homes I'd lived in had punishments. Beatings. Beratings. Withholding food. Scrubbing floors and pots until they shined. Whatever fit the environment and the master of the house.

Father wasn't like any other master.

For Wicker's sins, I paid the price.

All over a fucking game.

I'd had this problem back then–funny to imagine it now–of being afraid of the dark. So he locked me in at night, the room already absent of any light. I eventually found the cot and huddled underneath, refusing to move even after I wet myself. You'd think that when Father came down, I would have been embarrassed about both, but I was just so relieved to see daylight—to see another human—I didn't care.

By the time I turned nine, things had changed. I grew used to the small, dark places. I made them my home, because that way, Father had no power over me. This room, even, with its squat walls, moldy ceiling, and frigid chill is as familiar to me as the locker room. I know every stone in the hard floor. I've memorized the drafts, the sounds of the house above me, even the scent of the air.

Eventually, it became almost soothing, like a vacation.

Where Wicker had practices and appearances, I had naps and solace. Where Lex had tutoring and camps, I had the bliss of a blank, unoccupied mind. There are no responsibilities down here. No appointments. No tests. No jobs or pretense. I'm unfiltered here, able to be entirely myself.

And even though these were lies I told myself to make it more bearable, Father resented the phony comfort. Punishments stopped being so scary. In fourth grade, we came home from boarding school over the holidays, our interim reports in hand. We lined up in front of Father's desk and handed them to him, one after the other.

Mine had two Ds.

After handing him the paper, I turned on my heel and walked myself down to the dungeon. It was the last time he bothered punishing me for my own deeds. After that, if I came home with an unsatisfactory grade, it'd be Lex kneeling in front of the fireplace—or worse, it'd be Wicker getting dressed in his finest tuxedo for a night out with the only woman I've ever wanted to kill.

So yeah, the isolation hurts, but it's not being alone that bothers me. That, I can handle. It's the way Wicker is probably feeling about it right now. It's the responsibilities I'm leaving behind in order to pay the debt. It's the thought of Effie in a silent cage, staring at a blank screen, waiting for me to come home and give her a glimpse of the sky.

It twists in my chest, and I lean against the cold wall, bloody forearm propped on my knee as I wait, just like her.

A bird in a cage.

～

I'M NOT sure how long I've been dozing when I hear footsteps on the stairs in the distance.

I'm up long before the door heaves open, hands gripping the bars of my cell. "Did you feed Effie?" I ask, before I see who's even entering. "Lex can do it. Or Wicker, even. But Danner knows if they're not around."

I hear the high-pitched panic in my voice against the stone walls.

But it's Frank who walks through the door, holding a tray. Naturally, Father would never send family down. When Frank looks at me, his eyes go to the bloody smear on my arm.

"Did you hear me?!" I shout. "Is someone feeding my bird?"

He says nothing, just opens the slot near the floor and shoves the tray through, before turning on his heel and walking out.

"Hey, motherfucker!" I snap. "If something happens to her, I'm coming for you!" I scream, kicking the tray across the cell. "It'll be on you, asshole! You'll be a murderer!"

It's only when the light pops on some time later–eight in the morning–that I realize the tray was breakfast.

I don't eat it.

THE FIRST TIME I saw Wicker, I knew he was going to be mine.

I didn't understand yet, six years old and coming out of a group home situation that the social worker explained '*isn't going to work out for you*'. I just remember seeing him and thinking that I've never seen anyone so pure and clean and *pretty*, and if life is about obtaining the very best things, then little Whitaker Ashby just became number one on my list.

And then he opened his mouth.

"Who the fuck are you?" he asked.

Just as snottily, I replied. "I'm Pace. Who the fuck are you?"

"Your worst nightmare." With his blue eyes narrowed, he buried a fist into his palm, and I laughed. The more I laughed, the more menacing he tried to look. He was just too cute to take seriously. As rosy-cheeked as the cherubs in the paintings lining the walls.

It was easier with Lex, who, even at eight years old, looked me up and down and said, "Hey. I guess I'm, like, your brother or some-thing." And he's never been anything less than that, as if protecting me was never a question for him. It's almost like whatever I felt when I looked at Wicker, Lex felt it about me. That I belonged to them.

Just like that.

I'm pretty sure it's the only reason Wicker decided to give me a shot. By my second week there, all of that bluster was gone, replaced with the eyes of a boy who *hurt*, but didn't want to show it.

I smile dimly at the memory, braiding three frayed threads from my shoelace together. "Your worst nightmare," I mutter, snorting.

And then I think of her.

Rosilocks.

Verity.

Because I got the same feeling the first time I saw her. Somehow, I just knew she was going to be mine.

If life is about obtaining the very best things...

Slowly, my smile fades. It was different when I was six and clueless, distrustful but fragile. Now, I think of Verity and I don't see something shiny and unique. I see danger.

Because lately, Wicker's begun looking at her without any of the bluster.

Lex has started protecting her.

I've let myself find comfort and solace in her.

Our worst fucking nightmare.

~

WHEN I WAKE, it's dark again.

There are three slashes on my arm. One is scabbed over. The other is gummy with old blood. The third is vivid and still bleeding, marking the third day. It's important. I learned it long ago, scratching hash marks into the wall beside me. Of course, over the years, it got confusing. Old marks, new marks–they all started blending together. Sometimes it was hard to know if I was on my fourth or fifteenth day. In prison, skin was just easiest. No one to steal it or smudge it, force me to clean it away.

When I rise from the fog of slumber, my senses are heightened to the smallest of sounds.

"Who's there?" I ask, disoriented and confused. My stomach rumbles. I rejected dinner, and then another breakfast, and now I'm starting to feel it in a bad way. Sleep is my only respite down here and I ignore the ache in my gut, rolling to my side.

The light blinks on, glaring and bright, and I slam a palm over my eyes, wincing as I peek through my fingers.

"Jesus Christ!" I jolt upright, squinting through the burn of the brightness. "You scared the shit out of me!"

"Get up." Lex's voice is gruff, his form looming above where I'm curled up on the floor. I see how he takes me in, eyes landing on the fresh cuts. Only three. The most I've ever had from a punishment was seventeen, but those scars are hidden under the tattoos now.

"Effie?" I ask, knowing it's stupid. The question I should be asking is why Lex is down here and not Father. Father is the one that releases me, no one else.

He doesn't answer, just says, "You need to get showered and change."

"Lex." Stumbling to my feet, I grab his arm. "How is she?"

Not Wicker. Not the Princess. The bird. I know how that seems. Like, logically, I know, but...

I promised her I wouldn't leave her again.

When I got back from prison, the day I came home and she refused to leave me, so distressed that she couldn't even string a word together, I told her I wouldn't go away again.

I *promised*.

His eyes flick over my shoulder, to the corner where the camera I installed records everything. Tensely, I exhale. Being nice to me, showing me *any* kindness, will result in further punishment—and maybe not against me.

"Hurry up." Lex pries my fingers from his arm, but not at the wrist. At the forearm. His fingertips tap over the tattoos–my tallies–and with a flick of his eyes, he says, "Always a mischief."

It takes me a second to decipher the code.

The collective noun for rats.

You've been gone before, he's saying. *We're sticking together.* Two nights and three days is nothing compared to nearly two years in the Pen.

The shower is in the corner of the outer room, and it's no more than a hose with an industrial grade nozzle hanging from a hook in the ceiling. Usually this is used to clean instruments, or hose down the floor. Occasionally, if we need to remove DNA, it can make a passable effort with some bleach.

I strip, stepping under the frigid water. Lex hands me a bar of soap that I use to wash my hair and body. I'm shivering by the time I'm finished, and when Lex tosses me a towel and a clean pair of shorts, I'm confused and disoriented.

This isn't a part of the routine.

Once dried and dressed, he says, "Give me your arm."

I thrust it out, only barely making out the low mutter of concern under his breath. He's quiet as he bandages my cuts, checking them for infection, and I sink into it like it's the darkness. Familiar. Comforting. One of life's greatest tragedies is that Lex's hands have been trained to hurt and maim, because the world will never know just how good he is at the opposite.

His fingertips are gentle as he lifts my arm toward the light, cleaning the newest slash with a puckered forehead. When he's finished, I expect him to put me back in the cell, but instead, he opens the door on the far side of the wall.

I look between it and him, even more lost. "Really?"

It's a small room adjacent to the dungeon, outfitted with a single bed. It's not exactly the height of luxury, but it's a big step up from the damp, cold stone floor. We've used it in the past to sleep in if we're watching a mark and need to sleep in shifts.

Suspicion rolls over me. "What's going on?" Every part of this is unusual, and the feeling building in the pit of my stomach is dread. Father is too consistent for this. What's changed?

"Wait here," he says, as if I have any other choice. I perch uneasily on the bed, wishing I had a sweatshirt or, god forbid, a blanket. Only a few minutes have passed before Lex returns.

He's not alone.

A blindfolded Verity stumbles clumsily ahead of him, her hands reaching out to pat the walls. She's in a sheer white night-dress, her hair wild from what I'm assuming was sleep.

"What the fuck?" I shoot to my feet. It hits me, and the laugh that claws its way from my chest is half-hysterical. "She's here for her deposit."

"You've got an hour," he tells me, palm dragging down her lower back. It's such a casually possessive gesture that I doubt he even realizes he's doing it. "Make the most of it."

My brother closes the door behind him.

Approaching her, I yank off the blindfold, catching her when the force sends her jerking into my chest.

"Pace!" Frightened green eyes dart around the room, taking it all in. Taking *me* in. "I was worried about—"

I cut her off with a hard, bruising kiss, gathering her up against me with a desperation I'll think to be ashamed of later. She's solid and warm and *human*, and the feel of her breath on my cheek has me trembling from restraint, because fuck. I want to crush her into my skin. I want to pull her open and climb inside her flesh. I want to make her a part of me just to steal the warmth and life from her blood.

Instead, I begin pulling at her clothes, stripping the gown off with short, impatient motions when I have to break the kiss to lift it over her head. When I do, her wide eyes blink back at me, welling up with tears.

"Pace, what's going on?" she asks, reaching for my face. "Why are you down here? Have you been here this whole time?"

I cut her off with another hard kiss, shoving at my boxers to free my erection. I don't answer her because I don't know how to. All I know is that the urge to fuck her, to feel her, to fill her up with my seed, is stronger now than it's ever been.

If Father gets his heir, all of this will stop. He'll leave me and Lex and Wick alone. He'll be focused on the future—on the Princess.

He'll give me back Effie.

"Against the wall." I spin her around, pressing her cheek against the cold stone. My voice is curt and rough, and she stiffens at the order. "Spread your legs."

There's no time for edging or mindfuckery. No time for the bed behind us. Not a single goddamn second for anything that isn't getting the job done.

I push her into the wall and reach for her panties, feeling between her legs.

"I'm wearing it," she gasps as I push aside the cloth. "Lex put it back in after he made his deposit."

"Good girl," I say, pushing my fingers into her folds and grabbing the base of the plug. "How does it feel?"

"Full." She swallows, a shiver wracking her body. "But not as good as it does when you're inside."

"Are you pregnant?" I say quietly, mouth close to her ear.

"I-I don't know."

Reaching down, I stroke my cock, getting it nice and thick. "Then let's keep trying."

With my hands on her hips, I tilt them back and tug at the plug, watching her shoulders tense as it pops past the resistance. I only get a brief second to think that we must all be in there—my cum, Wicker's, Lex's. One second to feel the white-hot shot of lust the knowledge shoots up my spine. One second to watch as it begins dribbling from her hole.

Then I grab my dick, slot it up against the mess, and slam inside.

I think she must seize at the sudden intrusion, but I hardly register it. I'm too busy feeling my brothers' release, all mingled with my own, slicking the way for me. I press a palm to the wall, using the other to slither around her neck, fingers resting gently on her throat.

I fuck her hard and close.

With my mouth pushed into her hair, I can hear every little hitch of breath she makes as I thrust inside. The sound of our skin when the flesh meets between us. The rasp of her fingertips against the rough stone as she struggles to anchor herself. The way I pant like a dog as I skate my palm down to her plump tit.

"Pace," she whimpers, feet shuffling as she spreads her legs wider for my hand, which is dipping lower, beneath her belly.

Teeth clenched, I stop just above her clit. "Say it," I demand, punching my hips into her.

She makes a low, frantic sound, rocking forward to seek my fingers. "I want it," she gasps, shuddering when my fingertips brush over her clit. "I–I want your baby inside of me. Please. *Please.*"

Grunting, I push my fingers into the swollen nub, matching the punishing rhythm of my hips. Her hair smells like roses and something else. Something sharper. Something masculine. Something that evokes a feeling of safety and calm.

She smells like my brothers.

That's what I'm thinking about as the first wave of orgasm takes me. I'm thinking that she must be sleeping with them. In Lex's bed? The thought makes me seize with such sudden fury that I pinch her clit, basking in the sound of her sudden, body-shaking cry.

She crumbles beneath me, tensing with the sudden, aggressive force of her release. I hold her there as I ride out my own, pinning her pelvis to the wall with my dick as I fill her up. Surge after surge. Pump after pump.

When I finish with a weak growl, I don't release her.

Breathing hard into her hair, I say, "I need you to do something for me." I run my hand up and down her arm, feeling the waves of her muscles clenching around me in these mesmerizing little beats.

"What?" Her legs quiver, and I push my hips into her harder, holding her up.

"Promise you'll take care of Effie. She gets upset when I'm gone, and you know her diet is—"

"She's fine, Pace." Dazed eyes peer at me when she glances over her shoulder. "We've all been watching her."

All.

It's too much to untangle here, wondering who it is I'm envious of. Her? Them? I search her eyes for the lie. She's done it before. Who says she won't now? "Promise me."

She nods slowly. "I promise."

"You're not just saying that to appease me?"

Her pussy gives a weak flutter around me. "No. Why would I do that?"

Because she's a liar. The accusation tickles the back of my mind. Covering me like a dark cloud.

"How's Wick?" It burns to ask her. I would have asked Lex, but I knew he couldn't tell me. Part of this punishment is the *not* knowing.

Body flat against the cold concrete, she whispers, "He has a concussion, but they say he'll be alright. He was walking today." Some of the tension in my shoulder ratchets down, and then she asks, "How long are we going to stay like this?

"Until I'm finished with you." If it was up to me, I'd make it last all day and into the night. But right now, we're on Father's time.

Her fingers fidget against the texture of the wall. "What about the plug?"

"*I'm* your fucking plug." My cock twitches, and I lick her neck before grazing the wet spot with my teeth. The tremor that runs through her brings my cock back to life, twitching deep in her pussy.

Pumping in twice, I get hard again before pulling her toward the bed, careful not to break the connection. She stumbles clumsily for a few steps, before just letting me drag her, her soft body going limp against me as I haul her backward.

When I reach the mattress, I pull her down with me, guiding her hips carefully. "Ride me," I demand, pressing my fingers into her thighs. It's almost better like this, watching the muscles in her back twist and shift as she hesitantly rises up, only to sink back down on my cock. I hiss as I feel my cum–our cum–dripping out around me, and I clamp her hips tighter, not letting her get too far away. Somewhere in the last week, however, the Princess has learned not just to take a deposit, but to fuck. She rocks back and forth in my lap in slow, fluid motions, her head canting to the side as she gets lost in the motion of taking me.

"Harder," I demand, reaching up to palm her tits. I feel the bounce of them as she rolls her hips more sharply. These little punched whimpers escape her lips, and I drown myself in them, rubbing my palms everywhere–tits, hips, shoulders, thighs. All the while, my nose never leaves the tangle of her hair, lungs swallowing the scent of her–of them.

My second deposit is ripped out of me more than anything. The motion of her hips is too sensual, too practiced to be anything other than deliberate. I clutch her in a tight, bruising embrace as I empty myself into her cunt, cock surging with a long series of hot pulses. It hurts to give it, this last part of myself, but I know I need to.

Father will be pleased I managed two.

I rest there for a long while after, inhaling her hair, stealing her warmth, wondering how much more time we have.

"Tell Wicker I'm fine."

Verity caught her breath a while ago, so when her fingers trail over my injured arm, her voice is even and small. "Lie?"

"Lie," I confirm, lifting her carefully from my cock. I'm there with the plug before I can leak out, pushing it in with zero regard to her wince. "Eventually, you might get good at it."

She shifts to face me. "Is something wrong?"

"No, Princess." I brush her hair off her shoulder. "The opposite actually. Being down here has a way of making me see things more clearly."

She bites down on her bottom lip, worrying it as the wave of insecurity washes over her. Good, join the club.

"And do something else for me?"

"Of course. What do you need?"

"Tell Lex I need to talk to Father."

ON THE FIFTH DAY, I make the slash numbly, tossing the spoon aside with a hard sigh. I rub at my temples, wondering how much longer it'll be. Father never says. There's school and hockey and security work, but if he really wanted to, he could draw this out for weeks, just sending the Princess in to make sure I fill that goddamn quota. Right now, it's the only thing that matters to him.

I spend hours thinking of Effie, talking to her like she's here. "Rain. Lightning. Hail. Raptors. The sky's not even all that great, anyway." I spend some time talking to Wicker and Lex, too. "Fucking iceberg. Hockey without a puck. No wonder we like skates."

Occasionally, I'll even talk to Rosilocks. "Biggest rat of all."

I can feel that lights-out is coming soon when I hear footsteps approaching. It's not my day for a deposit. Thursday. Free day.

Ironic choice of words.

It's Father who pushes through the door, and I scramble to my feet, making my back straight, even though it screams in protest. Three nights sleeping on this floor has given me a god awful crick.

"Father," I say, fighting the urge to fling myself at the bars. It stings to consider it, but in times like these, I think I'd even warm up to him if it meant having some company down here.

It wouldn't though. The only way out is through his approval.

Frank passes him, unlocking the cell door while Father sits in the metal chair Lex used when interrogating Bruce. He nods to the torture seat. "Sit."

My body feels alien as I walk across the room. I ease down, knowing the metal seat will be cold through the thin layer of my shorts. This is how I know what it's like to be in the chair. What it feels like to be under the harsh light hanging above, the scent of bleach and the cold tile floor under my feet.

This is how every punishment ends.

I wait for him to speak and when he does, he asks, "Do you understand why it's important to keep your brother level on the ice?"

"Yes, sir."

"Do you? Because it's not only a hardship on the team to be down a player, but it meant Whitaker couldn't fulfill other obligations."

I know these fundamentals are important to Father. It's why

we're so close. Why we share a bed and such small quarters. Why we play not just hockey but on the same line. It's important that we're cohesive in every aspect of our lives. It's why, when one of us fails, another is punished.

We are one.

Which is why I'm well-fucking-aware of the obligations Wicker was to attend to, and no matter what, it was worth it not to put him through that trauma again. That doesn't mean I don't want out of here though, and back upstairs to our bed and my videos... well, Effie.

"It's my fault," I say, reciting the lines I've prepared. "I should have kept him from losing his temper."

"The boys struggled while you were imprisoned. They're more settled now that you're back." His fingers peak into a triangle. "Together you provide a strong foundation of support. Broken apart..." He drops his thumbs. "Well, then you're just individuals. Royals were meant to be in threes. That's why there are three in every fraternity. Once a leader has ascended to the position of King, there can be one. And still.... we have to have the balance of those below us to hold us upright."

"I won't let them, or you, down again."

"I should hope not." He steps in front of me, hand gripping my chin. My skin recoils at his touch—any touch—other than my brothers' and more recently, the Princess'. "You're my eyes and ears, Pace, and until I'm sure you're ready for that responsibility, I can't allow you back upstairs."

"What?" I shake my head. "No."

"You're saying the right things," he starts toward the door, "but I'm not sensing you mean it."

"Wait!"

He doesn't stop, gesturing to Frank to open the door.

"Wait! I have something you need to see," I blurt. "Something you'll *want* to see."

He pauses, eyes narrowing. "Holding back on me son?"

Sweat coats my back. "No. I told Lex days ago I needed to talk to you. I had the information then."

His lip curves, like he's assuming this is some kind of Hail Mary. He's not wrong. "Go on, tell me what's so important."

"I planted a bug at the Dukes' gym last week—at the Fury."

"A bug?" I see the interest flicker in his eyes. My old man, he loves to spy. Lives for it.

"In the cutslut lounge. I figured we needed a way to monitor the Princess during her weekly visits."

"How innovative." He considers for a moment. "Have you found anything of use?"

"Just that the Princess has ties to the Duchess. They're friendly. It's not much but..."

But, I can tell, looking at Father, it's enough to get me out of here.

"Show me," he says.

"Now?"

"Immediately."

28

L ex

THE BEAD of sweat drips down my temple but I don't dare wipe it away. Wicker and I have been waiting for Father in his office, the two of us silent and in position, for thirty minutes. I don't dare look over at the fireplace.

Everything is a goddamn mess.

It's been five days since he sent Pace down to the dungeon, two since I told him Pace wanted to talk to him. In that time, it's been nothing but tension and obligations, the foremost of which has gotten a little lost in the fray.

I haven't fucked Verity in a week.

The knowledge nags at me. Wicker was beside me in my bed on Sunday, when the clock struck twelve, and I just couldn't bring myself to leave him. So I locked us in, and since no one was around to let me out, I didn't do it. Not the right way. The proper way.

Last night, I thought about it. Over and over, I'd imagine going to her, pulling out my cock, and giving her my seed like I should. All I would have had to do was keep my door open and lay down. But when the time came, I found myself engaging the lock.

"You still made your deposits," Wicker murmurs, as if he's reading my mind.

Down in the medical wing, with my syringes–yes, I made a deposit on each day. But one deposit is mediocre. Not excelling. And Wicker hasn't exactly been up to his usual sexual magnitude, either. With Pace in the dungeon, that means our week has been paltry in terms of deposits.

"Just let him," I say, picking at my cuticle. "If he wants to punish me, don't fight him on it."

Not that Wicker has the energy.

Tomorrow, his team is leaving for the All-Eastern tournament. I'm to accompany them as a volunteer medic, but Pace?

I guess he's not going.

Next to me, Wicker looks like he went—and lost—three rounds with a gorilla. The worst is his face having taken the brunt of #99's wrath. He's an abstract of purples, blues and yellows, swollen and tender on every sharp angle of his face. I know that underneath his shirt, the rest of him doesn't look much better.

But he'll be able to play. He has to.

Leaning forward, Wicker props his elbows on his knees, gripping his hair. "I fucked up," he says in a whisper. "I should have just gone to Mayfield."

He's been like this all week. Wracked with guilt about Pace. It's what makes Father's punishments so effective. It's never about just one of us.

Pitching closer, I hiss. "Don't fucking say that. If you think what Pace is going through is worse than bidding on a goddamn child, then you're losing perspective."

Still, when I dip down to eye him, there's agony in his expression. "I should have given him the choice."

"Wick, look at me." When he does, my jaw locks. His right eye has a subconjunctival hemorrhage that's still startling, even after a few days. The white has transformed to an eerie crimson around the blue of his iris. Exhaling, I insist, "There was no choice."

His throat shifts with a swallow, but just as his lips part to speak, the door to the office opens.

We both go instantly rigid, keeping our eyes forward.

That is, until we hear a second pair of footsteps.

I know it's him before I even turn. It's like there's a shift in the energy of the room, his presence a tangible hum. When I whip around to look, I see him shuffling through the door, head down, eyes hardened.

"Pace," I say, moving to stand.

One glance from Father makes me sink back into my chair.

The day Pace was released from prison, Father didn't go with us to pick him up. It was probably the kindest thing he's ever done, letting Wicker and I be the ones to greet our brother as he exited the building. There were no eyes on us. No pressure to perform. No urge to hold back.

I can't remember ever hugging anyone as hard as I did that day. The sound of his and Wicker's laughter was like balm to a wound. I was still shaky from withdrawal, wrung out and unsteady. But Pace held me up, grinning from ear to ear as he yanked on my ponytail.

Wicker just about tackled the poor guy, blue eyes sparkling. I've never seen him smile so genuinely, landing a playful punch to Pace's stomach. "Think the big house has made you tough, huh?" he said, and I laughed as I watched the two of them pretend to spar. We went out for steak afterward, and it didn't even matter that the conversation lulled in places, an awkward darkness settling over us.

Even with the nausea and itching, getting my brother back was probably the best day of my life.

Now, I can do nothing but sit back down, as though every cell of my being isn't compelled to go to him. And in the confusing avalanche of emotions, one thought comes to me loud and clear.

I wish Verity were here to see him.

She's not like us. She's had no reluctance in voicing her worry about Pace these last few days. Even during my lone, mediocre deposit yesterday, her legs spread wide in the stirrups, hands wringing against her belly, she was asking when Pace might be back.

But I only get a second to look at him before Father sweeps in, commanding the room.

"Pace, pull up the screen," he says, shoes echoing on the floor. In my periphery, I notice that Pace doesn't assume his position between us, instead walking to the computer on the other side of the room. With the press of a button, a TV screen rises from the floor, blocking the fireplace. "Your brother," Father says, finally regarding us, "apparently has something to show us."

Father moves to the leather chair that faces the screen. Wicker and I follow, taking our expected positions, flanking each side of his chair. Behind Father's back, we dare a look at one another, but Wick shrugs, also confused.

Pace is wearing the same clothes he was sent down there with: athletic shorts and a plain black tee. The mini twists in his hair were growing out even before he went into the dungeon, but now it's even more obvious, his textured hair beginning to loc. His skin has gone a concerning gray, the circles under his bloodshot eyes pronounced. The hollows of his cheeks are sharper, and if I had to guess, he hasn't been eating much off the trays I've been sending down with Frank.

There are two new cuts on his arm.

Gnashing my teeth, I try my best to put it out of my mind as I watch him click around on the computer.

"It's here," Pace says, voice rough as he squints at the screen. The TV blinks to life with an image of what I know is the computer screen. Pace navigates to the main directory before drilling down into folders labeled with location codes and dates. "The night of the Fury, I placed a bug in the cutslut's lounge. Motion activated," he says, only sparing Wicker and I the briefest glance. In it, I can see hesitation, like he's not sure this is something he should be sharing. Regardless, he explains, "With the Princess going to the gym every week, it just seemed like a good idea."

I'd be impressed with his ingenuity, except I know my brother. He didn't plant that bug there for intel. He just couldn't stand knowing his Princess was somewhere he couldn't surveil. "Did you find anything?" I ask.

"Yes." He presses play and a video appears on the TV. It's women–blatantly West End women–in various states of dress and undress. The volume is loud, unclear because of so many high-pitched voices all at once, but Pace walks over and uses his finger to point at the screen. "Verity's right here."

She walks in and greets the other women, her posture casual and relaxed. It makes sense—these are her friends and family. But one by one, the girls leave the room, until it's just Verity and one other woman: Lavinia Lucia. The Duchess.

Pace reaches down to the keyboard, pausing the video.

It freezes on a frame of Verity pitching forward, smiling at the Duchess.

"This is a violation of the covenants," Wicker says, scowling at the frozen image. "She was specifically told that engagement with other Royals—including the women–is off the table."

Father stares at it, expressionless. "This happened a week ago."

"I asked her about it, but before I could verify any of her answers, I was..." Pace clears his throat, giving our father a nervous glance. "Uh, made unavailable."

"What were her answers to this?" Father asks, tapping his finger methodically against his knee.

Pace flicks his dark gaze to us. "She blew it off. Said they weren't close at all. But obviously, she lied. As you can tell, they're... friendly. At the very least."

"Very friendly," I reply, seeing the smile they share. It isn't just the polite, casual smile of acquaintances either. It's wide and comfortable. *Intimate.*

Well. Fuck.

Pace allows the video to continue to run, and we watch as Verity and Lavinia leave the locker room.

"Thank you, Pace, for taking the initiative of placing that

recording device in the DKS facility." Father looks up to meet my brother's gaze, and my spine loosens at what I see there. He could have easily penalized Pace for taking so long to bring this up, but instead, he looks satisfied. Proud. *Forgiving.* Father nods at him. "That's exactly the kind of dedication I like to see from you."

For one, bright moment, it seems as though everything is going to be okay. Sure, the Princess has a friend in the Duchess, but that can be stamped out. Pace has made amends by discovering this. Wicker is on the mend. No one is getting any appointments, isolations, or dates.

The world rights itself.

And then the media program autoplays the next file.

We all snap forward as it begins, surprised. Pace is usually really good about archiving pointless activations, but Wicker's eyes are intent on the screen as it starts up. Of course. He can't resist a half-naked chick.

What we get is just the Lucia girl, entering the room and leaning up against the wall, like she's waiting. It's not long, though, before someone else enters.

"Wait, wait. Hit pause," Wicker says, pointing to the screen. "Is that *her*?"

Sure enough, Verity is frozen on the screen, her wide eyes fixed on Lavinia. She's wearing a different outfit than the one in the last video, and her hair is pulled up. In the last shot, her hair was down.

"What day is this?" I ask.

Pace checks the timestamp, brows knitting together. "... last Friday?"

Sweat prickles my back. "Friday. The day after her family dinner."

Pace stares hard at the screen, confusion furrowing his forehead. "That was in the morning, right after I made my second deposit. We should have both been asleep in her bed when this was made."

It's impossible, because there she is talking to Lucia. Wicker and I share a harried look, because the Princess doesn't just get to waltz about Forsyth wherever and whenever she wants. She's to have a chaperone. Security. Her fucking Princes.

Pace snaps upright, his panicked eyes fixed to Father. "I check her tracker every night, sir. As far as I know, she never left the Palace."

Father's eyes narrow. "Clearly, she did."

"But she must have–"

"Shut up!" Father barks, shooting him a glare. "Turn up the volume and press play." Stone-faced, Pace obeys, and the tinny sound of Verity's voice emerges from the speakers.

"Last night, when I was... with Pace, he was asking me all these questions..."

The Duchess' head tilts. *"What kinds of questions?"*

"About family dinner—and you."

Lucia asks, *"Me? Specifically?"*

Verity looks down. *"He thinks you're a traitor. I mean, he thinks I'm a traitor, so this is pretty on brand for him, but I don't know. He just wouldn't let it go."* Then, so quiet that I have to pitch forward to hear her, she adds, *"He freaked me out."*

Lucia's expression turns pensive. *"Pace just got out of prison, right?"*

"Yeah."

I glance over at Pace, watching his eyes harden as they talk about him, although it's hard to hear over my pulse throbbing in my ears. Pace's expression turns to stone as they discuss him and his paranoia, his hands balling into tight fists at his sides.

The fucked up thing is, a part of me is so goddamn happy about this recording. It's proof that Pace was telling the truth–that he was trying to dig deeper, find something to bring to Father. That should absolve him, shouldn't it?

But one look at Father's fiery eyes, trained to the girls on the screen, makes it clear that it doesn't matter. His ire is directed else-where now.

"Verity," Lavinia says, *"it's fine. What could they know? We barely talk. You've hardly given me any real intel anyway."*

Almost as one entity, our attention hones in on them.

"You're catching feelings for your Princes," Lucia says, *"that's why you haven't been telling us anything useful, because a part of you is protecting them."*

Has she? Has she been *protecting* us? From who? The Dukes?

I try to catch Wicker's eye, but he's staring hard at the screen.

"I do know something," Verity is suddenly saying. *"Wicker's father is a Kayes. He's the Baron legacy."*

My heart stops, but I still hear Lucia's reply. *"Well, yeah. We already know that."*

"Turn it off," Wicker says, voice barely heard. When Pace doesn't respond right away, he shouts, "Turn. It. The. Fuck. Off!"

I watch him with wide eyes and frozen lungs. My brother's secret isn't a secret. I keep repeating it in my head–just saw the evidence of this fact–but somehow I'm convinced it can't be real. This information we've protected so fucking doggedly since we first learned it, back in middle school, could destroy him. Kill him.

And it's known by our enemies.

My first impulse is to take Pace and Wicker and drag them away. Run. Hide. Those new lives we spent so much of high school dreaming up? Now's the time to make them–create them–to become people who won't be hunted or hurt.

My second impulse is red-hot fury.

I fucking knew it.

It screams in my eyes as I look at Pace. I knew we couldn't trust her. I knew it from the very start, that her loyalties would never be with us. I knew it, and along the way, I forgot.

I forgot that we were fucking a traitor.

"How did the Princess come to know about this information?" Father asks, his voice oddly calm as it cleaves the silence.

After a moment of his jaw working around an aborted attempt at speaking, Wicker admits, "I told her." His voice sounds thin and wrecked, eyes still glued to the image of Verity's face. "I fucked up. I told her. She had me cuntstunned and I just... spilled like a goddamn fucking rookie." His voice quivers, eyes darting between us. "I'm sorry. I'll—"

"We have to get rid of her," I say. This declaration is pure instinct, but the look Pace gives me suggests it's not without merit.

"Kill her?" he asks, forehead twisting in a strange way.

But Father shoots abruptly to his feet, his posture stiff and straight. "Absolutely not," he sneers, and when he meets our gazes, the only instinct I feel is to step between him and my brothers. "That girl is your vessel, and I'll hear nothing more about it. Is that understood?"

"But she knows," I point out.

"And so do the Dukes," Father snaps, gesturing angrily at Lavinia Lucia. "What will killing your vessel do to shut them up, hm?" When none of us answer, he reaches down to his white cardigan, snapping it straight. "There's only one course of retribution here. Only one way of ensuring they all keep quiet about this knowledge." He looks between us, jaw hardening. "You'll need to host a Royal Cleansing."

"A what?" Pace blurts. If possible, he's paler than before. "You didn't even order that when Piper got knocked up by someone other than her Princes."

No one else would know it except the three of us, but my suggestion of killing her was a mercy that we'd afford no one else. There are worse things than death–a lot of those available at our own hands–and no one knows that better than us.

This is one of the things worse than death.

"*Piper*," Father says, the word dripping with distaste, "didn't betray family secrets to the enemy."

"When?" I ask, dread pooling in my gut, but knowing that Father is right. Killing Verity will just make the Dukes lash out, and with them holding the ticking time bomb attached to my brother, this is going to require strategy.

And I remind myself of this, a litany on repeat in my mind, to avoid thinking of the other reason we can't kill her.

Soft, tender, green eyes gazing up at me, gentle lips, plush mouth, sweet-smelling and fertile, the perfect body to sink into, the way she looks at me when I give that piece of myself to her, the feather of her blink when it's over, like she wishes it could be more, the exhilarating quirk of her grin when we ate dinner together that one night...

I shut it all out, like I should have done at the very beginning, because Verity Sinclaire isn't one of us. No matter how worried she was about Pace, or how gentle she was with Wicker when she took his deposit, or the way she kissed him and then looked at me, as if she was asking me to reassure her that she was doing it right.

I shake it all from my head.

"We'll do it immediately." Father walks behind his desk as if he hasn't just announced the most impossible thing. "Justice should be swift. I'm calling an emergency meeting to have everyone assemble in the throne room in one hour. Pace, go set up the appropriate recording devices." He makes a few hard taps at his phone screen, mouth pressed into a tight, furious line. "The Dukes will need a reminder of what's at stake if they choose to speak, retaliate, or attempt to blackmail us."

Pace goes to the door, but stops when I dart forward. "Father, I..." I falter, unwilling to show weakness, even though that's exactly what this is. With a deep breath, I explain, "I've been making progress with my... issues, but under the pressure of performing in front of a crowd—"

"You *will* perform."

"I can't," I burst, seeing Wicker flinch at my side. "I've tried everything, but the only time I've even remotely managed an erection while awake is when me and her are... together."

Father's eyes tighten. "Together?"

"Creating," I clarify, feeling my cheeks heat. "*Intimately.* And even that's tenuous, at best." Shaking my head, I say the words that I've been avoiding for months now. "I can't do it. I'll humiliate our family. I'll make a fucking joke out of us."

Father stares at me unblinkingly, putting down his phone. "I'm glad to hear you finally say that, Lex." He reaches down to slide open his desk drawer, pinning me with his gaze. "Sometimes, our greatest strength is the ability to acknowledge our weaknesses."

With a smooth, measured motion, he places a clear baggy on the desktop.

It has a serpent printed on it.

I swallow around the sudden constriction in my throat. "What's that for?"

Father raises his chin. "You know what it's for."

"No." I can feel Pace's gaze on the back of my head like a branding iron. "Lex, *no.*"

"It's not your choice to make," Father snaps, effectively shutting that down. A look passes between them, but I don't see it. My eyes are glued to the white powder beneath the plastic. "You're strong enough to face up to your weaknesses, Lagan. Now we need you to be strong enough to overcome them."

The only thing big enough to tear my stare away is the feeling of Wicker turning to look at me. I meet his gaze, stomach twisting at the numbness in his stare.

He already looks disappointed in me. "Lex."

"I'll need it to do this," I insist, palms feeling damp.

"Bullshit," he says, blinking that bloody eye. "You don't even know if it'll work."

"Yes, I do." I know it like I know the earth orbits the sun. I know it like I knew Wicker and Pace belonged to me, and like I know Verity does too. I just can't face up to it.

But I can face up to this.

"I can beat it," I tell him, holding his gaze. "I beat it once, I can do it again."

"Father," Wicker says, turning his stare to the drugs on the desk. Pain and regret ooze off of him. "I'm the one she betrayed. Let me be the one to inflict the punishment."

Coldly, Father holds his eye as he opens the baggy, emptying a fine white line onto the polished wooden surface. "The criteria of a Royal Cleansing are clear. It requires all three Princes." The look he sends me brooks no argument.

Required.

A part of me suddenly realizes that this was never a choice. The pretense of me having a decision was a humiliation in and of itself. A show for my brothers. It's proof that Pace can endure days down in that cell, that Wicker can endure being treated like a piece of meat, that I can withstand lash after lash, and it doesn't matter if those punishments are ineffective.

There's infinite power over me *right here*.

A cold sweat breaks out on my forehead. Not because I don't want it, but because I do. God, the anticipation is as painful as a lash from Father's whip. Stepping forward, I ignore the way Wicker lurches toward me–sharp, like an instinct.

I bend, taking the first snort, letting the delicious, addictive feeling wash over me. I taste the salty chemical of it in the back of my throat before I've even pushed upright. "Fuck," I mutter as I swallow it down, fingers tweaking my nostril. I'd almost forgotten that flavor, acrid and sour, and how it'd be followed by a sudden rush of heat. "*Fuck.*"

Father re-seals the baggy. "You have one hour to prepare. I expect you to be thorough and exact. I expect you to be *ruthless* and *precise.*" He looks between us. "I expect you to be Princes–to be *Ashbys*–but above all, I expect you to show no mercy."

The three of us look at each other, and I realize that no matter what just went down here, that's the one thing we all agree on. I see it now, the Viper Scratch flowing wildly through my veins. It makes everything clearer, sharper, intellectual high definition.

Everything I've come to like about Verity Sinclaire was a lie.

"Wait," he says as we move to leave. Holding out the baggy, Father says, "Take the rest with you. Use it."

I look between the Scratch and him, still rubbing the powder from my nose, swallowing down the bitterness. A better man would tell him to shove it and turn his back.

I reach out and grab it.

Father hasn't just given me an excuse–given *us* an excuse–he's given us permission.

And that's so much more dangerous.

SHE'S CONFUSED.

Even with the blindfold covering her eyes, I can tell that much.

Stella, her handmaiden, is the one to walk her in, and she looks jumpy, glancing around the room with wide, nervous eyes.

Verity pauses, tilting her head. "... Pace?"

She thinks she's here for another conjugal visit.

"I'm here," Pace says, but he's not looking at her. He's looking at the camera mounted on the tripod. It sits between us and the rows of chairs, filled with forty PNZ members. The three of us are positioned in front of the throne, Wicker in the middle, me to his right.

I'm so juiced that I can't stand still, my finger tapping an errant rhythm on my thigh. My jaw aches from the way I'm grinding my teeth, but I can't help it. My chest is light, but somehow also full. My veins zing with energy, mind racing through a dozen thoughts per millisecond.

Her shoulders sink in relief at the sound of Pace's voice, which is actually pretty funny.

He looks like he wants to fucking murder her.

The worst part about it is that he probably *doesn't* want to murder her. That's where Verity Sinclaire fucked up. If she'd stabbed us in the back like this a month ago, it would have been so easy to wipe her ass off the map. But she's smarter than that. She got close–almost close enough to matter–and she used it against us.

Wicker's never told anyone but me and Pace about who his real father is. Him telling her? That's fucking terrifying. It means she clawed her way in. It means she could know more. It means she's an even bigger threat than I ever imagined.

"Take it off," Wicker tells the handmaid, jerking his chin toward the blindfold.

"Wicker?" Verity says, blindly searching for the source of his voice. "What's going on? We aren't in the basement."

"Astute observation," I utter, watching her head jerk toward the sound of my voice.

Slowly, the handmaid unknots the silk covering Verity's eyes, letting it slip away. She gives a series of blinks, orienting herself, before her gaze lands on us.

Immediately she springs for Pace, grabbing his face in her hands. "Oh my god, are you okay? No one would tell me anything about–" Her words cut off when she realizes he's not looking at her, his stony expression fixed on the room at her back. She stiffens, palms slipping from his jaw as she realizes where she is.

The throne room.

It sinks into her green eyes like a pit of black shadow, and she shrinks back. For the first time, she turns, jolting in shock at the sight that greets her.

It's almost funny how she backs into us, like she's expecting us to protect her from the room of men.

"What's going on?" she asks, voice reedy and panicked. "Wicker, why are we–"

"You can go now," Wicker tells the handmaid, jerking his chin at the door. She's frozen, looking reluctant to abandon her Princess, but when Pace shoots her a hot glare, she turns and scurries out of the door, closing it behind her.

Verity flinches at the sound.

"This is a Royal Cleansing," I announce, unable to stay silent any longer. I feel the heat of her stare on me as I address the room– the camera. My fists flex and release, flex and release. "Our Princess has broken the covenants of our house. Covenants that she agreed and swore to, in this very room."

"Wait," she says, her eyes zipping across the sea of faces. "I didn't break any–"

"She's disloyal," I bark, shooting her a warning look. "Fraternizing with other members of the Royalty behind our backs, and sharing sensitive information with them–information that endangers the lives of your Princes."

Her face slackens, paling. "Lex. I don't know what you've been told, but–"

"Even right now," I say, gesturing to her, "she's lying."

Her mouth clicks shut. "Tell me what this is about."

"Lavinia Lucia," Pace sneers, finally meeting her gaze. "Or did you really think there's anywhere in this town I can't watch you?"

She blanches. I can practically see the gears turning in her head as her green eyes search our faces. She's wondering if we can really know.

In a mocking voice, Wicker says, "Freedom means choice, Ver."

It's what Lavinia Lucia had said to her on that video, and right now, Verity Sinclaire is realizing she has none of those. *Choices.*

Her chest caves at Wicker's words, body going limp, like a doll whose strings have just been cut. "Wicker," she says, green eyes already welling up. "It's not what you think."

"Fuck you," he snaps. I've seen Wicker angry plenty of times. Shit, probably a dozen times a day. This is nothing like the usual, though. He looks like he's been fucking gutted, every line of his face strung tight as he glares her down. "Everything I told you that night–you just went behind my back and fed it right to our fucking enemies."

"Not everything," she rushes to say, a tear brimming over. "I never would have told them about... *that.* And the other thing–they already knew."

"You think that makes it better?" My bark of laughter is cold, sharp enough to watch it cut her with a flinch. "I knew about you from the start. I knew you'd be a disloyal cunt, stepping on the backs of anyone who got in the way of what you wanted." I bring my palms together in a slow clap. "I've gotta hand it to you. You were almost good at it."

But she's searching my face with a frightened frown. "Why do your eyes look like that? What's wrong with you?"

"Nothing is wrong with me. In fact," reaching out, I snatch her hair in my fist, "I've never been more right. I wanted to take your hands, you see. But Father says you'll need them to hold the baby we're going to put into you tonight." Wrenching her closer, I make sure she feels my hardness against her hip. "The jury's still out on your toes, though."

Her eyes get wider, not just at the threat. "You're high."

"And thinking more clearly than I have been in weeks." I release her, raking my fingernails down my left forearm, the itch already settling in. "And what I'm thinking is that I'm finally going to be able to scratch one itch in particular." My tongue darts out. "Get on the table."

Her eyes shift to the gilded table positioned in the front of the room. The same table Wicker bent her over on her throning night. "Lex–"

"Get on the fucking table!" I roar, my heart pounding like it could rip through my sternum.

She visibly jumps, but follows my orders, stepping to the table and easing up on the edge. "Like this?"

With my brothers behind us and the frat members in front of the table, I stalk forward, hyperaware of the thickening of my cock, the way it feels nudging at the seam of my fly, every sensation in every nerve heightened from the Scratch. It's when I unzip that panic flickers across her face.

"What is this?" she whispers, eyes zeroed in on my very hard, very thick erection.

"The Royal Cleansing is ordered when a Princess violates her contract." I step between her legs and give my cock a long stroke. "It's required that you're purified again, this time not by blood, but by seed."

Face falling, she turns her head, looking over at the frat, all forty of them waiting for a show. "In front of... everyone?"

"Something I always hated about being a PNZ member," Wicker says from behind me. "Everyone wants the Princess, don't they? We have to watch her get throned and claimed, fucked in public, right under our noses, but we can't touch her. It's like dangling a fat, juicy pork chop in front of a pack of well-trained, hungry Rottweilers." He sounds closer when he adds, "Every man in this room would love nothing more than to split you open on his cock. To be the one to fill you up. To know that our Princess–an icon of purity and innocence–is walking around with *his* creampie growing inside of her."

Wide-eyed, she peers over her shoulder at them, shaking now. None of them say anything. They can't. Royal Cleansings are much like the thronings in that way.

But at least three of them already have their dicks out.

Wicker lets her sweat it for a beat. "They can't, of course," he says, a cold smirk in his voice. "But they still have a role in this."

Grabbing her chin, I jerk her horrified gaze back to mine. "That's right, Princess. You belong to PNZ. You betray one of us, you betray all of us."

Her lip wobbles, watery eyes shining up at me. "Lex, please."

"Oh," I breathe, reaching out to run my knuckle along the soft cut of her jaw, "we'll definitely take more of the begging."

"They'll like that," Wicker agrees, and I don't need to turn around to know he's looking at the camera. "You'll like that, won't you, Perilini? My brother's about to show you what happens to our defective property."

Her head whips around, spine going rigid. "Simon?" It isn't until her eyes land on the camera that she realizes the King of West End isn't here.

Not physically.

"No." The word falls out of her in a long, agonized breath. She turns to us, eyes streaming with tears now. "I'll take the punishment. I'll be good." Her voice breaks. "They don't have anything to do with this."

Low and cutting, Wicker says, "Fuck her, Lex. I want my go at her."

"Patience, little brother." Grabbing her hips, I yank her forward, knocking her off balance. She falls back, but struggles to get upright, eyes filled with frantic panic.

"Wait!" she cries, and I grunt, grabbing her thighs. "I'm sorry, okay? I'm sorry!"

"Hold her down!"

My brothers each take a side. Wicker's hands clamp around her bicep while Pace's wrap tight around her throat. My cock is throbbing so badly that I feel it like a goddamn jackhammer in my pants. Idly, I wonder if this is what I'm like when I'm asleep.

"You know it only hurts worse when you fight, Princess."

Spreading her thighs, I shove her dress up her hips, clawing at her panties as she thrashes. A prickle of familiarity rolls over me. This is the same position we're always in downstairs. The difference is, I wasn't able to take her like I wanted to during all those nights with her in the stirrups.

Now, my cock surges with want.

The panties are white and pristine. Another lie. After wrestling them off her, I hand them to Wicker, gaze honing in on the glint of gold shining from her pussy. It's the plug holding in our deposits. Glare hardening, I wedge my finger in and *yank*.

"Ah!" she cries out, muscles tightening as the plug pops out. "Lex, please, wait!"

I hand the plug to Pace, ignoring her pleas. My dick weeps at the sight of her pretty pink cunt, begging to be filled back up, and when I take my cock in my hand, I feel the thing I've been searching for all this time.

Power.

Fuck, I'd forgotten that. The power in sex. The way my cock feels in my palm, hard and potent, the surge of animalistic lust that burns in the pit of my balls as I nudge the tip against her slick entrance. "Is there anything else you want to tell your Dukes?" I ask, nodding to the camera. "Any other secrets you want to reveal? Last words?"

"You can't show them this," she croaks, squirming against my brothers, a different sort of misery twisting her face. "You *can't*. They think I want this. They don't know..."

"Don't know what?" I ask, gathering the wetness on my head. "What your real duty is here? That you're a vessel for our seed? That your days and nights are spent on your back with the singular goal of creating an heir?" Without warning, I thrust in, stretching her with my girth. She gasps, and I grin coldly down at her. "You're nothing to us, Verity. Just an incubator for our future. And it seems you need to remember your place."

When I draw my hips back, the second punch inside is harder, my cock driving in with incredible force. Her body skitters up the table as she screams, but my brothers hold her in place, making her take the full brunt of it. My fingers dig into her flesh, keeping her still, while my hips hammer into her. The rush is so good, everything is amplified, from the blood pumping into my cock, to her little strangled cries as she takes me.

It's the rawness of it all that gets me. The notches my fingertips make in her soft thighs. The torn texture of her voice when she releases a sob. The way we look together, my skin rubbing roughly against hers with every brutal thrust. There's no bright light, no smell of antibacterial hand soap, no gleam of stainless steel instruments or crinkle of latex.

It's primal.

I remember nothing about those nights in her room, nothing about the way it felt to claim her, to pump my seed inside with the intent to make a baby. I hate not knowing, and at this moment I know why.

This feels like the most glorious goddam dream.

Wicker pulls roughly at her dress, freeing her tits, and his fingers find her nipple, pinching and twisting tight. She yelps, and her pussy tightens around me. "She likes it," I say, sniffling the flavor of residual Scratch into the back of my throat. "Makes her tighten up." Wicker does it again, and this time her teeth bear down on her bottom lip so hard that blood beads.

She doesn't know it, but directly behind her, Tommy Wright is slouched low in his seat, pumping his fist around his dick.

As I fuck into her, jolting her body with each slam of my hips, her green eyes catch mine, brimming with hurt and shame. Instantly, my balls fill, the urge to come intensifying.

Look at me.

I've made her do it every time I've put my seed into her. She's never pushed with the need to know why, which is good, because I'd never tell her. There are no facts or studies or clear analytical evidence attached to my reasons for it. The truth is, I do it because of where I come from—who I come from. I do it because if creating life is more than medical, then I want to be sure.

I want to be sure it's made with some kind of connection.

And suddenly, it's the last thing I want.

All those nights she watched me, watched *Lagan*, surrendering to her while I was lost in another world, somewhere tucked deep in my mind. No. Now it's my turn to watch.

"Cover her eyes," I grunt, barely holding back. "I don't want to look at this bitch's traitorous face."

It feels right that it's Wicker who smashes her face to the side, forcing her gaze to Pace's perversely bulging crotch. It's only then that I allow the floodgates open, grunting raggedly with the force of it. I yank her hips into my thrust and hold them, my cock jerking with a river of cum as I spill into her.

There's no better orgasm than one had while high on Scratch.

It spreads out like wings, heat rushing to every appendage. My thoughts scatter like fine sand, a complete interior annihilation. The neurons don't just fire, they shatter into millions of pinpricks of light. I coast on the crest of it for so long that by the time I come down, my muscles are twinging in protest. I look down as I pull out, my cock slipping free.

A glob of cum follows it.

Pace is there before it can fall, two of his slender fingers guiding it back inside.

Verity is quiet now, her chest heaving with these little hitched sobs. She's still looking away, her wet eyelashes clumped together as she stares unblinkingly into the distance. There's snot on her face. Red cheeks. That bead of blood smeared over her mouth. She already looks absolutely fucking wrecked, and my chest swells with an odd, primal pride—the pride of knowing I'm the one who did it.

Nodding at Pace, I say, "You're up."

 icker

I'VE NEVER HAD A GIRLFRIEND.

Probably the closest I've ever come was this chick in eighth grade who lived behind our boarding school. We saw each other five times, making out behind the batting cages until her porch light came on. A lot of second and third base references that spring. I never even knew her last name. She wasn't pretty. She was just available. For boarding school boys, that basically makes any girl the center of his universe.

But somehow Verity rose to the top of that very short list.

She's never been my girlfriend. She's my responsibility. My obligation. My duty. But there for a blink, I found myself wanting something from her besides sex, and I don't even know what that thing is. Comfort? An ally? A confidant?

No, I have my brothers for that.

I wanted something else from Verity–even sought her out that day I learned about Mayfield. I wanted to look at someone and feel that spark of optimism and promise. I wanted her to look back at me and see someone strong and... what was it?

Worthy.

That's it.

It's not that I liked Verity Sinclaire.

It's that, there for a second, I wanted her to like me. I wanted to know how it felt to have her on my arm. To know what the fuss is about at the end of the day, when a man sinks into a woman he shares a life with. To understand this spark of excitement in my chest at the thought of her wanting to know those things too.

And it was a lie.

Not just for her, but for me too.

The truth is, I'm not made for that. Never was. Those five times behind the batting cages with the groundskeeper's daughter were a fluke, and this last month with Verity was just the pathetic result of my own lapse in judgment.

Which is why, as I watch my brother shove the gold plug into Verity's mouth, saying, "Maybe we should've used this to keep your fucking mouth shut instead of your pussy," I feel nothing.

Well, in my heart. My cock is steel, because I'm still a man. And nothing gets me harder than a traitor getting what's coming to them. Especially when it's this personal.

He's been at it for at least twenty minutes already, his hips driving into her as she lays there on the table, thighs spread obscenely wide. Lex is on the other side of the table holding her down, her wrists clenched in his fists. Predictably, Pace is taking his time, drawing this out to last as long as possible. Not everyone is as refined at the art of denial as he is. Two guys in the front row grit their teeth, probably one stroke from spilling their load. They wouldn't dare, though. It's against the *rules* to waste their seed tonight, and it's beyond satisfying, watching the frat get a taste of what I've endured these last few weeks.

Pushing my resentment aside, I step next to my brother, looking down at her pussy. Lex's cum coats Pace's cock—nature's lube. Verity looks up at me, mouth stuffed with the gold plug, and I see her green eyes glazing over. "Stay with us, Red." I snap my fingers over her face, jolting her back to reality. "You don't get to fade out before I've had my turn."

But Verity's worn-out pussy getting hammered is something she's used to. Day in and day out, we pump into her, hoping our seed will take root, making this all come to an end. That's not the motive today, though. For once, *creation* isn't our primary focus.

Punishment is.

Unzipping my pants, I pull out my cock and pump my hand up and down as I take in the scene. It's a shame, really. Verity has a fantastic body, when she actually uses it. Right now, it's all scuffed up with red marks and her overworked flush. She's not fighting against Lex's grip anymore. She's just laying there like a fuck doll.

I step between her legs, hip to hip with my brother, and say, "Maybe this will wake you up and remind you who you belong to."

Pace makes room for me without needing to be asked, his cock dragging in and out as I nudge mine into her folds. I nearly come when I feel the slick heat brush against my tip. *Not yet*, I tell myself. Fuck no. This girl, this punishment–it all belongs to me.

I grab the base of Pace's dick to feel his rhythm, then I push in with my brother, stretching her with both of our cocks at once.

Eyes slamming shut, she screams, the sound muffled around the plug. Her body shudders, a conflict of tension and release, knowing if she fights us, it'll hurt so much more.

"Does that hurt?" I ask, tone bitter as I look down into her wet eyes. "Does it feel as sharp as a knife in the back?"

We thrust in again and her throat swells up with the shriek.

"Did you plan it all along?" I ask through gnashed teeth as I push deeper, wanting an answer.

Frantically, she shakes her head.

"What's that, *Princess*?" Lex, still jacked up on the Scratch, leans over and removes the plug from her mouth.

"No," she gasps. "It wasn't planned! Wicker, I wish I hadn't–"

"Liar!" Taking both of our cocks in one hand, I slam in again, rocking her up the table. She screams and Lex crams the plug back in again, cutting it off.

Pace grinds out, "God, you're such a terrible liar. Almost as bad as you are at getting knocked up."

It hits me then that I'm fucking glad she's defective and hasn't been able to take my seed. She's West End trash who can't be trusted to carry the Ashby heir, let alone the Kayes'. She can't be the creator of a life so precious. A double legacy.

A future King.

My brain turns fuzzy with anger and want. Next to me, Pace's hand lands on my shoulder like an anchor. He growls, cock sliding next to mine when he comes suddenly, an explosive burst, so powerful I almost lose traction. Jesus, I see now what she was meaning about the firehose, because Pace *pours* into her, one surge after another. I feel it in his cock next to mine, jolting with each wave as he grunts. I still to let him work through it, engulfed in the thick, hot flow of his release, so good and warm, surrounding both of us, and I know...

I know whoever comes for me–Duke, Lord, or Baron–my brothers will always have my back.

Pace's forehead drops next to his hand, resting on my shoulder as he heaves out a long shudder.

"You got this?" he asks, breathless.

I look down at her, glassy-eyed and emptied of fight as she takes it, head lolled to the side. "By the skin of my fucking teeth."

He pulls out and I catch the dribble of his come with my fingers, shoving three in next to my cock before drawing out. I catch Lex's eye. "Turn her around," I say, because looking at her–*humanizing her*–that's what led to this moment. "I should have never fucked this bitch face-to-face."

With a yank, Lex drags her up and flips her, my fingers never leaving her hole, keeping her plugged. Once her ass is in the air and she's flat on her stomach, I enter her again, fucking all of Pace's cum back in deep.

My hand thrusts out, snatching her shiny red hair, and I twist, leveraging her to look sideways, up at the camera. "Look at them," I say, bending to hiss the words into her wet cheek. "Let them see what happens when you try to get one over on PNZ. Actually, maybe we should give them a better look." I jerk my chin at Pace and he grabs the camera off the tripod, bringing it closer. When I ease back, spreading her cheeks, he zeros in on her wrecked pussy, oozing with our cum around my cock. "What's it like watching your little narc get fucked into oblivion?" I ask. Noticing the plug has slumped out of her mouth, I reach over to snatch it up, deciding none of her holes should be left unfilled tonight.

The sound she makes when I push it into her ass is raw and ragged, Pace making sure to get the full breadth of the shot.

As I shove it in, I growl, "Bet Maddox wishes he'd climbed that fence a little faster."

"Fucking right," Pace breathes, moving the camera to where her fingers are white-knuckling the edge of the table. "Ride her hard, Wick."

Being inside her makes my skin crawl. I'm used to this disgusted, *used* thing squirming beneath my skin. It's the same thing I feel whenever Father sends me off to please someone rich and well-connected and revolting. It's the feeling of being the means to someone's ends.

Verity Sinclaire used me.

And if I didn't have a point to make and pain to inflict, I'd do my duty, cream into her, and walk away without looking back.

"*You* did this to her," I grind out to the camera, balls tightening. "You and your viper whore. So when you get angry, when you want to retaliate, remember who really deserves your wrath."

I slam into her one last time, cum shooting out before I've reached the hilt. The action is so hard, so forceful, that it lurches her back to life.

"I'm sorry!" Verity cries. "*Stop!*"

"I'll stop," I tell her, cock twitching, adding the last of my cum to the deposit, "but you're not finished. Not even close."

She doesn't know it yet, but the cleansing has only just begun.

~

FIVE MINUTES LATER, she looks as stiff as a mannequin, pale but pink-cheeked, eyes swollen from crying. As the three of us take our places beside her throne, her chest jerks with these little breathless, involuntary gasps.

She's sitting on the same device that took her cherry, back straight, eyes forward, fingers clenched around the arms of the ornate chair.

Unlike last time, she doesn't fight.

For one, her pussy is accustomed to being invaded now. Secondly, she knows there's no use.

"You look so good like this," Pace tells her, petting her hair back. "Finally, a good little pet."

Decker and Wright dropped their dicks long enough to move the table, allowing space for our brotherhood to get a good view of what comes next.

"How..." Her voice cracks and she swallows. "How much longer?"

Lex is the one to step up, speaking more to the frat than to her. "Stage one of the cleansing is complete. Her womb has been purified before you. Now, it's your turn, PNZ. Do your duty to your Princess." His eyes are dilated into two black orbs. Tomorrow, we're going to have to deal with that. But tonight, I let him train those blown pupils on her as he sneers, "Bathe her in your seed."

Her gaze springs up to meet his, widening with a dejected sort of horror. "What?"

But the men in front of her are already clambering to their place in line, just like Monday offerings. There's a certain familiarity in the sounds in the room. The rustle of fabric, the low groan of desire. The intoxicating scent of hormones and sex. I've spent years surrounded by it, exposed to it in locker rooms and dorms with peeling beige paint on the walls. Listening to my brothers rub a quick one out before going to class, or helping one another out through a long night. There's no shame here. It's part of what makes us brothers. And this event will only seal the bond, ultimately making East End stronger.

She wants to cry. I can see it in the way her face crumbles. But her eyes flick to the room, and she doesn't. Even when Lex sets everything in motion by gesturing to the first in line, announcing, "Let the cleansing begin," Verity smashes her lips together, refusing to speak. The camera has been trained on her once again, but she won't look into it. If I had to guess, she's putting on a fake face for them—her Dukes.

No one in the room is buying it.

Wright is first to step up, an excited glint in his eye as he stops in front of the throne, cock in his hand. He jerks it roughly, jaw clenched as he stares at her tits. It's not often we get to see a Princess on this throne completely unclothed, and it seems to do it for him, because he's grunting with release before Verity even has a chance to prepare herself for the first hot splash of his nut.

She flinches.

Hard.

I can see it ripple through her, and when she whimpers, I know it's not because Wright is painting her chest. It's because the phallus inside of her is pushing against her insides. Eyes squinched shut, she turns her face away, chest jerking with another of those stifled sobs. A final ribbon of cum lands on her collarbone, and Wright groans as he watches it drip down to her tits.

"For my beautiful Princess," he says, breathless. "May she reign."

He stumbles away, hitching his pants back up.

Next is Decker. He's a big fucker—the team's meanest D-man. His hog is short but girthy, and when he towers over her, reaching over her shoulder to grab the back of the throne, it's just as much about dominance as it is strategy.

His cum lands on her chin.

"For my beautiful Princess," he says, smirking. "May she reign."

The next few are quick—some of the two-pump Freshmen who got started jerking their cocks before anyone else. They look excited and horny as fuck, pumping their cum onto her sloppily. One of them barely manages to hit her at all, twitching like a goddamn tweaker as his cum dribbles out of his cock like it's half-asleep.

Lex scoffs as he bumbles off. "Keep it quick," he demands, eyes narrowed down the line. "Get your cocks out and start jerking. We have other shit to do tonight."

By the tenth guy, Verity has stopped flinching.

Her eyes are empty as she takes another, a rope of cum painting a slash against her pale cheek. The room has grown hot with everyone's quick breaths and surging hormones, the scent of it already thick enough to choke me, let alone her.

But she's not crying anymore.

She's nothing.

I watch her take load after load from a brotherhood of panting breaths and slapping flesh, saliva being spat into palms, animalistic grunts and ragged groans, and I know that she's finally defeated.

It's the only thing that eases this ugly, gnarled thing that's been growing inside of me since I saw her on that video, giving up the part of me I'd so freely given to her–for *her* safety. The hardest thing to face is that it isn't just shame twisting me up inside. It isn't only the knowledge that I'm a fucking idiot for telling her. It's something worse than that. Something deeper. Something new, yet as old as the air I'm breathing.

For once, I get to hurt the person who hurt me.

30

erity

IT MUST BE COLD, but I can't feel it. I put one foot in front of the other, feeling the twinge in my center, but numb to it in some odd, fundamental way. On either side of me, the paintings of cherubs and old dead men watch my humiliating, slow march down the hall. Behind me are the footfalls of my three Princes, escorting me back to the suite. I don't need to listen to know they're there. I can feel them in every pang. Every bruise. Every ache. I can feel them deeper, into the very core of me, painful and knurled.

I keep walking, because if I don't, I'll fall.

And there will be no one to catch me.

My arms rub against my bare sides, just as sticky as the inside of my thighs. *This isn't my body.* I say it over and over again in my mind, like a mantra. *Not mine. Not mine. Not mine.*

This has been true since I walked in the front doors of this place, but it has a different slant now. Where these words used to be the angry, bitter curse that roiled in my gut like poison, I now clutch to them as the only source of comfort afforded to me.

This isn't my body, so I don't need to deal with it. Simple. Clean. I'm just a machine of ropes and pulleys and tangled gears. I'm the skeleton, but not the flesh. I'm the veins, but not the blood that pumps through them.

I'd forget to stop at my door, except when I round the corner, I see Stella down there, waiting, her body curled tight around itself. She takes a step forward when she sees me, face falling, but then stops when she notices I'm not alone.

I approach her as if I'm a ghost–someone invisible–because the other option isn't possible.

The Princes stop when I do.

Stella wrings her hands. "Er, I'm not familiar with the procedure," she says to them. "Can I clean her up?" It's only the tone of her voice that draws my eyes to hers. There's a thread of anguish there and I feel it like claws scraping at my lungs.

There's a sharp scoff behind me. *Wicker.* "Bathe her, parade her around the campus, push her off the balcony–do whatever you want with her." His voice is suddenly closer, hot breath washing across my ear. "We're done," he growls.

I hear them leave more than I see it, a door closing somewhere to my left. It reverberates as loudly as a gunshot, and when Stella's gaze moves to mine, she says, "Come on, Verity. We'll wash it away." Her voice is soft and coaxing–completely unlike her–but that's not what chips at the crack in my armor. It's not even that she uses my name instead of calling me 'Princess'.

It's that she reaches out to take my hand.

Despite the disgusting gunk clinging to me, she folds our hands together and gently pulls me into the room. She's uncharacteristically silent during the whole process of starting my shower and gathering my clothes. No dresses or silk gowns for tonight. No, she goes into the closet, drops to her knees, fiddles around behind a stack of boots, and pulls out a soft pair of leggings and a worn sweater. Clothing I'd brought with me.

That's the first time I really smell myself.

Acrid, musty, the thick scent of men clinging to me like a toxic cloud. It sticks to the back of my throat, and suddenly, I feel it everywhere: arms, belly, shoulders, thighs, neck, chin. It's the reason my vision is blurry, a mixture of semen and old tears gluing my eyelashes together. It's on my nose. It's *in* my nose.

No part of me isn't covered in them.

Stella jumps out of the way when I dart to the toilet, bending in half to heave.

My body seizes the contents from my gut in a hard, violent way. The muscles around my ribs spasm and clench as I toss it all up, sour and too hot.

A hand lands on my back, rubbing up and down my spine. "I'm sorry. I didn't know."

Stella's the one to flush, reaching over me with her clean-smelling hair, and it's all I can do to not sink into her. I jerk away instead, ignoring how her face falls. I want to apologize, but I don't. This revolting sickness all over me feels too infectious to risk spreading it.

The first thing I do when I climb into the shower–*a Royal Cleansing*, I think, feeling hysterical–is crank up the heat until it scalds me. The pain is as close to being purified as I can get. But no matter how hard I scrub my skin to stinging rawness, I'm filled with a certainty that makes the tears return in full force.

What happened tonight was more than a punishment.

It was the end.

An end to my family, who's going to see the full scope of what I've become. An end to whatever fragile, curious spark had been growing between me and the three men I'd only just begun to catch a real glimpse of. An end to the girl who thought she had what it took to hold them, and worst of all an end to the girl who first drove over that bridge, wide-eyed and painfully pure, the world spread out so hopefully ahead of her.

As I wash those forty-three men from my body, I grieve for her the hardest.

~

"Rise and shine!"

I flinch as Stella yanks open the drapes, expecting the explosion of bright, cheery sunlight.

None comes.

Listlessly, I swing my gaze toward the window, finding a cold, dreary sky.

"Oh." Stella pauses, the heavy brocade of the curtain still clutched in her hands. Outside, rain is pelting the window. She shrugs. "Okay then, rise and gloom, because it's almost three in the afternoon, and we've got a jam-packed evening! What do you say we begin with a trip to the solarium, hm?" When no response arrives, she turns to me, meeting my gaze.

Gradually, all of her chipper spirit plummets away.

"Hey," she begins, deflating as she perches on the side of the bed. "I know the other night was..." She glances down at her wringing hands. "Well, it was a nightmare. I'm not going to put any sugar on it. I managed to buy you some time with the King and his staff, but Verity," she says, eyes pleading. "You need to eat. You need to take care of yourself. And somehow, you have to find a way to plan this ridiculous Valentine's Day party, because there's only three days left. You can't just give up."

That's exactly what I've done, in fact.

I didn't even get dressed after the shower. I allowed her to tuck me into this bed, and aside from a few trips to the bathroom, more than once to dry heave into the toilet, I haven't moved since. I didn't even realize a day and a half had passed until just now.

"What are they gonna do?" I ask, voice full of gravel. "Kill me?" The smile I give her is flat, but feels utterly jagged, and from the flash of panic in her eyes, she sees it.

At this point, death would be a mercy.

"You listen to me, Verity Sinclaire," she says, the words hard. "You're no pampered little East End socialite. You're West End. You're a fighter!"

The laugh scratches its way from my throat, dry and rough. Those are the same words I used to bolster myself that first week in this Palace. "Who am I going to fight, Stella? My Princes? Their King? Myself, for stabbing them in the back?" Rolling over, I wrench the blanket up to my chin, putting my back to her. "You should go. He'll be here soon."

She touches my hair. "Who?"

"Wicker," I say. It makes sense that Pace didn't come yesterday. After all, he'd already made his second deposit this week. But Wicker? "If it's really Saturday, then he'll be coming."

After a pause, Stella's fingers catching on my knotted hair, she says, "Prince Wicker isn't here. None of them are."

My eyebrows knit together. "What?"

"They're at the All-Eastern tournament," she explains, picking through a mat in my hair. "They won't be back until late Monday."

I turn to peer up at her. "When did they leave?"

"Thursday night. Right after..." Her eyes shutter and she sighs, dropping my knotted lock of hair. "I'll try to clear the rest of your day today. But tomorrow, you'll have to leave this room. Perhaps we'll start with that trip to the solarium. You love the solarium!" Standing, she nods at the bedside table. "And please, eat?"

I follow her gaze to the covered tray I haven't even considered touching. "I can't." Every time I close my eyes, I swear I can still feel them on me, the hot splash of semen tickling like a phantom illness that sends me scurrying back to the bathroom.

In a hopeful tone, Stella adds, "Danner can have anything made. He wants to. He's been asking after you."

It's shame more than bile that rises up my throat. It takes me a long while to swallow it down, breathing through the urge to purge it. "I can't," I say again.

I can't look Danner in the eye. He'll know what happened to me. He'll know what I did to instigate it. That I did it on his watch. He'll look at me with those gentle eyes and see something less than Verity Sinclaire. He'll see a traitor. He'll see a victim.

I'm not sure which is worse.

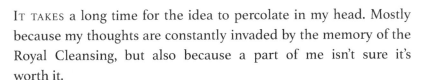

IT TAKES a long time for the idea to percolate in my head. Mostly because my thoughts are constantly invaded by the memory of the Royal Cleansing, but also because a part of me isn't sure it's worth it.

In the end, it's desperation that drives me from the bed that night, slipping into the soft, worn clothes Stella left here for me two nights ago. There isn't any hope behind it. No optimism. No *fight*.

It's just that if there's one thing that can be salvaged from all of this, then it has to be this.

It *has* to be.

I open my door and cringe against the sconces in the hallway. They're not bright, but my temples throb with the glow of them. Padding down to the door that leads to their rooms, my heart begins hammering frantically against my ribs. Stella said they were gone, but what if they aren't? What if I open that door and they're all inside, waiting?

What are they gonna do? Kill me?

It's become my new mantra, and no matter how concerned it made Stella to hear it, the general sentiment is true. Unless this works, I have nothing left to lose.

When I push the door open, I'm strung tight in anticipation of finding someone on the other side. Luckily, all that greets me is their dark, vacant sitting room. I tiptoe out of instinct toward Pace's room, the open door about as inviting as a guillotine.

I walk through it.

The space is illuminated by a single computer monitor that's showing a feed from the front gates. A moth flutters in front of the camera, sending a ghostly blur of a trail across the screen.

Squawk. "Hungry bird."

I yelp, practically jumping out of my skin as I whirl around, finding Effie peeking out of the bottom corner of her cage. There's a sheet over it, but one corner has caught on the gate, leaving her an opening.

"Jesus, Effie," I whisper, pressing a hand to my chest.

"*Gentle*," she croons, the sound of her wings flapping loud in the silence. "*Gentle pretty bird.*"

Hugging my middle, I cast my eyes about the space, searching for her treats. The bag isn't too far–maybe Danner feeds her while they're all away–and I pluck one out to give to her. "Quiet," I whisper as she takes it. Then, I fix the sheet, turning to the computer.

When I navigate to the directory, it's nothing like what I'm used to. The operating system looks old and complicated, and I don't know any of the keystrokes. It doesn't help that I'm trembling, and in my efforts to be swift, I'm just clicking around rabidly, hoping something catches my attention.

I force myself to pause and breathe, scanning the directory of oddly named folders. There are hundreds, with nothing but random letters and numbers. Then, it hits me. I sort by the most recently modified, scooting closer as I search the dates for Thursday night.

Unfortunately, the first folder I click prompts me for a password.

I bite back a groan, wracking my brain.

Ashby, I try.

Invalid passcode.

Wicker. Whitaker. Lex. Lagan. Pace. Kayes. WickerKayes. Whitaker-Kayes. PurplePalace.

Invalid passcode.

Biting my lip, I cast my eyes around the room before reluctantly trying: *Verity. VeritySinclaire. Princess. Rosilocks.*

Invalid passcode.

Stomach sinking, I know it's hopeless. Pace is paranoid. His passcode is probably fifty characters long and completely random, and I bet he could probably still recite it in his sleep. Then again, maybe that's what he'd expect an intruder to think. Maybe it's actually something simple.

Looking down at the keyboard, I intend to see if there are any particularly well-worn keys, which is when I see it. The F12 key is missing–as it usually is, because Effie likes to tear it off and run away with it. I've seen her do it a couple times, treating it like a game she's just won.

Pausing, I poise my finger over the little naked nub of a key.

Then I press it.

The room explodes with light and I gasp, shooting up from the chair. But it's not the overhead lights, nor the lamps. It's another monitor flaring to life, a directory of files appearing. Exhaling shakily, I sit back down, squinting at the bright screen as I read the contents.

They're videos, some recent, others much, much older.

The recent one is titled 'Evidence237-Deposits'.

With an unsteady hand, I open it.

An image of four people appears from a bird's eye view, as if in the corner of a room. One is King Ashby, sitting behind a desk, and the others are the Princes, on the opposite side of it. It takes me a long moment to realize the whispers I'm hearing are coming from a set of headphones sitting on the desk beside me.

Cautiously, I pick them up and put one of the cups to my ear.

"*And how is our mutual project coming along?*" a voice asks.

King Ashby.

Pace offers him a bounce of his chin. "*Slow but steady.*"

Ashby jabs the point of his pen in Pace's direction. "*That's the way it's done. A Princess like Verity will need a steady hand. Consistency, patience, reinforcement.*"

"*I agree,*" Pace replies, nodding. "*The Princess is everything you said she is. Willful, proud, combative. But she shows moments of... dedication. Being Princess is her own project. She wants to succeed.*"

The King's eyebrows tick up. "*Is that so?*"

Pace explains, "*She seemed disappointed that she isn't pregnant yet.*"

It's galling to hear these men talk about me–about the commitment I've shown to being their Princess. The thought of them sitting around, talking about how much I want their baby inside of me, makes my fucking skin crawl.

Ashby appears to take this in favorably before turning his gaze to Lex. "*And how many deposits did you make during this cycle, Lagan?*"

"*Four,*" Lex says, and then, "*No. Five.*"

Ashby leans back, a pause stretching on. "*Which is it? Four or five?*"

Lex stammers, "*Well, I–one of my deposits was comprised of two–*"

"You made four," Ashby snaps.

Lex's head bows. "*Yes, sir. One on each of my assigned days.*"

Ashby drags in a loud breath. "*I'd like to congratulate you as I have your brothers, but one deposit per day is the bare minimum. A disappointment. Mediocrity. It's unacceptable.*"

Lex tries, "*Father, I'm—*"

"*I thought you had your situation under control!*"

Even from the elevated view, Lex looks sick. "*I do. I've made strides to compensate for any physical failings by maximizing our efforts. In addition to my deposits, I've researched methods to encourage fertility and fertilization. I'm monitoring her diet, her hormone levels, and her ovulation cycles. I've begun genetic testing. Additionally, I'm keeping everyone on schedule and enforcing the adherence to the covenants.*"

Ashby stares at his son for a long, suspended moment. "*So what you're saying is that you're doing everything but giving the Princess a good, old-fashioned fucking.*" I flinch at the words, stomach churning.

Lex flounders. "*I—*"

"*Whitaker,*" the King says, "*get the box.*"

I watch, baffled as Wicker stands and strides across the room, opening the cabinet behind Ashby's desk. Lex stands next, unbuttoning his shirt before shrugging it off and hanging it neatly over the back of the chair. When he turns, I catch a glimpse of the scars etched into his back.

"*Father,*" Wicker says, "*Pace and I can contribute more deposits if—*"

Ashby rolls up his sleeves. "*This isn't about deposits, Whitaker. This is about Lagan giving me his word, and then failing to fulfill it. He's allowed a weakness to stand in the way of his purpose."* Then, Ashby commands, *"Fireplace."*

I watch in growing horror as Ashby–their father–extracts a long whip from the box. Lex's body is rigid, eyes staring into the fire as the King approaches him. Suddenly, there's a loud crack, the long strap landing on Lex's back.

The scars.

This is the source of them, I realize.

That night he came to me, asleep and animalistic, *these* were the wounds on his back, created by Ashby's whip. The look on his face as he does it is cold and unyielding.

"Four lashings for each of your deposits. And an additional four to get you to the same level as your brother. Be thankful I'm not holding you to Whitaker's standards."

"Yes, sir," Lex replies before the whip slices through the air and cuts into his skin once again. I can't see the pain on his face–not from the camera's vantage–but I can hear it in his voice. Maybe I should feel bad for him, but mostly what I feel is an oddly detached satisfaction. This was the man–the Prince–who held me down and fucked me in front of his frat. He's the man who held me down while his brothers did the same. He's the monster who stood aside and ordered the cleansing, watching as all those men spilled onto my body.

Still...

The whipping continues and I see the blood. The way Ashby slams his elbow back for a final, vicious lash, and the sound it makes when it connects, sharp and wet...

I feel bile rising in my throat once again, and throwing the headphones aside, I search frantically for somewhere to heave it. The trashcan under the desk becomes home to it, my back contracting as the vomit tears its way up my throat.

I'm only barely recovering, gasping shuddering breaths, when a low, metallic whine whips my attention to the outer room. Frantically, I begin closing out all the directories, my heart lodged in my throat as I hide the little bin with my puke in it.

"I know you're in there," a low, ominous voice calls. "Come out."

Frozen, I stare with terror at the open door, wondering if I can wait him out. Hide somewhere. Find another little, dark nook in the wall that can take me elsewhere. But if these recordings tell me anything, it's that there's no place, in or out of this palace, to hide.

In the end, I can do nothing but rise mechanically to my feet, shuffling out into the dim sitting room.

King Ashby is in the armchair, clad in a long, silk robe. "Everything my sons know, I've taught them." He lifts a foot, resting his ankle casually on his knee. He's wearing striped pajamas, which somehow startles me nearly as bad as the knowledge I've been busted. Sometimes it's too easy to forget this man lives here with us. He tilts his head. "Did you honestly believe Pace is the only one monitoring security in this house?"

I push my hand into my roiling stomach. "I'm sorry, sir. I was–"

"Snooping," he says, voice as sharp as a whip. "Trying to find something to send back to your Dukes. Is that it?"

The panic is swallowed by dread and certainty, and I repeat my mantra.

What are they gonna do? Kill me?

Deflating, I shrug. "The opposite actually. I was going to delete the video." That was the idea. If they left here right after what they did to me, then there's a possibility that the Dukes–my family–haven't seen it yet.

Ashby arches a brow. "And did you?"

"I couldn't get in," I admit.

His grin is joyless, patronizing. "Even if you had, it wouldn't matter. All our files are backed up. Plus," he sighs, tightening his robe, "it's already been sent."

My heart sinks. "What?"

He clarifies, "The video of your cleansing. The Dukes received it two nights ago." On his knee, his foot gives a rhythmic little shake. "It's been quite the controversy, I'm afraid. A lot of posturing and petty threats."

Hot tears sting my eyes as the hopelessness drags me under. I'm assaulted with the sudden vision of them watching it. Was it just Sy? Or was it all the Dukes? Lavinia? Did the whole of DKS need to see what I've been reduced to? The cutsluts?

My mother?

The sob claws free, and I struggle to push it back in, pressing a palm to my mouth.

Ashby's lips form a grim line. I'm not expecting his quiet, gentle voice when he asks, "You understand why your actions could have killed Whitaker, don't you?"

I suck in a hiccuping breath, forcing the anguish down. "Because he's the true Baron legacy," I say, sniffling. "It makes him a target."

He pins me with his eerie eyes, nodding. "More than you could even conceive. The Barons' enemies would find it advantageous to wipe out the last Kayes heir. Likewise, the Baron King's faithfuls are fanatical madmen. They'd eliminate Wicker as a show of devotion to their King. And to anyone *not* devoted..." The stare he gives me is heavy with significance. "Only two men in this town are capable of taking the title of Baron King, and our dear Wicker is the first."

First?

Dumbly, I ask, "Who's the second?"

If the probing nature of the question angers Ashby, then he does a good job of deflecting it. "Someone just as ill-suited to the position, I'm afraid." His expression suddenly shifts, a frown etching his forehead, and then he stands. "I must admit, it surprised me. I thought for sure Pace would be the first to trust you with something so sensitive. He's paranoid, but does tend to attach himself to anything that'll attach itself back. Wicker, however." Tsking, he approaches me, shaking his head. "You must have done quite a number on him. He's never let himself get that close to a girl before."

His dark eyes peer down at me. Within them, I can see perfectly clear the man who took that whip to his son's back. His gaze is worse than empty.

It's as penetrating as a knife.

"It's why I let Pace believe he was showing me that video of your treachery," he says, "when in actuality, I was showing it to them." At my slack expression, he grins, the evil smile making a shiver run up my back. "However closely you think my son is watching you, rest assured, I'm watching you ten times closer."

I gape through tear-blurred eyes, my question emerging like a plea. "Why?"

"Why did I order the Royal cleansing instead of dealing with you myself?" He holds my gaze for a long, unsteady moment. "Well, I can't have them feeling too attached to you, can I?" I'm too stunned to do more than stand stiffly when he reaches out, gathering my hand into his palm. "Nor can I have you feeling too attached to them."

Again, I wonder, "Why?" But I can already make a few guesses.

The four of us are better to manipulate and control when we're apart.

"Such beautiful, soft hands," he muses, ignoring the question. He looks down at it–my hand, cradled in his palm–and covers it with his other, giving my knuckles a slow, tender rub. "If I find you snooping like this again, I'll let Lagan take them."

I lurch back, yanking my hand from his grip. Maybe it's not the smart or safe thing to do, but when the thought rises to the surface, I release it without reservation. "You're the most terrible man I've ever met."

Ashby only gestures to the door, moving to let me through. "Then you haven't met very many men."

It's as I'm making my escape, fleeing for the hallway, that he stops me.

"Oh, and Princess?" When I freeze, not daring to look over my shoulder at him, he adds, "You have more than one duty in this Palace. A good Princess would already be mostly finished preparing for the Valentine's day party. It is being held in your honor, after all."

The laugh that threatens to erupt is more hysteria than humor, because I see how seriously he takes this. How he truly does think any and all of this is an honor, including my cleansing. His entire identity is wrapped around this world, and therefore by association, so are all of ours.

"No worries, my King," I say, because sometimes the only way to deal with a madman is to play on his level. "I have no doubt the party will be the most talked about in years."

I'm in the solarium before the sun has even completely risen.

It's cold and damp, the earth frozen beneath my fingers as I work, digging and cutting, even though it's useless. I haven't been able to get anything to grow in here. Not a single flower. Not one bulb. Not even a weed.

Angrily, I cull them all–the dead, frozen seedlings–my hands thrashing through soil even though there's a spade right beside my knee. I work my way down a long, stone planter, barely seeing what I'm doing, just knowing that I have to get rid of it. All of it.

No part of me should be in this place.

My movements turn frantic as I reach the urn, remembering the day Wicker had come down here. I was in the middle of transferring this dead rose bush, knowing it'd be useless, but bored enough to try. I remember him sitting on the steps, looking tired and sad and *haunted*. That was the look on his face–the one I couldn't place at the time. I see it with full clarity now.

"There you are," Stella calls, walking down the stone path. "I went to your room and was surprised to see you gone."

"You're the one that wanted me to come down here." I yank out a clump of brittle stalk and toss it to the ground in frustration. "And why, exactly? So I could see how I suck at this, too? That I can't even get a fucking flower to grow in this place? That my whole role here is a pointless, giant disaster?"

She freezes at the gate, frowning. "It's not pointless, Verity."

I turn and look at my handmaiden. "How did they find you?"

They. The Lady and Duchess.

She looks down, biting her lip. "At the Hideaway. I was working there–not as an escort–but cleaning rooms and whatever my sister needed. Story came in asking if there was anyone who might be a good handmaiden. I volunteered."

"Why?"

She shrugs, looking sad. "I guess you're not the only one who wanted to be something bigger than you were destined to be."

I exhale and sit on the stone wall, staring down at my dirty hands. "I'm a failure, Stella. I had two jobs. *Two*. The first one was to get pregnant, and the second was to secretly infiltrate the Palace for the Monarchs." I look at her. "Do you know how many deposits I've taken?"

She sits next to me and shakes her head.

"Forty-seven." I dig at the soil beneath my thumbnail. "I've been fucked every way you can do it. Missionary, cowgirl, reverse cowgirl, doggy-style, knees up, bent over a dozen surfaces, railed by a sleep-walking demon, and way too many times with my legs in stirrups." I look at her, scowling. "Not one single sperm has attached to my egg."

Her face falls. "Verity–"

"No," I cut her off. "If that's not pathetic enough, I not only got busted not-so-covertly fraternizing with the enemy, but I also got caught revealing the biggest secret in the Palace. *On* camera. And! *And!*" I shout, "Everyone already knew!" I drop my head in my hands, digging at my scalp. "Now everyone knows about what happened to me the other night. I've hurt my friends and family. I've lost every inch I've gained here. I'm a complete and utter failure."

There's a short pause before Stella's hand lands on my back. "So what do you want to do about it?"

I shoot up, pacing, unable to stay still. "Run away," I blurt, wiping my hands on my thighs. "Leave Forsyth and never come back." I feel how much of a relief it'd be, deep in my bones. I could. Stella and Ballsack could maybe smuggle me out. Although that idea hurts like a stab to the gut. Leaving my mom? The Dukes? The Monarchs?

She gives me a steady look. "If that's what you want, they can make it happen."

I barely hear her, a different idea spinning in my head. "Or, I could stay, do what I came here for. Get knocked up, try to raise a new generation where something like the Royal cleansing never happens again."

Stella nods, understanding shining in her eyes. "Whatever you want to do. They'll help you, no matter what you decide."

I explode, "You don't know that! And you... you can't risk it." I've seen the dungeon under the Palace. I know the Princes can make a man–or woman–disappear. They wouldn't blink at killing a girl like Stella.

"I do know it." Reaching out, she takes my hand, stilling me. "I think you can do whatever you set your mind to. Because the woman that I've watched over the last two months is so fucking strong, Verity. Way stronger than any woman over at the Hideaway, including my sister, and she's a boss bitch."

I sink down next to her, deflating. "She may be a boss bitch, but she still has a Lord and King she submits to." I stand again abruptly, grabbing and stabbing the spade into the dirt. "That's just how Forsyth works. I know it as well as anyone. Is it even possible for something good to come from so much evil?"

My mother warned me and I didn't listen. I wanted it too much. I wanted to be special. To be The One.

But all I am is another ordinary girl trying to be Princess in a long line of failures. I thrust my hand into the urn, pulling at the decaying leaves. But suddenly, I freeze, panting.

On the very tip of the stalk is a speck of impossible, vibrant green.

The shoot is tiny–barely a leaf–and looks frail, as if the vine it's attached to could snap at the slightest wind.

Slowly, I lower my hand, unsure if I should yank it out and keep it from taking root or do whatever I can to cultivate it. Is it fair to bring life into a place so cold and barren?

Should I run or should I do my duty?

"There was a reason I wanted you to come down here," Stella says, drawing me out of my thoughts.

I stare at the green, aware of my pulse quickening in my veins. "Why?"

"Because it's the only place we can speak freely," she answers.

Lex had said it himself. Pace couldn't find me down here. At a loss, I exhale. "Fine. So speak."

"I know these last few weeks have been one trial after another," she twists her braid around her finger, "but before you make any decisions, I have one last test I think you should take..."

I blink, trying to figure out why she's speaking in riddles if no one else can hear us, but then it clicks.

She's right.

There's only one test that really matters.

31

P ace

THREE DAYS, six games, one shiny ass trophy.

"Drink! Drink! Drink!"

The chant echoes off the bar's rafters, the whole room humming with a specific energy only reserved for undefeated champions.

Wicker holds the trophy over his head, champagne sloshing out of the wide rim. His tongue darts out and he drags it across the surface before taking a gulp. "Ahhh, the sweet taste of victory." My brother grins, his bottom lip freshly split. "Tastes better than pussy."

Some of the bruises from his ass-beating last week are still mottling his jaw, but you wouldn't know it from the way he's celebrating. To everyone else, he probably looks like the height of fucking satisfaction.

But I can see that gleam of defiant anger still swirling in his eyes.

"Twelve goals, and seven assists," Decker cheers, raising his bottle of cheap beer. "The Ashby brothers are the real MVPs of the game!"

Glancing around, the place is filled with pucksluts looking to bang a champion. Pitchers of beer and baskets of wings are piled on every table, all bought by fans wanting to give us a good night. It's a full-out celebration, but when the cup comes to me, I shake my head and wave it toward the next guy.

Just like with my Friday Night Fury victory, Father has given us permission to indulge until midnight. The text came just after the game, and something in my stomach still feels sour about it. The win belongs to the team—to me and Wick—but our father would never let us think so. Some part of it has to be his, just like everything else.

I look across the room to where Lex sits at a table with the other trainers, his drink untouched while his fingers tap on the table. We've barely spoken since the Royal Cleansing, the tournament occupying us in different scopes, but his quick temper and edginess have been obvious since the Scratch started wearing off days ago. There'd been no time to process what happened or to deal with whatever he's going through chemically. We dropped Verity off with her handmaiden and found out that Danner had packed for us while we were fire-hosing the Princess in cum. None of us spoke as we cleaned up, gathered our belongings, and got in the car waiting outside. Lex was lost in his head, fighting his own demons, Wicker wired like a trigger, ready to pop, and I couldn't stop mentally running the cleansing through my head over and over.

Rosi looked so defeated. So broken.

That's the only victory I care about tonight.

Tommy Wright's voice carries over the crowd. "Whatever the Princess did to get that public dicking-down should have happened weeks ago if that was going to be the result."

"What did you say?" A bar stool hits the floor seconds after Lex's voice cuts through the music and revelry.

Tommy's grin half-slips when he comes face-to-face with my brother's stone-cold expression. The room adopts a nervous hush. "Your brothers played like gods, Ashby. The whole team did. Like men who'd conquered and claimed. Just saying, maybe we need to have a go at your girl before every tournament."

Lex's hand snaps out and grabs Tommy by the collar, eyes swirling with that same edginess I've seen in them since that white powder went up his nose. His fingers twist, knuckles bearing into this throat. "What. Did. You. Say?"

Tommy gulps. "N-n-nothing."

I see the flicker in Lex's eye, the one that grows dark and focused down in the dungeon. He could end Tommy's life in two moves.

"That's what I thought." Lex pushes him back, releasing him with a thrust of the hand.

"Jesus," Tommy says, rubbing his throat, "you're a lot nicer on the Scratch."

Crack!

It's Wicker's fist that slams into Tommy's cheek. The second string forward shakes his head, taking a second to recover.

"What the fuck!" Tommy charges, shoving Wicker in the chest. My brother doesn't budge, just gives a cocky, terrifying grin and rolls his shoulders.

My eyes meet Lex's across the bar and the two of us are on the move in the space of a heartbeat. "Knock it off!" I shout, using the voice preferred by guards during a breakout. "Hands down."

Lex drags Wicker off toward a booth in the back corner, but I stay to square up to Tommy. "Mention our Princess one more time, and you'll end up without a tongue. Got it?"

Decker has a hand pressed against Tommy's shoulder, nudging him across the bar. He wisely answers for his friend. "He's got it, don't you, bro?"

Tommy nods, the heat of anger still flickering in his eyes, but he lets Decker lead him away.

I grab three glasses and a pitcher of beer off one of the tables and walk over to my brothers. "Jesus Christ." I slide them each a glass and fill them to the top. "Are you two done?"

"Maybe," Wicker says, grabbing the beer and pressing the cool side against his lip. "Fucking douche."

I take a moment to look over Lex. There are red marks on his arms but nothing that'll scar, and I don't miss the way his left eye twitches occasionally. "Are you okay? Because you're looking about five seconds from a relapse."

"I wish." He runs his hands through his hair, catching the band and letting the tresses fall to his shoulders. "I'd like to be fucking blitzed when the next part comes."

"What part?" Wick asks.

"The shitty part," Lex says, retying his hair. "The part where we have to face her and keep going, like she didn't put your life on the line."

Lex is a lot like me when it comes to hurting marks. Once we step into the dungeon, they're faceless, nameless. A job—nothing else.

What we did to Verity is different.

We didn't mean for it to be. Looking around the table, I see it in both of them in a way I never would have with Bruce. Before we were given the title of Prince, we watched or participated in a Royal Ceremony and then moved on. Those girls weren't our problem. Our *duty*. There's no getting out of this. The day we get back, the schedule will resume, our deposits will be made, and ultimately, if she doesn't get knocked up, there will be consequences.

"So we have to keep fucking our traitor," Wicker mutters, tipping the glass to his lips. "How exactly is that going to work?"

"A lot like it did the first time," I muse, glaring down at my phone. I've been tracking her movements, but she hasn't left the Palace once. "Maybe the two of you forgot she was a narc, but I never did. We'll have to keep her under lock and fucking key."

"Fantastic." Lex pushes his glass away. "Maybe the next video you bring to Father will put her into the dungeon. I prefer my maiming to be done without witnesses."

My stomach sinks. "Lex," I lean my elbows on the table, "I had no fucking idea Father would force you to—"

"You did what you had to," he says stiffly. "Just like we do. We all play our roles, and you were the only one with the clarity to plant that bug." He looks at Wicker. "To keep us safe."

"If anyone's to blame, it's me," Wicker says, his mouth forming a tight, grim line. "One good night with her, and I let down my guard like some pussy-whipped little..." He pauses, like he's trying to find the right word, his face screwing up when he does. "*Prince.*"

"She's really fucking good at that," Lex mutters.

"Or," Wicker's lip curves, "we're all just super deprived and seeking the kind of attention a woman like Verity has to give."

"Shut the fuck up with this bullshit." I glare at Wick, thrusting a finger in his direction. "She's the one at fault here. We did what we had to. She and the Dukes needed to understand the sensitivity of the information they have. There was no other way to do it."

Over at the bar, a puckslut wearing a jersey with my name on the back winks at me. For a moment, I wish I could walk over there and take it all out on her, but the covenants are still in place. I hold her gaze for a long moment before turning away.

"Neither of us are blaming you." Lex shreds a napkin in his fingers. "We all knew this would be a shit-show the second Father gave us the title."

"The Valentine's Day party is tomorrow." Wicker leans back, throwing his arm over the back of the booth. "We'll be expected to play the part."

"We play the part every fucking day," I reply. "How is this any different?"

But even I know that's bullshit. We didn't just destroy Verity, we annihilated her. That cleansing wasn't just a ritual. It wasn't even what we do in the dungeon.

It was personal.

L<small>EX SLEEPS</small> in our hotel room.

He doesn't need to–the sports medicine director puts the medics up in far calmer accommodations. But since Wicker and I are bunking together, it just makes sense that he fights through the celebration happening in the hallway and pushes through our door with a scowl.

"Fucking hate frat boys," he mutters, passing me as he enters.

I point out, "You are a frat boy."

Lex takes his shirt off with sharp, angry motions. "I don't see why I had to come to this thing. I'm beyond patching up split lips and talking babies through their boo-boos."

Wicker, who's just waltzing out of the steamy bathroom, towel slung low on his hips, scoffs. "Would you rather be home?"

We all share a look.

Fuck no.

If it weren't for the fact that Effie is alone in that godforsaken place, I'd say sayonara to the whole fucking island. But she is. All alone. In her cage.

"Whatever," Lex says, stalking into the bathroom.

I flop onto the bed, sighing, and grab my phone from the night-stand. Navigating my app to the webcam in her cage, I only let myself relax when I see her wing twitch. "How long will this last?" I ask Wicker, keeping half of my attention on the screen.

He's standing in front of the mirror above the little kitchenette, rubbing lotion onto his face. He stops to inspect one of the yellowing bruises. "You're referring to our sweet brother's glowing mood?" He prods the bruise, blue eyes narrowing. "Should be gone soon. It's not like he went on a bender. It was only a couple bumps."

"You think he wants more?"

"No." Wicker twists to meet my eye. "I *know* he wants more."

On the screen, Effie is preening her feathers. "Should we worry?"

"Yes," he says, and then, putting down the lotion, "No." He

pauses, propping his palms on the counter. His shoulders curl into a dejected line. "Fuck, I don't know. It seems like that's all we do, anyway." Twisting, he eyes my phone, dropping his towel. "You tracking her?"

"No. Effie," I clarify, but as soon as Wicker flops onto the bed beside me, I pull up the tracking app, showing him the screen. "She still hasn't left the island."

He watches Verity's little dot for a long moment, jaw hardening. "Show me."

I falter. Mostly because I know it'll just piss him off to see her face, but also because I haven't been able to bring myself to look at her yet, and I'm not sure why. Because I want to hold the image of her, defeated and cum-soaked, at the forefront of my mind? Or is it because of this displeasure I feel, deep down in my gut, at the memory of it?

In the end, I relent, going through all of the authentications to bring up the Palace's feeds. I check the front gates first, out of habit. Then the downstairs–dining room, kitchens, parlor–and the staircases.

Wicker, as impatient as ever, says, "Just look in her room."

My thumb pauses over the button, but I finally press it, bringing up the stream. I feel Wicker tense, just before he realizes it's empty. Her bed is rumpled, a tray sitting askew on the table beside it. There's a robe draped over the chaise, and a bra sitting on the top of the dresser.

But no one is there.

His eyes narrow. "Keep looking."

"What are you hoping to find, exactly?" Despite my question, I keep flipping through the cameras, but it's the next pick that does it.

She's in the bathroom.

Wicker and I both suck in a quiet breath when she comes on the screen. Part of it is that she's stark naked, standing at the vanity.

Part of it is that she's looking right at us.

Her hands are braced on the edge of the counter in such a

perfect mirror to Wicker's pose from moments ago that it's startling. Her hair is down, tumbling over her pale shoulders and perky tits. There are thumbprint bruises on her waist and dark circles beneath her eyes. Her nipples are erect, pink lips pressed together in a stoic line.

Her green eyes look right through me.

"You think she knows?" he asks, eyebrows pulled together.

"That the camera is in the mirror?" I shake my head, even though I can't know for sure. "She's just primping."

Only she keeps staring.

We watch her for a long while, the eerie sensation of being watched back tickling on the edge of my awareness. Her skin looks soft. That's the dangerous thing about Verity; she looks so goddamn inviting. Maybe Wicker had it right before. Maybe we're deprived of something she knows to give us. It's not just the softness or the sweetness. It's the way it feels to have that soft sweetness beneath our rough hands.

Suddenly, I realize why I haven't been able to see her yet. It's not even about the cleansing. Not about savoring the destruction, nor feeling remorse for it. It's because now I know.

I know that even after everything, I still want her.

In a low, gruff voice, Wicker asks, "Do you ever wish that she really could have been..."

"Ours?" I turn, meeting his gaze. I know my answer to that question. I feel it in the pull, because it's instinctive. There's no reason it should be. I only had her for a few weeks. But before I can begin trying to put that disappointment into words, I need to know, "Do you?"

It's not like Wicker.

Sex has always been easiest for him. Lex needs the perfect specimen—someone who'll understand that they're just body parts, chasing a biological high. I need something more complicated. The tug in my gut. The spark of curiosity. The flare of possessive fire, even if it's fleeting, that tells me she has to be mine.

Wicker's never needed more than a warm body, and from the

tinge of alarm in his eyes, he's realizing that Verity showed him something he wants, and it's more than a hot, slick pussy.

I'm not even surprised when he pushes his mouth to mine. It's not the first time we've kissed. It's not even the first time we've kissed since I got back from prison. The thing about Wicker is that he only knows two ways of coping with any given thing: hurt something or fuck it. And it's usually the latter–sometimes both. It's not his fault, it's just what being Father's product has shaped him into. I hate it. I've *always* hated it. From the first night he came back to boarding school and told Lex and I, smirking, about the sweet piece of ass he bagged over the weekend, I didn't feel jealous like Lex did. I felt fucking sick at the thought of someone owning him like that, because for all his boasting and bluster, I could see the uncertainty and hurt lurking beneath it.

Wicker didn't want it.

He doesn't want this, either.

He's just not ready to admit it.

So I kiss him back, threading my fingers through his damp hair, because fuck. It'd be easy–so much fucking easier–to want this instead of *her*. I lick into his mouth and he meets me with a determination that forces a grunt from my throat. He rolls into me, a hand grabbing for the waistband of my boxers, but when I palm his side, the muscles are flexed and strained, and when I cradle his jaw, it's all hard angles, his chest broad planes. There's no softness. No silky hair under my fingers. No plush lips or soft thighs, the sweet scent of roses distressingly absent.

It's nothing like our bored, drunken makeout sessions freshman year, our hands quick on each other's cocks as we raced to the finish line. It's not exactly a hardship. Wicker's always been a really fucking intense kisser, and it's not even really about his lack of having a pussy. It's that this is desperation without any of the fire. Need without any of the want. Bitter without any of the sweet.

We break away when we hear the shower cut off, blue eyes staring back at me instead of green, and the way my stomach plummets pretty much seals it.

I finally answer. "Yeah, I wish she could have really been ours." Glancing down at his cock, barely half-hard, I raise an eyebrow. "And I guess you do, too."

Wicker follows my gaze before flopping hard on his back, blue eyes gazing unblinkingly at the ceiling. "Fuck," he says, and then, clutching at his hair, "Fucking *fuck*."

I discreetly wipe my mouth. "Sounds about right."

"Trying to get me killed is one thing," Wicker bites out, scowling. "But Stockholming my dick? Are you fucking kidding me?"

"No." Wicker and I both swing our gazes to the bathroom door, where Lex is looking like a drowned rat, hair in his face. He glares at us. "You know the rules. No fooling around in the bed we sleep in. It's weird and annoying."

"Relax," I mutter as Wicker rolls his eyes, twisting to find some underwear. "We all have broken dicks now, apparently."

"Do we?" Lex's jaw hardens, teeth clenching as he yanks the towel around his hips off. "Because mine seems to have gotten with the program."

Wicker and I both gape at the sight of Lex's thick cock, which is currently standing at full pornographic salute.

Wicker's eyes narrow. "You said you flushed the rest of the–"

"I've been clean since Thursday night," Lex insists, eyes flashing.

"Christ." I pinch the bridge of my nose. "Like your fuse hasn't been short enough."

He climbs into bed with us minutes later, the tense silence settled around him like a storm cloud. It's only once we've all settled, some mundane sitcom playing on the TV, that he has anything to say. "Sorry I've been a shit."

I glance across Wicker's bare back, seeing the light play over Lex's furrowed brow. "It's not your fault." None of this is our fault. We didn't ask for it. We didn't even volunteer. We weren't created to be Princes, but Father made us ones anyway.

"For what it's worth," Lex adds, staring straight ahead, "It wasn't just you two. I thought she could be ours, too."

 erity

LOOKING OVER THE BALLROOM, I have to give my mother credit. She'd prepared me for this day. All those Family Dinners. All those fundraisers and Screw Year's Eve's.

Verity Sinclaire knows how to throw a party.

The grand room looks majestic, with soft lavenders against creamy whites. No gaudy hot pink, like the Princesses who came before me. No, the Princes are in love with love, but they're meant to be classy about it, just like the massive arch of white and pale purple roses over the door. There are fountains quietly bubbling over with French champagne, a dessert table covered in delicious confections, including trays of dark chocolate-covered strawberries and a six-tiered, ornate wedding cake. An orchestra tunes their instruments in the corner, and the crystal chandeliers have never sparkled more.

"It's perfect," Stella says from behind me. We're at the side door taking one last look, and she sounds stunned. "I can't believe you managed all this in just two days."

"I didn't," I tell her, watching as Danner brushes the wrinkle out of a tablecloth. "We did." Turning to send her a grateful look, I fret, "Do you think the photographers are too much? Is the photo booth area tacky?"

"No way, the girls will love it. Those, too." She nods at the men stationed by the front with baskets of roses. "It's elegant and sophisticated."

I exhale, scanning the ballroom one last time. "Good. I want everyone to like it."

She places a hand on my arm, giving me a soft, confident smile. "You made the right decision, Princess."

Satisfied, I nod. "Let's go get me dressed."

I SPEND a lot of time on my makeup, covering the dark circles beneath my eyes, accentuating my lips, trying to soften the hollows in my cheeks. The fading bruises on my neck get dabbed with concealer, and then I start on my hair, curling it into long, methodical ringlets.

I always thought being a Princess would be glamorous, and for once, that's true. The dress I slip into is a lot like the ballroom in that I've taken it up to a ten. It's unlike the ballroom in that I've forgone the illusion of purity and class, because it's siren red, sequined, and so tight that it fits like a second skin, the swell of my breasts peeking out the top. I may as well wear it while I can.

I look at myself in the mirror before reaching for the jewelry box, plucking out the golden chainmail choker.

"Allow me."

I freeze, eyes flicking to the reflection in the mirror.

Pace is blocking the bathroom doorway with a sleek, artful lean, dressed to kill in a black tuxedo. His hands are stuffed in his pockets, eyes searing through me like evil onyx orbs. "I did pick it out, after all."

He doesn't wait for my permission, but I don't expect him to. I square my shoulders and hold out the chain, refusing to think of what he looked like the last time I saw him. I fight back a shiver as his fingertips brush my neck, pulling my hair aside. I still remember the day I got this—a gift following a brutal deposit.

A collar.

There's a moment when his hands come around my throat and I'm assaulted by a flash memory of those fingers creating the bruises beneath my concealer.

Pace loops the choker around my neck and tugs it tighter than it should be, latching it with a hateful glint in his eye. "Now we just need a leash to attach to it."

In the mirror, I watch him blankly. With how tall he is, his head rises so high over mine that I can perfectly make out the strained tendon in his neck as he looks down, eyes fixed to a spot behind my ear. He tilts his head, searching.

Blandly, I ask, "What are you looking for?"

His black eyes meet mine in the mirror. "Anything you may have missed," he says, fingers combing my hair back. "Dried, flaky remnants..." The jab is just as obvious as his true intent.

He's probably checking to make sure my tracker is undisturbed. The leash.

I fix him with a cutting grin. "I clean up well."

He holds my eye. "I know. I watched every second of it." Dipping down, he whispers into my ear, "You're looking into my camera right now." I keep my expression carefully blank. It's not like I didn't know there was a camera in here already. At my lack of response, he drags his fingers down my arms. "I can't wait to replay the video from Thursday night. You, standing here, all slimy and fucked out—a walking testament to our creampie. I'd send that to your Dukes too, only I think I'll be greedy and keep it for myself." His smirk is sharp with malevolence when I jolt away.

"I need to be downstairs," I say, voice curt as I slip the hooks of two gold hoops in my ear. I don't worry too much. It isn't Pace's day.

It's Wicker's.

"I'm escorting you down to the others." He looks me up and down, lip curling back. "It's tradition."

"And what? You drew the short straw?" I reach for the last, and by far the biggest and shiniest, item of interest in the jewelry box.

The tiara.

I pick it up with both hands and place it on my head, watching Pace's reflection in my periphery.

He's staring at my tits. "I can't wait to watch Wicker and Lex fuck all of that crap off you tonight."

It's Wicker's night, but Lex's will roll over at midnight.

Grabbing my clutch purse, I coldly wonder, "Did anyone ever tell you that the three of you are incestuous freaks?"

When I'm ready, he's there, grabbing my hand and folding it around his forearm. "They're hungry, my brothers," he says, voice contemplative as he turns me to the door. "I think I'll hold you down for them again."

I let him guide me, allowing him to assume he has the power he so desperately needs to feel. Because I know the truth.

The Ashby brothers may be hungry, but I'm absolutely ravenous.

I SEE their backs before I see their faces.

Wicker and Lex.

They're waiting for me in front of the ballroom, gazing at the ornate maple door as the orchestra plays a saccharine, lilting melody in the room behind it. The sound of my heels on the floor must tip them off, because Wicker twists to look, his blue eyes finding mine with eerie, horrifying accuracy.

It's all I can do to not fold over and vomit again.

Pace clasps my hand around his forearm, tethering me, all but dragging my body to his brothers.

Lex is the next to look, his amber eyes not even deigning to meet mine. He looks at my tits first, then diverts his gaze to the tiara on my head, jaw tightening.

"They're about to announce us," Lex mutters, showing me his back.

It takes me a long moment to fight back the panic at seeing him, the memory of his drug-crazed, dilated eyes still fresh in my mind. The ghost of his fingertips, bruising my inner thighs. The way his teeth looked when his lips pulled back, feral and rabid.

I hold it close, important and precious.

As expected, Wicker's the one who can't stop looking at the dress, the way it accentuates my tits and falls over the curves of my ass.

Lex? He gave me the earrings, but he can't stop glancing at the tiara, while Pace eyes the choker around my neck as if he'd like to give it a sharp pull.

I'm wearing all of their gifts.

I could've brought the shears, but someone probably would have left without an appendage.

Without question, they look handsome as sin in their expensive suits, all broad shoulders and perfect posture. There's not a hair out of place on Lex's head, and no one would know the scars—the truth—hidden beneath that expensive tuxedo. Wicker's slouched against the wall, his healing lip giving him a rough, sexy vibe that manages to only make him look hotter. Their expressions are stone cold and indifferent. Exactly the way I feel inside, down deep in my chest.

Impassive.

"The party lasts three hours," I start, ignoring the nausea rolling in my stomach. "We'll mingle, eat some cake, smile for the camera." I look them each in the eye. "You'll flirt with me and pretend everything is normal."

"Perfect," Lex says, eyes still blazing on the tiara. For a second, I get the impression he wants to rip it off my head. I'm probably not too far off.

Locking my jaw, I ask, "So you agree?"

"No," Wicker says with an icy glance, "everything will be *perfect*, not normal."

"Princes never strive for normalcy," Pace adds, tone hard. "But I guess that's a concept that may be hard for West End trash to comprehend."

I second guess my decision to not bring the shears.

Wicker pushes off the wall and stiffly offers me the crook of his elbow, "The sooner we start, the sooner this joke of a party is over."

I catch his scent as I take his arm, and a warring emotion runs through me. He smells good, like bait on a line. Again my stomach threatens to revolt, and it takes a second to push it back as we walk through the door, Pace and Lex following close.

Danner stands on the other side of the rose arch, nodding his approval. "Good evening. You all look wonderful."

"Just announce us, Danner," Wicker says, running his hand through his hair, making it perfectly tousled.

"Of course." The room spreads in front of us like something out of a movie, packed with the PNZ boys and their dates. Music swells, the orchestra playing instrumental variations of popular music. Danner gives a signal that travels through the room until the music ceases. "Presenting the Princes of Forsyth and their beautiful Princess. May they reign."

Every eye turns to the doorway, voices echoing, "May they reign," and my first reaction is rage. There are no masks this time to hide the perpetrators and participants. Each of these men watched as I was assaulted all those weeks ago, and again on Thursday night. One by one, they defiled me. Do their dates know? No. The cleansing is a secret affair. The only ones outside of the people in the room that night who know are my family in West End.

We smile rigidly, giving everyone happy, solemn nods. This is the part I'm not good at. The acting. It's not in my blood—not what I was taught. A West Ender wouldn't think to hide their fury. They'd harness it. Tap it. Embrace it.

Which is why, once the spectacle is over, I slip away from Wicker's grip, his scent, his *everything*, and merge into the crowd with a fake smile plastered across my face. It burns to shake their hands, to be just as fake as I knew East End was, but I do it.

I do it because there will only be one outcome this evening.

Revenge.

A HAND BRUSHES against my lower back, and I stiffen. "Dance with me, Princess."

Unlike the last ball, Lex isn't asking, and I'm in no position to decline. Wordlessly, I let him take my hand and guide me to the dance floor, his movements smooth as he turns to clasp my waist, gently cradling my hand in his other.

With a grace our bodies haven't earned, we begin gliding with the other dancers, chins up, shoulders straight.

His amber eyes barely glance into mine. "You're different from the last ball," he says, his firm body spinning us. "Or maybe I am, because you look nothing like the doe-eyed girl you used to be."

He's right. I'm no longer the nervous potential Princess, unsure in my body and pedigree. I understand who I am better now. The power my body has over these men. But I'm also more aware of the vulnerabilities.

"You're exactly the same," I argue, allowing my body to move with his, following his precise but fluid steps. I can't help but see the dichotomy. The exacting, methodical Lex, versus the wild, feral Lagan.

One coin, two sides.

"Is that so?" he asks, eyes tightening at the corners. "You still think you know me."

"You still hate all the pretense," I say, noticing the way his gaze keeps slumping toward my cleavage. "All the pomp and circumstance–it bores you to tears. But you're still willing to make sacrifices just to please your father."

"That's the thing about parents," he says, spinning me around. Across the room, I see Pace watching us carefully, tracking my every move. Or so he thinks. "They know you even less than the people they're forcing you to form attachments to."

"Really." My voice is dry and cold. "What's that supposed to mean?"

He tilts his head until his mouth is close to my ear. "It means that your mother was CC'ed on the email we sent the Dukes, so she's going to see exactly what you are to us. Worse than a whore. A traitor to everyone, good for nothing but being stuffed full and thrown away."

We're not dancing anymore, my feet stuck like glue to the floor as my heart lodges in my throat.

Lex tucks my hair behind my ear, trailing his fingers down my cheek to the column of my neck. "My only regret is that she'll never get to hear how you always beg for it, willing to do anything to feel a cock deep inside."

I jolt back like I've been shocked. "You're bluffing," I say, even though the words are more of a hope than a certainty.

And from the dark, twisted smirk he gives me, he knows it. "I have this whole theory, you see. Nature or nurture. Are we who we become because of our DNA? Or does how we're raised determine our character and temperament? To what degree?" His eyes search mine, and for a moment, I'm bombarded with flashes of us, eyes meeting, sharing breaths, our lips against one another's. He pitches forward to whisper, "I hope she cried when she realized how much of a whore you've become."

In the end, I'm grateful for it.

Because Lex Ashby is someone I could have loved.

Until right this second.

I tear myself away, giving a loud clap to the room. "Can I have your attention, please?" I call out, my voice more even than it has any right to be.

"What are you doing?" he asks, clinging to my fingers.

I turn to flash him my iciest grin. "Oh, I have something special for my favorite Prince tonight."

His eyes narrow into hateful slits. "Do you, now?"

"It's a Valentine's Day gift." I tug him with me, leading him to the front of the room. "A gift for all of you, in fact."

I know I should be nervous—I can see King Ashby in the corner, cavorting with their hockey coach—but I'm not. In fact, as the King's gaze shifts to me, I've never felt more serene, even offering Tommy Wright's girlfriend a grin as I step up before the crowd.

Without having to do more than clear my throat, the dancing stops. The orchestra's sweet melody fades into silence. In the back, Pace is shifting, eyes darting around, as if searching for a threat. Wicker, currently bringing an hors d'oeuvres to Colby Harker's widow, halts in his steps, turning to peer at me through the crowd.

I lace my fingers, hands folded in front of me. "As your Princess, I'd like to thank you all for coming." There's a brief, quiet, dainty applause, and I gesture to Lex, who's still at the front of the audience, brows pulled down into a deep scowl. "I'd like to dedicate tonight to my Princes. There have never been three men more deserving of what you're about to see. For weeks, they've given me a home here. I mean," laughing, my hand flutters at my chest, "no door is closed to me in the Purple Palace. Never has a girl felt so welcome—so cherished—in the home of her intendeds."

In the audience, some of the girls 'aww', but within them, I also see the cruel, heartless men who derived such pleasure from degrading me. Men who are made to follow. Men who want strong, capable leaders.

"So what can I tell you about this generation of Princes?" I smile primly at the crowd. "For one, you should all know that Pace snores." There's a pause before they all give a surprised little laugh, and I nod along, all long-sufferingly. "And Wicker... well." Shrugging, I joke, "What can be said about Wicker Ashby that isn't already written on a bathroom stall, am I right?" The next round of laughter is colored by discomfort, eyes seeking Wicker out in the crowd. He's dropped the plate of food, glowering up at me. I hold out a palm, gesturing to his brother, his amber eyes like lasers. "And then there's Lex. You know, Lex was the first Prince I really felt comfortable with. It was probably just his forward nature. Plus, those hands?" I whistle. "Cold as ice, but super skilled."

Even as Lex shifts awkwardly, a few of the girls share glances, which tells me all I need to know about his history in the frat.

Sighing, I go on, "But tonight is about love. And what is love, really?" I ask, pacing toward the orchestra. "Well, we're in East End, where love means looking at the person next to you and thinking... 'Hey, I wouldn't mind procreating with this idiot.'" As the round of nervous titters that follow spreads around the room, I look anywhere but at the King in the corner. "But I want you to know that I'm not procreating with idiots. No. In fact, my Princes are exceedingly bright. And so tough, too. For example..." Sweeping a hand, I gesture to the screen behind me, currently filled with floating hearts, and text that happily declares, *"To create is to reign!"* "I've assembled this little tribute for you all. It's a true testament to what your Princes are." Smirking, I pull the little remote from my clutch, pressing a button.

The screen blinks, and suddenly, Ashby's office is on the screen.

"This isn't about deposits, Whitaker. This is about Lagan giving me his word, and then failing to fulfill it. He's allowed a weakness to stand in the way of his purpose." Then, Ashby commands, *"Fireplace."*

Casually, I watch Lex as he realizes what's coming, his mouth parting in shock. From someone so composed and aloof as him, it's truly a sight to see his face pale. "What–" he says haltingly. "How...?"

He barely even notices me moving next to him, straining up to whisper in his ear. "If you're wondering how it feels to have my friends and family see me so degraded–so fucking humiliated and broken?" I smile as his eyes turn to dark vacancy, the first strike of the whip resounding around the room. "It's a *little* like this."

On the screen, Ashby is hissing, *"Four lashings for each of your deposits. And an additional four to get you to the same level as your brother. Be thankful I'm not holding you to Whitaker's standards."*

The room erupts into shocked murmurs and instinctive yelps as the whip hits again.

"I should have killed you," Lex says, eyes fixed to the screen. He looks sick, like he's about to vomit all over his shiny shoes.

My God, revenge is delicious and sweet.

It's the final lash that does it, though I'm not sure why. Maybe it's the sound he makes through the speakers, low and pained, a whimper that seems to snap him into action.

He barrels at me, clamping my wrist in a vicious grip. "I should have killed you like I wanted to. I told them to! You fucking bitch!" His eyes are an inferno, but within them, I see a depthless hopelessness.

I grin back at him, showing my teeth. "Good. I'd rather be dead than create anything with you. Do you really think I ever wanted any of you twisted psychos to be the father of an innocent child?"

The insult, the truth of what I'm saying, lands. All those times I begged them to put a child in me...

It was nothing but lies.

A performance.

He lunges for me, catching me around the throat and squeezing. Gasping for air, I manage to drop the last of my arsenal. "You kill me now, and you'll also kill the baby."

There's a stretch of time where it feels like everyone in the room must be being strangled the same as me. There are no sounds, no breaths.

His amber eyes explode in alarm, grip tightening. "What did you say?"

I don't fight, wondering for a moment what it'd be like to let him squeeze the life out of me. If it was just me, I'd let him, but it's no longer just me.

"I'm pregnant."

Immediately, he insists, "You're lying."

I answer by clawing at my clutch, dipping a frantic hand inside to grab the plastic. I hold it up, head throbbing as I struggle to breathe. Lex's gaze snaps to it—the two bars indicating a positive test—and fixes there, dazed on it.

It's only a few seconds later that he's wrenched away, the action jarring and violent, causing me to sputter and stumble.

"You will not harm her," comes a snarled, frosty hiss. "No one will harm her!" King Ashby stands between me and Lex, his disconcerting gaze swinging to me. "Is this real?" he asks in an urgent, demanding voice. "You're with child?"

Grasping my throat, I nod, handing him the test. My voice emerges strained and uneven. "I took it yesterday. Ten of them, just to be certain. My handmaiden helped me."

Ashby clutches the test with wide, frantic eyes, reading the bars. "You're pregnant," he states, his crazed eyes meeting mine. "Their seed has taken root?"

Suddenly terrified, I nod, seeing Wicker in the distance, pushing through the bodies between us.

"This is it," Ashby breathes, glancing between me and the test. "You're carrying the heir to East End."

"Who cares?" Lex spits, murder still burning in his eyes. "She's a fucking fraud! A liar and traitor! We should throw her into the dungeon!"

Whirling on him, Ashby barks, "She's the Princess!"

Gaping, Lex flings a hand toward me. "She's a fucking hostage!"

But then Ashby roars, the rawness of it striking the entire ballroom into stunned silence. "*She's* my biological daughter!"

It reverberates like a gunshot, and the bullet finds a home in the middle of my chest when I realize this isn't meant symbolically. I can see it in the eyes of my Princes, heads snapping back in shock.

It's a lie.

It has to be.

There's no way that Rufus Ashby, King of East End, is my father. My father is a nameless DKS frat boy who left Forsyth before I was born. My mother told me this, time and time again.

Except...

My clutch tumbles to the floor, banging onto the marble with a *thud*.

Ashby turns to me, his crazed eyes as bright as spotlights. "You're my daughter, Verity. And you're carrying my grandchild." I'm useless to do more than stand here, still and stiff as a statue as he reaches out, palms framing my flat belly. "Through your womb, my legacy will endure."

He stares at it—my stomach, which will surely be swelling soon—and sinks to his knees, his expression all at once drawn and full of awe. "You don't just carry the heir to East End. You're carrying the heir to my crown."

AFTERWORD

Book 8 of the Royals of Forsyth Series, *Princes of Ash*, will be available later this year.

If you want to know about the two guests Wicker notices at the back of the cello performance and learn more about Micha and Michaela check out our book *Devil May Care*, part of the *Preston Prep* series.

∿

Angel:

I'm starting to think of the readers of Royals of Forsyth U as survivors. You're not just readers but witnesses to the darkness and depths of Samgel's mind. When we finished Lords everyone, including us, wanted to dive right into the Princes. We knew at the time that we hadn't prepared you all for what we wanted to do with a breeding story. We knew we weren't quite ready either. I don't think we knew why, but we felt it in our bones. To do the Princes justice we needed more time to build out the world of Forsyth, the Kings, and obviously find our Princess. Poor Verity. We didn't know the first time we wrote her name what we would do to her but... yeah, so goes life as a character in Forsyth.

Your support has meant so much to me during the last year. As I've said in the group, there has been a lot of household stress and health issues. These books and working with Sam allow me a place to go where I can just lose myself to reality and sink into another world. It may be awful, but there's always atonement and a happy ending. I promise, even if it doesn't look like it yet.

Thank you to our highest Queens: Lisa, Christina, Vicki, Nikki, Anna, Brittnay and everyone else that keeps us on the path. I always say it takes a village, apparently what it takes is a whole freaking Kingdom.

To the Victor-Angel

—

Sam:

My absolute biggest thanks goes out to Christina, who was there for me in the late/early hours when I felt like I was going to lose it. I always write at night, from midnight to 8am, which is good for me, because it means no interruptions. But it's also incredibly lonely and makes me very susceptible to brain worms, especially as I'm tapping my ids and traumas for inspiration and realism. Christina, you were the light in my tunnel and I can't thank you enough. I'm honestly not sure I could have done it without you. It truly does take a village!

Vicki, your feedback is what pushed me through at a time when I was unsure and floundering. So much of this is owed to your amazing and expert feedback and support. Lisa, you are always a rock in a wild river, and we'd be lost without you.

Also a huge thanks to my family, my super patient husband, and Crowley (my cat), who is the best employee a business owner could ask for, and thanklessly herded me up those steps every night.

To the readers who waited very many months for Chaos, this is all for you, and I hope with an intensity bordering on mortifying that you've enjoyed this book, or have at least gotten something from it. At the end of the day, it's all about making something you all have enjoyed, because as we all know:

To create is to reign.

Made in United States
North Haven, CT
16 October 2024

59065392R00350